MUSIC
AN APPRECIATION

BY THE AUTHOR

The Norton Scores: An Anthology for Listening

McGRAW-HILL BOOK COMPANY

New York St. Louis San Francisco Auckland Düsseldorf Johannesburg
Kuala Lumpur London Mexico Montreal New Delhi Panama Paris
São Paulo Singapore Sydney Tokyo Toronto

MUSIC

AN APPRECIATION / Roger Kamien

Queens College of the City University of New York

MUSIC: AN APPRECIATION

4567890 VHVH 7987

This book was set in Palatino and Helvetica Light by York Graphic Services, Inc.
The editors were Robert P. Rainier, Elysbeth Wyckoff, Robert Weber, and James R. Belser.
The indexer was Sylvia Kolb;
the designer was Jo Jones;
the production supervisor was Sam Ratkewitch.
The photo editor was Gabriele Wunderlich.
The drawings were done by ECL Art Associates, Inc.
Von Hoffmann Press, Inc., was printer and binder.

Library of Congress Cataloging in Publication Data

Kamien, Roger.
    Music: an appreciation.

    Bibliography: p.
    Discography: p.
    Includes index.
    1. Music—Analysis, appreciation. I. Title.
MT6.K22M9   780'.15 75-20067
ISBN 0-07-033266-5

See Acknowledgments on pages 558–559. Copyrights included on this page by reference.

Cover and title page photograph: Vienna's King of Waltz. Photograph by Dennis Stock, Magnum.

For Anita, David, Joshua, and Adina

CONTENTS

Contents
viii

Contents

ix

Contents
xiii

Contents
xvi

Contents

PREFACE

Why another music appreciation text? Fifteen years' experience with music appreciation courses and college students has shown me the need for an accurate, clear, and engaging book that takes students' interests and knowledge into account. My goal was to write a book that is useful both for study and in the classroom. This text provides an approach to perceptive listening and an introduction to musical elements, forms, and style periods. Its discussions of composers' lives, individual styles, and representative works aim to stimulate curiosity and enthusiasm, not merely to impart facts. The book was written to heighten a reader's love of music as well as to develop listening skills. The features outlined below will be attractive to students and teachers alike.

Readability

The biographical sketches and the descriptions of composers' individual styles attempt to give the flavor of each composer's personality and music. Anecdotal material and quotes from composers enliven the discussion.

Clarity of expression was a chief goal. This is a book that students can feel comfortable with. They will recognize that it was written for them by a musician who loves music and who wants to convey its essentials without confusion or boredom. Musical terms are defined simply and appear in bold type. Important terms and concepts are listed at the end of each section.

Flexibility

Music: An Appreciation takes a chronological approach but can adapt easily to individual teaching methods. Each style period is subdivided into short, relatively independent sections that can be studied in any order or even omitted.

While music examples are offered throughout the book, discussions of pieces require no knowledge of music notation. The examples provide visual aids for those who want them; students may prefer simply to read the text and skip the details of notation.

Organization

In addition to a comprehensive discussion of the musical style and sociological aspects of each historical period, the lives, individual styles, and representative works of many composers are examined in detail. Through repeated exposures to a variety of musical compositions, students are encouraged to listen for basic forms (such as A B A and theme and variations) as well as for elements of music (dynamics, tone color, rhythm, texture).

Part I of the book examines the elements of music both in general terms and with reference to illustrative pieces that are attractive, brief, and from a variety of style periods. Notation is used sparingly in this part—usually in connection with familiar tunes like "Home On the Range" that allow students first to analyze music they have known since childhood. Parts II through VII deal with specific periods of music history from the Middle Ages to the present. Each part opens with a discussion of the period's style characteristics, its cultural trends, and the roles of music and musicians in society. Jazz and rock are considered in Parts VIII and IX, and non-Western music is surveyed in Part X. These parts were written by individual specialists who also teach music appreciation.

Listening Outlines

A distinctive feature of this text is the use of "listening outlines" to enrich the discussion of many pieces. Meant to be followed while the composition is heard, each outline focuses attention on musical events as they unfold. The outlines can be followed easily and therefore are useful for outside listening assignments as well as for classroom work. However, since the text offers a general discussion of each composition represented, the listening outlines may be omitted.

Opera

The study of opera is aided in this text by extended excerpts from librettos, making it unnecessary for teachers to supply them. Opera texts appear with brief marginal notes that indicate the relationship between words and music and help readers follow the drama.

Supplementary Materials

To supplement *Music: An Appreciation,* appendixes provide an overall chronology, a reading list, a discussion of tone color and the harmonic series, and lists of key signatures and works represented in the recordings which accompany this book. Also available are a package of five related records for student use and a full teacher's manual with suggested tests.

Acknowledgments

Many musicians, teachers, and students were kind enough to read sections of the manuscript in rough draft and have earned my deep gratitude. Professors Lorna Adams, Benjamin Boretz, Andrew J. Broekema, Raoul F. Camus, Gordon F. Crain, Peter Gano, Henry J. Keating, James Kurtz, Robert Morgan, William V. Porter, Piero Weiss, and Franklin Zimmerman all contributed valuable suggestions. My colleagues in the music department of Queens College were extraordinarily generous and helpful. Stephen Elmer wrote the sections on jazz and rock, and Professor Ashenafi Kebede contributed the discussion of non-Western music. Henry Burnett, Charles Selzer, and Professors Charles Burkhart, Lawrence Eisman, Raymond Erickson, Hubert Howe, Joel Mandelbaum, Carl Schachter, and David Walker all read portions of the text. I am grateful for the expert assistance of Robert Weber as well as that of Elysbeth Wyckoff and her co-workers at McGraw-Hill.

My wife, Anita Kamien, contributed to every aspect of this book. She clarified ideas, helped choose representative pieces, and improved the listening outlines tirelessly. Her advice and encouragement were essential to the completion of *Music: An Appreciation.*

Roger Kamien

MUSIC
AN APPRECIATION

ELEMENTS

(Burk Uzzle, Magnum).

⟦1⟧ SOUND: PITCH, DYNAMICS, AND TONE COLOR

Sounds bombard our ears every day—the squeaks and honks of traffic noises, a child's laugh, the bark of a dog, the patter of rain. Through them we learn what's going on; we need them to communicate. By listening to the speech, cries, and laughter of others, we learn what they think and how they feel. But silence, an absence of sound, also communicates. When we hear no sound in the street, we assume no cars are passing. When someone doesn't answer a question or breaks off in the middle of a sentence, we quickly notice it, and we draw conclusions from the silence.

Sounds may be perceived as pleasant or unpleasant. Fortunately we can direct our attention to specific sounds, shutting out those that don't interest us. At a party we can choose to ignore the people near us and focus instead on a conversation across the room. We shut out most sounds, paying attention only to those of interest. The composer John Cage (b. 1912) may have meant to show this with his "composition" entitled 4'33", in which a musician sits at a piano for four minutes and thirty-three seconds—and does nothing. The silence forces the audience to direct attention to whatever noises, or sounds, they themselves are making. In a sense, the audience "composes" this piece. To get the effect, listen to the sounds that fill the silence around you right now.

What are these sounds that we hear? What *is* "sound"? What causes it, and how do we hear it?

Sound begins with the vibration of an object, say a table that is pounded or a string that is plucked. The vibrations are transmitted to our ears by a *medium*, which usually is air. As a result of the vibrations, our eardrums start vibrating too, and *impulses*, or signals, are transmitted to our brains. There the impulses are selected, organized, and interpreted.

Music is part of this world of sound, an art based on the organization of sounds in time. We distinguish music from other sounds by recognizing the four main properties of musical sounds: *pitch, dynamics* (loudness or softness), *tone color*, and *duration*. We'll look now at the first three of these properties. Duration—the length of time a musical sound lasts—is discussed in section 3, "Rhythm."

Pitch: The Highness or Lowness of Sound

Pitch is the relative highness or lowness that we hear in a sound. No doubt you've noticed that most men speak and sing in a lower range of pitches than women or children do. And when you sing the beginning of "The Star-Spangled Banner,"

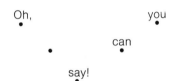

the pitch on *see* is higher than it is on *say*. Without differences of pitch, speech would be boring, and—worse—there would be no music as we know it.

The pitch of a sound is decided by the frequency of its vibrations. The faster the vibrations, the higher the pitch; the slower the vibrations, the lower the pitch. Vibration frequency is measured in cycles per second. On a piano the highest frequency tone is 4,186 cycles per second, while the lowest is about 27 cycles per second.

In general, the smaller the vibrating object, the faster its vibrations and the higher its pitch. All other things being equal, plucking a short string produces a higher pitch than plucking a long string. The relatively short strings of a violin produce higher pitches than do the longer strings of a double bass ("bass fiddle").

In music, sound that has a definite pitch is called a **tone.** It has a specific frequency, such as 440 cycles per second. The vibrations of a tone are regular and reach the ear at equal time intervals. On the other hand, noiselike sounds (the squeaking of brakes or a clash of cymbals) have an indefinite pitch and are produced by irregular vibrations.

Two tones will sound different because they have different pitches. The "distance" in pitch between any two tones is called an **interval.** When tones are separated by the interval called an **octave,** they sound very much alike. Sing the opening of "The Star-Spangled Banner" again. Notice that the tone you produce on *see* sounds like your tone on *say,* even though it's higher. (Sing the *say* and *see* tones several times.) An octave lies between them. The vibration frequency of the *say* tone is exactly half that of the *see* tone. If the *say* tone were 440 cycles per second, the *see* tone—an octave higher—would be 880 cycles per second. A tone an octave lower than the *say* tone would be half of 440, or 220 cycles per second. When sounded at the same time, two tones an octave apart blend so well that they almost seem to merge into one tone.

The interval of an octave is important in music. It is the interval between the first and last tones of the familiar scale:

do re mi fa sol la ti do

Sing this scale slowly and notice that you fill the octave with seven different pitches before arriving at the high *do,* which "duplicates" the low *do* you start on. You do not slide up as a siren does; you fill the octave with a specific number

Pitch: The Highness or Lowness of Sound

of pitches. If you start from the higher *do* and continue the scale upward, each of your original seven tones will be "duplicated" an octave higher. This group of seven tones was the basis of music in Western civilization for centuries. The seven are produced by the white keys of the piano keyboard.

As time passed, five pitches were added to the original seven. They are produced by the black keys of the keyboard. These twelve tones, like the original seven, are "duplicated" in higher and lower octaves. Every tone has "close relatives" one, two, three, or more octaves away. (In non-Western music, the octave may be divided into a different number of tones, say seventeen or twenty-two.)

The distance between the lowest and highest tones that a voice or instrument can produce is called its **pitch range** or, simply, range. The range of the average untrained voice is between one and two octaves, while a piano's range is over seven octaves. When men and women sing the same melody, they usually sing it an octave apart.

The organization of pitch is a composer's first resource. In sections 5 and 6, where melody and harmony are discussed, we will look at how pitch is organized. For now we'll simply observe that composers can create a special mood in their music by using very low or high pitches. For example, low pitches can intensify the sadness of a funeral march, while high pitches can make a dance sound lighter. And a steady rise in pitch often increases musical tension.

Though most music we know is based on definite rather than indefinite pitches, noiselike sounds—such as those made by a bass drum or cymbals—figure strongly in the rhythmic life of music. In parts of Africa, the indefinite pitches of drums are very important. And with recent electronic developments, indefinite pitches have come to play a vital role in Western music as well.

Dynamics

Degrees of loudness or softness in music are called **dynamics.** Loudness is related to the amplitude of the vibration that produces the sound. The harder a guitar string is plucked (the farther it moves from the fingerboard), the louder its sound. When instruments are played more loudly or more softly, or when there is a change in how many instruments are heard, a dynamic change results which may be either sudden or gradual. A gradual increase in loudness often creates excitement, particularly when the pitch rises, too. On the other hand, a gradual decrease in loudness can convey a sense of calm.

A performer emphasizes a tone by playing it more loudly than the tones around it. We call this a **dynamic accent.** Skillful, subtle changes of dynamics add spirit and mood to performances. Often these changes are not written in the music but are inspired by the performer's feelings about it.

Improvements in making musical instruments during the last 150 years have vastly increased our range of dynamics. In fact, today's electronic equipment has expanded it to the point where loudness can cause pain. (Did you ever sit near the speakers at a rock concert?) Probably no culture has used so wide a dynamic range as ours does today.

Elements

Dynamic Indications

When notating music for others to read, composers traditionally have used Italian words and abbreviations to show their intentions about dynamics. The usual abbreviations and their meanings are:

pp	*pianissimo*	very soft
p	*piano*	soft
mp	*mezzo piano*	moderately soft
mf	*mezzo forte*	moderately loud
f	*forte*	loud
ff	*fortissimo*	very loud

To indicate extremely soft or loud dynamic levels, a composer sometimes will use *ppp* or *pppp* and *fff* or *ffff*.

To show gradual changes in dynamics, the following symbols and words are used:

decrescendo (decresc.) or *diminuendo (dim.)*	gradually softer
crescendo (cresc.)	gradually louder

Like many elements of music, a dynamic indication is not absolutely precise. A tone has a dynamic level—is soft or loud—in relation to other tones around it. The loudest sound of a single violin is tiny compared with an entire orchestra's, and even further from an amplified rock group's. But it can be considered fortissimo (very loud) within its own context.

Tone Color

We can tell a trumpet from a flute even when they play the same tone at the same dynamic level. The quality of sound that distinguishes them is called **tone color,** or **timbre** (pronounced "tam'-ber"). Tone color is described by words like *bright, dark, brilliant, mellow,* and *rich.*[1]

As with dynamics, changes of tone color create variety and contrast. When the same melody is played by one instrument and then by another, it takes on different expressive effects because of each instrument's tone color. A contrast in tone color may be used to highlight a new melody: after violins play a melody, an oboe may present a contrasting one.

Tone colors also build a sense of continuity; it is easier to recognize the return of a melody when the same instruments play it each time. Specific instruments can reinforce a melody's emotional impact: the brilliant sound of a trumpet is suited to heroic or military tunes, while the soothing tone color

[1]An explanation of the physical basis of tone color appears in Appendix IV.

of a flute fits the mood of a calm melody. In fact, composers often invent a melody with a particular instrument's tone color in mind.

A practically unlimited variety of tone colors is available to composers. Combining different instruments—violin, clarinet, and trombone, for example—results in new colors. And tone color can be changed by varying the number of instruments or voices that perform a melody. Finally, new colors can be invented, as is the case with the electronic developments we are experiencing today.

Listening Outlines

Reading about pitch, dynamics, and tone color without hearing music is too abstract. To understand and recognize the properties of sound that we've considered, we must *listen for them.* In this book listening outlines will help focus your attention on musical events as they unfold. These outlines must be read *as you listen to the music;* otherwise, their value to you is limited.

Each item in a listening outline describes some musical sound. It may point out dynamics, instruments used, pitch level, or mood. (Remember that indications of mood in music are subjective. What one person calls "triumphant" another may call "determined.")

Before listening to a piece of music, it's helpful to glance over an entire listening outline. Then, while hearing one item, look ahead to learn what's next. For example, in the listening outline for the Prelude to Act III of Richard Wagner's opera *Lohengrin,* the first item (1a) is "Full orchestra, very loud (*ff*), main melody in violins, cymbal crashes." While listening to the music described by item 1a, glance at item 1b: "Brass melody, pulsating accompaniment in strings."

Sometimes not all the instruments playing are listed; instead, only those that are prominent at a given moment are shown. For example, item 2 in the *Lohengrin* Listening Outline reads "Soft (*p*), contrasting oboe melody. Melody repeated by flute. Clarinet and violins continue." While other instruments can be heard, this focuses attention on the instruments that play the melody.

Each listening outline is preceded by a description of the music's main features. Instrumentation, approximate duration, and recording notes (where important) are given also.

Lohengrin, Prelude to Act III, by Richard Wagner

Wagner makes wide and brilliant use of dynamic contrasts in this Prelude to set the scene for the wedding of the opera's hero and heroine. The Prelude opens with a feeling of exultation—great energy is conveyed by the massive sound of the full orchestra. Later the music suddenly becomes calm and gentle as we hear fewer instruments, playing softly. This is followed by another sudden contrast when Wagner again employs the full orchestra.

Elements

6

Lohengrin, Prelude to Act III (1848), by Richard Wagner (1813–1883)[2]

3 flutes, 3 oboes, 3 clarinets, 3 bassoons, 4 French horns, 3 trumpets, 3 trombones, bass tuba, timpani, triangle, cymbals, tambourine, violins 1, violins 2, violas, cellos, double basses

(About 3½ min)

1   *a.* Full orchestra, very loud (*ff*), main melody in violins, cymbal crashes.
     b. Brass melody, pulsating accompaniment in strings.
     c. Full orchestra, main melody in violins, cymbal crashes.
2   Soft (*p*), contrasting oboe melody. Melody repeated by flute. Clarinet and violins continue.
3   *a.* Full orchestra, very loud (*ff*), main melody in violins, cymbal crashes.
     b. Brass melody, pulsating accompaniment in strings.
     c. Cymbals. Becomes softer (decrescendo). Becomes very loud, brass proclamation at end.

Prelude in C Minor for Piano, Op. 28, No. 20, by Frédéric Chopin

In this Prelude, dynamic change is produced by a single instrument, the piano. A decrease in volume from very loud (*ff*) to soft (*p*), to very soft (*pp*) contributes to a feeling of emotional progression within this miniature lasting only a minute and a half; it's as though a majestic funeral march becomes increasingly personal.

Prelude in C Minor for Piano, Op.[3] 28, No. 20 (1839), by Frédéric Chopin (1810–1849)

(About 1½ min)

1   Heavy chords, very loud (*ff*).
2   New section, soft (*p*).
3   Very soft (*pp*) repeat of preceding section. Slows down toward the end.

Firebird Suite, Finale (1919 version), by Igor Stravinsky

In the Finale of the *Firebird Suite,* Stravinsky repeats one melody over and over, creating variety and contrast through changes in dynamics, tone color, and

---

[2] With concert ending, as performed on Columbia MS 6442.
[3] The abbreviation "Op." stands for *opus,* Latin for "work." An opus number is a way of identifying a piece or set of pieces. Normally, within a composer's output, the higher a composition's opus number, the later it was written.

rhythm. The *Suite* is a set of dances from *The Firebird* (1910), a ballet in which the hero marries a beautiful princess during the music of the Finale.

The Finale begins softly but becomes increasingly grand as the music gradually gets louder (crescendo), more instruments play, and the melody is repeated at higher pitches. After this slow build-up to a climax, there's a sudden quiet as all instruments but the strings stop playing.

LISTENING OUTLINE
To be read while music is heard

Firebird Suite, Finale (1919 version[4]), by Igor Stravinsky (1882–1971)

piccolo, 2 flutes, 2 oboes, 2 clarinets, 2 bassoons, 4 French horns, 2 trumpets, 3 trombones, tuba, timpani, bass drum, triangle, cymbals, harp, violins 1, violins 2, violas, cellos, double basses

(About 3½ min)

1   *a.* Melody in French horn, soft (*p*), quivering string accompaniment.
    b. Violins, soft, melody an octave higher. Flutes join.
    c. Gets louder (crescendo) as more instruments enter.
    d. Violins and woodwinds, loud, melody at an even higher octave, crescendo to
    e. Full orchestra, melody extremely loud (*fff*).
    f. Suddenly very soft (*pp*), strings, quick crescendo to
2   *a.* Brasses, very loud (*ff*), melody in quick detached notes, timpani (kettledrums). Melody slows down, full orchestra, *fff*, timpani.
    b. Cymbals, sustained brass chords, extremely loud (*fff*). Dynamic swell at end.

"Hotter Than That"
by Louis Armstrong and His Hot Five

A succession of different tone colors contributes to the variety within this music for jazz band. After an introduction played by the full band, we hear solos by the trumpet, clarinet, voice, guitar, and trombone. Louis Armstrong performs both as trumpeter and vocalist. His singing is like his trumpet playing in sound and style. Instead of lyrics he sings nonsense syllables like "dat-a bat-a dip-da." In one section the guitarist, Lonnie Johnson, imitates the melodic phrases sung by Armstrong, whose voice takes on a guitarlike twang.

Unlike the preceding compositions by Wagner, Chopin, and Stravinsky, this music was improvised by the performers. Their point of departure was the

Elements

8

  [4]Stravinsky composed three different versions of the *Firebird Suite.*

tune "Hotter Than That" by Lil Harding, the band's pianist (and Armstrong's wife at the time).

Within item 2 of the listening outline, the trumpet is momentarily heard alone, without its accompaniment of piano and guitar. This unaccompanied solo should not be mistaken for the entrance of the clarinet (item 3), which sounds like a high-pitched whine.

LISTENING OUTLINE
To be read while music is heard

"Hotter Than That" (1927), by Louis Armstrong and His Hot Five[5]

Voice, clarinet, trumpet, trombone, piano, banjo, guitar

(About 3 min)

1 All instruments, trumpet predominates.
2 Trumpet accompanied by piano and guitar. Trumpet briefly alone, piano and guitar rejoin.
3 Clarinet, high-pitched whine, piano and guitar accompany.
4 Voice, guitar accompaniment.
5 Voice imitated by guitar. Piano leads into
6 *a.* Muted trombone accompanied by piano and guitar.
  b. Trumpet, all instruments join. Guitar, trumpet, guitar at end.

Sound: Basic Terms

If you aren't sure what each of the following words means, look back at the text, where they appear in bold type. Additional information about some of them can be found by checking the index.

sound
pitch
tone
interval
octave
pitch range
dynamics
dynamic accent
tone color (timbre)

[5]Recorded on Columbia LP CL 851, *The Louis Armstrong Story*, Vol. 1, side 2, band 5, and *The Smithsonian Collection of Classic Jazz*, side 2, band 8.

[2] PERFORMING MEDIA: VOICES AND INSTRUMENTS

Voices

Throughout history, singing has been the most widespread and familiar way of making music. Ancient Greek drama included chanting choruses, and the Bible records that Moses and the Israelites sang to glorify the Lord. Singers seem always to have had a magnetic appeal, and even today adoring audiences imitate the looks and lifestyles of their favorites.

The exchange between singer and audience contains a bit of magic, something direct and spellbinding. Probably because the singer becomes an instrument, we identify with him or her especially—a human body like our own expressing emotions through sounds and words. (Trained dancers also make us realize how expressive our bodies can be.)

The voice's unique ability to fuse a word with a musical tone is the reason that poetry and singing have been inseparable in many cultures. Singing can make words easier to remember and heighten their emotional effect.

For many reasons it is difficult to sing well. In singing we use wider ranges of pitch and volume than in speaking. And we hold vowel sounds longer. Singing demands a greater supply and control of breath. Air is pushed from the lungs by the lower abdominal muscles and the diaphragm. The air makes the vocal cords vibrate, and the singer's lungs, throat, mouth, and nose come into play to produce the desired sound. The pitch of the tone varies with the tension of the vocal cords; the tighter they are, the higher the pitch.

The range of a singer's voice depends both on training and on physical make-up. Professional singers can command two octaves or even more, while an untrained voice is usually limited to about an octave and a half. Men's vocal cords are longer and larger than women's, and this difference produces a lower range of pitches. The classification of voice ranges for women and men follows, arranged from highest to lowest. (The four basic ranges are shown in bold type.)

Women	*Men*
soprano	**tenor**
mezzo soprano	baritone
alto (or contralto)	**bass**

Because of differences in taste, methods of singing vary widely from culture to culture. Oriental singing, for example, is more nasal than that of the West. While classical singers in our culture stand erect, singers in West Africa stand bending forward; and in India they sit on the floor. In fact, there are differences in performing styles in the West alone: classical, popular, jazz, folk, and rock music are all sung differently. Classical singers, for example, normally don't rely on microphones, but rock gets its point across partly by amplification.

Leontyne Price, soprano of the Metropolitan Opera, singing an aria from Verdi's *La Forza del Destino* (United Nations).

Until the late 1600s, most important music of Western culture was vocal. But by the end of the seventeenth century, instrumental music was greatly developed and had become as important as vocal music. Since then, vocal works—both solo and choral, with and without instrumental accompaniment—have made a major addition to the music we enjoy. Composers continue to write for solo voices, for small groups of voices, and for large choruses. And accompaniments range from single instruments like guitar or piano to entire orchestras.

Musical Instruments

People around the world use musical instruments that vary greatly in construction and tone color. An instrument may be defined as any mechanism —other than the voice—which produces musical sounds. Western musicians usually classify instruments in six broad categories:[6] **string** (such as guitar and violin); **woodwind** (flute, clarinet); **brass** (trumpet, trombone); **percussion** (bass drum, cymbals); **keyboard** (organ, piano); and **electronic** (synthesizer).

---

[6] The scientific classification of instruments, based on the way sound is made, has five categories: *chordophones* (a stretched string is the sound generator—our "string" category); *aerophones* (a column of air is the sound generator—our "woodwind" and "brass" categories); *idiophones* (instruments made of naturally sonorous material, such as cymbals, gongs, and bells—part of our "percussion" category); *membranophones* (instruments stretched with a skin or other membrane for the sound generator, such as drums—part of our "percussion" category); and *electrophones* (instruments generating their sounds by means of electricity—our "electronic" category).

An instrument often is made in different sizes that produce different ranges. For instance, the saxophone family includes soprano, alto, tenor, baritone, and bass saxophones—all in different sizes.

An instrument's tone color may vary with the **register** (part of the total range) in which it is played. A clarinet sounds dark and rich in its low register, but its high register is brilliant and piercing.

Instrumental performers try to match the beautiful, flexible tone of a singer's voice; a pianist, for example, is praised for a "singing" tone. Yet most instruments have a wider range of pitches than the voice does. While a trained singer's range is about two octaves, many instruments command three or four octaves, and some have six or seven. And instruments usually produce more rapid tones than the voice. When writing music for a specific instrument, composers have to consider its range of pitches and dynamics and how fast it can produce tones.

Instruments provide entertainment and accompany singing, dancing, religious rites, and drama. But they have served other functions, too. In some cultures, instruments are thought to have magic powers. Bells are worn to guard against harm, and rattles are witch-doctors' tools. In parts of Africa, drums are so sacred that religious rites are not performed without them, and special ceremonies and sacrifices are sometimes enacted when making them.

Instruments have been used for communication as well. Detailed messages were sent by drumbeats; hunters blew horns for signals; and musicians announced the time by sounding brass instruments from towers. Trumpets were used for military signals and to bolster soldiers' courage in battle. For centuries, trumpets and kettledrums announced kings and queens.

Musical instruments have even been status symbols. During the nineteenth and early twentieth centuries, the piano was a fixture in any home that aspired to be middle-class. "Proper" young ladies were expected to learn the piano as one of many "accomplishments." Such ideas lost their currency when women began to move more freely in the world (around the time of World War I), and when the radio and phonograph began to replace the piano as a source of home entertainment. Still, even today there are status implications in the type of record-playing equipment someone owns. Though a stereo is not a musical instrument, a connection can be made between the "parlor piano" of 1900 and the elaborate "home entertainment centers" found in many middle-class homes.

Today only a fraction of all known instruments are used. Their popularity rises and falls with changing musical tastes and requirements. However, twentieth-century interest in music of earlier times has led to the resurrection of long-forgotten instruments like the harpsichord, an ancestor of the piano, and the recorder, a relative of the flute. Modern replicas of ancient instruments are being built and played. In fact, modern musicians are flexible and far-ranging in their choice of instruments. Rock composers use non-Western instruments such as the Indian *sitar* (a plucked string instrument). Jazz musicians are turning to classical instruments like the flute, while classical composers are using instruments associated with jazz, such as the vibraphone.

Distribution of Instruments in a Modern Orchestra
(About 100 instrumentalists)

Woodwinds

3 flutes, 1 piccolo
3 oboes, 1 English horn
3 clarinets, 1 bass clarinet
3 bassoons, 1 contrabassoon

1 piano
2 harps

Brass

4 trumpets
6 French horns
4 trombones
1 tuba

Strings

18 first violins
16 second violins
12 violas
10 cellos
8 double basses

Percussion

4 timpani (1 player), bass drum, snare drum, cymbals, triangle, xylophone, celesta, glockenspiel, etc. (2 to 4 players)

Seating plan of the New York Philharmonic orchestra (The Friends of the New York Philharmonic).

Compositions are written for solo instruments, for small groups, and for orchestras with over one hundred musicians. Whatever the group, it may include instruments from only one category (say strings) or from several. Modern symphony orchestras contain string, woodwind, brass, and percussion instruments. (A typical seating plan for a large orchestra is shown on page 13, along with a photograph of the New York Philharmonic.) Keyboard instruments also find their way into the modern orchestra as needed.

Instruments commonly used for Western music are described in this chapter, by categories. Non-Western instruments are discussed in part X.

String Instruments

The **violin, viola, cello** (violoncello), and **double bass** ("bass fiddle") form the backbone of the symphony orchestra's string section. They vary in tone color as well as in size and range: the violin is the smallest and has the highest range; the double bass is the largest and has the lowest range. For symphonic music the strings usually are played with a **bow,** a slightly curved stick strung tightly with horsehair (see illustration). Symphonic strings are also plucked with the finger.

Of all the instrument groups, the strings have the greatest versatility and expressive range. They produce many tone colors and have wide ranges of pitch and dynamics. String players can produce tones that are brilliant and rapid or slow and throbbing; they can control tone as subtly as a singer. Orchestral works tend to rely more on the string instruments than any other group. Even with differing tone colors, the four string instruments blend beautifully. Here it will be helpful to consider the strings' construction and tone production; the violin can represent the entire family.

The hollow wooden body of the violin supports four strings made of gut or wire. The strings stretch, under tension, from a **tailpiece** on one end over a wooden **bridge** to the other end, where they are fastened around wooden **pegs.** The bridge holds the strings away from the **fingerboard** so that they can vibrate freely; the bridge also transmits the strings' vibrations to the **body,** which amplifies and colors the tone. Each string is tuned to a different pitch by tightening or loosening the pegs. (The greater the tension, the higher the pitch.)

The musician makes a string vibrate by drawing the bow across it with the right hand. The hair of the bow is rubbed with rosin (made from gum of turpentine) to increase its friction against the string. The speed and pressure of the bow-stroke control the dynamics and tone color of the sound produced. Pitch is controlled by the musician's left hand. In pressing a string against the fingerboard, the player varies the length of its vibrating portion and so changes its pitch. This is called *stopping* a string (because the vibrations are stopped at a certain point along the string's length). Thus a range of pitches can be drawn from each of the four strings.

Basically the viola, cello, and double bass are made in the same manner and produce sound by similar means. How the string instruments are played—

Elements

the string performance techniques—increases the musical effects that they can produce. The most frequently used techniques are listed here:

Pizzicato (plucked string): The musician plucks the string, usually with a finger of the right hand. In jazz, the double bass is played mainly as a plucked instrument, rather than being bowed.

Double stop (two notes at once): By drawing the bow across two strings, a string player can sound two notes at once. And by rotating the bow rapidly across three strings (**triple stop**) or four strings (**quadruple stop**), three or four notes can be sounded almost—but not quite—together.

Vibrato: The string player can produce a throbbing, expressive tone by rocking the left hand while pressing the string down. This causes small pitch fluctuations which make the tone warmer.

Mute: The musician can veil or muffle the tone by fitting a clamp (mute) onto the bridge.

Tremolo: The musician rapidly repeats tones by quick up-and-down strokes of the bow. This can create a sense of tension, when loud, or a shimmering sound, when soft.

Harmonics: Very high-pitched tones, like a whistle's, are produced when the string player lightly touches certain points on a string. (See Appendix IV.)

Though the violin, viola, cello, and double bass are similar, as in any family they have their differences. Study the photographs and captions in this section to see why each adds something distinctive to the orchestra's total sound.

Some string instruments are not played with a bow but are plucked instead. The most important of these are the **harp** and the **guitar.** The harp is the only plucked-string instrument that has gained wide acceptance in the symphony orchestra.

Right–Violin. The violin is often used as a solo instrument. In the orchestra, the violins are divided into first and second violins, with the former frequently playing the main melody (H. Armstrong Roberts).

Below left–Cello. While eighteenth-century composers generally used the cello in its bass and baritone registers, composers later exploited its upper registers as well (Suzanne Szasz).

Below right–Double bass. The double bass (or bass) has a very heavy tone and is less agile than other string instruments. It is often heard with the cello, but an octave lower (Gabriele Wunderlich).

Above–Harp. With the fingers of both hands, the harpist plucks forty-seven strings stretched on a triangular frame. The harp has a wide range of 6½ octaves.

Left–Guitar. The guitar's six strings are plucked with the fingers of the right hand. Frets mark the places where strings are pressed by fingers of the left hand (Gabriele Wunderlich).

Woodwind Instruments

The woodwind instruments are so named because they produce vibrations of air within a tube that traditionally was made of wood. During the twentieth century, however, piccolos and flutes came to be made of metal. All the woodwinds have little holes along their length that are opened and closed by the fingers or by pads controlled by a key mechanism. By opening and closing these holes, the woodwind player changes the length of the vibrating air column and so varies the pitch.

The woodwind instruments of the symphony orchestra are listed below, arranged from highest (piccolo) to lowest (contrabassoon) in range. (The pairing indicates closely related instruments; the more important one of each pair is starred.)

piccolo	clarinet*
flute*	bass clarinet
oboe*	bassoon*
English horn	contrabassoon

Woodwind instruments are great individualists and much less alike in tone color than the various strings. The flute, with its silvery tone, differs more from the nasal-sounding oboe than the violin does from the viola (see illustrations). These unique tone colors result largely from the different ways in which vibrations are produced. Flute and piccolo players blow across the edge of a mouth hole much as one makes sounds by blowing across the top of an empty bottle. The rest of the woodwind instruments rely on a vibrating reed. A **reed** is a very thin piece of cane, about $2\frac{1}{2}$ inches long, that is vibrated by a stream of air. There are single- and double-reed woodwinds. In **single-reed woodwinds** the reed is fastened over a hole in the mouthpiece and vibrates when the player blows into his or her instrument. The clarinet and bass clarinet are single-reed woodwinds.

In **double-reed woodwinds** two narrow pieces of cane are held between the musician's lips. The oboe, English horn, bassoon, and contrabassoon are double-reed woodwinds.

Heard by itself, a reed produces only a squawklike sound. While the tone color of reed woodwinds is mainly determined by the bore of the instrument's tube, the reed does affect the tone color somewhat. Professional woodwind players spend much time soaking and shaping their supply of reeds to ensure the best possible tone.

Tone colors also differ greatly among the various registers of each woodwind instrument. In general, low registers tend to be breathy and thick, and top registers are more penetrating. Unlike the strings, which can double stop, the woodwinds can only produce a single note at a time. In symphonic music they frequently are given melodic solos. Woodwind instruments are well suited for outdoors (shepherds have played simple woodwinds for thousands of years). They are often featured in music that evokes a rustic mood.

Elements

Above left–Piccolo. "Piccolo" is short for *flauto piccolo* ("small flute"). It plays an octave higher than the flute and is half its size. The piccolo's high register is shrill and whistlelike (Costa Manos, Magnum).

Above right–Flute. The flute has a high range and is extremely agile, capable of producing rapid successions of tones. Its tone is full and velvety in the low register and bright and sparkling in the top (Gabriele Wunderlich).

Left–Oboe. The oboe's tone is nasal, intense, and expressive. Because the instrument's pitch is difficult to adjust, the entire orchestra is tuned to the oboe's A (High School of Performing Arts).

Woodwind Instruments

Above left–English horn. The English horn is neither English nor a horn, but simply a low, or alto, oboe (Gabriele Wunderlich).

Right–Clarinet. The clarinet can produce tones very rapidly and has a wide range of dynamics and tone color (United Press International).

Above right–Bassoon. The bassoon's tone is deeply nasal (J. Schefler, High School of Performing Arts).

Elements

Left–Contrabassoon. The contrabassoon can produce the lowest pitch in the orchestră (Gabriele Wunderlich).

Below left–Saxophone. The saxophone has a single-reed mouthpiece like a clarinet's, but its tube is made of brass. Its tone is rich, husky, and speechlike (Gabriele Wunderlich).

Above–Recorder. Like the flute and piccolo, the recorder has no reed. The recorder's tone resembles a flute's, but it is softer and gentler. Its five main sizes are sopranino, soprano, alto, tenor, and bass (Suzanne Szasz).

Woodwind Instruments

21

Brass Instruments

Ranging from high to low in register, the **trumpet, French horn, trombone,** and **tuba** are the main instruments of the symphony orchestra's brass section. Trumpets and trombones are often used in jazz and rock groups.

The vibrations of brass instruments come from the musician's lips as he or she blows into a cup or funnel-shaped **mouthpiece.** The vibrations are amplified and colored in a tube that is coiled (to make it easy to carry and play). The tube is flared at the end to form a **bell.** While modern brass instruments are made of brass, earlier ones were made of hollow animal horns, elephant tusks, wood, and even glass.

Pitch of brass instruments is regulated both by varying the lip tension and by using **slides** and **valves** to change the length of the tube through which the air vibrates. The trombone uses a slide, a U-shaped tube that fits into two parallel straight tubes (see photograph). By pulling the slide in or pushing it out, the player changes the length of tube and makes it possible to play different

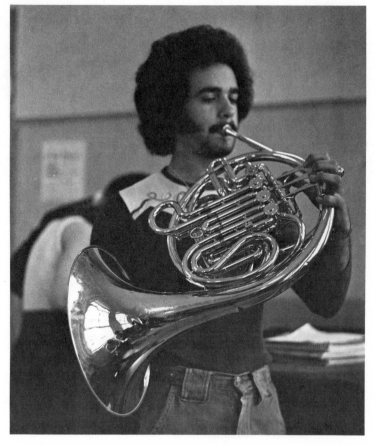

Above–Trumpet and mute. The trumpet sounds brilliant, brassy, and penetrating. (Gabriele Wunderlich).

Right–French horn. Its tone is less brassy, more mellow and rounded than the trumpet's (High School of Performing Arts).

Opposite page, left–Trombone. Its tone combines the trumpet's brilliance with the French horn's mellowness. It can suddenly swell or decrease in volume (Gabriele Wunderlich).

Opposite page, right–Tuba. Its thick heavy tone is used to add weight to the lowest orchestral register (Jan Lukas, Rapho/Photo Researchers).

pitches. The trumpet, French horn, and tuba use three or four valves to divert air through various lengths of tubing (see illustrations). The longer the length of tubing through which air is diverted, the lower the possible pitch. Valves came into common use around 1850. Before then, French horn and trumpet players would insert additional curves of tubing (called *crooks*) into their instruments to change the range of available pitches. When valves came into use these instruments could produce many more tones and became much more flexible. Brass players can also alter the tone of their instruments by inserting a **mute** into the bell. A mute is a hollow, funnel-shaped piece of wood or plastic.

Brasses are powerful instruments; when played loudly they can almost drown out the rest of the orchestra. Brasses are used at climaxes and for bold and heroic statements. They cannot play as rapidly as most of the string or woodwind instruments and serve less often as soloists. We often think of the brasses in terms of military marches or outdoor ceremonies. For many centuries they were simple instruments capable of producing only a few pitches and were used mainly for military signals, religious rites, or hunting calls.

Percussion instruments. Counterclockwise from bottom right: snare drum, timpani, cymbals and bass drum. The timpani are the only orchestral drums of definite pitch. One percussionist generally plays two to four timpani, each tuned to a different pitch (Constantine Manos, Magnum).

Percussion Instruments

Most percussion instruments of the orchestra are struck by hand, with sticks, or with hammers. Some are shaken or rubbed. They are subdivided into instruments of definite and indefinite pitch, depending on whether they produce a tone or a noiselike sound.

Definite Pitch		*Indefinite Pitch*	
timpani	xylophone	side drum	triangle
(kettledrums)	marimba	(snare drum)	cymbals
glockenspiel	celesta	bass drum	gong
vibraphone	chimes	tambourine	(tam-tam)

The vibrations of percussion instruments are set up by stretched membranes, like the calfskin of the kettledrum, and by plates or bars made of metal, wood, or other sonorous materials. Extremely loud sounds may be drawn from percussion instruments like the bass drum or cymbals. However, percussion sounds die away more quickly than those of other instruments. In a symphony orchestra, one percussionist may play several different instruments during a composition.

Elements

24

Percussion instruments have long been used to emphasize rhythm and to heighten climaxes. But until about 1900, they played a far less important role than strings, woodwinds, or brasses. Composers of our century have been more willing to exploit the special colors of the percussion group and have occasionally written entire pieces to show it off, such as *Ionisation* (1931) by Edgard Varèse. Jazz and rock musicians have, of course, made good use of percussion instruments. Yet, for all these recent explorations, Western musicians barely approach the incredibly varied use of percussion found in Africa and Asia, where subtle changes of tone color and dynamics are used with great imagination.

Keyboard Instruments

The **piano, harpsichord, organ,** and **accordion** are the best-known keyboard instruments. A keyboard permits the performer to play several tones at the same time with ease and rapidity. This capacity in common justifies grouping instruments that are otherwise quite different: The piano and harpsichord produce sounds through vibrating strings; the organ uses vibrating air columns. The piano and, to a lesser extent, the organ are sometimes used in modern symphony orchestras for coloristic effects. All keyboard instruments are played solo, as well.

During the last two centuries, more great music has been written for the **piano** than for any other solo instrument. It is exceptionally versatile. A pianist can play many notes at once, including both a melody and its accompaniment. The piano commands a wide range of pitches. Its eighty-eight keys span more than seven octaves. The dynamic range is broad, from a faint whisper to a powerful *fortissimo*. Because of its dynamic flexibility, the Italians named it *pianoforte* ("soft-loud").

When a pianist's finger strikes a key, a felt-covered hammer swings up against a string. The greater the force on the key, the more powerful the hammer's blow on the string, and the louder the tone produced. When the pianist releases the key, a felt *damper* comes down on the string to stop the vibrations and end the tone. The steel strings are held under tension by an iron frame. Below the strings is a wooden sounding board which amplifies and colors the strings' vibrations.

There are usually three pedals on a piano. Most important is the *damper pedal*, on the right, which allows a pianist to sustain tones even after the keys are released. The pedal on the left, commonly known as the *soft pedal*, veils the sound. The middle pedal is rarely used (and is often missing from upright pianos); it allows the pianist to sustain some tones without sustaining others.

Invented in 1709, the piano came into fairly wide use in the 1780s and was mechanically perfected by the 1850s. Today it is among the most popular instruments and is used for solos, for accompaniments, and in combination with one or many other instruments.

Top–Piano (Omikron).

Bottom–Harpsichord (Gabriele Wunderlich).

Elements

26

Above left–Pipe organ (The Bettmann Archive, Inc.).

Above right–Accordion (David Seymour, Magnum).

The **harpsichord** has strings that are plucked by a set of *plectra* (little wood, horn, leather, or plastic quills). These are controlled by one or two keyboards.

Pipe organs have many sets of pipes controlled from several keyboards, including a pedal keyboard played by the organist's feet. The keys control valves from which air is blown across or through openings in the pipes. Various sets of pipes are brought into play by pulling knobs called **stops.** Each set of pipes has a particular tone color which the organist uses alone or with others. The larger the organ, the more tone colors available. Organists, unlike pianists, cannot make subtle changes of dynamics by varying finger pressure. Instead, dynamic change is produced by adding or reducing the number of pipes being played or by opening and closing shutters (much like Venetian blinds) which surround some groups of pipes. The organ has a greater range of pitch, volume, and tone color than any other traditional instrument. Its tones last for as long as a finger or foot is held on a key or pedal.

The greatest period of organ music and organ building was from 1600 to 1750, when it was known as the "king of instruments." Although mostly connected with religious services, today the organ is found in many auditoriums and is used in concerts.

Keyboard Instruments

Electronic Instruments

An electronic instrument is one that produces or amplifies sound through electronic means. Invented as early as 1904 electronic instruments have had a great impact on music only since 1950.

Among the electronic instruments widely used in popular music and rock are the electric organ and guitar. A musician performs on these in public much as he or she would on a traditional nonelectronic concert instrument. Other electronic instruments are *not* usually played for an audience but are used by composers to produce sounds on audiotape. The three tools for creating such electronic music are the **tape studio,** the **synthesizer,** and the **computer.**

In a **tape studio,** the raw material consists of recorded sounds—definite pitches (tones) or indefinite pitches (noises). These sounds are either of electronic origin—from audio generators—or from nonelectronic sources—flutes, jet engines, water drips, bird calls, etc. The composer manipulates such raw material in several ways: by speeding the sounds up or slowing them down, or altering their pitch and duration. Thus a flute can be made to have the register of a bassoon. The tape can be played backwards, producing novel sound effects. A piano tone, for example, might consist of a gradual crescendo followed by a startling percussive sound, instead of the normal sharp attack followed by a gradual fading away. A sound may be given an echo, or it may be electronically filtered to change its tone color. The composer can place different sounds against each other by using several tape recorders or multitrack tape. Since audiotape can be cut and spliced, sounds can be played in any desired order. Rhythm can be fully controlled, too, since the duration of a sound depends only on the length of a tape segment.

Poème électronique ("Electronic Poem"), by Edgard Varèse

One of the most famous pieces of electronic music created in a tape studio is *Poème électronique* by Edgard Varèse. The eight-minute work was designed to be heard within the pavilion of the Philips Radio Corporation at the 1958 Brussels World Fair. Varèse obtained unique spatial effects by projecting sound from 425 loudspeakers placed all over the interior surfaces of the pavilion. The composer worked in collaboration with the architect Le Corbusier, who selected the series of images—photographs, paintings, and writing—that were projected on the walls as the music was heard. But there was no attempt to synchronize the sounds with the images, which included "birds and beasts, fish and reptiles . . . masks and skeletons, idols, girls clad and unclad, cities in normal appearance and then suddenly askew," as well as atomic mushroom clouds.

Varèse's raw sound material—tones and noises—came from a wide variety of sources, including electronic generators, church bells, sirens, organs, human voices, and machines. The sounds are often electronically processed in such a way that they cannot be precisely identified. In the listening outline, the effect

Elements

28

of such sounds is conveyed by words placed in quotation marks, like "wood-blocks" or "animal noises." Varèse organized his sounds into an electronic poem that seems weird, yet is amazingly logical and compelling.

Poème électronique is subdivided into two main sections, the first lasting two minutes thirty-six seconds and the second five minutes twenty-nine seconds. Each section begins with low bell-tolls and ends with sirens. Heard several times during the *Poème* is a distinctive group of three rising tones. Human voices and recognizable organ tones appear only during the second section. Varèse once remarked about the female voice heard toward the end of the *Poème:* "I wanted it to express tragedy—and inquisition."

Created in a tape studio, *Poème électronique* exists in only a single "perform-ance" whose duration is fixed on audiotape. Thus the listening outline can indicate the precise moment at which a sound occurs.

Tape studio (Columbia Records).

Top–RCA Sound Synthesizer (The Electronic Music Center of Columbia and Princeton Universities).

Bottom–Buchla Synthesizer (The Electronic Music Center of Columbia and Princeton Universities).

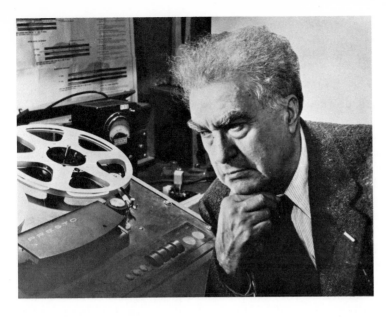

Edgard Varèse, composer of *Poème électronique,* using a tape recorder (The Bettmann Archive).

LISTENING OUTLINE
To be read while music is heard

Poème électronique ("Electronic Poem," 1958), by Edgard Varèse (1883–1965)

Tape studio

(8 min 5 sec)

0 sec	1 *a.*	Low bell-tolls. "Woodblocks." Sirens. Fast taps lead into high piercing sounds. 2-sec pause.
43 sec	*b.*	"Bongo" tones and higher grating noises. Short "squawks." Three-tone group stated three times.
1 min 11 sec	*c.*	Low sustained tones with grating noises. Sirens. Short "squawks." Three-tone group. 2-sec pause.
1 min 40 sec	*d.*	Short "squawks." High "chirps." Variety of "shots," "honks," "machine noises." Sirens. Taps lead to
2 min 36 sec	2 *a.*	Low bell-tolls. Sustained electronic tones. Repeated "bongo" tones. High and sustained electronic tones. Low tone, crescendo. Rhythmic noises lead to
3 min 41 sec	*b.*	Voice, "Oh-gah." 4-sec pause. Voice continues softly.
4 min 17 sec	*c.*	Suddenly loud. Rhythmic percussive sounds joined by voice. Low "animal noises," scraping, shuffling, hollow vocal sounds. Decrescendo into 7-sec pause.
5 min 47 sec	*d.*	Sustained electronic tones, crescendo and decrescendo. Rhythmic percussive sounds. Higher sustained electronic tones, crescendo. "Airplane rumble," "chimes," jangling.
6 min 47 sec	*e.*	Female voice. Male chorus. Electronic noises, organ. High taps. Swooping organ sound. Three-note group stated twice. Rumble, sirens, crescendo (8 min 5 sec).

Originating around 1951, the tape studio became the main tool of the electronic music composer of the 1950s. However, tape splicing and re-recording is a laborious and time-consuming process; as a result, many composers of the 1960s turned to synthesizers, which appeared around 1955.

Synthesizers are systems of electronic components which generate, modify, and control sound. They vary in size and capacity. The vacuum-tube RCA Sound Synthesizer is enormous, occupying an entire wall of the Columbia-Princeton Electronic Music Center in New York City. It remains one of a kind because—as composer Milton Babbitt has observed—"Nobody's going to build these monsters that cost about a quarter of a million dollars each." During the 1960s and 1970s, when transistor technology came into being, smaller, less expensive synthesizers such as the Moog and Buchla were developed and installed in electronic music studios at universities throughout the United States. They also appear in live concerts of electronic music and are used to create scores for movies and television shows. Their use in rock music is well known.

Synthesizers can generate a practically limitless variety of sounds, both musical tones and noises. They can simulate a group of conventional instruments or produce weird sounds that suggest outer space. The composer has complete control over pitch, tone color, loudness, and duration. Unlike the mechanisms of the tape studio, most synthesizers can be "played" by means of a keyboard. Usually, though, only one note can be played at a time. To get two melodies at once, a composer must combine two recordings. Some rock groups, however, use synthesizers with keyboards that can produce several tones at the same time.

Computers are the third and most recently developed means of producing sounds on audiotape. To understand this function of the computer, recall that any sound—musical tone, noise, or speech—is produced by vibrating waves. The characteristics of these waves can be represented by a series of numbers. With a computer program, a composer can feed musical specifications—numbers, words, and letters typed onto punch cards—into a computer. The computer then changes these specifications into a series of numbers that represent the final sounds. Later, these numbers are passed through a converter so that the music may be heard or recorded on audiotape. Of all electronic instruments, the computer gives composers the most precise control of sound. But since a computer does not directly produce sound—only numbers that are converted to sound on additional electronic equipment—a composer at present cannot instantly hear music he or she has programmed.

Performing Media: Basic Terms

If you aren't sure what each of the following words means, look back at the text, where they appear in bold type. Additional information about some of them can be found by checking the index.

Voices
- soprano
- alto
- tenor
- bass

Musical Instruments
- register

String Instruments

violin	guitar
viola	pizzicato
cello	stop (double, triple, quadruple)
double bass	vibrato
bow	mute
harp	tremolo
	harmonics

Woodwind Instruments

piccolo	contrabassoon
flute	saxophone
oboe	recorder
English horn	reed
clarinet	single-reed woodwinds
bass clarinet	double-reed woodwinds
bassoon	

Brass Instruments

trumpet	slides
French horn	valves
trombone	mute
tuba	

Percussion Instruments

timpani (kettledrums)	side drum (snare drum)
glockenspiel	bass drum
vibraphone	tambourine
xylophone	triangle
marimba	cymbals
celesta	gong (tam-tam)
chimes	

Keyboard Instruments

piano	organ
harpsichord	accordion

Electronic Instruments
- tape studio
- synthesizer
- computer

Performing Media:
Basic Terms

33

[3] RHYTHM

Rhythm is basic to life. We see it in the cycle of night and day, the four seasons, the rise and fall of tides. More personally, we feel rhythm as we breathe. We find it in our heartbeats and our walking.

The essence of rhythm is a recurring pattern of tension and release, expectation and fulfillment. This rhythmic alternation seems to pervade the flow of time. Time, as we live it, has fantastic diversity; it seems to speed by when we enjoy ourselves or are very busy, but it may drag when we wait for something or have nothing to do. Each hour has sixty minutes, but how different one may seem from another!

Rhythm forms the lifeblood of music, too; it orders the flow of music through time. Musical time is like lived time in its endless variety. It also seems to pass at varying speeds and intensities. Yet there is an essential difference between music and life. A composer can control the passage of time in music. In life, such order eludes us. We delight in surrendering to a musical time world that is ordered yet somehow related to our feelings and moods. We also enjoy letting the rhythm of music stimulate movement in our bodies.

Just as rhythm pervades our lives, so we find it everywhere in music—in pitch, tone color, and volume. How these elements change in time, and their rate of change, are concerns of **rhythm.** The many interrelated aspects of rhythm can be grasped more easily by considering them one at a time.

Beat

When you clap your hands or tap your foot to music, you are responding to its beat. The **beat** is a regular, recurrent pulsation that divides the music into equal units of time. Beats can be represented by marks on a time-line:

Beats

Time

In music, such beats may occur as often as every quarter second or as seldom as every second and a half. Sometimes the beat is powerful and easy to feel, as in march or rock music. Or it may be barely noticeable, suggesting feelings like floating or aimlessness.

The pulse of music is communicated in different ways. Sometimes the beat is explicitly pounded out, by a bass drum in a marching band, for instance. At other times the beat is sensed rather than actually heard. Sing the beginning of "America" up to the words *Land where my fathers died:*

My	coun- try,	'tis		of	thee,	Sweet land	of		lib-		er-	ty,
Of	thee		sing.			Land (etc.)						

Each of the marks represents a beat. Did you notice that you held *sing* for three beats automatically? You *sensed* the beat because you were aware of it and expected it to continue.

Beats form the background against which the composer places notes of varying lengths. Beats are basic units of time by which all notes are measured. Notes last either a fraction of a beat, an entire beat, or more than a beat. In the excerpt from "America," for example, each of the three syllables, *My coun-try,* lasts a beat; *'tis* lasts one beat and a half; and *of* lasts only a half beat. We already noted that *sing* is held for three beats. So in this song we have notes ranging in length from a half beat to three beats.

When we talk about the combination of different note lengths in "America," we are considering its *rhythm.* Earlier we spoke of rhythm as ordering the flow of music through time. Now we define **rhythm** as the specific arrangement of note lengths in a piece of music. The rhythm of a melody is an essential feature of its personality. Indeed, we might recognize "America" merely by clapping out its rhythm without actually singing the tones. "America"'s *beat* is an even, regular pulsation. But its *rhythm* flows freely, sometimes matching the beat, sometimes not.

Meter

While singing "America," you probably noticed that some beats felt stronger or more stressed than others. The stress comes regularly on the first of every three beats:

My	coun-	try,	'tis		of thee,
beat	beat	beat	**beat**	beat	beat

Therefore we count the beats of "America" as **1-2-3, 1-2-3**:

My	coun-	try,	'tis		of	thee,
1	2	3	**1**	2	3	

Sweet	land	of	lib-		er-	ty,
1	2	3	**1**	2	3	

Of	thee	I	sing.		
1	2	3	**1**	2	3

In much music we find a repeated pattern of a strong beat plus one or more weaker beats. The organization of beats into regular groups is called **meter.** Such a group containing a fixed number of beats is called a **measure.** Based on the number of beats in a measure, there are several types of meter.

When a measure has two beats, it is in **duple meter;** we count 1-2, 1-2, etc.:

Ma- ry	had a	lit- tle	lamb,	lit- tle	lamb,	lit- tle	lamb,
|**1**	2	|**1**	2	|**1**	2	|**1**	2 |

Meter

The vertical lines mark the beginning or end of the measure. The first, or stressed, beat of the measure is known as the **downbeat.**

A pattern of three beats to the measure is known as **triple meter.** As we have seen in "America," we count **1**-2-3, **1**-2-3, etc. All waltzes are in triple meter.

Another basic metrical pattern is **quadruple meter,** which contains four beats to the measure. As usual, the downbeat is strongest; but there is another stress on the third beat, which is stronger than the second and fourth beats, and weaker than the first: **1**-2-*3*-4, **1**-2-*3*-4. In the following example of quadruple meter the first word is on the **upbeat,** an unaccented pulse preceding the downbeat:

Mine	eyes	have	seen	the	glo-	ry	of	the	com-	ing	of	the	Lord;	He	is
1		2		3		4			**1**		2		3	4	

March, jazz, and rock music are usually in quadruple meter. Both duple and quadruple meter reflect the left-right, left-right pattern of walking or marching.

Sextuple meter contains six rather quick pulses to the measure. The downbeat is strongest, and the fourth beat also receives a stress: **1**-2-3-*4*-5-6.

Oh,	give	me	a	home		where the buf-	fa-	lo	roam,		where the
1	2	3	4	5	6	**1**	2	3	4	5	6

Note that the measure is subdivided into two groups of three beats each: 1-2-3/4-5-6. Thus sextuple meter is a combination of duple and triple meter. Melodies in sextuple meter often create a feeling of smooth flow, as in "Silent Night."

Like many elements of music, meter has been used differently throughout the history of music. While strongly emphasized in some periods, it has been less prominent and has even disappeared in others.

Accent and Syncopation

An important aspect of rhythm is the way individual notes are stressed—how they get "special emphasis." A note is emphasized most obviously by being played louder than the notes around it, that is, by receiving a dynamic **accent.** A note is sometimes especially accented when it is held longer or is higher in pitch than those near it. In "The Star-Spangled Banner," *see* is naturally accented by being longer and higher in pitch than *Oh, say can you.* In speech as well, we stress individual words through loudness, length, and pitch.

When an accented note comes where we normally would *not* expect it, the effect is known as **syncopation.** There is a syncopation when an "off-beat" note is accented, when the stress comes *between* two beats. In the following example, syncopation occurs on the accented *my,* which comes between beats 1 and 2:

Elements

36

Give	**my**	re-	gards	to	Broad-		way	
1	2	3	4	|1	2	3	4	|

A syncopation also occurs when a weak beat is accented, as in 1-**2**-3-4 or 1-2-3-**4**. Such contradictions of the meter surprise the listener and create rhythmic excitement. Syncopation is one of the most characteristic features of jazz.

Tempo

We've seen that the speed of the beat may be fast or slow. This speed of the beat is known as **tempo,** the basic pace of the music. A fast tempo is associated with a feeling of energy, drive, and excitement. A slow tempo often contributes to a solemn, lyrical, or calm mood. Such associations are rooted in the way we feel and act. When we're excited our hearts beat more rapidly than when we're calm; we tend to move and speak more quickly.

A **tempo indication** is usually given at the beginning of a piece. As in the case of dynamics, the terms that show tempo are in Italian:

largo	very slow, broad
grave	very slow, solemn
adagio	slow
andante	moderately slow, a walking pace
moderato	moderate
allegretto	moderately fast
allegro	fast
vivace	lively
presto	very fast
prestissimo	as fast as possible

Qualifying words are sometimes added to these indications to make them more specific. The two most commonly used are *molto* ("much") and *non troppo* ("not too much"). We thus get phrases like *allegro molto* ("very fast") and *allegro non troppo* ("not too fast").

As with dynamics, all these terms indicate only approximate tempos; they are relative. A piece marked *andante,* for example, might be played faster by one musician than another. With the markings as a guide, each performer chooses the tempo that seems appropriate for a piece. But there is no one "right" tempo. A piece can sound equally convincing at slightly different speeds.

The same tempo is not always used throughout a piece. A gradual quickening of tempo may be indicated by writing *accelerando* ("becoming faster"), and a gradual slowing-down of tempo by *ritardando* ("becoming slower"). An *accelerando,* especially when combined with a rise in pitch and volume, increases excitement, while a *ritardando* is associated with less tension and a feeling of conclusion.

Tempo

37

Since about 1816, composers have been able to indicate their preferred tempos by means of a **metronome,** an apparatus which produces ticking sounds or flashes of light at any desired musical speed. The metronome setting indicates the exact number of beats per minute. For example, *andante* might be represented by the metronome number 60 and *allegro* by the number 116.

Basic Terms

If you aren't sure what each of the following words means, look back at the text, where they appear in bold type. Additional information about some of them can be found by checking the index.

rhythm	downbeat
beat	upbeat
meter	accent
duple meter	syncopation
triple meter	tempo
quadruple meter	tempo indication
sextuple meter	metronome
measure	

[4] MUSIC NOTATION

We use written words to express our thoughts and communicate with others when we can't be with them. In music, ideas are also written down, or *notated,* so that a performer can play a piece unknown to him or her. **Notation** is a system of writing down music so that specific pitches and rhythms can be communicated. It's the alphabet of musicians.

Notation will be discussed here primarily to help you follow the short music examples from this book that your instructor may play in class. The aim is to help you recognize rising or falling melodic lines and long or short notes. It will be helpful for you to review pitch (section 1) and rhythm (section 3).

Notating Pitch

One way to indicate the general rise and fall of pitch is to "notate" the words of a familiar melody:

```
                                                        tle lamb,
        Ma-         lit- tle lamb,              lit-
          ry      a                   lit- tle lamb,
               had
```

But this is not exact. With music notation we can indicate *exact pitches* by the upward or downward placement of symbols.

Seven of the twelve pitches, or tones, that fill the octave in Western music are named after the first seven letters of the alphabet: A, B, C, D, E, F, G. This sequence of letters is repeated over and over to represent the "same" tones in higher or lower octaves (remember that one octave "duplicates" the tones in another octave). These seven tones correspond to the white keys of the piano keyboard:

The C nearest to the center of the keyboard is called **middle C.** This pitch is close to the middle of the piano's range.

Pitches are notated by the placement of *notes* on a *staff*. A **note** is a black or white oval to which a *stem* and *flags* can be added:[7]

A **staff** is a set of five horizontal lines:

Notes are positioned either on the lines or between them, in the spaces:

The higher a note is placed on the staff, the higher its pitch.

A **clef** is placed at the beginning of the staff to show the exact pitch of each line and space. The **treble clef** is used for relatively high pitch ranges, those played by a pianist's right hand.

[7]Whether a note is black or white or has a stem and flags determines its duration, which is explained under the next heading, "Notating Rhythm." For now, a note is an oval symbol that shows pitch by its position on a staff.

Notating Pitch

39

The **bass clef** is used for relatively low pitch ranges, those played by a pianist's left hand.

If a pitch falls above or below the range indicated by the staff, short horizontal **ledger lines** are used:

Keyboard music calls for a wide range of pitches to be played by both hands. When writing such music, composers use the **grand staff,** a combination of the treble and bass *staves* (plural of staff):

Notes on the grand staff are shown here in relation to their position on the piano keyboard:

To show how notation is applied, here are the pitches of "Mary Had a Little Lamb" as they might appear on the treble clef (the rhythm is not shown):

Ma - ry had a   lit - tle lamb, lit - tle lamb, lit - tle lamb,

and here is how we notate this melody to be sung by women and men at the same time, an octave apart:

Ma - ry had a   lit - tle lamb, lit - tle lamb, lit - tle lamb,

Notes placed exactly underneath one another mean that the pitches are heard at the same time.

So far, only seven tones within the octave have been named, those produced by the white keys of the piano. The other five tones, played on the black keys of the piano, are indicated by one of the same seven letters plus a **sharp sign** (♯) or a **flat sign** (♭). For example, the pitch between C and D may be called either C sharp (C♯)—higher than C—or D flat (D♭)—lower than D. The same is true of the other black keys:

Notating Pitch

41

Here are these additional five tones in music notation.

A **natural sign** (♮) is used in notation to cancel a previous sharp or flat sign (see above).

All twelve tones within the octave have now been shown in music notation.

Notating Rhythm

Music notation does not indicate the absolute duration of tones; instead, it shows how long one tone lasts in relation to others in the same piece. Under the preceding head, we have seen that the position of notes on a staff indicates their exact pitches. Now we will look at the notation system that indicates how long an exact pitch is to last compared with those around it.

A single note on the staff lasts longer or shorter depending on how it looks. It may be simply a white oval; or a white oval with a **stem** (vertical line); or a black oval with a stem; or a black oval with a stem and one or more **flags** (flying from the stem). Like any symbols, notes are easier to look at than to explain. Here are five duration symbols arranged from longest (left) to shortest (right):

Each note lasts half as long as the note to its left, or twice as long as the note to its right. For example, if a quarter note lasts one beat, a half note gets two, and a whole note gets four. In the same way, an eighth note lasts half as long as a quarter note; it gets a half beat. And a sixteenth note gets a quarter beat. This chart shows the relationships of the duration symbols used in notation:

1 whole note

= 2 half notes:

= 4 quarter notes:

= 8 eighth notes:

= 16 sixteenth notes:

From the chart we see that one whole note lasts as long as two half notes, or as long as four quarter notes, and so on. To make it easier to read crowded notation, the flags of several eighth notes or sixteenth notes that follow each other are usually joined by a horizontal **beam,** as the chart shows.

Having looked at the notation of both pitch and duration, we can apply it and get rhythm:

Baa, baa, black sheep, have you an-y wool? Yes sir, yes sir, three bags full.

Notice that the longer notes on *wool* and *full* are half notes; the quicker notes on *have you any* are eighth notes; the other notes are all quarter notes.

To lengthen the duration of a tone (and add rhythmic variety), we can make it a **dotted note.** By adding a dot (.) to the right of a note, we increase its duration by half. Ordinarily a quarter note equals 2 eighth notes: ♩=♫. But a dotted quarter note equals 3 eighth notes: ♩. = ♫♪. In "America," the longer notes on *'tis* and *lib-* are dotted quarter notes:

My coun-try, 'tis of thee, Sweet land of lib - er - ty,

Frequently, a dotted note is followed by one that is much shorter. For example, at the beginning of "The Battle Hymn of the Republic" each dotted eighth note is followed by a sixteenth note (♪. ♪):

Mine eyes have seen the glo - ry of the com - ing of the Lord; He is

Notating Rhythm

43

This long-short pattern is called **dotted rhythm.** Because the short note seems to rush to the next note on a beat, the dotted rhythm strongly emphasizes that beat. (This is why marches often use dotted rhythm.)

Another way to lengthen the duration of a note is by a **tie** (⌢). When two notes in a row are the same pitch and connected by a tie, the first note is lengthened by the duration of the second. In "The Farmer in the Dell," the two notes on *dell* are tied:

The farm - er   in   the dell,   The farm - er   in   the dell,

Thus the tone on *dell* lasts as long as a dotted quarter note plus a quarter note. The two tied notes become one continuous sound.

We can add rhythmic variety to music by shortening the duration of a note, too. We do this with a **triplet:** Three notes of equal duration are notated as a group within a curved line and the number 3 (). Such a three-note group lasts only as long as two notes of equal value usually do.

Silence (Rests)

Remember that silence in music can be as important as sound. We notate the duration of silence by using a symbol called a **rest.** Rests are pauses; their durations correspond to the types of notes we've already looked at:

whole rest	eighth rest
half rest	sixteenth rest
quarter rest	

Meter

To show the meter of a piece, composers use a **time signature.** This is stated as two numbers, one over the other, that appear at the beginning of the staff. (If the meter changes within the piece, two new numbers are given.) Don't confuse these numbers with fractions, though they look alike. In a **time signature** (or **meter signature**), the upper number tells how many beats fall in a measure; the lower number tells what kind of note gets the beat (a 2 = a half note; a 4 = a quarter note). A $\frac{2}{4}$ time signature, for example, shows that there are two beats to the measure (duple meter), and a quarter note gets one beat. Duple meter may also be shown by $\frac{2}{2}$ (or by its symbol, ₵). The most common triple meter is $\frac{3}{4}$. Quadruple meter is usually $\frac{4}{4}$ (or, symbolized, C). Compound meters, which contain groupings of three beats, are indicated by $\frac{6}{8}$, $\frac{9}{8}$, $\frac{12}{8}$. A $\frac{6}{8}$ meter, for instance, is counted 1-2-3-4-5-6, with each eighth note having a beat.

Basic Terms

If you aren't sure what each of the following words means, look back at the text, where they appear in bold type. Additional information about some of them can be found by checking the index.

The Notation of Pitch	*The Notation of Rhythm*
notation	stem
middle C	flag
note	beam
staff	dotted note
clef (treble and bass)	dotted rhythm
ledger lines	tie
grand staff	triplet
sharp sign (♯)	rest
flat sign (♭)	time signature
natural sign (♮)	

MELODY [5]

For a lot of us, music means melody. We've sung in schools, cars, camps, and the shower. After hearing music, we usually remember its melody best. Familiar melodies have the power to recall past emotions and experiences. Words and instruments aren't required, we don't need singers and large orchestras—just a few notes. How can they communicate so much?

Melody is easier to recognize than to define. Yet it must have something special; melody is common to music of all times and all peoples. Probably the elusive "something" that evokes so much feeling will never be trapped for a dictionary. We do know that a **melody** is a series of single tones that add up to a recognizable whole. A melody begins, moves, and ends; it has direction, shape, and continuity. The up and down movement of its pitches conveys tension and release, expectation and arrival. This is the melodic curve, or line.

A melody moves by small intervals called **steps** or by larger ones called **leaps.** A step is the interval between two adjacent tones in the *do-re-mi* scale (from *do* to *re*, *re* to *mi*, etc.). Any interval larger than a step is known as a

Melody

45

leap (*do* to *mi*, for example). A melody's range, or the distance between its lowest and highest tones, may be wide or narrow. "Mary Had a Little Lamb" moves mostly by step within a narrow range; "Rock-a-Bye Baby" has a wider range and lots of leaps as well as steps. Melodies written for instruments tend to have a wider range than those for voices, and they often contain wide leaps and rapid notes that would be difficult to sing.

The specific order of a melody's long and short notes is important. A well-known melody can be almost unrecognizable if it is not sung in proper rhythm. Note durations, as well as pitches, contribute to the distinct character of a melody. For example, the smooth, even rhythm of "Twinkle, Twinkle, Little Star" is calm, while the snappy dotted (long-short) rhythm of the "The Battle Hymn of the Republic" is exciting. Try reversing these rhythms: the first melody will lose its calmness, and the second will lack excitement.

How the tones of a melody are performed can vary its effect, too. Sometimes they are sung or played in a smooth, connected style called **legato.** Or they may be performed in a short, detached manner called **staccato.**

Many melodies are made up of shorter parts called **phrases.** These short units may have similar pitch and rhythm patterns that help unify a melody. On the other hand, contrasting phrases can furnish variety. Phrases often appear in balanced pairs; a first phrase of rising pitches may be followed by a second phrase of falling pitches. The second phrase may partly repeat the first one but have a more conclusive ending, a point of arrival. Such a resting place at the end of a phrase is called a **cadence.**

As you get further into the music explored in this book, you'll find a wealth of melodies: vocal or instrumental, long or short, simple or complex. To help sort them, let's see how some basic melodic principles apply to four familiar tunes. These are short melodies, easy to sing and remember.

"Row, Row, Row Your Boat" is first. Sing the tune only up to the word *stream.*

Row,   row,   row   your boat,   Gent - ly down   the stream.

Mer - ri - ly, mer - ri - ly, mer - ri - ly, mer - ri - ly, Life   is   but   a dream.

Notice that on *stream* the melody comes to a point of arrival, a resting place. This ends the first phrase of the melody. But the melody seems incomplete, as though it posed a question. Now sing the rest of the melody, the second phrase, beginning on *Merrily.* It ends conclusively and seems to answer the question. Each phrase has a point of arrival, a cadence. The first phrase ends with an **incomplete cadence** that sets up expectations; the second phrase ends with a **complete cadence** that gives an answer, a sense of finality.

Each phrase of "Row, Row, Row Your Boat" is the same length, a formula typical of many melodies called tunes. The two phrases create a feeling of symmetry and balance. The first moves upward by step (C-D-E-F-G—"Row, row, row your boat, Gently down the stream"); the second moves downward by leap (C-G-E-C—"Merrily, merrily, merrily, merrily"); and finally by step (G-F-E-D-C—"Life is but a dream"). Often the highest tone of a melody will be the **climax,** or emotional focal point. In this song the climax comes on the first *Merrily* at the beginning of the second phrase. The leaps create a carefree quality in the quick notes on the repeated *merrily.*

The two contrasting phrases of the song can be symbolized by the letters *a* and *b*. In discussing music it's helpful to let letters represent various sections of a piece. Lowercase letters (a, b, etc.) are used for phrases and relatively short sections while capital letters (A, B, etc.) are used for longer sections. When the phrases or sections of the music differ significantly, as in this song, we use different letters: a b. When one section exactly repeats another, the letter is repeated: a a. When a section is a varied repetition of a previous one, the previous letter is repeated but with a prime mark: a a'.

Now sing the entire nursery tune "Mary Had a Little Lamb":

As in "Row, Row, Row Your Boat," this melody has two balancing phrases, the first ending up in the air with an incomplete cadence, and the second ending conclusively with a complete cadence. However, the two songs also differ from each other. In "Mary" the second phrase begins exactly like the first. It starts over again but proceeds to a different, more conclusive ending. This partial repetition serves to unify the melody. "Mary Had a Little Lamb"'s phrases may be symbolized as a a'. We will see that melodic repetition, both exact and varied, plays an important unifying role in all kinds of music.

Both repeated and contrasting phrases can be heard in the cowboy song "Home on the Range":

Melody

b Home, home on the range, where the deer and the an - te - lope play,

a' Where sel - dom is heard a dis - cour - ag - ing word, and the skies are not cloud - y all day.

A yearning quality is projected here through a longer and more complex form than that of the two other tunes. There are four phrases, and, as in "Mary Had a Little Lamb," the second phrase is a repetition of the first but has a more conclusive ending. (Sing the first two phrases a few times, comparing the note on *play* with that on *day*.) The first two phrases may be outlined a a' (varied). Contrast is introduced in the third phrase of the melody, the climactic refrain "Home, home on the range." This phrase begins in a new way—on the highest pitch of the melody—and may be labeled b. The concluding fourth phrase ("Where seldom is heard") is a repetition of the beginning but with a final ending. Thus the song as a whole is outlined a a' b a'. The principle of *statement* (a a'), *departure* or *contrast* (b), and *return* (a') that governs "Home on the Range" is an essential one in the creation of form in music. We'll see it used often.

Our final example, "America," differs from the other songs in that its phrases are not of equal length:

a My coun - try, 'tis of thee, Sweet land of lib - er - ty, Of thee I sing.

b Land where my fa - thers died, Land of the Pil - grims' pride,

From ev - 'ry moun - tain - side, Let free - dom ring.

The second phrase (starting from *Land*) is longer than the first and creates a feeling of continuation rather than one of balance or symmetry. An interesting aspect of "America" is the way a repeated rhythmic pattern is used to unify the melody. The rhythmic pattern for "My country 'tis of thee" is repeated for "Sweet land of liberty," "Land where my fathers died," and "Land of the Pilgrims' pride."

Notice that the melody for "Land of the Pilgrims' pride" is simply a repetition a little lower of the preceding "Land where my fathers died." Such a repetition of a melodic pattern on a higher or lower pitch is called a **sequence.**

This is an impelling device of repetition that gives a melody a strong sense of direction.

We've considered tunes that are complete in themselves. Frequently, a melody will serve as the starting point for a more extended piece of music and, in stretching out, will go through all kinds of changes. This kind of melody is called a **theme.**

The concepts and vocabulary introduced in this chapter can be used to study melodies of any style. Try using them to examine your favorite songs. You may pinpoint parts that you like and, consequently, enjoy the melodies a bit more because you know what makes them tick.

Basic Terms

If you aren't sure what each of the following words means, look back at the text, where they appear in bold type. Additional information about some of them can be found by checking the index.

melody	cadence
step	incomplete cadence
leap	complete cadence
legato	climax
staccato	sequence
phrase	theme

HARMONY [**6**]

When folk singers accompany themselves on a guitar, they add support, depth, and richness to the melody. We call this "harmonizing." Most music in Western culture is such a blend of melody and harmony.

Harmony refers to the way chords are constructed and how they follow each other. A **chord** is a combination of three or more tones sounded at once. Essentially, a chord is a group of simultaneous tones, while a melody is a series of individual tones heard one after another. As a melody unfolds, it provides clues for harmonizing—some of the tones of the melody are usually included in the chords of the accompaniment. But a melody does not always dictate a specific series, or **progression,** of chords. A melody may be harmonized in several musically convincing ways. A musician such as a folk singer will experiment and choose the chords that best fit a melody's mood. Chord progressions will enrich a melody by adding emphasis, surprise, suspense, or finality. In today's popular music, a song writer often composes the melody, while an arranger supplies the accompanying chords. Composers of classical music create both the melody and harmony, often at the same time.

Harmony

Folk singer Joan Baez blends melody and harmony by accompanying herself on the guitar (Suzanne Szasz).

There is a tendency to think that a melody is composed first and that the chords are added later. Actually, it's often the other way around. For centuries repeated chord progressions have given rise to improvised melodies. In jazz, for example, a pianist may play the same basic progression of chords over and over again while a trumpet player invents a continually changing melody to fit the piano's pattern. When several jazz musicians improvise different melodies at once, their music is held together by the organized chordal background—by the harmony.

As different as Bach, Beethoven, jazz, folk, and rock may seem, some of the same chord progressions can be heard in all. While new chords and new progressions continually enter the language of music, the basic chordal vocabulary has remained fairly constant. We'll look now at a few principles of harmony that have proved so useful for so long.

Elements

50

Consonance and Dissonance

Some chords have been considered stable and restful, others unstable and tense. A tone combination that is stable is called a **consonance.** Consonances are the points of arrival, rest, and resolution. (Whoever coined the phrase "living in harmony with others" had consonance in mind.) A tone combination that is unstable is called a **dissonance.** Its tension demands an onward motion to a stable chord. A dissonance has its **resolution** when it moves to a consonance. When this resolution is delayed or accomplished in unexpected ways, a feeling of drama, suspense, or surprise is created. In this way a composer plays with the listener's sense of expectation. Dissonant chords are active and move music forward. Traditionally they have been considered harsh and have colored music that expresses pain, grief, and conflict.

Having defined consonance and dissonance, it's well to warn that they have various degrees. Some consonant chords are more stable than others, just as dissonant ones vary in the levels of their tension. Dissonant chords have been used with increasing freedom over the centuries, so that a chord considered intolerably harsh in one period may seem rather mild in a later one.

The Triad

A great variety of chords have been used in music. Some consist of three different tones, others have four, five, or even more. Depending on their make-up, chords sound simple or complex, calm or tense, bright or dark.

The simplest, most basic chord is the **triad** (pronounced "try-ad"), which consists of three tones. To indicate that a triad's three tones are played at one time, it is notated:

A triad may be made up of alternate tones of the scale, such as the first (*do*), third (*mi*), and fifth (*sol*) tones. The bottom tone is called the root; the others are a third and a fifth above the root. (From *do* to *mi* in the scale is an interval of a third, while from *do* to *sol* is the interval of a fifth.)

A triad built on the first, or tonic note of the scale (*do*) is called the **tonic chord** (*do-mi-sol*); it is the main chord of a piece, the most stable and conclusive. Traditionally, the tonic chord would usually begin a composition and almost always end it.

The triad built on the fifth note of the scale (*sol*) is next in importance to the tonic. It is called the **dominant chord** (*sol-ti-re*). The dominant chord is strongly pulled toward the tonic chord. This attraction has great importance in music. A dominant chord sets up tension that is resolved by the tonic chord. The progression from the dominant to the tonic gives a strong sense of con- clusion, and that's why it is used so often at the end of a phrase, melody, or entire piece. In "America," for example, the next to last syllable is harmonized by a dominant chord, while the last word is harmonized by the tonic chord:

A progression from the dominant chord to the tonic chord is called a **cadence.** The word *cadence* means both the resting point at the end of a melodic phrase (as we said in section 5) and a chord progression that gives a sense of conclusion.

Broken Chords, or Arpeggios

We have described a chord as a group of tones played together, as a block of sound. But the tones of a chord may be presented in other ways, too. When the individual tones of a chord are sounded one after another, it is called a **broken chord,** or **arpeggio.** Arpeggios may appear in the melody or in the accompaniment. "The Star-Spangled Banner" is a melody that begins with such a broken chord, or arpeggio. The notes of the tonic chord are heard one after another instead of together:

As we go on with our study of music in this book, the importance of harmony will become more and more apparent. You'll see that chord progressions can produce powerful emotional effects and be more than simply a background for melody. Sometimes a melody depends on the accompanying harmony for its expressiveness, as in Chopin's *Prelude in E Minor,* discussed below.

Harmony helps give music variety and movement. There's a relaxation of tension when a dissonant chord resolves to a consonant chord, a sense of conclusion when the dominant chord moves to the tonic. The effects of harmony are endless, varying with the style of a particular era and the desires of individual composers.

Elements

52

Prelude in E Minor for Piano, Op. 28, No. 4 (1839), by Frédéric Chopin

Chopin's harmony makes a vital contribution to the brooding quality of this miniature lasting less than two minutes. Without the pulsating chords of its accompaniment, the melody might seem aimless and monotonous. It hardly moves, alternating obsessively between a long note and a shorter one right above it.

But the returning long note seems to change in color because each time there is a different dissonant chord below it. The dissonant chords underscore the melancholy of this Prelude, which is meant to be played *espressivo* ("expressively").

Toward the end of the piece, a mildly dissonant chord is followed by a brief pause. This silence is filled with expectancy, as we wait for the dissonance to resolve. Finally the tension is released in the three solemn chords of the closing cadence.

Basic Terms

If you aren't sure what each of the following words means, look back at the text, where they appear in bold type. Additional information about some of them can be found by checking the index.

harmony	dissonance	dominant chord
chord	resolution	cadence
progression	triad	broken chord (arpeggio)
consonance	tonic chord	

KEY

Practically all familiar melodies are built around a central tone. The other tones of the melody gravitate toward this central one. Since the central tone is especially stable and restful, a melody usually ends on it. To feel the gravitational pull of a central tone, sing "America" and stop after the next-to-last word, *freedom;* then, after a few seconds, sing the ending tone of *ring.*

My coun-try, 'tis of thee, Sweet land of lib - er - ty,

Key

Of thee I sing. Land where my fa - thers died,

Land of the Pil - grims' pride, From ev - 'ry

moun - tain - side, Let free - dom ring.

You probably felt uneasy until you supplied that last tone. This central tone is the **keynote,** or **tonic,** of the melody. When a piece is in the key of C, for example, C is the keynote, or tonic. The keynote can also be E, A, or any of the twelve tones that fill the octave in Western music.

Key involves not only a central tone, but a central scale and chord as well. A piece in the key of C has a basic scale, *do-re-mi-fa-sol-la-ti-do,* with C as its *do,* or tonic. And the basic chord of a piece in C is a tonic triad with C as its root, or bottom tone. As we've seen in section 6, the tonic triad is made up of *do-mi-sol,* or the first, third, and fifth tones of the basic scale. Just as familiar melodies generally end on the keynote, compositions traditionally end with the restful tonic chord. Key, then, refers to the presence of a central note, scale, and chord within a piece. All other tones of a composition are heard in relationship to the central ones. Another term for key is **tonality.** After 1900, some composers abandoned the traditional system, but even today much of the music we hear is built around a central tone, chord, and scale.

The Major Scale

So far, we've referred to the *do-re-mi-fa-sol-la-ti-do* scale as a main element of key, but have not actually defined what a scale is. A **scale** is made up of the basic pitches of a piece of music arranged in order from low to high or from high to low. Many different scales have been used in various eras and cultures. The basic scales of Western music from the late 1600s to 1900 were the *major* and *minor*. And these scales have continued to be widely used during our own century.

Let's first consider the **major scale,** the familiar *do-re-mi-fa-sol-la-ti-do.* Sing this scale and note that you produce seven different pitches and then arrive at the high *do*—the eighth tone—which is really a duplication of the first tone an octave higher. As we've seen in section 1, the octave is the distance or interval between the first and eighth tones of the major scale. The major scale has a specific pattern of intervals between its successive tones. Two kinds of intervals are found in this scale: *half steps* and *whole steps*. The **half step** is the smallest interval traditionally used in Western music. The **whole step** is twice

Elements

54

as large as the half step. Here is the pattern of whole and half steps that makes up the major scale:

| whole | whole | half | whole | whole | whole | half |
| step | step | step | step | step | step | step |

do   re   mi   fa   sol   la   ti   do

There is an especially strong pull from *ti* to *do* because the interval is small, a half step. You'll feel this pull when you sing the scale and stop on *ti*.

Here is a major scale with C as the beginning tone:

The C-major scale uses only the white keys of the piano. There are half steps between E and F, and between B and C; these pairs of tones are not separated by black keys. As notated above, "America" is based on the C-major scale; it is in the key of C major.

We can construct similar major scales by starting on any one of the twelve tones that fill an octave. The same pattern of intervals can begin on any of these tones, so there are twelve possible major scales. To understand this better, imagine the major scale as a ruler on which eight marks are spaced irregularly

The Major Scale

(as shown in the *do-re-mi* diagram on page 55). The pattern of marks stays the same no matter where the "ruler" is placed. Similarly, the pattern of whole and half steps that makes up a major scale sounds the same even when the scales start on different keynotes.

To us the important point is not the technicality of half and whole steps but the idea of a scale as a pattern of intervals. Also important is the idea of the keynote (or beginning, or tonic), of the major scale; it is the scale's central tone toward which all others seem to pull. The conclusive quality we hear in the keynote is not a result of any law of nature—it's rooted in cultural conditioning.

The Minor Scale

Along with the major scale the minor scale is fundamental to Western music. "Joshua Fought the Battle of Jericho" is a tune based upon a minor scale.

Josh-ua fought the bat-tle of Jer-i-cho, Jer-i-cho, Jer-i-cho;

Josh-ua fought the bat-tle of Jer-i-cho, and the walls came tum-bl-ing down.

The **minor scale**—like the major—consists of seven different tones and an eighth tone that duplicates the first an octave higher; but it differs from the major scale in its pattern of intervals. The minor scale's pattern can also begin on any of the twelve tones in an octave, so there are twelve possible minor scales. As notated above, "Joshua Fought the Battle of Jericho" is based upon a minor scale beginning on C; it is in the key of C minor. Here is a comparison between a major and a minor scale both starting on C:[8]

C-major scale	whole step		whole step		half step	whole step		whole step		whole step		half step
	C		D		E	F		G		A		B C

C-minor scale	whole step		half step	whole step		whole step		half step	whole step		whole step	
	C		D	E♭		F		G	A♭		B♭		C

Elements

56

[8] The minor scale shown in this example is the *natural minor*, one of three kinds of minor scales. The other two kinds are the *harmonic minor* and the *melodic minor* scales. The three types of minor scales have slight variations in their patterns of intervals, but all can begin on any tone of the octave, and all will produce a sound that contrasts with the major scale as described above.

The crucial difference between major and minor is that in the minor scale there is only a half step between the second and third tones. A major scale has a whole step here. This small difference greatly changes the sound of a scale and the mood of music using that scale. Music based on minor scales tends to sound serious or melancholy. Almost all funeral marches, for example, are in minor keys. Also, the tonic triad built from a minor scale is a minor chord, while one built from a major scale is a major chord. Minor chords sound darker than major ones. Composers use the differences between minor and major to create contrasts of mood. A serious or agitated melody in C minor may be followed by a brighter tune in C major. We learn to tell the difference between minor and major as we learn to distinguish one color from another, by repeated exposure. In discussing music, we'll frequently point out shifts between minor and major scales.

The Key Signature

When a piece of music is based on a major scale with D as its keynote, we say that the piece is in the key of D major. Similarly, if a composition is based on a minor scale with the keynote F, the composition is in the key of F minor. Each major and minor scale has a specific number of sharps or flats ranging from none to seven. To indicate the key of a piece of music, the composer uses a **key signature,** sharp or flat signs immediately following the clef sign at the beginning of the staff. To illustrate, here is the key signature for D major, which contains two sharps:

By using a key signature a composer avoids the problem of having to write a sharp or a flat sign before every sharped or flatted note in a piece. (The seven sharps in the key of C-sharp major and the seven flats in the key of C-flat major would otherwise make notation very complicated!) Appendix V shows the key signatures for the different major and minor scales.

The Chromatic Scale

The twelve tones of the octave—*all* the white and black keys in one octave on the piano—form the **chromatic scale.** Unlike the major or minor scales, the chromatic scale's tones are all the same distance apart. Each tone is a half step away from the next one:

The Chromatic Scale

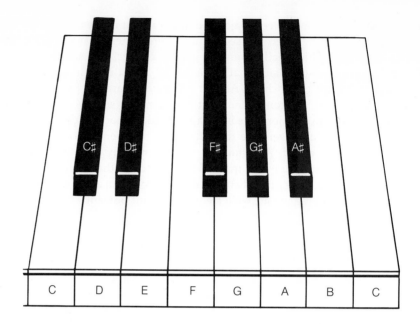

The word *chromatic* comes from the Greek word *chroma*, "color." Its derivation provides a clue to the chromatic scale's traditional function, which is to color or embellish the tones of the major and minor scales. The chromatic scale is not like the major and minor: it does not define a key. Its tones contribute a sense of motion and tension. Composers throughout history have used it to evoke strong feelings of grief, loss, and sorrow. We'll see that in the twentieth century it has become independent of major and minor scales and is used as the basis for entire compositions.

Modulation: Change of Key

Most short melodies we know remain in a single key from beginning to end. However, in longer pieces of music, variety and contrast are created by using more than one key. A composition may begin in the key of C major, for example, and then proceed to G major. A shift from one key to another within the same piece is called a **modulation.** A modulation is like a temporary shift in the center of gravity. When the music starts out in the key of C major, C is the central tone, and the C-major scale and chord predominate. With the modulation to G major, G temporarily becomes the central tone, and the G major scale and chord are now the main ones. By modulating between two such keys, a composer makes the music move and change in time. Though modulations are sometimes subtle and difficult to spot, they produce subconscious effects that increase the listener's enjoyment of the music.

Tonic Key

No matter how often a piece changes key, there usually is one main key, called the **tonic** or **home key.** The tonic key is the central key around which the whole piece is organized. Traditionally, a piece would usually begin in the home key and practically always end in it. A composition in the key of C major, for example, would begin in the home key, modulate to several other keys—say, G major and A minor—and finally conclude in home key of C major. The other keys are subordinate to the tonic.

Modulating away from the tonic key is like visiting: we may enjoy ourselves during the visit, but after a while we're glad to go home. In music, modulations set up tensions that are resolved by returning to the home key. For centuries, the idea of a central key was a basic principle of music. But after 1900, some composers wrote music that ignored the traditional system. The results of this revolutionary step are explored in Part VII, The Twentieth Century.

Basic Terms

If you aren't sure what each of the following words means, look back at the text, where they appear in bold type. Additional information about some of them can be found by checking the index.

keynote (tonic)   minor scale
key (tonality)   key signature
scale   chromatic scale
major scale   modulation
half step   tonic key (home key)
whole step

MUSICAL TEXTURE [**8**]

Elements

At a particular moment within a piece, we may hear one unaccompanied melody, several simultaneous melodies, or a melody with supporting chords. To describe these various possibilities, we use the term **musical texture;** it refers to how many different layers of sound are heard at once, to what kind of layers they are (melody or harmony), and to how they are related to each other. Like fabric, musical texture is described as transparent, dense, thin, thick, heavy, or light. Composers can vary the textures within their music to create contrast and drama. We'll look now at the three basic musical textures—*monophonic, polyphonic,* and *homophonic.*

Monophonic Texture

The texture of a single melodic line without accompaniment is **monophonic,** meaning literally "one sound." If you sing alone, you would make monophonic music. Performance of a single melodic line by more than one instrument or voice is playing or singing in **unison** and results in a fuller, richer-sounding monophonic texture. Examples of unison singing, where men and women sing the same notes in different octaves, appear in the "Hallelujah Chorus" by George Frideric Handel, which is analyzed on pages 62–63.

Polyphonic Texture

Simultaneous performance of two or more melodic lines of relatively equal interest produces the texture called **polyphonic,** meaning "many-sounding." In polyphony several melodic lines compete for attention. (When several jazz musicians improvise different melodies at once, they produce polyphony.) Polyphony adds a dimension that has been compared to perspective in painting: each line enriches and heightens the expression of the other. This mutual enhancement points up a difference between music and speech. If many people are saying different things at one time, the result can be confusing. But when several different melodies are sung together, highly expressive sounds may be created. This technique of combining several melodic lines into a meaningful whole is called **counterpoint.** (The term *contrapuntal texture* is sometimes used in place of polyphonic.)

To fully enjoy the simultaneous flow of several melodic lines you may have to hear a piece of music a few times. Repeated hearings lead to a satisfying awareness of how the whole is woven from its parts. It's often helpful first to listen for the top line, then for the bottom, and then for the middle lines. Such selective listening increases our appreciation of contrasting rhythms and melodic shapes and gives us a chance to hear how different lines are emphasized at any given moment.

Polyphonic music often contains **imitation,** which occurs when a melodic idea is presented by one voice or instrument and then restated immediately by another voice or instrument. It's as though different lines of texture play "follow the leader." Imitation is familiar to anyone who has sung "Row, Row, Row Your Boat."

This familiar tune is a *round*, a song in which several people sing the same melody, but each starts at a different time. By the time the first singer has reached *Merrily, merrily,* etc., the second singer is only at *Gently down the stream,* and the third is just beginning *Row, row, row your boat.* At any one time, all the voices are singing different parts of the same tune.

A round like "Row, Row, Row Your Boat" is an example of strict imitation; the different voices play "follow the leader" with exactly the same melody. But imitation is usually freer—the imitating line begins like the first one but then goes off on its own. A delightful feeling of give-and-take results when a short melodic idea is quickly passed from one voice or instrument to another. This happens often in polyphonic texture.

Homophonic Texture

When we hear *one main melody accompanied by chords,* the texture is **homophonic.** Attention is focused on the melody, which is supported and colored by sounds of subordinate interest. Homophonic texture is familiar to anyone who has heard a folk singer accompany himself or herself on a guitar. Though the accompaniment may be quite distinctive, it is there primarily to help carry the sound and meaning of the melody. "Row, Row, Row Your Boat," when harmonized by chords, is an example of homophonic texture.

Homophonic Texture

Mer - ri - ly, mer - ri - ly, mer - ri - ly, mer - ri - ly, Life   is but   a dream.

A hymn is another example of homophony. The hymn's tune is sung by the voice on top, while other voices have lower lines that harmonize, or blend, with the tune but are less individual. Generally, these lower voices sing notes that are different from the main tune but move in the same rhythm. All the voices moving together produce a progression of chords, one for each syllable of the hymn's text.

Accompaniments in homophonic music vary widely in character and importance. They range from subdued background chords to surging sounds that almost hide the main melody. An expressive quality in the melody can be strengthened by the rhythm or harmony that accompanies it. Sometimes a subordinate line may assert its individuality briefly and compete for the listener's attention. At such times the texture is probably best described as being between homophonic and polyphonic.

Changes of Texture

A composer can create variety and contrast by changing textures within a composition. He or she might begin with a melody and a simple accompaniment and later weave the melody into a polyphonic web. Or the composer might create drama by contrasting a single voice with massive chords sung by a chorus. A good example of textural variety is George Frideric Handel's "Hallelujah Chorus," analyzed here.

"Hallelujah Chorus" from *Messiah* (1741), by George Frideric Handel (1685–1759)

One of the world's famous choral pieces is the "Hallelujah Chorus" from *Messiah* by Handel. In this vigorous chorus Handel offers sweeping variety by sudden changes among monophonic, polyphonic, and homophonic textures. The monophonic texture is very full-sounding as all the voices and instruments perform in unison at the proclamation "for the Lord God Omnipotent reigneth." The texture becomes polyphonic when this majestic proclamation is set against joyful repeated exclamations of *Hallelujah* in quick rhythms. Polyphony gives way to homophony as the chorus sings "The kingdom of this world . . ." to hymnlike music.

Elements

In the "Hallelujah Chorus," words and phrases are repeated over and over, as has been common practice in choral music for several centuries. (In the following text, brackets connect lines which are sung at the same time.) Handel took his text from the Revelation of St. John, which celebrates God as the Almighty and Everlasting Ruler.

	Orchestral introduction
Hallelujah!	Chorus joins, homophonic, quick exclamations
for the Lord God Omnipotent reigneth;	Monophonic, longer notes
Hallelujah!	Homophonic, quick exclamations
for the Lord God Omnipotent reigneth;	Monophonic, longer notes
Hallelujah!	Homophonic, quick exclamations
⸢for the Lord God Omnipotent reigneth; ⸤Hallelujah!	Longer-note melody against quick exclamations, polyphonic
The kingdom of this world is become the Kingdom of our Lord and of His Christ:	Hymnlike in longer notes, homophonic
and He shall reign for ever and ever,	Bass melody, monophonic
	Other voices imitate, polyphonic
⸢King of Kings, and Lord of Lords. ⸤for ever and ever, Hallelujah, Hallelujah!	Long repeated tones against quick exclamations; phrases repeated at higher pitches
and He shall reign for ever and ever,	Polyphonic, imitation
⸢King of Kings, and Lord of Lords, ⸤for ever and ever, Hallelujah, Hallelujah!	Long repeated tones against quick exclamations
and He shall reign for ever and ever,	Polyphonic
King of Kings, and Lord of Lords.	Homophonic
and He shall reign for ever and ever,	Polyphonic
⸢King of Kings, and Lord of Lords, ⸤for ever and ever, for ever and ever, Hallelujah, Hallelujah, Hallelujah, Hallelujah!	Quick exclamations
	Pause
Hallelujah!	Sustained chords, homophonic

Basic Terms

If you aren't sure what each of the following words means, look back at the text, where they appear in bold type. Additional information about some of

Basic Terms

63

them can be found by checking the index.

musical texture   imitation
monophonic texture   homophonic texture
unison
polyphonic texture
counterpoint

MUSICAL FORM

The word *form* is associated with shape, structure, organization, and coherence. Form calls to mind the human body or the balanced arrangement of figures in a painting.

Form in music is the organization of musical ideas in time. Music exists only in time; there its sounds begin, vary, repeat, and end. In this time flow, a composer creates something cohesive out of all the musical elements we've looked at in the previous sections—pitch, tone color, dynamics, rhythm, melody, harmony, and texture. In a logically organized piece of music one thought grows from another, and all the parts are interrelated. Our memories let us perceive the overall form by recalling the various parts and how they relate. As awareness and recall of these parts are developed through repeated listening, the form becomes clearer and takes on an emotional meaning of its own.

Techniques That Create Form

Form has already been discussed in connection with simple tunes like "Mary Had a Little Lamb" and "Home on the Range" (see section 5). These tunes have phrases that are repeated—exactly or with variation—and phrases that are contrasted. *Repetition, contrast,* and *variation* are essential techniques in short tunes as well as in compositions lasting much longer. **Repetition** creates a sense of unity; **contrast** provides variety; and **variation,** in keeping some elements of a musical thought while changing others, gives a work unity and variety at the same time.

Repetition

Musical repetition appeals to the pleasure we get in recognizing and remembering something. In a play, a scene or act is rarely repeated, but in music the repetition of melodies or extended sections is a technique widely used for binding a composition together. Through repetition a melody is engraved in the memory.

The passage of time in music, as in life, influences the way we react to events. When a musical idea returns during a piece, the effect produced is not duplication but balance and symmetry.

Contrast

Forward motion, conflict, and change of mood all come from contrast. Opposition—of loud and soft, strings and woodwinds, fast and slow, major and minor—propels and develops musical ideas. Sometimes a common element will exist between the opposing ideas to establish a sense of continuity. At other times the contrast will be complete. (The contrast between black and white is different from the contrast between black and gray.) The separate identities of such contrasting ideas are heightened by being near each other. A composer can emphasize the power and excitement of a musical idea by contrasting it with one that is calm and lyrical, much as a photographer can show the height of a building by including a human figure in the photograph.

Variation

In the variation of a musical idea, some of its features will be retained while others are changed. For example, the melody might be restated with a different accompaniment. Or the pitches of a melody might stay the same while its rhythmic pattern is changed. A whole composition can be created from a series of variations on a single musical idea.

Types of Musical Form

In discussing form as the organization of musical ideas in time, it was mentioned that a composition is made up of ideas that are interrelated. And we looked at the basic techniques for combining these ideas into a coherent whole—repetition, contrast, and variation are used constantly in music of different styles and times. In section 5 you studied several such patterns. (Remember that lowercase letters represented phrases or relatively short sections, and capital letters represented longer sections.) "Home on the Range," for example, was outlined as a a' b a'. Other songs could be outlined by the same pattern of letters. (Think of "Oh, Susanna" or "Deck the Halls with Boughs of Holly.") These songs are said to have the same form, or to be of the same formal type. It's important to note, however, that two compositions having the same form may be different in every other respect.

Composers have used certain forms or patterns to organize their musical ideas. As listeners, we can respond more fully to music when we appreciate its form. We'll look now at some of the basic types of musical form.

Types of Musical Form

Three-part (Ternary) Form: A B A

During the last few centuries **three-part form, A B A,** has probably been used most frequently. This form can be represented as *statement* (A); *contrast* or departure (B); return (A). When the return of A is varied, the form is outlined A B A'. Wagner's Prelude to Act III of *Lohengrin,* analyzed in section 1, is in A B A' form. In the Prelude, the A and A' sections are very loud, played by full orchestra (items 1 and 3 in the outline), while the B section (item 2 in the outline) is softer, played by fewer instruments. But contrast, we noted above, can be of *any* kind. The A section might be softer than the B, not louder, as in Wagner's Prelude. Or the relative lengths of the three sections might vary; section B might be shorter or longer than A.

The way in which A returns after B also differs from piece to piece. Sometimes, as in the Prelude by Wagner, A returns suddenly; it's unexpected. More often, the return of A is clearly signaled. The B section will come to a definite end with a cadence and pause. The listener is thus alerted for what happens next. Or a transition might smoothly link B with A and lead into the return.

The sections of a composition in A B A form can be subdivided. One possible subdivision might be:

A   B   A
a b a c d c a b a

In this case, each large A section is divided into three subsections, a b a. And the large B section is divided into c d c. Depending on the piece, a listener might mistake the subsection b within the first large A section for the arrival of B. But as the music progresses, the greater contrast one hears with B will make it clear that b is a subsection within A.

Dance of the Reed Pipes from the *Nutcracker Suite* by Peter Ilyich Tchaikovsky

The *Nutcracker Suite* is a set of dances from Tchaikovsky's fairy tale ballet, *The Nutcracker.* The *Dance of the Reed Pipes* is a particularly clear example of A B A' form. Section A features three flutes playing a staccato melody which conveys a light, airy feeling and is repeated several times. The B section contrasts in tone color, melody, and key—it features a trumpet melody accompanied by brasses and cymbals. This melody moves by step within a narrow range, in contrast to the opening flute melody, which has a wide range and lots of leaps as well as steps. The F-sharp minor key of the middle section contrasts with the D major key of the opening section. The concluding A' section, in D major, is a shortened version of the opening A section.

Elements

LISTENING OUTLINE

To be read while music is heard

Dance of the Reed Pipes from the *Nutcracker Suite* (1892), by Peter Ilyich Tchaikovsky (1840–1893)

Three-part (ternary) form: A B A′

Moderato assai (very moderate), duple meter ($\frac{2}{4}$), D major

3 flutes, 2 oboes, English horn, 2 clarinets, bass clarinet, 2 bassoons, 4 horns, 2 trumpets, 3 trombones, tuba, timpani, cymbals, violins 1, violins 2, violas, cellos, double basses

(About 2½ min)

A   1   a. Low pizzicato strings, *p*, introduce
          b. 3 flutes, staccato melody in major, pizzicato strings accompany. Melody repeated.
          c. English horn melody, legato, flutes accompany, staccato.
          d. 3 flutes, staccato melody, pizzicato strings accompany. Melody repeated. Cadence.
B   2   a. Trumpet melody in minor, brasses and cymbals accompany.
          b. Strings repeat trumpet melody. Flutes lead back to
A′   3   3 flutes, staccato melody in major, strings accompany. Melody repeated. Cadence.

Two-part (Binary) Form: A B

A composition subdivided into two large sections is in **two-part form, A B.** Two-part form gives a sense of *statement* (A) and *counterstatement* (B). A composition in A B form might be represented by A A B or A B B or A A B B if either or both of its large sections are immediately repeated. For example, Chopin's Prelude No. 20 in C Minor, analyzed in section 1, is in two-part form and is outlined A B B (items 1, 2, and 3 in the outline). Again, differences between A and B may be of any kind, and the two sections may be equal or unequal in length. Like three-part form, the large sections of two-part form may be divided into subsections. The B section almost always returns to the home key and gives a sense of finality.

Prelude in C Minor from *The Well-Tempered Clavier,* Book 2, by Johann Sebastian Bach

Bach's Prelude in C Minor is in two-part (binary) form. It is outlined A A B B because each part is repeated. Parts A and B are similar in rhythm and texture but differ in key. Both sections feature a continuous rhythmic flow and two-voice texture. The first part begins in C minor and then modulates to E-flat major, while the second part begins in E-flat major and then modulates back to the tonic key of C minor. Section B opens with the same rhythmic pattern as section A but is slightly higher in pitch. Each section is rounded off by a complete cadence.

Types of Musical Form

This short piece was originally written for either harpsichord or clavichord (a stringed keyboard instrument). Today, it is often played on the piano as well.

LISTENING OUTLINE

To be read while music is heard

Prelude in C Minor from *The Well-Tempered Clavier*, Book 2 (1744), by Johann Sebastian Bach (1685–1750)

Two-part (binary) form: A A B B

Quadruple meter ($\frac{4}{4}$)

Harpsichord, clavichord, or piano

(About 2½ min)

A 1 Minor key, continuous rhythmic flow, two-voice texture. Cadence in major key. Section A repeated.

B 2 Major key, beginning higher in pitch than A, continuous rhythmic flow, two-voice texture. Cadence in minor key. Section B repeated.

Theme and Variations

In both two- and three-part form we've noticed two different musical units, A and B. The form called **theme and variations** generally uses only one idea that is repeated over and over and is changed each time. This can be outlined as theme (A)–variation 1 (A')–variation 2 (A'')–variation 3 (A'''), etc.; each prime mark indicates a variation of the basic idea. The Finale of Stravinsky's *Firebird Suite*, analyzed in section 1, is an example of theme and variations. Changes of instruments, dynamics, and rhythm are used to vary the repetitions of a core idea.

The core idea, or theme, may be a melody, a set of chords, or a series of notes in the bass line. Each variation is usually about the same length as the theme. Changes of melody, rhythm, harmony, accompaniment, dynamics, or tone color may be used to give a variation its own identity. The core melody may appear in the bass, or in minor instead of in major. The variations may be separated by pauses or connected to each other. A composer may invent an original theme or borrow someone else's. Beethoven once borrowed a little waltz tune and put it through thirty-three brilliant variations. More modest examples of theme and variations have as few as three variations.

Second Movement from Symphony No. 94 in G Major ("Surprise"), by Joseph Haydn

Elements

The second movement (Andante) of Haydn's "Surprise" Symphony is a theme and variations. The folklike, staccato theme begins softly but is punctuated

68

by a sudden loud chord. This is the "surprise" of the symphony. There are four variations, in which the theme is changed in tone color, dynamics, rhythm, and melody. Sometimes the original melody is accompanied by a new one called a countermelody. Such combinations of two distinctive melodies result in polyphonic texture. In one variation the theme is presented in minor instead of major. The last variation is followed by a closing section in which a gently dissonant accompaniment momentarily darkens the mood of the carefree theme.

The theme is composed of two parts, sections *a* and *b*, which are each repeated. This pattern is usually retained in the variations.

LISTENING OUTLINE

To be read while music is heard

Second Movement from Symphony No. 94 in G major ("Surprise"; 1791), by Joseph Haydn (1732–1809)

Theme and variations

Andante, duple meter ($\frac{2}{4}$), C major

2 flutes, 2 oboes, 2 bassoons, 2 French horns, 2 trumpets, timpani, violins 1, violins 2, violas, cellos, double basses

(About 5½ min)

Theme
    Section *a*   Violins, *p*, staccato theme.

                Section *a* repeated, *pp*, with pizzicato string accompaniment. Surprise chord, *ff*.
    Section *b*   Violins, *p*, continuation of theme.

                Section *b* repeated with flute and oboe.
Variation 1   *a.* Theme begins *f*, higher countermelody in violins, *p*. Section *a* repeated.

b. Violins, *p*, continuation of theme and higher countermelody. Section *b* repeated.

a. Theme in minor, *ff*, violin phrase in major, *p*. Section *a* repeated.

Variation 3

b. Violins, *f*, rapid downward scales, orchestra *f*. Violins alone, *p*, lead into

a. Oboe, *p*, theme in faster repeated notes, major key.

Flute and oboe, *p*, legato countermelody above staccato theme in violins, *p*.

Variation 4

b. Continuation of theme and countermelody. Section *b* repeated.

a. Theme in brasses and woodwinds, *ff*, fast notes in violins, *ff*.

Violins, *p*, legato version of theme, dotted rhythm (long-short).

Closing section

b. Violins, *p*, continuation of theme, dotted rhythm. Full orchestra, *ff*, triumphant continuation of theme leads to suspenseful chord, *ff*, sudden *p*.

Theme in oboe, *p*, gently dissonant chords in strings, flute joins, *pp* conclusion.

Listening for Form

The musical patterns discussed in this section fall into clearly defined units. But music is continuous in its flow, and sometimes can't be subdivided quite so easily. Short pieces often fall into this elusive category. And some music seems to fit none of the patterns we've looked at. Such music is not without form; it has a unique form that the listener can discover through repeated hearings.

Again, it's important to lean on memory when listening to music. Spotting musical ideas when they occur is fine, but it's only the beginning. The goal is to put the related ideas together by recognizing and remembering them. Find their relationships. Through alert, repeated listening their overall shape will be made clear, and your response to music will be more satisfying.

Elements

Basic Terms

If you aren't sure what each of the following words means, look back at the text, where they appear in bold type. Additional information about some of them can be found by checking the index.

form
repetition
contrast
variation

three-part form (A B A)
two-part form (A B)
theme and variations

PERFORMANCE

Elements

[**10**]

Music would remain soundless on a page without a performer. Unlike books and paintings, music speaks to us through a re-creator, a musician who makes the printed music sound. A composition, even a familiar one, can be a fresh experience each time it's performed.

It's the job of the **performer** to bring life to the printed symbols laid out by a composer. Just how loud is a chord marked *f*? How fast is a section labeled *allegro*? No matter how many specific indications of rhythm, dynamics, or accent are on a page, much is left to the performer. Like that of an actor, his or her interpretation is full of subtle timings and inflections. Performers project to an audience a mixture of their own feelings and the composer's intentions. Critics sometimes say about a particularly convincing interpretation that a performer is "identified" with a work and its composer. That's how close their relationship can be.

Music created directly and at the same time it's performed is called **improvisation.** Bach at the organ and Beethoven at the piano were brilliant improvisers; their musical ideas flowed instantly from brain to fingers. Improvisation today is a vital aspect of jazz and non-Western music.

Before the nineteenth century, performers were expected to add certain *ornaments,* or *embellishing notes,* not indicated in the printed music. Such **embellishments** offered variety and a sense of the performer's individuality. The many musicians today who perform music of the seventeenth and eighteenth centuries have made a point of learning these devices from the past. With such knowledge they can play the music as the composer intended it to be played. Music composed before 1600 presents the challenge of deciding what instruments to use. Often these were not specified by early composers, and to make things more difficult, some of the original instruments are not readily available today.

Performance styles change from generation to generation. Some performers today believe in making a work sound as it did when composed; a keyboard artist will play Bach on the harpsichord rather than on the piano. The size of an orchestra or chorus will be reduced to what was available to a church in 1630, or to a castle in 1760. Others believe that we need now to reinterpret a past work in a contemporary spirit. Today's audiences are used to a much wider range of dynamics, and they listen in larger concert halls. These performers choose to use all our modern resources to make the composer's message come alive.

The Performer

Outstanding performers of music, nearly always, have had special talents since childhood—a beautiful voice, unusual manual dexterity, an excellent ear for pitch, or a keen memory. Like athletes, they have exceptional coordination, strength, and competitive drive. Most pianists and violinists play professionally before the age of ten. Singers and woodwind players wait longer for serious training because their bodies need to mature.

Natural gifts are not enough. A developing performer studies for years with fine teachers, practices many hours a day, and cultivates musical taste and a sense of style. Out of all this may come a **virtuoso,** an artist of extraordinary technical mastery. The great solo performers are a breed alone. Above and beyond their natural gifts and training, they project a personal magnetism that can draw cheers from an audience. These rare few are constantly renewed by the challenge of performance and can make their hundredth playing of a work as exciting as the first. Discomforts of constant travel and the drain on their energies are minor matters—they thrive on communication through music.

What happens to the many fine instrumentalists who are not among the "rare few"? They teach, or play in orchestras, or both. Until fairly recently, wages for orchestral musicians were notoriously low. After lengthy and expensive training, instrumentalists were making less than sanitation workers. The musicians formed orchestral committees and improved their lives through collective bargaining. But even with higher pay and increased benefits, players must engage in additional free-lance work. Many feel that they're subsidizing their art, but they're willing to do so. As a member of their audience, one does well to appreciate that performers today—however glamorous they may seem—do not have an easy life.

The Conductor

A leader of musicians, the **conductor** represents responsibility and authority. The conductor's "instruments" are the orchestra, band, and chorus. He or she holds performers together and makes them translate the piece into a meaningful whole. Many, but not all, conductors use a thin stick called a **baton** to beat time and indicate pulse and tempo. With the other hand they control the balance among the instruments or voices so that the most important musical ideas will be brought out. Conducting styles vary greatly among these powerful individuals, but usually a conductor will use the left hand to indicate expression and to cue musicians.

Elements

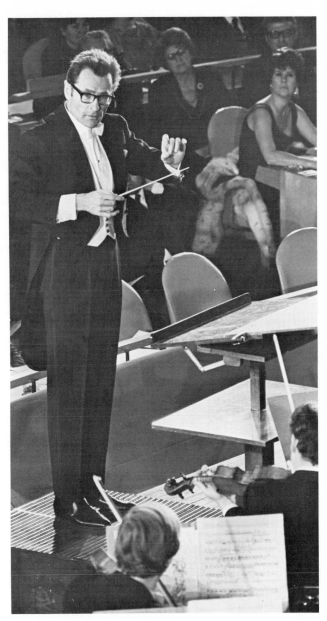

Above–The virtuoso cellist Pablo Casals—an artist of extraordinary technical mastery (Columbia Records).

Right–Stanslaw Skrowaczewski conducting the Minnesota Orchestra (Omikron).

The Conductor

Most of the conductor's work is done in rehearsal, where technical problems and expressive possibilities are worked over to his or her satisfaction. When a hundred instruments or voices sound at once, the conductor must be able to detect mistakes and performers who are out of tune. Conductors read, and "hear" in their minds, an orchestral **score** that may show more than twenty different staves of notation, one for each instrumental or vocal category. Often conductors memorize the score so that they will be free to hold the eyes of the musicians and thus control fine points of interpretation. In performance, different conductors seem flamboyant, reserved, graceful, or angular. But however he or she looks, the conductor is trying to project an overall concept of a musical work.

The experience of most conductors includes mastery of at least one instrument and extended study of orchestration, music theory, and composition. Conductors are, as needed, diplomats, dictators, and teachers; their role traditionally has been thought of as the most glamorous in the music profession. In the early nineteenth century, composers began to write increasingly complex music that demanded more and more musicians. This trend fostered the rise of the virtuoso conductor—one who can hold all the forces together and make interpretive sense of their sounds.

Before the nineteenth century, the time beat was given either by the first violinist or by the keyboard player, or both. From this early custom came a title still used today—*concertmaster*. In a modern symphony orchestra the **concertmaster** is the principal first violinist, who sits on the conductor's immediate left. Solo violin music that occurs in symphonic works is played by the concertmaster. He or she also serves as the conductor's assistant by seeing that the players' music contains special markings and by checking the tuning of the orchestra before the conductor appears.

Recorded and Live Performance

Recorded performance is a sensational innovation of our time. Our homes resound with medieval music, rock, Beethoven, and Indian *ragas.* The living room is a new kind of concert hall where we can hear and repeat what we want. Performances heard on record may never have existed "live," played through from beginning to end. Instead, they are often made up of spliced tape from several performances. It's understandable that performers who have smudged some notes would like them cleaned up by the splicing process. However, too much cleaning of a tape results in a loss of natural vitality, and the long interpretive line can be destroyed.

Through **dubbing,** records have made available new listening experiences not possible in live performance. Beeps, clangs, whistles, never-ending gongs, etc., can be added to music at a composer's electronic whim. Echo chambers and other equipment have given a new dimension to tone.

It's only in the last two hundred years or so that concert-hall listening developed. Before that, music was heard in church or palace, street or home. Much music was intended for amateurs to enjoy around their fireplaces. In church, at dances, or on ceremonial occasions, the listener often was also a performer.

In a live performance artists put themselves on the line; training and magnetism must overcome technical difficulties to involve the listeners' emotions. What is performed, how it sounds, how the artist feels about it that evening—all can never be repeated; they exist for a fleeting moment. An audience responds to the excitement of such a moment, and in responding, feelings are exchanged between stage and hall.

Despite the special electricity of a live performance, there are those who object to coughs and sneezes, the price of tickets, and the fact that seats don't recline in a concert hall. They prefer the living room, where they can choose in comfort from a staggering variety of music and performers on records. In the living room, however, be careful. Recorded music can become background sound. Carried to extremes, this can lessen the ability to concentrate. Total satisfaction from music requires that we focus attention as we would at a live performance.

Although records have wooed some people away from concert halls, it's also true that they have helped to build audiences for live performances. Enthusiasm for a record has filled innumerable seats in concert halls. So even though it's a very individual matter, most alert listeners will try to strike a happy balance between the voltages offered by the concert hall and by the wall socket.

Judging Performance

If you have listened to two music lovers arguing after a concert about the merits of what they had just heard, you know how much heat can be generated. Our response to a musical composition or an artist is subjective to a large extent and is rooted in deep feeling. Even professional critics can differ strongly in their evaluations of a performance. One will be bowled over by how clearly an artist has revealed the structure of a piece, and another will find the performance cold and unrewarding. There is no one "truth" about what we hear and feel.

Is a concept, an overall idea, projected by the performer? Do some sections of a piece communicate something to you, while others do not? Can you figure out why? Subtle effects of phrasing, dynamics, tone color, and tempo become more noticeable after listening to a number of performers. Listen to the same work played by three different musicians—say, pianists. At first, you may like the second pianist best, but by the third hearing you may decide that it was the first pianist who made the most of what the composer tried to say. All three pianists have played the same notes and yet made three different statements. This is what "molding an interpretation" means.

To a large extent, it's up to us as listeners to evaluate the performance of music. We can do that in the most sensitive way by being alert and open-minded. These qualities will enhance our ability to compare performances and judge music so that we can get full enjoyment from it.

Judging Performance

Basic Terms

If you aren't sure what each of the following words means, look back at the text, where they appear in bold type. Additional information about some of them can be found by checking the index.

performer
improvisation
embellishments
virtuoso
conductor

baton
score
concertmaster
dubbing

[11] MUSICAL STYLE

We use the word "style" in reference to everything from clothing to cooking, automobiles to paintings. The term is applied to individual behavior, too, as when we speak of a person's "life-style."

In music, **style** refers to a characteristic way of using melody, rhythm, tone color, dynamics, harmony, texture, and form. The particular way these elements are combined can result in a total sound that's distinctive or unique. When we hear an unfamiliar piece on the radio and identify it as jazz, Italian opera, or as a symphony by Beethoven, we are responding to its style. We speak of the musical style of an individual composer, a group of composers, a country, or a particular period in history. Compositions created in the same geographical area or around the same time are often similar in style. Yet, composers using the same musical vocabulary can create a personal manner of expression just as people dressed in a similar style can have an individual look.

Like most other things, musical styles change from one era in history to the next. These changes are continuous, so any boundary line between one style period and the next can only be an approximation. Though sudden turning points do occur in the history of music, even the most revolutionary new styles are usually foreshadowed in earlier compositions. And few changes of style sweep away the past entirely. Even after a new style has become established, elements of the previous style are usually preserved in the musical language.

The history of Western art music can be subdivided into the following style periods:

Middle Ages (450–1450)
Renaissance (1450–1600)
Baroque (1600–1750)
Classical (1750–1820)
Romantic (1820–1900)
Twentieth Century to 1950
1950 to the Present

In the following chapters, we'll describe the general features of each style period and show how it differs from the preceding one. An awareness of the characteristics of a style helps you to know what to listen for in a composition written in that particular period. And by knowing the common practice of a period, we can better appreciate the innovative or unique features of a particular composition.

Music is not created in a vacuum. To fully understand the style of a composition, one has to be aware of its function in society. Is a piece meant to provide entertainment in a nobleman's castle, a concert hall, or a middle-class home? Is it designed to accompany singing, dancing, religious rites, or drama? Musical style is shaped by political, economic, social, and intellectual developments as well. And often, similar features of style can be found in different arts of the same period.

The history of music is probably as old as the history of mankind itself. There is pictorial evidence of musical activity in Egypt as early as 3000 B.C. We know that music played an important role in the cultures of ancient Israel, Greece, and Rome. But hardly any notated music has survived from these ancient civilizations. The first style period to be considered in this book is the European Middle Ages, from which notated music has come down to us. Through the power of notation, music created over a thousand years ago can come alive today.

MIDDLE AGES

In peacetime, medieval nobility amused themselves with hunting, feasting, and tournaments (Service de Documentation Photographique).

[1] MUSIC IN THE MIDDLE AGES (450–1450)

A thousand years of European history are spanned by the phrase "Middle Ages." Beginning around 450 with the disintegration of the Holy Roman Empire, this era witnessed the "Dark Ages," a time of migrations, upheavals, and wars. But the later Middle Ages (until about 1450) was a period of cultural growth: Romanesque churches and monasteries (1000–1150) and Gothic cathedrals (1150–1450) were constructed, towns grew, and universities were founded.

During the Middle Ages a very sharp division existed among three main social classes: nobility, peasantry, and clergy. Nobles were sheltered within fortified castles surrounded by moats. During wars, these knights in armor engaged in combat, while in peacetime they amused themselves with hunting, feasting, and tournaments. Peasants—the vast majority of the population—lived miserably in one-room huts. Many were serfs, bound to the soil and subject to feudal overlords. All segments of society felt the powerful influence of the Roman Catholic Church. In this age of faith, hell was very real, and heresy was the gravest crime. Monks in monasteries held a virtual monopoly on learning; most people—including the nobility—were illiterate.

Just as the cathedral dominated the medieval landscape and mind, so was it the center of musical life. Most important musicians were priests and worked for the church. An important occupation in thousands of monasteries was liturgical singing. Boys received music education in song schools associated with churches and cathedrals. With this preeminence of the church, it's no surprise that for centuries only sacred music was notated.

Most medieval music was vocal, though a wide variety of instruments served as accompaniment. Few music manuscripts of the time indicate specific instruments, but from paintings and literary descriptions we know they were used. The church frowned upon instruments because of their earlier role in pagan rites.

After about 1100, however, instruments were used increasingly in church. The organ was most prominent. At first, it was a primitive instrument; the keys were operated by heavy blows with the fists. It was so loud that it could be heard for miles around. Gradually it evolved into a flexible instrument that could play intricate polyphonic music. Throughout the period churchmen complained about noisy instruments that distracted the worshipers. "Whence hath the church so many Organs and Musical Instruments?" complained a twelfth-century abbot. "To what purpose, I pray you, is that terrible blowing of Bellows, expressing rather the cracks of thunder than the sweetness of a Voyce? . . . In the meantime, the common people standing by, trembling and astonished, admire the sound of Organs, the noise of the Cymballs and Musical Instruments." In the later Middle Ages instruments were a source of constant struggle between composers, who wanted to create elaborate compositions, and church authorities, who wanted music only as a discreet accompaniment to the religious service.

In the Middle Ages most of the peasantry were serfs, bound to the soil and subject to feudal overlords (Giraudon).

Above—The late Middle Ages brought feverish construction of churches, monasteries, cathedrals, and towns (Austrian National Library).

Right—This well-ordered scene of a fourteenth-century town shows tailors, furriers, a barber, and a druggist (Bulloz: Art Reference Bureau).

Architecture changed during the Middle Ages from the Romanesque style, seen in the eleventh-century nave above, to the Gothic, shown in the Cathedral of Rheims on the right (Lauros—Giraudon).

[2] GREGORIAN CHANT

For over a thousand years, the official music of the Roman Catholic Church has been **Gregorian chant,** a melody sung without accompaniment. (The chant is monophonic in texture.) Based on sacred Latin texts, the melodies of Gregorian chant were meant to enhance parts of religious services. They set the atmosphere for specific prayers and ritual actions. For centuries, composers have based original compositions on chant melodies. (Since the second Vatican Council of 1962–1965, most Roman Catholic services are celebrated in the native language of each country, and today Gregorian chant is not common.)

Gregorian chant conveys a calm, other-worldly quality; it represents the voice of the church, rather than of any single individual. Its rhythm is flexible, without meter, and has little sense of beat. The rhythm of these melodies is uncertain because precise time values were not notated. But the free-flowing rhythm gives Gregorian chant a floating, almost improvisational character. The melodies tend to move by step within a narrow range of pitches. Depending on the nature and importance of the text, they are simple or elaborate; some are little more than recitations on a single tone, while others contain complex melodic curves.

Gregorian chant is named after Pope Gregory I (The Great), who reorganized the Catholic liturgy during his reign from 590 to 604. Although medieval legend credits Pope Gregory with the creation of Gregorian chant, we know that it evolved over many centuries. Some of its practices, such as the singing of psalms, came from the Jewish synagogue of the first centuries A.D. Most of the several thousand melodies known today were created between 600 and 1300.

At first Gregorian melodies were passed along by oral tradition, but as the number of chants grew to the thousands, they were notated to ensure musical uniformity throughout the Western church. The earliest surviving chant manuscripts date from about the ninth century. The composers of Gregorian chant—like the sculptors who decorated early medieval churches—remain almost completely unknown.

The Church Modes

The "other-worldly" sound of Gregorian chant partly results from the unfamiliar scales used. These scales are called the *church modes.* Like major and minor scales, **church modes** consist of seven different tones and an eighth tone that duplicates the first an octave higher. However, their patterns of whole and half steps are different. The church modes were the basic scales of Western music during the Middle Ages and Renaissance and were used in secular music as well as sacred. Much Western folk music follows the patterns of the church modes. For example, the sea shanty "What Shall We Do with the Drunken

Although medieval legend credits Pope Gregory with the creation of Gregorian chant, we know that it evolved over many centuries (Bibliotheque Nationale).

Sailor?" is in a mode called *Dorian,* and the Civil War song "When Johnny Comes Marching Home" is in the *Aeolian* mode.

Alleluia: Dominus dixit (before 700 A.D.)

An elaborate and jubilant Gregorian chant is the Alleluia from the First Mass for Christmas. The word *alleluia* is a Latinized form of the Hebrew *hallelujah* ("praise ye the Lord"). In this chant many notes are sung to single syllables of text. The long series of tones on *ia* is an expression of wordless joy and religious ecstasy. The monophonic texture of the chant is varied by an alternation between a soloist and a choir singing in unison. The chant is in A B A form; the opening Alleluia melody is repeated after a middle section that is set to a psalm verse.

The Church Modes

Solo voice, *Alleluia* phrase. Chorus, *Alleluia* phrase   A
    repeated with long series of tones on *ia.*

Solo voice:[1]   *Domine dixit ad me*   The Lord said to me: B
               Filius meus es tu,   "You are my Son;
               ego hodie genuite.   this day I have begotten you."

Chorus, *Alleluia* phrase with long series of tones on *ia.*   A

Middle Ages

86

[1]In some recordings, the psalm verse is sung by the chorus.

A
Alleluia
[Choir]

Al - le - - -

lu - - ia.

SECULAR SONG IN THE MIDDLE AGES [3]

Despite the domination of Gregorian chant throughout the Middle Ages, there was much music outside the church too. Wandering minstrels (or *jongleurs*—"juggler" comes from this French word) performed music and acrobatic tricks in castles, taverns, and town squares. Without civil rights and on the lowest social level with prostitutes and slaves, only a few were lucky enough to find steady work in the service of the nobility. But they were an important source of information in a time with no newspapers. They usually sang songs written by others and played instrumental dances on harps, fiddles (ancestors of the violin), and lutes (plucked-string instruments).

The first large body of secular songs that survives in decipherable notation was composed during the twelfth and thirteenth centuries by French noblemen called troubadours and *trouvères*. During this age of chivalry, knights gained great reputations as musical poets, as they might have done earlier by fighting bravely. Many of the love songs they sang have been preserved because nobles had clerics write them down. These songs were usually performed by court minstrels, and most of them deal with love; but there are also songs about the Crusades, dance songs, and spinning songs.

Some 1650 troubadour and trouvère melodies have been preserved. The notation does not indicate rhythm, but it's likely that many had a regular meter with a clearly defined beat. They thus differ from the free, nonmetrical rhythm of Gregorian chant.

Secular Song in the Middle Ages

87

Above—Most secular songs in the Middle Ages dealt with love. The illustration shows two plucked-string instruments of the period, a harp and a lute (The Bettmann Archive).

Opposite page—Medieval secular music was performed by wandering minstrels in castles, taverns, and town squares (Bärenreiter–Bild–Archiv).

THE DEVELOPMENT OF POLYPHONY: ORGANUM [**4**]

For centuries Western music was basically monophonic, having a single melodic line. But sometime between 700 and 900, the first steps were taken in a revolution that eventually transformed Western music. Monks in monastery choirs began to add a second melodic line to Gregorian chant. In the beginning, this second line was improvised, not written down; it duplicated the chant melody at a different pitch. The two lines were in parallel motion, note-against-note, at the interval of a fourth or a fifth. (The interval from *do* to *fa* is a fourth; from *do* to *sol* is a fifth.)

Sit glo - ri - a Do - mi - ni in se - cu - la

Medieval music that consists of Gregorian chant and one or more additional lines is called **organum.** Between 900 and 1200 organum became truly polyphonic, and the melody added to the chant became more independent. Instead

The Development of
Polyphony: Organum

89

of moving strictly parallel to the chant, it developed a melodic curve of its own. Sometimes this line was in contrary motion to the chant, moving up as the original melody moved down. The second line became even more independent around 1100, when the chant and the added melody no longer were restricted to a note-against-note style. Now the two lines differed rhythmically as well as melodically. The chant, on the bottom, was sung in very long notes, while the added melody, on top, moved in shorter notes. Medieval listeners must have been startled to hear religious music in which the added melody was more attractive than the chant. At times the chant tones were so slow and dronelike that the original melody was hardly recognizable. Nonetheless, the chant represented the authority of the church. And respect for the church was so great that for centuries most polyphonic music was created by placing new melodic lines against known chants.

The School of Notre Dame: Measured Rhythm

After 1150, Paris—the intellectual and artistic capital of Europe— became the center of polyphonic music. The University of Paris attracted leading scholars, and the Cathedral of Notre Dame (begun in 1163) was the supreme monument of Gothic architecture. Two successive choirmasters of Notre Dame, Leonin and Perotin, are the first notable composers known by name. They and their followers are referred to as the "School of Notre Dame."

From about 1170 to 1200, Notre Dame composers developed rhythmic innovations. Earlier polyphonic music was probably performed in the free, unmeasured rhythms of Gregorian chant. But the music of Leonin and Perotin used *measured rhythm,* with definite time values and a clearly defined meter. For the first time in music history, notation indicated precise rhythms as well as pitches. At first the new notation was limited to only certain rhythmic patterns, and the beat had to be subdivided into threes, the symbol of the Trinity. Despite these limitations, much fine polyphonic music was composed during the late twelfth and thirteenth centuries.

Modern listeners sometimes find medieval polyphony hollow and thin, probably because it has relatively few triads, which in later periods became the basic consonant chords. The triad contains two intervals of a third; medieval music theorists considered this interval a dissonance. (An interval of a third separates *do* and *mi*, and *mi* and *sol*.) But as the Middle Ages advanced, triads and thirds were used more often, and polyphonic music gradually became fuller and richer by our standards. As an example of Notre Dame polyphony, we'll listen to *Alleluya Nativitas,* an organum in three voices by Perotin (late twelfth century–early thirteenth century).

Alleluya Nativitas (1200?), by Perotin

Middle Ages

Perotin was the first known composer to write polyphonic music with more than two voices. *Alleluya Nativitas* is based on a Gregorian alleluia melody which Perotin placed in the lowest voice.

A chant that is used as the basis for polyphony is known as a **cantus firmus** ("fixed melody"). Above the *cantus firmus,* or preexisting melody, Perotin wrote two additional lines that move much more quickly. As many as sixty-six tones of the upper voices are sung against one long sustained tone of the chant. But only three chant tones—the first, second, and last—are treated in this dronelike way. In the middle of the piece, the chant tones are speeded up so that only about three tones are sung above each chant tone. (This speeding up was a practical necessity, since a chant sung entirely in long notes seems endless, and church services were already long enough!)

The top voices of *Alleluya Nativitas* have a clearly defined meter, which we would notate today as a fast $\frac{6}{8}$ (1-2-3-4-5-6). They relentlessly repeat rhythmic patterns: long-short-long, long-short-long. The rhythmic contrast between bottom and top voices is typical of medieval polyphony. The narrow range of the three voices is also characteristic; they are never more than an octave apart. When sung together, the tones of the different parts produce chords that have a hollow ring. As the three voices of *Alleluya Nativitas* resounded under the vaulted ceilings of Notre Dame, they must have seemed like a cathedral of tones.

FOURTEENTH-CENTURY MUSIC: THE "NEW ART" IN FRANCE AND ITALY [5]

The fourteenth century, an age of disintegration, suffered through the Hundred Years' War (1337–1453) and the Black Death—a bubonic plague that destroyed one-fourth of Europe's population around 1350. Both the feudal system and the authority of the church had been weakened by this time. From 1378 to 1417, two rival popes claimed authority, and at one time there were three. Even devout Christians were confused. Literature of the time, such as Chaucer's *Canterbury Tales* (1387–1400) and Boccaccio's *Decameron* (after 1348), stressed graphic realism and earthy sensuality, rather than virtue and heavenly reward.

Given this atmosphere, it's not surprising that secular music became more important than sacred in the fourteenth century. Composers wrote polyphonic music that was *not* based upon Gregorian chants, including drinking songs and pieces in which bird calls, dog barks, and hunting shouts are imitated.

Fourteenth-century Music: The "New Art" in France and Italy

By the early fourteenth century, a new system of music notation had evolved, and a composer could specify almost any rhythmic pattern. Now beats could be subdivided into two as well as three. Syncopation—rarely used earlier—became an important rhythmic practice. Changes in musical style in the fourteenth century were so profound that music theorists referred to French and Italian music as the "new art" (*ars nova* in Latin). As examples of fourteenth-century music we'll study an Italian song about hunting, and a love song and Mass by the leading French composer of the time.

Tosto che ll'alba ("As soon as the dawn"; Fourteenth Century), by Gherardello da Firenze

Tosto che ll'alba by Gherardello da Firenze (?–1363?) is a musical depiction of a deer hunt, an aristocratic pastime in fourteenth-century Italy. The text describes the hunter awakening, the calling out of the dogs, and the pursuit and capture of the deer. The music consists of a supporting part—probably for an instrument—and two lively vocal lines which sometimes suggest shouts and hunting-horn fanfares. The two voices are in strict imitation throughout as they play "follow the leader" with exactly the same melody. A composition like *Tosto che ll'alba* is appropriately called a *caccia*, which is Italian for "hunt" or "chase." We must emphasize that apart from the *caccia* (and its French counterpart, the *chace*), imitation was only rarely used in fourteenth-century music. In this piece, the imitation may be a bit difficult to spot on first hearing because it takes a while for the second voice to join the first. It's helpful to listen for exclamations like "Aiò! Aiò!" and for the vocal "horn calls" toward the end of the piece.

Tosto che ll'alba del bel giorno appare	As soon as the dawn of a fine day appears
Isveglia (gl)i cacciator.—Su, ch'egli è tempo!—	It wakens the hunters. "Get up! It is time!"
—Alletta (gl)i can!—Tè, Viola! tè, Primera!—	"Rouse the dogs!" "Up, Viola! Up, Primera!"
—Sus' alto al monte co' buon cani a mano	"Up to the mountain now, with the good dogs on their leashes,
E gli bracheti al piano,	And the hounds down on the plain,
Et nella piaggia ad ordine ciascuno!—	And on the side of the mountain every one in his place, in good order!"
—I' vegio sentir uno	"I see that one
De' nostri miglior brachi.—	Of our best hounds
—Star' avisato.—	Is on the alert.
—Bussate d'ogni lato	Watch out!
Ciascun le machie, che Quaglina suona!—	Beat the bushes on every side; The Horn is sounding!

—Aiò, aiò! a tte la cerbia vene!	Hey, hey! The deer is coming your way!
Carbon l'à pres' e in bocca la tene!—	Carbon has caught it in his mouth and is holding it!"
Del monte que' che v' era su gridava:	The man who was up on the mountain called out:
—All' altra! all' altra!—e suo corno sonava.	"Now to the other deer!" And he blew his horn.

Guillaume de Machaut

The leading composer of fourteenth-century France was Guillaume de Machaut (about 1300–1377), famous as both musician and poet. Born in the French province of Champagne, he studied theology and took holy orders. Though a priest, Machaut spent most of his life as a court official for various royal families. In 1323, he became secretary to John, King of Bohemia, whom he accompanied on trips and military campaigns throughout Europe. After the king died in battle, Machaut served the royal family of France. And in later years he lived mainly in Reims as an important church official.

Machaut traveled to many courts and presented beautifully decorated copies of his music to noble patrons. These copies make Machaut the first great composer whose works have survived. The decline of the church in the fourteenth century is reflected by Machaut's output, which consists mainly of love songs for one or two voices and instrumental accompaniment. We'll consider, first, one of his secular songs and then the Notre Dame Mass, the best-known composition of the fourteenth century.

Je puis trop bien ("I Can All Too Well"; Fourteenth Century)

Machaut wrote both the music and the poetry for this courtly love song about a hard-hearted beauty. A tender vocal melody stands out above two instrumental parts that move in longer time values. The long, subtly balanced vocal phrases sometimes contain many tones sung on one syllable. Typically, the accompanying instruments are not specified.

Je puis trop bien is a **ballade,** a French poetic and musical form that was introduced by the troubadours. It may be outlined A A' B. The intimate, almost sentimental mood of the music recreates the vanished world of chivalry.

Je puis trop bien ma dame comparer	I can all too well compare my lady	A
A l'ymage que fist Pymalion.	To the image which Pygmalion made.	
D'yvoire fu, tant belle et si sans per	It was of ivory, so beautiful, without peer,	A'

Guillaume de Machaut

93

Que plus l'ama que Medee Jazon.	That he loved it more than Jason did Medea.
Li folz toudis la prioit,	Out of his senses, he prayed to B it unceasingly,
Mais l'ymage riens ne li respondoit.	But the image answered him not.
Einssi me fait celle qui mon cuer font,	Thus does she treat me who makes my heart melt,
Qu'ades la pri et riens ne me respont.	For I pray her ever, and she answers me not.

The Notre Dame Mass (Mid-fourteenth Century)

One of the finest compositions known from the Middle Ages, Machaut's Notre Dame Mass is of great historical importance: It is the first polyphonic treatment of the Mass Ordinary by a known composer.

The **Mass Ordinary** consists of texts that remain the same from day to day throughout most of the church year. The five sung prayers of the Ordinary are the Kyrie, Gloria, Credo, Sanctus, and Agnus Dei. Starting in the fourteenth century, these five texts have often been set to polyphonic music and have inspired some of the greatest choral works. In each age, composers have responded to the Mass in their own particular style. This thousand-year tradition of the Mass gives invaluable insight into the long span of music and its changing styles.

The Notre Dame Mass is written for four voices, some of which were probably performed by instruments. How Machaut wanted his Mass performed and which instruments were used to support the voices are unknown. We also do not know when or why the Mass was composed. Scholars once thought it was written for the coronation of Charles V in 1364; it is now believed to have been composed for the building of Notre Dame at Reims, France, sometime after 1337. We'll examine the Kyrie of the Mass as an example of fourteenth-century polyphony.

Machaut's music for the Kyrie—a prayer for mercy—is solemn and elaborate. Complex rhythmic patterns contribute to the Kyrie's intensity. The two upper parts are rhythmically active and contain syncopation, a characteristic of fourteenth-century music. The two lower parts move in longer notes and play a supporting role. Machaut divides the beat into two or four notes rather than three (as was the rule during the earlier Middle Ages).

The harmonies of the Kyrie include stark dissonances, hollow-sounding chords, and full triads. The Kyrie sounds fuller than Perotin's *Alleluya Nativitas*, which we studied as an example of earlier medieval polyphony. Here there are four parts rather than three, and the total range of pitch is wider.

The Kyrie is based on a Gregorian chant which Machaut furnished with new rhythmic patterns and placed in the tenor, one of the two lower parts. Since it is rhythmically altered and within a polyphonic web, the chant *cantus firmus* is more a musical framework than a tune to be recognized.

Like the chant melody on which it is based, the Kyrie is composed of three sections which are divided into three subsections:

Kyrie	Christe	Kyrie
A	B	C
a a a	b b b	c c c′

This division into three is thought to symbolize the Trinity. In Machaut's time, music was meant to appeal as much to the mind as to the ear.

Kyrie eleison. (three times)	Lord, have mercy upon us.
Christe eleison. (three times)	Christ, have mercy upon us.
Kyrie eleison. (three times)	Lord, have mercy upon us.

Basic Terms

If you aren't sure what each of the following words means, look back at the text, where they appear in bold type. Additional information about some of them can be found by checking the index.

Gregorian chant	cantus firmus
church modes	ballade
organum	Mass Ordinary

THE RENAISSANCE

Ioan. Stradanus invent. Phls Galle excud.

The development of music printing during the Renaissance helped spread secular music, and thousands of song collections became available (The Metropolitan Museum of Art, Harris Brisbane Dick Fund, 1953).

[1] MUSIC IN THE RENAISSANCE (1450–1600)

The fifteenth and sixteenth centuries in Europe have come to be known as the Renaissance. People then spoke of a "rebirth," or "renaissance," of human creativity. It was a period of exploration and adventure—consider the voyages of Christopher Columbus (1492), Vasco da Gama (1498), and Ferdinand Magellan (1519–1522). The Renaissance was an age of curiosity and individualism, too, as can be seen in the remarkable life of Leonardo da Vinci (1452–1519), great painter, sculptor, architect, engineer, scientist, and a fine musician as well.

During the Renaissance the dominant intellectual movement, called *humanism,* focused on human life and its accomplishments rather than on an afterlife in heaven or hell. Though devout Christians, the humanists were captivated by the pagan cultures of ancient Greece and Rome. They became intoxicated by the beauty of ancient languages—Greek and Latin—and by the literature of antiquity. Humanism strongly influenced art throughout the Renaissance. Sculptors and painters once again depicted the nude human body, a favorite theme of antiquity, but a subject of shame and concealment during the Middle Ages. They no longer treated the Madonna as a childlike, unearthly creature; they showed her as a beautiful young woman.

The Catholic Church was far less powerful in the Renaissance than during the Middle Ages, for the unity of Christendom was exploded by the Protestant Reformation led by Martin Luther (1483–1546). No longer did the Church monopolize learning. Aristocrats and the upper middle class now considered education a status symbol, and they hired scholars to teach their children. The invention of printing with movable type (around 1450) accelerated the spread of learning. Before 1450, books were rare and extremely expensive, because they were copied entirely by hand. But by 1500, 15 to 20 million copies of 40,000 editions had been printed in Europe.

Music and Renaissance Society

The Renaissance in music occurred between 1450 and 1600. (Some historians place the beginning of the Renaissance as early as 1400.) As with the other arts, musical horizons were expanded greatly. The invention of printing widened the circulation of music, too, and the number of composers and performers increased.

In keeping with the Renaissance ideal of the "universal man," every educated person was expected to be trained in music. "I am not pleased with the courtier if he be not also a musician," Castiglione wrote in *The Book of the Courtier* (1528).

Renaissance sculptors and painters once
again depicted the nude human body, a
subject of shame and concealment during the
Middle Ages: Left–Michelangelo's *David* and
below–*The Birth of Venus* by Botticelli
(Omikron; Alinari-Scala).

The Madonna was no longer treated as a childlike, unearthly creature; Leonardo da Vinci painted her as a beautiful young woman in *Virgin on the Rocks* (Giraudon).

Shakespeare's stage directions call for music over three hundred times, and the plays are full of beautiful tributes to the art:

> The man that hath no music in himself,
> Nor is not mov'd with concord of sweet sounds,
> Is fit for treasons, stratagems and spoils.

The Merchant of Venice

As in the past, musicians worked in churches, courts, and towns. Church choirs grew in size. (The Papal Choir in Rome increased from ten singers in 1442 to twenty-four in 1483.) Although polyphonic church music in the Middle Ages was usually sung by several soloists, during the Renaissance it was performed by an entire (male) choir. The church remained an important patron of music, but musical activity gradually shifted to the courts. Kings, princes, and dukes competed for the finest composers. The number of court musicians ranged from ten to sixty and included singers as well as instrumentalists. A court music director composed secular pieces to entertain the nobility and sacred works for the court chapel. Noblemen often brought along their musicians when traveling from one castle to another.

The Renaissance

100

Renaissance town musicians played for civic processions, weddings, and religious services. They inherited the work of medieval minstrels, who finally had won respectability. In general, Renaissance musicians enjoyed higher status and pay than ever before. Composers no longer were happy to remain unknown; like other artists, they sought credit for their work.

Many leading Renaissance composers came from the Netherlands, an area which now includes parts of Holland, Belgium, and northern France. These Flemish composers were regarded highly and held important positions throughout Europe, but especially in Italy, which became the leading music center. Other countries with vibrant musical lives in the Renaissance were Germany, England, and Spain.

Words and Music

In the Renaissance, as in the Middle Ages, vocal music was more important than instrumental music. The humanistic interest in language influenced vocal music, creating a close relationship between words and music. A Renaissance composer wrote music to enhance the meaning and emotion of the text. "When one of the words expresses weeping, pain, heartbreak, sighs, tears and other similar things, let the harmony be full of sadness," wrote Zarlino, a leading music theorist of the sixteenth century. By contrast, medieval composers had been relatively uninterested in expressing the emotions of a text.

Renaissance composers often used **word-painting,** a musical representation of specific poetic images. For example, the words *descending from heaven* might be set to a descending melodic line, and *running* might be heard with a series of rapid notes. Yet, despite this emphasis on capturing the emotion and imagery of a text, Renaissance music may seem calm and restrained to us. While there *is* a wide range of emotion in Renaissance music, it usually is expressed in a moderate, balanced way. Extreme contrasts of dynamics, tone color, and rhythm do not characterize the style.

Renaissance Texture

The texture of Renaissance music is chiefly polyphonic. A typical choral piece has four, five, or six voice parts of nearly equal melodic interest. Imitation among the voices is common: each presents the same melodic idea in turn, as in a round. Homophonic texture, with successions of chords, is also used, especially in light music, like dances. The texture may vary within a piece to provide contrast and bring out aspects of the text as it develops.

Renaissance music sounds more full than medieval music. The bass register is used for the first time, expanding the pitch range to more than four octaves. With this new emphasis on the bass line came richer harmony. Composers began to think in terms of chords as well as of individual melodic lines. Now all the melodic lines were conceived at the same time. Earlier, during the Middle Ages, a complete melodic line was conceived, then another was added on top of it, with relatively little attention paid to the total harmonic effect. Renaissance

Renaissance Texture

101

music sounds mild and relaxed because stable, consonant chords are favored; triads occur often, while dissonances are played down.

Renaissance choral music did not need instrumental accompaniment. For this reason, the period is sometimes called the "golden age" of *a cappella*, unaccompanied choral music. Even so, instruments were often combined with voices. They might duplicate the vocal lines to reinforce the sound, or they might take the part of a missing singer. But parts written exclusively for instruments are rarely found in Renaissance choral music.

Renaissance Rhythm and Melody

In Renaissance music, rhythm is more a gentle flow than a sharply defined beat. This is because each melodic line has great rhythmic independence: when one singer is at the beginning of his melodic phrase, the others may already be in the middle of theirs. This technique makes singing Renaissance music both a pleasure and a challenge, for each singer must maintain an individual rhythm. But pitch patterns in Renaissance melodies are easy to sing. The melody usually moves along a scale with few large leaps.

Renaissance

[2] SACRED MUSIC IN THE RENAISSANCE

Two main forms of sacred Renaissance music are the *motet* and the *Mass*. They are alike in style, but the Mass is a longer composition. The Renaissance **motet** is a polyphonic choral work set to a sacred Latin text. The Renaissance **Mass** is a polyphonic choral composition made up of five sections: Kyrie, Gloria, Credo, Sanctus, and Agnus Dei.

Josquin des Prez and the Renaissance Motet

Josquin des Prez (about 1440–1521), a contemporary of Leonardo da Vinci and Christopher Columbus, was a master of Renaissance music. Like many Flemish composers, his career was international. Born in the province of Hainaut—today part of Belgium—Josquin spent much of his life in Italy, serving in dukes' private chapels and in the Papal Choir at Rome. In later years, he worked for Louis XII of France and held several church posts in his native land.

Josquin's compositions, which include Masses, motets, and secular vocal pieces, strongly influenced composers and were praised enthusiastically by music lovers. Martin Luther, for example, remarked: "God has His Gospel preached also through the medium of music; this may be seen from the compositions of Josquin, all of whose works are cheerful, gentle, mild, and lovely; they flow and move along and are neither forced nor coerced and bound by rigid and stringent rules, but, on the contrary, are like the song of the finch."

Ave Maria . . . virgo serena ("Hail, Mary"; 1502)[1]

Josquin's four-voice motet *Ave Maria* is an outstanding Renaissance choral work. This Latin prayer to the Virgin is set to delicate and serene music. The opening uses polyphonic imitation, a technique typical of the period.

The short melodic phrase on *Ave Maria* is presented by the soprano voice and then imitated in turn by the alto, tenor, and bass. The next two words, *gratia plena* ("full of grace"), have a different melody which also is passed from voice to voice. Notice that each voice enters while the preceding one is in the middle of its melody. This overlapping creates a feeling of continuous flow. Josquin adapted the melody for the opening phrases from a Gregorian chant, but the rest of the motet was not based on a chant melody.

[1] Because Josquin composed other works entitled *Ave Maria*, this motet is identified by the words *virgo serena*, which come later in the text.

Josquin des Prez and the Renaissance Motet

Josquin skillfully varies the texture of this motet; two, three, or four voices are heard at one time. In addition to the imitation among individual voices, there is imitation between pairs of voices: duets between the high voices are imitated by the two lower parts. Sometimes the texture almost becomes homophonic, as at the words *Ave, vera virginitas*. Here, also, is a change from duple to triple meter, and the tempo momentarily becomes more animated. But soon the music returns to duple meter and a more peaceful mood. *Ave Maria* ends with slow chords that express Josquin's personal plea to the Virgin, "O Mother of God, remember me. Amen."

Ave Maria	Hail Mary,	Each soprano phrase imitated in turn by alto, tenor, and bass.
gratia plena	full of grace,	
dominus tecum,	the Lord is with thee,	
virgo serena.	serene Virgin.	Duple meter.
Ave, cuius conceptio,	Hail, whose conception,	High duet imitated by three lower voices.
solemni plena gaudio,	full of great jubilation,	All four voices. Increased rhythmic animation reflects "new joy."
coelestia terrestria	fills Heaven and Earth	
nova replet laetitia.	with new joy.	
Ave, cuius nativitas	Hail, whose birth	High duet imitated by low duet.
nostra fuit solemnitas,	brought us joy,	
ut lucifer lux oriens	as Lucifer, the morning star,	Soprano phrase imitated by alto, tenor, and bass.
verum solem praeveniens.	went before the true sun.	
Ave, pia humilitas,	Hail, pious humility,	High duet imitated by low duet.
sine viro fecunditas,	fruitful without a man,	
cuius annuntiatio	whose Annunciation	High duet.
nostra fuit salvatio.	brought us salvation.	Low duet.
Ave, vera virginitas,	Hail, true virginity,	Triple meter.
immaculata castitas,	immaculate chastity,	
cuius purificatio	whose purification	
nostra fuit purgatio.	brought our cleansing.	
Ave, praeclara omnibus	Hail, glorious one	Duple meter, high duets imitated by lower voices.
angelicis virtutibus,	in all angelic virtues,	
cuius assumptio	whose Assumption	
nostra glorificatio.	was our glorification.	Brief pause.
O mater Dei,	O Mother of God,	Sustained chords.
memento mei. Amen.	remember me. Amen.	

Palestrina and the Renaissance Mass

During the sixteenth century, Italian composers attained the earlier excellence of such Flemish musicians as Josquin des Prez. Among the leading Italian Renaissance composers was Giovanni Pierluigi da Palestrina (about 1525–1594), who devoted himself to music for the Catholic Church. His career thus centered in Rome, where he held important Church positions, including music director for St. Peter's.

Palestrina's music includes 102 Masses and some 450 other sacred works; it is best understood against the background of the Counter-Reformation. During the early 1500s, the Catholic Church was challenged and questioned by the Protestants and, as a result, sought to correct abuses and malpractices within its structure, as well as to counter the move toward Protestantism. This need to strengthen the Church led to the founding of the Jesuit Order (1540) and the convening of the Council of Trent (1545–1563), which considered questions of dogma and organization.

During its deliberations the Council discussed Church music, which many felt had lost its purity. Years before this Council, the great scholar Desiderius Erasmus (about 1466–1536) had complained: "We have introduced an artificial and theatrical music into the church, a bawling and agitation of various voices, such as I believe had never been heard in the theaters of the Greeks and Romans. . . . Amorous and lascivious melodies are heard such as elsewhere accompany only the dances of courtesans and clowns." At the Council sessions, Church music was attacked because it used secular tunes, noisy instruments, and theatrical singing. Some complained that complicated polyphony made it impossible to understand the sacred texts; they wanted only monophonic music—Gregorian chant—for the Mass. The Council finally decreed that Church music should be composed not "to give empty pleasure to the ear," but to inspire religious contemplation.

The restraint and serenity of Palestrina's works reflect this emphasis on a more spiritual music. For centuries, Church authorities have regarded his Masses as models of church music because of their calmness and "other-wordly" quality. And even today the technical perfection of his style is a model for students of counterpoint.

Pope Marcellus Mass (1562–1563)

For a long time, the Pope Marcellus Mass was thought to have convinced the Council of Trent that polyphonic Masses should be kept in Catholic worship. While we now know that Palestrina's most famous Mass did *not* play this role, it does reflect the Council's desire for a clear projection of the sacred text. The Mass is dedicated to Pope Marcellus II, who briefly reigned in 1555 while Palestrina was a singer in the Papal Choir.

The Pope Marcellus Mass is written for an *a cappella,* or unaccompanied, choir of six voice parts: soprano, alto, two tenors, and two basses. We'll focus on the first two sections of the Mass, the Kyrie and the Gloria; the Credo, Sanctus, and Agnus Dei, which follow, are similar in style.

The Kyrie has a rich polyphonic texture. Its six voice parts constantly imitate each other, yet blend beautifully. This music sounds fuller than Josquin's *Ave Maria,* in part because six voices are used rather than four. Palestrina's elegantly curved melodies summon the spirit of Gregorian chant. They flow smoothly and can be sung easily. Upward leaps are balanced at once by downward steps, as in the opening melody:

Palestrina and the Renaissance Mass

The Kyrie of the Pope Marcellus Mass is written in three sections:

1. *Kyrie eleison.*   Lord, have mercy upon us.
2. *Christe eleison.*   Christ, have mercy upon us.
3. *Kyrie eleison.*   Lord, have mercy upon us.

This text is short, and words are repeated with different melodic lines to express calm supplication. The rhythm flows continuously to the end of each section, when all voices come together on sustained chords. Each of the three sections begins in a thin texture with only some of the voices sounding, but as the other voices enter, the music becomes increasingly full and rich.

The Gloria of the Mass has a much longer text than the Kyrie, and so Palestrina does not repeat words. Here the texture is mostly homophonic, and the voices usually sing the same words at the same time. This projects the text clearly and contrasts with the imitative polyphony of the Kyrie. Palestrina brings variety to the Gloria through subtle changes in the number of parts heard at one time and through shifts between higher and lower voices. The Gloria's opening words are sung as Gregorian chant by a priest; then the choir enters with Palestrina's music. The Gloria is divided into two sections. Here is the text for the opening section:

Gloria in excelsis Deo. Et in terra pax hominibus bonae voluntatis.	Glory to God in the highest and on earth peace to men of good will.
Laudamus te, benedicimus te, adoramus te, glorificamus te.	We praise Thee; we bless Thee; we adore Thee; we glorify Thee.
Gratias agimus tibi propter magnam gloriam tuam.	We give thanks to Thee for Thy great glory.
Domine Deus, rex coelestis, Deus Pater omnipotens.	O Lord God, heavenly King, God the Father almighty.
Domine Fili unigenite, Jesu Christe, Domine Deus, Agnus Dei, Filius Patris.	O Lord the only begotten Son, Jesus Christ, O Lord God, Lamb of God, Son of the Father.

[3] SECULAR MUSIC IN THE RENAISSANCE

Vocal Music

During the Renaissance, secular vocal music became increasingly popular. Throughout Europe music was set to poems in various languages, including Italian, French, Spanish, German, Dutch, and English. The development of music printing helped spread secular music, and thousands of song collections became available. Music was an important leisure activity; every educated

During the Renaissance music was an important leisure activity; every educated person was expected to play an instrument and read notation. This painting shows a lute player accompanying himself and two other singers (Omikron, Original in National Gallery, London).

person was expected to play an instrument and read notation. The Elizabethan composer Thomas Morley (1557–1603) vividly describes the embarrassment of being unable to participate in after-dinner music making: "But supper being ended, and Musicke bookes (according to the custome) being brought to the tables, the mistresse of the house presented me with a part, earnestly requesting me to sing. But when, after many excuses, I protested unfainedly that I could not: every one began to wonder. Yea, some whispered to others, demaunding how I was brought up."

Renaissance secular music was written for groups of solo voices and for solo voice with the accompaniment of one or more instruments. Word-painting —musical illustration of a text—was common. Composers delighted in imitating natural sounds such as bird calls and street cries. In a famous piece entitled *La Guerre* ("The War"), the Frenchman Clément Janequin (about 1485–1560)

Vocal Music

107

vividly imitated battle noises, drumbeats, and fanfares. Secular music contained more rapid shifts of mood than sacred music did. As Morley advised the composer, "You must in your music be wavering like the wind, sometimes wanton, sometimes drooping, sometimes grave and staid . . . and the more variety you show the better shall you please."

The Renaissance Madrigal

An important kind of secular vocal music during the Renaissance was the **madrigal,** a piece for several solo voices set to a short poem, usually about love. A madrigal, like a motet, combines homophonic and polyphonic textures. But it more often uses word-painting and unusual harmonies.

The Renaissance madrigal began in Italy around 1520, along with a creative explosion in Italian poetry. Madrigals were published by the thousands in sixteenth-century Italy, where they were sung by cultivated aristocrats. Among the many Italian madrigalists were Luca Marenzio (1553–1599) and Carlo Gesualdo (about 1560–1613), infamous Prince of Venosa who had his wife and her lover murdered after finding them in bed.

In 1588—the year of the Spanish Armada—a volume of translated Italian madrigals was published in London. This triggered a spurt of madrigal writing by English composers, and for about thirty years there was a steady flow of English madrigals and other secular vocal music. The time of Queen Elizabeth (1533–1603) and William Shakespeare (1564–1616) was as much a golden age in English music as it was in literature. The impetus for both arts arose in Italy. But the English madrigal became lighter and more humorous than its Italian model, and its melody and harmony were simpler.

"As Vesta Was" (1601), by Thomas Weelkes

Among the finest English madrigalists was Thomas Weelkes (about 1575–1623), an organist and church composer. Weelkes's "As Vesta Was" comes from *The Triumphes of Oriana* (1601), an anthology of English madrigals written to honor Queen Elizabeth, who often was called "Oriana." The text of this six-voice madrigal pictures Vesta (Roman goddess of the hearth) coming down a hill with her attendants, "Diana's darlings." (Diana was the Roman goddess of chastity, hunting, and the moon.) At the same time, the "maiden queen," Oriana (Elizabeth), is climbing the hill with her shepherd gallants. Vesta's attendants desert her and race down the hill to join Oriana.

"As Vesta Was" has the light mood typical of English madrigals. Word-painting is plentiful. For example, the word *descending* is sung to downward scales, and *ascending* to upward ones.

b)

She spied   a   maid - en Queen the same a - scend - - - ing,

When Vesta's attendants run down the hill "first *two* by *two*, then *three* by *three* together, leaving their goddess all *alone*," we hear first *two* voices then *three* voices, and finally a *solo* voice. In the extended concluding section, "*Long* live fair Oriana," a joyous phrase is imitated among the voices. And in the bass this phrase is sung in long notes, with the longest note on the word *long*.

As Vesta was from Latmos hill descending,	Descending scales.
she spied a maiden queen the same ascending,	Ascending scales.
attended on by all the shepherds swain,	
to whom Diana's darlings	Rapid descending
came running down amain.	figures.
First two by two,	Two voices.
then three by three together,	Three voices; all voices.
	Solo voice.
leaving their goddess all alone, hasted thither,	
and mingling with the shepherds of her train	
with mirthful tunes her presence entertain.	
Then sang the shepherds and nymphs of Diana,	
Long live fair Oriana!	Brief joyful phrase imitated among voices; long notes in bass.

Lute Song: "It Was a Lover and His Lass" by Thomas Morley

A simpler type of secular music than the madrigal was the song for solo voice and lute. The lute is a plucked-string instrument with a body shaped like half a pear. Its versatility made the lute the most popular instrument in the Renaissance home. It could play solos or accompaniments, chords, melodies, rapid scales, and even polyphonic music. In England, the lute song—called a lute "ayre"—was widely cultivated from the 1590s to about 1620. In contrast to much Renaissance music, a lute song was mostly homophonic in texture: the voice sang the melody, and the lute provided chordal support—an arrangement still practiced by folk singers today.

Perhaps the most popular of all lute songs, "It Was a Lover and His Lass" was written by Thomas Morley, (1557–1603), an English composer best known for madrigals. Lyrics from Shakespeare's *As You Like It* (act V, scene 3) provided the words for Morley's song. His lilting, tuneful melody evokes the delight of love and springtime that Shakespeare described in the poem. Each of the poem's four stanzas is set to the same music, which has a clear beat and the

The Renaissance Madrigal

swing of an English folk song or dance. The vocal line spins out of short melodic patterns that are repeated on different pitches. Listen for the rollicking scale figures on *hey ding-a-ding-a-ding.* "It Was a Lover and His Lass" was originally printed so that a singer could accompany the song on a lute; and there also was an optional part for bass viol, a bowed string instrument of the Renaissance.

It was a lover and his lass,
With a hey, with a ho, and a hey nonie no,
That o'er the green cornfields did pass
In Springtime, the only pretty ring time,
When birds do sing, hey ding-a-ding-a-ding.
Sweet lovers love the Spring.

Between the acres of the rye,
With a hey, with a ho, and a hey nonie no,
These pretty country fools would lie
In Springtime, the only pretty ring time,
When birds do sing, hey ding-a-ding-a-ding.
Sweet lovers love the Spring.

This carol they began that hour,
With a hey, with a ho, and a hey nonie no,
How that a life was but a flower
In Springtime, the only pretty ring time,
When birds do sing, hey ding-a-ding-a-ding.
Sweet lovers love the Spring.

Then pretty lovers take the time,
With a hey, with a ho, and a hey nonie no,
For love is crowned with the prime
In Springtime, the only pretty ring time,
When birds do sing, hey ding-a-ding-a-ding.
Sweet lovers love the Spring.

Instrumental Music

Through subordinate to vocal music, instrumental music did become more important during the Renaissance. Traditionally instrumentalists accompanied voices or played music intended for singing. Even in the early 1500s instrumental music was largely adapted from vocal music. Instrumental groups performed polyphonic vocal pieces, such as motets, which were often published with the indication, "to be sung or played." Soloists used the lute, harpsichord, or organ to play simple arrangements of vocal works.

During the sixteenth century, however, instrumental music gradually became free of vocal models. More music was directly conceived for instruments. Renaissance composers began to exploit the special capacities of the lute or organ when writing instrumental solos. They developed new instrumental forms such as theme and variations. Much of this instrumental music was intended for dancing, a popular Renaissance entertainment. But little Renaissance dance music has survived, because it was usually not written down, but improvised, like jazz.

The many instruments used in the Renaissance produced softer, less brilliant sounds than we hear today; most came in families of from three to eight instruments, ranging from soprano to bass. Recorders (instruments related to the flute) and viols (bowed string instruments) were among the most important Renaissance instruments. Often several members of the same instrumental family were played together, but Renaissance composers did not specify the instruments wanted. A single work might be performed by recorders, viols, or several different instruments, depending on what was available. Today's standardized orchestra did not exist. Large courts might employ, say, thirty instrumentalists of all types. And on state occasions such as a royal wedding, guests might be entertained by woodwinds, plucked and bowed strings, and keyboard instruments all playing together.

Ricercar in the Twelfth Mode (Sixteenth Century), by Andrea Gabrieli

St. Mark's Cathedral in Venice became a center of instrumental music during the sixteenth century. Colorful and wealthy, it employed many instrumentalists to participate in elaborate musical performances in St. Mark's Square. The Cathedral was noted for two widely separated choir lofts, each with an organ—an architectural feature that delivered "stereophonic music" for several choruses and groups of instruments.

Andrea Gabrieli (about 1520–1586) was organist at St. Mark's from 1564 until his death. He was a leading composer of both sacred and secular vocal music, and of instrumental music. Gabrieli's *Ricercar* in the Twelfth Mode was written for four unspecified instruments (soprano, alto, tenor, and bass). It sounds particularly exciting when played by the brasses that were prominent in Venetian processions. (A **ricercar** is a polyphonic instrumental composition employing imitation. That this one is "in the Twelfth Mode" means that it is based on a scale corresponding to C major.)

This short, lively piece is composed of several contrasting sections: A B CC A. Gabrieli unifies the *Ricercar* by bringing back the opening material (A) after the two middle sections. Most of section C is in triple meter and contrasts with the duple meter of sections A and B. The work features imitation among the individual instruments and rapid echoes between the two lower and upper parts. Though relatively simple, the piece is an early step toward more elaborate instrumental music that developed in the Baroque period.

Basic Terms

If you aren't sure what each of the following words means, look back at the text, where they appear in bold type. Additional information about some of them can be found by checking the index.

word-painting   Mass   ricercar
motet   madrigal

THE BAROQUE PERIOD

Baroque painters, sculptors, and architects became interested in forming a total illusion, like a stage setting. Shown here is Lully's opera *Alceste* being performed at the Palace of Versailles (The Metropolitan Museum of Art, Harris Brisbane Dick Fund, 1930).

BAROQUE MUSIC (1600–1750)

Though the word *baroque* has at various times meant bizarre, flamboyant, and elaborately ornamented, modern historians use it simply to indicate a particular style in the arts. An oversimplified, but useful, characterization of Baroque style is that it fills space—canvas, stone, or sound—with action and movement. Painters, sculptors, and architects became interested in forming a total illusion, like a stage setting. Artists such as Bernini, Rubens, and Rembrandt exploited their materials to expand the potentials of color, detail, ornament, and depth; they wanted to create totally structured worlds.

Such a style was very well suited to the wishes of the Baroque aristocracy, who also thought in terms of completely integrated structures. In France, for example, Louis XIV held court in the Palace of Versailles, a magnificent setting that fused Baroque painting, sculpture, and architecture into a symbol of royal wealth and power. The Baroque style was also shaped by the needs of churches, which used the emotional and theatrical qualities of art to make worship more attractive. The middle class, too, influenced the development of the Baroque style. In Holland, for example, prosperous merchants and doctors called for realistic depictions of landscapes and scenes from everyday life.

It's also helpful to think of Baroque style against the backdrop of seventeenth-century scientific discovery. Galileo (1564–1642) and Newton (1642–1727) represented a new approach to science based on the union of mathematics and experiment; they discovered mathematical laws governing bodies in motion. Such scientific advances led to new inventions and the gradual improvement of medicine, mining, navigation, and industry during the Baroque era. Baroque art is a complex mixture of rationalism, sensuality, materialism, and spirituality.

In music, the Baroque style flourished during the century and a half from 1600 to 1750. The two giants of Baroque composition were George Frideric Handel and Johann Sebastian Bach. Bach's death in 1750 marks the end of the period. Other Baroque masters—Claudio Monteverdi, Henry Purcell, Arcangelo Corelli, Antonio Vivaldi—were largely forgotten until the twentieth century. But the appearance of long-playing records in the late 1940s spurred a "Baroque revival" that made these long-forgotten musicians household names for many music lovers.

The Baroque period has three phases: early (1600–1640), middle (1640–1680), and late (1680–1750). Though the Baroque music best known today comes from the latest phase, the earliest period was one of the most revolutionary in music history. Monteverdi (1567–1643), for instance, strove to create unprecedented passion and dramatic contrast in his works. In Italy, especially, music was composed for texts conveying extreme emotion, and the text ruled the music. With this stress on drama and text, it is not surprising that Italian composers

The Baroque Period

Bernini's *Throne of St. Peter* fills space with action and movement (Anderson—Art Reference Bureau).

Peter Paul Rubens, *Henry IV Receiving the Portrait of Maria de'
Medici.* Baroque artists exploited their materials to expand the
potentials of color, ornament, detail, and depth (Alinari—Art
Reference Bureau).

of the early Baroque created opera—a drama sung to orchestral accompaniment.
Their melodic lines imitated the rhythms and inflections of speech.

During the early Baroque period, composers favored homophonic texture:
they often used one main melody with a chordal accompaniment. The polyphonic texture of Renaissance music tended to obscure the words. But note
that this new emphasis on homophonic texture characterizes only the *early*
Baroque; by the *late* Baroque period, polyphonic texture returned to favor.

To depict the extreme emotions of their texts, early Baroque composers used
dissonances with a new freedom. Never before were unstable chords so prominent and emphatic. Contrasts of sound were stressed—one or more solo singers
against a chorus, or voices against instruments. In Renaissance choral music,
instruments—if used at all—duplicated a singer's melody. But in the early
Baroque, voices were accompanied with melodic lines designed for instruments.

The French Academy of Science by Sébastien LeClerc. During the Baroque period, there was a new approach to science based on the union of mathematics and experiment (Omikron).

During the middle phase of the Baroque (1640–1680), the new musical style had spread from Italy to practically every country in Europe. The medieval or church modes—scales which had governed music for centuries—gradually gave way to major and minor scales. By about 1680, major or minor scales were the tonal basis of most compositions. Another feature of the middle Baroque phase was the new importance of instrumental music. Many compositions were written for specific instruments, the violin family being most popular.

We will focus mainly on the late Baroque period (1680–1750), which yielded most of the Baroque music heard today. Many aspects of harmony—including the emphasis of the dominant chord's attraction to the tonic—arose in this period. During the late Baroque, instrumental music became as important as vocal music for the first time. Early Baroque composers had emphasized homophonic texture; late Baroque composers gloried in polyphony. Let's look

Baroque Music (1600–1750)

117

more closely at some features of late Baroque style. (From now on the word *Baroque* will pertain to the late Baroque phase.)

Baroque Unity of Mood

A Baroque piece usually expresses one basic mood—what begins joyfully will remain joyful throughout. Emotional states like joy, grief, and agitation were represented. (At the time, these moods were called "affections.") Composers molded a musical language to depict the affections; specific rhythms or melodic patterns were associated with specific moods. This common language gives a family resemblance to much late Baroque music.

The prime exception to this Baroque principle of unity of mood occurs in vocal music. Drastic changes of emotion in a text may inspire corresponding changes in the music. But even in such cases, one mood is maintained at some length before it yields to another.

Baroque Rhythm

Unity of mood in Baroque music is conveyed, first of all, by continuity of rhythm. Rhythmic patterns heard at the beginning of a piece are repeated throughout it. This rhythmic continuity provides a compelling drive and energy—the forward motion is rarely interrupted. The beat in Baroque music is emphasized far more than in most Renaissance music, for example.

Baroque Melody

Baroque melody also creates a feeling of continuity. An opening melody will be heard again and again in the course of a Baroque piece. And even when a melody is presented in varied form, its character tends to remain constant. There is a continuous expanding, unfolding, and unwinding of melody. This sense of directed motion is frequently the result of a melodic sequence, that is, successive repetition of a musical idea at higher or lower pitch levels. Many Baroque melodies sound elaborate and ornamental, and they are not easy to sing or remember. Tunes constructed like "Mary Had a Little Lamb"—with its a a' form—are *not* typical of this period. The Baroque melody gives the impression of dynamic expansion rather than of balance and symmetry. A short opening phrase is often followed by a longer phrase with an unbroken flow of rapid notes.

Terraced Dynamics

Paralleling continuity of rhythm and melody in Baroque music is a continuity of dynamic level: the volume tends to stay constant for a stretch of time. When the dynamics do shift, it's sudden, as though one had physically stepped from one level to another. This alternation between loud and soft is called **terraced dynamics.** *Gradual* changes of crescendo and decrescendo are *not* prominent features of Baroque music. However, singers and instrumentalists no doubt made some subtle dynamic inflections for expressive purposes.

The main keyboard instruments of the Baroque period were the organ and harpsichord, both well suited for continuity of dynamic level. An organist or harpsichordist could not obtain a crescendo or decrescendo by varying finger pressure, as pianists today can. A third keyboard instrument, the **clavichord,** could make gradual dynamic changes, but only within a narrow range—from about *ppp* to *mp*. Sound was produced by means of brass blades striking the strings. The clavichord usually was not used in large halls, as its tone was too weak. But for home use by amateurs it was ideal; its cost was low and its expressive sound satisfying. It had especially wide popularity in Germany.

Baroque Texture

We've noted that late Baroque music is predominantly polyphonic in texture: two or more melodic lines compete for the listener's attention. Usually, the soprano and bass lines are the most important. Imitation between the various lines or "voices" of the texture is very common. A melodic idea heard in one voice is likely to make an appearance in the other voices as well.

However, not all late Baroque music was polyphonic. A piece may shift in texture, especially in vocal music, where changes of mood in the words demand musical contrast. Also, Baroque composers treated musical texture differently. Bach inclined toward a consistently polyphonic texture; Handel used much more contrast between polyphonic and homophonic sections.

Chords and the Basso Continuo (Figured Bass)

Chords became increasingly important during the Baroque period. In earlier times, there was more concern with the beauty of individual melodic lines than with chords formed when the lines were heard together. In a sense, chords were mere by-products of the motion of melodic lines. But in the Baroque period chords became significant in themselves. As composers wrote a melodic line, they thought of chords to mesh with it. Indeed, sometimes they composed a melody to fit a specific chord progression. This interest in chords gave new prominence to the bass part, which served as the foundation of the harmony. The whole musical structure rested on the bass part.

The new emphasis on chords and the bass part resulted in the most characteristic feature of all Baroque music, an accompaniment called the **basso continuo,** or **figured bass.** This is made up of a bass part together with numbers (figures) which specify the chords to be played above it. The basso continuo is usually played by at least two instruments: an organ or a harpsichord and a low melodic instrument like the cello or bassoon. With the left hand, the organist or harpsichordist plays the bass part, which is also performed by the cello or bassoon. With the right hand, the keyboard player improvises chords or even a melodic line, following the indications of the numbers. These numbers specify only a basic chord, not the exact way in which the chord should

Chords and the
Basso Continuo
(Figured Bass)

119

be played. Thus, the performer is given a great deal of freedom. (This shorthand system is similar in principle to the chord indications found on modern song sheets, from which jazz pianists improvise.)

The basso continuo offered the advantage of emphasizing the all-important bass part as well as a steady flow of chords. Practically, the use of numbers, rather than chords with all their notes written out, saved time for busy Baroque composers. It also saved paper at a time when it was expensive.

The Baroque Orchestra

During the Baroque period the orchestra evolved into a performing group based on instruments of the violin family. By modern standards the Baroque orchestra was small, consisting of from ten to thirty or forty players. Its instrumental make-up was flexible and could vary from piece to piece. At its nucleus was the basso continuo (harpsichord plus cello, double bass, or bassoon) and upper strings (first and second violins and violas). Use of woodwind, brass, and percussion instruments was variable. To the strings and continuo could be added recorders, flutes, oboes, trumpets, horns, trombones, or timpani. One piece might use only a single flute, while another would call for two oboes, three trumpets, and timpani. Trumpets and timpani joined the orchestra mainly when the music was festive. This flexibility contrasts with the standardized orchestra of later periods, composed of four sections: string, woodwind, brass, and percussion.

The Baroque trumpet (like the early French horn) had no valves but was given rapid, complex melodic lines to play in a high register. Because the instrument was difficult to play and had a traditional association with royalty, the trumpeter was the aristocrat of the Baroque orchestra. When prisoners of war were exchanged, trumpeters were treated like military officers.

Bach, Handel, Vivaldi, and others chose their orchestral instruments with care and obtained beautiful effects from specific tone colors. They loved to experiment with different combinations of instruments. However, in the Baroque period tone color was distinctly subordinate to other musical elements—melody, rhythm, and harmony. Tone color was considered secondary, and composers frequently rearranged their own or other composers' works for different instruments. A piece for string orchestra might become an organ solo, losing little in the process. Often, one instrument was treated like another. An oboe would play the same melody as the violins, or the flute and trumpet would imitate each other for extended sections of a piece.

Words and Music

Like their Renaissance predecessors, Baroque composers used music to represent the meaning of specific words. *Heaven* was set to a high tone, and *hell* to a low one. Rising scales represented upward motion, while descending scales depicted the reverse. Descending chromatic scales were associated with pain and grief. This descriptive musical language was quite standardized: a lament for a lost love might call forth the same descending chromatic scale used to depict suffering in the *Crucifixus* of the Mass.

Baroque composers emphasized words by writing many rapid notes for a single syllable of text. This also displayed a singer's virtuosity. The individual words and phrases are repeated over and over as the music continuously unfolds.

Baroque Forms

We have said that a piece of Baroque music—particularly instrumental music—usually has unity of mood. Yet many Baroque compositions include a set of pieces, or movements that contrast. A **movement** is a piece that sounds fairly complete and independent but is part of a larger composition. Usually, each movement has its own themes, comes to a definite end, and is separated from the next movement by a brief pause. Thus, a Baroque composition in three movements may contain contrasts between a fast and energetic opening, a slow and solemn middle, and a conclusion that is quick, light, and humorous.

All the form types described in Elements section 9, "Musical Form," appear in Baroque music. Three-part form (A B A), two-part form (A B), theme-and-variations form, and continuous or undivided form are all common. We'll consider examples of these and other forms in the following sections.

Regardless of form, Baroque music features contrasts between bodies of sound. Often there is a quite regular alternation between a small and large group of instruments, or between instruments and voices with instrumental accompaniment. This exploration of contrasting sounds was pursued with great imagination and provides a key to the understanding and enjoyment of Baroque music.

Basic Terms

If you aren't sure what each of the following words means, look back at the text, where they appear in bold type. Additional information can be found by checking the index.

terraced dynamics   basso continuo (figured bass)
clavichord   movement

MUSIC IN BAROQUE SOCIETY [2]

Baroque

Before 1800 most music was written to order, to meet a specific demand that came mainly from aristocratic courts and churches. Opera houses and municipalities also required a constant supply of music. In every case, the demand was for *new* music; Baroque audiences did not want to listen to pieces in an "old-fashioned" style.

The Baroque ruling class was enormously rich and powerful. While most of the population eked out a bare existence, European rulers surrounded themselves by luxury. Germany alone was subdivided into about three hundred territories governed separately. And each ruler proclaimed greatness by means of splendid palaces and magnificent court entertainments. Indeed, entertainment was necessary; most courtiers did no real work and tried to avoid boredom as much as possible.

Music was a main source of diversion. One court might employ an orchestra, a chapel choir, and opera singers—the size of the musical staff depending on the court's wealth. Bach directed about eighteen players in the orchestra of a small German court in 1717; but a large court might have more than eighty performers, including the finest opera singers of the day. The music director supervised performances and composed much of the music required, including operas, church music, dinner music, and pieces for court concerts. This overworked musician also was responsible for the discipline of other musicians, and for the upkeep of the instruments and music library.

The music director's job, like most, had good and bad features. Pay and prestige were quite high, and anything the composer wrote would be performed. But no matter how great, the composer was still a high-class servant who could neither quit nor take a trip without the patron's permission. Once, Bach was too forceful in asking permission to resign, and his duke put him in jail for a month. Like everyone in Baroque society, musicians had to curry favor with the aristocracy. It is in this light that we must understand dedications like the one which Bach addressed to a nobleman along with his *Brandenburg Concertos:* "Begging Your Highness most humbly not to judge their imperfection with the rigor of the fine and delicate taste which the whole world knows Your Highness has for musical pieces; but rather to infer from them in benign Consideration the profound respect and the most humble obedience which I try to show Your Highness." Yet sometimes musicians formed personal friendships with their patrons, as did Arcangelo Corelli, who thus gained a private apartment in a palace.

Some rulers were themselves good musicians. Frederick the Great, King of Prussia during the mid-eighteenth century, was a flutist and good composer, as well as a feared general. At his nightly court concerts, Frederick played his own works and some of the hundreds of pieces supplied by his flute teacher, Johann Quantz. (Quantz was "granted the privilege" of shouting "Bravo!" after a royal performance.)

Churches also needed music, and this often was very grand. Along with an organ and choir, many Baroque churches had an orchestra to accompany the service. Indeed, church was where most ordinary citizens heard music. There were few public concerts, and the populace was rarely invited to the palace. The music director of a church, like his court counterpart, had to produce a steady flow of new music. He also was responsible for the music training of choirboys in the church school. Fine church music contributed to the prestige of cities, which often competed to attract the best musicians.

Church musicians earned lower pay and status than court musicians. Their meager income was supplemented by allotments of firewood and grain and by irregular fees for weddings and funerals. They suffered a financial pinch when "a healthy wind" blew and there were fewer funerals than usual, a situation Bach once complained about.

Large towns employed musicians to perform a variety of functions—to play in church, in processions, in concerts for visiting dignitaries, and for university graduations. These town musicians often played with amateurs in music clubs or university music societies, getting together at private homes, coffeehouses, and taverns.

Some Baroque musicians earned money by writing operas for commercial opera houses located mainly in Italy. In Venice, a city of 125,000 people, six opera companies performed simultaneously between 1680 and 1700. In London, Handel became music director of a commercial opera company in 1719. Backed by English nobles, this company was a corporation with shares listed on the London stock exchange. When the company went bankrupt in 1728, Handel formed his own company, for which he wrote operas and served as conductor, manager, and impresario. In filling these many roles, Handel became one of the first great "free-lance" musicians.

How did one become a musician in the Baroque period? Often the art was handed from father to son; many leading composers—Bach, Vivaldi, Purcell, Couperin, and Rameau—were sons of musicians. Or boys sometimes were apprenticed to a town musician and lived in his home. In return for instruction, the boy did odd jobs, such as copying music. Many Baroque composers began their studies as choirboys, learning music in the choir school. In Italy, music schools were connected with orphanages. (Conservatory comes from the Italian for "orphans' home.") Orphans, foundlings, and poor children were given thorough musical training, and some became the most sought-after opera singers and instrumentalists in Europe. Eminent composers such as Vivaldi were hired to teach and direct concerts in these schools.

To get a job, musicians usually had to pass a difficult examination, performing and submitting compositions. Sometimes there were nonmusical job requirements, too. An applicant might be expected to make a "voluntary contribution" to the town's treasury, or even to marry the daughter of a retiring musician. Both Bach and Handel turned down the same job because one of the conditions was marriage to the organist's spinster daughter. In general, Italian musicians held the best posts in most European courts and were frequently paid twice as much as local musicians.

Composers were an integral part of Baroque society, working for courts, churches, towns, and commercial opera houses. And even though they wrote music to fit specific needs, its quality is so high that it has become a standard element in today's concert repertory.

Music in Baroque Society

Music was a main source of diversion for the Baroque ruling class, and many aristocrats were themselves good musicians (National Gallery, Washington).

THE CONCERTO GROSSO AND RITORNELLO FORM [**3**]

We've seen that the contrast between loud and soft sounds—between large and small groups of performers—is a basic principle of Baroque music. It governs the concerto grosso, an important form of orchestral music in the late Baroque period. In the **concerto grosso,** a small group of soloists is pitted against a larger group of players called the **tutti** ("all"). Usually between two and four soloists play with anywhere from eight to twenty or more musicians for the tutti. The tutti is mainly string instruments, with a harpsichord as part of the basso continuo. A concerto grosso sounds like a competition between the tutti and the soloists, who assert their individuality and appeal for attention through brilliant and fanciful melodic lines. The soloists were the best and highest-paid members of the Baroque orchestra because their parts were more difficult than those of the other players. Concerti grossi were frequently performed by private orchestras in aristocratic palaces.

The concerto grosso consists of *several movements that contrast in tempo and character.* Most often there are three movements: (1) fast, (2) slow, (3) fast. The opening movement is usually vigorous and determined, clearly showing the contrast between tutti and soloists. The slow movement is quieter than the first, often lyrical and intimate. The last movement is lively and carefree, sometimes with a dancelike character.

The first and last movements of concerti grossi are often in **ritornello form,** an important musical procedure of the Baroque period. This form features the alternation between tutti and solo sections. In ritornello form the tutti opens with a theme called the **ritornello** ("refrain"). This ritornello, played by the tutti, returns in different keys throughout the movement. But it usually returns in fragments, not completely. Only at the end of the movement does the entire ritornello return in the home key. Although the number of times a ritornello (tutti) returns varies from piece to piece, a typical concerto grosso movement might be outlined:

1 *a.* Tutti (*f*), ritornello in home key.
   b. Solo.
2 *a.* Tutti (*f*), ritornello fragment.
   b. Solo.
3 *a.* Tutti (*f*), ritornello fragment.
   b. Solo.
4 Tutti (*f*), ritornello in home key.

In contrast to the tutti's ritornello, the solo sections offer fresh melodic ideas, softer dynamics, rapid scales, and broken chords. Soloists may also expand short melodic ideas from the tutti. The opening movement of Bach's Brandenburg Concerto No. 5 is a fine example of ritornello form in the concerto grosso.

The Concerto Grosso and Ritornello Form

125

First Movement from Brandenburg Concerto No. 5 in D Major (1721), by Johann Sebastian Bach

With his set of six *Brandenburg Concertos,* Bach brought immortality to a German aristocrat, the Margrave of Brandenburg. Bach met the Margrave in 1718, when he was music director for another patron. The Margrave loved music and asked Bach to send him some original compositions. About three years later, Bach sent him the *Brandenburg Concertos* with the flattering dedication quoted in section 2, probably hoping for money or favors in return. (We don't know whether he got any.) These concertos had actually been composed for, and performed by, the orchestra of Bach's employer, the Prince of Cöthen. Each of the concertos is written for a different and unusual combination of instruments.

Brandenburg Concerto No. 5 uses a string orchestra and a group of soloists consisting of a flute, violin, and harpsichord. This was the first time that a harpsichord had been given the solo role in a concerto grosso. In 1719, the Prince of Cöthen bought a new harpsichord; Bach probably wanted to show off this instrument (as well as his skill as a keyboard player), and so he gave it a solo spot. The tutti is written for violins, violas, cellos, and double bass. During the tutti sections the solo violinist plays along, as does the harpsichordist, who supplies the figured bass.

The allegro movement opens with the ritornello, which is an almost continuous flow of rapid notes. After the ritornello ends very definitely, the soloists present short melodic ideas, with the flute and violin imitating each other playfully. The appearance of the soloists brings a lower dynamic level and the new tone color of the flute. After a while the tutti returns loudly with a brief fragment of the ritornello, only to give way again to the soloists. This alternation between brief, loud ritornello fragments by the tutti and longer, softer solo sections continues throughout the movement.

The soloists' music tends to be brilliant, fanciful, and personal compared with the more vigorous and straightforward tutti sections. Solo sections are also more polyphonic in texture than the tutti and stress imitation between the flute and violin. The soloists play new material of their own or varied fragments from the ritornello. These solo sections build tension and make the listener anticipate the tutti's return. Listen especially for the suspenseful solo section that begins with a new theme in minor and ends with the fluttery sound of trills in the flute and violin. (A **trill** is an ornament consisting of the rapid alternation of two tones that are a whole or half step apart.)

Only the harpsichord plays during the long final solo section. And it is spectacular! Bach builds a tense high point for the movement through irresistible rhythm and dazzling scale passages that require a virtuoso's skill. (He made the most of the new instrument *and* himself.) His audience must have marveled at this brilliant harpsichord solo within a concerto grosso. Audiences still do.

Basic Terms

If you aren't sure what each of the following words means, look back at the text, where they appear in bold type. Additional information about some of them can be found by checking the index.

concerto grosso   ritornello form
tutti   ritornello
                       trill

LISTENING OUTLINE
To be read while music is heard

Brandenburg Concerto No. 5 in D Major (1721), by Johann Sebastian Bach

First Movement: Allegro
Ritornello form, duple meter ($\frac{2}{2}$), D major
Flute, violin, harpsichord (solo group), string orchestra, continuo (tutti)

(About 11 min.)

     Tutti   1   *a.* Strings, *f,* ritornello.

     Solo   *b.* Flute, violin, harpsichord, major key.
     Tutti   2   *a.* Strings, *f,* ritornello fragment.
     Solo   *b.* Flute, violin, harpsichord, varied ritornello fragment.
     Tutti   3   *a.* Strings, *f,* ritornello fragment.
     Solo   *b.* Violin, flute, harpsichord.

Tutti	4	a. Strings, *f*, ritornello fragment, minor.
Solo		b. Harpsichord, flute, violin.
Tutti	5	a. Strings, *f*, ritornello fragment, major.
Solo		b. Flute, harpsichord, violin, varied ritornello fragment, *pp*. New theme in minor, *pp*, tossed between flute and violin, tension mounts.

Trills in flute and violin lead to

Tutti	6	a. Strings, *f*, ritornello fragment, major.
Solo		b. Violin, flute, harpsichord.
Tutti	7	a. Strings, *f*, longer ritornello fragment.
Solo		b. Violin, harpsichord, flute, varied ritornello fragment.
Tutti	8	a. Strings, *f*, ritornello fragment.
Solo		b. Violin and flute play carefree idea with rapid harpsichord scales in background.
		c. Long harpsichord solo featuring virtuoso display. Mounting tension resolved in
Tutti	9	Strings, *f*, ritornello.

[4] THE FUGUE

One cornerstone of Baroque music is the *fugue*. It is written for a group of instruments or voices, or for a single instrument like an organ or harpsichord. The **fugue** is a polyphonic composition based on one main theme, called a **subject.** Throughout a fugue, different melodic lines, or "voices," imitate the subject. The top melodic line—whether sung or played—is the soprano voice, and the bottom is the bass. A fugue's texture usually includes three, four, or five voices. Though the fugue's subject remains fairly constant throughout, it takes on new meanings when shifted to different keys or combined with different melodic and rhythmic ideas.

The form of a fugue is extremely flexible; in fact, the only constant feature of fugues is how they begin—the subject is almost always presented in a single, unaccompanied voice. By thus throwing a spotlight on the subject, the composer tells us what to remember and listen for. In getting to know a fugue, try to follow its subject through the different levels of texture. After its first presentation, the subject is imitated in turn by all the remaining voices.

The opening of a fugue in four voices may be represented as follows:

Soprano
voice Subject .... etc.

Alto
voice   Subject .... etc.

Tenor
voice   Subject .... etc.

Bass
voice   Subject .... etc.

In this case the top voice announces the subject and then the lower voices imitate it. However, the subject may be announced by *any* voice—top, bottom, or middle—and the order in which the remaining voices imitate it is also completely flexible.

This may seem reminiscent of a round like "Row, Row, Row Your Boat," but in a fugue the game of "follow the leader" (exact imitation of the subject) does not continue indefinitely. The dotted lines in the fugue diagram show that *after a voice has presented the subject, it's free to go its own way with different melodic material.* A fugue's opening differs from a round's in another way: In a round, each voice presents the melody on the same tones. If the melody begins with the tones C-D-E, each voice will begin with these tones, whether at a higher or lower register. But in the opening of a fugue, *the subject is presented in two different scales.* First, it is based on the notes of the *tonic scale.* But when the second voice presents the subject, it is in the *dominant scale*—five scale steps higher than the tonic—and it is called the **answer.** A subject beginning with the notes C-D-E, for example, would be imitated by an answer five steps higher, on G-A-B. This alternation between the two scales of subject and answer creates variety.

In many fugues, the subject in one voice is constantly accompanied in another voice by a different melodic idea called a **countersubject.** A constant companion, the countersubject always appears with the subject, sometimes below it, sometimes above it.

After the opening of a fugue, when each voice has taken its turn at presenting the subject, a composer is free to decide how often the subject will be presented, in which voices, and in which keys. Between presentations of the subject, there are often transitional sections called **episodes,** which offer either new material or fragments of the subject or countersubject. Episodes do *not* present the subject in its entirety. They lend variety to the fugue and make reappearances of the subject sound fresh. Bach called one composer of fugues "pedantic" because he "had not shown enough fire to reanimate the theme by episodes."

The Fugue

129

Several musical procedures commonly appear in fugues. One is **stretto,** in which a subject is imitated before it is completed; one voice tries to catch the other. Another common procedure is **pedal point** (or **organ point**), in which a single tone, usually in the bass, is held while the other voices produce a series of changing harmonies against it. (The term is taken from organ music, where a low, sustained tone is produced by the organist's foot on a key of the pedal keyboard.)

A fugue subject can be varied in four principal ways:

1. It can be turned upside down, a procedure known as **inversion.** If the subject moves *upward* by leap, the inversion will move *downward* the same distance; if the subject moves *downward* by step, the inversion will move *upward* by step. In inversion, each interval in the subject is reversed in direction.

2. The subject may be presented **retrograde,** that is, by beginning with the last note of the subject and proceeding backward to the first.

3. The subject may be presented in **augmentation,** in which the original time values are lengthened.

4. The subject may appear in **diminution,** with shortened time values.

Fugues usually convey a single mood and a sense of continuous flow. They are written as independent works or as single movements within larger compositions. Very often an independent fugue is introduced by a short piece called a **prelude.**

Bach and Handel each wrote hundreds of fugues which represent the peak of that Baroque procedure. In the Baroque period, as a friend of Bach observed, "Skill in fugue was so indispensable in a composer that no one could have attained a musical post who had not worked out a given subject in all kinds of counterpoint and in a regular fugue." Fugal writing has continued into the nineteenth and twentieth centuries, but is not used as frequently as in the Baroque period. To this day musicians must learn how to write fugues as part of their training.

Organ Fugue in G Minor ("Little" Fugue; about 1709), by Johann Sebastian Bach

One of Bach's best-known organ pieces is the "Little" Fugue in G minor, so called to differentiate it from another, longer fugue in G minor. The opening section of this fugue corresponds to the diagram on page 129. Each of the fugue's four voices takes its turn at presenting the subject, which is announced in the top voice and then appears in progressively lower voices, ending in the bass (played by the organist's feet on the pedal keyboard). The subject is tuneful and easy to remember. Like many Baroque melodies, it gathers momentum as it goes along, beginning with relatively long time values (quarter notes) and then proceeding to shorter ones (eighth and sixteenth notes).

Starting with its second appearance, the subject is accompanied by a counter-subject that moves in short time values.

After the opening section, the subject appears five more times, each time preceded by an episode. The first episode uses both new material and a melodic idea from the countersubject.

This episode contains downward sequences, which are melodic patterns repeated in the same voice but at lower pitches.

For harmonic contrast, Bach twice presents the subject in major, rather than minor keys. The final statement of the subject—in minor—exploits the powerful bass tones of the pedal keyboard. Though the fugue is in minor, it ends with a major chord. This was a frequent practice in the Baroque period; major chords were thought more conclusive than minor.

Organ Fugue in G Minor ("Little" Fugue; about 1709), by Johann Sebastian Bach

131

Basic Terms

If you aren't sure what each of the following words means, look back at the text, where they appear in bold type. Additional information about some of them can be found by checking the index.

fugue	pedal point (organ point)
subject	inversion
answer	retrograde
countersubject	augmentation
episode	diminution
stretto	prelude

Baroque

[5] THE ELEMENTS OF OPERA

The Baroque era witnessed the development of a major innovation in music—**opera, drama that is sung to orchestral accompaniment**. By combining music, acting, poetry, dance, scenery, and costumes, this unique fusion of many arts creates a theatrical experience of overwhelming excitement and emotion. Since its beginnings in Italy around 1600, opera has spread to many countries, and even today it remains a powerful form of musical theater. We'll look closely at the operatic aspects of the Baroque period in the next section; but first, a general discussion of opera is in order.

An opera's characters and plot are revealed through song, rather than the speech used in ordinary drama. Once we accept this convention, opera offers great pleasure; its music both delights the ear and heightens the emotional effect of the words and story. Music makes even a complicated plot believable by depicting mood, character, and dramatic action. It's the flow of the music that carries the plot forward. In opera, the music *is* the drama.

Opera demands performers who can sing and act simultaneously. On stage are star solo singers, secondary soloists, a chorus, and sometimes dancers—all in costume. Besides the chorus of professional singers there may be "supers" (supernumeraries, or "extras"), who don't sing but who carry spears, fill out crowds, drink wine, and generally add to the opera's effect. Scenery, lighting, and stage machinery are intricate. They're called upon to create fires, floods, storms, and supernatural effects. In the orchestra pit are the instrumentalists and the conductor, whose awesome responsibility it is to hold everything together. A large opera's personnel—from conductor to stage director and assorted vocal coaches, rehearsal accompanists, technicians, and stagehands—may reach a startling total of several hundred people.

The capacity of this combined force to create spectacle and pageantry accounts for much of opera's appeal. Historically, opera has been associated with high social status. It originated in the courts of kings and princes (who

could afford it) and long continued as a form of aristocratic entertainment. But as opera became more concerned with "real" people and less with royal figures, it attracted popular audiences. Today, radio and TV broadcasts and recordings have changed opera's image as an exotic and expensive diversion for the very rich. Millions of people from every economic background know opera for what it is: a powerful and pleasurable emotional experience.

The creation of an opera results from the joint efforts of a composer and a dramatist. The **libretto,** or text of the opera, is usually written by the **librettist,** or dramatist, and then set to music by the composer. But the composer often collaborates with the dramatist to ensure that the text meets his musical needs as well as telling the story. W. H. Auden has said that a good libretto "offers as many opportunities as possible for the characters to be swept off their feet by placing them in situations which are too tragic or too fantastic for words. No good opera plot can be sensible, for people do not sing when they are feeling sensible." And it is true—opera characters are overwhelmed by love, sex, hatred, and revenge. They wear fantastic disguises and commit extraordinary acts of violence. Yet the music makes them human and real. It evokes the haughtiness of a countess or the simplicity of a peasant girl. It creates a dramatic entrance for an outraged father; depicts the tension behind sword thrusts in a duel; and portrays the bleakness of a winter dawn. A great opera composer is a master of musical timing and characterization and has a keen sense of the theater. He knows just when to have a character sing a simple phrase or a soaring melody, when to provide a stirring chorus or a graceful dance. Through his music, the composer paces the drama; he controls the speed of gestures, entrances, exits, and stage movements.

Some operas are serious, some comic, some both. They may contain spoken dialog, but most are sung entirely. (Spoken dialog is used mainly in comic opera, where stage action must be performed quickly for the most humorous effect.) Since it normally takes longer to sing words than to speak them, the text of a three-hour opera is shorter than that of a three-hour play. The librettist allows time for the composer's musical elaboration.

The range of characters found in opera is broad and varied; gods, empresses, dukes, servants, priests, prostitutes, peasants, clowns, hunchbacks, and cowboys all make an appearance. Opera soloists must create all these characters and need acting skill as well as vocal artistry. During rehearsals the stage director coaches the singers to move well, gesture meaningfully, and identify with their characters.

The basic voice ranges (soprano, alto, tenor, bass) are divided more finely in opera. Some of the **voice categories of opera** are:

Coloratura soprano	Very high range; able to execute rapid scales and trills
Lyric soprano	Rather light voice; sings roles calling for grace and charm
Dramatic soprano	Full, powerful voice; capable of passionate intensity
Lyric tenor	Relatively light, bright voice

Dramatic tenor	Powerful voice; capable of heroic expression
Basso buffo	Takes comic roles; can sing very rapidly
Basso profundo	Very low range, powerful voice; takes roles calling for great dignity

Like plays, operas have from one to five acts subdivided into scenes. An act presents a variety of vocal and orchestral contrasts. For example, a tenor solo might be followed by a duet for soprano and bass, then a chorus, or an orchestral interlude. A section may end definitely—and provide an opportunity for applause—or be linked with the next section to form a continuous flow of music within an act.

The main attraction for many opera fans is the **aria, a song for solo voice with orchestral accompaniment.** It's an outpouring of melody that expresses an emotional state. In an aria, "I love you" may be sung ten times to accommodate the expansion of the idea. Often the action stops while the character's feelings are revealed through music. Lasting several minutes, an aria is a complete piece with a definite beginning, high point, and end. If the performance of an aria is brilliant, the audience responds with an ovation at its conclusion. Though this breaks the dramatic flow, it allows the audience to release its feelings through applause and shouts of "Bravo!"

Opera composers often lead into an aria with a **recitative, a vocal line that imitates the rhythms and pitch fluctuations of speech.** In a recitative (Italian for "recite") words are sung quickly and clearly, often on repeated tones. There's usually only one note to each syllable, as opposed to an aria, where one syllable may be stretched over many notes. Used for monologs and dialogs, the recitative connects the more melodic sections of the opera. It carries the action forward and quickly presents routine information.

Besides arias, soloists sing compositions for two or more singers: duets (two), trios (three), quartets (four), quintets (five), and sextets (six). When three or more singers are involved, the composition is called an **ensemble.** In a duet or ensemble, the performers either face the audience or move through action that develops the plot. Each character expresses his own feelings. Conflicting emotions like grief, happiness, and anger can be projected simultaneously when different melodies are combined. This special blend of feelings is the glory of opera and is possible only through music; it cannot be duplicated in spoken drama.

An opera chorus generates atmosphere and comments on the action. Its members are courtiers, sailors, peasants, prisoners, ballroom guests, and so on. Their sound creates a kind of tonal background for the soloists.

Rising just over the edge of the center stage, near the footlights, is the prompter's box. In this cramped space, invisible to the audience, is the **prompter,** who gives cues and reminds the singers of words or pitches if they momentarily forget. Occasional memory lapses are inevitable with so much activity on stage.

Dance in opera is generally incidental. It provides an ornamental interlude that contrasts with and relaxes the thrust of the plot. By and large, dance occurs as part of the opera's setting—in a ballroom, at a country fair, in a pagan court—while the soloists, downstage, advance the plot's action and work out their destinies.

The nerve center for opera in performance is the orchestra pit—a sunken area directly in front of the stage. An opera orchestra has the same instruments as a full symphony orchestra, but usually it has a smaller string section. Covered lights attached to the players' music stands leave the orchestra in a deep shadow that doesn't interfere with the audience's view of the stage. The orchestra not only supports the singers but depicts mood and atmosphere and comments on the stage action. During the performance, the conductor shapes the entire work. He sets tempos, cues in singers, and indicates subtle dynamic gradations.

Most operas open with a purely orchestral composition called an **overture,** or **prelude.** Since the eighteenth century, the music for the overture has been drawn from material heard later in the opera. The overture is thus a short musical statement that involves the audience in the overall dramatic mood. Orchestral introductions to later acts in the opera are always called preludes. We've already discussed one of these, the Prelude to Act III of *Lohengrin,* where Wagner anticipates the wedding of the opera's hero and heroine. Because overtures and preludes, like arias, are complete compositions, they frequently appear on symphony orchestra programs.

The battle continues about translating opera. Most of the best-loved operas are in Italian, German, or French. Champions of their translation into English argue that an audience should be able to understand the plot as it develops. Why tell jokes in a comic opera if they can't be understood? On the other hand, a composer takes pains to make a special fusion of pitch and the original word. This results in a tonal color that seems absolutely right. But no matter how well a singer articulates, some words are bound to be lost, in whatever the language. For example, a sung melody can stretch one vowel over many notes; it takes a while to get to the end of a word. If the melody is placed in a soprano's highest range, the listener is really only aware of the silvery vowel and not of the word as a whole. Some operas seem to work well in translation, others don't. Much depends on the style of the opera and on the sensitivity of the translator.

Before a live opera performance in any language, it's a good idea to read the libretto or a synopsis of the plot. Even better, listen to a recording while following the libretto. This way, without worrying about what happens next, you're free at the performance to become involved with the quality of production and interpretation.

Basic Terms

If you aren't sure what each of the following words means, look back at the text, where they appear in bold type. Additional information about some of them can be found by checking the index.

opera	librettist	aria	ensemble	overture (prelude)
libretto	voice categories of opera	recitative	prompter	

135

[**6**] OPERA IN THE BAROQUE ERA

Opera is a legacy from Italy. Its way was prepared by musical discussions among a small group of noblemen, poets, and composers who began to meet regularly in Florence around 1575. This group was known as the **Camerata** (Italian for "fellowship" or "society") and included the composer Vincenzo Galilei, father of the astronomer Galileo.

The Camerata members wanted to create a new vocal style modeled on the music of ancient Greek tragedy. Since no actual dramatic music had come down to them from the Greeks, they based their theories on literary accounts that had survived. It was believed that the Greek dramas were sung throughout in a style that was midway between melody and speech. The Camerata members wanted the vocal line to follow the rhythms and pitch fluctuations of speech. Because it was modeled after speech, the new vocal style became known as recitative ("recite"). It was sung by a soloist with only a simple, chordal accompaniment. The new music was therefore homophonic in texture. Polyphony was rejected by the Camerata because different words sounding simultaneously would obscure the all-important text.

Euridice by Jacopo Peri is the earliest opera that has been preserved. It was composed for the wedding of King Henri IV of France and Marie de' Medici and was performed in Florence in 1600. Seven years later Monteverdi composed *Orfeo*—the first *great* opera—for the court of the Gonzaga family in Mantua. Both these operas are based on the Greek myth of Orpheus descending into Hades to bring back his beloved Eurydice.

Much Baroque opera was composed for ceremonial occasions at court and was designed to display magnificent extravagance. The subject matter of these operas was drawn from Greek mythology and ancient history. Not only were aristocratic patrons of the Baroque fascinated by the classical civilizations of Greece and Rome, they identified with their heroes and divinities. Opera did indeed reflect the creative urge of composer and librettist, but it also was a way to flatter the aristocracy. The radiant appearance of Apollo (god of poetry, music, and the sun) in the last act was meant to represent the prince's enlightened rule.

In Venice in 1637, the first public opera house opened; now anyone with the price of admission could attend an opera performance. Between 1637 and 1700 there were seventeen opera houses in Venice alone, as well as many in other Italian cities—ample evidence that opera was born in the right place at the right time. Hamburg, Leipzig, and London had public opera houses by the early 1700s, but, on the whole, public opera outside Italy took longer to develop.

Venetian opera became a great tourist attraction. An English traveler wrote in 1645 about the opera and its "variety of scenes painted and contrived with no less art of perspective, and machines for flying in the air, and other wonderful motions; taken together, it is one of the most magnificent and expensive diversions the wit of man can invent." The stage machinery of Baroque opera bordered on the colossal. Stage effects were spectacular—gods descending on clouds or riding across the sky in chariots, ships tossing, boulders splitting. And set design was an art in itself. Painters turned backdrops into cities with arches and avenues that stretched into the distant horizon.

Baroque opera marked the rise of the virtuoso singer. Chief of these was the **castrato,** a male singer who had been castrated before puberty. Castrati combined the lung power of a man with the vocal range of a woman. Their agility, breath control, and unique sound (which was not like a woman's) intrigued listeners. Castrati received the highest fees of any musician. With their soprano or alto vocal ranges, they played male roles such as Caesar and Nero—Baroque audiences evidently were more interested in vocal virtuosity than dramatic realism. Some Baroque operas cannot be done today because contemporary singers aren't able to manage the fiendishly difficult castrato parts. (The castration of boy singers was common in Italy from 1600 to 1800; this was usually done with the consent of impoverished parents who hoped that their sons would become highly paid opera stars.)

During the late Baroque, operas consisted largely of arias that were linked by recitatives. All action stopped during the aria, when the singer faced the audience, expressed the feelings of the character, and displayed vocal virtuosity. The form of a typical late Baroque aria is A B A. An aria in A B A form is called a *da capo* **aria:** after the B section, the term *da capo* is written; this means "from the beginning" and indicates a repetition of the opening A section. However, the repetition was usually not literal because the singer was expected to embellish the returning melody with ornaments.

Combining virtuosity, nobility, and extravagance, Baroque opera perfectly expressed the spirit of a grand age.

Basic Terms

If you aren't sure what each of the following words means, look back at the text, where they appear in bold type. Additional information about some of them can be found by checking the index.

Camerata   castrato   *da capo* aria

CLAUDIO MONTEVERDI [7]

Claudio Monteverdi (1567–1643), one of the greatest composers of the early Baroque era, was born in Cremona, Italy. He served at the court of Mantua for twenty-one years, first as a singer and violist, then as music director. For this court Monteverdi created opera's earliest masterpiece, *Orfeo* ("Orpheus," 1607). Though widely recognized as a leading composer in Mantua, Monteverdi received little pay or respect: "I have never suffered greater humiliation," he wrote, "than when I had to go and beg the treasurer to obtain what was due me."

Life improved for Monteverdi in 1613, when he was appointed music director at St. Mark's in Venice, the most important church position in Italy. He stayed at St. Mark's for thirty years, until his death in 1643. There he composed not only the required sacred music but also secular vocal music for the aristocracy. He wrote operas for Venice's San Cassiano, the first public opera house in Europe. In this section we'll study part of *L'incoronazione di Poppea* ("The Coronation of Poppea," 1642), written when Monteverdi was seventy-five.

Monteverdi is a monumental figure in the history of music. His works form a musical bridge between the sixteenth and seventeenth centuries and greatly influenced composers of the time. All his music—madrigals, church music, opera—is for voices, ordinarily supported by a basso continuo and other instruments.

Monteverdi wanted to create music of emotional intensity. He felt earlier music had conveyed only moderate emotion, and he wanted to extend its range to include agitation, excitement, and passion. To achieve this intensity, he used dissonances with unprecedented freedom and daring. And to evoke the angry or warlike feelings in some of his texts, he introduced new orchestral effects, including pizzicato and tremolo.

Monteverdi was the first composer of operatic masterpieces. Only three of the twelve operas he wrote are preserved, but they truly blend music and drama. His vocal lines respond marvelously to the inflections of Italian while maintaining melodic flow. He used the opera orchestra to establish atmosphere, character, and dramatic situation. And he created variety by using many kinds of music in his operas—recitatives, arias, duets, choruses, dances, and instrumental interludes.

The Coronation of Poppea was recently revived with tremendous success in the United States, even though it's an Italian opera over three hundred years old. Sections of this opera use a variation form found in many other Baroque works—a *ground bass*.

Ground Bass

Often, in Baroque works, a musical idea in the bass is repeated over and over while the melodies above it constantly change. The repeated musical idea is called a **ground bass,** or **basso ostinato** ("obstinate" or "persistent" bass). The ground bass pattern may be as short as four notes or as long as eight measures. In this variation form, the constant repetition of the bass pattern gives unity, while the free flow of the melodic lines above it results in variety. Composers use a ground bass in both vocal and instrumental music. We'll hear a ground bass in an excerpt from *The Coronation of Poppea,* as well as in Purcell's opera *Dido and Aeneas* (section 8) and in Bach's B-minor Mass (section 12).

Claudio Monteverdi. The composer's work formed a
musical bridge between the sixteenth and seventeenth
centuries and greatly influenced composers of the time
(Ashmolean Museum).

The Coronation of Poppea (1642)

The Coronation of Poppea is an operatic tribute to love's power. Its plot, set in Rome in 65 A.D., is scandalous and amoral. The young emperor Nero passionately loves voluptuous Poppea and plans to make her empress in place of his wife. When his trusted old teacher Seneca opposes the plan, Nero orders him to commit suicide. An unsuccessful attempt on Poppea's life gives Nero a convenient excuse to divorce and banish his wife. The opera ends as Poppea is crowned Empress of Rome.

With the simplest of musical means, Monteverdi makes a wide range of characters come alive. Through vocal line alone he quickly characterizes a sensual and ambitious mistress, a despairing empress, and a stoic philosopher. Monteverdi sets his text in a very flexible way, freely alternating recitatives with more melodious passages, depending on the meaning of the words.

Act III: Coronation Scene

At the climax of the opera, Poppea is crowned by Roman consuls and tribunes, and she joins Nero in an ecstatic love duet built on a ground bass. The entrance of the consuls and tribunes is announced by a short, brilliant instrumental interlude with trumpets. The consuls and tribunes (tenors and basses) sing a two-voice chorus that is dignified and ceremonial. Notice that a single word (*imperial*) may be emphasized through a long series of notes or repetitions of a single tone.

After another brief instrumental interlude, the mood completely changes, and Nero and Poppea—their desires fulfilled—sing one of the most sensuous love duets in all opera. The duet is in ternary form: A B B A. In section A, the descending ground bass consisting of four notes is repeated over and over by the basso continuo. Above this repeated pattern are the melodic lines of Poppea and Nero.

Ground bass

Their ecstatic exclamations echo, pursue, and intertwine. Nero responds to his beloved Poppea with erotic delight. A rigidly repeated ground bass is used to govern some of the most free-sounding music of the Baroque period. With the middle section (B B) the pace quickens, and phrases rush from the lovers' lips ("you are my idol," "yes, my heart"). Then section A returns, and the opera ends on a note of rapture.

Nero's royal palace.

Consuls and Tribunes

Instrumental interlude, trumpets
Chorus, tenors and basses

A te, sovrana augusta,	August sovereign
con il consenso universal	with the universal consent
di Roma	of Rome
indiademiam la chioma;	we crown your locks;
a te l'Asia, a te	before you, Asia and
l'Africa s'atterra;	Africa kneel;
a te l'Europa, e il mar	to you, Europe and the
che cinge e serve	sea which surrounds and serves
questo impero felice,	this fortunate empire,
ora consacra e dona	now devote and offer
questa del mondo imperial	the imperial crown of
corona.	the world.

Nero and Poppea

Instrumental interlude, trumpets
Duet (ternary form: A B B A)
A: ground bass

Pur ti miro, pur ti godo,	I gaze at you, I rejoice in you,
pur ti stringo, pur	I embrace you, I
t'annodo,	enchain you,
più non peno,	no more do I suffer,
più non moro,	no more do I die,
o mia vita, o mio tesoro.	O my life, O my treasure.
Io son tua, tuo son io,	I am yours, you are mine,
speme mia dillo, dì,	O my hope, say it, say,
tu sei pur l'idol mio	you are my idol,
sì mio ben, sì mio cor, mia	yes my love, yes my
vita, sì,	heart, yes my life, yes.
Pur ti miro, pur	I gaze at you, I
ti godo,	rejoice in you,
pur ti stringo, pur	I embrace you, I enchain
t'annodo,	you,
più non peno, più non	no more do I suffer, no
moro,	more do I die,
o mia vita, o mio tesoro.	O my life, O my treasure.

B B: pace quickens

A: original tempo, ground bass

Basic Term

If you aren't sure what this term means, look back at the text, where it appears in bold type.

ground bass (basso ostinato)

[8] HENRY PURCELL

Henry Purcell (about 1659–1695), called the greatest of English composers, was born in London to a musician in the king's service. At about age ten, Purcell became a choirboy in the Chapel Royal, and by the late teens his extraordinary talents were winning him important music positions. In 1677, at about eighteen, he became composer to the king's string orchestra; two years later he was appointed organist of Westminster Abbey; and in 1682, he became an organist of the Chapel Royal. During the last few years of his short life, Purcell was also active composing music for plays.

Acclaimed as *the* English composer of his day, Purcell died in his thirty-sixth year and was buried beneath the organ in Westminster Abbey. He was the last native English composer of international rank until the twentieth century.

Purcell mastered all the musical forms of late seventeenth-century England. He wrote church music, secular choral music, music for small groups of instruments, songs, and music for the stage. His only true opera is *Dido and Aeneas* (1689), which many consider the finest ever written to an English text. His other dramatic works are spoken plays with musical numbers in the form of overtures, songs, choruses, and dances.

Few composers have equaled Purcell's handling of the English language. His vocal music is faithful to English inflection and brings out the meaning of the text. Purcell developed a melodious recitative that seems to grow out of the English language. His music is filled with lively rhythms and a fresh melodic style that captures the spirit of English folk songs. He treated the chorus with great variety and was able to obtain striking effects through both simple homophonic textures and complex polyphony. His music is spiced with dissonances that seemed harsh to the generation of musicians that followed him. Purcell built many of his finest songs on ground basses and, like Monteverdi, was able to make them flow with striking melodies and rhythmic freedom.

Dido and Aeneas (1689)

Dido and Aeneas, a masterpiece of Baroque opera, was written for students at a girls' boarding school. The opera lasts only an hour, is scored for strings and harpsichord continuo, and requires no elaborate stage machinery or virtuoso soloists. Most solo roles are for women. Purcell used many dances in this opera because the director of the school was a dancing master who wanted to display the students' accomplishments. The chorus plays a prominent role, both participating in the action and commenting on it.

The libretto of *Dido and Aeneas*, by Nahum Tate, was inspired by the *Aeneid*, the epic poem by the Roman poet Virgil (70–19 B.C.). As its title makes obvious, the opera's main characters are Dido, queen of Carthage, and Aeneas, king of the defeated Trojans. After the destruction of his native Troy, Aeneas was ordered by the gods to seek a site for the building of a new city. He sets out on the search with twenty-one ships. Landing at Carthage, a North African seaport, Aeneas falls in love with Dido. A sorceress and two witches see this as an opportunity to plot Dido's downfall. (In Purcell's time, people really believed in witches: nineteen "witches" were actually hanged in Massachusetts in 1692, three years after *Dido's* first performance.) A false messenger tells Aeneas that the gods command him to leave Carthage immediately and renew his search. Aeneas agrees but is desolate at the thought of deserting Dido.

Act III

In the last act, which takes place at the harbor, Aeneas's sailors sing and dance before leaving, and the witches look on in glee. Dido, arriving with courtiers and her friend Belinda, has an emotional scene with Aeneas. She calls him a hypocrite and refuses his offer to stay. After Aeneas sails, Dido sings a magnificient lament and kills herself. The opera concludes with the mourning of the chorus.

In these last twenty minutes of his opera, Purcell created an amazing range of emotions. He accomplished quick changes of mood through rapid alternation of brief arias, recitatives, choruses, and dances. Throughout, important words in the vocal line are illustrated vividly.

The climax of *Dido and Aeneas* is *Dido's Lament,* an aria built upon a chromatically descending ground bass that is stated eleven times. (Such chromatic ground basses were commonly used to show grief in the Baroque period.) Dido's melody moves freely above this repeated bass line, creating touching dissonances with it.

Dido and Aeneas (1689)

143

Dido's repeated "Remember me" reaches the highest note of the aria and haunts the listener.

(The harbor. Sailors are loading their ships.)

	Orchestral prelude, *Allegro spiritoso* (spirited allegro). Theme anticipates melody of following song.
Sailor: Come away, fellow sailors, come away, your anchors be weighing, Time and tide will admit no delaying; Take a boozy short leave of your nymphs on the shore, And silence their mourning With vows of returning, But never intending to visit them more.	Lively sailor song.
Chorus: (Text as above)	Chorus repeats sailor's melody with fuller harmony.
	Orchestral interlude: *The Sailors' Dance.*
(Sorceress and witches enter.) Sorceress: See, see the flags and streamers curling, Anchors weighing, sails unfurling! First Witch: Phoebus' pale deluding beams Gilding o'er deceitful streams. Second Witch: Our plot has took, The Queen's forsook!	Recitative.
First Witch and Second Witch: Elissa's ruin'd! Ho ho ho ho ho ho ho Elissa's ruin'd Our plot has took, The Queen's forsook!	Short duet, lively interplay between voices. ("Elissa" is another name for Dido.)

Sorceress:
Our next motion
Must be to storm her lover on the
 ocean.
From the ruin of others our
 pleasures we borrow;
Elissa bleeds tonight, and Carthage
 flames tomorrow!

Chorus:
Destruction's our delight,
Delight our greatest sorrow;
Elissa dies tonight,
And Carthage flames tomorrow!
Ho ho ho ho ho ho ho!

Brief song, dotted rhythms illustrate
 "storm."

Witches' chorus, allegro.
Chordal phrases alternate with rapid
 scales on "ho, ho."

Orchestral interlude: *The Witches'
 Dance.*

(*Dido, Belinda, and women enter.*)
Dido:
Your counsel all is urg'd in vain,
To earth and heaven I will
 complain;
To earth and heaven why do I call?
Earth and heaven conspire my fall.
To Fate I sue, of other means bereft,
The only refuge for the wretched
 left.
(*Aeneas enters*)
Belinda:
See, madam, see where the Prince
 appears!
Such sorrow in his look he bears
As would convince you still he's
 true.
Aeneas:
What shall lost Aeneas do?
How, how, royal fair, shall I impart
The gods' decree, and tell you we
 must part?
Dido:
Thus on the fatal banks of Nile
Weeps the deceitful crocodile;
Thus hypocrites that murder act
Make heav'n and gods the authors
 of the fact!

Recitative.

Dido and Aeneas (1689)

145

Aeneas:
By all that's good . . .
Dido:
By all that's good, no more!
All that's good you have forswore.
To your promised empire fly,
And let forsaken Dido die.
Aeneas:
In spite of Jove's commands I'll
  stay,
Offend the gods and Love obey.
Dido:
No, faithless man, thy course
  pursue,
I'm now resolved as well as you.
No repentance shall reclaim
The injur'd Dido's slighted flame;
For 'tis enough, what-e'er you now
  decree,
That you had once a thought of
  leaving me.
Aeneas:
Let Jove say what he please, I'll
  stay!
Dido:
Away, away! No, no, away, away!   Rapid exchanges between voices;
To Death I'll fly if longer you delay.   then they sing together.
Aeneas:
No, no, I'll stay, and Love obey.
(*Exit Aeneas*)
Dido:
But Death, alas! I cannot shun,   Recitative.
Death must come when he is gone.

Chorus:
Great minds against themselves   Chorus, begins in major, but ends
  conspire,   in minor.
And shun the cure they most desire.

Dido:
Thy hand, Belinda; darkness shades   Recitative, downward melody.
  me,
On thy bosom let me rest;
More I would but Death invades
  me;
Death is now a welcome guest.

When I am laid, am laid in earth,
    may my wrongs create
No trouble, no trouble in thy breast.
Remember me! But ah! forget my
    fate.

Dido's Lament (aria), melody unfolds over descending ground bass in low strings.

Orchestral postlude.

Chorus:
With drooping wings ye Cupids
    come,
And scatter roses on her tomb,
Soft and gentle as her heart;
Keep here your watch and never
    part.

Chorus, "drooping wings" illustrated by downward scale.

THE BAROQUE SONATA [9]

Instrumental music dramatically and rapidly gained importance during the Baroque period. A main development of instrumental music was the **sonata,** a composition in several movements for one to eight instruments. (In later periods, the term *sonata* took on a more restricted meaning.)

Composers often wrote **trio sonatas,** so called because they had three melodic lines: two high ones and a basso continuo. Yet the word *trio* is misleading, because the "trio" sonata actually involves *four* instrumentalists. There are two high instruments (commonly violins, flutes, or oboes) and two instruments for the basso continuo—a keyboard instrument (organ or harpsichord) and a low instrument (cello or bassoon).

The sonata originated in Italy but spread to Germany, England, and France during the seventeenth century. Sonatas were played in palaces, homes, and even in churches—before, during, or after the service. Sometimes composers differentiated between "church sonatas" (*sonata da chiesa*), which had a dignified character and were suitable for sacred performance, and "chamber sonatas" (*sonata da camera*), which were more dancelike in character and intended for court performance.

Basic Terms

If you aren't sure what the following terms mean, look back at the text, where they appear in bold type.

sonata   trio sonata

[10] ARCANGELO CORELLI

Around 1700, the leading Italian violinist and composer of string music was Arcangelo Corelli (1653–1713). He studied in Bologna but spent most of his adult life in Rome. He was friend and music director to Cardinal Ottoboni, in whose palace he lived. There he mingled with the intellectual and aristocratic elite of Rome.

As a teacher, Corelli instructed some of the most eminent musicians of his time and laid the foundations of modern violin technique. He was one of the first to write double stops and chords for the violin and is unique among Italian composers in that he wrote only instrumental music: sixty sonatas and twelve concertos, all for strings.

Though little is known about Corelli's personality, he generally is described as gentle and calm. But when he played, he seemed transformed. According to a contemporary report, "Whilst he was playing on the violin it was usual for his countenance to be distorted, his eyes to become as red as fire, and his eyeballs to roll as in an agony."

Trio Sonata in E Minor, Op. 3, No. 7 (1689)

This work is a fine example of the Baroque trio sonata. The basso continuo is for organ and cello, while upper lines are taken by two violins that play in the same high register. The violins are the center of attention; they seem to be rivals, each taking turns at the melodic ideas, intertwining, and sometimes rising above each other in pitch. Though the bass line is subordinate to the two upper voices, it is no mere accompaniment. It imitates melodic ideas presented by the violins.

The sonata consists of four short movements: (1) slow, (2) fast, (3) slow, (4) fast. All are in the same key, but they differ in meter, mood, and tempo. Each movement alone, however, has only a single mood, as is typical in Baroque instrumental music.

A solemn, dignified Grave opens the sonata in quadruple meter. The main motive is presented by the first violin and immediately imitated in turn by the other instruments before it has been completed. It's as though one instrument tries to catch the others. (See top of next page.)

The second movement, a vigorous Allegro, is fuguelike and written in duple meter. Fugal second movements were characteristic of Baroque trio sonatas.

The third movement is songlike and soulful, an Adagio in triple meter.

The lightest movement of the sonata is the concluding Allegro, a dancelike piece in triple meter. This movement is in two-part form, and each part is repeated: A A B B. Section B is almost twice as long as A. At the end of section B, Corelli uses his only dynamic change in the sonata: the concluding phrase is repeated softly, like an echo.

Violin 1

Violin 2

Continuo
(Cello and
Organ)

ANTONIO VIVALDI [11]

Antonio Vivaldi (1678–1741), a towering figure of the late Italian Baroque, was born in Venice, son of a violinist at St. Mark's Cathedral. Along with his musical training, he prepared for the priesthood and took holy orders at the age of about twenty-five. But poor health caused him to leave the ministry after a year. Because of this religious background and his red hair, Vivaldi was known as "the red priest" (*il prete rosso*).

For most of his life, Vivaldi was a violin teacher, composer, and conductor at the music school of the Pietà, an institution for orphaned or illegitimate girls in Venice. Every Sunday and holiday, about forty young women presented a concert of orchestral and vocal music in the chapel. They were placed in a gallery, "hid from any distinct view of those below by a lattice of ironwork." For this all-female group—considered one of the finest orchestras in Italy—Vivaldi composed many of his works. He also wrote for Venetian opera houses and sometimes took leave to visit foreign courts.

Vivaldi was famous and influential as a violinist and composer. Bach arranged some of his concertos. And the Emperor Charles VI, a passionate music lover, was said to have talked longer to Vivaldi "alone in fifteen days, than he talked to his ministers in two years."

But Vivaldi's popularity waned shortly before his death in 1741, and he died in poverty. Acclaimed during his lifetime, he was almost forgotten for two hundred years. The Baroque revival of the 1950s reclaimed his reputation with modern music lovers.

Although Vivaldi composed operas and fine church music, he is best known for his 450 or so concerti grossi and *solo concertos*. A solo concerto is for a *single* soloist and an orchestra. Vivaldi exploited the resources of the violin as well as other instruments. (There are concertos for solo flute, piccolo, cello, bassoon, and even mandolin.) His fast movements feature tuneful themes in vigorous rhythms, and his slow movements have impassioned, lyrical melodies that would fit an opera aria.

Antonio Vivaldi

149

Concerto Grosso in A Minor, Op. 3, No. 8 (1712)

This concerto for two violins and string orchestra comes from a collection entitled "The Harmonic Whim" (*L'Estro armonico*). Like most of Vivaldi's concertos, it has three movements: (1) fast, (2) slow, (3) fast.

First Movement: Allegro

The vigorous Allegro begins with a fairly long orchestral ritornello containing several melodic ideas.

After the ritornello comes to a clear end, the dynamic level drops, and the two solo violins play a new idea which is lightly accompanied by violins and violas. But the solo section soon yields to the tutti playing the last idea of the opening ritornello. The entire movement alternates between fairly loud tutti sections presenting fragments of the ritornello theme and somewhat softer solo sections. But the solo and tutti sections contrast more in character than in loudness or tone color. The soloists seem to be improvising as they play new ideas, motives from the ritornello, or continuous successions of short notes. After a while, the solo sections offer melodies spun from a tiny ritornello motive that is repeated on different pitches.

A sense of hesitation is created by the rests within the melodies. While one soloist plays these melodies, the other has a continuous run of short notes.

Despite the constant shifting between solo and tutti sections, this movement has a wonderful continuity of motion and mood. Its light, homophonic texture makes it simple and direct.

Second Movement: Larghetto e spiritoso (Slow and spirited)

The tender lyricism of this slow movement breathes the spirit of an operatic love duet. Only at the beginning and end do we hear the tutti, playing a serious descending phrase in unison. These two tutti sections frame a duet between the solo violins which alternate, interweave in imitative dialog, or harmoniously sing the same melody a third apart. The soloists are accompanied quietly by the orchestral violins and violas which constantly repeat the tutti theme or motives from it.

Third Movement: Allegro

Like the opening movement, the concluding Allegro features alternations between tutti and solo sections. But here Vivaldi uses contrasting thematic material in an unusual way. The first hint of something extraordinary comes with a sudden pause, followed by a series of repeated loud and soft chords, broken by rests. This dramatic break in the rhythmic motion signals an even more original stroke.

The second violin, like an opera singer addressing an audience, sings a very long legato melody accompanied softly by the rest of the orchestra. Then Vivaldi returns to the bustling motion of the tutti-solo alternation. Such contrast of thematic material was uncommon in instrumental music until the late eighteenth century. Vivaldi's use of it may well be why Bach chose to arrange this concerto grosso for organ.

Baroque

JOHANN SEBASTIAN BACH [**12**]

The masterpieces of Johann Sebastian Bach (1685–1750) mark the high point of Baroque music. Bach came from a long line of musicians: his father, grandfather, and great-grandfather were all church organists or town musicians in Germany. In fact, so many members of the family were musicians that their name became synonymous with "town musician." Annual family gatherings might assemble over one hundred Bachs to celebrate and make music. And Johann Sebastian Bach passed on this musical heritage—he was father to twenty children, nine of whom survived him, four to become well-known composers.

In Eisenach, his birthplace, Bach probably received his first musical training from his father, the town musician, and cousin, the church organist. But when

Johann Sebastian Bach

151

he was nine both his parents died and Johann went to live with his oldest brother, the organist in a nearby town. At fifteen, Bach left his brother's crowded home and moved to yet another town, where he went to school and supported himself by singing in the church choir and playing the organ and violin. By this time his enthusiasm for music was so great that he would walk up to thirty miles to hear a famous organist.

When he was eighteen, Bach became church organist in Arnstadt, a town not far from his birthplace. Here he came into conflict with church authorities because they felt his music was too complicated; they also questioned his meeting "a strange maiden" in the empty church to accompany her singing. Bach resolved both issues when he was twenty-three by finding a better position at Mühlhausen and by marrying "the strange maiden," his cousin Barbara. His reputation as an organist was growing steadily through his virtuoso performances, which included improvising elaborate fugues and, reportedly, playing with his feet (on the pedal keyboard) better than many performers could with their fingers.

After these two jobs as church organist, Bach obtained a more important post in 1708 as court organist in Weimar. He stayed there for nine years, becoming concertmaster of the court orchestra, but decided to leave when he was passed over for promotion. The Duke of Weimar was so annoyed at Bach's obstinacy in requesting dismissal that he put him in jail for a month! Such was the power of a minor German aristocrat. But Bach demanded his rights all his life, never fearing controversy.

Bach's most lucrative and prestigious post was as court conductor for the Prince of Cöthen. His salary equaled that of the Marshal of the Court, the second highest official. But more importantly, this was the first time in Bach's career that he was not involved with church or organ music. The prince belonged to the Reformed (Calvinistic) Church, and only simple psalm singing was permitted in the service. For the six years from 1717 to 1723, Bach directed the prince's small orchestra of about eighteen players and composed music for it. The *Brandenburg Concertos* grew out of this productive period.

In 1720 Bach's wife died, leaving him with four young children. The next year, at thirty-six, he married a twenty-one-year-old singer at the Cöthen court, and the second marriage was apparently as happy as the first.

Because he was an ardent amateur musician, the Prince of Cöthen treated Bach as a friend. However, the prince's interest began to wane when he married a young princess who did not like music, and Bach decided to look for a new job.

He found it in 1723, as Cantor (director of music) of St. Thomas Church in Leipzig, a position that involved responsibility for four main municipal churches. Bach remained here for the last twenty-seven years of his life. Though one of the most important church posts in Germany, the position carried less prestige and paid less than the one with the Prince of Cöthen. But Bach probably was interested because it was in Leipzig, a comparatively large city of 30,000, where his children could receive a good Lutheran education and go to

At the Church of St. Thomas, in Leipzig, Bach was cantor
for the last twenty-seven years of his life
(Bärenreiter-Bild-Archiv).

Johann Sebastian Bach

153

the University. Then, too, Bach was a deeply religious man. At the beginning of each sacred composition he wrote the letters *J.J.*, for *Jesu Juva* ("Jesus help"), and at the end he put *S.D.G.*, for *Soli Deo Gloria* ("to God alone the glory").

At Leipzig, Bach rehearsed, conducted, and usually composed an extended composition for chorus, soloists, and orchestra for each Sunday and holiday of the church year. He was responsible for the musical education of some fifty-five students in the St. Thomas school. Later he became director of the Leipzig *Collegium Musicum*, a student organization that gave concerts every Friday night at a coffee house. He was also an eminent teacher of organ and composition, gave organ recitals, and was often asked to judge the construction of organs. It's hard to imagine how he did all this while surrounded by children, relatives, and students. And he lived in the school building next to a classroom!

A year before his death in 1750, Bach was almost blind. His last composition, the organ piece, "Before Thy Throne I Step, O Lord" had to be dictated. It breaks off before the end, as though death had kept him from finishing it.

Though recognized as the most eminent organist, harpsichordist, improviser, and master of fugue, Bach was by no means considered the greatest composer of his day. He was little known outside Germany, and even his Leipzig offer came only after two other noted musicians had turned it down. By the time of Bach's maturity, the Baroque style had begun to go out of fashion, and people wanted light, uncomplicated music. Many thought his works too heavy, complex, and polyphonic.

Bach's music was largely forgotten and remained unpublished for years after his death. But a few composers of the following generations knew some of his compositions and were aware of his genius, and a Bach revival took place. In 1829, Felix Mendelssohn performed the *St. Matthew Passion*, and Bach's music has been the daily bread of every serious musician since then.

Bach's Music

Bach created masterpieces in every Baroque form except opera. Throughout, he fused technical mastery and emotional depth. His instrumental music includes pieces for orchestra, for small groups, and for solo organ, harpsichord, clavichord, violin, and cello. The excellence and number of these works show how prominent instrumental music became in the Baroque period. Bach's vocal music—the bulk of his output—was written mostly for the Lutheran church and often was based on hymns familiar to the congregation.

In forming his personal style, Bach drew on musical resources of three different lands. He avidly studied Italian concertos and French dance pieces, as well as the church music of his native Germany.

Bach's music is unique in its combination of polyphonic texture and rich harmony. Several melodic lines of equal importance occur at once; and so many things go on at the same time that the music conveys an awesome complexity and elaboration. Even with the great interest of individual voices, it is the progression of chords that directs the musical motion. More imaginatively than

Though recognized as the most eminent organist,
harpsichordist, improviser, and master of fugue, Bach was
by no means considered the greatest composer of his day;
his music was largely forgotten and remained unpublished
for years after his death (Bärenreiter-Bild-Archiv).

his contemporaries, Bach used complex and dissonant harmonies. His works show an astounding mastery of harmony and counterpoint, and they are used as models by music students today.

Baroque music leans toward unity of mood, and this is particularly true of Bach, who liked to elaborate a single melodic idea in a piece. Such melodies can be intricate, unpredictable, and highly embellished, but unity of mood is created by an insistent rhythmic drive. Whether slow or fast, Bach's works generate perpetual motion.

By Bach's time there was little difference in style between secular and sacred music. In fact, he often created sacred music simply by rearranging instrumental pieces or works originally written for secular texts. His church music also uses operatic forms like the aria and recitative.

Bach liked to illustrate religious or pictorial ideas through musical symbolism. In an organ piece based upon the hymn tune "Old Adam's Fall" (*Durch Adams Fall*), Bach represents the serpent by twisting inner voices, and man's fall by downward leaps in the bass. And in one called *The Ten Commandments*, Bach used the theme exactly ten times.

Sometimes Bach composed music to demonstrate what he could do with a specific musical form. His *Art of the Fugue,* for example, is a collection which displays all the resources of fugue writing. He also explored with unprecedented thoroughness a system of tuning that was being developed at the time. This system, called *equal temperament,* allowed a composer to write in any key, not just simple ones. So Bach used every major and minor key in his collection of forty-eight preludes and fugues, *The Well-Tempered Clavier* (which roughly means "The Well-tuned Keyboard Instrument"). The collection is in two volumes (1722, 1744), each with twenty-four preludes and fugues, one in each major and minor key. Today, the pieces are basic to the repertoire of keyboard players.

Brandenburg Concerto No. 5 in D Major (1721)

Second Movement: Affettuoso (Affectionately, tenderly)

We have already discussed the opening movement (Allegro) in section 3, "The Concerto Grosso and Ritornello Form." Here we'll study the two remaining movements of this concerto grosso for flute, violin, harpsichord, and orchestra.

The *Affettuoso* is in marked contrast to the vigorous opening movement; it's slow, in a minor key, and much quieter. It uses only the three solo instruments and a cello, which duplicates the bass line (left hand) of the harpsichordist. The harpsichord has both an accompanying and a solo role in the movement. Sometimes, as at the beginning, it serves merely as a basso continuo accompaniment to a duet between the violin and flute. In these sections, there is no notated part for the right hand; the harpsichordist is expected to improvise chords as guided by Bach's figured bass. (In modern performing editions, the editor supplies these chords for the player.) In other sections, Bach gives the harpsichordist's right hand a melody of its own, and the instrument becomes a center of attention.

The *Affettuoso* projects a single rather serious mood throughout and is woven entirely from two brief motives that are constantly passed among the instruments. Bach creates melodic variety by turning his motives upside down. The following example shows the two motives, marked *a* and *b*, and their inversions.

Third Movement: Allegro

The concluding Allegro is dancelike in character. It is in A B A form; the A sections are in major, and the B section is in minor. The movement begins like a fugue, with a rollicking subject introduced by the solo violin then imitated by the flute and harpsichord.

After a while, the instruments of the tutti—not heard since the opening movement—join in playing the subject.

The middle section, in minor, begins softly with a lyrical melody by the flute.

This melody starts like the main subject but contains long notes which give it a songlike character. After the flute, the violin and harpsichord take turns playing this melody. The main subject also has a prominent role throughout the middle section and can be heard in a harpsichord solo. Bach achieves both unity and variety by combining within the middle section both the main subject and the new lyrical melody related to it.

A loud tutti signals the conclusion of the middle section. Then the solo violin, imitated by the flute, announces the return of the opening section A. The major key and lively rhythms seem even more joyful after the minor key and reflective quality of the middle section.

Mass in B Minor (begun 1733)

Over a period of years, Bach, a pious Lutheran, composed what is probably the most monumental setting of the Roman Catholic Mass. In 1733, he wrote

Mass in B Minor
(begun 1733)

the first two sections (Kyrie and Gloria) and sent them to a Catholic monarch with a request for the honorary title of court composer. Years later, he finished the Mass by composing new music and by fitting the Latin text to some of his earlier Lutheran church pieces. Bach probably never heard the entire work performed. Since it is far too long to be used in the Catholic service, Bach's reasons for creating it are unknown. He may simply have wanted to show what he could do with this ancient and imposing form.

Bach's B-minor Mass contrasts strikingly with the Renaissance Masses we studied. It has specific orchestral accompaniments for the voices. And each major section of the Mass—like the Kyrie or Credo—is subdivided into arias, duets, and choruses. Thus this Mass has more variety within each large section than corresponding sections of a Renaissance Mass. Each part of Bach's B-minor Mass expresses the meaning and emotion of the text.

Here are two contrasting movements from the Credo: the *Crucifixus*, a profound expression of grief at Christ's crucifixion, and *Et resurrexit*, which expresses joy at Christ's resurrection.

Crucifixus

The *Crucifixus* is scored for four-voice chorus and a small orchestra of strings, two flutes, and continuo. It is built upon a chromatically descending ground bass, or basso ostinato, the traditional symbol of grief in Baroque music (which we heard in *Dido's Lament*, by Purcell).

Over the constantly repeating ground bass, the four voices sing ever-changing melodic lines that produce dissonant harmonies. Minor key, slow tempo, and hushed dynamics—together with the generally downward-moving melodies—contribute to a feeling of infinite sorrow. One of the sublime moments in all music occurs at the very end of this movement, when there is an unexpected shift from minor to major, and the sopranos chromatically descend to their lowest tone. At this point of deepest sorrow, the major key implies hope.

Crucifixus etiam pro nobis sub Pontio Pilato, passus et sepultus est.	And was crucified also for us under Pontius Pilate. He suffered and was buried.

Et Resurrexit

The jubilant *Et resurrexit* fulfills the hope implied in the *Crucifixus*. Now Bach uses a full orchestra, including three trumpets, timpani, and two oboes. The movement is in major; a fast tempo and bright-sounding trumpets make it festive. Typically Baroque is the rising melodic line on the words *Et resurrexit* ("and He rose").

Et re-sur-re — xit, re-sur-re - xit,

Variety is achieved through repeated alternations between orchestral sections and those using voices and instruments.

Et resurrexit tertia die secundum scripturas. Et ascendit in coelum, sedet ad dexteram Dei Patris, et iterum venturus est cum gloria judicare vivos et mortuos, cujus regni non erit finis.

And the third day he rose again according to the scriptures. And ascended into Heaven. And sitteth at the right hand of God the Father. And he shall come again with glory to judge both the living and the dead; Whose kingdom shall have no end.

THE BAROQUE SUITE [**13**]

Instrumental music has always been closely linked with dancing; much of it was written for use in palace ballrooms. During the Renaissance, dances often came in pairs—a dignified dance in quadruple meter was followed by a lively one in triple meter. In the Baroque and later periods, music was written that—while meant for listening, not dancing—was related to specific dance types in tempo, meter, and rhythm.

Baroque composers wrote **suites,** which are sets of dance-inspired movements. Whether for solo instruments, small groups, or orchestra, the movements of a Baroque suite are all written in the same key but differ in tempo, meter, and character. They also have a variety of national origins: the moderately paced *allemande* from Germany might be followed by a fast *courante* and moderate *gavotte* from France, a slow and solemn *sarabande* from Spain, and a fast *gigue* (jig) from England and Ireland. Suites were played at private homes, at court concerts, or as background music for dinner and outdoor festivities.

Dance pieces have a diverse past. Some began as folk dances, while others sprang from aristocratic ballrooms. Even the character of a dance might show dramatic evolution. The slow, solemn sarabande grew out of a sexy song and dance that a sixteenth-century moralist condemned as "so lascivious in its words, so ugly in its movements, that it is enough to inflame even very honest

The Baroque Suite

people." In the seventeenth century, however, the sarabande became respectable enough to be danced by a cardinal at the French court!

The movements of a suite are usually in two-part form with each section repeated: A A B B. The A section, which opens in the tonic key and modulates to the dominant, is balanced by the B section, which begins in the dominant and returns to the tonic key. Both sections use the same thematic material, and so they contrast relatively little except in key.

Suites frequently begin with a movement that is *not* dance-inspired. One common opening is the *French overture,* which is also heard at the beginning of baroque oratorios and operas. Usually written in two parts, the **French overture** first presents a slow section with dotted rhythms that is full of dignity and grandeur. The second section is quick and lighter in mood, often beginning like a fugue. Sometimes part of the opening section will return at the end of the overture.

The suite is an important instrumental form of the Baroque. Even compositions not called "suite" often have several dance-inspired movements. Music influenced by dance tends to have balanced and symmetrical phrases of the same length, because formal dancing has a set of steps in one direction symmetrically balanced by a similar motion in the opposite direction.

Bach wrote four orchestral suites called "overtures," after the French overture that begins each one. We don't know when they were composed, but it seems likely that the *collegium musicum* performed them in a Leipzig coffee house.

Suite (Overture) No. 3 in D Major, by Johann Sebastian Bach

2 oboes, 3 trumpets, timpani, strings, continuo

First Movement: Overture

The suite opens with a majestic French overture, which exploits the bright sounds of trumpets. After a slow opening section with dotted rhythms, we hear the energetic fast section. This begins like a fugue, with an upward-moving theme introduced by the first violins then imitated by the other instruments.

The fast section is like a concerto grosso in its alternation of solid tutti passages with lightly scored ones highlighting the first violins. At the end of the French overture, the slow tempo, dotted rhythms, and majestic mood of the opening return.

Second Movement: Air

The second movement contains one of Bach's best-loved melodies. Scored for only strings and continuo, the Air is serene and lyrical in contrast to the majestic and bustling French overture. The title suggests that the movement is written in the style of an Italian aria. Like the opening movement, the Air is not related to dance. Its A A B B form has a B section that is twice as long as the A section. The Air combines a steadily moving bass (which proceeds in upward and downward octave leaps) with a rhapsodic and rhythmically irregular melody in the violins.

Third Movement: Gavotte

After the Overture and Air, all the movements are inspired by dance, beginning with the Gavotte. Written in duple meter and in a moderate tempo, it uses the full orchestra again. It may be outlined: Gavotte I (A A B B); Gavotte II (C C D D); Gavotte I (A B). Notice the contrast between the sections for full orchestra and those without trumpets and timpani.

Fourth Movement: Bourrée

The Bourrée is an even livelier dance, also in duple meter. Its form is A A B B, and it is the shortest movement of the suite.

Fifth Movement: Gigue

The Suite concludes with a rollicking Gigue in $\frac{6}{8}$ time, also in the form A A B B. This is Bach being simple and direct. Listen for the splendid effect when timpani and trumpets periodically join the rest of the orchestra.

Basic Terms

If you aren't sure what each of the following words means, look back at the text, where they appear in bold type. Additional information can be found by checking the index.

    suite   French overture

Baroque

THE CHORALE AND THE CHURCH CANTATA [**14**]

In the Leipzig of Bach's day, the Lutheran church service on Sunday was the social event of the week: it started at seven in the morning and lasted about four hours. The sermon alone could take an hour.

    Music was a significant part of the Lutheran service. While most religious services today use no more than a chorus and organ, Bach's church had a small orchestra of between fourteen and twenty-one players to accompany the twelve or so men and boys of the choir. The service was filled with music; single compositions might last half an hour.

To further direct communication that Lutheranism stressed between the believer and Christ, the rite was largely in the vernacular—German. Each service included several hymns called *chorales.* The **chorale,** or hymn tune, was sung to a German religious text. These tunes were easy to sing and remember, having only one note to a syllable and moving in steady rhythm. They had been composed in the sixteenth and seventeenth centuries, or had been adapted from folk songs and Catholic hymns. The congregation had sung these tunes since childhood, and each tune carried religious associations. Congregational singing of chorales was an important way for people to participate directly in the service. These melodies were often harmonized for church choirs. The hymn melody was sung in the top part, and the tones of the supporting harmonies were sung by the three lower parts. New church music was often based on traditional melodies written as far back as two centuries. Before the congregation began to sing a hymn, the organist might play a **chorale prelude** a short composition based upon the hymn tune that reminded the congregation of the hymn's melody. By using traditional tunes in their works, composers could involve the congregation and enhance the religious associations.

The Church Cantata

The principal musical expression in the Lutheran service, and one which employed chorales, was the church **cantata.** *Cantata* originally meant a piece that was *sung,* as distinct from the sonata, which was *played.* While many kinds of cantatas were used in Bach's day, we shall focus on the one designed for the Lutheran service in Germany in the early 1700s. Usually written for chorus, vocal soloists, organ, and a small orchestra, it had a German religious text. The text was either newly written or drawn from the Bible or familiar hymns. In the Lutheran services, there were different Gospel and Epistle readings for each Sunday and holiday, and the cantata text was related to the lesson of the day. In a sense, the cantata was a sermon in music which reinforced the minister's sermon, also based on the Gospel and Epistle reading. The cantata of Bach's day might last twenty-five minutes and include several different movements—choruses, recitatives, arias, and duets. We'll see that in its use of aria, duet, and recitative, the cantata closely resembled the opera of the time, and it is typical of Baroque fusion of sacred and secular elements in art and music.

The cantor, or music director, had to provide church cantatas for every Sunday and holiday. Bach wrote about 295; about 195 are still in existence. In his first few years as cantor in Leipzig, he composed them at the staggering rate of almost three a month. During the remaining twenty-five years of his tenure, he was inclined to reuse cantatas, and so his output dropped.

Cantata No. 140: Wachet auf, ruft uns die Stimme ("Åwake, a Voice Is Calling Us"; 1731)

This is Bach's best-known cantata. To fully appreciate it, we perhaps should imagine ourselves as pious Lutherans of his time. Cantata No. 140 was composed for the twenty-seventh Sunday after Trinity Sunday, when the Gospel reading was the parable of the wise and foolish virgins (Matthew, 25). The Christian believers are represented by virgins, and Christ by the Bridegroom:

> Then shall the kingdom of heaven be likened unto ten virgins, which took their lamps and went forth to meet the bridegroom. And five of them were wise, and five were foolish. . . . And at midnight there was a cry made, Behold the bridegroom cometh; go ye out to meet him. Then all those virgins arose, and trimmed their lamps. And the foolish said unto the wise, Give us of your oil; for our lamps are gone out. But the wise answered, saying, Not so; lest there not be enough for us and you: but go ye rather to them that sell, and buy for yourselves. While they were away the bridegroom arrived; and those who were ready went in with him to the wedding; and the door was shut. . . . Keep awake then; for you never know the day or the hour. . . .

Bach based his cantata on the chorale tune *Wachet auf* because its text was inspired by this Sunday's Gospel. The text and melody of the chorale were written by Philipp Nicolai (1556–1608) in about 1597—over 130 years before Bach used it. This was a widely known chorale tune that had been used by other composers before Bach. The hymn has three stanzas, and each is sung to the same melody. Bach used the chorale melody as well as one stanza of its text in three of the seven movements in the cantata:

Movement	Use of Chorale	Content of Text
1 Chorus with orchestra	Chorale, stanza 1	Virgins awakened by the watchmen announcing the coming of the Bridegroom.
2 Recitative for solo tenor with continuo		The Bridegroom is coming.
3 Duet for soprano and bass with violino piccolo and continuo		Dialog between a longing Soul (soprano) and Jesus (bass).
4 Tenors of chorus sing chorale in unison; strings and continuo	Chorale, stanza 2	Zion (Christian believers) rejoices at the arrival of Lord Jesus, God's Son.
5 Recitative for bass, accompanied by strings and continuo		Jesus lovingly greets the bride.

Cantata No. 140: Wachet auf, ruft uns die Stimme ("Awake, a Voice Is Calling Us"; 1731)

163

| 6 | Duet for soprano and bass with oboe and continuo | | Joyous union between Christ (bass) and Christian (soprano). |
| 7 | Chorus doubled by orchestra | Chorale, stanza 3 | Christians praise God and rejoice in union with Him. |

According to a Protestant theologian and music scholar, the chorale text interprets the relationship of the Bridegroom and bride "as a picture of the union of God with his people, of Christ with the Church." The cantata's other texts, for duets and recitatives, were written by an unknown author and depict "the relationship between Jesus and the pious individual soul." They are based on the sensuous Song of Songs (Solomon) in the Bible.

Before listening to all of Cantata No. 140, it's helpful to become acquainted with the chorale tune, which the last movement presents unadorned. The melody has the form A A B.

There are nine melodic phrases, of which the first three are repeated immediately (A A). The last phrase of the A section (phrase 3) reappears at the end of the B section (phrase 9) and beautifully rounds off the chorale melody.

First Movement: Chorus and Orchestra

2 oboes, English horn, French horn, violins 1, violins 2, violas, continuo (organ, bassoon, cello)

In the chorale text of the first movement, watchmen on the towers of Jerusalem call on the wise virgins (Christians) to awake because the Bridegroom (Christ) is coming. The movement opens with an orchestral ritornello which may have been intended to suggest a procession or march. There are dotted rhythms (long-short, long-short), a rising figure with syncopation, and a series of rising scales.

At the ritornello's closing cadence the sopranos enter and sing the chorale's first phrase in long notes. Soon the three lower voices engage in an imitative dialog based on a new motive in shorter note values. Throughout, the orchestra continues to play still shorter notes.

Cantata No. 140: Wachet auf, ruft uns die Stimme ("Awake, a Voice Is Calling Us"; 1731)

165

Thus there are three layers of sound: the chorale phrases in long notes in the soprano; the imitative dialog in shorter note values in the three lower voices; and the ever-busy orchestra playing motives from the ritornello in even shorter notes. The chorale tune (in the soprano) is not presented as a continuous whole but rather phrase by phrase, with breaks between. After each phrase, the voices pause while the orchestra continues to play interludes of either the whole ritornello or sections from it. Sometimes the motives in the three lower voices illustrate the text, as when they have rising scale figures at the word *high* (*hoch*) and exclamations at the repeated *where* (*wo*).

Once during the movement, the three lower voices become emancipated from the soprano and jubilantly sing a melody in rapid notes on *Alleluja*. This, perhaps, is the most exciting moment in the movement.

		Orchestral ritornello.
Wachet auf,	"Awake,"	
ruft uns die Stimme	the voice of watchmen	
		Brief orchestral interlude.
der Wächter sehr	calls us from	
hoch auf der Zinne,	high on the tower,	Rising scales in lower voices depict *high* (*hoch*).
		Brief orchestral interlude.
wach auf,	"Awake,	
du Stadt Jerusalem!	you city of Jerusalem!"	
		Orchestral ritornello.
Mitternacht	Midnight	
heisst diese Stunde;	is this very hour;	
		Brief orchestral interlude.
sie rufen uns	they call to us	
mit hellem Munde:	with bright voices:	
		Brief orchestral interlude.
wo seid ihr	"Where are you,	
klugen Jungfrauen?	wise virgins?"	
		Long orchestral interlude.
Wohl auf,	Take cheer,	
der Bräut'gam kömmt,	the Bridegroom comes,	
		Brief orchestral interlude.
steht auf,	arise,	
die Lampen nehmt!	take up your lamps!	
Alleluja!	Hallelujah!	Altos, jubilant melody in rapid notes. Imitation by tenors, then basses.
Alleluja!	Hallelujah!	Sopranos, chorale in long notes.
		Orchestral interlude.

Macht euch bereit	Prepare yourselves	
		Orchestral interlude.
zu der Hochzeit	for the wedding,	
		Brief orchestral interlude.
ihr müsset ihm	you must go forth	
entgegen gehn.	to meet him.	
		Orchestral ritornello.

Second Movement: Recitative for Tenor

Continuo

Third Movement: Duet for Bass (Jesus) and Soprano (Soul)

Violino piccolo, continuo

When Bach was hired as cantor by the Leipzig town council, he specifically agreed to compose church music that would *not* "make an operatic impression." These two movements, which would be appropriate for a love scene in a Baroque opera, show that Bach did not take his contract literally. The second movement, a recitative in minor, uses only a solo tenor and continuo and contrasts sharply with the brilliant opening movement in major. This is a **secco** ("dry") **recitative,** in which a speechlike melody has a single note to each syllable.

The third movement, a dialog between Jesus and a faithful Soul, conveys a sense of tender longing. This duet begins with a ritornello using the violino piccolo, a small violin tuned higher than the usual instrument. (Today a standard violin plays this part.) After a touching opening phrase, the violin's melody dissolves into a series of tones with rapid time values.

In the vocal sections, the Soul (soprano) has short questioning phrases which are answered by the reassuring Jesus (bass). Throughout, the violin's melody intertwines with the voices, while the continuo provides a steady rhythmic pulse.

Er kommt, er kommt, der Bräut'gam kommt!	He comes, he comes, the Bridegroom comes!
Ihr Töchter Zions, kommt heraus,	Daughters of Zion, come forth,
sein Ausgang eilet aus der Höhe	he is hurrying from on high
in euer Mutter Haus.	into your mother's house.

Cantata No. 140: Wachet auf, ruft uns die Stimme ("Awake, a Voice Is Calling Us''; 1731)

167

Der Bräut'gam kommt, der einem Rehe	The Bridegroom comes, who like a roe
und jungem Hirsche	and a young hart
gleich auf denen Hügeln springt	leaping upon the hills
und euch das Mahl der Hochzeit bringt.	brings you the wedding meal.
Wacht auf, ermuntert euch!	Wake up, bestir yourselves!
der Bräut'gam zu empfangen;	to receive the Bridegroom;
dort, sehet, kommt er hergegangen.	there, look, he comes along.
Wann kommst du, mein Heil?	Soul: When will you come, my salvation?
Ich komme, dein Teil.	Jesus: I am coming, your own.
Ich warte mit brennendem Öle:	Soul: I am waiting with burning oil.
Eröffne den Saal	Throw open the hall
zum himmlischen Mahl!	to the heavenly banquet!
Ich öffne den Saal	Jesus: I open the hall
zum himmlischen Mahl.	to the heavenly banquet.
Komm Jesu!	Soul: Come, Jesus!
komm, liebliche Seele!	Jesus: Come, lovely Soul!

Fourth Movement: Tenor Chorale

Violins and violas in unison, continuo

The chorale tune returns in the fourth movement, the most popular of the cantata. Bach liked this section so much that toward the end of his life he rearranged it as a chorale prelude for organ. With miraculous ease, he sets two contrasting melodies against each other. First we hear the unison strings supported by the continuo playing a warm, flowing melody that Bach may have intended as a dancelike procession of the maidens as they "all follow to the joyful hall and share in the Lord's supper." This melody is repeated and varied throughout while the tenors sing the chorale tune against it.

The chorale tune moves in faster rhythmic values than it did in the opening movement, but here, too, it is broken into component phrases linked by the instrumental melody. It's helpful to listen several times to this movement, first focusing on the rapid rhythms of the graceful string melody; then on the sturdy, slower rhythms of the chorale tune; and finally on all lines at once.

Zion hört die Wächter singen,	Zion hears the watchmen singing,
das Herz tut ihr vor Freuden springen,	for joy her very heart is springing,
sie wachet und steht eilend auf.	she wakes and rises hastily.
Ihr Freund kommt von Himmel prächtig,	From heaven comes her friend resplendent,
von Gnaden stark, von Wahrheit mächtig,	sturdy in grace, mighty in truth,
Ihr Licht wird hell, ihr Stern geht auf.	her light shines bright, her star ascends.
Nun komm, du werte Kron,	Now come, you worthy crown,
Herr Jesu, Gottes Sohn.	Lord Jesus, God's own Son,
Hosianna!	Hosanna!
Wir folgen all'	We all follow
zum Freudensaal	to the joyful hall
und halten mit das Abendmahl.	and share the Lord's Supper.

Fifth Movement: Recitative for Bass (Jesus)

Strings, continuo

Sixth Movement: Duet for Bass (Jesus) and Soprano (Soul)

Oboe, continuo

An operatic atmosphere is again suggested in movements 5 and 6, a recitative and duet that balance movements 2 and 3. The fifth movement is called an **accompanied recitative,** because the voice is supported by strings as well as continuo. The dancelike, joyful duet (sixth movement) depicts the happy union of Christ and the Soul—but it could well suggest the bliss of any newlywed couple. A solo oboe first plays an opening ritornello and then intertwines with the voices almost throughout. Perhaps to suggest "union," the soprano and bass imitate each other and often sing together harmoniously. The movement is in A B A form.

So geh herein zu mir,	Come enter in with me,
du mir erwählte Braut!	my chosen bride!
Ich habe mich mit dir	I have pledged my troth
in Ewigkeit vertraut.	to you in eternity!

Cantata No. 140:
Wachet auf, ruft uns
die Stimme ("Awake, a
Voice Is Calling Us";
1731)

169

Dich will ich auf mein Herz,	I will set you as a seal upon my heart,
auf meinen Arm *gleich wie ein Siegel setzen,* *und dein betrübtes Aug'ergötzen.*	and as a seal upon my arm and restore delight to your sorrowful eye.
Vergiss, o Seele, *nun die Angst, den Schmerz,* *den du erdulden müssen;* *auf meiner Linken sollst du ruh'n,* *und meine Rechte soll dich küssen.*	Forget now, o soul, the anguish, the pain which you had to suffer; on my left you shall rest, and my right shall kiss you.

Mein Freund ist mein!
Und ich bin dein!
Die Liebe soll nichts
scheiden.
Ich will mit dir in
Himmels Rosen weiden,
Du sollst mit mir in
Himmels Rosen weiden,
da Freunde die Fülle,
da Wonne wird sein!
	Soul: My friend is mine!
	Jesus: and I am his!
	Both: Love shall separate
	  nothing!
	Soul: I will feed with you
	  among heaven's roses,
	Jesus: You shall feed with
	  me among heaven's roses,
	Both: There fullness of joy,
	  there rapture shall be!

Seventh Movement: Chorale

Chorus doubled by orchestra

Bach rounds off Cantata No. 140 by bringing back the chorale once more. For the first time since movement 1, all voices and instruments take part. Here the chorale is set in a relatively simple, homophonic texture for four voices, with the instruments simply doubling them, not playing melodies of their own. Now the chorale is heard as a continuous melody, without interludes between its phrases. The rich sound, full harmonies, and regular rhythms express praise of God, faith in Him, and joy in being in His Kingdom. No doubt the congregation joined in the singing of this final chorale, which so firmly expressed their unity and belief.

Gloria sei dir gesungen *mit Menschen- und englischen Zungen,* *mit Harfen und mit Cymbeln schon.*	Gloria be sung to you with men's and angels' tongues, with harps and beautiful cymbals.
Von zwölf Perlen sind die Pforten *an deiner Stadt; wir sind Konsorten* *der Engel hoch um deinen Thron.*	Of twelve pearls are the gates at your city; we are consorts of the angels high about your throne.

Kein Aug' hat je gespürt,	No eye has ever sensed,
kein Ohr hat je gehört	no ear has ever heard
solche Freude.	such a delight.
Des sind wir froh,	Of this we rejoice,
io, io!	io, io,
ewig in dulci jubilo.	forever in sweet joy.

Basic Terms

If you aren't sure what each of the following words means, look back at the text, where they appear in bold type. Additional information about some of them can be found by checking the index.

chorale
chorale prelude
cantata

secco recitative
accompanied recitative

THE ORATORIO [15]

With the opera and cantata, the oratorio stands as a major development in Baroque vocal music. Like opera, the **oratorio** is a large-scale composition for chorus, vocal soloists, and orchestra; it usually is set to a narrative text. Oratorio differs from opera in that it has no acting, scenery, or costumes. Most oratorios are based on biblical stories, but usually they are not intended for religious services. Today they are performed either in concert halls or churches.

An oratorio contains a succession of choruses, arias, duets, recitatives, and orchestral interludes. The chorus is especially important and serves either to comment on or to participate in the drama. A narrator's recitatives usually relate the story and connect one piece with another. Oratorios are longer than cantatas (sometimes over two hours) and have more of a story line.

Oratorios first appeared in early seventeenth-century Italy as musical dramatizations of biblical stories and were performed in prayer halls called "oratorios." During the Baroque period, the oratorio spread to other countries and assumed many forms. *Messiah* by George Frideric Handel has been for decades the best-known and most-loved oratorio.

Basic Term

If you aren't sure what this word means, look back at the text, where it appears in bold type.

oratorio

Basic Term

171

[16] GEORGE FRIDERIC HANDEL

George Frideric Handel (1685–1759), master of Italian opera and English oratorio, was born in Halle, Germany, one month before J. S. Bach. But Handel was not from a musical family; his father was a barber-surgeon who wanted his son to study law, not music. By nine, Handel's musical talent was so outstanding that his father relented somewhat and permitted him to study with the local organist, who also was a composer. By eleven, he was able not only to compose but also to give organ lessons. Perhaps to honor the wishes of his father, who had died when Handel was twelve, he entered Halle University to study law at seventeen. But a year later he left the university and set out for Hamburg.

Handel was drawn to Hamburg's renowned opera house. There he became a violinist and harpsichordist in the orchestra, and when he was twenty, one of his operas was successfully produced.

Handel was a man of temperament and conviction. At the Hamburg opera an incident almost cost him his life. The company was performing an opera by one of Handel's friends, who insisted that he, not Handel, would play the harpsichord. Handel refused to give up his post, and their argument led to a duel. A metal button on Handel's coat broke his opponent's sword. It was a button's great contribution to posterity.

Handel's good fortune continued. At twenty-one he went to Italy for three highly productive years to establish his career. There he wrote Italian operas that were acclaimed far and wide. And he mingled with princes and leading musicians; even cardinals wrote librettos for him to set to music.

Returning to Germany in 1710, Handel took a well-paid position as music director for the Elector Georg Ludwig of Hanover. After just a month, he asked for a leave to go to London, where his opera *Rinaldo* was being produced. *Rinaldo* was a triumph, and he returned to Hanover. A year later Handel again asked the Elector for an English leave. It was granted on condition that Handel stay only a reasonable length of time in London.

This turned out to be the next half-century (1712–1759). Handel's fame in England grew as rapidly as it had in Italy. He became England's leading composer and a favorite of Queen Anne, who gave him a subsidy of two hundred pounds a year. On Queen Anne's death, a complicated royal blood arrangement made the Elector of Hanover, Georg Ludwig, King George I of England (1714). Evidently the King had not taken great offense at Handel's absence; the composer's subsidy was increased to four hundred pounds annually, and he taught music to the King's granddaughters.

Italian opera in London was an exotic entertainment for the pleasure of the aristocracy. Middle-class audiences had little desire to see works with plots they considered absurd; mythology and historic figures of the Mediterranean world did not appeal. So a few aristocrats provided the base of support for opera in London. They ran a commercial opera company called the Royal Academy of Music, and in 1719 Handel became its music director. After nine seasons the company folded because of inadequate support. But in that period Handel had composed a number of brilliant operas for outstanding prima donnas and castrati.

Handel's reputation continued to grow, and after the collapse of the Royal Academy, he decided to form a company to produce his works. (For years he had a triple career as impresario, composer, and performer.) Opera had become a political weapon. To spite him, a company called The Opera of the Nobility was formed. Its backers opposed the party in power, and Handel—friend of the King and an Establishment composer—became a scapegoat.

Both opera companies went bankrupt as a result of the competition, and Handel suffered a breakdown. He went to Germany to recuperate, and his condition moved the future King of Prussia to write, in 1737, "Handel's great days are over, his inspiration is exhausted, and his taste behind the fashion."

But the King of Prussia was mistaken. Handel recovered, returned to London, and—though heavily in debt—managed again to produce operas on his own. To these he added his oratorios, and a glowing new chapter had opened.

For the English public, oratorios were a novelty. But they knew the Old Testament and liked hearing English on stage. Handel offered his oratorios during Lent, when operas were prohibited. Oratorios, unlike opera, required no expensive sets, stage machinery, or costumes, and were thus cheaper to produce. Even though Handel charged high prices, he attracted a new middle-class audience.

In 1741, the year he composed *Messiah,* Handel stopped writing operas entirely. Oratorios poured from his pen. At first, some people were scandalized that biblical words were sung in a public theater. One newspaper received a letter asserting that "the People of England were arriv'd to such a Height of *Impiety* and *Prophaneness,* that the most sacred *Things* were suffer'd to be us'd as *publick Diversions.*"

Despite sniping, the oratorio seasons were acclaimed; they had the added attraction of Handel himself performing his organ concertos between acts. But too much success can bring trouble. Some aristocrats again began to plot Handel's ruin. To them, the idea of a foreign-born musician's attaining power and prominence was too much. Concert posters were torn down, hired hoodlums robbed and assaulted concertgoers, and aristocrats made a point of giving private concerts and balls on oratorio evenings. Gradually, all this simmered down, but not before Handel had another breakdown. Again, he recovered rapidly and went on producing oratorios.

By 1753, Handel was still conducting and giving organ concerts, though he was almost blind. During his lifetime a statue of him was erected in a public park, and when he died in 1759, three thousand mourners attended his funeral in Westminster Abbey. He was stubborn, wealthy, generous, and cultivated. But above all, he was a master composer whose dramatic sense has rarely been equaled.

George Frideric Handel

Handel's triple career as impresario, composer, and performer
brought him success and fame but led to political in-fighting and
two nervous breakdowns (The Bettmann Archive).

Handel's Music

Handel shares Bach's stature among composers of the late Baroque. Although he wrote a great deal of instrumental music—suites, organ concertos, concerti grossi—the core of his huge output consists of English oratorios and Italian operas.

Handel's English oratorios usually are based on stories from the Old Testament and have titles like *Israel in Egypt, Saul, Joshua,* and *Judas Maccabaeus.* They are *not* church music, however; they were composed to entertain paying audiences in public theaters. Most have plots and characters, even though they are performed without acting, scenery, or costumes. As we'll see, *Messiah* is an exception, in that it deals with a New Testament subject and is without a plot.

The chorus is the focus of the Handelian oratorio. Sometimes it participates in the narrative, representing the Israelites or their heathen enemies. But it also comments on the action, lamenting or exulting. Handel treats the combination of chorus and orchestra with flexibility and imagination. In his hands, a chorus can project delicacy, drama, or grandeur. Even Beethoven marveled at Handel's ability "to achieve great effects with simple means."

Handel never hesitated to reinforce an idea in his text by interrupting a polyphonic flow with a series of chords. Changes in texture are more frequent in his music than in Bach's. And he liked to present two different melodic ideas, then combine them polyphonically. Handel achieved sharp changes of mood by shifting between minor and major keys.

Handel's thirty-nine Italian operas, almost all written in London, are less well known today than the oratorios. But after two centuries of neglect, these operas are being revived successfully by modern opera companies. Handel's operas are nearly all serious, and they are based on ancient Greek and Roman history or mythology. The heroes and heroines are royal figures like Julius Caesar and Cleopatra. Most noteworthy in Handel's opera are the arias, which are connected by long passages of recitative in which the plot develops. The arias show Handel's outstanding ability to evoke a mood or emotion. They often were written to display the virtuosity of singers, some of whom were castrati. As examples of Handel's style, we'll listen to an aria from *Julius Caesar* and a section from *Messiah.*

"I Shall Lament My Fate" (*Piangerò la sorte mia*) from *Julius Caesar* (*Giulio Cesare*; 1724)

Julius Caesar met acclaim both in Handel's lifetime and in recent revivals by American, English, and German opera companies. Like many Baroque opera plots, this one is based on ancient history. Caesar loves Cleopatra, who is fighting her brother Ptolemy for the Egyptian throne. At the end of the opera, Caesar and the young queen are joyfully united.

"I Shall Lament My Fate" (*Piangerò la sorte mia*) from *Julius Caesar* (*Giulio Cesare*; 1724)

Handel's ability to express emotion is shown in Cleopatra's aria "I shall lament my fate," from act III.[1] Cleopatra has been captured by Ptolemy and sings to herself while in chains. The aria has the ABA form typical of late Baroque opera. In section A, Cleopatra expresses grief; in section B she vows that her ghost will torment her tyrant brother. These different emotions in the text call for dramatic musical contrasts. The slow opening section (A), in major, is in triple meter. Cleopatra's melody is marked by upward leaps, as is the string accompaniment. The gentle tone color of a flute doubles the first violin.

The B section, in minor, is faster and in quadruple meter. Cleopatra's rage is depicted by brilliant coloratura passages and rapid rhythms.

With the return of section A, Cleopatra again expresses grief. This return is made more touching by the singer's ornamentation of the melody, a common Baroque practice.

Piangerò la sorte mia, *sì crudelo e tanto ria,* *finchè vita in petto avrò.*	I shall lament my fate, so cruel and so wicked, as long as there is life in my breast.	A	Slow, triple meter, major
Mà poi morte d'ogn'intorno *il tiranno e notte e giorno* *fatta spettro agiterò.*	But when I am dead, from every side, both night and day, I, become a specter, will torment the tyrant.	B	Allegro, quadruple meter, minor; brilliant coloratura passages
Piangerò la sorte mia, *sì crudelo e tanto ria,* *finchè vita in petto avrò.*	I shall lament my fate, so cruel and so wicked, as long as there is life in my breast.	A	Slow, triple meter, major; singer adds ornaments

Messiah (1741)

Messiah lasts about 2½ hours and was composed in just twenty-four days. Handel wrote it before going to Ireland, where a concert hall was being dedicated by performances of his works. About five months after arriving in Dublin (1742), Handel first performed *Messiah* to benefit those lingering in debtors' prisons. Rehearsals attracted wide attention: one newspaper commented that *Messiah* was thought "by the greatest Judges to be the finest Composition of Musick that ever was heard." Normally, the concert hall held 600 people; but to increase the capacity, women were asked not to wear hoopskirts, and men were asked to leave their swords at home.

[1] In the RCA Victor recording of *Julius Caesar,* the aria is moved to act I.

Although the premiere was a success, the first London performance (1743) was poorly received, mainly because of the religious opposition to the use of a Christian text in a theater. It took *Messiah* almost a decade to find popularity in London. Not until it was performed yearly at a benefit for a London orphanage did it achieve its unique status. A contempory wrote that *Messiah* "fed the hungry, clothed the naked, fostered the orphan."

In three parts, the oratorio starts with the prophecy of the Messiah's coming and makes celestial announcements of Christ's birth and man's redemption through His appearance. Part II is aptly described by one Handel scholar as "the accomplishment of redemption by the sacrifice of Jesus, mankind's rejection of God's offer and mankind's utter defeat when trying to oppose the power of the Almighty." Part III expresses faith in the certainty of eternal life through Christ as Redeemer.

Unlike most of Handel's oratorios, *Messiah* is meditative rather than dramatic; it lacks plot action and specific characters. *Messiah* is Handel's only English oratorio that uses the New Testament as well as the Old. Millionaire Charles Jennings, an amateur literary man, compiled the text by taking widely separated passages from the Bible—Isaiah, Psalms, and Job from the Old Testament; Luke, I Corinthians, and The Book of Revelations from the New.

Over the years, Handel rewrote some movements in *Messiah* for different performers and performances. Initially, the orchestra and chorus were smaller than we are used to: the chorus included twenty singers, all male, and the small orchestra had only strings and continuo, with trumpets and timpani used in some sections. Today we sometimes hear arranged versions (Mozart made one) played by orchestras of one hundred and choruses of several hundred.

When discussing texture (p. 62) we studied the famous *Hallelujah Chorus*, which ends part II of *Messiah*. Now we will focus on the opening twelve pieces of part I, dealing with the prophecy of the Messiah's coming. (The whole oratorio has over fifty movements.) Handel ensures variety by skillfully contrasting movements and groups of them. He achieves profound effects through simple alternation of major and minor.

1. Sinfonia for Orchestra (French Overture)

Grave; Allegro moderato (Moderate allegro)

Messiah opens with a French overture in minor. As is customary, a slow section featuring dotted rhythms is followed by a quite rapid section beginning like a fugue. A lively subject is passed from higher to lower instruments.

Messiah (1741)

177

After this, the imitation mainly involves fragments of this subject. Near the end of the movement is a feature typical of Handel: in the midst of bustling motion, the orchestra, quite unexpectedly, sustains a chord, and after a brief pause, there is a closing cadence of slow chords. It's as though Handel applied a brake to bring the music to a decisive end.

The three vocal pieces following the overture form a group consisting of an accompanied recitative, an aria, and a chorus.

2. "Comfort ye, my people"

Accompanied Recitative for Tenor and Orchestra

Larghetto (Slow, but less so than largo)

The second movement opens with an orchestral ritornello in major that seems "comforting" after the overture's minor key. This material returns throughout. The second movement is an arioso—the vocal line is between a recitative and an aria, more lyrical than one, less elaborate than the other. At the end, however, a heavenly voice is heard ("The voice of him that crieth in the wilderness"), and the vocal line becomes completely recitative.

high - way   for our God.

The tenor's opening "Comfort ye" motive (long-short-long) is echoed by the strings, which repeat it reassuringly throughout.

Isaiah XL, 1-3   Comfort ye, comfort ye my people, saith your God. Speak ye comfortably to Jerusalem, and cry unto her, that her warfare is accomplish'd, that her iniquity is pardon'd. The voice of him that crieth in the wilderness, Prepare ye the way of the Lord, make straight in the desert a highway for our God.

3. "Ev'ry valley shall be exalted"

Aria for Tenor

Andante

This aria is striking in its vivid word-painting, so characteristic of Baroque music. On a single syllable of *exalted* (raised up), forty-six rapid notes form a rising musical line.

Shall be_____ ex-alt - - - - - - - - - - - - ed,

Notice, too, the rising and falling direction of the phrase "and every mountain and hill made low."

and ev-'ry moun-tain and hill_____ made low;

Messiah (1741)

179

"The crooked straight" is represented:

the crook - ed   straight,

Plain (smooth or level), in the line "and the rough places plain," is expressed by sustained tones and a long, legato melodic line.

Isaiah XL, 4   Ev'ry valley shall be exalted, and ev'ry mountain and hill made low, the crooked straight, and the rough places plain.

4. "And the glory of the Lord shall be revealed"

Chorus

Allegro

In quick succession Handel gives us the altos alone, the whole chorus in a chordal assertion, and then the various voices imitating each other. Four different melodic ideas are contrasted and intertwined. The solemn repeated-note idea, "For the mouth of the Lord hath spoken it," is heard against the more rhythmically active "and all flesh shall see it together."

Isaiah XL, 5   And the glory of the Lord shall be revealed, and all flesh shall see it together, for the mouth of the Lord hath spoken it.

Then the mood changes as Handel's text evokes the awesomeness, rather than comfort, of the Lord's coming. The Lord shall "shake the heav'ns and the earth"; He is "like a refiner's fire"; and "shall purify the sons of Levi." As in the first three vocal pieces, an accompanied recitative is followed by an aria and chorus. But in keeping with the different character of the text, Handel emphasizes minor, rather than major, keys.

5. "Thus saith the Lord of Hosts"

Accompanied Recitative for Bass

Andante

Fierce determination is suggested by the dotted rhythms of the orchestral accompaniment and the bass's long series of quick notes which graphically *"shake* the heavens."

Haggai II, 6-7   Thus saith the Lord of Hosts: Yet once, a little while, and I will shake the heav'ns, and the earth, the sea, and the dry land, and I will shake all nations, and the desire of all nations shall come.

Malachi III, 1   The Lord, whom ye seek, shall suddenly come to His temple, ev'n the messenger of the Covenant, whom ye delight in, behold, He shall come, saith the Lord of Hosts.

6. "But who may abide the day of His coming?"

Aria for Bass[2]

Larghetto

The text in this aria is set in contrasting ways. "But who may abide the day of His coming, and who shall stand when He appeareth?" is set to slow, calm music in triple meter. "For He is like a refiner's fire," in sharp contrast, is *prestissimo,* with the "refiner's fire" stoked by furiously rushing rhythms in both voice and orchestra. The aria may be outlined A(slow), B(fast), A'(slow), B'(fast).

Malachi III, 2	But who may abide the day of His coming, and who shall stand when He appeareth? For He is like a refiner's fire.

7. "And He shall purify the sons of Levi"

Chorus

Allegro

Handel created much of this chorus from music he originally wrote for an Italian secular duet to the words, "Life too is a flower; it comes with the morning and dies with the spring of a single day." This origin accounts for the unusually light texture of music for so stern a text as "And He shall purify the sons of Levi." In some places only one or two voices are heard. But for the line "that they may offer unto the Lord an offering in righteousness," Handel created music that is more powerful, emphatic, and chordal.

Malachi III, 3	And He shall purify the sons of Levi, that they may offer unto the Lord an offering in righteousness.

8. "Behold, a virgin shall conceive"

Recitative for Contralto

This tender narration is the first *secco* recitative in *Messiah.* Other recitatives are accompanied by the orchestra, but here only the basso continuo is heard.

Isaiah VII, 14	Behold, a virgin shall conceive, and bear a son, and shall call his name Emmanuel: "God with us."

9. "O thou that tellest good tidings to Zion"

Contralto Aria and Chorus

Andante

Handel here combines a contralto aria and a chorus into one. After the extended aria, the chorus enters (without a break), singing the same thematic material

---

[2]Handel wrote several versions of this aria.

Messiah (1741)

181

to identical words. This produces a contrast of sound rather than mood. The cheerful aria flows in $\frac{6}{8}$ meter (1-2-3-4-5-6), and the unison violins often echo vocal phrases. After opening in imitative texture, the chorus is largely homophonic. Notice the exclamations on *arise* and *behold*, which are playfully echoed by the orchestra.

| Isaiah XL, 9 | O thou that tellest good tidings to Zion, get thee up into the high mountain, O thou that tellest good tidings to Jerusalem, lift up thy voice with strength, lift it up, be not afraid, say unto the cities of Judah: Behold your God! |
| Isaiah LX, 1 | O thou that tellest good tidings to Zion, arise, shine, for thy light is come, and the glory of the Lord is risen upon thee. |

10.   "For behold, darkness shall cover the earth"

Accompanied Recitative for Bass

Andante larghetto

11.   "The people that walked in darkness"

Aria for Bass

Larghetto

The accompanied recitative and aria bring yet another change of mood as darkness covers the earth. They eclipse the brightness of the chorus in major which came before; this "dark" music is in a minor key, low register, and relatively slow tempo.

The text of the accompanied recitative features an opposition between the lines "For, behold, darkness shall cover the earth, and gross darkness the people," and "but the Lord shall arise upon thee, and His glory shall be seen upon thee." Handel depicts this by a sudden shift from minor to major, and a long ascending line on "but the Lord shall *arise.*"

In the aria, too, minor and major are used to separate darkness and light. Handel suggests people groping in darkness by a winding vocal line that is in stark unison with the orchestra. The words "have seen a great light" bring a change from minor to major and a vocal melody that is more independent of the orchestra.

| Isaiah LX, 2-3 | For behold, darkness shall cover the earth, and gross darkness the people: but the Lord shall arise upon thee, and His glory shall be seen upon thee. And the Gentiles shall come to thy light, and kings to the brightness of thy rising. |
| Isaiah IX, 2 | The people that walked in darkness have seen a great light. And they that dwell in the land of the shadow of death, upon them hath the light shined. |

12.   "For unto us a Child is born"

Chorus

This is some of Handel's most joyful music. The major key sounds fresh after the minor in the preceding pieces. The texture is light, often with only one or two voices singing at a time. After the sopranos announce a motive, it is imitated by the tenors, then both voices—with different rhythms—are combined.

The words "and the government shall be upon His shoulder" bring a new melodic idea in dotted rhythm.

Handel keeps the dynamics subdued until the magnificant chordal outburst on "Wonderful, Counsellor." This change of texture and dynamics is a master's stroke.

With such a close fusion of words and music, it may be disconcerting to learn that most of the melodic ideas in this chorus came from Handel's Italian duet for the words "No, I will not trust you, blind love, cruel Beauty! You are too treacherous, too charming a deity!" (The musical idea for *Wonderful* is new.) But remember that in Handel's time there was little difference in style between sacred and secular music. Amorous and religious joy could therefore be conveyed in the same manner.

Isaiah IX, 6   For unto us a Child is born, unto us a Son is given, and the government shall be upon His shoulder, and His Name shall be called: Wonderful, Counsellor, the Mighty God, the Everlasting Father, the Prince of Peace!

Messiah (1741)

183

THE CLASSICAL PERIOD

Mozart playing a duet with his sister, Maria Anna, while their father, Leopold, listens (The Bettmann Archive).

[1] THE CLASSICAL STYLE (1750–1820)

In looking at the Baroque era, we found that the scientific methods and discoveries of geniuses like Galileo and Newton had vastly changed man's view of the world. By the middle of the eighteenth century, faith in the power of reason was so great that it began to undermine the authority of the social and religious establishment. Philosophers and writers—especially Voltaire (1694–1778) and Denis Diderot (1713–1784)—saw their time as a great turning point in history and referred to it as the "Age of Enlightenment." They believed in progress, holding that reason, not custom or tradition, was the best guide to human conduct. Their attacks on the privileges of the aristocracy and clergy reflected the outlook of the middle class, which struggled for its rights. This new climate of opinion prepared the way for the American and French Revolutions at the end of the eighteenth century.

Revolutions in thought and action were paralleled by shifts of style in the visual arts. During the early eighteenth century, the heavy, monumental Baroque style gave way to the more intimate rococo style, with its light colors, curved lines, and graceful ornaments. Painters Antoine Watteau (1684–1721) and Jean Honoré Fragonard (1732–1806) depicted an enchanted world peopled by elegant men and women in constant pursuit of pleasure. But by the later eighteenth century there was yet another change in taste, and rococo art was thought frivolous, excessively ornamented, and lacking in ethical content. The rococo style was superseded by the neoclassical style, which attempted to recapture the "noble simplicity and calm grandeur" of ancient Greek and Roman art. Neoclassical artists emphasized firm lines, clear structures, and moralistic subject matter. The painter Jacques Louis David (1748–1825), who took part in the French Revolution, sought to inspire heroism and patriotism through his scenes of ancient Rome.

Artistic response to the decline of traditional power is evidenced further by English painter William Hogarth (1697–1764), whose socially conscious paintings satirized the manners and morals of the British aristocracy and middle class, and by the Spaniard Francisco Goya (1746–1828), whose highly personal vision lashed out against hypocrisy, oppression, and inhumanity.

In music history, the transition from the Baroque style to the full flowering of the Classical is called the "pre-Classical" period; it extends from roughly 1730 to 1770. The shift in musical taste parallels the similar, earlier trend in the visual arts. It was developing even as Bach and Handel were creating Baroque masterpieces. Among the important pioneers of this new style were Bach's sons, Carl Philipp Emanuel (1714–1788) and Johann Christian (1735–1782). Around the middle of the eighteenth century, composers concentrated on simplicity and clarity, discarding much that had enriched late Baroque

The Classical Period

186

The rococo painter Jean Honoré Fragonard depicted the
game of love in *The Meeting* (The Frick Collection).

William Hogarth satirized the manners and morals of society in *Election Entertainment* (Sir John Soane's Museum).

music. Polyphonic texture was neglected in favor of tuneful melody and simple harmony. Carl Philipp Emanuel Bach described music with strict polyphonic imitation as "dry and despicable pieces of pedantry." Mid-eighteenth-century composers entertained their listeners with music offering contrasts of mood and theme. The term *gallant style* (*style galant*) was applied to this light, graceful music.

The term *Classical* is confusing because it has so many different meanings. It may refer to an aspect of Greek or Roman antiquity, or it may be used for any supreme accomplishment of lasting appeal (as in the expression "movie classic"). Many people take "classical music" to mean anything that is *not* rock, jazz, folk, or popular music.

Music historians have borrowed the term *Classical* from the field of art history, where it is more appropriate. Painting, sculpture, and architecture of the late eighteenth and early nineteenth centuries were often influenced by Greek and Roman models. But the music of this period shows little direct relationship to antiquity. The significant parallel between "Classical" music and "neoclassical" art is a common stress on balance and clarity of structure. These traits can be found in the fully developed Classical style in music which we will focus on. The style flourished from about 1770 to 1820, and its master composers are Joseph Haydn (1732–1809), Wolfgang Amadeus Mozart (1756–1791), and Ludwig van Beethoven (1770–1827). First, we'll study some characteristics of their work.

Classical Contrast of Mood

Great variety and contrast of mood received new emphasis in Classical music. While a late Baroque piece may convey a single emotion, a Classical composition will fluctuate in mood. Dramatic, turbulent music may lead into a carefree dance tune. Not only are there contrasting themes within a movement, but there also may be striking contrasts within a single theme.

Mood in Classical music may change gradually or suddenly, expressing conflicting surges of elation and depression. But such conflict and contrast are under the firm control of the Classical composer. Great masters like Haydn, Mozart, and Beethoven were able to impart unity and logic to music of wide emotional range.

Classical Rhythm

Flexibility of rhythm adds variety to Classical music. A Classical composition has a wealth of rhythmic patterns, while a Baroque piece contains a few that are reiterated throughout. Baroque works convey a sense of continuity and perpetual motion, so that after the first few bars one can predict pretty well the rhythmic character of an entire movement. But the Classical style includes unexpected pauses, syncopations, and frequent changes from long notes to shorter ones. And the change from one pattern of note-lengths to another may be either sudden or gradual.

Classical Texture

In contrast to the polyphonic texture of late Baroque music, Classical music is basically homophonic. However, texture is treated as flexibly as rhythm. Pieces shift smoothly or suddenly from one texture to another. A work may begin homophonically with a melody and simple accompaniment, but then tension and excitement are created by a change to a more complex polyphonic texture that features two simultaneous melodies or melodic fragments imitated among the various instruments.

Classical Melody

Classical melodies are among the most tuneful and easy to remember. The themes of even highly sophisticated compositions may have a folk or popular flavor. Occasionally, composers simply borrowed popular tunes. (Mozart did, in his variations on "Twinkle, Twinkle, Little Star," which he knew as the French song *Ah, vous dirai-je, maman*.) More often, they wrote original themes with a popular character.

Classical melodies often sound balanced and symmetrical because they are made up of two phrases of the same length. The second phrase may begin like the first, but it ends more conclusively. Such a melodic type, which may be diagrammed a a', is easy to sing (it frequently is found in nursery tunes such as "Mary Had a Little Lamb"). Baroque melodies, on the contrary, tend to be less symmetrical, more elaborate, and harder to sing.

Classical Dynamics and the Piano

The Classical composers' interest in expressing shades of emotion led to widespread use of gradual dynamic change—crescendo and descrescendo. They did not restrict themselves to the terraced dynamics (abrupt shifts from loud to soft) characteristic of Baroque music. Crescendos and decrescendos were an electrifying novelty, and audiences sometimes rose excitedly from their seats.

The Classical desire for gradual dynamic change led to the replacement of the harpsichord by the piano. By varying the finger pressure on the keys, a pianist can play more loudly or softly. Although the piano was invented in 1709, it began to replace the harpsichord only in the 1780s and 1790s. Almost all the mature keyboard compositions of Haydn, Mozart, and Beethoven were written for the piano, rather than for the harpsichord, clavichord, or organ featured in Baroque music.

The End of the Basso Continuo

The basso continuo was gradually abandoned during the Classical period. In Haydn's or Mozart's works, a harpsichordist did not need to improvise an accompaniment. The basso continuo became obsolete because more and more music was written for amateurs, who could not master the difficult art of improvising from a figured bass. Also, Classical composers wanted more

The End of the Basso Continuo

191

control; they preferred to specify an accompaniment rather than to trust the judgment of improvisers.

The Classical Orchestra

A new orchestra evolved during the Classical period. Unlike the Baroque orchestra, it was a standard group of four sections: strings, woodwinds, brass, and percussion. In the late instrumental works of Mozart and Haydn, an orchestra might consist of the following:

Strings: violins 1, violins 2, violas, cellos, double basses
Woodwinds: 2 flutes, 2 oboes, 2 clarinets, 2 bassoons
Brass: 2 French horns, 2 trumpets
Percussion: 2 timpani

Notice that woodwind and brass instruments are paired and that clarinets are added. On the other hand, trombones were used by Haydn and Mozart only in opera and church music, not in solely instrumental works.

The number of musicians in a Classical orchestra was greater than in a Baroque group, but practice varied considerably from place to place. Haydn directed a private orchestra of only twenty-five players from 1761 to 1790. But for public concerts in London in 1795, he led a large orchestra of sixty musicians.

Classical composers exploited individual tone colors of orchestral instruments. Unlike Baroque composers, they did not treat one instrument like another. Classical composers would not let an oboe duplicate the violin melody for the entire length of a movement. A Classical piece has greater variety of tone color, and more rapid changes of color. Strings alone may begin, followed by a shift to woodwinds, and then the whole orchestra will be heard.

Each section of the Classical orchestra had a special role. The strings were the most important section, with the first violins taking the melody most of the time, and the lower strings providing an accompaniment. The woodwinds added contrasting tone colors and were often given melodic solos. Horns and trumpets brought power to loud passages and filled out the harmony, but they did not usually play the main melody. Timpani were used for rhythmic bite and emphasis. As a whole, the Classical orchestra had developed into a flexible and colorful instrument to which composers could entrust their most powerful and dramatic musical conceptions.

Classical Form

Instrumental works of the Classical period usually consist of several movements that contrast in tempo and character. Usually four movements are arranged as follows: (1) fast movement, (2) slow movement, (3) dance-related movement, and (4) fast movement. Classical symphonies and string quartets usually follow this four-movement pattern, while Classical sonatas may consist of two, three, or four movements. A *symphony* is written for orchestra; a *string quartet* for two violins, viola, and cello; and a *sonata* for one or two instruments. (The Classical symphony, string quartet, and sonata are more fully described in sections 3 to 6 and 8.)

In writing an individual movement of a symphony, string quartet, or sonata, a Classical composer could choose from several different forms. One movement of a composition might be in A B A form, while another might be a theme and variations. The following sections will describe some other forms used in Classical movements, but now we'll look at a few general characteristics of Classical form.

Classical movements often contrast themes vividly. A movement may contain two, three, or even four or more themes of different character. This use of contrasting themes distinguishes Classical from Baroque music, which often uses only one main theme. The Classical composer sometimes signals the arrival of a new theme with a brief pause.

The larger sections of a Classical movement balance each other in a satisfying and symmetrical way. Unstable sections that wander from the tonic key are balanced by stable ones that confirm it. By the end of a Classical movement, musical tensions have been resolved.

Though we speak of the Classical style, we must remember that Haydn, Mozart, and Beethoven were three individuals with dissimilar personalities. While Haydn's and Mozart's works at first may sound similar, deeper involvement reveals striking personal styles. Beethoven's music seems more powerful, violent, and emotional when compared with the apparently more restrained and elegant works of the earlier masters. But Haydn and Mozart also composed music that is passionate and dramatic. We'll see that all three composers employed similar musical procedures and forms; yet their emotional statements bear the particular stamp of each.

COMPOSER, PATRON, AND PUBLIC IN THE CLASSICAL PERIOD [2]

Haydn, Mozart, Beethoven—three of the world's greatest composers—worked during a time of violent political and social upheaval. The seventy-year period from 1750 to 1820 was convulsed by the American and French Revolutions and by the Napoleonic wars. Political and economic power shifted from the aristocracy and the church to the middle class. Social mobility increased to a point where a low-born genius like Napoleon could become Emperor of

Composer, Patron, and Public in the Classical Period

The Spanish painter Francisco Goya lashed out at the inhumanity of war in *The Third of May*, 1808, which shows the execution of Spanish hostages by soldiers of Napoleon's army (Omikron).

France. "Subversive" new slogans like "Liberty, equality, fraternity!" sprang from the people's lips. All established ideas were being reexamined, including the existence of God.

Like everyone else, musicians were strongly affected by such changes, and in the careers of the three Classical masters we can trace the slow emancipation of the composer. First came Joseph Haydn (1732–1809), content to spend most of his life serving a wealthy aristocratic family. His contract of employment (1761) shows he was considered a skilled servant, like a gardener or game-keeper. He had to wear a uniform and "compose such music as His Highness shall order"—and was warned to "refrain from vulgarity in eating, drinking, and conversation." Born just twenty-four years later, Wolfgang Amadeus Mozart (1756–1791) could not bear being treated as a servant; he broke from his court position and came to Vienna to try his luck as a free-lance musician. But his personality was unsuited to the struggles of such a career, and he died tragically in poverty. Ludwig van Beethoven (1770–1827) succeeded where

Mozart failed. Only a few years after Mozart's death, Beethoven was able to work as an independent musician in Vienna. His success was gained through a wider middle-class market for music and a commanding personality that prompted the nobility to give him gifts and treat him as an equal.

As the eighteenth century advanced, more people made more money. Merchants, doctors, and government officials could afford larger homes, finer clothes, and better food. But the prospering middle class wanted more than material goods; it also sought aristocratic luxuries like theater, literature, and music. In fact, during the Classical period, the middle class had a great influence on music. Because palace concerts were usually closed to the townsman, he organized public concerts where, for the price of admission, he could hear the latest symphonies and concertos. Following the success of a famous concert series in Paris, the *Concert spirituel* (1725), public concerts mushroomed throughout Europe. But the merchant or lawyer was not content to hear music only in concerts. He wanted to be surrounded by music at home. He felt his own children deserved music lessons as much as did the children of aristocrats. Indeed, if his children played instruments well enough, they might be invited to palaces and eventually marry into the aristocracy. In any event, demand for printed music, instruments, and music lessons had vastly increased.

Composers in the Classical period took middle-class tastes into account. They wrote pieces that were easy for amateur musicians to play and understand. They turned from serious to comic opera, from heroic and mythological plots dear to the nobility to middle-class subjects and folklike tunes. Their comic operas sometimes even ridiculed the aristocracy, and their minuets became less elegant and courtly, more vigorous and rustic.

Serious composition was flavored by folk and popular music. The Classical masters sometimes used familiar tunes as themes for symphonies and variations. Mozart was delighted that people danced to waltzes arranged from his opera melodies. Haydn, Mozart, and Beethoven all wrote dance music for public balls in Vienna.

Vienna

Vienna was one of the music centers of Europe during the Classical period, and Haydn, Mozart, and Beethoven were all active there. The seat of the Holy Roman Empire (which included parts of present-day Austria, Germany, Italy, Hungary, and Czechoslovakia), it was a bustling cultural and commercial center with a cosmopolitan character. Its population of almost 250,000 (1800) made Vienna the fourth largest city in Europe. All three Classical masters were born elsewhere, but they were drawn to Vienna for study and for recognition. In Vienna Haydn and Mozart became close friends and influenced each other's musical style. Beethoven traveled to Vienna at sixteen to play for Mozart; at twenty-two, he returned to study with Haydn.

Princes, dukes, and counts from all over the Empire spent the winter in Vienna, sometimes bringing their private orchestras. Music was an important

The old Burgtheater in Vienna where Mozart's operas were first performed (Austrian National Library).

part of court life, and a good orchestra was a symbol of prestige. Many of the nobility were excellent musicians. For instance, Empress Maria Theresa had sung in palace musicales when she was young; Emperor Joseph II was a competent cellist, and Archduke Rudolf was Beethoven's long-time student of piano and composition.

Much music was heard in private concerts, where aristocrats and wealthy commoners played alongside professional musicians. Mozart and Beethoven often earned money by performing in these intimate concerts. The nobility frequently hired servants who could double as musicians. An advertisement in the *Vienna Gazette* of 1789 reads: "Wanted, for a house of the gentry, a manservant who knows how to play the violin well."

In Vienna there was also outdoor music, light and popular in tone. Small street bands of wind and string players played at garden parties or under the windows of people likely to throw down money. A Viennese almanac reported that "on fine summer nights you may come upon serenades in the streets at all hours." Haydn and Mozart wrote many outdoor entertainment pieces, which they called *divertimentos* or *serenades*. Vienna's great love of music and its enthusiastic demand for new works made it the chosen city of Haydn, Mozart, and Beethoven.

SONATA FORM

3

An astonishing amount of great music from the Classical period to the twentieth century is composed in *sonata form* (sometimes called *sonata-allegro form*). The term **sonata form** refers to the form of a *single* movement. It should not be confused with the term sonata, which is used for a whole composition made up of *several* movements. The opening fast movement of a Classical symphony, sonata, or string quartet is usually in sonata form. This form is also used in slow movements and in fast concluding movements.

A sonata-form movement consists of three main sections: the *exposition*, where the themes are presented; the *development*, where themes are treated in new ways; and the *recapitulation*, where the themes return. These three main sections are often followed by a concluding section, the *coda* (Italian for "tail"). Remember that these sections are all within *one movement*. A sonata-form movement may be outlined as follows:

Exposition
First theme in tonic (home) key
Bridge containing modulation from home key to new key
Second theme in new key
Closing section in key of second theme

ONE MOVEMENT

Development
New treatment of themes; modulations to different keys

Recapitulation
First theme in tonic key
Bridge
Second theme in tonic key
Closing section in tonic key

(*Coda* in tonic key)

A movement in sonata form is sometimes preceded by a slow introduction that creates a strong feeling of expectancy.

Exposition

The **exposition** sets up a strong conflict between the tonic key and the new key, between the first theme (or group of themes) and the second theme (or group of themes). It begins with the first theme in the tonic, or home, key. There follows a **bridge,** or *transition,* leading to the second theme in a new key. Such modulation from the home key to a new key creates a feeling of harmonic tension and forward motion. The second theme often contrasts in mood with the first theme. A closing section ends the exposition in the key of the second theme. At the end of a Classical exposition there usually is a repeat sign (:‖) indicating that the whole exposition is repeated.

Exposition

197

Development

The **development** is often the most dramatic section of the movement, keeping the listener off balance as the music moves restlessly through several different keys. Through these rapid modulations, the harmonic tension is heightened. In this section, themes are *developed,* or treated in new ways. They are broken into fragments or **motives,** which are short musical ideas developed within a composition. A motive may take on different and unexpected emotional meanings. A fragment of a comic theme, for example, may be made to sound aggressive and menacing through changes of melody, rhythm, or dynamics. Themes can be combined with new ideas or changed in texture. A complex polyphonic texture can be woven by shifting a motive rapidly among different instruments. The harmonic and thematic searching of the development builds a tension that demands resolution.

Recapitulation

The beginning of the **recapitulation** brings resolution as we again hear the first theme in the tonic key. In the recapitulation, the first theme, bridge, second theme, and concluding section are presented more or less as they were in the exposition, with one crucial difference: All the principal material is now in the tonic key. Earlier, in the exposition, there had been strong contrast between the first theme in the home key and the second theme and closing section in a new key; that basis for tension is resolved in the recapitulation by presenting the first theme, second theme, and closing section all in the tonic key.

Coda

An even more powerful feeling of conclusion is attained by following the recapitulation with yet another section. The **coda** rounds off a movement by repeating themes or developing them further. It always ends in the tonic key.

The amazing durability and vitality of sonata form results from its capacity for drama. The form moves from a stable situation toward conflict (the exposition), to heightened tension (the development), then back to stability and resolution of conflict (the recapitulation and coda). Here is an outline:

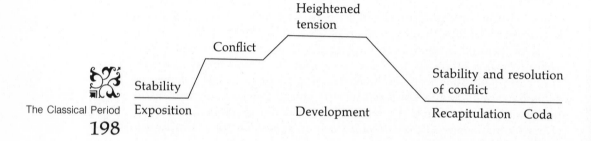

Heightened tension

Conflict

Stability

Stability and resolution of conflict

Exposition   Development   Recapitulation   Coda

Sonata form is exceptionally flexible and subject to endless variation. It is not a rigid mold into which musical ideas are poured. Rather, it may be viewed as a set of principles that serve to shape and unify contrasts of theme and key. Haydn, Mozart, and Beethoven repeatedly used sonata form, yet each maintained individuality. Movements in sonata form may differ radically in character, length, and in the number and treatment of themes. Sonata form is so broad and useful that it's no surprise to find it spanning two hundred years.

Fourth Movement from Symphony No. 40 in G Minor, K. 550, by Wolfgang Amadeus Mozart

This rapid sonata-form movement from Mozart's Symphony No. 40 in G Minor conveys a feeling of controlled tension. The opening theme, in the tonic key of G minor, offers brusque contrasts of dynamics and rhythm. A soft upward arpeggio (broken chord) alternates repeatedly with a loud rushing phrase.

Excitement is maintained throughout the long bridge, which is based on the loud rushing phrase of the first theme. The bridge ends clearly with a brief pause, as do other sections in this movement.

The tender second theme is in the new key of B-flat major. A lyrical contrast to the brusque opening theme, it is softer, flows more smoothly, and uses longer notes.

Mozart weaves almost the entire development section from the upward arpeggio of the first theme. During the opening few seconds, there is an eruption of violence as the orchestra in unison plays a variation of the arpeggio and a series of jagged downward leaps. As the development continues, the texture becomes polyphonic and contrasts with the homophony of the exposition. Arpeggios press upon each other in quick imitation. Rapid shifts of key create restless intensity.

In the recapitulation, both the first and second themes are in the tonic key, G minor. This minor key now adds a touch of melancholy to the tender second theme, which was heard in major before. The passion and violence of this movement foreshadow the Romantic expression to come during the nineteenth century.

Fourth Movement from Symphony No. 40 in G minor, K. 550 by Wolfgang Amadeus Mozart

LISTENING OUTLINE

To be read while music is heard

Symphony No. 40 in G Minor, K. 550 (1788), by Wolfgang Amadeus Mozart

Fourth Movement: Allegro assai (very fast)

Sonata form, duple meter ($\frac{2}{2}$), G minor

flute, 2 oboes, 2 clarinets, 2 bassoons, 2 French horns, violins 1, violins 2, violas, cellos, double basses

(About 4½ min)

EXPOSITION

First theme   1   Upward arpeggio, *p*, explosive rushing phrase, *f*, minor key.

		High repeated tones, *f*, upward arpeggio, *p*, rushing phrase, *f*, leads into
Bridge	2	Long passage of continuously rushing notes, strings, *f*.
Second theme	3	*a.* Tender melody in violins, *p*, major key.

		b. Clarinet, *p*, tender melody somewhat varied.
Closing section	4	Suddenly loud, continuously rushing notes in strings, *f*. (Exposition' may be repeated.)

DEVELOPMENT

1   Orchestra in unison, *f*, upward arpeggio, jagged downward leaps.

          2   Suddenly soft, upward arpeggio lightly tossed between violins and woodwinds.

          3   Suddenly loud, string arpeggios interwoven with rushing notes. Arpeggios press upon each other in quicker imitation. Woodwinds rejoin imitative dialog.

RECAPITULATION

First theme   1   Upward arpeggio, *p*, explosive rushing phrase, *f*, minor key. High repeated tones, *f*, upward arpeggio, *p*, rushing phrase, *f*, leads into

Bridge   2   Passage of continuously rushing notes, strings, *f*.

Second theme   3   *a*. Tender melody in violins, *p*, minor key.

                    b. Woodwinds, *p*, tender melody somewhat varied.

Closing section 4   Suddenly loud, continuously rushing notes, full orchestra. Cadence.

Basic Terms

If you aren't sure what each of the following words means, look back at the text, where they appear in bold type. Additional information about some of them can be found by checking the index.

sonata form	motive
exposition	recapitulation
bridge (transition)	coda
development	

MINUET AND TRIO

Classical

[4]

The form known as **minuet and trio,** or **minuet,** is employed as the third movement of Classical symphonies, string quartets, and other works. Like the movements of the Baroque suite, the minuet originated as a dance. It first appeared at the French court of Louis XIV around 1650 and was danced by aristocrats throughout the eighteenth century. The minuet was a stately, dignified dance in which the couple exchanged curtsies and bows.

The minuet movement of a symphony or string quartet is written for listening, not dancing. It is in triple meter ($\frac{3}{4}$ time) and usually in a moderate tempo. The movement is in A B A form: minuet (A), trio (B), minuet (A). The trio (B) is usually quieter than the minuet (A) section and requires fewer instruments. It often contains woodwind solos. The trio section got its name during the Baroque period, when a set of two dances would be followed by a repetition of the first dance. The second dance was known as a "trio" because it usually was played by three instruments. Classical composers did not restrict themselves to three instruments in the B sections of their minuets, but the name "trio" remained.

The A (minuet) section includes smaller parts a, b, and a' (variation of a). In the opening A (minuet) section, all the smaller parts are repeated, as follows:

Minuet and Trio

a (repeated) ba' (repeated). [In the musical score, the repeat sign (:‖) indicates each repetition.] The B (trio) section is similar in form: c (repeated) dc' (repeated). At the close of the B (trio) section, the repetition of the entire A (minuet) section is indicated by the words *da capo* ("from the beginning"). This time, however, the minuet is played straight through without the repetitions: a ba'. The whole movement can be outlined like this:

Minuet	*Trio*	*Minuet*
A	B	A
a (repeated) ba' (repeated)	c (repeated) dc' (repeated)	a ba'

With its A B A form and many repeated parts, the minuet is structurally the simplest movement of a symphony or string quartet.

In many of Beethoven's compositions, the third movement is not a minuet but a related form called a *scherzo*. Like a minuet, a **scherzo** is usually in A B A form and triple meter, but it moves more quickly, generating energy, rhythmic drive, and rough humor. (*Scherzo* is Italian for "joke.")

Third Movement (Minuet) from *Eine kleine Nachtmusik*, K. 525 ("A Little Night Music"), by Wolfgang Amadeus Mozart

Mozart's *Eine kleine Nachtmusik* is a **serenade,** a work that's usually light in mood, meant for evening entertainment. It is written for a small string orchestra or for a string quartet plus a double bass. (The double bass plays the cello part an octave lower.) The third movement is a courtly minuet in A B A form. The A (minuet) section is stately, mostly loud and staccato, with a clearly marked beat. In contrast, the B (trio) section is intimate, soft, and legato. Its murmuring accompaniment contributes to the smooth flow of the music.

LISTENING OUTLINE
To be read while music is heard

Eine kleine Nachtmusik, K. 525 (1787), by Wolfgang Amadeus Mozart

Third Movement: Menuetto (Allegretto)

A B A form, triple meter ($\frac{3}{4}$), G major

violins 1, violins 2, violas, cellos, double bass

(About 2 min)

    Minuet (A)   1   Stately melody, *f*, predominantly staccato. Repeated.

Allegretto

Legato phrase, *p*, leads to stately staccato phrase, *f*. Repeated.

Trio (B)   2   Gracious legato melody, *p*, mumuring accompaniment. Repeated.

Climbing legato phrase, *f*, leads to legato melody, *p*. Repeated.

Minuet (A)   3   Stately melody, *f*, predominantly staccato.
Legato phrase, *p*, leads to stately staccato phrase, *f*.

Basic Terms

If you aren't sure what each of the following words means, look back at the text, where they appear in bold type. Additional information about some of them can be found by checking the index.

minuet and trio (minuet)
serenade
scherzo

RONDO [5]

Many classical movements are in *rondo* form. A **rondo** features a tuneful main theme (A) which returns several times in alternation with other themes. Common rondo patterns are A B A C A and A B A C A B A. The main theme is usually lively, pleasing, and simple to remember, and the listener can easily recognize its return. Because the main theme is usually stated in the tonic key, its return is all the more welcome. A rondo appears both as an independent piece and as one movement of a symphony, string quartet, or sonata. It often serves as a finale, because its liveliness, regularity, and buoyancy bring a happy sense of conclusion.

Rondo

Rondo form is often combined with elements of sonata form to produce the *sonata-rondo*. The **sonata-rondo** contains a development section similar to that in sonata form and is outlined A B A—development section—A B A.

The popularity of the rondo did not end with the Classical period. It has been used by twentieth-century composers such as Igor Stravinsky and Arnold Schoenberg.

Fourth Movement (Rondo) from String Quartet in C Minor, Op. 18, No. 4, by Ludwig van Beethoven

The exciting rondo movement from Beethoven's String Quartet in C minor, Op. 18, No. 4 may be outlined A B A C A B A. Its main theme, A, is a lively gypsy dance made up of two repeated parts: a a b b. An unexpected held tone in part b suggests the improvisatory playing of a gypsy fiddler. The main theme, in minor, contrasts with the other themes, which are in major. Theme B is a lyrical legato melody, while theme C is playful, with quick upward rushes. At its final return, the main theme (A) has a faster tempo, prestissimo, and leads into a frenzied concluding section.

LISTENING OUTLINE

String Quartet in C Minor, Op. 18, No. 4 (1798–1800) by Ludwig van Beethoven

Fourth Movement: Rondo (Allegro)

Duple meter ($\frac{2}{2}$), C minor

violin 1, violin 2, viola, cello

(About 4½ min)

A   1   Lively main theme in violin 1, minor key.

B   2   Lyrical melody, legato, major key.

A	3	Lively main theme, minor key. Theme becomes more agitated.
C	4	Upward rushes in each instrument, playful downward phrase in violin 1, major key.
A	5	Lively main theme, minor key. Crescendo to held chord, *ff*.
B	6	Lyrical melody, legato, major key. Melody repeated an octave higher. Playful phrases in violins, crescendo to *f*, sustained tones in violin 1.
A	7	Lively main theme, *ff*, faster tempo (prestissimo), minor key. Concluding section builds, downward staccato scale, high repeated tones, *p*. Upward rushes, *ff*, at end.

Basic Terms

If you aren't sure what each of the following words means, look back at the text, where they appear in bold type. Additional information can be found by checking the index.

> rondo
> sonata-rondo

THE CLASSICAL SYMPHONY [**6**]

The great contribution of the Classical period to orchestral music is the symphony. Haydn wrote about one hundred and four symphonies, Mozart over forty, and Beethoven nine. Most of Haydn's symphonies were composed for his employers, who required a steady flow of works for their palace concerts. Beethoven, on the other hand, wrote a symphony only when inspired. His symphonies are longer than Haydn's or Mozart's and were conceived for performance in large concert halls.

A **symphony** is an extended, ambitious composition lasting between twenty and forty-five minutes, exploiting the expanded range of tone color and dynamics of the Classical orchestra. A Classical symphony usually consists of four movements which evoke a wide range of emotions through contrasts of tempo and mood. A typical sequence is (1) a vigorous, dramatic fast movement; (2) a lyrical slow movement; (3) a dancelike movement (minuet or scherzo); and (4) a brilliant or heroic fast movement.

The opening movement is almost always fast and in sonata form. It is usually the most dramatic movement and stresses exciting development of short motives. Sometimes a slow introduction leads to the opening fast movement and creates a feeling of anticipation.

It is in the slow second movement that we are most likely to find broad, songlike melodies. This movement, by and large, is either in sonata form, A B A

The Classical Symphony

205

form, or theme-and-variations form. Unlike the other movements in the symphony, the slow movement is generally *not* in the tonic key. For example, if the first, third, and fourth movements are in the tonic key of C major, the second movement may be in F major. The new key points up the expressive contrast of the slow movement.

In the symphonies of Haydn and Mozart, the third movement is generally a minuet and trio, which may be in a moderate or fairly quick tempo. This movement varies in character from a courtly dance to a peasant romp to a vigorous piece that is hardly dancelike. Beethoven liked fast, energetic scherzos for his third movements.

The fourth, concluding movement of a Haydn or Mozart symphony is fast, lively, and brilliant, but somewhat lighter in mood than the opening movement. (The agitated final movement of Mozart's Symphony No. 40 in G minor is not typical.) Beethoven's concluding movement tends to be more triumphant and heroic in character and sometimes is meant as the climax of the whole symphony. The final movement of a Classical symphony is most often in sonata or sonata-rondo form.

In most Classical symphonies, each movement is a self-contained composition with its own set of themes. A theme in one movement will only rarely reappear in a later movement. (Beethoven's Fifth and Ninth Symphonies are exceptions.) But a symphony is unified partly by the use of the same key in three of its movements. More important, the movements balance and complement each other both musically and emotionally.

The importance of the symphony has lasted into the middle of the twentieth century. Its great significance is reflected in such familiar terms as "symphonic music," "symphony hall," and "symphony orchestra."

Basic Term

If you aren't sure what the following word means, look back at the text, where it appears in bold type. Additional information can be found by checking the index.

symphony

[7] THE CLASSICAL CONCERTO

A Classical **concerto** is a three-movement work for an instrumental soloist and orchestra. It combines the soloist's virtuosity and interpretative abilities with the orchestra's wide range of tone color and dynamics. Emerging from this encounter is a contrast of ideas and sound that is dramatic and satisfying. The soloist is very much the star, and all of his or her musical talents are needed in this challenging dialog.

The Classical love of balance can be seen in the concerto, for soloist and orchestra are equally important. Together, there's an interplay of melodic lines and a spirit of give and take. One moment the soloist plays the melody while the orchestra accompanies. Then the woodwinds may unfold the main theme against rippling arpeggios (broken chords) by the soloist. Mozart and Beethoven—the greatest masters of the Classical concerto—often wrote for themselves as piano soloists, and the piano is the favored solo instrument. But other solo instruments include violin, horn, trumpet, clarinet, bassoon, and cello.

Like symphonies, concertos can last anywhere from twenty to forty-five minutes. But instead of the symphony's four movements, a concerto has three: (1) fast, (2) slow, and (3) fast. A concerto has no minuet or scherzo.

In the first movement and sometimes in the last movement, there is a special unaccompanied showpiece for the soloist, the **cadenza** (Italian for "cadence"). Near the end of the movement, the orchestra suspends forward motion by briefly sustaining a dissonant chord. This is indicated in the score by a *fermata* sign (⌒), meaning "pause," which is placed over the chord. The suspense announces the entry of the soloist's cadenza. For several minutes, the soloist, *without orchestra,* displays virtuosity by playing dazzling scale passages and broken chords. Themes of the movement are varied and presented in new keys. At the end of a cadenza, the soloist plays a long trill followed by a chord that meshes with the reentrance of the orchestra.

In the Classical era, the soloist, who was often the composer, generally improvised the cadenzas. In this case, the score contained only the fermata sign, indicating that a cadenza should be inserted at that point. But after the eighteenth century, the art of improvisation declined, and composers began to write cadenzas directly into the score. This gave them more control over their compositions.

Today, performers of eighteenth-century concertos may have a choice of cadenzas. For some concertos the composer may have written cadenzas for his own performance or for that of a student. And many nineteenth- and twentieth-century musicians later provided cadenzas for Classical concertos. These are best when their style matches that of the concerto. For example, the cadenzas Beethoven composed for Mozart's D-minor Piano Concerto are so strong and in the spirit of the work that pianists today still use them.

A Classical concerto begins with a movement in sonata form, but it is different—there are *two* expositions. The first is played by the orchestra, which presents several themes in the home key. This opening section sets the mood for the movement and leads us to expect the soloist's entrance. The second exposition begins with the soloist's first notes. Music for the solo entry may be powerful or quiet, but its effect is dramatic because suspense has been built. With the orchestra, the soloist explores themes from the first exposition and introduces new ones. After a modulation from the home key to a new key,

The Classical Concerto

the second exposition then moves to a development section, followed by the recapitulation, cadenza, and coda. The slow middle movement may take any one of several forms, but the finale is usually a quick rondo or sonata-rondo.

Basic Terms

If you aren't sure what each of the following words means, look back at the text, where they appear in bold type. Additional information can be found by checking the index.

concerto
cadenza

[8] CLASSICAL CHAMBER MUSIC

Classical **chamber music** is designed for the intimate setting of a room (chamber) in a home or palace, rather than for a public concert hall. It is performed by a small group of two to nine musicians, with one player to a part. Chamber music is lighter in sound than Classical orchestral music. During the Classical period, it was fashionable for an aristocrat or a member of the well-to-do middle class to play chamber music with friends and to hire professional musicians to entertain guests after dinner.

Chamber music is subtle and intimate, intended to please the performer as much as the listener. A chamber music group is a team. Each member is essential, and each may have a share of the important thematic material. This calls for much give and take among the instruments. Classical chamber music does not need a conductor; instead, each musician must be sensitive to what goes on and coordinate dynamics and phrasing with the other musicians. In this respect, a chamber ensemble is like a small jazz group.

The most important form of Classical chamber music is the **string quartet,** written for two violins, a viola, and a cello. Haydn, Mozart, and Beethoven wrote some of their most important music in this form. The string quartet can be compared with a conversation among four lively, sensitive, and intelligent people. And it's not surprising that the string quartet evolved when conversation was cultivated as a fine art.

Like the symphony, the string quartet usually consists of four movements: (1) fast, (2) slow, (3) minuet or scherzo, (4) fast. (Sometimes the second movement is a minuet or scherzo, and the slow movement is third.)

Other popular forms of Classical chamber music are the sonata for violin and piano, the piano trio (violin, cello, and piano), and the string quintet (two violins, two violas, and cello).

Today, as in the eighteenth century, much chamber music is performed by amateurs. By consulting the directory *Amateur Chamber Music Players,* one can find partners for chamber music almost anywhere in the United States.

Basic Terms

If you aren't sure what each of the following words means, look back at the text, where they appear in bold type. Additional information can be found by checking the index.

chamber music
string quartet

JOSEPH HAYDN [9]

The first of three Classical masters, Joseph Haydn (1732–1809) was born in a tiny Austrian village called Rohrau. His father made wagon wheels, and until the age of six, Haydn's musical background consisted of folksongs his father loved to sing and the peasant dances that whirled about him on festive occasions. (This early contact with folk music later had an influence on his style.) Haydn's eager response to music was recognized, and he was sent to live with a relative who gave him basic music lessons for two years. At eight, he went to Vienna to serve as a choirboy in the Cathedral of St. Stephen. There, though his good voice was appreciated, he had no chance for composition lessons or for perfecting an instrumental technique. And when his voice changed, Haydn was dismissed from St. Stephen's and turned out on the street without a penny. "I barely managed to stay alive by giving music lessons to children for about eight years," he wrote. Throughout those years he struggled to teach himself composition and also took odd jobs, including playing violin in the popular Viennese street bands that offered evening entertainment.

Gradually, aristocratic patrons of music began to notice Haydn's talent. For a brief time he was music director at the court of a Bohemian count, but the orchestra was dissolved because of his patron's financial problems. At the age of twenty-nine, Haydn's life changed for the better, forever.

In 1761, Haydn entered the service of the Esterházys, the richest and most powerful of the noble Hungarian families. For almost thirty years, from 1761 to 1790, most of his music was composed for performance in the palaces of the family. Haydn spent much of his time at Esterház, a magnificent but isolated palace in Hungary that contained an opera house, a theater, two concert halls, and 126 guest rooms.

As a highly skilled servant, Haydn was to compose all the music requested by his patron, conduct the orchestra of about twenty-five players, coach singers, and oversee the condition of instruments and the operation of the music library.

Joseph Haydn

209

Haydn rehearsing at the Esterházy Palace (The Bettmann Archive).

He also was required to "appear daily in the antechamber before and after midday and inquire whether His Highness is pleased to order a performance of the orchestra." The amount of work demanded of Haydn as assistant music director and later as music director was staggering; there were usually two concerts and two opera performances weekly, as well as daily chamber music in the prince's apartment. Since Nicholas Esterházy played the baryton (a complicated stringed instrument now obsolete), Haydn wrote over 150 pieces with a baryton part.

Though today it seems degrading for a genius to be dependent on the will of a prince, in the eighteenth century patronage was taken for granted. Composers had definite advantages in that they received a steady income and their works were performed. And though Haydn felt restricted by his job from time to time, he later wisely said, "My prince was always satisfied with my works. Not only did I have the encouragement of constant approval, but as conductor of an orchestra I could make experiments, observe what produced an effect and what weakened it, and was thus in a position to improve, alter, make additions or omissions, and be as bold as I pleased. I was cut off from the world; there was no one to confuse or torment me, and I was forced to become original."

Joseph Haydn (Royal College of Music).

Despite an unhappy marriage, Haydn was good-humored and unselfish. He was conscientious about professional duties, and he cared about the personal interests of his musicians. Prince Nicholas loved Esterház and once stayed at the palace longer than usual. The orchestra members came to Haydn and asked to return to Vienna; they were tired of being isolated in the country, away so long from their wives and children. Haydn obliged them by composing a symphony in F-sharp minor, now known as the "Farewell." At its first performance for the prince, the musicians followed the indications in the score. During the last movement, one after another stopped playing, put out his candle, and quietly left the hall. By the time that only Haydn and the first violinist remained, Nicholas took the hint; the next day he ordered the household to return to Vienna.

Haydn met the younger Mozart in the early 1780s and they became close friends. To someone finding fault with one of Mozart's operas, Haydn replied, "I cannot settle this dispute, but this I know: Mozart is the greatest composer the world possesses now." Between 1782 and 1785, Mozart wrote six string quartets which were dedicated to Haydn.

Over a period of twenty years, word spread about the Esterházys' composer, and Haydn's music became immensely popular all over Europe. Publishers and concert organizations sent commissions for new works. After the death of

Joseph Haydn

211

Prince Nicholas Esterházy in 1790, Haydn was free to go to London where a concert series was planned around his compositions. He'd been asked by concert manager Johann Peter Salomon to write and conduct new symphonies for performance at public concerts. Six were composed for a first visit in 1791–1792 and six more for a second visit in 1794–1795. These twelve became known as the "Salomon Symphonies" or "London Symphonies."

Reports of the time say that Haydn's appearances were triumphs. By the end of the eighteenth century, London was the largest and richest city in the world. Its concert life was unusually active and attracted many foreign musicians. Acclaim at Haydn's concerts was so overwhelming that some symphony movements had to be repeated. One listener noted that there was "an electrical effect on all present and such a degree of enthusiasm as almost amounted to a frenzy."

And so, a servant had become a celebrity. Haydn was wined and dined by the aristocracy, given an honorary doctorate at Oxford, and received by members of the royal family. And, as though to balance out earlier personal unhappiness, he had a love affair with a rich English widow. After thirty years of service to the Esterházys, Haydn's reception by the English moved him to write, "How sweet is some degree of liberty. The consciousness of no longer being a bond servant sweetens all my toil."

Rich and honored, Haydn returned to Vienna in 1795 and maintained good relations with Esterház. The new Prince, Nicholas II, did not have his father's wide musical interests and liked only religious music. Haydn's agreement specified that he would compose a Mass a year. There are six, and all reflect the mature, brilliant writing of the London Symphonies. In this period of his late sixties, Haydn composed two oratorios, *The Creation* (1798) and *The Seasons* (1801). They were so popular that choruses and orchestras were formed at the beginning of the nineteenth century for the sole purpose of performing them.

Haydn died in 1809, at the age of seventy-seven, while Napoleon's army occupied Vienna. A memorial service indicated the wide recognition of Haydn's greatness: Joining the Viennese were French generals and an honor guard of French soldiers.

Haydn's Music

Haydn was a pathfinder for the Classical period, a pioneer in the development of the symphony and string quartet. Both Mozart and Beethoven were influenced by his style. Haydn's music, like his personality, is robust and direct; it radiates a healthy optimism. Haydn never forgot the peasant dances and songs of his childhood in a small village, and many of his works have a folk flavor. He quotes actual peasant tunes and composes original melodies in a folklike style. The minuets often romp and stomp rather than bow and curtsey. *The Creation* (1798) and *The Seasons* (1801), his late oratorios, reflect Haydn's love of nature. There are vivid and humorous musical descriptions of storms, hail, animals, birds, and fish.

Haydn is a master at developing themes. He splits them into small fragments that are quickly repeated by the different instruments. His skill at development made it possible for him to build a whole movement out of a single main theme. In such movements, contrast of mood results from changes in texture, key, rhythm, dynamics, and orchestration. In the "Drum Roll" Symphony (No. 103), which we'll study, Haydn takes a short dancelike tune and uses it to propel an exciting finale. The contagious joy that springs from his lively rhythms and vivid contrasts makes it clear why London went wild.

"I prefer to see the humorous side of life," Haydn once said. He produces comic effects from unexpected pauses and tempo changes and from sudden shifts in dynamics and pitch. We've heard one of his musical jokes in the second movement of the "Surprise" Symphony, where a soft theme is suddenly punctuated by a loud chord.

Haydn's enormous output revolves around the 104 symphonies, which span a period of over thirty-five years, from about 1758 to 1795. For a long time, the last twelve symphonies (Nos. 93 to 104), composed for public concerts in London during the 1790s, were the only ones regularly performed. Now, thanks to venturesome scholars and performers, the earlier symphonies composed for Esterház and other castles are heard more often. Many of Haydn's popular symphonies have nicknames, such as "Surprise" (No. 94), "Military" (No. 100), "Clock" (No. 101), and "Drum Roll" (No. 103).

Along with the symphonies, the sixty-eight string quartets are considered Haydn's most important works. Some scholars believe Haydn invented the form. He began writing string quartets for good reason—only three other musicians were on hand during the summer of 1757, when he was invited to take part in chamber music performances at a castle. The steward of the aristocratic host and the parish priest each played a violin, and there was a cellist named Albrechtsberger. Spurred by necessity, the twenty-five-year-old Haydn tried his hand at the first of the lifelong series of string quartets.

Haydn's output also includes piano sonatas, piano trios, divertimentos, operas, and Masses. The variety in his works is astounding. He was a great innovator and experimenter who hated arbitrary "rules" of composition. "What is the good of such rules? Art is free, and should be fettered by no such mechanical regulations. The educated ear is the sole authority in all these questions, and I think that I have as much right to lay down the law as anyone."

Symphony No. 103 in E-flat Major ("Drum Roll"; 1795)

Haydn composed his next-to-last symphony in 1795, during his second visit to London. It was performed at a public concert by an orchestra of sixty players, an unusually large group for the time. The London *Morning Chronicle* reported that the new symphony "had continual strokes of genius. The Introduction excited the deepest attention, the Allegro charmed, the *Andante* encored." The minuet was "playful and sweet, and the last movement was equal, if not superior to the preceding."

Symphony No. 103 in E-flat Major ("Drum Roll"; 1795)

213

The nickname "Drum Roll," coined by a publisher, comes from the mysterious timpani roll at the very beginning of the symphony. No symphony had ever opened so strangely. Typical of Haydn are the musical surprises, folklike tunes, and vivid contrasts of tone color and dynamics in Symphony No. 103.

First Movement:
Adagio (slow introduction); Allegro con spirito
(spirited allegro)

Haydn begins Symphony No. 103 with an extended slow introduction that is serious and expectant: the opening timpani roll leads to a solemn low theme played in unison by the bassoon, cellos, and basses.

Haydn integrated this material into the following Allegro in inventive and imaginative ways.

The rollicking dance tune of the Allegro contrasts delightfully with the serious introduction.

This tune is the first theme of a sonata-form movement and is followed by a long bridge section that's loud and energetic. The bridge is built mostly from fragments of the opening theme.

A lilting waltz melody serves as the second theme of the exposition.

It is played softly by the first violins with an "oom-pa-pa" accompaniment in the other strings. Soon, the remaining instruments join in and bring the exposition to a rousing finish. (The exposition may be repeated.)

The development begins softly as Haydn reveals the potential of his rollicking first theme. Tiny fragments of the theme are tossed among the string instruments, and there's a crescendo to loud chords. Then, Haydn cleverly presents a quickened version of the introduction theme in the low strings.

After further development of the opening theme, the lilting waltz melody (second theme) returns and leads into the recapitulation.

For a while, all is "normal" in the recapitulation; we hear the first theme, the bridge, and the second theme. But Haydn saves his biggest surprise for the coda—he dramatically brings back the slow introduction and its mysterious timpani roll. His audience must have been astounded! But the solemn mood doesn't last long. As if in a burst of laughter, Haydn speeds up the introduction theme, and the movement rushes to a jubilant conclusion.

Second Movement:
Andante più tosto Allegretto
(andante, somewhat allegretto)

Haydn's love of folk music and the countryside are reflected in the second movement. This is a set of variations based on two themes adapted from East European folk tunes. (Remember Haydn's long service in Hungary with the Esterházys.) The first theme (A), presented softly by the strings, is serious and in minor.

In contrast, the second theme (B) is festive, fuller in sound (horns and woodwinds join the strings), and in major.

Each theme is quite long and consists of repeated parts. The entire second movement may be outlined as follows:

Themes		*Variations*				
A	B	A¹	B¹	A²	B²	Coda
minor	major	minor	major	minor	major	major

Haydn embellishes tunes for variety, adding countermelodies and changing dynamics and orchestration. When he adds plaintive woodwind countermelodies in variation A^1, the theme sounds more melancholy. The melody in variation B^1 is presented in a gracefully decorated version by a solo violin, while loud brass fanfares make variation A^2 triumphant. The really rustic section is variation B^2, which features hopping bassoons and chirping flutes. An unexpected dark cloud appears in the coda, as a string tremolo and a rapid crescendo create a momentary feeling of uncertainty. But the cloud soon passes, and a lovely solo for flute and oboes leads to an exultant conclusion.

Symphony No. 103 in E-flat Major ("Drum Roll"; 1795)

215

Third Movement: Menuetto

With its heavily accented downbeats, the minuet of Symphony No. 103 sounds more like a boisterous peasant romp than an elegant court dance. This movement is written in the minuet's customary A B A form:

Minuet		Trio		Minuet
A		B		A
a (repeated)	ba' (repeated)	c (repeated)	dc' (repeated)	a ba'

The opening melody (a) of the minuet ends comically as Haydn tosses a three-note fragment from low to high instruments.

The trio (B) section is flowing and gentle, with softer dynamics, fewer instruments, and a less strongly emphasized beat.

Fourth Movement: Finale (Allegro con spirito)

From a single dance tune, Haydn produces the symphony's brilliant finale, in sonata-rondo form. In this movement, Haydn gets a maximum of contrast from a minimum of material.

The finale opens with two unaccompanied French horns playing a short phrase which Haydn's contemporaries associated with hunting and the outdoors. The violins present the main theme, a carefree dance tune, with the French-horn phrase serving as an accompaniment.

Instantly, Haydn plays polyphonic games as fragments of the tune are tossed from one instrument to another. These fragments can be recognized by their repeated-note beginning. With great mastery, Haydn uses polyphonic texture in this movement to convey both humor and dramatic excitement. The "Drum Roll" Symphony is an example of Haydn's genius at making rich, complex music from the simplest phrases and themes.

WOLFGANG AMADEUS MOZART [**10**]

One of the most amazing child prodigies in history, Wolfgang Amadeus Mozart (1756–1791) was born in Salzburg, Austria, the son of a court musician. By the age of six, he could play the harpsichord and violin, improvise fugues, write minuets, and read music perfectly at first sight. At eight, he wrote a symphony; at eleven, an oratorio; and at twelve, an opera. By his early teens, Mozart had behind him many works that would have brought credit to a composer three times his age.

Mozart's father, Leopold, was understandably eager to show him off and went to great lengths to do so. Between the ages of six and fifteen, Mozart spent almost half his life on tour in Europe and England. He played for Empress Maria Theresa in Vienna, for Louis XV at Versailles, for George III in London, and for innumerable aristocrats along the way. On his trips to Italy he was able to study and master the operatic style which he later put to superb use. At fourteen, Mozart was in Rome during Holy Week, and he went to the Sistine Chapel to hear the famous choir performing a work that was its treasured property. Anyone caught copying this choral piece was to be punished by excommunication. Mozart heard it once, wrote it out afterward almost completely, returned with his manuscript to make a few additions—and was discovered. That anyone should copy the music was a crime; that Mozart should hear and remember it accurately was incredible. He not only escaped punishment but was knighted by the Pope for his musical accomplishments.

At fifteen, Mozart returned to Salzburg, which was ruled by a new Prince-Archbishop, Hieronymus Colloredo. The Archbishop was a tyrant who did not appreciate Mozart's genius, and he refused to grant him more than a subordinate seat in the court orchestra. With his father's help, Mozart tried repeatedly over the next decade to find a suitable position, but there were never any vacancies.

The tragic irony of Mozart's life was that he won more acclaim as a boy wonder than as an adult musician. Partly, his upbringing and personality were to blame. As a child, his complete dependence on his father gave little opportunity to develop initiative. Even when Mozart was twenty-two, his mother tagged along when he went to Paris to seek recognition and establish himself. A Parisian observed that Mozart was "too good-natured, not active enough,

Wolfgang Amadeus Mozart

217

By the age of six, Mozart could play the harpsichord and violin, improvise fugues, write minuets, and read music perfectly at first sight (Omikron).

The Classical Period

218

too easily taken in, too little concerned with the means that may lead him to good fortune."

Unlike Haydn, Mozart began life as an international celebrity, pampered by kings. He could not tolerate being treated like a servant and eating with valets and cooks, and his relations with his patron went from bad to worse. Mozart became totally insubordinate when the Prince-Archbishop forbade him to give concerts or perform at the houses of the aristocracy. After an ugly confrontation, Mozart wrote: "He lied to my face that my salary was five hundred *gulden,* called me a scoundrel, a rascal, a vagabond. At last my blood began to boil, I could no longer contain myself, and I said, 'So Your Grace is not satisfied with me?'" He was answered with, "What, you dare to threaten me—you scoundrel? There is the door!" On his third attempt to request dismissal, Mozart was thrown out of the room by a court official and given a kick.

By 1781, when he was twenty-five, Mozart could stand it no longer. He broke free of provincial Salzburg and traveled to Vienna, intending to be a free-lance musician. To reassure his father, he wrote, "I have the best and most useful acquaintances in the world. I am liked and respected in the best houses, and all possible honors are given me, and moreover I get paid for it. I guarantee you I'll be successful."

Indeed, Mozart's first few years in Vienna were successful. His German opera *The Abduction from the Seraglio* (1782) was acclaimed. Concerts of his own music were attended by the Emperor and nobility. Pupils paid him high fees, his compositions were published, and his playing was heard in palace drawing rooms. He even went against his father's wishes by marrying Constanze Weber, who had no money and was as impractical as he. Contributing to the brightness of these years was Mozart's friendship with Haydn, who told his father, "Your son is the greatest composer that I know, either personally or by reputation; he has taste and beyond that the most consummate knowledge of the art of composition."

Then, in 1786, came his opera *The Marriage of Figaro.* Vienna loved it, and Prague was even more enthusiastic. "They talk about nothing but *Figaro.* Nothing is played, sung, or whistled but *Figaro,*" Mozart joyfully wrote. This success led a Prague opera company to commission *Don Giovanni* the following year. *Don Giovanni* was a triumph in Prague, but it pushed the Viennese too far. The Emperor Joseph II acknowledged that it was a masterwork, but not appropriate for his pleasure-loving subjects. Dark qualities and dissonance did not appeal.

Mozart's popularity in Vienna began to decline. It was a fickle city; one was society's darling for a few seasons, then suddenly ignored. And Mozart's music was considered complicated and hard to follow, too "highly spiced" with dissonance. A publisher warned him: "Write in a more popular style, or else I can neither print nor pay for any more of your music!" His pupils dwindled, and the elite snubbed his concerts. In desperate financial straits, he wrote to friends, "Great God, I would not wish my worst enemy to be in this position. . . . I am coming to you not with thanks but with fresh entreaties."

Wolfgang Amadeus Mozart

Wolfgang Amadeus Mozart (Omikron, original in Mozartium).

Many of Mozart's letters have been published. These span his life, and it is sad to move from the colorful, witty, and keenly observant notes of a prodigy on tour through his initial optimism about Vienna to the despair of "I cannot describe what I have been feeling. . . . A kind of longing that is never satisfied."

The events of Mozart's last year would have been good material for a grim opera plot. Though his health was failing in 1791, Mozart was delighted to receive a commission from a Viennese theater for a German comic opera, *The Magic Flute.* While hard at work, Mozart was visited by a stranger dressed entirely in gray who carried an anonymous letter commissioning a Requiem, a Mass for the Dead. Unknown to Mozart, the stranger was a servant of an unscrupulous nobleman who meant to claim the Requiem as his own composition. Mozart's health grew worse, and the Requiem took on ominous implications; he believed it to be for himself and rushed to finish it while on his deathbed. A final bit of happiness came to him two months before his death. *The Magic Flute* was premiered to resounding praise in Vienna. Its success probably would have brought large financial rewards, but it came too late. Mozart died shortly before his thirty-sixth birthday, and the final sections of the Requiem were not his. The work was completed from his sketches by Süssmayr, his favorite pupil.

Mozart's funeral was the poorest possible. His body was laid in a common grave assigned to paupers.

Mozart's Music

Mozart is among the most versatile of the great composers; his masterpieces represent all the musical forms of his time. The symphonies are as profound as the string quartets, the piano concertos as dramatic and lyrical as the operas. All his music sings. Even his instrumental melodies seem to grow out of the human voice. His works convey a feeling of ease, grace, and spontaneity, as well as balance, restraint, and perfect proportion. Yet mysterious harmonies bring dark moods that contrast with the lyricism. Mozart uniquely fuses power and elegance. However passionate and intense, his works are always sensuous and beautiful. He believed that music "must never offend the ear, but must please the hearer, or in other words, must never cease to be *music.*"

Mozart's compositions not only sound effortless, they were created with miraculous ease and rapidity. For example, he completed his last three symphonies in only six weeks! And he composed extended works completely in his mind. Notating the music was a mechanical task for Mozart, a little like taking dictation from audiotape. He could even converse while notating a score.

Mozart's more than six hundred compositions were cataloged during the nineteenth century by Ludwig von Köchel. Hence, it is customary to refer to a Mozart work by the "K" number that indicates its chronological place in his output. For example, his Piano Concerto in D minor (1785) is K.466, while his Symphony No. 40 in G minor (1788)—composed three years later—is K. 550.

In Mozart's hands, the Classical concerto was raised to its highest level. Many of his greatest works take this form. Particularly important are the more than twenty piano concertos that Mozart—a brilliant virtuoso—composed mainly for his own performances. He also wrote several violin and horn concertos, two flute concertos, and a concerto each for bassoon, oboe, and clarinet. The concertos, as well as his other works, show a sensitivity to woodwind tone colors that is unmatched by earlier composers. The clarinet, especially, came into its own through Mozart. The Concerto for Clarinet, K. 622 (1791), written in the last year of his life, remains the finest ever composed for that instrument.

Mozart was a master of opera, and few composers have matched his ability to coordinate music and stage action. His dramatic works reveal a keen sense of theater, an inexhaustible gift of melody, and a genius for creating characters through tone. Most of his operas are comedies, composed to librettos in German or Italian, then the international language of music. While the Italian operas are entirely sung, the German operas include spoken dialog, the custom at the time. Mozart's three masterpieces of Italian comic opera are *The Marriage of Figaro* (1786), *Don Giovanni* (1787), and *Così fan tutte* (1790); they all were composed to librettos by Lorenzo da Ponte. Mozart's finest German work is *The Magic Flute* (1791); its wide range of style embraces folk song and fugue, farcical comedy, and solemn hymns about the brotherhood of man.

The comic operas contain both humorous and serious characters who are not mere stereotypes; they are human beings who think and feel. Even when six characters sing together in a complex ensemble, the individuality of each shines through. Mozart once tried to explain how he depicted emotion in an aria: "Would you like to know how I have expressed it—and even indicated his throbbing heart? By two violins playing octaves. You feel the trembling—the faltering—you see how his throbbing breast begins to swell; this I have expressed by a crescendo. You hear the whispering and sighing—which I have indicated by the first violins with mutes and a flute playing in unison." Emotions in Mozart's arias and ensembles are not static; they continuously evolve and change. A character may feel one way at the beginning of an ensemble and a different way at its end. In a duet from *Don Giovanni*, we'll watch the feelings of a peasant girl change as she gradually gives in to the charm of a noble Don Juan.

Throughout his life, Mozart learned from other composers. As a boy, he was influenced by Italian operas and the graceful style of one of Bach's sons, Johann Christian Bach. The strongest influence on his later works came from Bach the father, dead and nearly forgotten, and from Haydn, the most famous composer at the time. From Bach, Mozart learned to write intricate polyphonic textures that flow smoothly. He arranged Bach's and Handel's works for performances at private concerts sponsored by Baron Gottfried van Swieten, a passionate Viennese music lover. From Haydn's works, he learned ways to develop themes. But his musical relationship with Haydn was not one-sided. Some compositions by Haydn show traces of Mozart's melodic and orchestral style.

"I am never happier," Mozart once wrote his father, "than when I have something to compose, for that, after all, is my sole delight and passion." Mozart's "delight and passion" are communicated in his works, which represent late eighteenth-century musical style at its highest level of perfection.

Don Giovanni (1787)

Don Giovanni is a unique blend of comic and serious opera, combining seduction and slapstick with violence and the supernatural. The old tale of Don Juan, the fabulous Spanish lover, had attracted many playwrights and composers before Mozart. Mozart's Don is an extremely charming but ruthless nobleman who will stop at nothing to satisfy his sexual appetite. Don Giovanni's comic servant, Leporello, is a grumbling accomplice who dreams of being in his master's place.

The Don attempts to rape a young noblewoman, Donna Anna, and her father, the Commandant, challenges him to a duel. Don Giovanni kills the old man, causing Donna Anna and her fiancé, Don Ottavio, to swear revenge. Pursued by his enemies, the Don deftly engages in new amorous adventures. During one of them, he hides in a cemetery, where he sees a marble statue of the dead Commandant. The unearthly statue utters threatening words, but Don Giovanni brazenly invites it to dinner. When the statue appears at the banquet hall, it orders the Don to repent his sins. Don Giovanni defiantly refuses and is dragged down to hell.

Overture

Mozart plunges us into a dark atmosphere at the beginning of the overture with awesome D-minor chords, anxious syncopations, and sinister scale passages. There is a hair-raising effect when this slow, ominous music returns at the end of the opera for the statue's confrontation with Don Giovanni in the banquet hall. The overture continues with a fast sonata-form movement in D major, which has the energy and swagger of the opera's leading character. This contrast of minor and major, mystery and brilliance, foretells the tremendous range of emotions to come.

Act I: Introduction

The Overture leads directly into the opening scene, which is one of the most action-packed in all opera. In breathless succession we witness Leporello keeping guard, Don Giovanni struggling with Donna Anna, the Commandant dueling with the Don, and the Commandant's agonized last gasps. Mozart's music breathes life into the characters and pushes the action forward. (In the following libretto, brackets indicate that characters sing at the same time. "Etc." indicates that previous lines of text are repeated.)

Don Giovanni (1787)

Late evening outside the Commandant's palace in Seville.
Don Giovanni, concealing his identity, has stolen into Donna
Anna's room for an amorous adventure. Leporello paces back
and forth.

Orchestral introduction, Molto allegro; sudden *fortes* suggest pacing and abrupt turns.

Leporello

Notte e giorno faticar,	Night and day I slave
per chi nulla sa gradir;	For one who does not appreciate it.
Piova e vento sopportar,	I put up with wind and rain,
Mangiar male e mal dormir!	Eat and sleep badly.
Voglio far il gentiluomo,	I want to be a gentleman
E non voglio più servir,	And to give up my servitude.
No, no, no, no, no, no,	No, no, no, no, no, no,
Non voglio più servir!	I want to give up my servitude.
O che caro galantuomo!	Oh, what a fine gentleman!
Voi star dentro colla bella	You stay inside with your lady
Ed io far la sentinella!	And I must play the sentinel!
Voglio far il gentiluomo, ecc.	Oh, what a fine gentleman, etc.
Ma mi par che venga gente . . .	But I think someone is coming!
Non mi voglio far sentir, ecc.	I don't want them to hear me, etc.

Leporello hides to one side. Don Giovanni and Donna
Anna come down the palace stairs struggling. The Don
hides his face to prevent her from recognizing him.

Orchestral crescendo.

Donna Anna

Non sperar, se non m'uccidi.	There's no hope, unless you kill me
Ch'io ti lasci fuggir mai!	That I'll ever let you go!

Don Giovanni	
Donna folle, indarno gridi:	Idiot! You scream in vain.
Chi son io tu non saprai.	Who I am you'll never know!
Donna Anna	
Non sperar, ecc.	There's no hope, etc.
Don Giovanni	
Donna folle! ecc.	Idiot! etc.
Leporello	
Che tumulto! Oh ciel, che gridi!	What a racket! Heaven, what screams!
Il padron in nuovi guai.	My master in another scrape.
Donna Anna	
Gente! Servi! Al traditore!	Help! Everyone! The betrayer!
Don Giovanni	
Taci, e trema al mio furore!	Keep quiet! Beware my wrath!
Donna Anna	
Scellerato!	Scoundrel!
Don Giovanni	
Sconsigliata!	Fool!
Donna Anna	
Scellerato!	Scoundrel!
Don Giovanni	
Sconsigliata!	Fool!
Leporello	
Sta a veder che il malandrino	We will see if this rascal
Mi farà precipitar.	Will be the ruin of me!
Donna Anna	
Gente! Servi!	Help! Everyone!
Don Giovanni	
Taci, e trema!	Keep quiet!
Donna Anna	
Come furia disperata	Like a desperate fury
Ti saprò perseguitar! ecc.	I'll know how to pursue you! etc.
Scellerato! Gente! Servi!	Scoundrel! Help! Everyone!
Come furia disperata, ecc.	Like a desperate fury, etc.

Don Giovanni (1787)

225

Don Giovanni

Questa furia disperata	This desperate fury
Mi vuol far precipitar!	Is aimed at destroying
ecc.	me!
Sconsigliata! Taci, e trema!	Fool! Keep quiet!
Questa furia disperata,	This desperate fury,
ecc.	etc.

Leporello

Che tumulto! Oh ciel, che gridi!	What a racket! Heavens, what screams!
Sta a veder che il malandrino, ecc.	We will see if this rascal, etc.

Donna Anna hears the Commandant: she leaves Don Giovanni and goes into the house. The Commandant appears.

String tremolo, *ff*, shift to minor key.

Commandant

Lasciala, indegno! Battiti meco!	Leave her alone, wretch, and defend yourself.

Don Giovanni

Va, non mi degno di pugnar teco.	Go away! I disdain to fight with you.

Commandant

Così pretendi da me fuggir?	Thus you think to escape me?

Leporello

Potessi almeno di qua partir.	If I could only get out of here!

Don Giovanni

Va, non mi degno, no!	Go away! I disdain you!

Commandant

Così pretendi da me fuggir?	Thus you think to escape me!

Leporello

Potessi almeno di quà partir!	If I could only get out of here!

Commandant

Battiti!	Fight!

Don Giovanni

Misero! Attendi, se vuoi morir!	So be it, if you want to die!

They duel. The Commandant is fatally wounded.

Dueling music, upward sweeps in strings.
Death blow, suspenseful, held chord.

Commandant

Ah, soccorso! son tradito!	Help! I've been betrayed!
L'assassino m'ha ferito,	The assassin has wounded me!
E dal seno palpitante	And from my heaving breast
Sento l'anima partir.	I feel my soul escaping!

Andante, *pp*, pathetic minor phrases.

Don Giovanni

Ah! già cade il sciagurato!	Ah, already the wretch has fallen,
Affannosa e agonizzante	And he gasps for air.
Già dal seno palpitante	From his heaving breast I already
Veggo l'anima partir, ecc.	See his soul escaping, etc.

Leporello

Qual misfatto! Qual eccesso!	What a misdeed! What a crime!
Entro il sen dallo spavento	I can feel my heart
Palpitar il cor mi sento!	Beating hard from fright!
Io non sò che far, che dir, ecc.	I don't know what to do or say, etc.

The Commandant dies, and the music fades into a recitative that is accompanied by a harpsichord. Leporello's sarcastic, "Good job! Raping the daughter and killing the father," comes as a shocking contrast to the preceding death scene.

Act I: Leporello's "Catalogue Aria" (*Madamina*)

Not long after the opening scene, Leporello sings his famous "Catalogue Aria" (*Madamina*) to Donna Elvira. In mocking "consolation," Leporello tells her that she is but one of many and displays a fat catalog of his master's conquests. The music bubbles with Leporello's delight as he reels off the amazing totals: "640 in Italy, 231 in Germany, 100 in France, 91 in Turkey" and "in Spain, 1003!" Mozart makes the most of comic description as Leporello proceeds to list the Don's seduction techniques for different types of girls:

Don Giovanni (1787)

227

Italian	English	Music
Madamina, il catalogo è questo	My dear lady, this is a list	Allegro.
Delle belle, che amò il padron mio;	Of the beauties my master has loved,	
Un catalogo egli è, che ho fatt'io	A list which I have compiled.	
Osservate, leggete con me.	Observe, read along with me.	
In Italia seicento e quaranta,	In Italy, six hundred and forty;	Staccato woodwind chuckles.
In Almagna duecento a trentuna,	In Germany, two hundred and thirty-one;	
Cento in Francia, in Turchia novantuna,	A hundred in France; in Turkey ninety-one.	
Ma in Ispagna son già mille e tre!	In Spain already one thousand and three!	Longer notes.
V'han fra queste contadine,	Among these are peasant girls	Shorter notes.
Cameriere, cittadine,	Maidservants, city girls,	
V'han contesse, baronesse,	Countesses, baronesses,	
Marchesine, principesse,	Marchionesses, princesses,	
E v'han donne d'ogni grado,	Women of every rank,	
D'ogni forma, d'ogni età.	Every shape, every age.	
In Italia seicento e quaranta, ecc.	In Italy six hundred and forty, etc.	
Nella bionda egli ha l'usanza	With blondes it is his habit	Andante con moto, courtly minuet.
Di lodar la gentilezza;	To praise their kindness;	
Nella bruna, la costanza;	In brunettes, their faithfulness;	Mock heroic flourish.
Nella bianca la dolcezza	In the very blonde, their sweetness.	Suave melodic phrase.
Vuol d'inverno la grassotta,	In winter he likes fat ones,	
Vuol d'estate la magrotta;	In summer he likes thin ones.	
È la grande maestosa,	He calls the tall ones majestic.	Crescendo, melody slowly rises to high held tone.
La piccina è ognor vezzosa;	The little ones are always charming.	Spritely quick notes.

Delle vecchie fa conquista	He seduces the old ones	
Pel piacer di porle in lista.	For the pleasure of adding to the list.	
Sua passion predominante	His greatest favorite	
È la giovin principiante.	Is the young beginner.	
Non si picca se sia ricca,	It doesn't matter if she's rich,	
Se sia brutta, se sia bella,	Ugly or beautiful;	
Se sia ricca, brutta, se sia bella;	If she is rich, ugly or beautiful.	
Purchè porti la gonnella,	If she wears a petticoat,	
Voi sapete quel che fa!	*You* know what he does.	
Purchè porti la gonnella, ecc.	If she wears a petticoat, etc.	

Act I: Duet: *Là ci darem la mano* ("There you will give me your hand")

The Don's seduction technique is put to use in this lovely duet. Don Giovanni convinces the pretty peasant girl Zerlina to come to his palace, promising to marry her and change her life. The music magically conveys his persuasiveness and her gradual surrender, as the voices become more and more intertwined. Forgetting her fiancé, Masetto, Zerlina throws herself into the Don's arms and they sing together, "Let us go, my beloved."

	Don Giovanni	
Là ci darem la mano,	There you will give me your hand,	Andante, $\frac{2}{4}$, legato melody.
Là mi dirai di sì.	There you will tell me "yes".	
Vedi, non è lontano;	You see, it is not far;	
Partiam, ben mio, da qui.	Let us leave, my beloved.	
	Zerlina	
Vorrei e non vorrei;	I'd like to, but yet I would not.	Legato melody repeated.
Mi trema un poco il cor.	My heart trembles a little.	
Felice è ver, sarei,	It's true I would be happy,	
Ma può burlarmi ancor.	But he may just be tricking me.	
	Don Giovanni	
Vieni, mio bel diletto!	Come, my dearly beloved!	Quicker interchange between voices.

Don Giovanni (1787)

229

	Zerlina	
Mi fa pietà Masetto!	I'm sorry for Masetto.	
	Don Giovanni	
Io cangierò tua sorte.	I will change your life!	
	Zerlina	
Presto, non son più forte!	Soon I won't be able to resist.	
	Don Giovanni	
Vieni! Vieni!	Come! Come!	
Là ci darem la mano!	There you will give me your hand.	Legato melody now shared by both voices.
	Zerlina	
Vorrei, e non vorrei!	I'd like to, but yet I would not.	
	Don Giovanni	
Là mi dirai di sì.	There you will tell me "yes".	
	Zerlina	
Mi trema un poco il cor!	My heart trembles a little.	
	Don Giovanni	
Partiam, mio ben, da qui!	Let us leave, my beloved.	
	Zerlina	
Ma può burlarmi ancor!	But he may just be tricking me.	
	Don Giovanni	
Vieni, mio bel diletto!	Come, my dearly beloved!	
	Zerlina	
Mi fa pietà Masetto!	I'm sorry for Masetto.	Voices overlap.
	Don Giovanni	
Io cangierò tua sorte.	I will change your life.	
	Zerlina	
Presto, non son più forte!	Soon I won't be able to resist.	
	Don Giovanni	
Andiam! Andiam!	Let us go!	
	Zerlina	
Andiam!	Let us go!	
	Don Giovanni and Zerlina	
Andiam, andiam, mio bene,	Let us go, let us go, my beloved,	Allegro, $\frac{6}{8}$; together they sing a new joyous tune.
A ristorar le pene	To soothe the pangs	
D'un innocente amor! ecc.	Of an innocent love, etc.	

Act II: Finale

The finale opens with Don Giovanni enjoying good food and music; it closes with a sextet celebrating his horrible punishment. Mozart's genius fuses these dissimilar events into a coherent whole. Don Giovanni dines in his banquet hall while watching Leporello's comic antics and listening to his private band play three hit tunes. The third tune is from Mozart's *Marriage of Figaro,* and Leporello comments, "This I know only too well." The frivolous mood evaporates when Donna Elvira bursts in and begs the Don to mend his ways. Terror strikes as the Commandant's marble statue enters, accompanied by the awesome music of the overture. Mozart uses this return to weld a powerful sense of unity within the opera. As the orchestra plays the dueling music from Act I, the statue commands, "Repent, change your life, it is your last moment!" Defiant to the end, Don Giovanni shouts, "No, no, I do not repent!" Flames and smoke surround the Don. He cries out in agony as a chorus of demons sing of his eternal damnation. With a hideous shriek, Don Giovanni is engulfed by the flames of hell.

An epilog in a lighter mood follows this scene of terror. The other characters, learning of the Don's fate, form a sextet and jubilantly sing a moral to the audience: "This is how evil-doers end up!" This moral ending fools no one. Mozart's music has made a sinner seem very attractive.

Symphony No. 40 in G Minor, K. 550 (1788)

Symphony No. 40 in G minor is the most passionate and dramatic of Mozart's symphonies. While Classical in form and technique, the work is almost Romantic in emotional intensity. It staggers the imagination that Mozart could compose the G minor and two other great symphonies—No. 39 in E flat and No. 41 in C ("Jupiter")—during the incredibly short period of six weeks. They are his last three symphonies.

Like most Classical symphonies, the Symphony No. 40 in G minor has four movements: (1) fast, (2) slow, (3) minuet, (4) fast.

First Movement: Molto Allegro

A quiet but agitated opening theme in the violins sets the mood for the entire first movement, which is in sonata form. A throbbing accompaniment in the violas contributes to the feeling of unrest. Dominating the violin melody is the rhythmic pattern short-short-long, first heard in the opening three-note motive.

Symphony No. 40 in G Minor, K. 550 (1788)

The persistence of this rhythmic pattern gives the music a sense of urgency. Yet the melody is balanced and symmetrical. Questioning upward leaps are answered by downward scales, and the second phrase of the melody is a repetition of the first, one step lower. The exposition continues with a bridge section that presents a new staccato motive played loudly by the violins.

The lyrical second theme, in B-flat major, contrasts completely with the agitated G-minor opening. Mozart exploits the expressive resources of tone color by dividing the theme between strings and woodwinds. In the closing section of the exposition, Mozart uses a fragment from the opening theme to achieve a different emotional effect. The three-note motive now sounds gentle and plaintive as it is passed between clarinet and bassoon with a sighing string background.

In the development, the movement becomes feverish. The opening theme is led into different keys and is cut into smaller and smaller pieces. The development begins mysteriously as the opening phrase ends in an unexpected way and sinks lower and lower. Then a sudden explosion of polyphonic texture increases the excitement and sense of complication. Mozart brusquely shifts the opening phrase between low and high strings while combining it with a furious staccato countermelody. Soon after, he demolishes the opening phrase: we hear the beginning of the theme without its upward leap.

Then the final note is lopped off.

Finally, we are left with the irreducible minimum of the original theme, the three-note motive.

The tension resolves only with the entrance of the entire opening theme in the tonic key.

In the recapitulation, exposition material is given new expressive meaning. The bridge is expanded and made more dramatic. The lyrical second theme, now in G minor, is touching and sad.

LISTENING OUTLINE

To be read while music is heard

Symphony No. 40 in G Minor, K. 550 (1788) by Wolfgang Amadeus Mozart

First Movement: Molto Allegro

Sonata form, duple meter ($\frac{2}{2}$), G minor

flute, 2 oboes, 2 clarinets, 2 bassoons, 2 French horns, violins 1, violins 2, violas, cellos, double basses

(About 7½ min)

EXPOSITION

First theme   1   *a.* Main theme in violins, *p*, throbbing accompaniment in violas, minor key.

           b. Full orchestra, *f.*

Bridge   2   *a.* Violins, *p*, main theme takes new turn to

           b. Full orchestra, *f*, major key, staccato motive and insistent upward scales in violins. Pause.

Second theme   3   *a.* Lyrical melody, *p*, major key, strings and woodwinds.

           b. Woodwinds and strings, *p*, lyrical melody somewhat varied. Crescendo in full orchestra.

           c. Staccato phrase, *f*, downward scale to

Closing section   4   *a.* String sighs, *p*, three-note motive in woodwinds, violins, *f.* Varied repetition of string sighs and three-note motive.

           b. Downward scales, *f*, full orchestra, cadence in major key.

           (Exposition may be repeated.)

DEVELOPMENT   1   *a.* High woodwinds, *p*, lead to

           b. Violins, *p*, main-theme phrase repeated on lower pitches.

    2   Sudden *f*, full orchestra, main theme phrase combined with rapid countermelody.

    3   *a.* Sudden *p*, high violins and woodwinds, three-note motive.

           b. Sudden *f*, full orchestra, three-note motive.

           c. Sudden *p*, high flutes and clarinets, three-note motive carried down to

RECAPITULATION

First theme   1   *a.* Main theme in violins, *p*, throbbing accompaniment in violas, minor key.

           b. Full orchestra, *f.*

Bridge   2   *a.* Violins, *p*, main theme takes new turn to

           b. Full orchestra, *f*, staccato motive in violins and cellos. Insistent upward scales in violins, *f.* Pause.

Second theme	3	*a.*	Lyrical melody, *p*, minor key, strings and woodwinds.
		b.	Woodwinds and strings, *p*, lyrical melody somewhat varied. Crescendo in full orchestra.
		c.	Staccato phrase, *f*, downward scale to
Closing section	4	*a.*	String sighs, *p*, three-note motive in woodwinds, violins, *f*. Varied repetition of string sighs and three-note motive.
		b.	Downward scales, *f*, full orchestra.
CODA	1	*a.*	Sudden *p*, main-theme motive in strings.
		b.	Full orchestra, *f*, cadence in minor key.

Second Movement: Andante

The mood of the Andante hovers between gentleness and longing. Written in sonata form, the Andante is the symphony's only movement in major (E-flat). This movement develops from a series of gently pulsating notes in the opening theme.

As the theme continues, the violins introduce an airy two-note rhythmic figure which will transform almost every section of the Andante by being, at different times, graceful, insistent, and forceful.

Later, Mozart uses the airy figures as a delicate countermelody to the repeated-note idea. Floating woodwinds interwoven with strings reveal Mozart's sensitivity to tone color as an expressive resource.

Third Movement: Menuetto (Allegretto)

This G-minor minuet is serious and intense; it does not sound like an aristocratic dance. The form of the minuet is A B A:

Minuet		Trio		Minuet
A		B		A
a (repeated)	ba' (repeated)	c (repeated)	dc' (repeated)	a ba'

Powerful syncopations give a fierce character to the A section (minuet), which is predominantly loud and in minor.

Later, Mozart increases the tension through polyphonic texture and striking dissonances. And at the end of the A section, there is a sudden drop in dynamics; the flute, supported by oboes and a bassoon, softly recalls the opening melody of the minuet.

The trio section (B) brings a shift from minor to major, from fierce energy to graceful relaxation.

This change of mood is underscored by a soft dynamic level and pastoral woodwind interludes. After the trio, a sudden *forte* announces the return of the fierce A section.

Fourth Movement: Allegro assai

Mozart ends the symphony with the tense movement already discussed in section 3.

Piano Concerto in D Minor, K. 466 (1785)

The highly dramatic, demonic nature of the D-minor Piano Concerto made it a favorite among musicians of the Romantic period and one of the works that convinced the world of Mozart's greatness shortly after his death. Only this and one other of Mozart's more than twenty piano concertos are in a minor key. Mozart associated the particular key of D minor with moods of foreboding, conflict, and tragedy. (You'll remember that he used it for the somber opening of the Overture of *Don Giovanni* and for the appearance of the Commandant's statue at the end of the opera.)

Like all Classical concertos, this one has three movements. The middle movement is a point of repose between the tense opening movement and the finale.

Mozart composed the D-minor Piano Concerto for a concert in Vienna in 1785. At the time he was very popular, and his concerts were well attended by aristocratic music lovers eager to hear his latest works. The concerto was completed only one day before the concert, and there was not enough time for Mozart to rehearse the concluding movement with the orchestra. Nevertheless, the performance was a success. "Wolfgang played an excellent new piano concerto," wrote Father Leopold to his daughter in Salzburg. Ten years later, in 1795, Beethoven played this concerto at a benefit for Mozart's impoverished widow.

Piano Concerto in
D Minor, K. 466 (1785)

235

First Movement: Allegro

The Allegro does not begin with a melody, but with syncopated throbbing in the violins and violas and hushed upward rushes in the cellos and double basses. This highly original opening creates a restless atmosphere that explodes into violence with a sudden *forte* in the whole orchestra. After several orchestral themes, the piano enters, unaccompanied, with a melancholy melody that sounds almost like an improvisation. Since this melody is played only by the piano, we will call it the "solo theme." In the development section, the piano and orchestra confront each other. The piano sings its melancholy solo theme, and the orchestra responds with the restless idea heard at the opening of the movement. Toward the end of the Allegro is a cadenza, or unaccompanied showpiece for the soloist. Mozart did not notate cadenzas for this concerto, and so the pianist either supplies one or uses those written by other composers (including two that Beethoven wrote for a student).

LISTENING OUTLINE
To be read while music is heard

Piano Concerto in D Minor, K. 466 (1785) by Wolfgang Amadeus Mozart

First Movement: Allegro

Sonata form, quadruple meter ($\frac{4}{4}$), D minor

piano, flute, 2 oboes, 2 bassoons, 2 French horns, 2 trumpets, timpani, violins 1, violins 2, violas, cellos, double basses

(About 13 min)

FIRST
EXPOSITION

    1 Strings, *p*, syncopated throbbing, low upward rushes, minor key.

    2 *a.* Sudden *f*, full orchestra, upward rushes climb in violins.
        b. Violins, *p*, echoed by oboes.
        c. Sudden *f*, full orchestra. Brief pause.
    3 Oboes, *p*, alternate with flute, dialog theme.

Strings, *p*, lead to
4   Sudden *f*, agitated passages in full orchestra repeatedly alternate with sighing phrase in strings, *p*. High repeated tones in violins, *f*, sudden *p* followed by
5   Tender closing theme in strings, *p*.

SECOND
EXPOSITION

1   Piano alone, solo theme in minor.

Piano joined by winds, *p*.
2   Strings, *p*, syncopated throbbing, low upward rushes. Piano joins with faster rhythm, melody gradually climbs, crescendo to climactic full orchestra, *f*. Brief pause.
3   Oboes, *p*, alternate with piano, dialog theme. Running notes in piano. Brief pause.
4   *a*. Piano, graceful theme in major, strings accompany.

    b. Oboe and flute repeat graceful theme, piano scales accompany.
5   Piano, long passage of running notes, scales, broken chords, trills, strings accompany. End of piano trill meshes with entrance of
6   *a*. Full orchestra, *f*, upward rushes climb in violins.
    b. Violins, *p*, echoed by oboes.
    c. Strings, *p*, tender closing theme.

DEVELOPMENT

1   *a*. Piano alone, solo theme in major. Running notes in piano lead to
    b. Strings, *p*, full orchestra, *f*, upward rushes.
2   *a*. Piano alone, solo theme in minor, running notes.
    b. Strings, *p*, full orchestra, *f*, upward rushes.
3   Piano alone, solo theme in major, downward running notes.
4   Piano, rapid broken chords, joined by strings, upward rushes. Piano alone, low register.

RECAPITULATION

1   Strings, *p*, syncopated throbbing, low upward rushes. Piano joins with running notes.
2   *a*. Sudden *f*, full orchestra, upward rushes climb in violins.
    b. Violins, *p*, piano joins, full orchestra, *f*. Brief pause.
3   Oboes, *p*, alternate with piano, dialog theme. Running notes in piano. Brief pause.
4   *a*. Piano, graceful theme in minor, strings accompany.
    b. Oboes repeat graceful theme, piano scales accompany.

CADENZA	5 Piano, long passage of running notes, scales, broken chords, trills, strings accompany. End of piano trill meshes with entrance of
	6 Full orchestra, *f*, upward rushes climb in violins. Briefly held chord.
	1 Extended piano solo.
CODA	1 Full orchestra, *f*, agitated passage, alternates with sighing phrase in strings, *p*. High repeated tones in violins, *f*. Sudden *p* followed by
	2 Strings, *p*, tender closing theme, winds join, *p*, repeated chords at end, *pp*.

Second Movement: Romance

The Romance, in B-flat major, is a slow, lyrical movement in three-part form. The piano introduces the tender main theme, which the orchestra repeats.

We then hear an arialike melody by the piano with a discreet orchestral accompaniment. A return to the main theme rounds off the opening section of the second movement.

This movement's serene mood is shattered by a stormy middle section in G minor. Rapid rhythms and abrupt shifts from high to low pitches recall the turbulence of the first movement. After a while the agitation subsides, and the rhythm gradually slows down. This is a beautifully smooth transition to the peaceful concluding section, which begins with the tender main theme. The Romance ends as gently as it began.

Third Movement: Rondo (Allegro assai)

The last movement, in D minor, is a sonata-rondo; its fury recalls the atmosphere of the first movement. The piano announces the fiery main theme, which begins with an upward arpeggio similar to the one in the finale of Mozart's Symphony No. 40 in G minor.

After several agitated ideas in minor, Mozart lightens the mood with a carefree F-major theme that is introduced by the woodwinds and repeated by the piano.

This theme returns in the D-major coda, which concludes the movement brilliantly and gaily. It's typical for late eighteenth-century music to end happily.

LUDWIG VAN BEETHOVEN [**11**]

For many people, Ludwig van Beethoven (1770–1827) represents the highest level of musical genius. His unique stature is comparable to Shakespeare's in literature and Michelangelo's in art. He opened new realms of musical expression that profoundly influenced composers throughout the nineteenth century.

Beethoven was born on December 16, 1770, in Bonn, Germany. Like Bach and Mozart before him, he came from a family of musicians. His grandfather, also named Ludwig, was music director of the court at Bonn. His father, Johann, was a tenor who held a low position in the court and who saw his talented son as a profitable prodigy like Mozart. It's told that Johann Beethoven and a musician friend would come home from the local tavern late at night, rouse young Ludwig from sleep, and make him practice at the keyboard until morning. At eleven, Beethoven served as assistant to the court organist, and by thirteen he had published several piano compositions.

Beethoven went to Vienna when he was sixteen to improvise for Mozart, who said, "Keep your eyes on him; some day he will give the world something to talk about." He then returned to Bonn because his mother was critically ill. She died shortly after, and his father, who became an alcoholic, was dismissed from the court choir. Beethoven, at eighteen, became legal guardian of two younger brothers. At court he was organist and violist, composing and practicing; suddenly, he was also head of a family.

Shortly before his twenty-second birthday, Beethoven left Bonn to study with Haydn in Vienna, where he spent the rest of his life. In 1792, Haydn was at the height of his fame, too busy composing to devote much time or energy to teaching. As a result, he overlooked errors in Beethoven's counterpoint exercises, and his pupil felt forced to go secretly to another teacher. (Haydn never learned of this.) Beethoven's drive for thoroughness and mastery—evident throughout his life—is shown by his willingness to subject

Ludwig van Beethoven

239

himself to a strict course in counterpoint and fugue even after he had composed fine works.

Beethoven's first seven years in Vienna brought hard work, growing confidence, a strong sense of identity, and public praise. His letters of introduction from Bonn noblemen opened the doors of the social and cultural elite in this music-loving city. He dazzled everyone with his piano virtuosity and moved them with his improvisations. "He knew how to produce such an impression on every listener," reports a contemporary, "that frequently there was not a single dry eye, while many broke out into loud sobs, for there was a certain magic in his expression." A rebel against social convention, Beethoven asserted that an artist deserved as much respect as nobles. Once, while playing in an aristocratic drawing room, he was disturbed by the loud conversation of a young count. Beethoven jumped up from the piano, exclaiming, "I will not play for such swine!" For a long time he was a guest of Prince Carl Lichnowsky, who told his personal servant that if ever he and Beethoven rang at the same time, Beethoven should be served first. The same aristocrats who had allowed Mozart to die in poverty a few years before showered Beethoven with gifts. He earned good fees from piano lessons and private concerts. Publishers were quick to buy his compositions, even though some critics complained they were "bizarre" and "excessively complicated."

Disaster struck during his twenty-ninth year: Beethoven felt the first symptoms of deafness. Doctors could do nothing to halt the course of his physical and emotional torment. In 1801 he wrote despairingly, "For two years I have avoided almost all social gatherings because it is impossible for me to say to people 'I am deaf.' If I belonged to any other profession it would be easier, but in my profession it is a dreadful state." On October 6, 1802, Beethoven was in Heiligenstadt, a village outside Vienna where he sought solitude during the summer. That day his feelings were expressed in what is now known as "The Heiligenstadt Testament," a long agonized letter addressed to his brothers. Beethoven wrote, "I would have ended my life—it was only my art that held me back. Ah, it seemed to me impossible to leave the world until I had brought forth all that I felt was within me."

Beethoven's victory over despair coincided with an important change in his musical style. Works created after his emotional crisis have a new power and heroism. From 1803 to 1804, he composed the gigantic Third Symphony, the *Eroica*, a landmark in music history. At first, he planned to name it "Bonaparte," after the First Consul of the French Republic. Beethoven saw Napoleon as the embodiment of heroism and the champion of the principles underlying the French Revolution. "Liberty, equality, fraternity" were stirring words that expressed Beethoven's democratic ideals. But when he learned that Napoleon had proclaimed himself Emperor of the French, Beethoven "flew into a rage and cried out, 'He too is nothing but an ordinary man! Now he will trample under foot all the rights of man and only indulge his ambition. He will exalt himself above all others and become a tyrant!'"Seizing his score, Beethoven

The German poet Goethe described Beethoven as "an
utterly untamed personality" (Omikron).

Ludwig van Beethoven
241

tore out the title page bearing Napoleon's name and threw it on the floor. On a new title page, later, Beethoven wrote, "Heroic Symphony composed to celebrate the memory of a great man."

In 1812, Beethoven met Johann Wolfgang von Goethe, the great German poet he had long worshiped. He played for Goethe and the two artists walked and talked together. Shortly after this meeting, Goethe described Beethoven to a friend as "an utterly untamed personality." To his wife the poet wrote, "Never before have I seen an artist with more power of concentration, more energy, more inwardness." Despite such descriptions by people who knew him, Beethoven remains a mystery. He was self-educated and had read widely in Shakespeare and the ancient classics, but he was weak in elementary arithmetic. He claimed the highest moral principles, but he was often unscrupulous in dealing with publishers. Orderly and methodical when composing, Beethoven dressed sloppily and lived in incredibly messy apartments. During his thirty-five years in Vienna, he changed dwellings about forty times.

Beethoven fell in and out of love with several women, mostly of noble birth, but never was able to form a lasting relationship. To a woman now referred to as "The Immortal Beloved," he wrote a passionate letter that was found in a drawer after his death. No one has been able to conclusively establish her identity. Beethoven took consolation for disappointments in his personal life from nature. Ideas came to him while walking through the Viennese countryside. His Sixth Symphony, the *Pastoral,* beautifully expresses his recollections of life in the country.

Beethoven was never in the service of the Viennese aristocracy. A growing musical public made it possible for him to earn a fairly good income by selling compositions to publishers. His stature was so unique that when he threatened to accept a position outside Austria in 1809, three nobles made a special arrangement to keep him in Vienna. Prince Kinsky, Prince Lobkowitz, and Archduke Rudolf—the Emperor's brother and Beethoven's pupil—obligated themselves to give Beethoven an annual income. Their only condition was that Beethoven continue to live in the Austrian capital—an unprecedented arrangement in music history.

As Beethoven's hearing weakened, so did his piano playing and conducting. By the age of forty-four, this once brilliant pianist was forced to stop playing in public. But he insisted on conducting his orchestral works long after he could do it efficiently. The players would become confused by his wild gestures on the podium, and performances were often chaotic. His sense of isolation grew with his deafness. Friends had to communicate with him through an ear trumpet, and during his last eight years he carried notebooks in which people would write questions and comments.

In 1815, his brother Caspar died, and Beethoven and the widow became coguardians of the nine-year-old son. Young Carl was the object of a savage tug-of-war. For five years, Beethoven fought legal battles for exclusive custody of his nephew; he finally won. This "victory" was a disaster for everyone.

Growing up in the household of a deaf, eccentric bachelor uncle is not easy at best, and for Carl it was complicated by Beethoven's craving for love and companionship. The young man attempted suicide, a crushing event for Beethoven, whose health was already poor.

During the first three years of legal battles over Carl, Beethoven composed less, and the Viennese began to whisper that he was finished. Beethoven heard the rumor and said, "Wait a while, they'll soon learn differently!" It was true. After 1818, Beethoven's domestic problems did not prevent a creative outburst that produced some of his greatest works: the late piano sonatas, string quartets, the *Missa solemnis,* and the Ninth Symphony—out of total deafness, new realms of sound.

Beethoven's Music

"I must despise the world which does not know that music is a higher revelation than all wisdom and philosophy." For Beethoven, music was not mere entertainment, but a moral force capable of creating a vision of higher ideals. His music directly reflects his powerful, tortured personality. In both art and life, his heroic struggle resulted in victory over despair.

Beethoven's demand for perfection meant long and hard work. Unlike Mozart, he couldn't dash off three great symphonies in six weeks. Sometimes he worked years on a single symphony, writing other works at the same time. He carried music sketchbooks everywhere, jotting down new ideas, revising and refining old ones. These early notes often seem crude and uninspired when compared with their final versions, which were hammered out through great labor.

Beethoven mostly used Classical forms and techniques, but he gave them new power and intensity. The musical heir of Haydn and Mozart, he bridged the Classical and Romantic eras. Many of his innovations were used by composers who came after him.

In his works, great tension and excitement are built up through syncopations and dissonances. The range of pitch and dynamics is greater than ever before, so that contrasts of mood become more pronounced. Accents and climaxes seem titanic. Tiny rhythmic ideas are often repeated over and over to create momentum. Greater tension called for a larger musical framework, and so Beethoven expanded his forms. For example, the Third Symphony (*Eroica*) is far longer than any symphony by Haydn or Mozart and takes almost fifty minutes to unfold. Beethoven was a musical architect who was unsurpassed in his ability to create large-scale structures in which every note seems inevitable. In describing Beethoven's music, it is perhaps too easy to give the impression that all of it is stormy and powerful. A lot is; but much is gentle, humorous, noble, or lyrical. His range of expression is enormous. Tempo, dynamic, and expressive indications are marked far more extensively in his scores than in those of earlier composers. For example, one direction reads, "Rather lively with the most intimate feeling." Characteristic of his explicit dynamic markings is ⎯ p, a gradual increase in loudness followed by a sudden softness.

More than his predecessors, Beethoven tried to unify the contrasting movements of a symphony, sonata, or string quartet. Musical continuity is heightened in several ways. Sometimes a movement leads directly into the next, instead of ending traditionally with a pause. In the Fifth Symphony, for example, the last two movements are linked by a suspenseful bridge section. A musical bond between different movements of the same work is also created when their themes resemble each other. In a few compositions (Fifth and Ninth Symphonies), a theme from one movement is quoted in a later movement.

Like Haydn and Mozart, Beethoven wrote many movements in sonata form. The development section is greatly expanded and becomes even more dramatic. It often contains a powerful crescendo that leads to the climactic return of the first theme (recapitulation). The coda is also expanded and serves to develop themes still further. Its length balances what came before and affirms the victory of the tonic key over the many new keys in the development section.

As the third movement of a symphony or string quartet, Beethoven most often used a scherzo rather than the traditional minuet. He transformed the courtly dance into a rapid movement with rhythmic drive. The character of this scherzo is flexible. In the Fifth Symphony it's an ominous force, while in the Sixth Symphony ("Pastoral") it depicts peasant merrymaking. Beethoven's works often have climactic, triumphant finales, toward which the previous movements seem to build. This marks an important departure from the light, relaxed ending movement favored by Haydn and Mozart.

Beethoven's most popular works are the nine symphonies, which were conceived for larger orchestras than Haydn's or Mozart's. For greater power and brilliance, Beethoven sometimes added the trombone, piccolo, and contrabassoon—instruments that were not used previously in symphonies. All the orchestral instruments have to play difficult music. For example, the French horn is assigned prominent melodies, and the timpani participate in the musical dialog, rather than merely mark the beat.

Each of Beethoven's symphonies is unique in character and style. There is a curious alternation of mood between odd-numbered symphonies (3, 5, 7, and 9), which tend to be forceful and assertive, and even-numbered ones (4, 6, 8), which are calmer and more lyrical. In the finale of the Ninth Symphony ("Choral"), Beethoven took the unprecedented step of using a chorus and four solo vocalists. They sing the text of Schiller's "Ode to Joy," an exalted poem about human brotherhood.

A feeling for the virtuosity and improvisation that so astounded the Viennese can be gotten from Beethoven's thirty-two piano sonatas. Far more difficult than the sonatas of Haydn and Mozart, they exploit the stronger, tonally improved piano of Beethoven's time. He drew many new effects from the piano, ranging from massive chords to the hollow, mystical sounds produced when the right and left hands play far apart on the keyboard. These sonatas were

The Classical Period

244

experimental grounds for the compositional techniques he later expanded in the symphonies and string quartets.

Beethoven's sixteen string quartets are among the greatest music composed. Spanning the composer's entire career, they are unsurpassed in sheer invention, thematic treatment, and heart-rending expressiveness. In three of the last quartets, Beethoven again stepped beyond the conventions of classical form: He used five, six, and seven movements (Op. 132, Op. 130, Op. 131) which are connected in subtle ways. And he wrote five superb piano concertos, each remarkable in its individuality. In the fourth and fifth concertos, the opening movement begins with a brief piano solo rather than the traditional orchestral exposition.

While most of Beethoven's great works are for instruments, his sense of drama was also expressed in vocal music. In his only opera, *Fidelio*, a wife's heroism enables justice to triumph over tyranny. Beethoven also composed two Masses. The *Missa solemnis* ("Solemn Mass"; 1819–1823) is one of the most monumental and expressive settings of this sacred text.

Beethoven's total output is usually divided into three periods: early (up to 1802), middle (1803–1814), and late (1815–1827). Haydn and Mozart influence some works of the early period, while other pieces clearly show Beethoven's personal style. The compositions of the middle period are longer and heroic in tone. And the sublime works of the last period well up from the depths of a man almost totally deaf. During this period he often used the fugue to express new musical conceptions. These late works contain passages that sound surprisingly harsh and "modern." When a violinist complained that the music was very difficult to play, Beethoven reportedly replied, "Do you believe that I think of a wretched fiddle when the spirit speaks to me?"

Symphony No. 5 in C Minor, Op. 67 (1808)

The Fifth Symphony opens with one of the most famous rhythmic ideas in all music, a short-short-short-long motive. Beethoven reportedly interpreted this four-note motive as "Fate knocking at the door." It dominates the first movement and plays an important role later in the symphony, too. The entire work can be seen as an emotional progression from the conflict and struggle of the first movement, in C minor, to the exultation and victory of the final movement, in C major. The finale is the climax of the symphony; it is longer than the first movement and more powerful in sound, employing three trombones. This was the first time that a trombone was used in a symphony.

Through several different techniques, Beethoven brilliantly welds four contrasting movements into a unified work. The basic rhythmic motive of the first movement (short-short-short-long), is used in a marchlike theme in the third movement. And this third-movement theme is later quoted dramatically within the finale. The last two movements are also connected by a bridge passage.

Symphony No. 5 in
C Minor, Op. 67 (1808)

245

Beethoven worked on the Fifth Symphony off and on from 1804 to 1808. During this period, he also composed other great works. The individual movements of this famous symphony are:

First Movement: Allegro con brio (allegro with vigor)

The Allegro con brio is an enormously powerful and concentrated movement in sonata form. Its character is determined by a single rhythmic motive, short-short-short-long, from which Beethoven creates an astonishing variety of musical ideas. Tension and expectation are generated from the very beginning of the movement. Three rapid notes of the same pitch are followed by a downward leap to a held, suspenseful tone. This powerful idea is hammered out twice by all the strings in unison; the second time it is a step lower in pitch.

As the opening theme continues in C minor, Beethoven maintains excitement by quickly developing his basic idea. He crowds varied repetitions of the motive together and rapidly shifts the motive to different pitches and instruments.

The second theme, in E-flat major, dramatically combines different ideas. It begins with an unaccompanied horn call that asserts the basic motive in a varied form (short-short-short-long-long-long).

This horn-call motive announces a new legato melody which is calm and contrasts with the preceding agitation. Yet even during this lyrical moment, we are not allowed to forget the basic motive; now it is muttered in the background by cellos and double basses.

Beethoven generates tension in the development section by breaking the horn-call motive into smaller and smaller fragments until it is represented by only a single tone. Supported by a chord, this tone is echoed between woodwinds and strings in a breathtaking decrescendo. The recapitulation comes as a tremendous climax as the full orchestra thunders the basic motive. The recapitulation also brings a new expressive oboe solo at the end of the first theme. The heroic closing section of the recapitulation, in C major, moves without a break into a long and exciting coda in C minor. This coda is like a second development section in which the basic motive creates still greater power and energy.

LISTENING OUTLINE

To be read while music is heard

Symphony No. 5 in C Minor, Op. 67 (1808) by Ludwig van Beethoven

First Movement: Allegro con brio

Sonata form, duple meter ($\frac{2}{4}$), C minor

2 flutes, 2 oboes, 2 clarinets, 2 bassoons, 2 French horns, 2 trumpets, timpani, violins 1, violins 2, violas, cellos, basses

(About 6½ min)

EXPOSITION

First theme   1   *a.* Basic motive, *ff*, repeated a step lower, strings in unison.

         b. Sudden *p*, strings quickly develop basic motive, minor key, powerful chords, high held tone.

Bridge   2   *a.* Basic motive, *ff*, orchestra in unison.

         b. Sudden *p*, strings quickly develop basic motive, crescendo, *ff*, powerful chords.

Second theme   3   *a.* Solo French horns, *ff*, horn-call motive.

         b. Violins, *p*, lyrical major melody. Basic motive accompanies in low strings.

         Crescendo to

     4   *a.* Triumphant melody, *ff*, violins.

b. Woodwinds and horns, basic motive rushes downward. Cadences in basic
           rhythm. Pause.
        (Exposition may be repeated.)

DEVELOPMENT

    1 *a.* Basic motive, *ff*, horns, strings.
       b. Sudden *p*, strings and woodwinds, basic motive quickly developed. Motive
          climbs to rapidly repeated chords, *ff*.
    2 *a.* Violins, *ff*, horn-call motive, low strings, descending line.

        b. High woodwinds, *ff*, in dialog with lower strings, *ff*. Horn-call motive broken
          into tiny fragments. Decrescendo to *pp*.

        c. Sudden *ff*, horn-call rhythm.
        d. Sudden *pp*, woodwinds echoed by strings.
        e. Sudden *ff*, repeated motive drives into

RECAPITULATION

First theme   1 *a.* Climactic basic motive, full orchestra, *ff*, repeated a step lower.
        b. Sudden *p*, strings quickly develop basic motive, minor key, chords lead
          to
        c. Oboe solo.

Bridge	2	Basic motive quickly developed in strings, crescendo to *ff*, full orchestra.
Second theme	3	*a.* Horn-call motive, solo bassoons, *ff* (horns sometimes added).
		b. Lyrical major melody, *p*, violins and flutes alternate. Basic motive accompanies in timpani, *p*. Crescendo to
	4	*a.* Triumphant melody, *ff*, violins.
		b. Woodwinds, basic motive rushes downward.
		Cadences in basic rhythm.

CODA

1   *a.* Rapidly repeated chords, *ff*.
      b. Horn-call motive, lower strings, *f*, with higher violin melody, minor.

Descending violin melody, staccato, leads to

3   *a.* New, rising theme in strings, legato and staccato.

      b. High woodwinds, *ff*, answered by lower strings in powerful interchange. Rapidly repeated notes lead to

4   *a.* Basic motive, *ff*, repeated a step lower, full orchestra.
      b. Sudden *p*, basic motive quickly developed in strings and woodwinds.
      c. Sudden *ff*, powerful concluding chords.

Second Movement: Andante con moto
(moderately slow but not too slow)

The second movement, in A-flat major, is mostly relaxed and lyrical, but it includes moments of tension and heroism. It is an extended set of variations based on two themes. The main theme (A), softly introduced by the cellos and violas, is a long legato melody of great nobility. The second theme (B) begins very gently in the clarinets but soon brings a startling contrast of mood. The full orchestra suddenly bursts in, and the clarinet melody is transformed into a triumphant trumpet fanfare. A hushed transitional passage then leads back to the main theme, presented now in quicker notes.

After several variations, there is a middle section in which fragments of the themes are treated in new ways. Woodwind instruments are featured, and there is a brief episode in minor. The movement concludes with a final variation of the main melody—now majestically proclaimed by the full orchestra—and a coda that poetically recalls what has come before.

Symphony No. 5 in
C Minor, Op. 67 (1808)

LISTENING OUTLINE

To be read while music is heard

Symphony No. 5 in C Minor, Op. 67 (1808) by Ludwig van Beethoven

Second Movement: Andante con moto

Theme and variations, triple meter ($\frac{3}{8}$), A-flat major

2 flutes, 2 oboes, 2 clarinets, 2 bassoons, 2 French horns, 2 trumpets, timpani, violins 1, violins 2, violas, cellos, double basses

(About 10 min)

THEME A

     1   Lyrical melody, violas and cellos, *p*.

     Melody continues in higher register, violins alternate with flute.

THEME B

     2   *a*. Clarinets, *p*, rising phrases.

     Violins, *pp*, sudden *ff*, full orchestra.
     b. Trumpets, *ff*, rising phrases.

     Violins, *pp*, sustained notes.

VAR. A¹

     3   Violas and cellos, *p*, lyrical melody in even-flowing rhythm.

     Melody continues in higher register, violins alternate with flute.

VAR. B¹

4   *a.* Clarinets, *p*, rising phrases. Violins, *pp*, sudden *ff*, full orchestra.
     b. Trumpets, *ff*, rising phrases. Violins, *pp*, sustained notes, cellos, low repeated notes.

VAR. A²

5   *a.* Violas and cellos, *p*, lyrical melody decorated by quick, even-flowing notes.

     b. Violins, *pp*, repeat decorated melody in higher register.
     c. Loud repeated chords, decorated melody in cellos and double basses. Upward scales lead to high held tone.

MIDDLE SECTION

6   Sudden *pp*, repeated string chords, clarinet phrase passed to bassoon and flute. High woodwind interlude leads to
7   *a.* Full orchestra, *ff*, rising phrases, timpani rolls.
     b. Strings, *p*, repeated short figure.
8   *a.* Woodwinds, *p*, staccato variation of lyrical melody, minor key.
     b. Rising scales in flute, strings. Crescendo.

VAR. A³

9   Full orchestra, *ff*, lyrical melody in high register, major key, rising scales. Flute and violins, *p*, continue melody.

CODA

10   *a.* *Più mosso* (faster tempo), bassoon, *p*, variation of lyrical phrase. Violins, crescendo.
      b. Original tempo, flute and strings, *p*, conclusion of lyrical melody.
      c. Clarinets, *p*, variation of lyrical phrase, low strings, crescendo. Cadence in full orchestra, *ff*.

Third Movement: Allegro (scherzo)

The rapid third movement is a scherzo, in C minor, composed of three sections: A (scherzo) B (trio) A′ (scherzo). The scherzo opens with a hushed, mysterious theme played by cellos and double basses in a low register.

Soon, in sharp contrast, a bold repeated-note theme is hammered out loudly by the horns.

Symphony No. 5 in
C Minor, Op. 67 (1808)

251

This theme is dominated by the rhythmic pattern short-short-short-long and recalls the basic motive of the first movement.

The B section (trio), in major, brings a gruff, hurried theme, played by cellos and double basses.

This theme is imitated, in the style of a fugue, by each of the higher strings. The bustling rhythmic motion of the B section has a feeling of energy and rough humor.

When the scherzo section (A') returns, it is hushed and ominous throughout, sounding like a ghost of its former self. The mysterious opening theme is now played pizzicato rather than legato. The repeated-note theme is completely transformed in mood; it no longer is proclaimed by horns but is whispered by clarinets, plucked violins, and oboe.

One of the most extraordinary passages in the symphony follows the scherzo section (A'): a bridge leading from the dark, mysterious world of the scherzo to the bright sunlight of the finale. It opens with a feeling of suspended animation as the timpani softly repeat a single tone against a sustained chord in the strings. Over the timpani pulsation, the violins hesitantly play a fragment of the mysterious scherzo theme. Tension mounts as this fragment is carried higher and higher, until a sudden crescendo climaxes with the heroic opening of the finale.

Fourth Movement: Allegro

The fourth movement, in sonata form, is the climax of the symphony. It brings the victory of C major over C minor, of optimism and exultation over struggle and uncertainty. For greater power and brilliance, Beethoven enlarged the orchestra to include three trombones, a piccolo, and a contrabassoon. Brass instruments are especially prominent and give a marchlike character to much of the movement.

The exposition is rich in melodic ideas; even the bridge has a theme of its own, and there is also a distinctive closing theme. The triumphant opening theme begins with the three tones of the C-major triad, brilliantly proclaimed by the trumpets.

A bridge theme, similar in mood to the opening one, is announced by the horns and continued by the violins.

Triplets lend a joyous quality to the second theme, which contrasts loud and soft phrases.

Two powerful chords and a brief pause announce the closing theme of the exposition. Composed of descending phrases, this melody is first played by the strings and woodwinds and then forcefully repeated by the entire orchestra.

The development focuses mainly on the second theme and its triplet rhythm. A huge climax at the end of the development is followed by one of the most marvelous surprises in all music. Beethoven dramatically quotes the whispered repeated-note theme (short-short-short-long) of the preceding scherzo movement. This ominous quotation is like a sudden recollection of past anxiety, and it creates a connection between the last two movements. Leading into a powerful recapitulation, it renews the victory over uncertainty.

During the finale's long coda, earlier themes are heard in altered and quickened versions. Several times, the music keeps going even though the listener thinks it's coming to an end. Over and over, Beethoven affirms the tonic key and resolves the frenzied tensions built up during the symphony. Such control over tension is an essential element of Beethoven's genius.

Piano Sonata in F Minor, Op. 57 ("Appassionata"; 1804–1805)

The title "Appassionata," though not coined by Beethoven, suggests the passionate, stormy, almost violent character of the F-minor Piano Sonata.

Piano Sonata in F Minor, Op. 57 ("Appassionata"; 1804–1805)

Beethoven's impetuous playing and masterful improvisational powers are mirrored in the sonata's extreme dynamic contrasts, explosive accents, crashing chords, and rapid sweeps up and down the keyboard.

First Movement: Allegro assai

The dramatic opening movement, in F minor, is in sonata form. Its first theme begins mysteriously with an F-minor arpeggio played two octaves apart by both hands at the same time.

The large interval between these high and low tones produces a haunting, hollow sound. As the opening theme continues, we hear a low, four-note figure, short-short-short-long, similar to the basic motive in Beethoven's Fifth Symphony. This generates tension and explodes into a downward rush of tones and a series of powerful chords.

A complete contrast of mood comes with the lyrical and consoling second theme, a legato melody in the new key of A-flat major.

But this relaxation is only a brief interlude. Trills and a long downward scale soon lead to the stormy third theme, in minor. In this agitated section the short-short-short-long motive is asserted in the bass.

As the first movement continues, the motives undergo striking transformations. For example, during the extended development section, the lyrical second theme is made to sound tense and threatening. Its altered opening phrases are repeated at higher and higher pitches and lead to a climax during which the four-note motive is violently hammered out. Within the long coda, the second theme is played at a faster tempo and sounds almost desperate. At the end of the movement, the arpeggio figure from the first theme makes a final appearance in a new guise. It briefly rises, then sinks five octaves to the lowest register of the piano as the sound dies away.

Second Movement: Andante con moto

The second movement—a theme and variations in D-flat major—is an oasis of calm between the stormy outer movements. The theme is quiet, hymnlike, and in a low register. Each of its two parts is repeated: a a b b. Within the three variations that follow, the mood shifts gradually from contemplation to exultation. Each variation is presented in a successively higher register, so that at the climax the melody is almost at the top note of the piano keyboard. At the same time, the rhythm is quickened. Each variation of the theme is ornamented by increasingly rapid notes. The closing section brings a sense of resolution as the theme returns in its original hymnlike form.

   The Andante ends suspensefully with an inconclusive broken chord. This mysterious chord is repeated louder and higher, and the rapid concluding movement follows without a break.

LISTENING OUTLINE

To be read while music is heard

Piano Sonata in F Minor, Op. 57 ("Appassionata"; 1804–1805) by Ludwig van Beethoven

Second Movement: Andante con moto

Theme and variations, duple meter ($\frac{2}{4}$), D-flat major

Piano

(About 6 min)

THEME

   Section a   Hymnlike theme, *p*, low register, legato. Section a repeated.

   Section b   Hymnlike theme continues, melody reaches upward, slight crescendo and decrescendo. Section b repeated.

VAR. 1

    a. Detached melody tones, bass tones on off beats. Repeated.

    b. Detached melody reaches upward, crescendo, to *f*, sudden *p*. Repeated.

VAR. 2

    a. Flowing legato melody, octave higher than Var. 1. Repeated.

    b. Flowing melody reaches upward, slight crescendo and decrescendo. Repeated.

VAR. 3

    a. Syncopated melody tones, octave higher than Var. 2, running-note accompaniment below melody.

    Running-note melody above syncopated chords.
    b. Repeated-note melody, running-note accompaniment below melody. Running-note melody above syncopated chords. Crescendo to *ff*, decrescendo to

CODA

    a. Hymnlike theme divided between low and higher register, *p*.
    b. Hymnlike theme continues, melody reaches upward, slight crescendo and decrescendo. Suspenseful broken chord, *pp*, chord repeated *ff*, octave higher. (Rapid introduction to next movement follows without a pause.)

Third Movement: Allegro ma non troppo
(fast, but not too fast)

In contrast to the exultant ending of the Fifth Symphony, the Appassionata concludes with a movement—in F minor—that conveys tragedy and desperation. Loud repeated chords and a descending passage lead into the first theme, which is composed of a continuous flow of rapid notes in the bass register.

The opening theme dominates every section of this sonata-form movement; its rushing rhythm, maintained almost throughout, builds enormous tension. Beethoven saves his most striking new theme for the Presto coda: two crashing chords launch a breathless staccato melody. This climactic idea brings a fresh surge of energy and ushers in a faster version of the opening theme—and so the Appassionata comes to a furious conclusion.

Piano Sonata in
F Minor, Op. 57
("Appassionata";
1804–1805)

257

THE ROMANTIC PERIOD

John Constable captured the Romantic view of nature in *Cathedral from the Bishop's Garden* (The Frick Collection).

[1] ROMANTICISM IN MUSIC

The early nineteenth century brought the flowering of Romanticism, a cultural movement that stressed emotion, imagination, and individualism. In part, Romanticism was a rebellion against the neoclassicism of the eighteenth-century Age of Reason. Romantic writers broke away from time-honored conventions and emphasized freedom of expression. Painters used bolder, more brilliant colors and preferred dynamic motion to gracefully balanced poses.

But Romanticism was too diverse and complex to be defined by any single formula. It aimed to broaden all human horizons and encompass the totality of our experience. The Romantic movement was international in scope and influenced all the arts.

Emotional subjectivity was a basic quality of Romanticism in art. "All good poetry is the spontaneous overflow of powerful feelings," wrote William Wordsworth, the English Romantic poet. And "spontaneous overflow" made much Romantic literature autobiographical; authors projected their personalities in their work. Walt Whitman, the American poet, expressed this subjective attitude beautifully when he began a poem, "I celebrate myself, and sing myself."

In exploring their inner lives, the Romantics were especially drawn to the realm of fantasy: the unconscious, the irrational, the world of dreams. Romantic fiction includes tales of terror and the supernatural, such as "The Cask of Amontillado" by Edgar Allan Poe and *Frankenstein* by Mary Shelley. The writer Thomas De Quincey vividly describes his drug-induced dreams in the *Confessions of an English Opium-Eater:* "I was buried, for a thousand years, in stone coffins, with mummies and sphinxes. I was kissed, with cancerous kisses, by crocodiles." The visual arts also depict nightmarish visions. In an etching called *The Sleep of Reason Breeds Monsters,* Spanish painter Francisco Goya shows bat-like monsters surrounding a sleeping figure. The realm of the unknown and the exotic also interested the French artist Eugène Delacroix, who often depicted violent scenes in far-off lands.

Romantic fascination with fantasy was paired with enthusiasm for the Middle Ages, that time of chivalry and romance. While neoclassicists had thought of the medieval period as the "dark ages," the Romantics cherished it. They were inspired by medieval folk ballads, tales of fantasy and adventure. Romantic novels set in the Middle Ages include *Ivanhoe* (1819) by Sir Walter Scott and *The Hunchback of Notre Dame* (1831) by the French writer Victor Hugo. Gothic cathedrals, which had long gone unappreciated, now seemed picturesque and mysterious. A "gothic revival" in architecture resulted in the construction of buildings such as the Houses of Parliament in London (1836–1852) and Trinity Church in New York (1839–1846).

Of all the inspirations for Romantic art, none was more important than nature. The physical world was seen as a source of consolation and a mirror

Delacroix's *The Death of Sardanapalus* (1827) shows a defeated
Assyrian tyrant who has his wives killed before taking his own life.
This violent and sensuous painting reflects the Romantic
preoccupation with the exotic (Giraudon).

Romanticism in Music

The nineteenth century was the age of grand opera. Construction
of the Paris Opera House was begun in 1861 (Giraudon).

The Industrial Revolution spurred an interest in the working class. *The Stone Breakers* by Gustave Courbet illustrates this trend toward a new realism in the arts (Deutsche Fotothek, Dresden).

Romanticism in Music

of the human heart. Wordsworth, for example, thought of nature as "the nurse,/ the guide, the guardian of my heart, and soul." One of his poems begins:

There was a time when meadow, grove, and stream,
   The earth, and every common sight,
      To me did seem
  Apparelled in celestial light,
The glory and the freshness of a dream.

Romantic sensitivity to nature is revealed in landscape painting, which attained new importance. Artists like John Constable and William Turner in England were masters in conveying the movement of nature: rippling brooks, drifting clouds, stormy seas. In Turner's seascapes, the sweep of waves expresses not only the grandeur of nature, but human passion as well.

Romanticism coincided with the Industrial Revolution, thus producing an interest in the working class and the poor. The novels of Charles Dickens and the paintings of Gustave Courbet reflect this interest.

Subjectivity, fantasy, enthusiasm for nature and the Middle Ages are only a few aspects of Romanticism in literature and painting. We'll now focus on Romanticism in music.

The Romantic Period in Music (1820–1900)

The Romantic period in music extended from about 1820 to 1900. Great Romantic composers include Franz Schubert, Hector Berlioz, Felix Mendelssohn, Frédéric Chopin, Robert Schumann, Franz Liszt, Richard Wagner, Giuseppe Verdi, Johannes Brahms, and Peter Ilyich Tchaikovsky. The length of this list—even with many important composers omitted—testifies to the richness and variety of Romantic music and proves its continuing impact on today's concert and operatic repertory.

Composers of the Romantic period continued to use the musical forms of the preceding Classical era. The emotional intensity associated with Romanticism was already present in the work of Mozart and particularly in that of Beethoven, who greatly influenced composers after him. The Romantic preference for expressive, songlike melody also grew out of the Classical style. Nonetheless, there are many differences between Romantic and Classical music. Romantic works tend to have greater ranges of tone color, dynamics, and pitch. Also, the Romantic harmonic vocabulary is broader, with more emphasis on colorful, unstable chords.

Romantic music is linked more closely to other arts, particularly to literature. New forms developed, and in all forms there was greater tension and less balance and resolution. But Romantic music is so diverse that generalizations are apt to mislead. Some Romantic composers, such as Mendelssohn and Brahms, created works that were deeply rooted in Classical tradition, while others, such as Berlioz, Liszt, and Wagner, were more revolutionary.

The Romantic Period

264

Individuality of Style

Romantic music puts unprecedented emphasis on self-expression and individuality of style. There is "not a bar which I have not truly felt and which is not an echo of my inner-most feelings," wrote Tchaikovsky of his Fourth Symphony. "A new world of music" was the goal of young Chopin. Many Romantics created music that sounds unique and reflects their personalities. Robert Schumann observed that "Chopin will soon be unable to write anything without people crying out at the seventh or eighth bar, 'That is indeed by him.'" And today, with some listening experience, a music lover can tell within a few minutes whether a piece is by Schumann or Chopin, Tchaikovsky or Brahms.

Expressive Aims and Subjects

The Romantics explored a universe of feeling that included flamboyance and intimacy, unpredictability and melancholy, rapture and longing. Countless songs and operas glorify romantic love. Often the lovers are unhappy and face overwhelming obstacles. Fascination with the fantastic and diabolical is expressed in music like "Dream of a Witches' Sabbath" from Berlioz's *Fantastic Symphony*. All aspects of nature attracted Romantic musicians. In this chapter we'll study music that depicts shepherd's pipes and distant thunder (Berlioz's *Fantastic Symphony*), a wild horseback ride on a stormy night (Schubert's *Erlking*), the flow of a river (Smetana's *Moldau*), and a spectacular fire and flood (Wagner's *Twilight of the Gods*). Romantic composers also dealt with subjects drawn from the Middle Ages and from Shakespeare's plays.

Nationalism and Exoticism

Nationalism was an important political movement that influenced nineteenth-century music. Musical **nationalism** was expressed when Romantic composers deliberately created music with specific national identities, using folk songs, dances, legends, and histories of their homelands. This national flavor of Romantic music—whether Polish, Russian, Bohemian, or German—contrasts with the more universal character of Classical music.

Fascination with national identity also led composers to draw on colorful materials from foreign lands, a trend known as musical **exoticism.** For instance, some wrote melodies in an oriental style or used rhythms and instruments associated with distant lands. The French composer Georges Bizet wrote *Carmen*, an opera set in Spain; the Italian Giacomo Puccini evoked Japan in *Madame Butterfly*; and the Russian Rimsky-Korsakov suggested an Arabian atmosphere in his orchestral work *Scheherazade*. Musical exoticism is in keeping with the Romantics' attraction to things remote, picturesque, and mysterious.

Program Music

The nineteenth century was the great age of **program music,** instrumental music associated with a story, poem, idea, or scene. Usually the nonmusical element

The Romantic Period
in Music (1820–1900)

265

is specified by a title or by explanatory comments called a **program.** A programmatic instrumental piece can represent the emotions, characters, and events of a particular story, or it can evoke the sounds and motions of nature. For example, in Tchaikovsky's *Romeo and Juliet,* an orchestral work inspired by Shakespeare's play, agitated music depicts the feud between the rival families, a tender melody conveys young love, and a funeral-march rhythm suggests the lovers' tragic fate. And in *The Moldau,* an orchestral work glorifying Czechoslovakia's main river, Smetana uses musical effects that call to mind a flowing stream, a hunting scene, a peasant wedding, and the crash of waves.

While program music in some form or another has existed for centuries, it became particularly prominent in the Romantic period, when music was closely associated with literature. Composers—Berlioz, Schumann, Liszt, Wagner—were often prolific authors as well. Artists in all fields were intoxicated by the idea of a "union of the arts." Poets wanted their poetry to be musical, and musicians wanted their music to be poetic.

Expressive Tone Color

Romantic composers reveled in rich and sensuous sound, using tone color to obtain variety of mood and atmosphere. Never before had timbre been so important.

In both symphonic and operatic works, the Romantic orchestra was larger and more varied in tone color than the Classical orchestra. Toward the end of the Romantic era, an orchestra might include close to one hundred musicians. (There were twenty to sixty players in the Classical ensemble.) The constant expansion of the orchestra reflected composers' changing needs as well as the growing size of concert halls and opera houses. The brass, woodwind, and percussion sections of the orchestra took on a more active role. Romantic composers spectacularly increased the power of the brass section, calling for trombones, tubas, and more horns and trumpets. In 1824, Beethoven broke precedent by asking for nine brasses in the Ninth Symphony; and in 1894, German composer Gustav Mahler demanded twenty-five brass instruments for his Second Symphony. The addition of valves had made it easier for horns and trumpets to cope with intricate melodies.

The woodwind section took on new tone colors as the contrabassoon, bass clarinet, English horn, and piccolo became regular members of the orchestra. Improvements in the construction of instruments allowed woodwind players to perform more flexibly and accurately. Orchestral sounds became more brilliant and sensuously appealing through increased use of cymbals, the triangle, and the harp.

New sounds were drawn from all instruments of the nineteenth-century orchestra. Flutists were required to play in the breathy low register, and violinists were asked to strike the strings with the wood of their bows. These demands compelled performers to attain a higher level of technical virtuosity.

New ways of blending and combining tone colors were sought to achieve the most poignant and intense sound. In 1844, Hector Berlioz's *Treatise on Modern Instrumentation and Orchestration* signaled the recognition of orchestration as an art in itself.

The piano, the favorite instrument of the Romantic age, was improved vastly during the 1820s and 1830s. A cast-iron frame held the strings under greater tension, and the hammers were covered with felt. Thus the piano's tone became more "singing," and its range was extended. With a stronger instrument, the pianist could produce more sound. And use of the damper ("loud") pedal allowed a sonorous blend of tones from all registers of the piano.

Colorful Harmony

In addition to exploiting new tone colors, the Romantics explored new chords and novel ways of using familiar chords. Seeking greater emotional intensity, composers emphasized rich, colorful, and complex harmonies. There was more prominent use of **chromatic harmony,** chords containing tones not found in the prevailing major or minor scale. Such chord tones come from the chromatic scale (which has 12 tones), rather than from the major or minor scales (which have seven different tones). Chromatic chords add color and motion to Romantic music. Dissonant, or unstable, chords were also used more freely than during the Classical era. By deliberately delaying the resolution of dissonance to a consonant, or stable, chord, Romantic composers created feelings of yearning, tension, and mystery.

A Romantic piece tends to have a wide variety of keys and rapid modulations, or changes from one key to another. Due to the nature and frequency of these key shifts, the tonic key is somewhat less clear than in Classical works. The feeling of tonal gravity tends to be less strong. By the end of the Romantic period, even more emphasis was given to harmonic instability and less to stability and resolution.

Expanded Range of Dynamics, Pitch, and Tempo

Romantic music also calls for a wide range of dynamics. It includes sharp contrasts between faint whispers and sonorities of unprecedented power. Classical dynamic extremes of *ff* and *pp* didn't meet the needs of Romantics, who sometimes demanded *ffff* and *pppp*. Seeking more and more expressiveness, nineteenth-century composers used frequent crescendos and decrescendos, as well as sudden dynamic changes.

Range of pitch was expanded, too, as composers reached for extremely high or low sounds. In search of increased brilliance and depth of sound, the Romantic exploited instruments like the piccolo and contrabassoon, as well as the expanded keyboard of the piano.

The Romantic Period in Music (1820–1900)

Mood changes in Romantic music are often underlined by accelerandos, ritardandos, and subtle variations of pace: there are many more fluctuations in tempo than there were in Classical music. To intensify the expression of the music, Romantic performers made use of **rubato,** the slight holding back or pressing forward of tempo.

Form: Miniature and Monumental

The nineteenth century was very much an age of contradictions. Romantic composers characteristically expressed themselves both in musical miniatures and in monumental compositions. On one hand are piano pieces by Chopin and songs by Schubert that last but a few minutes. Such short forms were meant to be heard in the intimate surroundings of a home; they met the needs of the growing number of people who owned pianos. These miniatures were a perfect outlet for the Romantic genius at creating an intense mood through a melody, a few chords, or an unusual tone color. In contrast, there are gigantic works by Berlioz and Wagner that call for a huge number of performers and last for several hours. Mammoth compositions, of course, were designed for large opera houses or concert halls.

Romantic composers continued to write symphonies, sonatas, string quartets, concertos, operas, and choral works, but their individual movements tended to be longer than Haydn's and Mozart's. For example, a typical nineteenth-century symphony may last about forty-five minutes, as opposed to twenty-five minutes for an eighteenth-century symphony. And as the Romantic period drew to a close, compositions tended to become even more extended, more richly orchestrated, and more complex in harmony.

New techniques were used to unify such long works. The same theme or themes might occur in several different movements of a symphony. Here composers followed the pioneering example of Beethoven's Fifth Symphony, where a theme from the scherzo is quoted within the finale. When a melody returns in a later movement or section of a Romantic work, its character may be transformed by changes in dynamics, orchestration, or rhythm—a technique known as **thematic transformation.** A striking use of thematic transformation occurs in Liszt's Piano Concerto in E-flat major, where a lyrical, intimate melody from the slow movement becomes a jaunty march tune in the finale.

Different movements or sections of a Romantic work can also be linked through transitional passages; one movement of a symphony or concerto may lead directly into the next. Here, again, Beethoven was the pioneer. And nineteenth-century operas are unified by melodic ideas that reappear in different acts or scenes, some of which may be tied together by connecting passages.

In dealing with an age that so prized individuality, generalizations are especially difficult. The great diversity found in Romantic music can best be appreciated, perhaps, by approaching each piece as the composers did—with an open mind and heart.

Basic Terms

If you aren't sure what each of the following words means, look back at the text, where they appear in bold type. Additional information about some of them can be found by checking the index.

nationalism   chromatic harmony
exoticism   rubato
program music   thematic transformation
program

ROMANTIC COMPOSERS AND THEIR PUBLIC

[**2**]

The composer's role in society had changed radically during Beethoven's lifetime (1770–1827). In earlier periods, part of a musician's job was composing works for a specific occasion and audience. Thus Bach wrote cantatas for weekly church services in Leipzig, while Haydn composed symphonies for concerts in the palaces of the Esterházy family. But Beethoven, we have seen, was one of the first great composers who worked as a free-lance musician outside the system of aristocratic or church patronage.

The image of Beethoven as a "free artist" inspired Romantic musicians, who composed to fulfill an inner need rather than a nobleman's commission. Romantic composers were interested not only in pleasing contemporaries, but also in the judgment of posterity. The young Berlioz wrote to his father, "I want to leave on this earth some trace of my existence." It became common for Romantics to create extended works with no immediate prospects for performance. For example, Wagner wrote *The Rhine Gold,* a 2½-hour opera, and then had to wait fifteen years before seeing its premiere.

Sometimes the Romantic composer was a "free artist" by necessity rather than choice. Because of the French Revolution and Napoleonic Wars (from 1789 to 1814), many aristocrats could no longer afford to maintain private opera houses, orchestras, and "composers in residence." Musicians lost their jobs when many of the tiny princely states of Germany were abolished as political units and merged with neighboring territories. (In Bonn, Germany, the court and its orchestra were disbanded; Beethoven could not return to his position there even if he had wanted to.) Many composers who would have had modest but secure incomes in the past had to fight for their livelihood and sell their wares on the marketplace.

Romantic composers wrote primarily for a middle-class audience whose size and prosperity had increased because of the Industrial Revolution. During the

Romantic Composers
and Their Public

269

nineteenth century, cities expanded dramatically, and a sizable number of people wanted to hear and play music.

The needs of this urban middle class led to the formation of many orchestras and opera groups during the Romantic era. While public concerts had developed during the eighteenth century, only in the nineteenth century did regular subscription concerts become common. The London Philharmonic Society was founded in 1813, the Paris *Société des Concerts du Conservatoire* in 1828, the Vienna *Philharmonische Konzerte* and the New York Philharmonic in 1842.

The middle-class public was captivated by virtuosity. Musical heros of the 1830s were the pianist Franz Liszt and the violinist Niccolò Paganini, who toured Europe and astonished audiences with their feats. Never before was instrumental virtuosity so acclaimed. After a concert by Liszt in Budapest, Hungarian nobles presented him with a jeweled sword, and a crowd of thousands formed a torchlight parade to escort the virtuoso to his dwelling. Following Liszt's example, performers began to give solo recitals in addition to their customary appearances with orchestras.

Private music making also increased during the Romantic era. The piano became a fixture in every middle-class home, and there was great demand for songs and solo piano pieces. Operas and orchestral works were transcribed, or arranged, so that they could be played on pianos in the home.

Romantic composers came from the social class that was their main audience. Berlioz was the son of a doctor; Schumann was a bookseller's son; and Mendelssohn was the son of a banker. This was a new situation. In earlier periods, music, like cabinet making, was a craft passed from one generation to another. Bach, Mozart, and Beethoven were all children of musicians. But the Romantics often had to do a great deal of persuading before their parents permitted them to undertake a musical career. Berlioz wrote to his reluctant father in 1824: "I am voluntarily driven towards a magnificent career (no other term can be applied to the career of an artist) and I am not in the least headed towards damnation. This is the way I think, the way I am, and nothing in the world will change me."

Middle-class parents had reason for concern when their children wanted to be musicians. Few Romantic composers were able to support themselves through composition alone. Only a successful opera composer like Verdi could become wealthy by selling music to opera houses and publishers. Most composers were forced to work in several areas at once. Some were touring virtuosos like Paganini and Liszt. Many taught. Chopin charged high fees for piano lessons given to rich young women in Paris. Music criticism was a source of income for Berlioz and Schumann. (And Berlioz bitterly resented having to waste time reviewing compositions of nonentities.) Some of the finest conductors of the Romantic period were composers like Mendelssohn and Mahler. Tchaikovsky and Wagner were among the few fortunates with wealthy patrons to support them while they created. And lastly, some composers, like Schubert, never really earned a livelihood, leading a Bohemian existence and dying in poverty.

THE ART SONG [3]

One of the most distinctive forms of Romantic music is the **art song, a composition for solo voice and piano.** The accompaniment is an integral part of the composer's conception, and it serves with the voice as an interpretive partner. Now performed in concert halls, Romantic songs were written to be sung and enjoyed at home.

Poetry and music are intimately fused in the art song. It is no accident that this form flowered with the emergence of a rich body of Romantic poetry in the early nineteenth century. Many of the finest song composers—Schubert, Schumann, Brahms—were German or Austrian and set poems in their native language. Among the poets favored by these composers were Johann Wolfgang von Goethe (1749–1832) and Heinrich Heine (1797–1856). The German word *Lied* ("song") is commonly used for a song with German text. (*Lied* is pronounced "leet"; its plural, *Lieder*, is pronounced as in "leader.")

Yearning—over a lost love, toward nature, legend, other times and places—haunted the imagination of Romantic poets. Thus art songs are filled with the despair of unrequited love, the beauty of flowers, trees, and brooks, and the supernatural happenings of folk tales. There are also songs of joy, wit, and humor. But by and large, Romantic song was a reaching out of the soul.

Song composers interpreted a poem, translating its mood, atmosphere, and imagery into music. They created a vocal melody that is musically satisfying and perfectly molded to the text. Important words are emphasized by stressed tones or melodic climaxes.

The voice shares this interpretive task with the piano. Emotions and images of the text get added dimension from the keyboard commentary. Arpeggios suggest the splashing of oars or the motion of a mill-wheel. Chords in a low register depict darkness or a lover's torment. The mood is often set by a brief piano introduction and summed up at the end by a piano section called a **postlude.**

Strophic and Through-composed Form

When a poem has several stanzas, the musical setting must accommodate their total emotional impact. Composers can use **strophic form, repeating the same music for each stanza of the poem.** This makes the song easy to remember. Strophic form is used in almost all folksongs. Or composers might use **through-composed form,** writing new music for each stanza. ("Through-composed" is a translation of the German term *durchkomponiert.*) Through-composed form allows music to reflect a poem's changing moods.

The art song is not restricted to strophic or through-composed form. There are many ways that music can be molded to the structure and feeling of a poem. A three-stanza poem is frequently set as follows: A (stanza 1) B (stanza

Stropic and Through-composed Form

271

2)   A (stanza 3). This might be called a **modified strophic form,** since two of the three stanzas are set to the same music.

The Song Cycle

Romantic art songs are sometimes grouped in a set, or **song cycle.** A cycle may be unified by a story line that runs through the poems, or by musical ideas linking the songs. Among the great Romantic song cycles are Schubert's *Die Winterreise* ("The Winter Journey," 1827) and Schumann's *Dichterliebe* ("Poet's Love," 1840).

In the art song, Romantic composers achieved a perfect union of music and poetry. They created an intensely personal world with a tremendous variety of moods. These miniatures contain some of the most haunting melodies and harmonies in all music.

Basic Terms

If you aren't sure what each of the following words means, look back at the text, where they appear in bold type. Additional information about some of them can be found by checking the index.

art song   through-composed form
postlude   modified strophic form
strophic form   song cycle

Romantic

FRANZ SCHUBERT

The career of Franz Schubert (1797–1828), the earliest master of the Romantic art song, was unlike that of any great composer before him. He never held an official position as musical director or organist, and he was neither a conductor nor a virtuoso. "I have come into the world for no other purpose but to compose," he told a friend. The full measure of his genius was recognized only years after his death at the tragically early age of thirty-one.

Schubert was born in Vienna, the son of a schoolmaster. Even as a child, his musical gifts were astounding. "If I wanted to instruct him in anything new," recalled his amazed teacher, "he knew it already. Therefore I gave him no actual instructions but merely talked to him and watched him in silent astonishment." At eleven, Schubert became a choirboy in the court chapel and won a scholarship to the Imperial Seminary, an exclusive boarding school where he played first violin and occasionally conducted the orchestra. Schubert so loved music that he once sold his school books to buy a ticket for Beethoven's opera *Fidelio.*

Schubert managed to compose an extraordinary number of masterpieces in his late teens while teaching at his father's school, a job he hated. His love of poetry led him to the art song, a form that Haydn, Mozart, and Beethoven had only touched on. Inflamed by the poetry and passion of Goethe's *Faust*, seventeen-year-old Schubert composed his first great song, "Gretchen at the Spinning Wheel." The next year he composed 143 songs, including "The Erlking." At nineteen his productivity rose to a peak: he composed 179 works, including two symphonies, an opera, and a Mass.

When he was twenty-one, Schubert gave up teaching school to devote himself entirely to music. He associated with a group of Viennese poets and artists who admired his compositions. "We often wandered about town until three in the morning," recalled a friend. "One of us not seldom would sleep in the apartment of another. We were not particular about comfort in those days. Whoever happened to have money paid for us all." Schubert often lived with friends because he did not have money to rent a room of his own.

Working with incredible speed, Schubert turned out one piece after another. He worked from seven in the morning until one or two in the afternoon; then he spent his afternoon in cafes, drinking coffee, playing billiards, reading newspapers, and talking with friends. His evenings were spent at "Schubertiads," parties where only his music was played. He accompanied the songs and played his delightful waltzes while friends danced. Most of his works were composed for performance in the homes of Vienna's cultivated middle class. Unlike Beethoven, Schubert did not mingle with the aristocracy. He was even too timid to introduce himself to Beethoven, his musical hero.

At twenty-five Schubert contracted venereal disease, becoming moody and prone to despair. "Think of a man," he wrote of himself, "whose health can never be restored . . . of a man whose brightest hopes have come to nothing, to whom love and friendship are but torture. . . ." Several times during his last years he applied for musical positions but never received them. Inept when it came to money, Schubert sold publishers masterpieces for next to nothing. The publication and performance of his songs brought some recognition, but he was less well known than many contemporaries who are now forgotten. His two greatest symphonies, the "Unfinished" and the "Great" C major, went unperformed during his lifetime. Only in his last year was a public concert devoted to his works.

Schubert was thirty-one when he died of typhoid fever in 1828, a year after Beethoven's funeral. His reputation was mainly that of a fine song composer, until the "Unfinished" Symphony was performed almost forty years later. Then the world could recognize Schubert's comprehensive greatness.

Schubert's Music

It is amazing how original, varied, and numerous are the works of this composer who died at thirty-one. Along with over six hundred songs, Schubert left

Franz Schubert did not mingle with the aristocracy, preferring instead the company of other musicians, poets, and painters (Omikron).

symphonies, string quartets, chamber music, piano sonatas, short piano pieces for two and four hands, Masses, and operatic compositions.

The songs embrace an incredible variety of moods and types. Some are very short, others very long; their forms include strophic, modified strophic, and through-composed. Many deal with nature—the flow of a brook, the mystery of the night—or with unhappy love. These songs amply display Schubert's melodic genius. His melodies range from simple, folklike tunes to complex lines that suggest impassioned speech. And his piano accompaniments are equally rich and evocative. Many songs draw emotional power from the relentless repetition of a rhythmic idea or from a shattering climax.

Schubert's imaginative harmonies provide some of the most poetic moments in music. He uses unexpected dissonances to capture a mood, and he shifts abruptly to contrasting keys. In Schubert's hands, even the simple change from minor to major can evoke a sudden thought of love or an illusion of light breaking through clouds.

The spirit of song permeates Schubert's instrumental music, too. Many of his symphonies and chamber works have long lyrical melodies, and often Schubert writes variations on his own songs. For instance, the fourth movement of the "Trout" Quintet, for piano and strings, is a set of variations on his song "The Trout" (*Die Forelle*). And his short piano pieces such as the *Moments musicaux* ("Musical Moments") and *Impromptus* are true "songs without words."

Schubert wrote a number of symphonies and chamber works that are comparable in power and emotional intensity to those of his idol, Beethoven. The "Unfinished" Symphony (1822) and the "Great" C-major Symphony (1828) employ horns, trombones, and woodwinds with a new feeling for their poetic capacities. The "Unfinished" Symphony, Schubert's most popular orchestral work, was written six years before his death. We probably will never learn why it contains two rather than the usual four movements. The "Great" C-major Symphony was discovered ten years after Schubert's death by Robert Schumann, who was ecstatic about the work. "It is not possible to describe it to you," he wrote his fiancée. "All the instruments are human voices . . . and this length, this heavenly length. . . ." Reviewing the first performance of this symphony, Schumann made an observation that is true of much of Schubert's music: "It bears within it the seeds of everlasting youth."

"The Erlking" (*Erlkönig;* 1815)

Schubert's song "The Erlking" is one of the earliest and finest examples of musical Romanticism. A friend of Schubert tells how he saw the eighteen-year-old composer reading Goethe's narrative ballad of the supernatural. "He paced up and down several times with the book; suddenly he sat down, and in no time at all (just as quickly as you can write) there was the glorious ballad finished on the paper." Goethe's ballad, in dialog almost throughout, tells of a father riding on horseback through a storm with his sick child in his arms. The delirious boy has visions of the legendary Erlking, the king of the elves who symbolizes death.

"The Erlking"
(*Erlkönig;* 1815)

Schubert employs a through-composed setting to capture the mounting excitement of the poem. The piano part, with its rapid octaves and menacing bass motive, conveys the tension of the wild ride.

The piano's relentless triplet rhythm unifies the episodes of the song, and suggests the horse's gallop.

By imaginatively varying the music, Schubert makes one singer sound like several characters in a miniature drama. The terrified boy sings in a high register in minor. Three times during the poem he cries out, "My father, my father." Each time, the boy sings a musical outcry that is intensified through dissonant harmonies.

Mein Va - ter, mein Va - ter,

To convey mounting fear, Schubert pitches the boy's outcry higher and higher each time. The reassuring father sings in a low register that contrasts with the high-pitched outcries of his child. The Erlking, who tries to entice the boy, has coy melodies in major keys.

"Du lie - bes Kind,komm,geh mit mir! gar schö - ne Spie -le spiel' - ich mit dir;

The deeply moving climax of "The Erlking" comes when father and son arrive home and the galloping accompaniment gradually comes to a halt. In a bleak, heart-breaking recitative that allows every word to make its impact, the narrator tells us, "In his arms the child was dead!"

The Romantic Period

276

Piano intro-
duction, rapid
octaves, *f*,
bass
motive,
minor
key.

Narrator

Wer reitet so spät durch Nacht und Wind?	Who rides so late through the night and the wind?
Es ist der Vater mit seinem Kind;	It is the father with his child;
Er hat den Knaben wohl in dem Arm,	he folds the boy close in his arms,
Er fasst ihn sicher, er hält ihn warm.	he clasps him securely, he holds him warmly.

Father

"Mein Sohn, was birgst du so bang dein Gesicht?"	"My son, why do you hide your face so anxiously?"	Low register.

Son

"Siehst, Vater, du den Erlkönig nicht?	"Father, don't you see the Erlking?	Higher regis-ter.
Den Erlenkönig mit Kron' und Schweif?"	The Erlking with his crown and his train?"	

Father

"Mein Sohn, es ist ein Nebel-streif."	"My son, it is a streak of mist."	Low register.

Erlking

"Du liebes Kind, komm, geh mit mir!	"Dear child, come, go with me!	Coaxing tune, *pp*,
Gar schöne Spiele spiel' ich mit dir,	I'll play the prettiest games with you.	higher reg-ister,
Manch bunte Blumen sind an dem Strand,	Many colored flowers grow along the shore;	major.
Meine Mutter hat manch gülden Gewand."	my mother has many golden garments."	

Son

"Mein Vater, mein Vater, und hörest du nicht,	"My father, my father, and don't you hear	Outcry, *f*, minor.
Was Erlenkönig mir leise verspricht?"	the Erlking whispering promises to me?"	

Father

"Sei ruhig, bleibe ruhig, mein Kind:	"Be quiet, stay quiet, my child;	Low register.
In dürren Blättern säuselt der Wind."	the wind is rustling in the dead leaves."	

"The Erlking"
(*Erlkönig;* 1815)

277

Erlking

"Willst, feiner Knabe, du mit mir gehn?	"My handsome boy, will you come with me?	Playful tune, *pp*, major.
Meine Töchter sollen dich warten schön;	My daughters shall wait upon you;	
Meine Töchter führen den nächtlichen Reihn	my daughters lead off in the dance every night,	
Und wiegen und tanzen und singen dich ein."	and cradle and dance and sing you to sleep."	

Son

"Mein Vater, mein Vater, und siehst du nicht dort	"My father, my father, and don't you see there	Outcry, *f*, higher than before, minor.
Erlkönigs Töchter am düstern Ort?"	the Erlking's daughters in the shadows?"	

Father

"Mein Sohn, mein Sohn, ich seh' es genau:	"My son, my son, I see it clearly;	Lower register.
Es scheinen die alten Weiden so grau."	the old willows look so gray."	

Erlking

"Ich liebe dich, mich reizt deine schöne Gestalt;	"I love you, your beautiful figure delights me!	
Und bist du nicht willig, so brauch' ich Gewalt."	And if you are not willing, then I shall use force!"	

Son

"Mein Vater, mein Vater, jetzt fasst er mich an!	"My father, my father, now he is taking hold of me!	Outcry, *f*, highest yet.
Erlkönig hat mir ein Leids getan!"	The Erlking has hurt me!"	

Narrator

Dem Vater grauset's, er reitet geschwind,	The father shudders, he rides swiftly on;	
Er hält in Armen das ächzende Kind,	he holds in his arms the groaning child,	
Erreicht den Hof mit Mühe und Not;	he reaches the courtyard weary and anxious:	
In seinen Armen das Kind war tot.	in his arms the child was dead.	Piano stops. Recitative.

"Gretchen at the Spinning Wheel" (*Gretchen am Spinnrade;* 1814)

"Gretchen at the Spinning Wheel," written when Schubert was seventeen, was the composer's first great song and his first song to a text by Goethe. The poem, from the play *Faust*, depicts a tormented young girl who is thinking of her absent lover while spinning. Like "The Erlking," this song is a perfect marriage of words and music; piano and voice contribute equally to the musical expression.

The song's form follows the poem's as Schubert returns to the haunting opening melody with each recurrence of the poetic refrain, "My peace is gone, my heart is heavy. . . ." This song is a modified through-composed setting. Continuously running notes in the piano give a feeling of perpetual motion, depicting the revolving spinning wheel and Gretchen's unrest.

Schubert's song is a miracle of psychological insight; it captures Gretchen's passionate outbursts and moments of depression. When she thinks of her lover's "noble walk," the music shifts from minor to major. As the melody rises ever higher, she remembers his look, his words, the pressure of his hand. At Gretchen's "and oh, his kiss!" the climax is heightened by dissonant piano chords. Gretchen is so overwhelmed that she momentarily stops spinning. Two faltering starts of the spinning piano figuration show Gretchen gradually regaining composure. As she resumes spinning, she again sings her pathetic refrain. The music builds to yet another climax at "under his kisses I should die!" Then Schubert lets the song fade away with the melancholy refrain, "My peace is gone, my heart is heavy."

Meine Ruh ist hin,	My peace is gone,
Mein Herz ist schwer,	my heart is heavy;
Ich finde sie nimmer	never, never again
Und nimmermehr.	will I find rest.
Wo ich ihn nicht hab,	Where I am not with him
Ist mir das Grab,	I am in my grave,
Die ganze Welt	the whole world
Ist mir vergällt.	turns to bitter gall.
Mein armer Kopf	My poor head
Ist mir verrückt,	is in a whirl,
Mein armer Sinn	my poor thoughts
Ist mir zerstückt.	are all distracted.
Meine Ruh ist hin,	My peace is gone,
Mein Herz ist schwer,	my heart is heavy,
Ich finde sie nimmer	never, never again
Und nimmermehr.	will I find rest.

"Gretchen at the Spinning Wheel" (*Gretchen am Spinnrade*; 1814)

279

Nach ihm nur schau' ich	I seek only him when I look
Zum Fenster hinaus,	out of the window,
Nach ihm nur geh' ich	I seek only him when I leave
Aus dem Haus.	the house.
Sein hoher Gang,	His noble walk,
Sein' edle Gestalt,	His fine stature,
Seines Mundes Lächeln,	the smile of his lips,
Seiner Augen Gewalt,	the power of his eyes,
Und seiner Rede	and the magic flow
Zauberfluss,	of his speech,
Sein Händedruck,	the pressure of his hand,
Und ach, sein Kuss!	and oh, his kiss!
Meine Ruh ist hin,	My peace is gone,
Mein Herz ist schwer,	my heart is heavy;
Ich finde sie nimmer	never, never again
Und nimmermehr.	will I find rest.
Mein Busen drängt	My bosom yearns
Sich nach ihm hin;	towards him.
Ach dürft' ich fassen	If only I could seize him
Und halten ihn,	and hold him
Und küssen ihn,	and kiss him
So wie ich wollt',	to my heart's content—
An seinen Küssen	under his kisses
Vergehen sollt'!	I should die!
Meine Ruh ist hin,	My peace is gone,
Mein Herz ist schwer. . .	My heart is heavy. . . .

"Who Is Sylvia?" (*An Sylvia;* 1826)

One of Schubert's many charming love songs, "Who Is Sylvia?" was inspired by a German translation of a lyric poem in Shakespeare's *Two Gentlemen of Verona*. This strophic song shows Schubert's genius at inventing a melody that is both beautiful in itself and perfectly matched to its text. The opening phrase is a seed from which the entire melody grows.

A particularly beautiful moment comes in the last phrase of the song when the melody leisurely skips up an octave and down another:

Though distinctly subordinate to the voice in this case, the piano part contributes to the joyful mood of the song. Continuously repeated chords in the right hand probably represent the strumming of a lute, while the staccato left-hand notes suggest a plucking of its strings. Delicate piano echoes at the end of the vocal phrases enhance the charm of this eternally fresh song.

Was ist Silvia, saget an,	Who is Silvia? What is she,	A
Dass sie die weite Flur preist?	That all our swains commend her?	
Schön und zart seh' ich sie nah'n;	Holy, fair, and wise is she;	
Auf Himmels Gunst und Spur weis't,	The heaven such grace did lend her,	
Dass ihr Alles untertan.	That she might admired be.	
Ist sie schön und gut dazu?	Is she kind as she is fair?	A
Reiz labt wie milde Kindheit;	For beauty lives with kind-ness.	
Ihrem Aug' eilt Amor zu,	Love doth to her eyes repair	
Dort heilt er seine Blindheit,	To help him of his blindness,	
Und verweilt in süsser Ruh.	And, being help'd, inhabits there.	
Darum Silvia tön', o Sang,	Then to Silvia let us sing	A
Der holden Silvia Ehren;	That Silvia is excelling;	
Jeden Reiz besiegt sie lang,	She excels each mortal thing	
Den Erde kann gewähren:	Upon the dull earth dwelling.	
Kränze ihr und Saitenklang.	To her let us garlands bring.	

ROBERT SCHUMANN [5]

Robert Schumann (1810–1856) in many ways embodied musical Romanticism. His works are intensely autobiographical, and they usually are linked with descriptive titles, texts, or programs. He expressed his essentially lyrical nature in startlingly original piano pieces and songs. A gifted writer and critic, he discovered and made famous some of the leading composers of his day.

Schumann was born in Zwickau, Germany. His father was a bookseller, from whom he acquired a love of literature. As a youth, Schumann wrote poetry, composed short pieces, and played the piano fairly well. To please his mother, he studied law at Leipzig University; but he rarely attended lectures and devoted his time instead to literature and music.

Schumann decided to become a piano virtuoso at the late age of twenty. To hasten his progress, he used a mechanical gadget that promoted finger

Robert Schumann

independence by allowing four fingers to exercise while one was kept stiff. As a result, one finger was permanently crippled, dashing all hopes of becoming a virtuoso. "Don't be uneasy about the finger," he wrote his mother, "I can compose without it." Indeed, in his twenties he composed many poetic piano works which are a basic part of the pianist's repertory even today. In Schumann's time, however, many considered his compositions too unconventional, too personal. Schumann admitted that his works were autobiographical: "I am affected by everything that goes on in the world—politics, literature, people—I think it over in my own way, and then I long to express my feelings in music."

During his twenties, too, Schumann founded and edited the *New Journal of Music* to promote musical originality and combat the commercial trash that flooded the market. In his essays, Schumann invented an imaginary "League of David" fighting against musical "Philistines," lovers of the conventional. He often signed his articles with the names "Florestan" or "Eusebius," characters who represented, respectively, the out-going and introspective sides of his personality. The twice-weekly journal grew to be influential and contained Schumann's appreciative reviews of young "radical" composers like Chopin and Berlioz. In its pages, Schumann described his discovery of Schubert's "Great" C-major Symphony, which had been previously unknown.

While studying piano, Schumann became acquainted with his teacher's daughter and prize pupil, Clara Wieck. Schumann was eighteen when they met, and Clara was a nine-year-old prodigy who was already a well-known pianist. The two were engaged when Clara was seventeen, despite bitter opposition from her father, who did not want his daughter's brilliant career to be hampered by marriage to an impoverished musician. Since Clara was not of age, the couple fought bitter court battles against Wieck before they could be married. Their marriage turned out to be a happy one that produced eight children. Clara was the ideal interpreter of her husband's piano works and introduced many of them to the public.

Apart from his gifts as a writer and editor, Schumann was temperamentally ill-suited for a regular musical position. He taught for a short time in the newly established Leipzig Conservatory of Music. He was a failure as municipal music director at Düsseldorf because of his inability to control an orchestra and chorus. During later years his mental and physical health progressively deteriorated, and in 1854 Schumann attempted suicide by throwing himself from a bridge into the Rhine. At his own request, he was committed to an asylum, where he died two years later.

Schumann's Music

Schumann's genius is most characteristically expressed in his songs and short piano pieces, which he usually organized into sets or cycles. The titles of these sets—*Carnaval, Scenes of Childhood, Night Pieces, Poet's Love, Fantasy Pieces*—provide insight into his imagination. Schumann thought of music in emotional, literary, and autobiographical terms; his work is full of extramusical references.

Clara Wieck Schumann was an ideal interpreter
of husband Robert Schumann's piano works and
introduced many of them to the public (Omikron).

Schumann's Music
283

During the first ten years of his creative life, Schumann published only piano pieces. His basic musical style seems to grow out of piano improvisation, and these short pieces are like mosaics of vivid musical fragments. Each expresses a single mood through an intensely sensitive melody. Dance rhythms like the waltz are prominent, as are syncopations and dotted rhythms. Schumann's cycles of short pieces are unified through a story or title, or by thematic connections.

In 1840, the year of his marriage, Schumann composed many art songs. The songs, like the piano pieces, reveal Schumann's great gift for melody. Many of the songs have piano postludes which sum up the message of the text. Schumann's song texts suit his feelings, and he often changes a poem by repeating words, lines, and even whole stanzas.

After 1840, Schumann turned to symphonies and chamber music. This direction may well have resulted from Clara's influence, for she wrote in her diary, "I am infinitely delighted that Robert has at last found the sphere for which his great imagination fits him." Schumann's four symphonies are Romantic in their emphasis on lyrical second themes, their use of thematic transformation, and their connections between movements. A Romantic attitude colors his remarks about the First Symphony ("Spring"): "I wrote the symphony in that flush of spring which carries a man away even in his old age. Description and painting were not part of my intention but I believe that the time when it came into existence may have influenced its shape and made it what it is."

"Dedication" (*Widmung*), Op. 25, No. 1, from Myrtles (*Myrthen;* 1840)

This song, from a poem by Friedrich Rückert, expresses Schumann's "Dedication" to and love for Clara, his bride-to-be. In it, both sides of Schumann's literary personality are expressed, the ardent Florestan and the tender Eusebius. The song has the form A B A' postlude. In the opening section, the rapturous vocal melody and animated piano arpeggios convey the outpouring of love, "You my soul, you my heart." The middle section is calmer, to underscore the words, "You are rest, you are peace." The rhythms are slower, the vocal melody is in a lower register, and the music dissolves into a contrasting key. Schumann's text for the concluding A' section is simply a repetition of the first four lines and the concluding line of the poem. After the singer's concluding tones, we hear a brief piano postlude containing a new melodic idea that seems to sum up the song's message of tenderness.

Du meine Seele, du mein Herz,	You my soul, you my heart,	A
Du meine Wonn', o du mein Schmerz,	you my joy, oh you my grief;	
Du meine Welt, in der ich lebe,	you my world in which I live,	
Mein Himmel du, darein ich schwebe,	my heaven you, into which I soar;	

O du mein Grab, in das hinab	O you my grave in which	
Ich ewig meinen Kummer gab!	I bury forever my sorrows.	

Du bist die Ruh, du bist der Frieden,	You are rest, you are consolation;	B
Du bist vom Himmel mir beschieden,	you are given to me by heaven;	
Dass du mich liebst, macht mich mir wert,	that you love me makes me worthy in my own eyes;	
Dein Blick hat mich vor mir verklärt,	your glance transfigures me in my own sight;	
Du hebst mich liebend über mich,	you raise me lovingly above myself—	
Mein guter Geist, mein bessres Ich!	my guardian spirit, my better self.	

Du meine Seele, du mein Herz,	You my soul, you my heart,	A'
Du meine Wonn', o du mein Schmerz,	you my joy, oh you my grief;	
Du meine Welt, in der ich lebe,	you my world in which I live,	
Mein Himmel du, darein ich schwebe,	my heaven you, into which I soar;	
Mein guter Geist, mein bessres Ich!	my guardian spirit, my better self.	

Postlude

Träumerei ("Dreaming") from Scenes of Childhood (*Kinderscenen*), Op. 15 (1838)

In this poetic miniature, Schumann magically weaves a spell of reverie. *Träumerei*—German for "dreaming"—is one of the Scenes of Childhood, a set of short pieces with titles like "Strange Story," "Entreating Child," and "At the Fireside." Like many other Romantics, Schumann was nostalgic for his lost childhood and attempted to recapture the past in his works.

The enchantment of this tender piece comes from the flowing legato melody, composed of phrases which arch up to high tones, linger for a moment—in wonder—then gradually drift downward.

Träumerei ("Dreaming") from Scenes of Childhood (*Kinderscenen*), Op. 15 (1838)

Schumann creates a touching mood with music that is moderate in tempo and subdued in dynamics. The imaginative harmonies of the accompaniment add to the melody's haunting quality. Toward the end, there's an especially evoca-

285

tive moment when the melody rises to a held tone that forms a mild dissonance with the chord below it. Then the melody floats downward, and *Träumerei* ends as simply and quietly as it began.

[6] FRÉDÉRIC CHOPIN

Frédéric Chopin (1810–1849), called the poet of the piano, was the only great composer who wrote exclusively for the piano.

Chopin was brought up in Warsaw, the son of a Polish mother and a French father. At an early age his highly original style of playing and composing astonished the Polish aristocracy. After graduating from the Warsaw Conservatory, he toured Austria and Germany playing his own compositions. While he was away, the Poles revolted against the Russians. Upon learning that the Russians had conquered Warsaw, Chopin was filled with despair and guilt: "They have burnt down the town . . . and here I am—doing nothing, only heaving sighs and pouring out my grief at the piano." In 1831, the twenty-one-year-old Chopin arrived in Paris, his home for the rest of his short life.

In the 1830s Paris was a center of Romanticism and the artistic capital of Europe. Chopin met great writers like Victor Hugo, Balzac, and Heine. The painter Delacroix was a close friend, as were Liszt and Berlioz. Chopin's playing quickly gained him access to the aristocratic salons of Paris. "I have found my way into the very best society," he wrote in 1833. Liszt provides a vivid description of the kind of people who attended Chopin's rare concerts: "Numerous carriages brought . . . the most elegant ladies, the most fashionable of young men, the richest financiers, the most illustrious great lords . . . an entire aristocracy of birth, fortune and beauty."

Chopin was a shy, reserved man who disliked crowds and preferred to play in salons rather than in public concert halls. It was for such intimate gatherings that he conceived short pieces like the nocturnes, preludes, and waltzes.

Chopin's frail physique made it difficult for him to draw big sounds from the piano. The fascination of his playing lay, rather, in his beautiful tone,

Frederic Chopin was a shy, reserved man who disliked crowds
and preferred to play in salons rather than in public concert halls
(Omikron).

rhythmic flexibility, atmospheric use of the pedal, and poetic subtleties of
dynamics. Chopin is the only pianist in history to achieve a legendary reputation on the basis of only thirty or so public performances. He earned a good
living by teaching piano to the daughters of the rich. An elegant and fashionable
man of the world, Chopin lived in luxury.

Chopin's life took an increasingly productive turn after he met Madame
Aurore Dudevant, the well-known novelist whose pen-name was George Sand.
She was a feminist who often wore men's clothing, smoked cigars, and fought
for sexual freedom. Chopin and Sand became lovers when he was twenty-eight
and she thirty-four. He thrived on the mothering she provided, composing
many of his greatest works during the nine years they lived together. After
they separated, his health declined rapidly and he stopped composing.

Frédéric Chopin

287

Before dying of tuberculosis at thirty-nine, Chopin asked that Mozart's *Requiem* be played at his funeral. The mourners also heard his own Funeral March from the Piano Sonata in B-flat minor.

Chopin's Music

By the age of eighteen, Chopin had evolved an utterly personal and original style. Compared with other great composers, he wrote relatively few works, but almost all of them remain in the pianist's repertory. Most of the pieces are short. But in these exquisite miniatures, Chopin evokes an infinite variety of moods, from melancholy to heroism. His music is always elegant and graceful. Even the virtuoso passages are melodic, not intended merely for display.

Chopin expressed his love of Poland in mazurkas and polonaises. In these stylized dances, he captured the spirit of the Polish people without actually using folk tunes. Unlike Schumann, Chopin did not attach literary programs or titles to his pieces.

No composer has made the piano sound so beautiful as Chopin. His unique melodic gift creates the illusion that the piano sings. In repeating a melody, Chopin adds delicate and graceful ornamental tones, similar to vocal decorations in the Italian opera of his time. Many of Chopin's most poetic effects come from the sensitive exploitation of the damper ("loud") pedal. He blends harmonies like washes of color. The pedal connects widely spaced tones in the left-hand accompaniment. Chopin's treatment of harmony was highly original and influenced later composers.

His compositions allow a pianist to heighten expression by slightly speeding up or slowing down the tempo, or by holding a note longer than the music actually indicates. This use of *rubato* lends a poetic and improvisatory quality to Chopin's music.

Nocturne in E-flat Major, Op. 9, No. 2 (1830–1831)

Chopin composed this popular nocturne when he was about twenty. A **nocturne,** or "night piece," is a slow, lyrical, and intimate composition for piano. Like much of Chopin's music, this nocturne is tinged with melancholy. It opens with a legato melody containing graceful upward leaps which become increasingly wide as the line unfolds.

This melody is repeated three times during the piece. With each repetition, it is varied by ever more elaborate decorative tones and trills.

A sonorous foundation for the melody is provided by the widely spaced accompaniment notes connected by the damper ("loud") pedal.

The music is reflective in mood until near the end, when it suddenly becomes passionate. The melody rises to a high register and is played forcefully in octaves. Then, after a brilliant trill-like passage, the excitement subsides, and the nocturne ends calmly.

Étude in C Minor, Op. 10, No. 12 ("Revolutionary"; 1831?)

The Russian takeover of Warsaw in 1831 may have inspired Chopin to compose the blazing and furious "Revolutionary" étude. An **étude** is a study piece designed to help a performer master specific technical difficulties. The "Revolutionary" étude, for example, develops speed and endurance in a pianist's left hand, which must play rapid passages throughout. Chopin's études reach beyond mere exercises in technique to become masterpieces of music exciting to hear as well as master.

This étude begins with a dramatic outburst. High dissonant chords and downward rushing passages lead to the main melody, marked *appassionato* ("impassioned"), which is played in octaves by the right hand. Tension mounts because of the melody's dotted rhythms and its tempestuous accompaniment. Toward the end of the piece, after a climax, the tension momentarily subsides. Then a torrential passage sweeps down the keyboard to come to rest in powerful closing chords.

Étude in C Minor, Op. 10, No. 12 (Revolutionary"; 1831?)

289

Polonaise in A-flat Major, Op. 53 (1842)

The **polonaise,** in triple meter, originated as a stately processional dance for the Polish nobility. Chopin's heroic polonaises evoke the ancient splendor of the Polish people.

The A-flat polonaise is majestic and powerful, with moments of lyrical contrast. It may be outlined: introduction—A B A'—coda. Its main theme makes a grand entrance.

This theme's majesty is enhanced by intervals of thirds in the right hand and by the resonant, wide-ranging accompaniment. After the main theme is repeated twice with an even richer texture, Chopin offers the contrasting middle section (B). This is a marchlike melody accompanied by relentlessly repeated rapid octaves in the left hand. This section tests a pianist's strength and endurance. Powerful crescendos bring mounting excitement. Then Chopin gradually relaxes the mood to prepare for the final return of the heroic main theme (A').

Basic Terms

If you aren't sure what each of the following words means, look back at the text, where they appear in bold type. Additional information about some of them can be found by checking the index.

nocturne   polonaise

étude

FRANZ LISZT [**7**]

During the 1840s, a handsome, long-haired, magnetic young man performed superhuman feats at the piano and overwhelmed the European musical public. Irresistible to women and an incredible showman, Franz Liszt (1811–1886) left a trail of broken hearts from Paris to Moscow. Musicians were equally impressed. Brahms said, "Whoever has not heard Liszt cannot speak of piano playing." Chopin wished he could play his own piano études the way Liszt did. Schumann wrote that Liszt "enmeshed every member of the audience with his art and did with them as he willed. Within a few seconds tenderness, boldness, exquisiteness, wildness succeed one another; the instrument glows and flashes under the master's hands."

Franz Liszt, an outstanding pacesetter in the history of music, was born in Hungary in 1811. His father was an administrator for the same Esterházy family that Haydn had served. As a boy of eleven, Liszt studied in Vienna, where he met Schubert and Beethoven.

Paris, city of Romanticism and a mecca for virtuoso performers, was Liszt's home during his teens and twenties. Already acclaimed as a brilliant pianist, nineteen-year-old Liszt was overwhelmed by the virtuosity of the great violinist Paganini. The unheard-of effects Paganini drew from his violin drove audiences into a frenzy; people half suspected he had been taught by the devil. And young Liszt was determined to become the Paganini of the piano. He withdrew from the concert stage for a few years, practiced from eight to twelve hours a day, and emerged as probably the greatest pianist of his time.

To display his incomparable piano mastery, Liszt composed the *Transcendental Études* and piano transcriptions of Paganini's violin pieces. "My piano," he wrote, "is my very self, my mother tongue, my life. . . . A man's ten fingers have the power to reproduce the harmonies which are created by hundreds of performers." Following an orchestral performance of a movement from Berlioz's *Fantastic Symphony*, Liszt played his own piano arrangement of the movement and made a more powerful effect than the entire orchestra. He toured Europe tirelessly between 1839 and 1847, playing mainly his own piano music and receiving unprecedented public adulation.

But Liszt wanted recognition as a serious composer, too. At thirty-six, he abandoned his career as traveling virtuoso to become court conductor for the Grand Duke in Weimar. He composed many orchestral pieces during the following years, and developed a new form of program music that influenced later composers. Weimar had become a center for modern music, and Liszt conducted works by such contemporaries as Berlioz, Schumann, and Wagner. One of the most unselfish and generous musicians who ever lived, Liszt provided the musical and financial support crucial to Wagner's success. Hundreds of gifted pianists flocked to Weimar, and he taught them free of charge.

Franz Liszt

291

Franz Liszt—handsome, long-haired, magnetic—performed superhuman feats at the piano and overwhelmed the European musical public (Omikron).

Liszt was also an active writer about music, publishing music criticism as well as books on Chopin and gypsy music. His literary efforts were aided by two women with whom he had long-term relationships. Both were aristocrats and writers. The first, Countess Marie d'Agoult, left her husband to live with Liszt. One of their three children, Cosima, later left her own husband to marry Richard Wagner. Liszt's companion in Weimar was the Russian Princess Carolyne Sayn-Wittgenstein, a deeply religious woman who wrote a twenty-four-volume study entitled "Interior Causes of the External Weakness of the Church."

Liszt's many-sided career took another abrupt turn in 1861. Dissatisfied with conditions at Weimar, he resigned and went to Rome to pursue religious studies. In 1865 he took minor holy orders, becoming Abbé Liszt. Contemporaries were stunned by the seeming incongruity: a notorious Don Juan and diabolical virtuoso had become a churchman. One commented, "Yesterday I saw Liszt clad as an Abbé . . . his black silk cassock fluttering ironically behind him. Mephistopheles disguised as an Abbé." During his period in Rome, Liszt composed oratorios and Masses, feeling a mission to reform and renew church music.

During the last seventeen years of his life, Liszt traveled between Rome, Weimar and Budapest, where he was president of the new Academy of Music. Now he began to write curious, experimental piano pieces that foreshadowed features of twentieth-century music. Though these late works went unappreciated, Liszt was a living legend. The grand duke who had once employed him said, "Liszt *was* what a prince *ought* to be."

Liszt's Music

Liszt's music is controversial. Some consider it vulgar and bombastic; others revel in its extroverted Romantic rhetoric. Yet few would deny Liszt's originality, influence, and importance as the creator of the symphonic poem.

Liszt found new ways to exploit the piano; under his hands it could give the impression of an entire orchestra. In the *Hungarian Rhapsodies,* which influenced a generation of nationalist composers, Liszt made the piano sound like a cimbalom (a Hungarian instrument in which strings are struck by hammers held in the hand) and an entire gypsy band. Liszt's piano works demand an unprecedented range of dynamics, from a whispered *ppp* to a thunderous *fff*. He requires a pianist to play rapid octaves in both hands and make daring leaps across the keyboard. Lyrical melodies are embellished with rapid runs, and melodies in the middle register are sometimes surrounded by garlands of arpeggios which create the impression that three hands are playing, not two. Before phonograph records and frequent concerts, Liszt's transcriptions of operas and symphonies made it possible for people to play great orchestral works on their own pianos.

Liszt created the **symphonic poem,** or **tone poem,** a one-movement orchestral composition based to some extent on literary or pictorial ideas. In these and

Liszt's Music

293

other works, Liszt unified contrasting moods through thematic transformation. A single theme recurs throughout a work but is varied so that its character is transformed. For example, in his most famous symphonic poem *Les Préludes* ("The Preludes," 1854), a basic motive is treated as a majestic melody in one section, a love theme in another, a pastoral tune in a third, and a march in the finale. Liszt's music can stand by itself without a program, as can most program music. However, he no doubt felt that particular influences from literature should be cited to make his musical process very clear. Liszt broke away from the standard four-movement symphony and from the sonata form as it was used by the Classical masters.

Among Liszt's favorite inspirations were the literary works of Goethe (the Faust Symphony, 1854) and Dante (Dante Symphony, 1856). Many of his compositions are concerned with the devil or death and bear titles like *Mephisto Waltz, Dance of Death* (*Totentanz*), or *Funérailles.* Constant changes of tempo and mood and alternations between diabolical fury and semireligious meditation contribute to a feeling of improvisation.

Liszt's music influenced many composers, including Wagner, who admitted to him: "When I compose and orchestrate, I always think only of you." As a stupendous performer, innovative composer, and charismatic personality, Liszt typified the Romantic movement.

Concerto No. 1 for Piano and Orchestra in E-flat Major (1849; revised 1853, 1856)

This blazing virtuoso concerto was first performed in 1855 with Liszt as soloist and Berlioz as conductor—a combination that is the essence of Romantic personality and performance. Berlioz described Liszt's playing as "dazzling with verve and power." Liszt composed the concerto in Weimar, after he stopped making concert tours in order to compose, conduct, and promote contemporary music. The soloist of this concerto needs enormous power and technical mastery; he is a Romantic hero who must project massive sounds that match and sometimes triumph over the entire orchestra.

In many ways, this concerto breaks with traditional principles. Instead of three separate movements, as is customary in a concerto, there are four movements combined into one. The last three movements are played without pause, an example of the Romantic trait of linking movements of a composition. Even greater unity results from the thematic relationships among the movements. Themes from the first two movements reappear in the third movement. And in the finale, no new themes are introduced; it is based entirely on transformations of ideas heard earlier in the concerto.

Liszt was the first composer to use a triangle in a concerto. A Viennese critic was so affronted by this "lowly" instrument, which first appears in the third movement, that he contemptuously referred to the composition as "the triangle concerto." The critic's mockery was enough to keep the concerto from being heard again in Vienna for twelve years.

THE RENAISSANCE

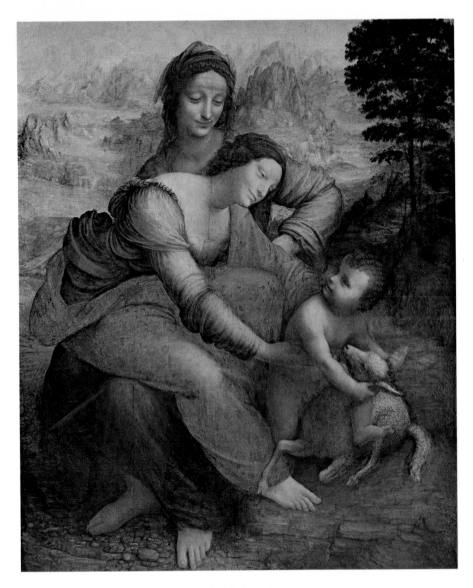

Plate 1—Leonardo da Vinci, *Saint Anne, the Virgin and Child,* 1506–1510 (Scala, New York/Florence).

Plate 2—Michelangelo, *Creation of Adam,* 1508–1512 (Alinari).

Symmetry, harmony, and rationalism characterized the art of the Renaissance. Unlike artists of the previous Gothic era with its God-centered art, Renaissance artists emphasized the power and beauty of human beings. Not only did the Renaissance in art mean the rebirth of Greek and Roman art, it actually aimed at surpassing the ancients by combining their innovations with Christianity and an abiding faith in the strength of man's abilities.

Leonardo da Vinci's *Saint Anne, the Virgin and Child,* 1506–1510 (Plate 1), set an example for many later Renaissance artists with its strongly pyramidal composition, its use of *chiaroscuro* (modeling in light and dark shadows), and its inclusion of scientifically accurate geological and botanic details.

Michelangelo's *Creation of Adam* from the Sistine Chapel ceiling (Plate 2) depicts a strong, muscular, but lethargic man about to be given life by the Divine spark from the hand of God. Adam represents the very embodiment of Renaissance man—strong, proud, and capable, but powerless without God's will.

THE BAROQUE PERIOD

Plate 3—Rembrandt van Rijn, *Night Watch*, 1642 (Rijksmuseum, Amsterdam).

Plate 4—Antoine Watteau, *Les Plaisirs du Bal,* 1719 (Dulwich College Picture Gallery, London).

The Baroque period in art laid great stress on drama, illusion, turbulence, and emotion. The calm horizontals and verticals of Renaissance art gave way to diagonals and to twisting and frenzied movement.

Rembrandt van Rijn's controversial *Night Watch,* 1642 (Plate 3), uses strong contrast, diagonal movement, and unequal emphasis of parts for a highly unconventional group portrait.

The term Rococo best characterizes eighteenth-century art, which transformed Baroque art into a frivolous, light, decorative art of the "salon." The French artist Antoine Watteau's *Les Plaisirs du Bal,* 1719 (Plate 4), typifies the airy, graceful *fêtes galantes,* showing the nobility enjoying themselves in games of flirtation. One can almost hear in the background the light, delicate mid-eighteenth-century music referred to as *style galant.*

THE CLASSICAL PERIOD

Plate 5—Jacques Louis David, *Oath of the Horatii,* 1784–1785
(Three Lions, Inc.)

Classicism in eighteenth- and early nineteenth-century art refers to Neo-Classicism, an
end to Rococo superficiality, and an emphasis on severity, strength, and heroism. Neo-
Classical artists often used Greek and Roman examples. Jacques Louis David in France, for
example, painted the *Death of Socrates,* 1787, and the *Oath of the Horatii,* 1784–1785
(Plate 5), proclaiming an end to rule by the aristocracy and a transfer of power to the
middle classes. David, known sometimes as the "Robespierre of the brush," looked to
Republican Rome as an example to the embattled people of France.

THE ROMANTIC PERIOD

Plate 6—Joseph Turner, *The Slave Ship,* 1839 (Museum of Fine Arts, Boston).

Romanticism refers more to a way of thinking and feeling than to a specific chronological period or style in art. In fact, the predominant characteristics of Romanticism such as freedom from rules, individuality, and personal emotion prohibit a formal grouping. The first half of the nineteenth century did see a golden age of Romanticism, including such giants as Eugène Delacroix in France, Joseph Turner and John Constable in England, and Francisco Goya in Spain. Turner embodied Romanticism in *The Slave Ship,* 1839 (Plate 6), in which he abstracted the forces of nature into a dynamic symbol.

THE TWENTIETH CENTURY

Plate 7—Pablo Picasso, *Ma Jolie,* 1911–1912 (Collection, The Museum of Modern Art, New York, acquired through the Lillie P. Bliss Bequest).

Plate 8—Hans Hofmann, *Memoria in Aeternum,* 1962 (Collection, The Museum of Modern Art, New York, gift of the artist).

At the beginning of the twentieth century painters depicted real objects in a very different way from their predecessors. The Expressionists, for example, distorted reality in order to portray the inner essence of their subject. The Expressionists were intensely emotional, whereas the Cubists stressed a more intellectual geometric approach. In *Ma Jolie,* 1911–1912 (Plate 7), Pablo Picasso distorted the reality of his subject by breaking form into geometric planes.

In the later part of the twentieth century, a variety of painting styles developed. These include such diverse approaches as the Abstract Expressionism of Hans Hofmann's *Memoria in Aeternum,* 1962 (Plate 8); the "pop art" of Andy Warhol's Campbell Soup cans; and the "op art" of Victor Vasarely's visual illusions.

First Movement: Allegro maestoso (majestic allegro)

The opening movement presents the orchestra and piano as two contrasting personalities that repeatedly confront each other. While the orchestra concentrates on the decisive main theme and holds a strict tempo, the soloist has various themes and a rhythmic freedom that suggests improvisation. The movement is in a very free A B A' form. Structurally, it bears little resemblance to the first movement of a Classical concerto.

All the strings open in unison with the main theme of the entire concerto. This is a descending, staccato idea, built from a fragment of a chromatic scale and punctuated by high chords in the woodwinds and brasses.

The piano immediately enters with a virtuoso passage of loud, rapid octaves that establish it as a formidable rival to the orchestra. After the unaccompanied piano briefly varies the opening theme and sweeps up to the highest register, the orchestra reenters to quietly restate the main idea. The movement alternates between orchestral restatements of the theme and cadenzalike solo passages that are brilliant, lyrical, or dramatic.

The brief middle section (B) is an intimate dialog between piano, clarinet, and violin. A new legato melody is introduced by the piano, then imitated by the clarinet.

Liszt has the soloist play with rubato, slight fluctuations of tempo that express a sense of freedom. Soon the music becomes louder and faster, building to a climactic return of the main theme in the full orchestra (A' section). Again, the piano and orchestra alternate, followed by a quiet concluding section in which the orchestra murmurs a variation of the main theme while the soloist plays running notes.

The movement trails off into silence.

Second Movement: Quasi Adagio

The slow movement of the concerto is an intimate interlude that introduces two new melodies. This is the only movement in which neither the full orchestra nor the powerful main theme are heard. Muted strings present a lyrical theme which the piano soon extends:

Concerto No. 1 for Piano and Orchestra in E-flat Major (1849; revised 1853, 1856)

295

The dreamy mood of this legato melody is suddenly broken as the piano dramatically declaims over an accompaniment of tremolo strings. The agitation subsides as quickly as it started. A calm new woodwind melody is presented in turn by the flute, clarinet, and oboe, with a high piano trill in the background.

Both this woodwind theme and the opening lyrical melody will be greatly transformed when they return in the finale. After a brief recollection of the lyrical theme by the clarinet, the Adagio leads without pause into the third movement, a scherzo.

Third Movement: Allegretto vivace (scherzo)

Light triangle strokes accompany the sparkling and playful scherzo theme.

This staccato idea makes the brilliant top register of the piano ring with elfin spriteliness. After several dazzling variations of the scherzo theme, Liszt unexpectedly brings back the main theme of the first movement. This ominous recollection is played in a low register by the solo piano. Then a powerful crescendo climaxes in a proclamation of the main theme by the full orchestra. As at the beginning of the concerto, the orchestra is immediately confronted by the virtuoso piano passage of loud, rapid octaves. The woodwind theme from the slow movement is recollected, and the powerful piano passage leads directly into the finale.

Fourth Movement: Allegro marziale animato (martial and animated allegro)

The finale of the concerto is built entirely from variations of themes heard in earlier movements. It begins with a joyful march theme that is a complete transformation of the lyrical theme from the opening of the second movement. A melody that was originally slow, soft, and legato is now fast, loud, and staccato.

Triangle strokes heighten the orchestra's brilliance.

Soon the trombones, then the piano, loudly assert the second phrase of the lyrical theme in an altered form that sounds defiant and threatening.

The mood then lightens as the piano in a higher register presents a graceful, animated transformation of the woodwind theme from the end of the second movement.

Virtuoso running passages in the piano lead to the march theme, then to the scherzo theme with its accompanying triangle. Liszt speeds up the tempo and uses the concerto's main theme to build a triumphant conclusion.

Basic Term

If you aren't sure what the following word means, look back at the text, where it appears in bold type. Additional information can be found by checking the index.

symphonic poem (tone poem)

[8] FELIX MENDELSSOHN

Felix Mendelssohn (1809–1847) was a Romantic whose music was rooted deeply in Classical tradition. Born in Hamburg, Germany, he came from a wealthy and famous family. His father was a banker, and his grandfather was the distinguished Jewish philosopher Moses Mendelssohn. He, a brother, and two sisters were raised in the Protestant faith.

Mendelssohn's talent was as phenomenal and precocious as Mozart's. By the age of nine, he was a brilliant pianist; and by thirteen, he had written symphonies, concertos, sonatas, and vocal works. And the quality of this youthful work is more astounding than its quantity. His Overture to *A Midsummer Night's Dream* (1826), composed at seventeen, is a masterpiece of startling originality. As a teenager, Mendelssohn tried out his compositions with a private orchestra in his family dining room. Sunday musicales there were attended by the intellectual and artistic elite of Berlin, where the family settled.

In 1829, at twenty, Mendelssohn conducted Bach's *St. Matthew Passion*, the first performance since the Baroque master's death. This historic concert rekindled interest in Bach's music and earned an international reputation for Mendelssohn. He often performed as pianist, organist, and conductor in Germany and in England, where his music was especially popular. When only twenty-six, Mendelssohn became conductor of the Leipzig Gewandhaus Orchestra and transformed it into one of the finest performing groups in Europe. He directed the posthumous premiere of Schubert's "Great" C-major Symphony, which his friend Schumann had discovered, as well as the first performances of two Schumann symphonies. As though all these accomplishments weren't enough, Mendelssohn founded the Leipzig Conservatory when he was thirty-three.

Besides his musical achievements, Mendelssohn was a talented painter, a fine writer, and a brilliant conversationalist in four languages. Extremely polished and charming, he was at ease in aristocratic salons. In England, he often visited the young Queen Victoria, who sang his songs while Mendelssohn accompanied her on the piano. His personal life was more conventional than that of many Romantics; he was happily married and the father of four children.

The high point of Mendelssohn's career was the triumphant premiere of his oratorio *Elijah* in Birmingham, England, in 1846. The London *Times* reported that "the last note of 'Elijah' was drowned in a long-continued unanimous volley of plaudits, vociferous and deafening. . . . Never was there a more complete triumph—never a more thorough and speedy recognition of a great work." But constant travel and exhausting work had sapped Mendelssohn's strength, and the death of a beloved sister in 1847 was a violent shock. He died five months later at the age of thirty-eight.

Besides his musical achievements, Felix Mendelssohn was a talented painter, a fine writer, and a brilliant conversationalist in four languages (The Metropolitan Museum of Art, The Crosby Brown Collection of Musical Instruments, 1901).

Mendelssohn's Music

Mendelssohn's music radiates the elegance and balance of his personality. It evokes a variety of moods but avoids emotional extremes. His typical pieces convey an elfin quality through rapid movement, lightness, and transparent orchestral texture. He was a musical landscapist who could depict a particular atmosphere in orchestral program works. For example, the *Hebrides Overture* (1830–1832; also called *Fingal's Cave*) suggests an agitated sea through swells and surges of sound. But even when Mendelssohn evokes something extramusical, his compositions have a logical form and can be enjoyed without knowing their sources of inspiration.

Mendelssohn wrote an enormous amount of music in all the forms of his day except opera. Today, few of his works are in the concert repertory, but they are extremely popular. Among his best-known compositions are the violin concerto—which we'll study—the *Midsummer Night's Dream* and *Hebrides* overtures, the Italian and Scotch symphonies (1833, 1842), the oratorio *Elijah*, and the Trio in D minor for violin, cello, and piano (1839). His collection of short piano pieces, *Songs without Words* (1829–1845), is now returning to favor after a period of neglect. They convey youthful dash and vigor as well as lyricism tinged with melancholy, basic qualities of Mendelssohn's art.

Concerto for Violin and Orchestra in E Minor, Op. 64

This concerto was inspired by Mendelssohn's friendship with the concertmaster of his orchestra, the famous violinist Ferdinand David. "I should like to make a violin concerto for you next winter," Mendelssohn wrote. "One in E minor runs in my head and its beginning gives me no rest." With David as soloist, Mendelssohn's violin concerto met great success at its premiere in 1845. Ever since, the work's unique fusion of lyricism and virtuosity has made it one of the best-loved concertos.

The concerto's three movements are played without pause, a characteristic linking technique of Romantic composers. Mendelssohn's love of balance is reflected in the cooperation and interplay between soloist and orchestra. Themes pass from one to another, producing a beautiful contrast of tone color and expression. At one moment, the violinist plays a melody while the orchestra discreetly accompanies; at another, the woodwinds present thematic fragments while the soloist has dazzling running passages.

First Movement: Allegro molto appassionato (very impassioned allegro)

Though Mendelssohn usually is considered a conservative composer, a "Classical Romantic," his opening movement departs from Classical concerto form. Traditionally, the opening movement of a concerto began with an extended section for orchestra. But Mendelssohn's violin concerto begins with the soloist, who presents the main theme. This ardent, expansive melody is heard high above a murmuring string accompaniment. The orchestra then expands the violin's theme and introduces a new, flowing melody that begins the bridge section of this sonata-form movement. Toward the end of the bridge the excitement is gradually relaxed to prepare for the second theme, a tranquil woodwind melody which the soloist accompanies with a single sustained tone. This unusual combination of instruments produces a delicate, intimate sound. Following this, the violin reclaims the spotlight and sings the tranquil theme while the woodwinds support.

The cadenza has new function in this movement. In Classical concertos, it was improvised by the soloist and played near the end of the movement. Here, the composer has written it out and placed it at the end of the development section as a transition to the recapitulation. Mendelssohn wanted the cadenza to be an integral part of the movement, not merely tacked on to display the soloist's virtuosity. Listen for the magical moment when the violinist's rapid arpeggios are joined by the orchestra softly playing the first theme of the recapitulation.

LISTENING OUTLINE
To be read while music is heard

Concerto for Violin and Orchestra in E Minor, Op. 64 (1844) by Felix Mendelssohn

First Movement: Allegro molto appassionato

Sonata form, duple meter ($\frac{2}{2}$), E minor.

solo violin, 2 flutes, 2 oboes, 2 clarinets, 2 bassoons, 2 horns, 2 trumpets, timpani, violins 1, violins 2, violas, cellos, double basses

(About 13 min)

EXPOSITION

First theme   1   a. Strings, p, introduce solo violin. Main melody in minor, high register, legato.

b. Running notes in solo violin. Crescendo, climbing phrases.
c. Orchestra, ff, main melody. Increased rhythmic motion leads to cadence.

Bridge   2   a. Violins, flowing bridge theme. Solo violin repeats bridge theme an octave higher.

Violins

p

  b. Solo violin phrases sweep downward and upward through wide range. Flute joins. Crescendo. Running passage rises and falls. Decrescendo, mood calms.

Second theme 3 *a.* Clarinets and flutes, *pp*, calm melody in major. Solo violin accompanies with sustained tone.

Clarinet

pp *tranquillo*

  b. Solo violin, *pp*, calm theme expanded. Woodwinds, then strings accompany.

  4 *a.* Main melody in solo violin, major. Brilliant running passages, pizzicato accompaniment. Crescendo.

  b. Climactic orchestral trills alternate with solo violin, opening of main melody. Decrescendo.

DEVELOPMENT

  1 *a.* Solo violin, *p*, flowing bridge theme. Violins, *f*.

  b. Running passage in solo violin and fragments of main melody in orchestra.

  2 Solo violin, *p*, main melody varied. Decrescendo. Violin melody slowly descends. Orchestral crescendo to *ff*.

CADENZA

  3 Unaccompanied solo violin, broken chords. Ascents to high tones, trills, fragment of main melody. Rapid broken chords lead into

RECAPITULATION

First theme 1 Main melody in orchestra, *p*. Broken chords continue in solo violin. Crescendo.

Bridge 2 *a.* Orchestra, *ff*, bridge theme.

  b. Solo violin, *mf*, bridge theme carried downward. Decrescendo.

Second theme 3 *a.* Woodwinds, *pp*, calm melody in major. Solo violin accompanies with sustained tone.

  b. Solo violin, *pp*, calm theme expanded. Woodwinds, then strings accompany.

  4 *a.* Brilliant running passages in solo violin. Pizzicato accompaniment. Crescendo.

  b. Climactic orchestral trills alternate with solo violin, opening of main melody. Decrescendo.

CODA

  5 Solo violin, bridge theme. Tempo becomes faster. Crescendo. Brilliant running passages. Full orchestra, *ff*. Sustained tone in bassoon connects with second movement.

Second Movement: Andante

A single bassoon tone links the brilliant opening movement with the hushed introduction to the slow second movement. The C-major Andante is a songlike, intimate piece in A B A' form. Its opening section (A) features a warm, expansive melody in the solo violin's high register; a string accompaniment gently emphasizes the $\frac{6}{8}$ meter (**1**-2-3-**4**-5-6). The middle section (B) becomes more agitated, and the accompaniment is rhythmically more active. The orchestra plays a more important role as it engages in dialog with the soloist. Mendelssohn requires the solo violinist to play both a melody and a trembling accompaniment figure at the same time. The soloist also presents the melody in full-sounding octaves. The transition to the concluding A' section is very smooth because the trembling accompaniment figure is maintained. The Andante ends quietly with a tender epilog for solo violin and woodwinds.

Third Movement: Allegretto non troppo (transitional section); Allegro molto vivace (very lively allegro)

A pensive transitional section for solo violin and strings connects the Andante with the concluding movement of the concerto. This very rapid movement, in sonata form, creates the lightness, joy, and brilliance so typical of Mendelssohn's art. Forceful chords in the woodwinds and upward solo figures usher in the opening theme of the exposition. Playful and mostly staccato, it is presented by the solo violin and high woodwinds.

A dazzling series of running passages and a long upward scale lead directly into the second theme, which is also a carefree one. With great effect, it combines a loud, marchlike phrase by the full orchestra with a softer motive from the opening theme.

In the development, the woodwinds softly present the marchlike phrase while the soloist plays brilliant running passages. A highlight of the development comes when the violinist presents a new legato melody which the strings lightly accompany with fragments of the opening theme.

Concerto for Violin and Orchestra in E Minor, Op. 64

303

Then there is a reversal of roles; the strings sing the lyrical melody while the soloist gracefully presents the opening theme fragment.

At the beginning of the recapitulation, the two themes are combined once again. The horn and lower strings play the warm, legato melody while the soloist brings back the sparkling first theme. After a return of the second theme, the movement builds to an exciting climax in the coda, which is fuller in sound than anything that has come before.

PROGRAM MUSIC

Romantic composers were particularly attracted to **program music,** or instrumental music associated with a story, poem, idea, or scene. Programmatic orchestral works such as Berlioz's *Fantastic Symphony,* Tchaikovsky's *Romeo and Juliet,* and Smetana's *The Moldau* depict emotions, characters, and events of particular stories, or the sounds and motions of nature. Such nonmusical ideas are usually specified by the title or by the composer's explanatory comments (**program**) in the concertgoer's program.

Program music draws on music's capacity to suggest and evoke. It is obvious that music can imitate certain sounds—bird songs, the rumble of thunder, bells clanging, or the howling wind. But "sound effects" are only part of music's descriptive resources. A composer can also exploit the correspondence between musical rhythm and objects in motion. A continuous flow of rapid notes, for example, can evoke a running stream or the rise and fall of waves. Most important, though, is music's capacity to create mood, emotion, and atmosphere. An agitated theme can represent a feud between rival families, just as a lyrical melody can symbolize youthful love.

Apart from the "sound effects" mentioned above, music alone makes no definite reference to ideas, emotions, and objects. Music cannot identify anything. It is the title or a verbal explanation that lets us fully grasp a composer's source of inspiration. We know that the agitated theme in Tchaikovsky's *Romeo and Juliet* is meant to suggest the feud between rival families, but in another piece, the same theme could as easily evoke a king's rage or a cavalry charge.

The aim of most program music is expression more than mere description. Beethoven explicitly stated this aim when he referred to his *Pastoral* Symphony (No. 6) as "an expression of feeling rather than painting." Even the most "realistic" episodes in program music can also serve a purely musical function, as in the *Pastoral's* slow movement, "By the Brook," where the songs of a nightingale, quail, and cuckoo are realistically imitated. (The names of these birds are even written into the score.) These bird calls provide a point of rest near the end of the movement and flow logically from what has come before.

Generally, one can appreciate a descriptive piece as pure music, without knowing its title or program. We can enjoy the lyrical theme of Tchaikovsky's *Romeo and Juliet,* for example, without associating it with young love. The forms used for program music are similar to those for nonprogram music, or **absolute music.** A programmatic work can be heard simply as an example of rondo, fugue, sonata form, or theme and variations. But our pleasure may be greater when we can relate music to literary or pictorial ideas. Romantic composers were well aware that verbal explanations helped listeners follow the flow of music. Occasionally, they even added titles or programs to finished works. Musicians and audiences in the Romantic period liked to read stories into all music, whether the composer so intended or not.

Clearly, the distinction between program music and absolute music is not always useful. A composition simply entitled Symphony No. 6 may have a program that its composer chooses not to reveal. Here are Tchaikovsky's comments about his Sixth Symphony ("Pathétique"): "This time a program symphony—but with a program which shall remain an enigma for everyone—let them puzzle their heads over it. This program is subjective through and through, and during my journey, while composing it in my mind, I often wept bitterly."

Most Romantic program music was written for piano or for orchestra. Schumann's *Carnaval* (1835) and Mussorgsky's *Pictures at an Exhibition* (1874)—each a set of short pieces— are well-known descriptive compositions for piano. But program music found its most varied expression in the coloristic resources of the Romantic orchestra. The main forms of orchestral program music are the *program symphony,* the *concert overture,* the *symphonic (tone) poem,* and *incidental music.*

A **program symphony** is a composition in several movements—as its name implies, a symphony with a program. Each movement usually has a descriptive title. For example, Berlioz's *Fantastic Symphony* has five movements: (1) "Reveries, Passions," (2) "A Ball," (3) "Scene in the Country," (4) "March to the Scaffold," and (5) "Dream of a Witches' Sabbath." (This work is discussed in section 10.)

A **concert overture** has one movement, usually in sonata form. The Romantic concert overture was modeled after the opera overture, a one-movement composition that establishes the mood of an opera. But the concert overture is *not* intended to usher in a stage work; it is an independent composition. Well-known concert overtures are Mendelssohn's *Hebrides* Overture and Tchaikovsky's *Overture 1812* and *Romeo and Juliet* Overture, discussed in section 12.

A **symphonic poem,** or **tone poem,** is also a one-movement composition. Symphonic poems take many traditional forms—sonata form, rondo, or theme and variations—as well as irregular forms. This flexibility of form separates the symphonic poem from the concert overture, which usually is in sonata form.

Program Music

Franz Liszt developed the symphonic poem in the late 1840s and 1850s, and it became the most important type of program music after 1860. Well-known tone poems include *Les Préludes* by Liszt, *Don Juan* (1888) and *Till Eulenspiegel* (1895) by Richard Strauss, and *The Sorcerer's Apprentice* (1897) by Paul Dukas. During the late nineteenth century, symphonic poems became an important expression of nationalism in music. In section 13, we'll study a nationalistic tone poem, Smetana's *The Moldau*, which depicts Czechoslovakia's main river as it winds through the countryside.

Incidental music is intended to be performed before or during a play. It is "incidental" to the staged drama, but it sets the mood for certain scenes. Interludes, background music, marches, and dances are all incidental music (as are today's movie scores). Mendelssohn's incidental music for *A Midsummer Night's Dream* includes his famous *Wedding March*.

Basic Terms

If you aren't sure what each of the following words means, look back at the text, where they appear in bold type. Additional information about some of them can be found by checking the index.

program music
program
absolute music
program symphony
concert overture
symphonic poem (tone poem)
incidental music

[**10**] HECTOR BERLIOZ

Hector Berlioz (1803–1869), the first French Romantic composer and a daring creator of new orchestral sounds, was born in a small town near Grenoble. Berlioz was twenty before he could devote himself to music. His father, a physician, sent him to Paris to study medicine, but Berlioz was "filled with horror" by the dissecting room. He shocked his parents by abandoning his medical studies to pursue a career in music.

It did not take long for Berlioz to fill the gaps in his musical knowledge. He studied at the Paris Conservatory, analyzed musical scores, haunted the opera house, and composed. He memorized many operas and became furious if a conductor tampered with the orchestration. This fiery young fanatic would stand during a performance and shout, "Not two flutes, you scoundrels! Two piccolos! Two piccolos!"

At twenty-three, Berlioz was overwhelmed by Shakespeare. He also fell madly in love with Harriet Smithson, a Shakespearean actress whose portrayals of

Ophelia and Juliet had captivated the Parisian public. Berlioz wrote Harriet letters that were so wild and impassioned that she thought he was a lunatic and refused to see him. He grieved: "If she could for one moment conceive all the poetry, all the infinity of such a love, she would fly into my arms." Instead, Harriet Smithson left Paris without meeting Berlioz. That came later.

To depict his "endless and unquenchable passion," Berlioz wrote the *Fantastic Symphony* in 1830. Parisians were startled by the sensationally autobiographical program for the symphony, its amazingly novel orchestration, and its vivid depiction of the weird and diabolical. At twenty-six, Berlioz had become the musical counterpart of revolutionary French Romantics like Victor Hugo and Delacroix.

In 1830, too, Berlioz won the Prix de Rome (Rome prize), the highest award of the Paris Conservatory. It subsidized two years' study in the Eternal City. When he returned to Paris, Berlioz presented a concert featuring his *Fantastic Symphony*. In the audience was Harriet Smithson. When she realized that Berlioz's music depicted her, "she felt the room reel about her; she heard no more but sat in a dream." The next day they met, and a year later they were married. Alas; the fantasy was more successful than reality—they separated after only a few years.

Berlioz's unconventional music irritated the directors of the main Paris opera house and concert society. To get a hearing for his work, Berlioz arranged concerts at his own expense. This involved hiring a hall, rounding up hundreds of musicians, writing publicity, getting the music copied, and countless other petty chores; it drained Berlioz financially, physically, and emotionally. "The main reason for the long war against me," he wrote at fifty-four, "lies in the antagonism existing between my musical feeling and that of the great mass of the Parisian public." He complained that "all music off the beaten track . . . seemed to these people the music of madness." But Berlioz was not completely unappreciated in Paris. He had a following of about 1,200 who faithfully bought tickets to his concerts. Nevertheless, this was not enough support for a composer of difficult and monumental works requiring much rehearsal time and hundreds of performers. To support his family, Berlioz turned to musical journalism. He was one of the most brilliant and witty music critics who ever lived. He made it his mission to convince the Parisian public that music was not merely a form of entertainment but a dramatic emotional expression.

Outside France, Berlioz's stock was higher. Liszt directed a German orchestra in several "Berlioz weeks," performing nothing but his works. After 1840, he was in demand throughout Europe, conducting his own music and that of others. As one of the first great orchestral conductors, he influenced a whole generation of musicians. In 1860, Wagner wrote to Liszt, saying that the three greatest composers of the time were Wagner, Liszt, and Berlioz.

Berlioz's later years were bitter. He was repeatedly passed over for important conducting positions and academic honors. He composed very little during the six years before his death at sixty-five.

Hector Berlioz

Berlioz's Music

"The prevailing qualities of my music," wrote Berlioz, "are passionate expressiveness, inner fire, rhythmic drive, and unexpectedness." Above all, Berlioz's music sounds unique. It includes abrupt contrasts between high woodwinds and low strings, snarling brass, and rumbling percussion. The dynamics fluctuate constantly, and the tempo changes many times.

Berlioz was extraordinarily imaginative in treating the orchestra, creating tone colors never before heard. At a time when the average orchestra contained about sixty players, Berlioz often assembled hundreds of musicians to achieve an enormous range of power and instrumental timbre. More than any earlier composer, he made tone color a basic part of his musical language. A list of orchestral effects in the *Fantastic Symphony* alone would include four kettle drums combining to play a chord, bells combined with brasses, and violinists striking the strings with the bow-stick.

Berlioz's compositions are full of long melodies that take unexpected turns and are irregular and asymmetrical in construction. To critics who complained that his works lacked melodies, Berlioz replied, "To deny their existence is unfair and absurd. But as they are often on a large scale, an immature or unappreciative mind cannot appreciate their forms."

Most of Berlioz's works are for orchestra, or for orchestra with chorus and vocal soloists. All his major works are dramatic in nature and relate either to a literary program or to a text. He invented new forms: his "dramatic symphony" *Romeo and Juliet* (1839) is for orchestra, chorus, and vocal soloists, and his "dramatic legend" *The Damnation of Faust* (1846) combines opera and oratorio. Berlioz wrote three operas, *Benvenuto Cellini* (1838), *The Trojans* (1856–1858), and *Beatrice and Benedict* (1860–1862). Some of his works are grandiose and monumental, such as his *Requiem* (1837). He knew he was a pioneer in this territory: "In the *Requiem,* for example, I employ four distinct brass orchestras, answering each other at certain distances around the main orchestra and chorus. The result of this immensity of form is that either one entirely misses the drift of the music or is crushed by a tremendous emotion. . . . I have seen one man listening in terror, shaken to the depths of his soul, while his next neighbor could not catch an idea, though trying with all his might to do so."

Fantastic Symphony (Symphonie fantastique; 1830)

This astonishing program symphony by the twenty-six-year-old Berlioz is a Romantic manifesto. Both the symphony and Berlioz's program reflect the young composer's unrequited passion for the actress Harriet Smithson:

> A young musician of extraordinary sensibility and abundant imagination, in the depths of despair because of hopeless love, has poisoned himself with opium. The drug is too feeble to kill him but plunges him into a heavy sleep accompanied by weird visions. His sensations, emotions, and memories, as they pass through his affected mind, are transformed into

musical images and ideas. The beloved one herself becomes to him a melody, a recurrent theme (*idée fixe*) which haunts him continually.

A single melody which Berlioz called the *idée fixe*, or "fixed idea," is used to represent the beloved. It appears in all five movements and unifies the contrasting episodes of the symphony. This recurrence of the same theme in every movement of a symphony was a striking novelty in Berlioz's day. The theme changes in character during the work, sounding, in turn, exultant, waltzlike, and vulgar.

Another innovation of the symphony is its requirement of a very large and colorful orchestra: piccolo, 2 flutes, 2 oboes, English horn, 2 clarinets, 4 bassoons, 4 horns, 2 cornets, 2 trumpets, 3 trombones, 2 tubas, 4 timpani, bass drum, snare drum, cymbals, bells, 2 harps, and strings. Beethoven had not used the English horn, tuba, bells, cornet, or harp in his symphonies. Berlioz saves the heaviest orchestration for the last two movements, where he depicts the fantastic and diabolical. Though the macabre and supernatural had long been dealt with in opera (in Mozart's *Don Giovanni*, for example), this is its first expression in an important symphony.

First Movement: Reveries, Passions. Largo (slow introduction); Allegro agitato e appassionato assai (agitated and very impassioned allegro)

> First he remembers that weariness of the soul, that indefinable longing, that somber melancholia and those objectless joys which he experienced before meeting his beloved. Then, the volcanic love with which she suddenly inspired him, his delirious suffering, his return to tenderness, his religious consolations.

The symphony opens with an extended slow introduction—almost a movement in itself—in which fluctuations of tempo and mood help create a dreamlike atmosphere. A long muted violin melody expresses, in Berlioz's words, "the overpowering sadness of a young heart first caught in the toils of a hopeless love." Berlioz took this melody from a sad song he wrote when, as a boy of twelve, he was in love with an unapproachable "older woman" of eighteen.

The allegro movement following the introduction is written in a modified sonata form. Its first theme, played by the violins and flutes, is the *idée fixe* ("fixed idea"). Berlioz described this expansive, upward-groping melody as "passionate but at the same time noble and shy."

Fantastic Symphony (Symphonie fantastique; 1830)

309

In the development, Berlioz uses a fragment of the *idée fixe* and builds tension through rising and falling chromatic scales played by staccato strings. A shattering climax is followed by a pregnant moment of silence. Yet another climax occurs toward the end of the movement when the full orchestra plays the *idée fixe* in a hysterically jubilant transformation. The movement concludes with slow chords that evoke the "religious consolations" mentioned in the program.

Second Movement: A Ball. Allegro non troppo

He finds his beloved again at a ball in the midst of the tumult of a brilliant party.

The second movement is a waltz, the most popular dance of the Romantic era. Its form may be outlined: introduction—A B A'—coda. A shimmering atmosphere is created in the introduction by string tremolos and delicate harp arpeggios. The lilting waltz theme is introduced by the violins (A section).

The B section brings a return of the *idée fixe,* now transformed into a waltz played by woodwinds.

The *idée fixe* is soon joined by an oom-pah-pah accompaniment and intertwined with fragments of the lilting waltz theme.

In the coda, Berlioz builds to a climax that is suddenly interrupted by yet another reminiscence of the *idée fixe*—this time played soulfully by a solo clarinet. The movement concludes brilliantly.

Third Movement: Scene in the Country. Adagio

On a summer evening in the country, he hears two herders calling each other with their shepherd melodies. The pastoral duet in such surroundings, the gentle rustle of the trees softly swayed by the wind, some reasons for hope which had come to his knowledge recently—all unite to fill his heart with a rare tranquility and lend brighter colors to his ideas. But his beloved appears anew, spasms contract his heart, and he is filled with dark premonitions. What if she were deceiving him? One of the shepherds resumes his rustic tune, the other does not reply. The sun sets. Far away there is rumbling thunder—solitude—silence.

Like the preceding waltz movement, the Adagio has the form: introduction—A B A'—coda. In the introduction, Berlioz evokes a mood of loneliness in the midst of nature: a solo English horn is echoed by an oboe an octave higher. No previous symphonic movement had ever begun with a duet between these two instruments. The A section opens with an extended melody for flute and violins—"delightful reverie."

The *idée fixe* returns in the B section. Played by the oboe and flute, it is now set against an agitated low countermelody in the cellos and basses. This combination of contrasting melodies in widely separated registers and different tone colors is a typically brilliant stroke. At the end of the coda, we again hear the English horn solo, but this time the oboe does not answer. Instead, four timpani suggest "the rumbling of distant thunder." Berlioz explains that his aim is not merely to imitate thunder, "but rather to make silence more perceptible, and thus to increase the impression of uneasy sadness and painful isolation."

Fourth Movement: March to the Scaffold. Allegretto non troppo

He dreams that he murdered his beloved, that he has been condemned to death and is being led to execution. A march that is alternately somber and wild, brilliant and solemn, accompanies the procession. . . . The tumultuous outbursts are followed without transition by the muffled sound of heavy steps. At the end, the fixed idea returns for a moment, like a last thought of love interrupted by the death blow.

"The March to the Scaffold is fifty times more frightening than I expected," Berlioz gleefully observed after the first rehearsals of the *Fantastic Symphony*. It is not until this fiendish fourth movement that all the brass and percussion instruments enter the action. Berlioz creates a menacing atmosphere with the opening orchestral sound, a unique combination of muted horns, timpani tuned a third apart, and basses playing pizzicato chords. The first theme, stated by the cellos and basses, moves steadily downward for two octaves.

Fantastic Symphony (Symphonie fantastique; 1830)

This idea is repeated several times with countermelodies in the bassoons. Then we hear a syncopated march tune blared by the brasses and woodwinds.

At the end of the march a solo clarinet begins to play the *idée fixe* but is savagely interrupted by a very loud chord representing the fall of the guillotine's blade.

Fifth Movement: Dream of a Witches' Sabbath. Larghetto; Allegro

> He sees himself at a witches' sabbath in the midst of a hideous crowd of ghouls, sorcerers, and monsters of every description, united for his funeral. Strange noises, groans, shrieks of laughter, distant cries, which other cries seem to answer. The melody of the loved one is heard, but it has lost its character of nobleness and timidity; it is no more than a dance tune, ignoble, trivial, and grotesque. It is she who comes to the sabbath! . . . A howl of joy greets her arrival. . . . She participates in the diabolical orgy . . . the funeral knell, burlesque of the *Dies irae*. Witches' dance. The dance and the *Dies irae* combined.

The "Dream of a Witches' Sabbath" is the most "fantastic" movement of the symphony; it depicts a series of grotesque events. Its slow, hushed introduction (Larghetto) immediately draws the listener into the realm of the macabre and supernatural, evoking "strange noises, groans, shrieks of laughter" and "distant cries." Eerie tremolos in high muted strings and menacing low tones of cellos and basses begin a succession of fragmentary ideas in starkly contrasting tone colors, registers, and dynamics. In the exploratory spirit of his Romantic age, Berlioz dared to create sounds that are weird rather than conventionally pleasing.

In the Allegro section, the beloved is revealed to be a witch. Her theme, the once "noble and timid" *idée fixe,* is transformed into a dance tune that is "trivial and grotesque." Played shrilly by a high-pitched clarinet, the tune moves in quick notes decorated by trills.

A "funeral knell" of sonorous bells lends an awesome atmosphere to the next part of the movement. Tubas and bassoons intone a solemn low melody in long even notes.

This melody is the medieval chant *Dies irae* ("Day of Wrath"), traditionally sung in the Mass for the Dead. Berlioz quotes it here as a symbol of eternal damnation. Soon the chant melody is shifted up to a high register and played by woodwinds and pizzicato strings in a quick dancelike rhythm.

Thus Berlioz dared to parody a sacred chant by transforming it into a trivial tune, as he did earlier with the *idée fixe*.

Berlioz conveys the frenzy of a witches' dance in a fuguelike section. The fugue subject (witches' dance) is introduced by the lower strings and then imitated by other instruments.

A crescendo builds to a powerful climax in which the rapid witches' dance is set against the slower-moving *Dies irae* proclaimed by the brasses and woodwinds. This musical nightmare ends in an orgy of orchestral power.

Fantastic Symphony (Symphonie fantastique; 1830)

313

[**11**] NATIONALISM IN NINETEENTH-CENTURY MUSIC

During the nineteenth century all Europeans felt their homelands merited loyalty and self-sacrifice. These nationalistic feelings were awakened during the upheavals of the French Revolution and Napoleonic Wars (1789–1814), when French armies invaded much of Europe. In many countries, military resistance to Napoleon aroused the citizens' sense of national identity. Common bonds of language, culture, and history were strengthened, since now battles were fought by soldiers drawn from the general population, not by mercenaries, as in the past. Patriotic feeling was intensified, too, by Romanticism, which glorified love for one's national heritage.

As a revolutionary political movement, nationalism led to the unification of lands—like Germany and Italy—that had previously been divided into tiny states. It spurred revolts in countries under foreign rule, such as Poland and Bohemia (now part of Czechoslovakia).

Nationalism was a potent cultural movement, as well, particularly regarding language. In lands dominated by foreign powers, the national language was used increasingly in textbooks, newspapers, and official documents. For example, in Bohemia there was a revival of the Czech language, which before 1800 had lost ground to the German spoken by Austrian rulers. By the 1830s and 1840s, important textbooks on astronomy and chemistry were written in Czech, and there were many collections of Czech folk poetry. In every land, the "national spirit" was felt to reside in the "folk," the peasantry. The national past became a subject of intense historical investigation, and there was new enthusiasm for folk songs, dances, legends, and fairy tales.

Nationalism influenced Romantic music, as composers deliberately gave their works a distinctive national identity. They used folk songs and dances and created original melodies with a folk flavor. Nationalist composers wrote operas and program music inspired by the history, legends, and landscapes of their native lands. Their works bear titles like *Russian Easter Overture* (Rimsky-Korsakov), *Finlandia* (Sibelius), and *Slavonic Dances* (Dvořák). But a genuine feeling of national style does not come merely through the use of folk songs or patriotic subjects. A piece of music will *sound* French, Russian, or Italian when its rhythm, tone color, texture, and melody spring from national tradition. There had been regional traits in music before the Romantic period, but never had differences of national style been emphasized so strongly or consciously.

In these revolutionary times, musical compositions symbolized nationalist yearnings and sometimes stirred audiences to violent political demonstrations. The Italian opera composer Giuseppe Verdi deliberately chose librettos that fanned public hatred for Austrian overlords. And censors constantly pressured him to change scenes that might be interpreted as anti-Austrian or antimon-archical. In the twentieth century, the Nazis banned performances of Smetana's *The Moldau* in Prague, the composer's home city.

Nationalism's strongest impact was felt in lands that had been dominated by the music of Italy, France, Germany, or Austria. During the Romantic period, Poland, Russia, Bohemia, and the Scandinavian countries produced important composers whose music has a national flavor. Early in the nineteenth century, Chopin transformed his native Polish dances into great art. After about 1860, groups or "schools" of composers consciously declared their musical inde-pendence and established national styles. Among the leading musical nation-alists were Mussorgsky, Rimsky-Korsakov, and Borodin from Russia; Smetana and Dvořák from Bohemia; Grieg from Norway; and Sibelius from Finland. We will focus on the most important of the national schools, the Russian.

"The Russian Five"

The most distinctive national music arose in Russia, where folk songs pervaded daily life. "Every muzhik, carpenter, bricklayer, doorkeeper, cabman; every peasant woman, laundry-maid and cook, every nurse and wet-nurse—all bring the folk songs of their villages with them to Petersburg, Moscow, to each and every city, and we hear them the whole year round," wrote a Russian music critic of the nineteenth century. The folk music of Russia sounds different from that of Western Europe. It is often based on ancient church modes, rather than on major or minor scales. (Like major and minor scales, church modes consist of eight tones within an octave, but they have different patterns of whole and half steps.) Russian folk tunes also tend to be irregular in meter. A measure may contain five beats ($\frac{5}{4}$ time), instead of the customary two, three, four, or six. And the meter may change within a song so that two bars in $\frac{3}{4}$ time will be followed by one in $\frac{5}{4}$. Russian nationalist composers thus were able to draw on folk music that was both distinctive and highly varied.

Before 1800 there had been no important Russian composers of art music. Tsars imported Italian and German composers to provide court music. But in the early 1800s a composer emerged who is considered the father of Russian music—Mikhail Glinka (1804–1857). His opera *A Life for the Tsar* (1836) incor-porated peasant and folk tunes in a convincing way and laid the groundwork for the development of a national style.

But it was only in the 1860s that a true "school" of national music came into being. (This decade saw the appearance of the great Russian novels *Crime and Punishment* by Dostoevsky and *War and Peace* by Tolstoy.) Five young men, now known as "The Russian Five," met together in St. Petersburg with the aim of creating a truly Russian music. They criticized each other's works and asserted the necessity of breaking from some of the traditional techniques of German, Italian, and French composers. Remarkably, all but one began as am-ateurs; most had nonmusical jobs and could compose only in their spare time. At first, the only professional musician was Mily Balakirev (1837–1910). The

"The Russian Five"

315

other members were César Cui (1835–1918), an army engineer; Alexander Borodin (1833–1887), a chemist; Nikolai Rimsky-Korsakov (1844–1908), a naval officer; and Modest Mussorgsky (1839–1881), a civil servant. Mussorgsky was most original and probably the greatest of the "Russian Five." We'll focus on his opera *Boris Godunov,* a masterpiece of musical nationalism.

Boris Godunov (1874), by Modest Mussorgsky

The son of a wealthy landowner, Modest Mussorgsky (1839–1881) was educated in a military academy, becoming an army officer at seventeen. After two years he left the army to devote himself to music. But the emancipation of the Russian serfs in 1861 caused financial hardship to his family, and Mussorgsky had to find a job. He became a government clerk in St. Petersburg and remained in that position for most of his life.

Though a competent pianist, Mussorgsky had little training in composition. He taught himself, except for occasional advice from Balakirev—one of the Russian Five. Mussorgsky was plagued by severe psychological problems and eventually became an alcoholic. When he died at forty-two, he left relatively few compositions: These include *Boris Godunov,* some songs, the symphonic poem *Night on Bald Mountain,* and the piano piece *Pictures at an Exhibition,* which Maurice Ravel later arranged for orchestra.

Mussorgsky's highly original music is imbued with the spirit of Russian folk music. His melodies reflect the rhythms, accents, and pitch fluctuations of everyday Russian speech. "I should like to make my characters speak on the stage exactly as they do in real life," he wrote. Contemporaries condemned Mussorgsky's unconventional chord progressions as "crude" and "incorrect." Today, we can appreciate their color, strength, and originality.

Mussorgsky adapted the libretto of *Boris Godunov* (1874) from a drama by Alexander Pushkin, the Russian Romantic poet. The opera deals with a violent chapter in Russian history and centers around the powerful personality of Tsar Boris, who reigned from 1598 to 1605. Boris gained the throne by causing the murder of its rightful heir, the child Dimitri. In a series of episodes, Mussorgsky vividly depicts Boris's coronation, his anguished feelings of guilt, his political enemies, his love of family and country, and his tragic death.

While the opera's central character is Tsar Boris, the Russian people emerge as its real "hero." In 1873 Mussorgsky wrote, "It is the people I want to depict. When I sleep I see them, when I eat I think of them, when I drink—I can visualize them, integral, big, untainted, and without any tinsel." Through massive choruses and vocal solos, he offers realistic portraits of the Russian peasant, nobleman, nursemaid, soldier, policeman, vagabond monk, and village idiot. In this "musical folk-drama" (as *Boris* is subtitled), Mussorgsky's aim was not merely to create a work of art, but to reveal the depth and variety of the Russian character.

Boris was acclaimed by the Russian public during Mussorgsky's lifetime, but it was dropped from the repertory not long after his death in 1881. In 1896 and again in 1908, the score was revised by Rimsky-Korsakov, who edited and published Mussorgsky's works. Rimsky changed many passages and made the orchestration more brilliant. Though scholars debate the merits of Rimsky's revision, it is the one usually performed today. We'll focus on the spectacular *"Coronation Scene"* from the Prologue to Act I.

Prologue to Act I: "Coronation Scene"

Set in the courtyard of the Kremlin in Moscow, this dazzling scene calls up the splendor, pageantry, and religious fervor of ancient Russia. The Cathedral of the Archangels, burial place of tsars, is on one side of the stage; on the other side is the Cathedral of the Assumption, where tsars are crowned. The courtyard is filled with a mass of common people, kneeling, who are watched by police.

In a brilliant and highly original orchestral introduction, Mussorgsky depicts the tolling of all the great bells of the Kremlin. Bells were a characteristic feature of ancient Russia and were linked with events that marked the passing of time—births, deaths, weddings, and coronations. The orchestral introduction is built entirely from the repeated alternation of just two dissonant chords.

This particular succession of chords was highly unusual in Mussorgsky's day, and no other composer has repeated it to create such a special atmosphere. Mussorgsky's technique of repetition was to have profound influence on twentieth-century composers such as Igor Stravinsky.

A solemn procession of nobles moves toward the cathedral for the coronation of Boris. From the porch of the cathedral, Prince Shuisky, Boris's adviser, exclaims, "Long live Tsar Boris." Then the chorus sings an exultant hymn of praise which Mussorgsky based on a Russian folk song.

To the sun in all splen - dor ris - en be glo - ry, glo - ry!

As the tsar's procession emerges from the cathedral, the music builds to a climax. When Boris appears, the mood changes dramatically. Clad in magnificent royal garb and followed by his two children, Boris at first voices "dark foreboding" about his fate and prays for God's blessing. Then he invites everyone present—nobles and lowly poor—to a feast, and his melody becomes powerful and determined. The bell-chords and choral hymn of praise recur as Boris's procession continues to the Cathedral of the Archangels to pay homage before the tombs of Russia's tsars.

Boris Godunov (1874), by Modest Mussorgsky

Prince Shuisky

Da zdrávstvuyet Tsar Borís Feódorovich!   Long live Tsar Boris Feodorovich!

Chorus

Zhiví i zdrávstvui, Tsar násh bátyushka!   Long live the Tsar, our little father!

Prince Shuisky

Slávte!   Glory to you!

Chorus

Uzh kák na nébe sólntsu krásnomu,
Sláva!
Uzh i sláva no Rusí Tsaryú Borísu!
  Sláva!

Even as glory to the radiant sun in the sky, so glory to Tsar Boris in Russia!

(*An imperial procession from the Cathedral. Police officers keep the people in line on both sides of the procession.*)

Zhivi i zdrávstvui!
Ráduisya, veselísya pravoslávnyi lyud!
Velichái Tsaryá Borísa i sláv!

Long live the Tsar! Rejoice and make merry, all ye faithful of the Russian church, and glory to the great Tsar Boris.

(*from the porch*)

Nobles

Da zdrávstvuyet Tsar Borís Feódorovich!   All hail to Tsar Boris Feodorovich!

Chorus

Da zdrávstvuyet!   All hail!

(Boris *now appears and crosses the stage.*)

Uzh, kák na Rusí Tsaryú Borísu!
Sláva, sláva Tsaryú!
Sláva, sláva, sláva!

Glory to Tsar Boris in all Russia! Glory, glory to the Tsar! Glory, glory, glory!

Boris

Skorbít dushá!
Kakói-to strákh nevólnyi
Zlovéschim predchúvstviyem
Skovál mne sérdtse.
O právednik, o mói otéts derzhávnyi!
Vozzrí s nebés na slyózy vérnykh slug
I nisposhlí ty mné svyaschénnoye na vlást
Blagoslovénye.
Da búdu blag i práveden kak tý,
Dá v sláve právlyu svói naród.
Tepér poklónimsya pochíyuschim
Vlastítelyam Rusíyi.
A tám szyvát naród na pir,
Vsekh, ot boyár do níschevo sleptsá,
Vsem vólnyi vkhod, vse gósti dorogíye.

My soul is torn with anguish! Involuntary fears and sinister forebodings clutch my heart. Oh, righteous and sovereign Father, look down from heaven and behold the tears of these your faithful servants! Bestow Thy sacred blessings upon me and my dominion! Help me to be kind and just like Thyself, and rule over my people in glory! And now let us bow in homage to the great departed rulers of Russia. Then let us summon the people, from the noble to the blind beggar, to a feast. All are free to come and be my dear and welcome guests.

(*Bells are rung on stage as the procession continues to the Archangels Cathedral.*)

Chorus

Zhiví i zdrávstvui Tsár nash bátyushka.   Long live the Tsar, our little father!

(*Police officers try to restore order, but the people break away and dash towards the Archangels Cathedral.*)

Uzh kák na nébe sólntsu krásnomu,   Even as glory to the radiant sun in the
Sláva, sláva!   sky, so glory to Tsar Boris in Russia!
Uzh, kák na Rusí Tsaryú Borísu,   Glory, glory and a long life!
Sláva, sláva i mnógaya léta!

(*Great commotion. The police officers struggle with the people. Boris emerges from the Archangels Cathedral and proceeds to his chambers.*)

Basic Term

If you aren't sure what the following word means, look back at the text, where it appears in bold type. Additional information can be found by checking the index.

nationalism

PETER ILYICH TCHAIKOVSKY [**12**]

Peter Ilyich Tchaikovsky (1840–1893), the most famous Russian composer, came from the small town of Votkinsk, where his father was a mining inspector. At ten, he and his family moved to St. Petersburg (Leningrad), where he studied at the School of Jurisprudence. Graduating at nineteen, Tchaikovsky became a government clerk. He began to study music theory at the relatively late age of twenty-one. While keeping his government position, he entered the newly established St. Petersburg Conservatory, the first college-level music school in Russia. Two days after the opening of the conservatory, he wrote to his sister: "Sooner or later I shall abandon my present job for music. . . . Of course, I won't resign from my present job till I'm certain that I'm no longer a clerk, but a musician." The next year he did just that. So rapid was his progress in music that after graduating he became professor of harmony at the new Moscow Conservatory, a position he held for twelve years. As though to make up for his late start, Tchaikovsky composed furiously; a symphony, an opera, and a tone poem flowed from his pen, and by the age of thirty, he had composed his first great orchestral work, *Romeo and Juliet*.

Peter Ilyich
Tchaikovsky

319

Peter Ilyich Tchaikovsky, the first Russian composer to gain fame internationally (The Granger Collection).

The year 1877 was bitterly dramatic. He took the disastrous step of marrying a twenty-eight-year-old conservatory student who adored him and his music. Tchaikovsky seems to have married only to conceal his homosexuality. A few days after the wedding, he was writing of "ghastly spiritual torture." Two weeks later he waded into the icy Moscow River, intending to commit suicide by getting pneumonia. But a strong constitution saved him, and he fled to St. Petersburg, where a nervous collapse resulted in a coma for two days. He separated from his wife, never seeing her again.

In 1877 Tchaikovsky also acquired a benefactress, Nadezhda von Meck. A very rich widow of forty-six with eleven children, she passionately loved Tchaikovsky's music. Madame von Meck gave him an annuity that allowed him to quit his conservatory position and devote himself to composition. For fourteen years they corresponded, but they agreed never to meet. "I prefer to think of you from afar," she wrote, "to hear you speak in your music and to share your feelings through it." After so many years of this curious but intimate friendship, Tchaikovsky was deeply hurt when she abruptly cut off the annuity and stopped corresponding. "This situation lowers me in my own eyes," he wrote her son-in-law, "it makes the memory of the money I accepted from her almost unbearable. . . ."

During these years, Tchaikovsky more and more conducted his own works, achieving successes throughout Europe. Yet success did not bring spiritual peace. His brother observed, "The weariness and suffering which sprang up in Tchaikovsky's soul . . . reached their greatest intensity at the moment of his greatest triumphs." In 1891 he was invited to the United States, where he participated in four concerts inaugurating Carnegie Hall in New York and two concerts of his music in Baltimore and Philadelphia. He also visited Niagara Falls and Washington, where he was guest of honor at the Russian Embassy.

On October 28, 1893, Tchaikovsky conducted the premiere of his last great work, the Symphony No. 6 ("Pathétique"), which ends unconventionally with a slow, despairing finale. An epidemic of cholera was then rampant in St. Petersburg, and people were cautioned against drinking unboiled water. Tchaikovsky disregarded the warning, caught the infection, and died at fifty-three.

Tchaikovsky's Music

"I grew up in the backwoods, filling myself from earliest childhood with the inexplicable beauty of the characteristic traits of Russian folk music. . . . I passionately love the Russian element in all its manifestations." Tchaikovsky thought of himself as "*Russian* in the fullest sense of the word." But Russian folk song was only one influence on his art. His style also contains elements of French, Italian, and German music.

Tchaikovsky's works are much more in the Western tradition than are the compositions of his contemporaries, the "Russian Five." He fused national and international elements to produce intensely subjective and passionate music.

Tchaikovsky's Music

"At the moment of composing," Tchaikovsky wrote, "when I am aglow with emotion, it flashes across my mind that all who will hear my music will experience some reflection of what I am feeling myself." And indeed, the brooding melancholy that plagued Tchaikovsky is a prominent feature in much of his music.

Tchaikovsky was a prolific composer of both instrumental and vocal works. Among his most popular orchestral compositions are the Fourth, Fifth, and Sixth ("Pathétique") Symphonies (1877, 1888, 1893), the Piano Concerto No. 1 in B-flat minor (1875), the Violin Concerto (1878), and the overture-fantasy *Romeo and Juliet* (1869), which we'll study. Tchaikovsky wrote some of his best music for ballet: *Swan Lake* (1876), *Sleeping Beauty* (1889), and *The Nutcracker* (1892). He reworked these ballet scores into concert suites, of which *The Nutcracker* is best known. The spirit of ballet permeates much of Tchaikovsky's music. Of his eight operas, *Eugene Onegin* (1877–1878) and *Pique Dame* (*The Queen of Spades;* 1890) are performed with some frequency. There also are the orchestral showpieces *Marche slave* and *Overture 1812.*

All of Tchaikovsky's music contains beautiful melodies that stretch and leap widely, like dancers. He repeats melodies over and over, sometimes transforming an intimate, lyrical utterance into an intense outcry by means of louder dynamics and fuller orchestration. His treatment of the orchestra is extremely colorful, marked by striking contrasts and alternations of strings, woodwinds, and brasses. The emotional quality of his music results from sharp contrasts of tempo, dynamics, and thematic material, as well as from ever more powerful climaxes.

Romeo and Juliet, Overture-Fantasy

Romantic composers felt an artistic kinship to Shakespeare because of his passionate poetry, dramatic contrast, and profound knowledge of the human heart. Shakespeare's plays inspired many of the finest nineteenth-century compositions. Among these were *Macbeth* and *Othello,* set as operas by Verdi, and *A Midsummer Night's Dream,* depicted in incidental music by Mendelssohn. *Romeo and Juliet* inspired both a "dramatic symphony" by Berlioz and a concert overture by Tchaikovsky.

Tchaikovsky composed *Romeo and Juliet* at twenty-nine, near the beginning of his musical career. Now one of the best-loved orchestral works, *Romeo and Juliet* was a dismal failure at its premiere in 1870. "After the concert we dined. . . . No one said a single word to me about the overture the whole evening. And yet I yearned so for appreciation and kindness." Tchaikovsky decided to revise the overture. He composed a new theme to represent Friar Laurence, adopting the suggestion of his friend Balakirev. Despite this, the work remained unappreciated. Only about twenty years later, after further revisions, did *Romeo and Juliet* achieve worldwide popularity.

Like Shakespeare's play, Tchaikovsky's *Romeo and Juliet* glorifies a romantic love powerful enough to triumph over death. He captures the essential emotions of Shakespeare's play without defining each character or the exact course of events. Highly contrasted themes are used to express the conflict between family hatred and youthful love. Tchaikovsky also depicts the gentle and philosophical Friar Laurence, intermediary between the lovers and the harsh outside world.

Romeo and Juliet is a concert overture consisting of a slow introduction and a fast movement in sonata form. (Tchaikovsky's title, "Overture-Fantasy," implies that he treated the musical material in a free and imaginative way.) We can enjoy *Romeo and Juliet* as an exciting orchestral piece without knowing the play. However, a new dimension is added to our listening experience when we associate the music with the drama.

Tchaikovsky opens the overture with the Friar Laurence theme, a solemn hymnlike melody. As the slow introduction unfolds, brooding strings set an atmosphere of impending tragedy. The clash of swords and the anger of the feud between the Montagues and the Capulets is suggested by the violent first theme of the Allegro. Syncopations, rushing strings, and massive sounds create enormous excitement. The second theme of the exposition, a tender love theme, is expressively scored for English horn and muted violas. When the love theme returns in the recapitulation, it has a new exultant character, as Tchaikovsky envelops the listener in waves of opulent orchestral sound. There are long crescendos as the melody is led higher and higher to ever more passionate climaxes.

In the coda, Tchaikovsky transforms the love theme into a song of mourning, while timpani softly beat the rhythm of a funeral march. Then, a new hymn and a tender reminiscence of the love theme suggest that Romeo and Juliet are reunited in death.

LISTENING OUTLINE

To be read while music is heard

Romeo and Juliet, Overture-Fantasy (1869) by Peter Ilyich Tchaikovsky

Andante non tanto quasi Moderato (andante, almost a moderate tempo; slow introduction); Allegro giusto (moderate allegro)

Sonata form, quadruple meter ($\frac{4}{4}$), B minor

piccolo, 2 flutes, 2 oboes, English horn, 2 clarinets, 2 bassoons, 4 horns, 2 trumpets, 3 trombones, tuba, timpani, cymbals, bass drum, harp, violins 1, violins 2, violas, cellos, basses.

(About 18½ min)

Andante non tanto
quasi moderato
(slow introduction)   1   *a.* Low clarinets and bassoons, *p*, hymnlike Friar Laurence theme.

b. Strings and horns, *p*, sustained tones. Basses.
    c. Woodwinds and strings, crescendo. Harp, *mf,* flutes, *p*.
2 *a.* Pizzicato strings accompany high woodwinds, *p*, Friar Laurence theme.
    b. Strings and horns, *p*, sustained tones. Basses.
    c. Strings and woodwinds, crescendo, Harp, *mf*, violins, *p*.
3 *a.* Strings answered by high woodwinds, *mf*. Crescendo to *ff*, full orchestra,
       accelerando. Timpani roll, decrescendo, much slower tempo.
    b. Strings, *p*, answered by woodwind chords, *pp*. Crescendo and accelerando
      to

Allegro giusto
EXPOSITION

First theme   1 *a.* Orchestra, *f*, feud theme, minor.

    b. Cellos imitated by piccolo, *f*, feud motive.
    c. Cymbal crashes against rushing notes in strings. Crescendo to *ff*.
    d. Full orchestra, *ff*, feud theme. Cymbal crashes.
Bridge   2 Suddenly soft, woodwinds. Basses and horns, *pp*, rhythm slows.
Second theme   3 *a.* English horn and muted violas, love theme, major.

    b. Muted violins, *pp*, gently pulsating melody.

    Crescendo.
    c. High woodwinds, *p*, love theme extended.
Closing section   4 Harp, *p*, accompanies muted strings, bassoon, English horn, *p*.

DEVELOPMENT

                      1 Strings, woodwinds, *p*, feud motive. Crescendo, rushing notes in strings, *f*.
                      2 *a.* Horns, *p*, Friar Laurence theme, strings accompany. Violins, *pp*, high
                         repeated notes, brass, woodwind chords, *pp*.

    b. Horns, *p*, Friar Laurence theme. Crescendo, rushing notes in strings, *f.*

    c. Horns, *p*, Friar Laurence theme, strings accompany. Violins, *pp*, high repeated notes, brass, woodwind chords, *pp.*

    d. Horns, *p*, Friar Laurence theme

3 Low strings, *f*, answered by woodwinds, *f*, feud motive. Crescendo to *ff*, cymbal crashes.

4 *a.* Trumpets, *ff*, Friar Laurence theme.

    b. Strings, *ff*, rushing notes, cymbal crashes.

RECAPITULATION

First theme   1 Full orchestra, *ff*, feud theme, minor, cymbal crashes. Downward rushing notes in strings.

Second theme   2 Oboes, *p*, gently pulsating melody, major. Violins accompany, *pp*, Crescendo.

3 *a.* Strings, *f*, love theme extended. Crescendo to *ff*. Love theme repeated. Decrescendo.

    b. Cellos, woodwinds, *mf*, love-theme phrases. Horn. Crescendo.

    c. Strings, *ff*, love theme. Feud motive, cymbal crashes.

4 *a.* Full orchestra, *ff*, feud theme, cymbal crashes.

    b. Brasses, *ff*, Friar Laurence theme.

    c. Full orchestra, *ff*, feud theme, cymbal crashes.

    d. Brasses, *ff*, Friar Laurence theme.

    e. Full orchestra, *ff*, cymbal crashes. Cellos and basses, timpani roll, decrescendo to *p.*

CODA

1 Timpani, *p*, funeral-march rhythm. Strings, *mf*, love theme transformed into song of mourning. Very moderate tempo.

2 Woodwinds, *pp*, hymnlike melody. Harp.

3 Violins, *mf*, love theme varied. Timpani roll, crescendo.

4 Full orchestra, *ff*, repeated chords.

Romantic

BEDŘICH SMETANA [13]

Bedřich Smetana (1824–1884) is the founder of Czech national music. His works are steeped in the folksongs, dances, and legends of his native Bohemia (now part of Czechoslovakia). Smetana grew up when Bohemia was under Austrian domination, and the official language in Prague schools and government bureaus was German, not Czech. Young Smetana's feelings of national identity were inflamed during the revolutions of 1848, when Czech radicals fought for political freedom and the abolition of serfdom. As a member of the armed Citizen Corps, he probably manned the barricades when the Austrians bombarded Prague. The insurrection was a failure and resulted in a harsh reaction from Austria; censorship was increased and patriots were imprisoned.

In this repressive atmosphere, Smetana's musical nationalism could make little headway. Though he was recognized as a pianist, his compositions were scorned by those opposed to nationalism or "modernity" of any variety. In 1856, Smetana emigrated to Sweden, where he taught, conducted, and composed symphonic poems in the style of Franz Liszt. He returned to Prague only in 1862, when Austria's military defeats had resulted in some liberal concessions. Political prisoners were released, Czech-language newspapers were established, and there were Czech theaters for drama and opera. For one of these theaters Smetana wrote *The Bartered Bride,* his most famous opera, based on Bohemian legend and folk material. Smetana was active in Prague not only as a composer, but as a pianist, conductor, teacher, and tireless propagandist for Czech musical nationalism.

At the age of fifty, Smetana suffered the same fate as Beethoven—he became completely deaf. Yet some of his finest works followed, including *My Country* (*Má Vlast;* 1874–1879), a cycle of six symphonic poems glorifying Bohemian history and legend, the fertile Czech countryside, and peasant songs and dances. Smetana's last ten years passed in acute physical and mental torment caused by syphilis. He died in an insane asylum at the age of sixty.

The Moldau (*Vltava*)

"Today I took an excursion to the St. John Rapids where I sailed in a boat through huge waves. . . . The view of the landscape was both beautiful and grand." Smetana's trip inspired his famous symphonic poem, *The Moldau* (*Vltava*), which depicts Bohemia's main river as it flows through the countryside. This orchestral work, part of the cycle *My Country,* is both a Romantic representation of nature and a display of Czech nationalism. It was written in three weeks shortly after Smetana became deaf. *The Moldau's* fresh, optimistic mood gives no hint of the composer's anguish and despair. Smetana wrote the following program to preface his score:

> The composition depicts the course of the river, beginning from its two small sources, one cold the other warm, the joining of both streams into one, then the flow of the Vltava (Moldau) through forests and across meadows, through the countryside where merry feasts are celebrated; water nymphs dance in the moonlight; on nearby rocks can be seen the outline of ruined castles, proudly soaring into the sky. Vltava swirls through the St. John Rapids and flows in a broad stream toward Prague. It passes Vyšehrad [where an ancient royal castle once stood] and finally the river disappears in the distance as it flows majestically into the Elbe.

The Moldau falls into contrasting musical sections that represent different scenes and episodes described in the program. Hunting at the river bank is suggested by horn fanfares, a peasant wedding by a rustic polka—the Bohemian dance; and a moonlit night is represented by shimmering woodwinds and a serene melody in high muted strings. An expansive folklike theme that recurs several times symbolizes the river. Smetana unifies the symphonic poem by running notes evoking the movement of water, sometimes rippling, sometimes turbulent.

LISTENING OUTLINE
To be read while music is heard

The Moldau (Vltava; 1874) by Bedřich Smetana

Allegro commodo non agitato (unhurried allegro, not agitated), sextuple meter ($\frac{6}{8}$), E minor

piccolo, 2 flutes, 2 oboes, 2 clarinets, 2 bassoons, 4 horns, 2 trumpets, 3 trombones, tuba, timpani, bass drum, triangle, cymbals, harp, violins 1, violins 2, violas, cellos, basses

(About 11½ min)

Two springs   1   *a.* Flutes, *p*, running notes. Harp, pizzicato violins.

             Clarinets, *p*, join, running notes.
             b. Lower strings, *p*, running notes lead to

The river   2   Violins, songlike river theme, minor key. Running-note accompaniment in strings.

             River theme extended.

Forest hunt   3   *a.* Horns and trumpets, *f*, hunting calls. Strings, running notes. Crescendo to *ff*.
             b. Decrescendo to *ppp*.

Peasant wedding   4   *a.* Strings, *p*, polka.

             Crescendo to *f*, triangle strokes.
             b. Decrescendo to *ppp*, melody descends.

Moonlight: dance
of water nymphs   5   *a.* Woodwinds, *pp*, sustained tones. Flutes, *p*, running notes lead to
             b. High muted violins, *pp*, serene legato melody. Harp, *p*.
             c. Brasses, *pp*. Staccato chords join accompaniment to violin melody.
             d. Crescendo. Woodwinds, running notes lead to

	6	Violins, river theme. Running-note accompaniment in strings.
The river		
The rapids	7	*a.* Full orchestra, *ff*. Brasses, timpani roll, piccolo, cymbal crashes.
		b. Strings, *pp*. Quick crescendo.
The river at		
its widest		
point	8	Full orchestra, *ff*, river theme in major key. Faster tempo.
Vyšehrad, the		
ancient castle	9	*a.* Brasses and woodwinds, *ff*, hymnlike melody. Cymbal crashes.
		b. Decrescendo. Violins, *ppp*. Full orchestra, *ff*, closing chords.

Romantic

[14] ANTONIN DVOŘÁK

Antonin Dvořák (1841–1904) followed Smetana as the leader of Czech national music. He infused his symphonies and chamber music with the spirit of Bohemian folk song and dance.

Dvořák's father was a poor innkeeper and butcher in a small town near Prague. After working in his father's butcher shop, the sixteen-year-old Dvořák left home to study music in Prague. For years he earned a meager living by playing in an opera orchestra under Smetana's direction. He was little known as a composer until his works came to the attention of Brahms. The German master recommended Dvořák to his own publisher: "I took much pleasure in the works of Dvořák of Prague. If you play them through, you will enjoy them as much as I have done. Decidedly he is a very talented man."

From this time on—Dvořák was about thirty-six—his fame spread rapidly. He was invited several times to England, where the melodiousness of his symphonies, chamber music, Slavonic dances, and choral works appealed to the English love for folk music and the countryside. Although Dvořák rarely quoted actual folk tunes, his works breathe a folk quality and express a cheerful and direct personality.

In 1892, Dvořák went to New York to spend almost three years as the Director of the National Conservatory of Music. He received a salary of 15,000 dollars, about twenty times what he was earning as a professor at the Prague Conservatory. Dvořák encouraged American composers to write nationalistic music. Besides his urban impressions, Dvořák learned about the American heartland by spending a summer in Spillville, Iowa, where there was a colony of Czechs.

Dvořák soon became interested in American Indian melodies and Negro spirituals, which he learned about from his student Henry T. Burleigh, a black composer and baritone. "In the Negro songs," Dvořák told a reporter from the New York *Herald,* "I have found a secure basis for a new national musical school. America can have her own music, a fine music growing up from her own soil and having its own character—the natural voice of a free and great nation." In 1895 Dvořák returned to his homeland and rejoined the faculty of the Prague Conservatory, becoming its director six years later.

Symphony No. 9 in E Minor, "From the New World"

The *New World Symphony* was written during Dvořák's first year in the United States. One of the best known of all symphonies, it glorifies the folk spirit of both America and Czechoslovakia. Its popular character grows out of Dvořák's use of syncopations, pentatonic (five-note) scales, and modal scales often found in folk music. Colorful orchestration and melodious thematic material add to the *New World Symphony*'s attractiveness. The symphony's four contrasting movements are unified through quotation of thematic material: themes from the first movement are recalled in the second and third, and the finale brings back themes from all three preceding movements.

First Movement: Adagio (slow introduction); Allegro molto

The slow introduction builds great tension and contains an ominous bass motive that foreshadows the opening theme of the energetic Allegro that follows. In the exposition of this sonata-form movement, there are three distinctive themes. The first begins in minor with a syncopated arpeggio motive that dominates the entire symphony. Also in minor, the dancelike second theme is gentler than the first and narrower in range. Dvořák shifts to a major key for the third theme, a gracious melody which resembles the spiritual, "Swing Low, Sweet Chariot." (In the Listening Outline this is called the "Swing Low theme," without implying that Dvořák meant it to recall the spiritual.) Between these themes come beautiful bridge passages that rise to a climax and then calm down to usher in new melodic material. In his development, Dvořák concentrates on the first and third themes, which he varies and combines. The recapitulation of all three themes is followed by a coda, which brings the movement to a climactic close.

LISTENING OUTLINE
To be read while music is heard

Symphony No. 9 in E Minor, "From the New World" (1893) by Antonin Dvořák

First Movement: Adagio (slow introduction); Allegro molto

Sonata form, duple meter ($\frac{2}{4}$), E minor

piccolo, 2 flutes, 2 oboes, 2 clarinets, 2 bassoons, 4 horns, 2 trumpets, 3 trombones, timpani, violins 1, violins 2, violas, cellos, basses

(About 11 min)

Adagio
(slow introduction)   1   *a.* Cellos, *pp*, downward phrases. Horns.

b. Flute, *p*, downward phrases.
2 *a.* Strings, *ff,* alternate with timpani, woodwinds, horns, *ff.*
   b. Cellos and basses, *pp.*
   c. High woodwinds alternate with low strings, bass motive.
   d. Full orchestra, crescendo, timpani roll, violin tremolo, *pp.*

Allegro molto
EXPOSITION

First theme   1 *a.* Horns, arpeggio motive. Woodwinds, *p*, playful rhythm, minor key.

b. Oboes, arpeggio motive. Woodwinds, playful rhythm.
c. Strings, *ff*, arpeggio motive developed. Crescendo.

Bridge   2 Brasses, *ff*, arpeggio motive. Strings, playful rhythm developed. Decrescendo.
Second theme   3 *a.* Flute and oboe, *p*, dancelike tune.

b. Violins, *ppp*, dancelike tune developed, crescendo to *f*. Decrescendo.

Third theme   4 *a.* Flute, *p*, "Swing Low" theme, major.

b. Violins, "Swing Low" theme. Crescendo to *ff*, full orchestra.
(Exposition may be repeated.)

DEVELOPMENT

1 Strings, decrescendo.
2 *a.* Horn, *p*, "Swing Low" motive, piccolo. Crescendo.
   b. Trumpets, *f*, "Swing Low" motive. Trombones, *f*, arpeggio motive. Horns,
      ff. Strings, *ff*.
   c. Trombones, *ff*, arpeggio motive. High violins, *ff*. Rhythm quickens.
3 Oboes, *p*, arpeggio motive, flute. Crescendo.

RECAPITULATION

First theme   1 *a.* Horns, *mf*, arpeggio motive. Woodwinds, *p*, playful rhythm, minor.
                        b. Oboes, arpeggio motive. Woodwinds, *p*, playful rhythm.
                        c. Strings, *ff*, arpeggio motive developed. Decrescendo.

<table>
<tr><td>Second theme</td><td>2</td><td>a.</td><td>Flute, p, dancelike tune.</td></tr>
<tr><td></td><td></td><td>b.</td><td>Woodwinds, p, dancelike tune. Strings, dancelike tune developed, crescendo to ff. Decrescendo.</td></tr>
<tr><td>Third theme</td><td>3</td><td>a.</td><td>Flute, p, "Swing Low" theme, major.</td></tr>
<tr><td></td><td></td><td>b.</td><td>Violins, "Swing Low" theme. Crescendo.</td></tr>
<tr><td>CODA</td><td></td><td></td><td></td></tr>
<tr><td></td><td>1</td><td>a.</td><td>Full orchestra, fff, "Swing Low" and arpeggio motives, minor.</td></tr>
<tr><td></td><td></td><td>b.</td><td>Repeated chords, ff, at end.</td></tr>
</table>

Second Movement: Largo

After introductory chords, we hear the famous Largo melody, which has a nostalgic quality heightened by the timbre of the English horn. Dvořák uses tone color expressively throughout the second movement, frequently passing musical ideas among different instruments. The Largo is in the form A B-bridge-A'. Its gentle mood is broken only in the bridge, which contains a climactic quotation of motives from the first movement.

LISTENING OUTLINE
To be read while music is heard

Symphony No. 9 in E Minor, "From the New World" (1893) by Antonin Dvořák

Second Movement: Largo

A B-bridge-A' form, quadruple meter ($\frac{4}{4}$), D-flat major

2 flutes, 2 oboes, English horn, 2 clarinets, 2 bassoons, 4 horns, 2 trumpets, 3 trombones, tuba, timpani, violins 1, violins 2, violas, cellos, basses

(About 14½ min)

Introduction	1		Brasses and woodwinds, pp, solemn chords. Crescendo and decrescendo.
	2		Muted strings, ppp.
A	1	a.	English horn, p, main melody, major key.

		b.	Clarinet, pp, repeats ending notes of melody.
	2		High woodwinds, pp, solemn chords, crescendo. Brasses, timpani, ff, decrescendo.
	3		Muted strings, ppp, extension of main melody.
	4	a.	English horn, p, concluding phrases of main melody. Clarinet, violins softly repeat ending notes of melody.
		b.	Muted horns, p, opening notes of melody.
B	1		Oboe and flute, pp, minor melody, a little faster tempo than before. Tremolo strings accompany.

2 a. Clarinets, *pp*, hymnlike minor melody, a little slower tempo. Pizzicato basses accompany.

    b. Flutes and oboes, *p*, hymnlike melody continued. Pizzicato basses accompany.

3 Muted violins, *pp*, minor melody, a little faster tempo. Countermelody in oboe and flute. Strings, decrescendo.

4 Muted violins, *pp*, hymnlike minor melody, a little slower tempo. Tremolo strings accompany. Strings, *pp*, major chord.

Bridge   5 *a.* Staccato oboe, *p*, flute trills, *p*.

    b. Crescendo to *ff*, full orchestra. Arpeggio and ''Swing Low'' motives from first movement combined with opening of Largo melody. Decrescendo.

A'   1 *a.* English horn, main melody, original tempo, major.

    b. Muted strings, *pp*, main melody broken up by pauses.

    c. Solo violin and solo cello, *pp*.

    d. Strings, concluding phrases of main melody. Clarinet, *p*, repeats ending notes of melody. Violins, decrescendo to *ppp*.

2 *a.* Brasses, *pp*, solemn chords. Crescendo. Decrescendo. Strings, *pp*, melody rises to high, sustained chord, *pp*. Ending chords in double basses, *pp*.

Third Movement: Scherzo (Molto vivace)

The exciting Scherzo breathes the spirit of dancing. Its form is outlined: A (scherzo)–bridge–B (trio)–bridge–A (scherzo)–coda. Motives from the first movement are recalled in the bridge to the trio and in the coda. The opening part of the scherzo (A) section, in minor, has great rhythmic drive and features a short motive which chases itself in close imitation.

Dvořák then relaxes the tension with a lilting legato melody in a major key; the charm is heightened by delicate strokes of the triangle.

In the bridge to the trio (B), the cellos recall the arpeggio motive from the first movement.

The trio (B) section, in major, features two staccato dance tunes that might be performed by a town band. The first is softly played by the woodwinds with the triangle accompanying.

The second tune, graced by delightful trills, alternates between violins and woodwinds.

The scherzo section (A) is played again, and then we hear a dramatic string tremolo that ushers in the coda. Horns vigorously recalling the arpeggio motive are whimsically answered by *p* woodwinds playing the scherzo motive. The movement fades into silence before ending with a powerful chord for full orchestra.

Fourth Movement: Allegro con fuoco (allegro with fire)

The *New World Symphony* ends with a sonata-form finale of great power and splendor. Dvořák skillfully combines finale themes with motives from the earlier three movements.

After a brief string introduction, the horns and trumpets proclaim the first theme, which sounds like a proud march song.

A solo clarinet presents the yearning second theme, accompanied by a cello countermelody in faster time values.

Symphony No. 9 in E Minor, "From the New World"

The third theme, jubilant and folklike, ends with a three-tone descending figure that resembles "Three Blind Mice."

Dvořák plays with the three-tone figure, shifting it from low to high instruments and embellishing it with humorous variations.

In the development, motives from preceding movements are quoted and varied. Flutes and clarinets softly recall the Largo melody, which is combined with the marchlike finale theme and reminiscences of the Scherzo. A crescendo builds to the opening of the recapitulation, as brasses proclaim the marchlike theme. The remainder of the recapitulation is subdued in dynamics, and from it the coda emerges as a passionate and triumphant summary of the whole symphony.

[15] JOHANNES BRAHMS

Johannes Brahms (1833–1897) was a Romantic who poured new life into Classical forms. He was born in Hamburg, Germany, where his father made a precarious living as a string bass player. At thirteen, Brahms led a double life: during the day he studied piano, music theory, and composition; at night he played dance music for prostitutes and their clients in waterfront bars. Brahms's first concert tour when he was twenty gave him a chance to meet two of the greatest living composers, Liszt and Schumann. The contact with Liszt was not helpful. Brahms, a product of conservative musical education, was repelled by what he considered the bombast and lack of form in Liszt's music.

Schumann, on the other hand, was to shape the course of Brahms's artistic and personal life. Moments after presenting himself at Schumann's home, Brahms began to play one of his own piano sonatas. At the end of the first movement, Schumann called his wife Clara, the famous piano virtuoso, and they listened enthusiastically to Brahms's music for hours. Four weeks later,

Schumann published a magazine article hailing young Johannes Brahms as a musical Messiah "called to give ideal expression to his time" (Omikron).

Schumann published a magazine article hailing young Brahms as a musical Messiah "called to give ideal expression to his time." Brahms was both over-joyed and apprehensive about his overnight fame. "The open praise which you gave me," he wrote Schumann, "has probably excited the expectations of the public to such a degree that I don't know how I can come anywhere near fulfilling them."

As Brahms was preparing new works for an eager publisher, Schumann had a recurrence of his nervous illness and tried to drown himself. He was com-mitted to an asylum, leaving Clara Schumann with six children to support. Brahms rushed to her aid and helped care for the children while she went on concert tours to earn money. For two years Brahms lived in the Schumann

Johannes Brahms

335

home, becoming increasingly involved with Clara, who was fourteen years older. "I love you desperately," he wrote her. The conflict between his loyalty to Robert and his passion for Clara may well have accounted for the stormy music he wrote at the time. Robert Schumann's death left Brahms and Clara Schumann free to marry, yet they did not. Since they destroyed many of their letters, we'll never know what passed between them. A few months later they separated, remaining lifelong intimate friends. Brahms never married; for him, Clara Schumann was "the most beautiful experience of my life."

Brahms desperately wanted to become conductor of the Philharmonic Orchestra in Hamburg, his birthplace. When he was passed over for the post in 1862, the disappointment was overwhelming. "For me this was much sadder even than you can possibly imagine," he wrote Clara Schumann, "perhaps even sadder than you can understand." He left his native city to settle in Vienna, where he spent the last thirty-five years of his life. For several years he conducted a Viennese musical society and introduced many forgotten masterpieces by Bach, Handel, and Mozart to the public. Brahms had a wide knowledge of older music; he edited Baroque and Classical compositions, and he was an ardent collector of music manuscripts. (He owned Mozart's original manuscript of the Symphony No. 40 in G minor.)

His intimate knowledge of past masterpieces made Brahms extremely critical of his own work. Once, after a violinist played a Bach piece, he threw his own music to the floor, exclaiming, "After that, how could anyone play such stuff as this!" Brahms was obsessed by Beethoven. "You have no idea," he told a friend, "how the likes of us feel when we hear the tramp of a giant like him behind us." He worked at his First Symphony on and off for twenty years and completed it only when he was forty-three. Brahms endlessly revised compositions and sent them to friends for advice and criticism. He sent some songs to Clara Schumann with the request, "Write me if possible one short word about each . . . such as: Op. 10, No. 5, bad, No. 6, shameful, No. 7 ridiculous."

In 1879 an honorary doctoral degree from Breslau University calling Brahms "the first among today's masters" provoked a venomous attack from Richard Wagner, who sneered, "Compose, compose, even if you don't have the slightest of ideas!" Music critics of the time pitted Brahms's fondness for traditional forms against Wagner's innovative music dramas. Actually, their musical paths hardly ever crossed; Brahms never wrote opera, Wagner's special territory.

Brahms always lived frugally, even though he earned a good income from publishers and from playing and conducting his works. He hid a shy, sensitive nature behind a mask of sarcasm and rudeness. On leaving a party, he reportedly announced, "If there is anyone here I have not insulted, I apologize!" Yet this gruff bear could be extremely generous to talented young musicians. He helped Dvořák find a publisher, and the grateful Czech composer wrote: "I am so overcome by his kindness that I cannot help but love him! What a warm heart and great spirit there is in that man!"

When Brahms's beloved Clara Schumann lay dying in 1896, his grief found expression in the haunting *Four Serious Songs,* set to biblical texts. Not long after, it was discovered that he had cancer; on March 7, 1897, he dragged himself to hear a performance of his Fourth Symphony. The audience and orchestra gave him a tremendous ovation. Less than a month later, at the age of sixty-four, he died.

Brahms's Music

Brahms created masterpieces in all the traditional forms except opera. His varied output includes four symphonies, two concertos for piano and one for violin, short piano pieces, over two hundred songs, and magnificent choral music such as the *German Requiem* (1868). Some of Brahms's finest music may be found in the two dozen chamber works written for many different instrumental combinations, including duo sonatas for cello and piano (Op. 38 and Op. 99), a trio for violin, horn, and piano (Op. 40), and a quintet for clarinet and strings (Op. 115).

Brahms's works, though very personal in style, are rooted deeply in the music of Haydn, Mozart, and Beethoven. They reinterpret Classical forms while using the harmonic and instrumental resources of Brahms's later time. Brahms was the greatest master of theme-and-variations form since Beethoven. He wrote variations which sound completely different from their thematic source, even while retaining the theme's basic structure. We'll study this aspect of Brahms's art in the *Variations on a Theme by Haydn* for orchestra (Op. 56a).

While Brahms's music embraces a range of moods, it particularly has an autumnal or world-weary feeling and a sense of lyrical warmth. Lyricism pervades even the rich polyphonic textures he was so fond of. One Brahms scholar has aptly observed, "It is possible to sing every Brahms movement from beginning to end as though it were a single, uninterrupted melody. Through all its polyphonic intricacies, the clear flow of invention always remains distinctly recognizable."

Among Romantics, Brahms is outstanding in his ability to make intricate polyphonic texture sound natural and spontaneous. In his twenties, he and a violinist friend gave each other difficult contrapuntal exercises to correct. "Why shouldn't we two serious and intelligent people," Brahms wrote, "be able to teach one another better than some professor could?"

All of Brahms's music is rhythmically exciting. Contrasting rhythmic patterns are set against one another; one instrument plays two even notes to the beat, while another plays three. The use of "two against three," as this rhythmic technique is called, is one of Brahms's trademarks. He also delights in all sorts of syncopations and in phrases of irregular length that push against the prevailing meter.

The quality of sound in Brahms's music is very special. He liked rich, dark tone colors. In his orchestral music, he usually blended the different instru-

Brahms's Music

337

mental choirs, favoring mellow instruments like the viola, clarinet, and French horn. (It's characteristic of Brahms's feeling for tradition that he preferred the old-fashioned hunting-type horn to the modern horn with valves.) The rich sound often results from his practice of doubling melodies in thirds and sixths; the same melody is duplicated at the interval of a third or sixth.

All of Brahms's music radiates the security and solidity of a complete master. He justified Schumann's prediction of greatness for the "young eagle."

Variations on a Theme by Haydn for Orchestra, Op. 56a (1873)

These Variations have an unusual history. One of Brahms's friends, an eminent music historian, showed him a score for wind instruments thought to be by Haydn. Brahms was fascinated by the second movement, entitled "Chorale St. Antoni," probably a traditional Austrian pilgrim song. He copied the Chorale into his notebook and three years later, in 1873, used it as the theme for a set of variations. Today scholars doubt that the Chorale really is by Haydn, but Brahms's composition is still called by its original title. Brahms wrote the Variations in two versions: one for orchestra, which we'll consider, and one for two pianos (Op. 56b).

The work consists of a theme, eight variations, and an extended finale. The theme is like a processional, with moderate tempo (Andante) and clear duple meter. Brahms based his orchestration on the original scoring for wind band. He uses woodwinds and brasses, with no strings except pizzicato cellos and double basses to reinforce the lowest line. The form of the theme may be outlined as: a (repeated) ba' (repeated). The opening phrases are each five measures, rather than the usual four.

dim.

Each variation is unique and differs in mood from the simple theme. Together, they vary in tempo, meter, rhythm, and orchestration. Two are in minor, though the theme is in major. Most astonishing is how Brahms disguises the original melody. Many variations sound completely new, though some original tones are retained. Brahms's delight in disguising a theme was noted by contemporaries. When he grew a beard one summer, a friend joked that Brahms's face was now as hard to recognize under the beard as the theme in his variations.

The variations maintain the basic form, harmonies, and phrase structure of the theme. Some concentrate on particular features of the theme, such as the dotted rhythm (long-short) of the opening notes, or the repeated chords of the closing bars. Though separated by brief pauses, each variation seems to arise naturally from what precedes, either through contrast or continuation of mood.

Variation 1: Poco più animato (a little more animated)

The woodwinds and brasses intone the series of repeated notes that rounded off the theme. In the strings, there is an interweaving of flowing melodic lines.

Variation 2: Più vivace

Variation 2 is based on the dotted rhythm (long-short) heard at the beginning of the theme. Patterns like long-short-long-short are heard throughout. A loud, abrupt idea is repeatedly followed by softer phrases that are dancelike or lyrical.

Variation 3: Con moto

Now the original theme is transformed into a legato, even-flowing melody introduced by the oboe and repeated by the violins.

p

The second part of the variation features a beautiful interplay among the horn, woodwinds, and strings.

Variation 4: Andante con moto

The mood darkens in Variation 4, which presents a new melody in a minor key. Throughout, a more quick-flowing countermelody accompanies the main melody, either below or above it.

Variations on a Theme by Haydn for Orchestra, Op. 56a (1873)

339

Variation 5: Vivace

This joking, rhythmically animated music, in major, provides emotional release from the melancholy of Variation 4. It contains much syncopation and is brightened by the sound of high, staccato woodwinds.

Variation 6: Vivace

The original theme is more easily recognized in this variation, which is festive like the preceding one. It opens with a horn phrase that is answered by the woodwinds. In the second part of this variation, the full orchestra is heard for the first time, producing a vibrant, heroic sound.

Variation 7: Grazioso (gracefully)

A relaxed feeling pervades this variation, which has a rocking sextuple meter ($\frac{6}{8}$; 1-2-3-4-5-6); it is subdued in dynamics. The graceful new melody played by strings and flute has a rhythm traditionally associated with pastoral scenes.

Variation 8: Presto non troppo

Hushed, mysterious, and in a minor key, this variation moves so quickly that it is over almost before we know it. Scurrying figures alternate between muted strings and high woodwinds.

Finale (ground bass, or passacaglia): Andante

In the extended Finale, Brahms uses the Baroque ground bass form (also called passacaglia) that we've heard in works by Monteverdi, Purcell, and Bach. (Brahms also used a ground bass to stunning effect in the Finale of his Fourth Symphony.) A five-bar musical idea derived from the theme is presented seventeen times in a row, mostly in the bass.

Over this repeated idea, Brahms weaves imaginative variations that flow smoothly into one another. Like the Baroque masters he revered, Brahms focuses the listener's attention on the ever-changing melodic lines, rather than on the repeated ground bass.

The finale begins in a calm, hymnlike mood and soon builds to a climax through a rise in pitch and dynamic level. After the climax, there is a relaxed, lyrical interlude in which a syncopated oboe solo is followed by a winding, legato melody in the flute. Then a shift from major to minor brings a momentary darkening of mood. The five-bar idea is transferred from the bass to a high register, where it is played in turn by the oboe and violins. The dark minor soon gives way to a bright major, as the main theme, the "Chorale St. Antoni," triumphantly returns in the full orchestra. Now embellished by triangle strokes and high woodwind scales, the theme brings the Finale to a brilliant and joyous conclusion.

GIUSEPPE VERDI [**16**]

The most popular of all opera composers, Giuseppe Verdi (1813–1901) was born in a tiny Italian village. His father was a poor tavern keeper who could neither read nor write. At the age of ten, Verdi went to live in a nearby town, Busseto, to study music and go to school. Every Sunday for nine years, he walked three miles barefoot to serve as church organist in his own village, carrying his shoes to preserve them. A wealthy music patron took Verdi into his home and later supported his studies in Milan. Finishing his music education at twenty-two, Verdi returned to Busetto and became municipal music director. Thus assured of a regular income, he was able to marry his patron's daughter, a young woman he had known and loved since childhood.

But the small town couldn't fulfill Verdi's needs for long. After three years he returned to Milan with the score of his first opera, *Oberto* (1839). With the help of an influential friend, the young provincial's work was produced at La Scala, Italy's most important opera house. Though response to *Oberto* was only modest, it was enough to win Verdi a contract for three more operas. Just when Verdi's future seemed bright, disaster struck. While he was working on his next opera—a comedy—his wife fell ill and died. This tragedy completed the destruction of his family, since two infant children had died within the previous two years. Verdi managed to complete the opera, but it understandably lacked inspiration and was greeted by boos and hisses. In despair, he vowed to compose no more.

He changed his mind after reading a libretto about the ancient Jews exiled from their homeland. Verdi was an ardent nationalist who yearned to see the Italian people free from Austrian domination and unified into one nation. For him, the ancient Jews symbolized the enslaved Italians. He quickly composed *Nabucco* (Nebuchadnezzar, King of Babylon), which was an enormous success. One melody, "Oh my country so beautiful and lost!" became a national liberation hymn sung by all Italian patriots. From that time on, Verdi and his operas symbolized a free and united Italy. A poet wrote that "the very soul of Italy . . . has today its voice in the name of Giuseppe Verdi." As Italy approached war with Austria, the cry "Viva Verdi" stood also for the patriotic slogan, *Vittorio Emmanuele Re D'Italia* (Victor Emmanuel, King of Italy).

In his late thirties, Verdi composed *Rigoletto* (1851), *Il Trovatore* (1853), and *La Traviata* (1853), the first of his operas which are now universally known. While the public loved these works, critics were often scandalized by their

Giuseppe Verdi

341

Giuseppe Verdi was one of the greatest opera composers and an ardent Italian nationalist (Brown Brothers).

subject matter. *Rigoletto* seemed to condone rape and suicide, while *La Traviata* glorified free love and made a heroine out of a kept woman. But Verdi was a fiercely independent man, who himself lived openly with his second wife for ten years before marrying her.

Now wealthy, Verdi bought an estate at Busseto. He was elected deputy to the first Italian parliament in 1861 after Italy had become a nation. Verdi was Italy's most famous native son when he wrote *Aïda* (1871), an opera originally meant to commemorate the completion of the Suez Canal. In 1887, the seventy-three-year-old Verdi had a triumphant success with *Otello*, one of his greatest operas. Even this masterpiece did not still his creative urge. At the incredible age of seventy-nine, Verdi completed *Falstaff* (1893), his first comedy since the failure of his second opera fifty years earlier.

Verdi's Music

"In the theater, lengthy is synonymous with boring, and of all styles the boring style is the worst." Verdi composed not for the musical elite, but for a mass public whose main entertainment was opera. Verdi wanted subjects that were "original, interesting . . . and passionate; passions above all!" An aria "needs the greatest variety of mood; irony, contempt, rage, all thrown into sharp profile." Almost all of Verdi's mature works are serious and end unhappily. The operas move fast and involve characters who are plunged quickly into extremes of hatred, love, jealousy, and fear. His powerful music summons up heroes and villains and vividly underlines dramatic situations.

Expressive vocal melody is the soul of a Verdi opera. No matter how elaborate or atmospheric the orchestral part, the musical center lies in the voice. There are many duets, trios, and quartets, in which each character is given melodies superbly tailored to the emotions depicted. Choruses—of gypsies, Egyptian priests, conspirators, and monks, for example—play an important role in his operas.

In the course of a long life, Verdi's style became less conventional, more subtle and flexible. His later works have greater musical continuity. He used fewer pauses between sections and lessened the difference between aria and recitative. His orchestration became more imaginative and the accompaniments richer.

Verdi's last three operas are perhaps the greatest. *Aïda* is a true "grand opera" with spectacular pageants, ballets, and choruses. Yet for all its spectacle, there are many scenes of tender and intimate beauty. *Otello* and *Falstaff*, the operas of Verdi's old age, have marvelous librettos based on the plays by Shakespeare. The librettist was Arrigo Boito, himself a gifted opera composer. For *Otello,* the seventy-three-year-old Verdi wrote sensuous, overpowering music that completely fuses with the poetry and action. The opera rivals Shakespeare's play in its dramatic force and lyricism. Verdi's last opera, *Falstaff*, is incomparably witty, imaginative, and sparkling. The aged composer ended this comic masterwork with a carefree fugue to the words, "All the world's a joke!"

Rigoletto (1851)

Verdi dared to create an operatic hero out of a hunchback, a court jester named Rigoletto, whose only redeeming quality is an intense love for his daughter Gilda. Rigoletto's master, the licentious Duke of Mantua, has won Gilda's love while posing as a poor student. He seduces the innocent girl, causing Rigoletto to plot his death. Gilda loves the Duke even after learning about his dissolute character, and she ultimately sacrifices her own life to save his. Vice triumphs in this powerful drama.

Rigoletto (1851)

343

Act III: *La donna è mobile* and Quartet

Act III of *Rigoletto* contains two of the most popular pieces in opera, the Duke's aria *La donna è mobile* and the Quartet. The scene is a run-down inn where the Duke has come to meet Maddalena, voluptuous sister of the cutthroat Sparafucile.

The gay and tuneful *La donna è mobile* ("Woman is fickle") perfectly expresses the Duke's pleasure-loving personality. Even before *Rigoletto's* premiere in Venice, Verdi knew that *La donna è mobile* would be a hit. Afraid that his catchy tune would leak out during rehearsals and be sung by every Venetian gondolier, he waited until the last possible moment before giving it to the tenor.

The Quartet is sung as Rigoletto and Gilda peer through a crack in the wall of the inn, observing the Duke flirting with Maddalena. Verdi projects four conflicting emotions at one time, characterizing each singer with an appropriate melodic line. The Duke attempts to seduce Maddalena with a suave and ardent legato melody. Maddalena coquettishly repels his advances with quick, staccato laughs. Outside the inn, Gilda laments her fate with anguished sobs punctuated by rests, while Rigoletto curses and mutters threats of vengeance in repeated notes. Verdi lets us hear each voice separately before combining them in a glorious ensemble.

The right bank of the river Mincio. Gilda and the uneasy Rigoletto are on the road. Sparafucile, inside the inn, is sitting at a table, polishing his belt. He can hear nothing of what happens outside. It is night.

Slow string introduction, *pp*.

Rigoletto

E l'ami?   And you love him?   Recitative.

Gilda

Sempre.   Forever.

Rigoletto

Pure tempo a guarirne t'ho lasciato.   Yet I gave you time to be cured of it.

Gilda

Io l'amo!   I love him!

Rigoletto

Povero cor di donna! . . .   Poor woman's heart! . . .
Ah il vile infame!   Ah, the vile wretch!
Ma ne avrai vendetta, o Gilda!   But you'll have revenge, O Gilda!

Gilda

Pietà, mio padre!   Have pity, Father!

Rigoletto

E se tu certa fossi	And if you were certain
Ch'ei ti tradisse, l'ameresti ancora?	He betrayed you, would you love him still?

Gilda

Nol so . . . ma pur m'adora.	I don't know . . . but anyway he adores me.

Rigoletto

Egli?	He?

Gilda

Sì.	Yes.

Rigoletto leads her to one of the crevices in the wall, and she looks inside.

Rigoletto

Ebben, osserva dunque.	Very well, watch then.

Gilda

Un uomo vedo.	I see a man.

Rigoletto

Per poco attendi.	Wait a little.

The Duke, in a simple cavalry officer's uniform, comes into the ground-floor room through a door at left.

Rapid string passage.

Gilda (*starting*)

Ah padre mio!	Ah, Father!

Duke (*to Sparafucile*)

Due cose, e tosto . . .	Two things, and quickly . . .

Sparafucile

Quali?	What?

Duke

Una stanza e del vino . . .	A room and some wine . . .

Rigoletto

(Son questi i suoi costumi!)	(These are his ways!)

Sparafucile

(Oh il bel zerbino!)	(Oh the handsome wastrel!)

He goes into the next room.

Aria. Orchestra introduces Duke's melody.

Duke

La donna è mobile	Woman is fickle
Qual piuma al vento,	Like a feather in the wind,

Rigoletto (1851)

345

Muta d'accento	She changes her words
E di pensiero.	And her thoughts.

Sempre un amabile	Always a lovable
Leggiadro viso,	And lovely face,
In pianto o in riso,	Weeping or laughing,
È menzognero.	Is lying.
La donna è mobil, ecc.	Woman is fickle, etc.

È sempre misero	The man's always wretched	Orchestra. Duke's melody repeated with different words.
Chi a lei s'affida,	Who believes in her,	
Chi le confida	Who recklessly entrusts	
Mal cauto il core!	His heart to her!	
Pur mai non sentesi	And yet one who never	
Felice appieno	Drinks love on that breast	
Chi su quel seno	Never feels	
Non liba amore!	Entirely happy!	
La donna è mobil, ecc.	Woman is fickle, etc.	

Sparafucile comes back in with a bottle of wine and two glasses, which he sets on the table; then he strikes the ceiling twice with the hilt of his long sword. At this signal, a laughing young girl, in a gypsy dress, leaps down the stairs: the Duke runs to embrace her, but she escapes him. Meanwhile Sparafucile has gone out into the road, where he says softly to Rigoletto: — Duke's melody in orchestra, decrescendo.

Sparafucile

È là vostr'uomo . . .	Your man is there . . .
Viver dee o morire?	Must he live or die?

Rigoletto

Più tardi tornerò l'opra a compire.	I'll return later to complete the deed.

Sparafucile goes off behind the house toward the river. Gilda and Rigoletto remain in the street, the Duke and Maddalena on the ground floor. — Brief pause.

Duke

Un dì, se ben rammentomi,	One day, if I remember right,	Allegro.

O bella, t'incontrai . . .	I met you, O beauty . . .
Mi piacque di te chiedere,	I was pleased to ask about you,
E intesi che qui stai.	And I learned that you live here.
Or sappi, che d'allora	Know then, that since that time
Sol te quest'alma adora!	My soul adores only you!

Gilda

Iniquo!	Villain!

Maddalena

Ah, ah! . . . e vent'altre appresso	Ha, ha! . . . And does it now perhaps
Le scorda forse adesso?	Forget twenty others?
Ha un'aria il signorino	The young gentleman looks like
Da vero libertino . . .	A true libertine . . .

Duke (*starting to embrace her*)

Si . . . un mostro son . . .	Yes . . . I'm a monster . . .

Gilda

Ah padre mio!	Ah, Father!

Maddalena

Lasciatemi, stordito.	Let me go, foolish man!

Duke

Ih, che fracasso!	Ah, what a fuss!

Maddalena

Stia saggio.	Be good.

Duke

E tu sii docile,	And you, be yielding,
Non fare tanto chiasso.	Don't make so much noise.
Ogni saggezza chiudesi	All wisdom concludes Rhythm slows.
Nel gaudio e nell'amore.	In pleasure and in love.

(*He takes her hand.*)

La bella mano candida!	What a lovely, white hand! Quick rhythm resumes.

Maddalena

Scherzate voi, signore.	You're joking, sir.

Duke

No, no.	No, no.

Maddalena

Son brutta.	I'm ugly.

Duke

Abbracciami.	Embrace me.

Rigoletto (1851)

347

	Gilda	
Iniquo!	Villain!	

	Maddalena	
Ebro!	You're drunk!	

	Duke	
D'amor ardente.	With ardent love!	

	Maddalena	
Signor l'indifferente,	My indifferent sir,	
Vi piace canzonar?	Do you enjoy teasing?	

	Duke	
No, no, ti vo'sposar.	No, no, I want to marry you.	

	Maddalena	
Ne voglio la parola.	I want your word.	

	Duke (*ironic*)	
Amabile figliuola!	Lovable maiden!	

	Rigoletto	
	(*to Gilda, who has seen and heard all*)	
E non ti basta ancor?	Isn't that enough for you yet?	

	Gilda	
Iniquo traditor!	Villainous betrayer!	Characters sing

	Maddalena	simulta-
Ne voglio la parola.	I want your word.	neously.

	Duke	
Amabile figliuola!	Lovable maiden!	

	Rigoletto	
E non ti basta ancor?	Isn't that enough for you yet?	Short pause.

	Duke	
Bella figlia dell'amore,	Beautiful daughter of love,	Quartet, Andante.
Schiavo son de' vezzi tuoi;	I am the slave of your charms;	
Con un detto sol tu puoi	With a single word you can	
Le mie pene consolar.	Console my sufferings.	

Duke

Bel - la fi - glia del - l'a - mo - re,   schia - vo son de'

vez - zi tuo - i;   con un det-to, un det - to sol   tu

puo   i le mie pe - ne le mie pe - ne con - so - lar.

Vieni, e senti del mio core	Come, and feel the quick beating
Il frequente palpitar . . .	Of my heart . . .
Con un detto sol tu puoi	With a single word you can
Le mie pene consolar.	Console my sufferings.

Maddalena

Ah! ah! rido ben di core,	Ha! Ha! I laugh heartily,
Chè tai baie costan poco.	For such tales cost little.

Ah! ah! ri - do ben di co - re, chè tai ba - ie cos - tan po - co;

Gilda

Ah! così parlar d'amore . . .	Ah! To speak thus of love . . .

Ah!_____ co - sì_____ par - lar_____ d'a - mo - re!

Maddalena

Quanto valga il vostro gioco,	Believe me, I can judge
Mel credete, so apprezzar.	How much your game is worth.

Gilda

. . . a me pur l'infame ho udito!	. . . I too have heard the villain so!

Rigoletto (*to Gilda*)

Taci, il piangere non vale.	Hush, weeping is of no avail.

Ta - ci,   il pian-ge - re non va - le;

Gilda

Infelice cor tradito,	Unhappy, betrayed heart.	Characters sing simultaneously.
Per angoscia non scoppiar.	Do not burst with anguish.	
Ah, no!	Ah, no!	

Rigoletto (1851)

349

	Maddalena
Son avvezza, bel signore,	I'm accustomed, handsome sir,
Ad un simile scherzare.	To similar joking.
Mio bel signor!	My handsome sir!
	Duke
Bella figlia dell'amore, ecc.	Beautiful daughter of love, etc.
Vieni!	Come!
	Rigoletto
Ch'ei mentiva sei sicura.	You are sure that he was lying.
Taci, e mia sarà la cura	Hush, and I will take care
La vendetta d'affrettar.	To hasten vengeance.
Sì, pronta fia, sarà fatale,	Yes, it will be swift and fatal,
Io saprollo fulminar.	I will know how to strike him down.
Taci, taci . . .	Hush, hush . . .

[17] GIACOMO PUCCINI

Some of the best-loved operas were created by Giacomo Puccini (1858–1924), who succeeded Verdi as the leading Italian opera composer of his time. Puccini came from a long line of composers and church organists. During his student years at the Milan Conservatory (1880–1883), he lived a hand-to-mouth existence, usually eating on credit at a restaurant fittingly named Aïda. The success of his first opera, written shortly after graduation, brought him to the attention of Italy's leading music publisher, who commissioned new works and gave him an annual income.

In 1893 Puccini became well known throughout Italy because of *Manon Lescaut*, and after 1896, he was wealthy and world-famous from the enormous success of *La Bohème*, which presents a "Bohemian" life similar to Puccini's as an impoverished music student. *La Bohème*, along with two other very popular operas, *Tosca* (1900) and *Madame Butterfly* (1904), was written in collaboration with the librettists Luigi Illica and Giuseppe Giacosa. Puccini was very concerned with the literary and dramatic qualities of his librettos, often demanding endless changes from his collaborators. He spent as much time polishing the librettos as he did composing the music. His last opera, *Turandot*, was based on a Chinese fairy tale. He died before finishing it; the work was completed from Puccini's sketches by a friend, Franco Alfano.

Giacomo Puccini became wealthy and world-famous from the enormous success of *La Bohème*, which presents a "Bohemian" life similar to his own as an impoverished music student (Brown Brothers).

Puccini's marvelous sense of theater has given his operas lasting appeal. He knew just when to introduce new musical material or a moment of silence, and he was able to provide smooth transitions from one scene or mood to another. His melodies have short easy-to-remember phrases and are intensely emotional. He uses the orchestra to reinforce the vocal melody and to suggest atmosphere, landscape, and mood. As Verdi did in his late works, Puccini minimized the difference between aria and recitative, thus creating a continuous flow of music. He got unity and continuity also by using the same material in various acts, particularly when characters reflect on past events or emotions.

Some of Puccini's operas—notably *Tosca*—reflect an artistic trend of the 1890s known as *verismo*, "realism" or the quality of being "true to life." Operas related to this realistic movement deal with ordinary people rather than kings, gods, or great heroes, and often contain many shockingly violent scenes with

Giacomo Puccini

351

music of raw emotional power. *Cavalleria rusticana* ("Rustic Chivalry," 1890) by Pietro Mascagni and *I Pagliacci* ("The Clowns," 1892) by Ruggiero Leoncavallo are other famous examples of *verismo*. Puccini's operas also feature exoticism. Not only is *Madame Butterfly* set in Japan and *Turandot* in China, but Puccini used melodic and rhythmic elements derived from Oriental music. His sentiment-producing melodies cast a Romantic glow over any subject matter, whether realistic or exotic.

La Bohème (1896)

La Bohème ("Bohemian life") takes place in the Latin Quarter of Paris around 1830. Its hero is Rodolfo, a young poet who shares a garret with Marcello, a painter, Colline, a philosopher, and Schaunard, a musician. Mimi, the heroine, is a poor tubercular seamstress who lives in the same building. The simple, touching plot has been aptly summarized as "boy meets girl, boy loses girl, boy and girl are reunited as girl dies of consumption in boy's arms and curtain falls." Everyone can relate to the characters and emotions of this enchanting opera. Though there are many realistic touches in this picture of "Bohemian" life, it is seen through a Romantic haze.

Act I: Scene between Rodolfo and Mimi

Toward the end of Act I, Mimi and Rodolfo meet and fall in love. Her candle has blown out, and she knocks on his door asking for a light. After a short musical conversation, Mimi realizes she has lost her key, and they both search for it in the dark. When their hands touch, Rodolfo sings the aria, *Che gelida manina* ("What a cold little hand"). He sings about himself, his dreams and his fantasies. Mimi responds with a poetic description of her simple life in the aria, *Mi chiamano Mimi* ("They call me Mimi"). Under the spell of their new-found love, they join in a duet which closes the act.

Puccini's sensuous melody casts a glow over the entire scene. His music has an improvisatory quality due to many fluctuations of tempo. When Mimi enters, the orchestra murmurs a touching phrase, the Mimi theme, which suggests her fragility and tenderness. Each aria begins simply, almost in conversation. Then the melody grows warmer until it reaches a climax in a broad, passionate phrase. The climactic phrase of Rodolfo's aria, sung to the word's, *Talor dal mio forziere* ("My hoard of treasure is robbed by two thieves: a pair of beautiful eyes"), is the love theme of the whole opera. Mimi's emotional high point is reached when she dreams about the end of winter (*ma quando vien la sgelo*), when "the first kiss of April" is hers. Returning to reality at the end of her aria, she sings in conversational repeated tones. The tension breaks momentarily as Rodolfo has a brief exchange with his friends in the courtyard—an example of Puccini's great theatrical timing, for he provides a moment of relaxation before the lovers join in the closing duet. First, Rodolfo sings alone, then both voices beautifully unite in a declaration of love.

Rodolfo closes the door, sets his light on the table, and tries to write. But he tears up the paper and throws the pen down.   Flute melody.

Rodolfo

Non sono in vena.   I'm not in the mood.

A timid knock at the door.

Chi è la?   Who's there?   Speechlike.

Mimi

Scusi.   Excuse me. . .

Rodolfo

Una donna!   A woman!

Mimi

Di grazia, mi si è spento   I'm sorry . . . my light   Mimi theme, *pp*,
Il lume.   Has gone out.   in orchestra.

Rodolfo

Ecco.   (*opens*) Here.

Mimi

                (*in the doorway, with a candle-*
                stick and a key)
Vorrebbe . . . ?   Would you . . . ?

Rodolfo

S'accomodi un momento.   Come in for a moment.

Mimi

Non occorre.   There's no need.

Rodolfo

La prego, entri.   Please . . . come in.

Mimi enters, has a fit of coughing.   Faster, agitated.

Rodolfo

Si sente male?   You're not well?

Mimi

No . . . nulla.   No . . . it's nothing.

Rodolfo

Impallidisce!   You're pale!

Mimi

È il respir . . . quelle scale . . .   I'm out of breath . . . the
                stairs . . .

She faints, and Rodolfo is just in time to support her and   Oboe.
help her to a chair. The key and the candlestick fall from her
hands.

Rodolfo

Ed ora come faccio?   Now what shall I do?

He gets some water and sprinkles her face.

La Bohème (1896)

353

Così.	So.	
Che viso d'ammalata!	How ill she looks!	
Mimi comes to.		Staccato muted
Si sente meglio?	Are you better now?	strings.

Mimi

Sì.	Yes.

Rodolfo

Qui c'è tanto freddo.	It's so cold here.
Segga vicino al fuoco.	Come and sit by the fire.

He helps her to a chair by the stove.

Aspetti . . . un po' di vino.	Wait . . . some wine.

Mimi

Grazie.	Thank you.

Roldolfo

A lei.	Here.

Mimi

Poco, poco.	Just a little.

Rodolfo

Così.	There.

Mimi

Grazie.	Thank you.

Rodolfo

Che bella bambina!	What a lovely creature!

Mimi

Ora permetta	Now, please,
Che accenda il lume.	Relight my candle.
È tutto passato.	I'm better now.

Roldolfo

Tanta fretta.	Such a hurry.

Mimi

Sì.	Yes.

Rodolfo lights her candle for her.

Mimi

Grazie. Buona sera.	Thank you. Good evening.

Rodolfo

Buona sera.	Good evening.

Mimi goes out, then reappears at the door.

Mimi

Oh! sventata, sventata,	Oh! foolish me! . . .	A little faster.
		Tuneful vocal
		melody.

La chiave della stanza	Where have I left
Dove l'ho lasciata?	The key to my room?

Rodolfo

Non stia sull'uscio:	Don't stand in the door:
Il lume vacilla al vento.	The wind makes your
	light flicker.

Her candle goes out.

Mimi

Oh Dio! Torni ad accenderlo.	Heavens! Will you relight
	it?

Rodolfo rushes to her with his light, but when he reaches the door, his candle goes out, too. The room is dark.

Rodolfo

Oh Dio! Anche il mio s'è	There. . . . Now mine's
spento.	out, too.

Mimi

Ah! E la chiave ove sarà?	Ah! And where can my
	key be?

Rodolfo

Buio pesto!	Pitch dark!

Mimi

Disgraziata!	Unlucky me!

Rodolfo

Ove sarà?	Where can it be?

Mimi

Importuna è la vicina. . .	You've a bothersome neigh-
	bor. . .

Rodolfo

Ma le pare!	Not at all.

Mimi

Importuna è la vicina . . .	You've a bothersome neigh-
	bor . . .

Rodolfo

Cosa dice, ma le pare!	What do you mean? Not
	at all.

Mimi

Cerchi.	Search.

Rodolfo

Cerco.	I'm searching.

They both grope on the floor for the key.

Mimi

Ove sarà?	Where can it be?

La Bohème (1896)

355

		Rodolfo	
Ah!		Ah! (*finds the key, pockets it*)	
		Mimi	
L'ha trovata?		Did you find it?	
		Rodolfo	
No.		No.	
		Mimi	
Mi parve . . .		I thought . . .	
		Rodolfo	
In verità!		Truthfully!	
		Mimi	
Cerca?		Are you hunting?	
		Rodolfo	
Cerco.		I'm hunting for it.	

Guided by her voice, Rodolfo pretends to search as he draws closer to her. Then his hand meets hers, and he holds it. Orchestra alone, tempo slows.

	Mimi	
Ah!	(*surprised*) Ah!	

They rise. Rodolfo continues to hold Mimi's hand.

	Rodolfo	
Che gelida manina,	What a cold little hand,	Rodolfo's aria.
Se la lasci riscaldar.	Let me warm it.	

Cercar che giova? Al buio	What's the use of searching?	
Non si trova. Ma per fortuna	We'll never find it now.	Harp.
È una notte di luna,	But luckily there's a moon,	
E qui la luna l'abbiamo vicina.	And she's our neighbor here.	
Aspetti, signorina,	Just wait, my dear young lady,	
Le dirò con due parole chi son,	And meanwhile I'll tell you	
Chi son, e che faccio, come vivo.	In a word who and what I am.	
Vuole?	Shall I?	

 Mimi is silent.

Chi son? Chi son? Son un poeta.	Who am I? I'm a poet.

Che cosa faccio? Scrivo.	My business? Writing.	
E come vivo? Vivo.	How do I live? I live.	
In povertà mia lieta	In my happy poverty	
Scialo da gran signore	I squander like a prince	
Rima ed inni d'amore.	My poems and songs of love.	
Per sogni e per chimere	In hopes and dreams	
E per castelli in aria	And castles in air,	
L'anima ho milionaria.	I'm a millionaire in spirit.	
Talor dal mio forziere	My hoard of treasure	Love theme.
Ruban tutti i gioielli	Is robbed by two thieves:	
Due ladri: gli occhi belli.	A pair of beautiful eyes.	

Ta - lor dal mio for - zie - re_____ ru - ban tut - ti‿i gio-
iel - li due la - dri: gli‿oc - chi bel - li.

V'entrar con voi pur ora	They came in now with you	
Ed i miei sogni usati,	And all my lovely dreams,	
Ed i bei sogni miei	My dreams of the past,	
Tosto si dileguar!	Were soon stolen away.	
Ma il furto non m'accora	But the theft doesn't upset me,	
Poichè, poichè v'ha preso stanza	Since the empty place was filled	
La speranza.	With hope.	
Or che mi conoscete	Now that you know me,	
Parlate voi. Deh parlate.	It's your turn to speak.	
Chi siete? Vi piaccia dir?	Tell me, please, who are you?	

Mimi

Sì.	Yes.	
Mi chiamano Mimì,	They call me Mimi,	Mimi's aria.
Ma il mio nome è Lucia.	But my real name is Lucia.	

Andante lento

Mi chia - ma - no Mi - mì, ma‿il mio no - me‿è Lu - ci - a___

La Bohème (1896)

357

La storia mia è breve.	My story is brief.
A tela o a seta	I embroider silk and satin
Ricamo in casa e fuori.	At home or outside.
Son tranquilla e lieta,	I'm tranquil and happy,
Ed è mio svago	And my pastime
Far gigli e rose.	Is making lilies and roses.
Mi piaccion quelle cose	I love all things
Che han si dolce malia,	That have a gentle magic,
Che parlano d'amor, di prima-	That talk of love, of spring,
vere,	
Che parlano di sogni e di	That talk of dreams and
chimere,	fancies—
Quelle cose che han nome	The things called poetry . . .
poesia . . .	
Lei m'intende?	Do you understand me?

Rodolfo

Sì.	Yes.

Mimi

Mi chiamano Mimì.	They call me Mimi—
Il perchè non so.	I don't know why.
Sola, mi fo il pranzo	I live all by myself
Da me stessa.	And I eat all alone.
Non vado sempre a messa,	I don't often go to church,
Ma prego assai il Signor.	But I like to pray.
Vivo sola, soletta,	I stay all alone
Là in una bianca cameretta;	In my tiny white room,
Guardo sui tetti e in cielo.	I look at the roofs and the sky.
Ma quando vien lo sgelo	But when the thaw comes
Il primo sole è mio,	The first sunshine is mine,
Il primo bacio	The first kiss
Dell'aprile è mio!	Of April is mine!
Il primo sole è mio!	The first sunshine is mine!
Germoglia in un vaso una	A rose blossoms in my
rosa,	vase,
Foglia a foglia l'aspiro.	I breathe in its perfume,
Così gentil è il profumo	Petal by petal. So lovely,
d'un fior.	
Ma i fior ch'io faccio, ahimè,	So sweet is the flower's perfume.
I fior ch'io faccio,	But the flowers I make,
Ahimè non hanno odore.	Alas, have no scent.
Altro di me non le saprei	What else can I say?
narrare.	

Sono la sua vicina	I'm your neighbor,
Che la vien fuori d'ora a	Disturbing you at this im-
importunare.	possible hour.

Schaunard

Eh! Rodolfo!	(*from below*) Hey! Rodolfo!

Colline

Rodolfo!	Rodolfo!

Marcello

Olà! Non senti?	Hey! Can't you hear?
Lumaca!	You snail!

Colline

Poetucolo!	You fake!

Schaunard

Accidenti al pigro!	To hell with that lazy one!

Rodolfo, impatient, goes to the window to answer. When the window is opened, the moonlight comes in, lighting up the room.

Rodolfo

Scrivo ancora tre righe a volo.	I've a few more words to write.

Mimi

Chi son?	Who are they?

Rodolfo

Amici.	Friends.

Schaunard

Sentirai le tue.	You'll hear about this.

Marcello

Che te ne fai lì solo?	What are you doing there alone?

Rodolfo

Non son solo. Siamo in due.	I'm not alone. There're two of us.
Andate da Momus, tenete il posto.	Go to Momus and get a table.
Ci saremo tosto.	We'll be there soon.

Marcello, Schaunard, Colline

Momus, Momus, Momus,	Momus, Momus, Momus.
Zitti e discreti andiamocene via.	Quietly, discreetly, we're off.
Momus, Momus, Momus.	Momus, Momus, Momus.
Trovò la poesia.	He's found his poem at last.

Turning, Rodolfo sees Mimi wrapped in a halo of moonlight. He contemplates her, in ecstasy.

La Bohème (1896)

359

Rodolfo

O soave fanciulla, o dolce viso	Oh! lovely girl, oh! sweet face	Duet.
Di mite circonfuso alba lunar,	Bathed in the soft moon-light.	
In te, ravviso il sogno	I see in you the dream	
Ch'io vorrei sempre sognar!	I'd dream forever!	
Fremon già nell'anima	Already I taste in spirit	Voices unite, love theme.
Le dolcezze estreme,	The heights of tenderness!	
Amor nel bacio freme!	Love trembles in our kiss!	

Mimi

Ah, tu sol comandi,   Ah! Love, you rule
  amore. . . .   alone. . . .
Oh! come dolci scendono   How sweet his praises
Le sue lusinghe al core. . . . Enter my heart. . . .
Tu sol comandi, amore!   Love, you alone rule!

Rodolfo kisses her.

Mimi
No, per pietà!   No, please!

Rodolfo
Sei mia!   You're mine!

Mimi
V'aspettan gli amici. . . .   Your friends are waiting.

Rodolfo
Già mi mandi via?   You send me away already?

Mimi
Vorrei dir . . . ma non oso. I daren't say what I'd like. . . .

Rodolfo
Di'.   Tell me.

Mimi
Se venissi con voi?   If I came with you?

Rodolfo
Che? Mimì!   What? Mimi!
Sarebbe così dolce restar qui. It would be so fine to stay here.
C'è freddo fuori.   Outside it's cold.

Mimi
Vi starò vicina!   I'd be near you!

Rodolfo
E al ritorno?   And when we come back?

Mimi
Curioso!   Who knows?

	Rodolfo	
Dammi il braccio,	Give me your arm, my	Melody from
o mia piccina. . .	dear. . .	Rodolfo's
		aria.
	Mimi	
Obbedisco, signor!	Your servant, sir. . .	
	Rodolfo	
Che m'ami . . . di' . . .	Tell me you love me!	
	Mimi	
Io t'amo.	I love you.	
	Rodolfo	
Amor!	My love!	
	Mimi	
Amor!	My love!	
	Rodolfo and Mimi	
Amor!	Beloved!	

RICHARD WAGNER [**18**]

Romantic

Few composers have had so powerful an impact on their time as Richard Wagner (1813–1883). During the last decades of the nineteenth century, his operas and artistic philosophy influenced not only musicians, but poets, painters, and playwrights, too. Such was his preeminence that an opera house of his own design was built in Bayreuth, Germany, solely for performances of his music dramas.

Born in Leipzig, Wagner grew up in a theatrical atmosphere. Both his stepfather and two sisters were actors, and another sister was an opera singer. His boyhood dream was to be a poet and playwright. But at fifteen he was overwhelmed by the power of Beethoven's music, and he decided to become a composer. The young Wagner taught himself by studying scores. He never tried to master an instrument and had only six months of formal training in music theory.

When he was seventeen, Wagner enrolled in Leipzig University, where he was more interested in riotous student club life than in academic studies. His family thought him good for nothing because of his dueling, drinking, and gambling. The pattern continued throughout his life; Wagner shamelessly lived off other people and accumulated enormous debts that he never repaid.

During his early twenties, Wagner conducted in small German theaters, wrote several operas, and married Minna Planer, a beautiful and well-known actress. In 1839 he decided to try his luck in Paris, then the center of grand opera. Unpaid debts prevented his getting a passport, and so he and Minna

Richard Wagner

361

illegally crossed the frontier. Their two years in Paris were miserable. Unable to get an opera performed, Wagner was reduced to musical hack work. He ran up such bills that he was briefly confined to a debtors' prison.

Wagner returned to Germany in 1842 to supervise the production of *Rienzi* at the Dresden opera. The work was immensely successful, and Wagner was appointed conductor of the Dresden opera, a lifetime position with a good salary. He spent six years there, becoming famous both as an opera composer and as a great conductor. Wagner demanded that his orchestra play with enormous dynamic subtlety and rhythmic freedom. "When he conducts," a musician observed, "he is almost beside himself with excitement. . . . Every sinew in his body speaks. His whole appearance is of arrogance and despotism personified."

The revolutions of 1848 swept across Europe like a forest fire and marked an important turning point in Wagner's career. His life in Dresden had become increasingly difficult because of debts he had again accumulated (he owed more than ten times his annual salary). Hoping that a new society would wipe out his debts and produce conditions favorable to his art, Wagner participated in the Dresden insurrection. He ordered hand grenades and tried to incite disobedience among the king's soldiers. When a warrant was issued for his arrest, Wagner fled to Switzerland.

For several years Wagner did no composing; instead he worked out theories of art in essays such as *Art and Revolution* (1849), *The Art Work of the Future* (1850), and *Opera and Drama* (1851). More important, he completed the librettos to *The Ring of the Nibelung,* a set of four operas based on Nordic mythology. *The Ring* was to occupy Wagner for a quarter of a century. He began the text in 1848 and finished the music in 1874. Wagner's amazing self-confidence and belief in his greatness enabled him to compose one gigantic opera after another, with no prospects for their performance. He composed the first opera of the *Ring* cycle, *The Rhine Gold* (1853–1854), then the second, *The Valkyrie* (1854–1856), and the first two acts of the third, *Siegfried* (1856–1857). Then he interrupted his work to compose *Tristan and Isolde* (1857–1859), which he hoped would have a better chance for performance. In this opera, sexual passion is musically presented with unprecedented power and vividness.

Wagner had several bad years after finishing *Tristan.* His opera *Tannhäuser* was a failure at the Paris Opera, and *Tristan* was abandoned by the Vienna Opera after many rehearsals. Creditors banged on his door, demanding payment for the silks, satins, laces, and perfumes he "needed" for his lifestyle.

In 1864 Wagner was rescued from his desperate situation by King Ludwig of Bavaria, an eighteen-year-old fanatical Wagnerite.

King Ludwig wrote, "Since the power is mine, I will use it to sweeten your life. The most beautiful moments of my life I have received from you, everything . . . every joy, every rapture!" The King was determined to help Wagner produce his operas and complete *The Ring.* All the resources of the Munich Opera were put at Wagner's disposal. *Tristan* and *The Mastersingers of Nuremberg* (1862–1867) were lavishly produced in Munich. Wagner completed *Siegfried*

Richard Wagner's operas and artistic philosophy had a powerful impact on his time (The Bettmann Archive).

(1869–1870) and composed the final opera of the *Ring*, *The Twilight of the Gods* (1869–1874).

During this period, Wagner fell in love with Cosima von Bülow. She was Liszt's daughter and the wife of Hans von Bülow, Wagner's close friend and favorite conductor. Cosima gave birth to two of Wagner's children while still married to von Bülow. Shortly after Wagner's first wife died, he married Cosima.

In Richard Wagner, towering musical genius was allied with utter selfishness, ruthlessness, and an absolute conviction about his place in history. A rabid German nationalist, he wrote in his diary, "I am the most German of beings.

Richard Wagner

363

I am the German spirit." He bent people to his will. Indeed, he forged an audience for his complex music dramas from a public accustomed to conventional opera.

Wagner designed a theater to suit performances of *The Ring*. With the help of King Ludwig and contributions from Wagner clubs which had been formed all over Germany, Wagner's festival theater was constructed in Bayreuth, a small Bavarian town. The premiere of the *Ring* cycle in 1876 was perhaps the single most important musical event of the century. Sixty newspaper correspondents from all over the world attended, including two from the United States. Though some critics still found his music too dissonant, heavily orchestrated, and long-winded, Wagner was generally acclaimed the greatest composer of his time. A year after completing *Parsifal* (1877–1882), his last opera, Wagner visited Venice, where he died at the age of sixty-nine.

Wagner's Music

For Wagner, an opera house was a temple in which the spectator was to be overwhelmed by music and drama. He wrote his own librettos, based on medieval Germanic legends and myths. His characters are usually larger than life—heroes, gods, demigods.

Wagner called his works "music dramas" rather than operas, to emphasize the close relationship between music and drama. He envisioned music drama as a "universal art work" (*Gesamtkunstwerk*) in which all the arts—music, drama, dance, painting—are fused. Today, however, many find Wagner's music more exciting than his rather static drama. For long stretches of time his characters exult, lament, or relate what has happened to them.

Within each act, there is a continuous musical flow which Wagner described as "unending melody." The music is not broken into traditional arias, recitatives, and duets. He achieves musical and dramatic continuity by smoothly connecting each section to the next. There are no breaks where applause can disturb the listener's concentration. Wagner conceived his vocal line as a "speech song" combining the speechlike quality of a recitative with the lyricism of an aria. The vocal line is inspired by rhythms and pitch fluctuations in the German text.

Wagner revolutionized opera by shifting the musical center of gravity from the voice toward the orchestra. His expanded and colorful orchestration brilliantly expresses the drama and reveals characters' thoughts and feelings. He treats the orchestra symphonically, constantly developing, transforming, and intertwining musical ideas. Many long orchestral interludes graphically depict scenic effects like floods, sunrises, and flames.

Wagner loved to exploit the rich power of the brasses. *The Ring* calls for eight horns and new brass instruments (called "Wagner tubas") that he designed. The orchestral sound is so full that only singers with unusually powerful voices, such as a "Wagnerian soprano" or a "heroic tenor," can cut through it.

Wagner spins an orchestral web out of recurrent musical ideas called *leitmotifs* or *leading motives*. **A leitmotif is a short musical idea associated with a person, object, or thought in the drama.** When the text refers to Siegfried, his leitmotif is usually heard in the orchestra. These motives are sometimes in the vocal parts, too. They are varied and transformed to convey the evolving dramatic situation and changes of character. When Siegfried is murdered, his leitmotif is set against strident dissonant harmonies. As Wagner develops his leitmotifs, he sets one against another to suggest the clash of two persons or ideas. Such leitmotifs unify Wagner's greatly extended music dramas.

The emotional tension of Wagner's music is heightened by chromatic and dissonant harmonies. He creates motion and color through rapid shifts from one key to another and through many chromatic chords in each key. The listener often expects a resolution to a stable chord only to hear yet another dissonance. Wagner's chromatic harmony ultimately led to the breakdown of tonality and to the new musical language of the twentieth century.

The Twilight of the Gods (*Götterdämmerung*, 1874)

The Twilight of the Gods is the fourth and concluding music drama in Wagner's gigantic cycle, *The Ring of the Nibelung*. With all its gods, giants, dwarfs, and magic fire, *The Ring* is really about Wagner's view of nineteenth-century society. He uses Nordic mythology to warn that society destroys itself through lust for money and power. It is fitting that Wagner first sketched the plot of *The Ring* in 1848, a year that brought Marx's *Communist Manifesto* and revolutions throughout Europe.

Act III: Immolation Scene

Wagner builds an overwhelming climax at the end of *The Ring* as men and gods are punished for their crimes by a spectacular fire and flood. To grasp this scene fully, it's helpful to know what has taken place in the three preceding music dramas.

A Nibelung dwarf has stolen gold belonging to the Rhinemaidens, mermaids in the Rhine river. From this gold, the dwarf fashions a ring that can bestow world power on anyone who wears it and is willing to renounce love. The dwarf, in turn, is robbed of his prize by Wotan, king of the gods. (Wednesday comes from "Wotan's day.") Furious, the dwarf casts a curse on the ring and anyone who wears it. Soon Wotan is forced to give up the ring; he lives in fear that someone will use it to destroy him. Hoping to protect himself, he surrounds his castle, Valhalla, with a bodyguard of heroes. His daughters, goddesses called Valkyries, swoop over battlefields on horseback bearing away the dead bodies of the bravest warriors.

Brünnhilde, one of the Valkyries, is Wotan's favorite daughter. Thinking she is following Wotan's inner feelings, Brünnhilde disobeys her father by saving Siegmund, a hero fated to die. She is punished by being turned into

The Twilight of the Gods (Götterdämmerung, 1874)

365

a mortal. Cast into a deep sleep by Wotan, she lies on a mountain surrounded by magic fire. The hero Siegfried, son of Siegmund, penetrates the fire, awakens Brünnhilde, and becomes her husband.

In the course of his adventures, Siegfried has gained possession of the ring, but he is unaware of its power. Shortly before the Immolation Scene, Siegfried is murdered through the treachery of Hagen, who wants the ring.

The Immolation Scene occurs in front of a castle on the Rhine. Brünnhilde sings an exalted farewell before sacrificing herself to join Siegfried in death. At her command, warriors build a huge funeral pyre of logs. As Siegfried's body is lifted onto the pyre, Brünnhilde takes the magic ring from him and puts it on, bequeathing it to the Rhinemaidens. The following excerpt begins as Brünnhilde addresses a pair of ravens, Wotan's messengers.

In this glorious conclusion to *The Twilight of the Gods,* Brünnhilde's soaring vocal line is matched by the powerful orchestra. Various leitmotifs are heard, sometimes together. After Brünnhilde rides into the funeral pyre, the orchestra magnificently depicts the flames and the overflowing of the Rhine. The opera ends as Valhalla, the castle of the gods, is engulfed in flames accompanied by the leitmotif "Redemption by love." Wagner seems to be expressing the feeling that despite the destruction of men and gods, a new world will be reborn through love. (In the following libretto, words in quotation marks—like "Law" and "Magic fire"—refer to specific leitmotifs. These leitmotifs are indicated where they can be most clearly heard.)

Brünnhilde has put the Ring on her finger and now takes a firebrand from one of the men.

Trumpets and trombones, *f,* "Law."

Brünnhilde

Fliegt heim, ihr Raben!	Fly home, ye ravens!
raunt es eurem Herren,	Tell your lord
was hier am Rhein ihr gehört!	what you heard here on the Rhine!

Full orchestra, *f,* "Magic fire," "Loge, god of fire."

An Brünnhildes Felsen	Fly past Brünnhilde's rock,
fliegt vorbei:	where Loge is still flaming,
der dort noch lodert,	and bid him go
weiset Loge nach Walhall!	to Valhalla!
Denn der Götter Ende	For the end of the gods
dämmert nun auf:	is now dawning.

so—werf' ich den Brand *in Walhalls prangende Burg.*	See—I throw the firebrand into Valhalla's glorious cita- del!	Cymbal crash.

She hurls the torch onto the pyre. Two ravens fly up and disappear in the background. She turns to her horse.

Strings surge upward as pyre bursts into flames.

Grane, mein Ross. *sei mir gegrüsst!*	Grane, my steed, greetings to you!

Horns, "Ride of the Valky-ries."

"Ride of the Valkyries"

Weisst du auch, mein Freund, *wohin ich dich führe?* *Im Feuer leuchtend*	My friend, do you know where I lead you? In the bright fire

Flute and voice, "Redemption by love."

Flute

"Redemption by love"

liegt dort dein Herr, *Siegfried, mein seliger Held.* *Dem Freunde zu folgen,* *wieherst du freudig?*	there lies your master, Siegfried, my blessed hero. Are you neighing, eager to follow your friend?
Lockt dich zu ihm *die lachende Lohe?* *Fühl' meine Brust auch,* *wie sie entbrennt;* *helles Feuer* *das Herz mir erfasst.* *Ihn zu umschlingen,* *umschlossen, von ihm,*	Do the laughing flames allure you? Feel my breast, too, how it is burning; bright flames seize on my heart. To clasp him to me, to be held fast in his arms,

The Twilight
of the Gods
(Götterdämmerung,
1874)

367

in mächtigster Minne	to be united with him	Trumpet, "Sieg-fried."
vermählt ihm zu sein!	by the power of love!	
Hei-a-ja-ho! Grane!	Hei-a-ya-ho! Grane!	
Grüss deinen Herren!	Greet your lord!	
Siegfried! Siegfried! Sieh!	Siegfried! Siegfried! See!	
selig grüsst dich dein Weib!	Your wife greets you joy-fully!	

She swings herself onto the horse and makes it leap into the burning pyre.

Brasses, "Ride of the Valk-yries."

Flames fill the whole space in front of the castle, which itself catches fire. Men and women press to the front of the stage in terror.

Full orchestra, *ff*, "Magic Fire."

"Magic Fire"

When all seems wrapped in flames, the glow is suddenly extinguished, so that only a cloud of smoke is seen.

Decrescendo, descending chromatic scale, "Magic sleep."

At the same time the Rhine upswells mightily and pours its waters over the pyre. The three Rhinemaidens ride the waves and appear by the pyre. At their appearance Hagen—Siegfried's murderer—is seized with alarm. He flings away his spear, shield, and helmet, and madly plunges into the flood, crying:

Strings, upward running-notes. Crescendo.

Hagen

Zurück vom Ring!	Away from the Ring!

Two Rhinemaidens grab Hagen around the neck and drag him down into the water. A Rhinemaiden exultantly holds up the recovered Ring.

Downward strings and decrescendo depict drowning. Oboes and clarinets, lilting "Rhine-maidens."

"Rhinemaidens"

Through the bank of clouds which lie on the horizon, a red glow breaks forth with increasing brightness.

Brasses, solemn "Valhalla."

"Valhalla"

In its light, the Rhine is observed to have returned to its bed, and the Rhinemaidens are circling and playing with the Ring in the calm water.

Interweaving of leitmotifs:
Oboes and clarinets, "Rhinemaidens"; violins, "Redemption by love"; brasses, "Valhalla."

From the ruins of the half-burned castle, the men and women perceive the red glow in the heavens, in which appears the castle of Valhalla, where the gods and heroes are sitting together.

Crescendo.
Trumpets and trombones, *f*, "Siegfried."

"Siegfried"

Bright flames seize Valhalla. The curtain falls as the gods become entirely hidden by the flames.

Violins, *p*, "Redemption by love."

Basic Term

If you aren't sure what the following word means, look back at the text, where it appears in bold type. Additional information can be found by checking the index.

leitmotif

THE TWENTIETH CENTURY

Joseph Wolins, *Trio 1942*. The years following 1900 brought radical new developments in the arts (Joseph Wolins).

[1] MUSICAL STYLES: 1900–1950

The years 1900 to 1913 brought radical new developments in science and art. During the period preceding World War I, discoveries were made that overturned long-held beliefs. Sigmund Freud explored the unconscious and developed psychoanalysis, and Albert Einstein revolutionized the view of the universe with his "Special Theory of Relativity." Pablo Picasso's painting and sculpture distorted human figures and objects with unprecedented daring, showing them from several angles at one time; Wassily Kandinsky's abstract paintings no longer tried to represent the visual world.

In music, too, the early twentieth century was a time of revolt. The years following 1900 saw more fundamental changes in the language of music than any time since the beginning of the Baroque era. There were entirely new approaches to the organization of pitch and rhythm and a vast expansion in the vocabulary of sounds used, especially percussive sounds. Some compositions so broke with tradition that they were met with violent hostility. The most famous riot in music history occurred in Paris on May 29, 1913, at the premiere of Igor Stravinsky's ballet *The Rite of Spring* (*Le Sacre du printemps*). Police had to be called in as hecklers booed, laughed, made animal noises, and actually fought with those in the audience who wanted to hear Stravinsky's evocation of primitive rites. One music critic complained that *The Rite of Spring* produced the "sensation of acute and almost cruel dissonance" and that "from the first measure to the last, whatever note one expects is never the one that comes. . . ." Another wrote, "To say that much of it is hideous in sound is a mild description. . . . It has no relation to music at all as most of us understand the word."

Today, we are amused by the initial failure of some music critics to understand this composition, now recognized to be a masterpiece. Chords, rhythms, and percussive sounds that were baffling in 1913 are now commonly heard in jazz, rock, and music for movies and television. But the hostile critics of the early 1900s were right in seeing that a great transformation in musical language was taking place.

From the late 1600s to about 1900, musical structure was governed by certain general principles. As different as the works of Bach, Beethoven, and Brahms may be, they share fundamental techniques of organizing pitches around a central tone. After 1900, however, no single system governs the organization of pitch in all musical compositions. Each piece is more likely to have a system of pitch relationships unique to that particular piece.

In the past, composers depended on the listener's awareness—conscious or unconscious—of general principles underlying the interrelationship of tones and chords. For example, they relied on the listener's expectation that a dominant chord would normally be followed by a tonic chord. By substituting another chord for the expected one, the composer could create a feeling of suspense, drama, or surprise. Twentieth-century music relies less on preestablished relationships and expectations. Listeners are guided by musical cues contained only within an individual composition. This new approach to the organization of sound makes twentieth-century music fascinating. When we listen openly, with no assumptions about how tones "should" relate, modern music is an adventure.

We'll now focus on music from 1900 to 1950. Music after 1950 is discussed in section 14.

1900–1950: An Age of Musical Diversity

The range of musical styles during the first half of our century was vast. The stylistic diversity in the works of Claude Debussy, Igor Stravinsky, Arnold Schoenberg, Alban Berg, Anton Webern, Béla Bartók, Charles Ives, and Aaron Copland—to name only composers studied here—is a continuation and intensification of the diversity we've seen in Romantic music. During the twentieth century, differences among styles are so great that it seems as though composers use different musical languages, not merely different dialects of the same musical language. Radical changes of style occur even within the works of individual composers.

Such great variety of musical styles reflected the diversity of life during the early twentieth century. More people were free to choose where to live, how to earn a living, and how to spend their time. The automobile, airplane, telephone, phonograph, movies, and radio all made the world seem smaller and expanded the range of experiences.

Through the work of scholars and performers, a wider range of music became available. Composers drew inspiration from an enormous variety of sources, including folk and popular music from all over the world, the music of Asia and Africa, and European art music from the Middle Ages through the nineteenth century.

Elements of folk and popular music were often incorporated within personal styles. Composers were attracted especially to unconventional rhythms, sounds, and melodic patterns that deviated from the common practice of Western music. Folk music was studied more systematically than ever before, and scholars now could record the actual sounds of peasant songs. One of the greatest twentieth-century composers, Béla Bartók, was also a leading scholar of the peasant music of his native Hungary and other parts of Eastern Europe. "Studies of folk music in the countryside," he wrote, "are as necessary to me as fresh air is to other people." Bartók's imagination was fired by Hungarian, Bulgarian, and Rumanian folk songs, and he believed that peasant music provided "the ideal starting point for a musical renaissance." Other composers stimulated by folklore were Stravinsky, who drew upon the folk songs of his native Russia, and Charles Ives, who used American revival hymns, ragtime, and patriotic songs.

1900–1950: An Age of Musical Diversity

NU DESCENDANT UN ESCALIER

Marcel Duchamp in *Nude Descending a Staircase No. 2* (1912) (left) and
Picasso in *Seated Woman, 1927* (above) distorted human figures and objects
with unprecedented daring (Philadelphia Museum of Art; Art Gallery of Ontario).

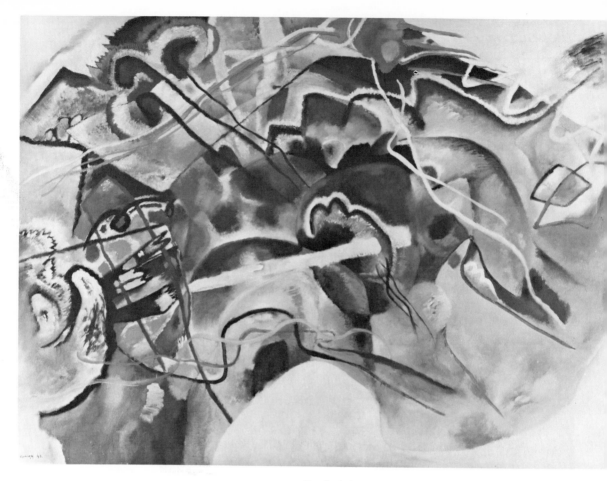

Kandinsky's abstract paintings, such as *Picture with White
Border, No. 173* (1913), no longer tried to represent the
visual world (The Solomon R. Guggenheim Museum).

During the early twentieth century, non-European music had a deep influence on the music of the West. Composers and painters were more receptive and sympathetic to Asian and African cultures than they had been earlier. For example, in 1862, Hector Berlioz could say that "the Chinese sing like dogs howling, like a cat screeching when it has swallowed a toad." But in 1889, Debussy was delighted by the Javanese music he heard at the Paris International Exhibition. "If we listen without European prejudice to the charm of their percussion," he wrote later, "we must confess that our percussion is like primitive noises at a country fair." Echoes of the gamelan (Indonesian orchestra) can be heard in the bell-like sounds and five-tone melodic patterns of Debussy's piano piece *Pagodes* (*Pagodas*, 1903). Another composer influenced by Asian culture is the Frenchman Olivier Messiaen (b. 1908), whose novel rhythmic procedures grew out of his study of Indian music.

American jazz is another non-European influence on twentieth-century composers. Musicians were fascinated by its syncopated rhythms and improvisational quality, as well as by the unique tone colors of jazz bands. Unlike a string-dominated symphony orchestra, a jazz band emphasizes woodwinds, brasses, and percussion.

Jazz elements were used in works as early as Debussy's "Golliwog's Cake Walk" (from the suite *Children's Corner*, 1908) and Stravinsky's "Ragtime" (from *The Soldier's Tale*, 1918). But the peak of jazz influence came during the "Jazz Age" of the 1920s, with works such as the ballet *The Creation of the World* (*La Création du monde*, 1923) by the Frenchman Darius Milhaud and *Piano Concerto* (1926) by the American Aaron Copland. For Americans, jazz idioms represented a kind of musical nationalism, a search for an "American sound." For European composers, it was a kind of musical exoticism. During the 1920s and 1930s, popular composers such as George Gershwin (1898–1937) used jazz and popular elements within "classical" forms. His *Rhapsody in Blue* (1924) and the opera *Porgy and Bess* (1934–1935) are well known.

Modern composers can also draw inspiration from a wider historical range of music. During the twentieth century, music from remote times has been unearthed by scholars and then published, performed, and recorded. There has been a rediscovery of earlier masters like Perotin and Machaut from the medieval period, Josquin des Prez and Gesualdo from the Renaissance, and Purcell and Vivaldi from the Baroque. Some leading modern composers have been music historians, like Anton Webern, or experts in the performance of "old" music, like Paul Hindemith.

Music from the past is a fruitful source of forms, rhythms, tone colors, textures, and compositional techniques. Baroque dances like the gavotte and gigue and forms like the passacaglia and concerto grosso are being used again. The long-forgotten harpsichord has been put to new use in compositions such as Elliott Carter's Sonata for Flute, Cello, Oboe and Harpsichord (1952), which we'll study. In the *Classical Symphony* (1917) by the Russian composer Sergei Prokofiev (1891–1953), a Classical orchestra is used, and the texture is light and transparent like much late eighteenth-century music. Occasionally a twentieth-century composer uses themes of earlier composers, as Stravinsky did in his ballet *Pulcinella* (1920), which is based on music by Giovanni Battista Pergolesi (1710–1736).

While modern compositions may be inspired by older music, they do not simply imitate past styles. Instead, a traditional form might be used with harmonies, rhythms, melodies, and tone colors that would have been inconceivable before the twentieth century.

Modern composers were also influenced by the music of the immediate past. Nineteenth-century composers such as Wagner, Brahms, Mahler, Richard Strauss, and Mussorgsky were musical points of departure for composers of the early twentieth century. Wagner's music, in particular, was as potent an influence as Beethoven's was for Romantic musicians. Composers took Wagner's style as a departure point or violently reacted against all he stood for.

Having reviewed some sources of inspiration for twentieth-century music, let's now examine some of its musical characteristics.

Tone Color

During the twentieth century tone color has become a more important element of music than ever before. Its role is often major, creating variety, continuity, and mood. In Webern's *Orchestral Piece*, Op. 10, No. 3 (1913), for example, the use of eerie, bell-like sounds at the beginning and end is vital to the form. If this composition were altered in tone color by being played on a piano, it would lose much. An orchestral work from an earlier period, say Beethoven's Fifth Symphony, suffers less in a piano arrangement.

In modern music, noiselike and percussive sounds are often used, and instruments are played at the very top or bottom of their ranges. Uncommon playing techniques have become normal. For example, the **glissando,** a rapid slide up or down a scale, is more widely used. Woodwind and brass players are often asked to produce a fluttery sound by rapidly rolling their tongues while they play. And string players frequently strike the strings with the stick, rather than with the hair of the bow.

Percussion instruments have become prominent and numerous, reflecting twentieth-century interest in unusual rhythms and tone colors. Instruments that have become standard during the 1900s include the xylophone, celesta, and wood block, to name a few. Composers occasionally call for noisemakers— typewriters, sirens, and automobile brake drums. A piano is often used to add a percussive edge to the sound of an orchestra. Modern composers often draw hard, drumlike sounds from the piano, in contrast to the Romantics, who wanted the instrument to "sing." Besides expanding the percussion section of the orchestra, early twentieth-century composers wrote works for unconventional performing groups in which percussion plays a major role. Well-known examples are Stravinsky's *The Wedding* (*Les Noces,* 1914–1923) for vocal soloists, chorus, four pianos, and percussion, Bartók's *Music for Strings, Percussion and Celesta* (1936), and Varèse's *Ionization* (1931), one of the first works for percussion ensemble.

Modern orchestral and chamber works often sound transparent; individual tone colors are heard clearly. To bring out the individuality of different melodic lines that are played simultaneously, a composer will often assign each line to a different timbre. In general, there is less emphasis on blended sound than during the Romantic period. Many twentieth-century works are written for nonstandard chamber groups made up of instruments with sharply contrasting tone colors. Stravinsky's *The Soldier's Tale* (*L'Histoire du soldat*, 1918) for example, is scored for violin, double bass, clarinet, bassoon, cornet, trombone, and percussion. Even orchestral works often sound as though they are scored for a group of soloists.

Harmony

Consonance and Dissonance

The twentieth century brought fundamental changes in the way chords are treated. Up to about 1900, chords were divided into two opposing types: consonant and dissonant. A consonant chord was stable; it functioned as a point of rest or arrival. A dissonant chord was unstable; its tension demanded onward motion, or resolution to a stable, consonant chord. Traditionally, only the triad, a three-tone chord, could be consonant. All others were considered dissonant. In the nineteenth century, composers came to use ever more dissonant chords, and they treated dissonances with increasing freedom. By the early twentieth century, the traditional distinction between consonance and dissonance was abandoned in much music. A combination of tones that earlier would have been used to generate instability and expectation might now be treated as a stable chord, a point of arrival. In Stravinsky's words, dissonance "is no longer tied down to its former function. Having become an entity in itself, it frequently happens that dissonance neither prepares nor anticipates anything. Dissonance is thus no more an agent of disorder than consonance is a guarantee of security."

This "emancipation of the dissonance" does not prevent composers from differentiating between chords of greater or lesser tension. Relatively mild-sounding chords may be goals of motion, while harsher chords are used for transitional sounds. But no longer is there a general principle that determines whether a chord is stable or not. It is now entirely up to the composer's discretion. "We find ourself confronted with a new logic of music that would have appeared unthinkable to the masters of the past," wrote Stravinsky. "This new logic has opened our eyes to riches whose existence we never suspected."

New Chord Structures

Before 1900, there were general principles governing chord construction: certain combinations of tones were considered chords, while others were not. At the core of traditional harmony is the triad. A triad might be made up of alternate tones of a major scale, such as the first (*do*), third (*mi*), and fifth (*sol*). Within a triad, there are two intervals of a third.

While the triad often appears in twentieth-century music, it no longer is so fundamental.

Some twentieth-century composers create fresh harmonies by placing one traditional chord against another. Such a combination of two chords heard at the same time is called a **polychord.**

Copland, *Appalachian Spring*

A polychord can be heard either as a single block of sound or as two distinct layers, depending on whether the two combined chords contrast in tone color and register.

Another development of twentieth-century music is the use of chordal structures *not* based on triads. One used commonly is the **fourth chord,** in which the tones are a fourth apart, instead of a third. (From *do* to *fa,* or from *re* to *sol,* is an interval of a fourth.)

Ives, *The Cage*

Harmonic resources have been extended also through the **tone cluster,** a chord made up of tones only a half step or a whole step apart. A tone cluster can be produced on a piano by striking a group of adjacent keys with the fist or forearm.

Ives, *The Majority*

Alternatives to the Traditional Tonal System

In addition to creating new chord structures, twentieth-century composers explored alternatives to the traditional tonal system. Known as tonality or key, this system of tonal gravity governed the organization of pitch from the 1600s to about 1900. By the late nineteenth century, the gravitational pull of a central tonality had been weakened by rapid and frequent key shifts. After 1900, some composers continued to use the traditional system, but others modified it greatly. Still others discarded it entirely.

Before looking at new approaches to pitch organization, recall the basic principles of the traditional tonal system. As we saw in the Elements section, *tonality,* or *key,* refers to the use of a central tone, scale, and chord within a composition. The central tone, called the *tonic* or *keynote* (*do*), is the composition's resting point. The tonic major or minor scale and the tonic triad are built on this tone. Since the tonic triad is stable and restful, compositions almost always ended with it. Next in importance to the tonic triad is the *dominant chord,* which is built on the fifth (*sol*) tone of the tonic scale. There is a special gravitational pull from the dominant chord toward the tonic chord, and the motion from dominant to tonic is the essential chord progression of the tonal system. This cadence provides a strong sense of conclusion, and traditionally it was used to round off melodies, sections, and entire pieces. In summary, the tonal system is based on a central tone, a major or minor scale, and a triad; and there is a special relationship between the tonic and dominant chords.

After 1900, this system was modified in many different ways. The new techniques of pitch organization are so varied as to resist easy generalization. We'll mention only a few of them. Some compositions have a central tone, but other traditional elements are missing, such as the tonic triad, the central major or minor scale, or the dominant-tonic relationship. This approach is reflected even in the titles of compositions, which are less likely to include the terms *major* or *minor.* For example, one Stravinsky piano piece is entitled *Serenade in A* to show that it revolves around the tone A but is not in a major or minor key.

To create fresh sounds, composers used scales other than major or minor. For example, they breathed new life into the ancient church modes, scales that had been used widely before 1600, as well as in folk songs of every period. Other scales were borrowed from the musical traditions of lands outside Western Europe, and still others were invented by composers.

Twentieth-century compositions are often organized around a central chord other than the triad. Thus, the basic chord may well be one that was considered a dissonance earlier. In some works, the traditional relationship between dominant and tonic triads is replaced by other chord relationships. Melodies, sections, or entire pieces are rounded off not by the usual dominant-tonic cadence, but by other chord progressions.

Another twentieth-century approach to pitch organization is **polytonality,** the use of two or more keys at one time. When only two different keys are used at once—as is most common—the technique is called **bitonality.** A famous bitonal passage occurs in Stravinsky's ballet *Petrushka,* when one clarinet plays in C major and another plays in F-sharp major.

Alternatives to the
Traditional Tonal
System

In general, the greater the contrast of tone color, register, and rhythm between the different layers of sound, the more we can hear the different keys.

A further departure from tradition is **atonality,** the absence of tonality or key. Atonality was foreshadowed in nineteenth-century works such as Wagner's *Tristan and Isolde,* where the pull of a central key is weakened by frequent modulations and by liberal use of all twelve tones in the chromatic scale. Arnold Schoenberg wrote the first significant atonal pieces around 1908. He avoided traditional chord progressions in these works and used all twelve tones without regard to their traditional relationship to major or minor scales. But atonality is not a specific technique of composition; each atonal work is structured according to its needs. (Though the word *atonality* is imprecise and negative, no other term has yet come into general use.)

Before long Schoenberg felt the need for a more systematic approach to atonal composition, and during the early 1920s he developed the *twelve-tone system,* a new technique of pitch organization. This system gives equal prominence to each of the twelve chromatic tones, rather than singling out one pitch, as the tonal system does. For about twenty years, only Schoenberg and a few disciples used the twelve-tone system, but during the 1950s it came to be used by composers all over the world.

Rhythm

The new techniques of pitch organization were accompanied by new ways to organize rhythm. Music's rhythmic vocabulary was expanded, with increased emphasis on irregularity and unpredictability. Rhythm is one of the most striking elements of twentieth-century music; it is used to generate power, drive, and excitement.

In the twentieth century, new rhythmic procedures are drawn from many sources, including folk music from all over the world, jazz, and European art music from the Middle Ages through the nineteenth century. Béla Bartók used the "free and varied rhythmic structures" of East European peasant music. The syncopations and complex rhythmic combinations of jazz fired the imagination of Stravinsky and Copland. And irregular phrase structures in Brahms's music inspired rhythmic innovations in Schoenberg's works.

Rapidly changing meters are characteristic of twentieth-century music, while Baroque, Classical, and Romantic music maintains a single meter throughout a movement or section. Before the twentieth century, beats were organized into regularly recurring groups; the accented beat came at equal time intervals. Rhythmic irregularities such as syncopations or accents on weak beats were heard against a pervasive meter. But in many twentieth-century compositions, beats are grouped irregularly, and the accented beat comes at unequal time intervals. In some modern music the meter changes with almost every bar, so that we might count *1–2–3, 1–2–3–4–5, 1–2–3–4–5, 1–2–3, 1–2–3–4, 1–2–3–4–5, 1–2–3–4–5–6, 1–2–3–4–5, 1–2, 1–2–3–4–5–6*.

Stravinsky, "The Game of Abduction" from *The Rite of Spring*

Count this again quickly and experience some of the rhythmic excitement of twentieth-century music, which often has a rapid and vigorous beat with jolting accents at unexpected times.

The rhythmic resources of twentieth-century music have also been expanded through the use of unconventional meters. Along with traditional meters such as duple and triple, modern composers use meters with five or seven beats to the measure. The pulses within a measure of any length may be grouped in irregular, asymmetrical ways. For example, eight quick pulses within a measure may be subdivided $3 + 3 + 2$, or *1–2–3–4–5–6–7–8, 1–2–3–4–5–6–7–8*. This meter, common in East European folk music, is used by Bartók in one of his *Six Dances in Bulgarian Rhythm*.

Twentieth-century music often uses two or more contrasting and independent rhythms at the same time; the procedure is called **polyrhythm.** Each part of the musical texture goes its own rhythmic way, often creating accents that are out of phase with accents in the other parts. Different meters are used at the same time. For example, one instrument may play in duple meter (*1–2, 1–2*), while another plays in triple meter (*1–2–3, 1–2–3*). While polyrhythm occasionally occurs in Classical and Romantic music, it became both more common and more complex after 1900. The polyrhythms of jazz strongly influenced composers in the 1920s and 1930s.

Rhythm
383

Rhythmic repetition of a group of pitches is a widely used unifying technique in twentieth-century music. Many modern compositions contain an **ostinato,** a motive or phrase that is repeated persistently at the same pitch throughout a section. The ostinato may occur in the melody or in the accompaniment. (The accompaniment for the last music example has an eight-note ostinato: 1–2–3–4–5–6–7–8.) Ostinatos can be found in music from various periods and cultures. In twentieth-century music, they usually serve to stabilize particular groups of pitches.

Melody

The new techniques of pitch and rhythmic organization that we've surveyed had a strong impact on twentieth-century melody. Melody no longer is necessarily tied to traditional chords or major and minor keys. It may be based on a wide variety of scales or freely use all twelve chromatic tones and not have a tonal center. Melody today often contains wide leaps that are difficult to sing. Rhythmic irregularity and changing meters tend to make twentieth-century melodies unpredictable. They often consist of a series of phrases that are irregular in length. In general, twentieth-century music relies less than Classical and Romantic music on melodies that are easy to sing and remember. Melody is as rich and varied as twentieth-century music itself; neither can be classified easily.

Basic Terms

If you aren't sure what each of the following words means, look back at the text, where they appear in bold type. Additional information about some of them can be found by checking the index.

| polychord | tone cluster | bitonality | polyrhythm | glissando |
| fourth chord | polytonality | atonality | ostinato | |

[2] MUSIC AND MUSICIANS IN SOCIETY

The twentieth century has seen dramatic changes in how music reaches its listeners. The living room has become the new "concert hall" through phonograph records, tape recordings, radio, and television. These technological advances have brought music to a larger audience than ever before, as well as vastly increasing the range of music available. Today's repertory of recorded music includes not only familiar classics but also Renaissance, early Baroque, non-Western, and unconventional twentieth-century works—music not often played in concert. Recordings of such lesser-known music multiplied with the appearance of long-playing discs in 1948. But as early as 1904, composers' interpretations of their own works were recorded, giving composers an unprecedented opportunity to communicate precisely their intentions about phrasing, dynamics, and tempo.

Radio broadcasts of live or recorded music began to reach a large audience during the 1920s. In the thirties, radio networks in several countries formed orchestras specifically to broadcast live music. The best-known American ensemble of this kind was the NBC Symphony Orchestra, directed by Arturo Toscanini. In addition to such radio-sponsored groups, regular broadcasts of the Metropolitan Opera's Saturday matinee performances have made opera available to millions of people.

With television, broadcast music performances can be seen as well as heard. Christmas Eve 1951 brought the premiere of the first opera created for television, *Amahl and the Night Visitors* by Italian-American composer Gian Carlo Menotti. Other television highlights included the appearances of Leonard Bernstein conducting the New York Philharmonic Orchestra. But apart from such notable exceptions, commercial television has devoted little time to opera and symphonic music.

In the first half of this century, the concert and operatic repertory was dominated by music from earlier periods rather than by contemporary works. This was a new situation in music history. In Mozart's time, audiences demanded and got the latest music, not operas by Handel or cantatas by Bach. Even during the Romantic period, when interest in past music was high, concert programs consisted mainly of recent works.

After 1900, however, listeners and performers were often baffled by the dissonances, percussive sounds, and irregular rhythms in some of the new music. (Remember the riot at the first performance of Stravinsky's *Rite of Spring*.) To avoid alienating audiences, many conductors chose not to perform "difficult" contemporary works, favoring those that were relatively accessible in style. One result was that some of the most innovative twentieth-century composers—Ives, Webern, and Varèse, for example—were neglected.

After World War I, organizations were formed for the specific purpose of giving the public a greater opportunity to hear new music. The International Society for Contemporary Music was the most influential, with branches in many countries.

During the 1950s and 1960s, major orchestras and opera companies began to program more twentieth-century music. Long-playing recordings gave access to works that had seemed incomprehensible; they could now be played repeatedly until they were understood and enjoyed. Musicians themselves grew more accustomed to intricate modern rhythms and thus were better able to perform them.

Many modern compositions were commissioned by ballet and opera companies, foundations, orchestras, performers, film studios, and wealthy music lovers. Developments in the dance had an especially strong impact on twentieth-century music. A single company, Sergei Diaghilev's Russian Ballet,

Music and Musicians
in Society

provided the impetus for masterpieces such as Stravinsky's *Petrushka* (1911), Ravel's *Daphnis et Chloé* (1912), and Debussy's *Jeux* (1913). Films provided a new stimulus for music, too. Though most film scores were merely background music, some, like Prokofiev's *Lieutenant Kije* (1934), were enjoyed apart from the movie. Philanthropic foundations have become significant music patrons in our time. One, most active in the field of chamber music, was established by Mrs. Elizabeth Sprague Coolidge in 1925 at the Library of Congress in Washington. Mrs. Coolidge's generosity spurred the creation of many fine compositions, including Bartók's *Fifth String Quartet* (1934) and Schoenberg's *Fourth String Quartet* (1936). Yet, however important commissions have been in our century, few serious musicians can live on them alone. Most modern composers are also teachers, conductors, or performers.

Like all people, musicians have been affected by the political, economic, and social upheavals of the twentieth century. Hitler's rise to power in Germany in 1933 had an especially dramatic impact on their lives and careers. Avant-garde, socialist, and Jewish musicians were abruptly ousted from their jobs, and their works were no longer performed. Dictatorship, persecution, and the onset of World War II (1939–1945) led to the largest migration of artists and intellectuals in history. Many leading composers, including Stravinsky, Bartók, Schoenberg, and Hindemith, left Europe for the United States. Such distinguished refugees made enormous contributions to America's musical culture. Schoenberg and Hindemith, for example, taught in universities and helped train some of America's finest composers.

During this century, the United States became a potent force in music. American jazz and popular music swept the world. With more first-rank symphony orchestras than any other country, after 1920 America produced a large group of composers representing a wide spectrum of contemporary styles.

American colleges and universities have played an unusually vital role in our musical culture. They have trained and employed many of our leading composers, performers, and scholars. Music courses have expanded the horizons and interests of countless students. And since midcentury, many universities have sponsored performing groups specializing in twentieth-century music. In addition, they housed most of the electronic music studios. Thus, American colleges and universities have indirectly become patrons of music, as the church and nobility were in earlier times.

Twentieth
Century

[**3**] IMPRESSIONISM AND SYMBOLISM

Many different musical styles coexisted around the turn of the century. Among the most important was impressionism, best represented by the music of French composer Claude Debussy (1862–1918). We'll look closely at musical impressionism in section 4; first, two related, but slightly earlier artistic movements in France demand our attention: impressionist painting and symbolist poetry.

French Impressionist Painting

In 1874, a group of French painters including Claude Monet (1840–1926), Auguste Renoir (1841–1919), and Camille Pissarro (1830–1903) had an exhibition in Paris. One Monet painting entitled *Impression: Sunrise*—a misty scene of boats in port—particularly annoyed an art critic, who wrote, "Wallpaper in its embryonic state is more finished than that seascape." Using Monet's title, the critic mockingly called the entire show "the exhibition of the impressionists." The term *impressionist* stuck, but it eventually lost its derisive implication.

Today most of us appreciate impressionist paintings, which colorfully depict the joys of life and the beauties of nature. But during the 1870s, they were seen as formless collections of tiny colored patches—which they are, when viewed closely. But from a distance, the brush strokes blend and merge into recognizable forms and shimmering colors. Impressionist painters were concerned primarily with effects of light, color, and atmosphere—with impermanence, change, and fluidity. Monet created a series of twenty paintings (1892–1894) showing Rouen Cathedral at different times of the day, from dawn to dusk. In this series, the cathedral's stone facade is desolidified and looks like colored mist. (In section 4, we'll study Debussy's piano piece *The Sunken Cathedral* (1910), which is a musical analogy to Monet's cathedral paintings.) Many impressionist painters preferred to work in the open air, rather than in a studio. They were fascinated by outdoor scenes from contemporary life, picnics in the woods, and crowds on Parisian boulevards. But most of all, the impressionists were obsessed by water. Using light, pastel colors, they depicted the ripples and waves of the ocean and sailboats on the river Seine.

French Symbolist Poetry

As impressionist painters broke from traditional depictions of reality, writers called *symbolists* rebelled against the conventions of French poetry. Like the painters, poets such as Stéphane Mallarmé (1842–1898), Paul Verlaine (1844–1896), and Arthur Rimbaud (1854–1891) emphasized fluidity and suggestion. "To *name* an object," insisted Mallarmé, "is to suppress three-quarters of the enjoyment of a poem, which is made up of gradually guessing; the dream is to *suggest* it." Symbolist writers emphasized the purely musical, or sonorous, effects of words.

Claude Debussy was a close friend of many symbolist poets, especially Mallarmé, whose poem *L'Après-midi d'un faune* (*The Afternoon of a Faun*) inspired Debussy's most famous orchestral work. Many poems by Verlaine became texts for Debussy's songs. (And, more personally, Verlaine's mother-in-law was his first piano teacher.) Both impressionist painting and symbolist poetry were

French Symbolist
Poetry

387

catalysts for many developments during the twentieth century. The next section describes their effect on music.

CLAUDE DEBUSSY

French impressionist composer Claude Debussy (1862–1918) linked the Romantic era with the twentieth century. He was born in St. Germain-en-Laye, a small town near Paris. At the early age of ten, he entered the Paris Conservatory, where he studied until he was twenty-two. Debussy's teachers regarded him as a talented rebel who improvised unorthodox chord progressions of dissonances that did not resolve. (While Debussy was at the Conservatory, the impressionists exhibited their paintings in Paris.)

In his late teens, Debussy worked summers as pianist for Mme. von Meck, the Russian patroness of Tchaikovsky. During these stays in Russia, Debussy's lifelong interest in Russian music took root. In 1884, he won France's highest award for composers, the Prix de Rome, which subsidized three years of study in the Eternal City. But he left Italy after only two years because he lacked musical inspiration away from his beloved Paris.

When Debussy returned to Paris in 1887, the music and ideas of Richard Wagner had a profound influence on French composers and writers. Many of Debussy's friends wrote articles for *The Wagnerian Review* (*La Revue Wagnérienne*), a periodical devoted to the German master. During the summers of 1888 and 1889, Debussy traveled to Bayreuth, Germany, to hear Wagner's music dramas. They were memorable events for the young Frenchman, who was both attracted and repelled by Wagner's music.

Oriental music performed at the Paris International Exhibition of 1889 also had a strong impact on Debussy. "Do you not remember the Javanese music," he wrote a friend, "able to express every shade of meaning . . . and which makes our tonic and dominant seem like ghosts."

For years Debussy led an unsettled life, earning a small income by teaching piano. His friends were mostly writers, such as Stéphane Mallarmé, whose literary gatherings he attended regularly. In cafes and cabarets he mingled with jockeys and entertainers like those immortalized in the paintings of Toulouse-Lautrec. Until the age of thirty-one, he was little known to the musical public and not completely sure of himself. "There are still things that I am not able to do—create masterpieces for example," he wrote in 1893. But that same year Debussy did complete a masterpiece, the *String Quartet*. And in 1894 he created another, the tone poem *Prelude to "The Afternoon of a Faun,"* which has become his most popular orchestral work.

A dramatic turning point in Debussy's career came in 1902, with his opera *Pelléas et Mélisande*. Critics were sharply divided. Some complained about the absence of melody and the harmonies that broke traditional rules; others were delighted by the poetic atmosphere and subtle tone colors. The opera soon caught on, and Debussy was recognized as France's leading composer. Musicians all over the world imitated his style.

This artistic triumph was surrounded by a personal life filled with financial and emotional crises. Debussy constantly borrowed money for luxuries he craved: fine food, beautiful clothes, and art works. The attempted suicides of two women in his life were major scandals in Paris. His longtime mistress shot herself when he left her for Rosalie Texier, a milliner who became his first wife. Then Rosalie Texier, in turn, shot herself when Debussy left *her* for Emma Bardac, an intelligent, talented, and rich society woman.

Debussy's marriage to Emma Bardac caused him to undertake concert tours to maintain their high standard of living. Though he was not gifted as a conductor and hated appearing in public, he presented his music throughout Europe. At fifty he developed cancer. The onset of World War I in 1914 heightened his sense of nationalism, and he began to sign his works "Claude Debussy, French musician." He died in Paris on March 25, 1918, while the city was being shelled by German artillery.

Debussy's Music

Like the French impressionist painters and symbolist poets, Debussy was a master at evoking a fleeting mood and misty atmosphere. His interest in the effects of fluidity, intangibility, and impermanence is mirrored even in his titles: *Reflections in the Water* (*Reflets dans l'eau*), *Clouds* (*Nuages*), and *The Sounds and the Perfumes Swirl in the Evening Air* (*Les sons et les parfums tournent dans l'air du soir*). Literary and pictorial ideas often inspired Debussy, and most of his compositions have descriptive titles. His music sounds free and spontaneous, almost improvised. He once wrote, "I am more and more convinced that music is not, in essence, a thing which can be cast into a traditional and fixed form. It is made up of colors and rhythms." This stress on tone color, atmosphere, and fluidity is characteristic of **impressionism** in music.

Tone color truly gets unprecedented attention in Debussy's works. His subtle changes of timbre are as crucial to his music as thematic contrasts are in earlier music. The sensuous, beautiful sound he sought is never harsh. The entire orchestra seldom plays together to produce massive sound. Instead, there are brief but frequent instrumental solos. The woodwinds are especially prominent and are used in unusual registers. (The velvety low register of the flute is featured in the *Prelude to "The Afternoon of a Faun."*) Strings and brasses are often muted; their sound seems to come from far off. Atmosphere is created through the shimmer of a string tremolo or the splash of a harp.

Debussy wrote some of his finest music for piano, again creating new sonorities. Frequent use of the damper pedal, which allows a pianist to sustain tones after the keys are released, results in hazy sounds. Chords are often blended together, and the pianist is directed to let the sounds vibrate. The rich variety of bell and gong sounds in Debussy's piano works may reflect the influence of Asian music he heard at the Paris International Exposition in 1889.

Debussy's treatment of harmony was a revolutionary aspect of musical impressionism. He tends to use a chord more for its special color and sensuous quality than for its function in a standard harmonic progression. He uses successions of dissonant chords that do not resolve. (When young, Debussy was asked which harmonic rules he followed; he replied, simply, "My pleasure.") He freely shifts a dissonant chord up or down the scale, and such parallel chords characterize his style.

Debussy, *The Sunken Cathedral*

Debussy's harmonic vocabulary is large. Along with traditional three- and four-note chords, he uses five-note chords with a lush, rich sound. Chord progressions that were highly unorthodox when Debussy wrote them soon came to seem mild and natural.

"One must drown the sense of tonality," Debussy wrote. While he never actually abandoned tonality, Debussy weakened it by deliberately avoiding chord progressions that strongly affirm the key. The traditional dominant-tonic cadence is relatively rare in his music. He also "drowns" tonality by using scales in which the main tone is less emphasized than in major or minor scales. He turned to the medieval church modes, which he knew from Gregorian chant. He also used the pentatonic, or five-tone, scales heard in Javanese music. These pentatonic scales lend an Oriental atmosphere to some of Debussy's music. (A pentatonic scale is produced by five successive black keys of the piano: F♯–G♯–A♯–C♯–D♯.)

Debussy's most unusual and tonally vague scale is the **whole-tone scale,** made up of six different notes each a whole step away from the next (C–D–E–F♯–G♯–A♯–C). Unlike major and minor, the whole-tone scale has no special pull from *ti* to *do*, since its tones are all the same distance apart. And because no single tone stands out, the scale creates a blurred, indistinct effect.

Debussy, *Voiles* (Sails)

The pulse in Debussy's music is sometimes as vague as tonality. "Rhythms cannot be contained within bars," he wrote. He avoids recurring strong accents that coincide with the bar line. His rhythmic flexibility reflects the fluid, unaccented quality of the French language. In fact, few composers have set French to music so sensitively as Debussy. He composed fifty-nine art songs, many of which are set to symbolist poems by Charles Baudelaire, Paul Verlaine, and Stéphane Mallarmé. His only opera, *Pelléas et Mélisande,* is an almost word-for-word setting of a symbolist play by the Belgian poet Maurice Maeterlinck. This great and highly original opera is the essence of musical impressionism. Its vague, mysterious plot includes characters who barely communicate with each other. There are no arias, and the melodic line is almost entirely speechlike. The play's dreamlike atmosphere is magically evoked by an orchestral accompaniment that is discreet and understated; it's as though Debussy consciously sought to avoid the powerful sound of Wagner's orchestral parts.

While not large, Debussy's output is remarkably varied. Along with his opera, he contributed masterpieces to the literature of the piano, orchestra, chamber ensemble, and art song. We have said that Debussy's music is tonally vague and has an improvisational, floating quality. It's not surprising, then, that he avoided sonata form, which traditionally calls for a clear contrast of keys and systematic development of themes. One section of Debussy's music melts into the next; melodic lines tend to be brief and fragmentary.

Echoes of Debussy's music can be heard in the works of many composers during the first two decades of the twentieth century. However, no other leading musician can so fairly be described as an impressionist. Even the composer most similar to Debussy, his younger French contemporary Maurice Ravel (1875–1937), wrote music with greater clarity of form. Debussy's impressionist style was both a final expression of Romanticism and the beginning of a new era. His use of tone color as a vital element of form and his novel harmonic techniques made him the immediate forerunner of later twentieth-century musicians. Igor Stravinsky was perceptive when he remarked, "I and the members of my generation owe most to Debussy."

Prelude to "The Afternoon of a Faun" (*Prélude à "L'Après-midi d'un faune"*)

"The music of this Prelude," wrote Debussy, "is a very free illustration of the beautiful poem by Stéphane Mallarmé, *The Afternoon of a Faun.*" This poem evokes the dreams and erotic fantasies of a pagan forest creature who is half man, half goat. While playing "a long solo" on his flute, the intoxicated faun tries to recall whether he actually carried off two beautiful nymphs or only dreamed of doing so. Exhausted by the effort, he falls back to sleep in the warm sunshine.

Debussy intended his music to suggest "the successive scenes through which pass the desires and dreams of the faun in the heat of this afternoon." The subtle, sensuous timbres of this miniature tone poem were new in Debussy's day. Woodwind solos, muted horn calls, and harp glissandos create a rich variety of delicate sounds. The dynamics are usually subdued, and the entire

Prelude to "The Afternoon of a Faun" (Prélude à "L'Après-midi d'un faune")

orchestra—from which trombones, trumpets, and timpani are excluded—rarely plays at one time. The music often swells sensuously, only to subside in voluptuous exhaustion.

The Prelude begins with an unaccompanied flute melody; its vague pulse and tonality make it dreamlike and improvisatory. This flute melody is heard again and again, faster, slower, and against a variety of lush chords. Though the form of the Prelude may be thought of as A B A', one section blends with the next. It has a continuous ebb and flow. The fluidity and weightlessness typical of impressionism are found in this music. We are never tempted to beat time to its subtle rhythms. The Prelude ends magically with the main melody, played by muted horns, seeming to come from far off. The bell-like tones of antique cymbals finally evaporate into silence. With all its new sounds and musical techniques, the piece has aptly been described as a "quiet revolution" in the history of music.

LISTENING OUTLINE
To be read while music is heard

Prelude to "The Afternoon of a Faun" (*Prélude à "L'Après-midi d'un faune"; 1894*) by Claude Debussy

At a very moderate tempo, A B A' form, E major

3 flutes, 2 oboes, 1 English horn, 2 clarinets, 2 bassoons, 4 horns, 2 harps, antique cymbals, violins 1, violins 2, violas, cellos, double basses

(About 10 min)

A   1   *a.* Solo flute, *p*, main melody.

       Harp glissando; soft horn calls. Short pause. Harp glissando; soft horn calls.
   b. Flute, *p*, main melody; tremolo strings in background. Oboe, *p*, continues melody. Orchestra swells to *f*. Solo clarinet fades into
   c. Flute, *p*, main melody varied and expanded; harp and muted strings accompany. Flute melody comes to quiet close.
  2   *a.* Clarinet; harp and cellos in background.
   b. New oboe melody.

Violins take up melody, crescendo and accelerando to climax. Excitement subsides. retardando. Clarinet, *p*, leads into

B   3   *a.* Woodwinds, *p*, legato melody in long notes. Crescendo.

          b. Strings repeat melody; harps and pulsating woodwinds in background, crescendo. Decrescendo. Horns, *p*, solo violin, *p*, clarinet, oboe.

A′   4   *a.* Harp accompanies flute, *p*, main melody in longer notes. Oboe, staccato woodwinds.

          b. Harp accompanies oboe, *p*, main melody in longer notes. English horn, harp glissando.

     5   *a.* Antique cymbals, bell-like tones. Flutes, *p*, main melody. Solo violins, *pp*, in high register.

          b. Flute and solo cello, main melody; harp in background.

          c. Oboe, *p*, brings melody to close. Harps, *p*.

          d. Muted horns and violins, *ppp*, beginning of main melody sounding far off. Flute, antique cymbals, and harp; delicate tones fade into silence.

The Sunken Cathedral (*La Cathédrale engloutie*), from *Preludes* for piano (Book I, 1910)

This piano piece was inspired by a French legend about the Cathedral of Ys, which had sunk beneath the sea. According to legend, the cathedral sometimes rises, its bells tolling and its priests chanting a hymn. Then it slowly sinks back beneath the waves.

Debussy uses the piano's damper pedal to create lingering vibrations that suggest different effects, including waves, mist, the murmur of the sea, and a variety of bells. The opening is "profoundly calm, in a softly sonorous mist." Mysterious bell-tolls merge with legato, upward-moving chords that have a hollow sound.

The Sunken Cathedral
(*La Cathédrale
engloutie*), from
Preludes for piano
(Book I, 1910)

393

The music "gradually comes out of the mist," as low rumbling sounds depict waves. With a crescendo the bell sounds grow richer and more sonorous. Then the cathedral is suggested by a majestic, hymnlike melody accompanied by deep, repeated bell-tolls in the bass.

In this hymnlike passage, the chords move in parallel motion; that is, the same chord structure is shifted to different pitch levels. This technique is characteristic of impressionist style.

Debussy suggests the cathedral's return to the ocean depths by a faint echo of the hymnlike melody. Now it is muffled, in a lower register, and accompanied by a murmuring repeated figure in the bass. The piece ends "in the sonority of the beginning" with legato upward-moving chords (now slightly dissonant) and quiet bell sounds.

 Basic Terms

If you aren't sure what each of the following words means, look back at the text, where they appear in bold type. Additional information can be found by checking the index.

impressionism
whole-tone scale

NEOCLASSICISM [5]

From about 1920 to 1950 the music of many composers, including Igor Stravinsky and Paul Hindemith, reflected an artistic movement known as **neoclassicism.** Neoclassicism is marked by emotional restraint, balance, and clarity; neoclassical compositions use musical forms and stylistic features of earlier periods, particularly of the eighteenth century. Stravinsky summed it up: "I attempted to build a new music on eighteenth-century classicism." Neoclassical music is not merely a revival of old forms and styles; it uses earlier techniques to organize twentieth-century harmonies and rhythms.

"Back to Bach" was the slogan of this movement that reacted against Romanticism and impressionism. (Since many neoclassical compositions were modeled after Bach's music, the term *neobaroque* might have been more appropriate.) Neoclassical composers turned away from program music and the gigantic orchestras favored at the turn of the century. They preferred absolute (nonprogrammatic) music for chamber groups. This preference for smaller performing groups partly reflected economic necessity: during the post-World War I period, economic conditions were so bad in parts of Europe that there was little money to hire large orchestras. Favoring clear polyphonic textures, composers wrote fugues, concerto grossos, and Baroque dance suites. Most neoclassical music was tonal and used major and minor scales. Still, neoclassicism was more an attitude than a style. Schoenberg wrote minuets and gigues using his twelve-tone system. And though neoclassical composers referred to many past styles, their works sound completely modern. They play on the delightful tension between our expectations about old forms and styles and the novel harmonies and rhythms. In section 6, we'll study a neoclassical work by Stravinsky, the *Symphony of Psalms* (1930).

Neoclassicism was an important trend in other arts, too. Poet T. S. Eliot often quoted and alluded to earlier writers. Picasso, who designed sets for Stravinsky's first neoclassical work, *Pulcinella* (1920), went through a phase where he created paintings that show the influence of ancient Greek art. Picasso described the neoclassical attitude by saying that artists "must pick out what is good for us where we find it. When I am shown a portfolio of old drawings, for instance, I have no qualms about taking anything I want from them."

Neoclassicism

395

Basic Term

If you aren't sure what the following word means, look back at the text, where it appears in bold type. Additional information can be found by checking the index.

neoclassicism

[6] IGOR STRAVINSKY

Even before his death in 1971 at the age of eighty-eight, Igor Stravinsky (1882–1971) was a legendary figure regarded as the world's greatest composer. His once revolutionary works were modern classics; he was a restless innovator who influenced three generations of composers and inspired many painters, writers, and choreographers. Cultural giants like Picasso and T. S. Eliot were his friends; President and Mrs. John F. Kennedy honored him at a White House dinner in his eightieth year.

Born in a small town near St. Petersburg (Leningrad), Russia, Stravinsky grew up in a musical atmosphere. His father was a leading singer at the St. Petersburg opera. Despite Stravinsky's obvious talent, his parents insisted that he study law at the University of St. Petersburg. Soon he began to neglect his studies and devote himself to composition. At twenty-one, he became a private student of Nikolai Rimsky-Korsakov.

Stravinsky's life took a sudden turn in 1909, when the great impresario Sergei Diaghilev heard his music at a concert in St. Petersburg. Diaghilev was director of the Russian Ballet. Based in Paris, this troupe had a powerful impact on both Stravinsky and the entire cultural scene in Europe from 1909 to 1929. It employed great masters in all arts. Its dancers included Vaslav Nijinsky, and choreographers Mikhail Fokine and George Balanchine created works for the troupe. It commissioned stage designs from great painters like Picasso and ballet music from outstanding musicians like Stravinsky, Debussy, Ravel, and Prokofiev. Diaghilev asked twenty-six-year-old Stravinsky to orchestrate piano pieces by Chopin as ballet music for the first season of the Russian Ballet in 1909. In 1910, Stravinsky was commissioned to compose an original ballet, *The Firebird*. Based on a Russian fairy tale, this ballet's immense success immediately established Stravinsky as a leading young composer. His second ballet, *Petrushka* (1911), was performed a year later, and at twenty-nine Stravinsky was hailed as a modern master. His incisive rhythms, witty musical satire, and brilliant orchestral colors delighted sophisticated Parisians.

Igor Stravinsky in a sketch by Picasso (Omikron).

A now-legendary riot erupted in the audience when Stravinsky's third ballet, *The Rite of Spring*, was performed in Paris in 1913. We've already described how spectators hissed and booed at the music's "primitive" evocation of pagan fertility rites, at its harshly insistent dissonance, at its percussiveness and pounding rhythms. One audience member reported that someone excitedly "began to beat rhythmically on top of my head with his fists. My emotion was so great that I did not feel the blows." Soon after, however, the ballet was recognized as a masterpiece; it influenced composers all over the world.

The outbreak of World War I in 1914 forced Stravinsky to seek refuge in neutral Switzerland, where he lived for six years with his wife and children. Since the Russian Revolution of 1917 ended his private income, he met financial difficulties for the first time in his life. To "escape from this alarming situation," Stravinsky wrote *The Soldier's Tale* (1918), a theatrical work that required few performers and was easy to present under wartime conditions.

Igor Stravinsky

397

After the armistice in 1918, Stravinsky moved to France, his home until the onset of World War II. Now Stravinsky was an international figure, constantly touring Europe and the United States to play and conduct his music. His voluntary exile from Russia coincided with his turning away from Russian folk music as a source of inspiration. Stravinsky's works in the twenties and thirties seemed excessively cool and objective to some music lovers, who preferred the early Russian-flavored ballets.

Unlike his great contemporaries Schoenberg and Bartók, Stravinsky got well-paying commissions for his work and was an astute businessman. He described himself as composing "every day, regularly, like a man with banking hours." Stravinsky's love of order and discipline was reflected in his studio, which had, in the words of a friend, "all the instruments needed for writing, copying, drawing, pasting, cutting, clipping, filing, sharpening, and gluing that the combined effects of a stationery and hardware store can furnish."

World War II caused Stravinsky to settle in yet another country, the United States. He lived outside Los Angeles not far from Arnold Schoenberg, but the two never visited. Their different musical philosophies created an unbridgeable gulf, and each had his group of loyal disciples. In 1948, Stravinsky engaged Robert Craft, a twenty-four-year-old conductor, as his musical assistant. Craft encouraged Stravinsky to become more familiar with the works of Schoenberg, Berg, and Webern. By the 1950s, all three composers were dead, and Stravinsky astonished his followers by adopting Schoenberg's twelve-tone system. And in his seventies and eighties, despite physical pain, this incredible man toured the world from Chile to Tahiti conducting his rich and intense late works. He also, for the first time in fifty years, returned to Russia and bared his soul to a group of Soviet composers: "The smell of the Russian earth is different. . . . A man has one birthplace, one fatherland, one country."

Stravinsky's Music

Stravinsky had an enormous influence on twentieth-century music. His innovations in rhythm, harmony, and tone color inspired musicians throughout the world. No contemporary contributed so many masterpieces to the international repertory. Stravinsky's extensive output includes music of almost every kind, for both voices and instruments. His many works for the stage include thirteen ballet scores.

Like his friend Picasso, Stravinsky's development shows dramatic changes of style. His three early ballets—*The Firebird* (1910), *Petrushka* (1911), and *The Rite of Spring* (1913)—call for very large orchestras and draw upon Russian folklore and folk tunes. During World War I, Stravinsky abandoned the large orchestra and wrote for small chamber groups with unconventional combinations of instruments. Ragtime rhythms and popular dances (for example, the tango) were used in such works as *The Soldier's Tale* (1918). During the period from about 1920 to 1951 (discussed earlier as the era of neoclassicism) he gradually turned from Russian folklore and drew inspiration largely from eighteenth-century music. First came the ballet *Pulcinella* (1920), based on the music of Giovanni Battista Pergolesi, an Italian composer of the early eighteenth century; the period ended with his opera *The Rake's Progress* (1951), modeled after Mozart's operas. Emphasizing emotional restraint, balance, and wit, Stravinsky's work at this time was far removed from the violence and "primitivism" of *The Rite*. Many pieces feature woodwind and brass instruments, which Stravinsky felt to be less "romantic" in sound than strings. Some works are based on subjects from antiquity, like the opera-oratorio *Oedipus Rex* (1927); others were inspired by religious works, like the *Symphony of Psalms* (1930).

Whatever Stravinsky's current style, he had always written music with a clear tonal center. So the musical world was startled when he shifted from tonality to the twelve-tone system. This dramatic change of approach came during the 1950s, when Stravinsky was in his seventies. Taking inspiration from the music of Anton Webern (1883–1945), Stravinsky now wrote brief works in which melodic lines were "atomized" into brief fragments in constantly changing tone colors and registers.

Despite such style changes, all of his music has an unmistakable "Stravinsky sound." His tone colors tend to be dry and clear, while the beat is strong and regular.

Stravinsky's rhythmic imagination was one of the most fertile in our century. His music abounds in changing and irregular meters; sometimes several meters are heard at once. Ostinatos, or repeated rhythmic patterns, frequently unify sections of a piece. They also accompany melodies with highly irregular phrase structures.

Stravinsky's treatment of musical form is also unique. Rather than connecting themes with bridge passages, he shifts abruptly from one section to the next. One idea is repeated and varied for a while, only to be broken off by something new. "Here, you see, I cut off the fugue with a pair of scissors," he remarked of a fugue that is repeatedly punctuated by contrasting material. But despite all the sudden changes, Stravinsky's music sounds unified and continuous.

Tone color is an integral part of his work. The effectiveness of his rhythms, chords, and melodies depends largely on how they are orchestrated. Much of his music is scored for unconventional groups of instruments. Highly contrasting tone colors are often combined: a violin is set against a trumpet, or a piano against a trombone. Instruments play in unusual registers, too. For example, *The Rite of Spring* opens with the highest tones of a solo bassoon. Stravinsky uses percussion instruments imaginatively, often giving them solo roles. (He even acquired percussion instruments so that he could personally try out his drum parts.) The writer with whom he collaborated on *The Soldier's Tale* reported that he and Stravinsky met almost daily "in the blue room . . . surrounded by side drums, kettle drums, bass drums, and every kind of percussion instrument."

Stravinsky's music has rich, novel harmonies, such as the famous "Petrushka chord," a bitonal combination of a C-major triad with an F♯-major triad. He makes even conventional chords sound unique through spacing, doubling, and the orchestration of their tones. The spirit of this composer's approach is seen in his exclamation about one such novel-sounding harmony: "How happy I was when I discovered this chord!"

Stravinsky often used known material to create original music. He drew on a vast range of styles, from Russian folk songs to Baroque melodies, from Renaissance madrigals to tango rhythms. Sometimes he gave another composer's melody new harmonies and orchestration. But more often, the music is entirely Stravinsky's, while vaguely suggesting a past style. Stravinsky spoke of a "lifelong need for outside nourishment." He believed that tradition is "a living force that animates and informs the present. . . . It appears as an heirloom, a heritage that one receives on condition of making it bear fruit before passing it on to one's descendants."

Petrushka (1911)

Petrushka was Stravinsky's second ballet score for the Russian Ballet in Paris. It is a fantasy that unfolds against the backdrop of a Russian street fair during the St. Petersburg Carnival in the 1830s. Its main characters are three life-sized puppets—Petrushka, the Moor, and the Ballerina—who are brought to life by an old magician. In Stravinsky's words, Petrushka is "the immortal and unhappy hero of every fair in all countries." In a way, he's the Russian counterpart of the puppet Pinocchio. Petrushka competes with the Moor for the affection of the Ballerina. In the fourth and last scene of the ballet, the Moor strikes Petrushka with a sword and kills him, to the crowd's astonishment.

Petrushka's music is, by turns, brilliant, grotesque, and humorous. It perfectly matches the story line. Stravinsky uses Russian folk songs as well as popular songs and dances to capture the atmosphere of the Russian street fair. The sheer color and imagination of the score make *Petrushka* as popular in the concert hall as it is in the theater. We'll now focus on the ballet's opening scene, which is divided into three sections: (1) The Crowds, (2) The Magic Trick, and (3) The Russian Dance.

Opening Scene

The curtain rises on a street fair with booths, a puppet theater, and a milling crowd. Soon an organ grinder and a street dancer compete with a music-box player and another dancer for the crowd's attention. The music is marvelously descriptive; trills and running notes match the lively activity on stage. The general confusion of a crowd is suggested through polyrhythm—the double basses play in one meter, while piccolos play in another. Woodwinds perfectly imitate the sound of a barrel organ.

The most important borrowed melody in the first section is an Easter song from the Smolensk region of Russia. The tune begins with a tone that is repeated several times. After its introduction by the double basses, the melody is played by the full orchestra as a group of drunken merrymakers dance across stage. There are two different barrel-organ tunes. The second was originally a French music-hall favorite, "She had a wooden leg," which Stravinsky actually heard outside his window while he was composing this scene.

The opening section of *Petrushka* is in three-part form: A (crowd) B (soloists: barrel organ and music box) A' (crowd). The two outer sections are more complex musically, with the many abrupt changes characteristic of Stravinsky—rapidly changing meters, irregular rhythms, and twentieth-century chord structures. In the contrasting middle section (B), the harmonies and rhythms are conventional, in keeping with the humble folk instruments shown playing them on stage.

The second and third sections of this scene—The Magic Trick and The Russian Dance—are much shorter than the first. An old magician appears at the puppet theater and brings the three puppets to life by playing a magic flute. The puppets then do a frantic Russian dance, first dangling on their strings in the theater and then out in the street among the amazed crowd.

Stravinsky uses a descending figure in the bassoon to represent the old magician. Strange chromatic harmonies and wisps of sound from the celesta and harp create a mysterious atmosphere.

The Russian Dance suggests the puppets' jerky movements by a rapid, powerful beat and bright, percussive tone colors. Piano, xylophone, and woodwinds often have solo parts. The main theme has a narrow range and is spun out of a small group of tones; these are repeated again and again with slight rhythmic variations. Repeated rhythmic figures occur in the accompaniment, too.

LISTENING OUTLINE

To be read while music is heard

Opening scene from *Petrushka* (original 1911 version) by Igor Stravinsky

2 piccolos, 2 flutes, 4 oboes, English horn, 4 clarinets, bass clarinet, 4 bassoons, contrabassoon, 4 horns, 2 cornets, 2 trumpets, 3 trombones, tuba, timpani, bass drum, cymbals, gong, triangle, tambourine, snare drum, xylophone, glockenspiel, 2 harps, piano, celesta, violins 1, violins 2, violas, cellos, double basses

(About 10 min)

Section 1: Crowds (Vivace)

Bustling crowd.   1   a. High flute, crowd theme; accompanying trills
                                          in clarinets and horns.

                                   b. Low basses, opening of Russian tune.

c. High flute, crowd theme; accompanying trills in
   clarinets and horns.
d. Low basses, Russian tune. High piccolos join,
   Russian tune in faster notes. Crescendo, trumpets.

A group of drunken merrymakers pass by, dancing.

2 a. Full orchestra, *fff*, Russian tune; powerful
     beat, cymbals.

b. Suddenly softer, Russian tune in woodwinds and
   violins, pizzicato. Brass chord crescendo.

The old showman of the fair entertains the crowd from the height of his booth.

3 a. Timpani; staccato repeated notes in strings;
     irregular accents. Staccato brasses, *f*.

b. High piccolos, crowd theme.

An organ-grinder with a street dancer appears in the crowd.

c. Timpani. Clarinets, opening of first
   barrel-organ tune.

d. Timpani; staccato repeated notes in strings.
   Staccato brasses, *ff*.
e. High violins, crowd theme.

Organ-grinder begins to play

4 a. Clarinets, first barrel-organ tune; slow
     "oom-pah-pah" accompaniment.

The street dancer dances, beating time on the triangle.

b. Triangle accompanies second barrel-organ tune
   in flutes and clarinets.

The organ-grinder, continuing to turn the crank with one hand, plays the cornet with the other.

Trumpet joins. Violins, crowd theme bursts in.

On the other side of the stage a music box begins to play.

c. Glockenspiel (bells), music-box tune; clarinets, first
   barrel-organ tune. Triangle accompanies
   second barrel-organ tune in flutes and

Another street dancer
dances around it.

clarinets. High violins, crowd theme
bursts in.

    d. Timpani; staccato repeated notes in strings;
irregular accents.

The barrel-organ
and the music box
stop playing. The
old showman again
entertains the crowd.

5   High crowd theme with bustling accompaniment.
Piccolos and trumpets join, crescendo.

The drunken
merrymakers return.

6 *a.* Russian tune, orchestra, *fff*, powerful beat;
cymbals.

    b. Suddenly softer, Russian tune in woodwinds and
violins, pizzicato. Brass chord crescendo.

7 *a.* Timpani; staccato repeated notes in strings,
irregular accents. Staccato brasses, *f.*

    b. High piccolo, crowd theme.

    c. Timpani; staccato repeated notes in strings, irregular
accents. Staccato brasses, *f.*

    d. High piccolo, crowd theme. Trumpets join,
crescendo to *fff* climax.

    e. Drum rolls.

Two drummers
standing in front
of the little theater
attract the attention
of the crowd by their
drum rolls.

Section II: The Magic Trick (Lento)

Out of the little
theater steps the
old magician.

1   Solo bassoon, *p*, low descending figure. High,
mysterious sounds in celesta, harp, and violins.
Chord in strings.

The magician plays
the flute.

2   Solo flute, *p*, upward and downward arpeggios.

The curtain of the
little theater
opens, and the
crowd sees three
puppets: Petrushka,
the Moor, and the
Ballerina.

3   Violins, *pp*, high descending figure. Mysterious
sounds in celesta, harps, and woodwinds.

The magician
animates them by
touching them with
his flute.

Solo flute, piccolo (two tones for each puppet).

Section III: The Russian Dance (Allegro, in strict time)

Petrushka, the
Moor, and the
Ballerina begin to
dance together, to
the great surprise
of all.

1 *a.* Main theme, *f.* Upward glissando to

Petrushka (1911)

403

b. Brief solos by cornet, clarinet, and oboe.
       Other instruments join on melody, crescendo.

2 *a.* Main theme, *ff*, full orchestra.
    b. Oboe solo punctuated by loud percussive sounds.

3 *a.* Piano solo, second theme. Solo violin takes
       second theme. Xylophone, main theme.
    b. Clarinet and English horn, *p*, main theme in slower
       tempo.

4 Solo piano, *f*, main theme in fast tempo. Other
    instruments join. Running notes punctuated by
    loud chords. Abrupt concluding cadence.

The Rite of Spring (Le Sacre du printemps; 1913)

Few compositions have had so powerful an impact on twentieth-century music as *The Rite of Spring,* Stravinsky's third ballet score for the Russian Ballet. Its harsh dissonances, percussive orchestration, rapidly changing meters, violent off-beat accents, and ostinatos fired the imaginations of many composers. The idea for *The Rite* came to Stravinsky as "a fleeting vision," while he was completing *The Firebird* in St. Petersburg in 1910. "I saw in imagination a solemn pagan rite: wise elders, seated in a circle, watching a young girl dance herself to death. They were sacrificing her to propitiate the god of spring." Later in life, Stravinsky revealed that "the most wonderful event" of every year of his childhood was "the violent Russian spring that seemed to begin in an hour and was like the whole earth crackling."

Stravinsky's interest in a so-called "primitive" or nonliterate culture was shared by many artists and scholars in the early 1900s. In 1907, Picasso's violent and path-breaking painting *Les Demoiselles d'Avignon* reflected the influence of African sculpture. In 1913—the same year as *The Rite of Spring*—Freud published *Totem and Taboo,* a study of the "resemblances between the psychic lives of savages and neurotics." But **primitivism**—the deliberate evocation of primitive power through insistent rhythms and percussive sounds—did not have a lasting impact on early twentieth-century music. Stravinsky never again wrote anything like *The Rite;* and with the exception of works like *Allegro barbaro* (1911), a piano piece by Bartók, few primitivistic compositions have entered the repertory.

The Rite of Spring consists of two large parts which are subdivided into sections with varying speeds. These subsections follow each other without pause. The titles of the dances suggest their primitive subject matter: Part I, The Adoration of the Earth: (1) Introduction; (2) Omens of Spring: Dances

In 1907, Picasso's painting *Les Demoiselles d'Avignon* reflected the influence of African sculpture (Collection, The Museum of Modern Art, New York. Acquired through the Lillie P. Bliss Bequest).

of the Youths and Maidens; (3) The Game of Abduction; (4) Spring Rounds; (5) Games of the Rival Tribes; (6) Procession of the Wise Elder; (7) Adoration of the Earth; (8) Dance of the Earth. Part II, The Sacrifice: (1) Introduction; (2) Mysterious Circles of the Young Girls; (3) Glorification of the Chosen Maiden; (4) Evocation of the Ancestors; (5) Ritual of the Ancestors; (6) Sacrificial Dance. Each of the two large parts begins with a slow introduction and ends with a frenzied, climactic dance.

The Rite of Spring is written for an enormous orchestra including eight horns, four tubas, and a very important percussion section made up of five timpani, bass drum, tambourine, tam-tam, triangle, antique cymbals, and a guiro (a notched gourd scraped with a stick). Though *The Rite* contains only one folk song, its melodies are folklike. They have narrow ranges like ancient Russian folk tunes and are made up of fragments that are repeated with slight changes in rhythm and pitch. Many individual chords are repeated, and each change of harmony produces a great impact. This melodic and harmonic repetition gives the music a ritualistic, hypnotic quality. Rhythm is a vital form-building element in *The Rite*; it has a life of its own, almost independent of melody and harmony. Today, *The Rite of Spring* is rarely presented as a ballet and is usually heard in the concert hall.

We shall now take a closer look at three sections of *The Rite:* the Introduction and Dances of the Youths and Maidens, which open Part I; and the Sacrificial Dance, which concludes Part II.

Part I: Introduction

For Stravinsky, the Introduction to Part I represented "the awakening of nature, the scratching, gnawing, wiggling of birds and beasts." It begins with the strangely penetrating sound of a solo bassoon straining at the top of its register. As though improvising, the bassoon repeats a fragment of a Lithuanian folk tune in irregular ways.

Soon other woodwind instruments join the bassoon with repeated fragments of their own. The impression of improvisation is strengthened by the absence of a clearly defined pulse or meter. Dissonant, unconventional chord structures are used. Toward the end of the Introduction, different layers of sounds— mostly from woodwinds and brasses—are piled on top of each other, and the music builds to a piercing climax. But suddenly, all sound is cut off; only the solo bassoon forlornly repeats its opening melody. Then the violins, playing pizzicato, introduce a repeated four-note figure.

This figure later serves as an ostinato in the Dances of the Youths and Maidens, which immediately follows the Introduction.

Omens of Spring: Dances of the Youths and Maidens

Sounding almost like drums, the strings pound out a dissonant chord. There are unexpected and irregular accents whose violence is heightened by jabbing sounds from eight horns. This is the way the passage might be counted (with a rapid pulse): 1-2-3-4, 1-2-3-4, 1-2-3-**4**, 1-2-3-4, 1-2-3-4, 1-2-3-4, 1-2-3-**4**, 1-2-3-**4**. The unchanging dissonant harmony is a polychord that combines two different traditional chords.

A succession of melodic fragments soon join the pounding chord and other repeated figures. Played by brass and woodwind instruments, the melodic fragments are narrow in range and are repeated over and over with slight variations.

The rhythmic activity is constant and exciting. Gradually more and more instruments are added, and the music builds to the frenzied opening of the next section, which is marked by violent strokes on the timpani and bass drum.

The Rite of Spring (Le Sacre du printemps; 1913)

407

It's interesting to compare Stravinsky's musical techniques in Dances of the Youths and Maidens with those of a Classical movement in sonata form. A Classical movement grows out of contrasts between different keys; this music is based almost entirely on the repetition of a few chords. The themes in a Classical movement are developed through different keys, varied and broken into fragments that take on new emotional meanings. Here, Stravinsky simply repeats melodic fragments with relatively slight variation. His novel techniques grew out of the Russian musical tradition of the nineteenth century. The Coronation Scene from *Boris Godunov* (1874), by Mussorgsky, also uses just a few chords that are repeated throughout a section. Like some of his Russian forebears, Stravinsky relies on variations of rhythm and tone color to create movement and growth.

Part II: Sacrificial Dance

The Sacrificial Dance is the overwhelming climax of the whole work. It consists of sections that can be outlined: A B A' C A" (very brief) C A'''. In the opening section (A), explosive, percussive chords fight brutal blows on the timpani. The time signature changes with almost every bar: $\frac{3}{16}$ $\frac{2}{16}$ $\frac{3}{16}$ $\frac{2}{8}$ $\frac{2}{16}$ $\frac{3}{16}$. The rapid pulse and irregular, jolting accents create intense excitement. The second section (B) begins with a sudden drop in dynamic level as a single chord is repeated obsessively. Brief silences between these repeated chords urge the listener to supply accents. Section C features brasses and percussive sounds from five timpani, a tam-tam (gong), and a bass drum. The Sacrificial Dance glorifies the power of rhythm, as does the entire *Rite of Spring*.

Symphony of Psalms (1930)

A masterpiece from Stravinsky's "neoclassical period," the *Symphony of Psalms* was written for the fiftieth anniversary of the Boston Symphony Orchestra in 1930. It has three movements and is scored for chorus and orchestra. The Latin text is taken from three psalms in the Vulgate Bible. Stravinsky chose the Latin version to evoke the feeling of an ancient and solemn ritual. An austere, archaic quality is also communicated through chantlike melodies that sometimes are restricted to one or two tones.

The neoclassical features of the *Symphony of Psalms* include its use of tonality, major and minor triads, fugue, and the deliberate evocation of the past. Yet the music sounds completely of this century. As in many works by Stravinsky, the orchestra is highly unconventional. There are no violins, violas, or clarinets; the sounds of woodwinds, brasses, and two pianos predominate. Stravinsky intended the voices and instruments to "be on an equal footing, neither of them outweighing the other." He uses the term "symphony" not in its usual sense, but simply to indicate a work in several movements that calls for an orchestra. The three movements are related motivically and are performed without interruption.

First Movement: Psalm 38 (Vulgate), verses 13–14[1]

Based on a psalm beginning "Hear my prayer, O Lord," the brief opening movement is a prelude to the successively longer movements that follow. First, a staccato orchestral chord repeatedly punctuates woodwind solos. Though a standard E-minor triad, this chord sounds unique because its tones are spaced and orchestrated in a novel way. After this orchestral introduction, the alto voices of the chorus sing a chantlike melody composed of just two notes that alternate.

E - xau - di_____ o - ra - ti - o - nem me-am, Do - mi - ne,_____

This chantlike theme is supported by ostinatos in the woodwinds.

The first part of the movement is marked by abrupt contrasts between the staccato chord, woodwind interludes, and brief passages for chorus and orchestra. The second part of the movement is more continuous as the chorus and orchestra are always heard together. The movement ends in triumph, with a sustained G-major triad that has a great impact because it is the movement's only *major* triad; it vividly contrasts with the staccato minor triads heard earlier.

		Orchestral introduction; loud staccato chord punctuates solos by oboe, bassoon.
		Piano. High cello.
Exaudi orationem meam, Domine,	Hear my prayer, O Lord,	Altos, chantlike theme.
et deprecationem meam;	and my supplication:	Full chorus.
		Oboe.

Symphony of Psalms (1930)

409

---

[1] Psalm 38 in the Vulgate is Psalm 39 in the King James version.

auribus percipe lacrymas meas.	give ear to my tears.	Altos, chantlike theme.
		Staccato chord.
Ne sileas,	Be not silent:	Tenors and altos, *f*; staccato chord.
quoniam advena ego sum apud te,	for I am a stranger with thee,	Altos, basses. Other voices join.
et peregrinus sicut omnes patres mei.	and a sojourner as all my fathers were.	Crescendo to *ff*.
Remitte mihi, (remitte mihi,)	O forgive me, (O forgive me,)	Suddenly softer, chantlike theme in tenors, sopranos.
ut refrigerer priusquam abeam et amplius non ero.	that I may be refreshed, before I go hence, and be no more.	Major chord, *ff*.

Second Movement: Psalm 39 (Vulgate), verses 2–4[2]

Stravinsky based the second movement on a psalm which he described as "a prayer that a new canticle (song) may be put into our mouths." The movement is a fugue with two different subjects, or themes. One is played by instruments only, while the other is entirely vocal. A solo oboe introduces the instrumental subject, a jagged melody with upward and downward leaps.[3]

This subject is imitated in turn by a flute, second flute, and second oboe. This use of only woodwind instruments in a high register is an unusual feature of the opening fugue. This music does follow certain traditions of fugue technique, but it has a twentieth-century sound due to its unconventional harmonies.

After the extended section for woodwinds, the sopranos of the chorus announce the vocal subject, which begins with a downward leap.

Ex - pec____ tans ex - pec - ta____ vi DO - MI-NUM,

---

[2] Psalm 39 in the Vulgate is Psalm 40 in the King James version.

[3] At the beginning of this subject, a series of four tones, C–E♭–B–D, is stated four times in succession. The repetition is disguised, however, by changes of rhythm and register. This succession of two upward thirds (from C to E♭ and B to D) was derived from one of the woodwind ostinatos (B–D–A♯–C♯) that accompany the chantlike melody in the opening movement. (See example on page 409.)

The vocal subject is imitated by the other chorus parts, while fragments of the instrumental subject appear in the background. Refreshing changes of tone color occur as a beautiful passage for unaccompanied chorus is followed by one for instruments alone. The words "And he put a new canticle into my mouth" bring the first fortissimo in the movement, and the chorus and orchestra are reunited. The movement ends calmly as the chorus sings a repeated tone while instruments recall the opening fugue subject.

		Solo oboe, instrumental fugue subject; imitation by flute, 2nd flute, 2nd oboe.
Expectans, expectavi Dominum,	With expectation I have waited for the Lord:	Sopranos, vocal fugue subject; imitation by altos, tenors, basses; instrumental fugue subject in background.
et intendit mihi.	and he was attentive to me.	
Et exaudivit preces meas,	And he heard my prayers,	
et eduxit me de lacu miseriae	and brought me out of the pit of misery	
et de luto faecis.	and the mire of dregs.	
Et statuit super petram pedes meos,	And he set my feet upon a rock,	Chorus alone, *p*.
et direxit gressus meos.	and directed my steps.	
		Orchestra alone, *p*, fragment of instrumental fugue subject imitated. Brief pause.
Et immisit in os meum canticum novum, carmen Deo nostro. Videbunt multi, et timebunt, et sperabunt in Domino.	And he put a new canticle into my mouth, a song to our God. Many shall see and shall fear: and they shall hope in the Lord.	Sudden *ff*, chorus and orchestra; dotted rhythms. Parts of both fugue subjects. Sudden *p*; chorus sings repeated tone while instruments recall opening fugue subject

Symphony of Psalms
(1930)

411

Third Movement: Psalm 150 (Vulgate)

The last movement—the longest, by far—is set to Psalm 150, which calls for universal praise of God through music. Despite the consistently joyful text, Stravinsky chose to evoke a variety of moods, from solemnity to exultation. There are frequent shifts between slow and fast tempos.

We first hear slow, soft music to the words *"Alleluia. Laudate Dominum"* ("Alleluia. Praise ye the Lord"). Stravinsky thought of this Alleluia as "the new song" which answered the prayer of the psalm in the preceding movement. The Alleluia motive recurs both in the middle of the movement and at the very end as a unifying refrain. After the slow opening, there is a rapid section described by Stravinsky as being "inspired by a vision of Elijah's chariot climbing the Heavens." The horns introduce a striking rhythmic figure composed of rapid repeated notes. Later, this repeated-note figure is sung on the syllables *Lau-da-te Do-mi-num.* The fast section contains a wild outburst of triplet rhythms which Stravinsky intended to "suggest the horses and chariot."

The feeling of suspended time has never been more beautifully evoked than by the extended slow section that concludes the movement. "The final hymn of praise," wrote Stravinsky, "must be thought of as issuing from the skies, and agitation is followed by 'the calm of praise.'" During this solemn processional, a melodic pattern of three beats is hypnotically repeated by the sopranos, accompanied by a four-beat ostinato in the timpani, pianos, and harp.

This polyrhythm of "three against four" helps create a magical quality in this processional. After the final appearance of the gentle Alleluia motive, the *Symphony of Psalms* ends serenely in C major.

Alleluia.
Laudate Dominum in sanctis ejus;
laudate eum in firmamento virtutis ejus.
(Laudate Dominum.)

Alleluia.
Praise ye the Lord in his holy places;
praise ye him in the firmament of his power.
(Praise ye the Lord.)

Slow tempo, sustained woodwind chord. Chorus, *p*, "Alleluia" motive.

		Orchestra alone. Faster tempo. Horns, rapid repeated notes; trumpet. Crescendo to *ff*, fast triplet rhythms.
Laudate eum in virtutibus ejus; (*Laudate Dominum in virtutibus ejus, laudate Dominum in sanctis ejus.*)	Praise ye him for his mighty acts; (Praise ye the Lord for his mighty acts, praise ye the Lord in his holy places.)	Sopranos and altos. Tenors and altos, *p*, rapid repeated notes.
laudate eum secundum multitudinem magnitudinis ejus. *Laudate eum in sono tubae;* [*laudate eum in psalterio et cithara.*]	praise ye him according to the multitude of his greatness. Praise him with sound of trumpet: [praise him with psaltery and harp.]	Basses. Other voices join, *f*.
		Slow tempo, sudden *p*. Sustained woodwind chords.
(*Alleluia.*	(Alleluia.	Chorus, *p*, "Alleluia" motive.
Laudate Dominum. *Laudate eum.*	Praise ye the Lord. Praise ye him.	Faster tempo, sudden *f*; chorus and orchestra. Orchestra alone, *p*.
Laudate Dominum, laudate eum.)	Praise ye the Lord, praise ye him.)	Chorus, rapid repeated notes. Crescendo. Orchestra, *ff*, triplet rhythms. Slower tempo, sudden *p*; repeated wind chords.
Laudate eum in tympano et choro; laudate eum in chordis et organo.	Praise him with timbrel and choir: praise him with strings and organs.	Sopranos, *p*, new lyrical melody. Basses imitate. Crescendo as

Symphony of Psalms (1930)

413

		other voices join.
Laudate eum in cymbalis benesonantibus; laudate eum in cymbalis jubilationibus.	Praise him on high sounding cymbals: praise him on jubilant cymbals.	Sudden *p*, still slower tempo; solemn processional. Sopranos repeat three-beat figure over instrumental ostinato.
(Laudate Dominum. Laudate eum.)	(Praise ye the Lord. Praise ye him.)	Basses and tenors. Other voices join, crescendo.
Omnis spiritus laudet Dominum!	Let every spirit praise the Lord!	Sopranos repeat three-beat figure over instrumental ostinato. Orchestra alone, *p*.
Alleluia. (Laudate Dominum.)	Alleluia. (Praise ye the Lord.)	Chorus, *p*, "Alleluia" motive.

Basic Term

If you aren't sure what the following word means, look back at the text, where it appears in bold type.

primitivism

[7] EXPRESSIONISM

Much twentieth-century music reflects an artistic movement called **expressionism,** which stressed intense, subjective emotion. It was largely centered in Germany and Austria from 1905 to 1925. Painters, writers, and composers explored inner feelings rather than depicting outward appearances. They used deliberate distortions to assault and shock their audience, to communicate the tensions and anguish of the human psyche. Expressionism grew out of the same intellectual climate as Freud's studies of hysteria and the unconscious. The German expressionist painters were reacting against French impressionism, with its pleasant subjects, delicate pastel colors, and shimmering surfaces.

The expressionists rejected conventional prettiness. Their works may seem "ugly" in their preoccupation with madness and death. Expressionist painters

Oskar Kokoschka, *Self Portrait*. German expressionist painters reacted against French impressionism; they often used jarring colors and grotesquely distorted shapes to explore the subconscious (Collection, The Museum of Modern Art, New York).

Expressionism

415

such as Ernst Ludwig Kirchner, Emil Nolde, and Oskar Kokoschka often use jarring colors and grotesquely distorted shapes. Expressionist art is fragmentary; the scenes of an expressionist play may be episodic and discontinuous. Expressionism is an art concerned with social protest. It movingly conveyed the anguish felt by the poor and oppressed. Many expressionists opposed World War I and used art to depict their horror of bloodshed.

There was close communication between expressionist writers, painters, and musicians. Many were creative in several different areas. Painter Wassily Kandinsky wrote essays, poetry, and plays, while the composer Schoenberg painted and even participated in the shows of expressionist artists.

Twentieth-century musical expressionism grows out of the emotional turbulence in the works of late Romantics like Wagner, Richard Strauss, and Gustav Mahler. In the following sections, we'll study four expressionistic compositions: *Five Pieces for Orchestra,* Op. 16 (1909), and *A Survivor from Warsaw,* Op. 46 (1947), by Schoenberg; the opera *Wozzeck* (1917–1922) by Alban Berg; and *Five Pieces for Orchestra,* Op. 10 (1911–1913), by Anton Webern. They share a stress on harsh dissonance, fragmentation, an exploitation of extreme registers, and unusual instrumental effects. All four pieces avoid tonality and traditional chord progressions. Both *A Survivor from Warsaw* and *Wozzeck* depict a nightmarish world and express a profound empathy with the poor and tormented.

Basic Term

If you aren't sure what the following word means, look back at the text, where it appears in bold type. Additional information can be found by checking the index.

expressionism

[8] ARNOLD SCHOENBERG

Arnold Schoenberg (1874–1951) was born in Vienna, the city of Mozart, Beethoven, and Brahms. Unlike such earlier masters, he was an almost entirely self-taught musician. "I began studying the violin at eight and almost immediately started composing," he later recalled. Schoenberg acquired his profound knowledge of music by studying scores, by playing in amateur chamber groups, and by going to concerts. His first musical hero was Brahms, then the greatest living German composer. He soon became "an equally confirmed addict" of Wagner; he saw each of Wagner's operas from twenty to thirty times.

When Schoenberg was sixteen, his father died and he had to work for several years as a bank clerk. When he lost this job at twenty-one, he decided to devote himself to music. He earned a poor living by conducting a choir of metal-

Arnold Schoenberg (Omikron).

workers in an industrial center outside Vienna. He also orchestrated operettas written by popular composers of the time. Performances of his own early works met with hostility from the conservative Viennese public. One music critic suggested that Schoenberg be put in an insane asylum without music paper.

Schoenberg began to teach music theory and composition in Vienna in 1904. His personality inspired love and loyalty among his students. Two of his disciples, Alban Berg and Anton Webern, themselves became leading composers.

Around 1908 Schoenberg took the revolutionary step of abandoning the traditional tonal system. "I already feel the opposition that I shall have to overcome," he wrote in a program note for his first atonal works. Schoenberg was a man possessed. "I have a mission. I have a task. . . . I am but the

Arnold Schoenberg

loudspeaker of an idea." His productivity between 1908 and 1915 was incredible. Besides creating many dazzlingly original works at lightning speed, he published a harmony textbook, wrote his own librettos, and entered his paintings in exhibitions of the German expressionists.

Following this fertile period came a span of eight years encompassing World War I and the difficult postwar period when Schoenberg published nothing. He searched for a way to organize the new musical resources he had discovered. Finally, in the summer of 1921, he told a student, "I have made a discovery which will insure the supremacy of German music for the next hundred years." From 1923 to 1925 Schoenberg published compositions using his newly developed twelve-tone system. While his music did not find a large audience, leading musicians respected it. At fifty-one, Schoenberg received an important academic post: director of the master class in musical composition at the Prussian Academy of Arts in Berlin.

This period of official recognition was cut short in 1933, when the Nazis seized power in Germany. Schoenberg was dismissed from the faculty of the Prussian Academy. This shattering experience caused him to return to Judaism. (He had converted to Protestantism when he was eighteen.) The same year he and his family left Germany for the United States, where he soon joined the music faculty at the University of California in Los Angeles. But Schoenberg felt neglected in his adopted country. His music was rarely performed, and he was refused a grant from the Guggenheim Foundation. At the age of seventy he was forced to retire from UCLA with a pension of less than forty dollars a month. "I am quite conscious," he wrote in 1947, "that a full understanding of my work cannot be expected before some decades . . . and I know that—success or not—it is my historic duty to write what my destiny orders me to write." But appreciation came earlier than Schoenberg anticipated. Since his death in 1951, the twelve-tone system has been used increasingly by composers throughout the world.

Schoenberg's Music

"I claim the distinction of having written a truly new music which, based upon tradition as it is, is destined to become tradition." This proud assertion by Schoenberg contains a great deal of truth. His musical language was indeed new, yet rooted in the past and the result of a gradual stylistic evolution. And his musical system *was* eventually adopted by many other composers.

Schoenberg's point of departure was the music of Wagner, Brahms, and Mahler. His early works, like the string sextet *Verklärte Nacht* ("Transfigured Night," 1899), show many features of the late Romantic style. The music is emotionally intense and often has a literary program. Some early compositions use the gigantic orchestras favored by late nineteenth-century composers. For example, the immense cantata *Gurre-Lieder* ("Songs of Gurre," 1901; orchestration, 1911) calls for five vocal soloists, a speaker-narrator, four choruses, and a greatly expanded orchestra including about fifty woodwind and brass players.

A feeling of subjectivity is generated through dissonances that resolve in unexpected ways and through angular melodies that have wide ranges and big leaps. There is prominent use of chromatic harmony, or chords with tones that do not belong to the prevailing major or minor scale. The pull of a central tonality is weakened because the music rapidly moves through keys remote from the main one.

During the years 1903 to 1907, Schoenberg moved farther from the harmonic language of the late Romantics. In compositions such as the *Chamber Symphony,* Op. 9 (1906), for fifteen solo instruments, he uses whole-tone scales and fourth chords.

Atonality

Around 1908, Schoenberg finally began to write atonal music. Though a revolutionary development, **atonality**—the absence of key—evolved from Schoenberg's earlier emphasis on chromatic harmony and liberal use of all twelve tones in the chromatic scale. But in his atonal works, all twelve tones are used without regard for their traditional relationship to major or minor scales. Dissonances are "emancipated" from the necessity of resolving to consonances. Schoenberg explained atonality as a style based on the "emancipation of the dissonance"; it "treats dissonances like consonances and renounces a tonal center. By avoiding the establishment of a key, modulation is excluded, since modulation means leaving an established tonality and establishing another tonality." In Schoenberg's atonal music from 1908 to 1914, triads and the traditional vocabulary of chord progressions are deliberately avoided, as are major and minor scales. But "atonality" does not imply a single system of composition. Each atonal composition has its own means of achieving unity. A piece usually grows out of a few short motives that are transformed in many different ways.

Among the best-known of Schoenberg's atonal compositions are the *Five Pieces for Orchestra,* Op. 16 (1909)—which we'll study—and *Pierrot lunaire,* Op. 21 ("Moonstruck Pierrot," 1912), a setting of twenty-one poems. The jagged melodies, novel instrumental effects, and extreme contrasts of dynamics and register in Schoenberg's music are like the distorted figures and shocking colors in expressionist paintings. The texture is polyphonic and very complex. Phrases are of irregular length, and melodic repetition is avoided. *Pierrot lunaire* and other Schoenberg works call for an unusual style of vocal performance halfway between speaking and singing. This is called **Sprechstimme,** which literally means "speech-voice" in German. The vocal part is written in music notation, but small *x*'s on the note stems indicate that the pitches are only approximate.

Schoenberg's atonal language was soon adopted by his students Berg and Webern. Their early atonal works, like Schoenberg's, tended to be extremely emotional and very short. Without a musical system like tonality, the three composers could create extended compositions only when they had a long text to serve as an organizing force.

The Twelve-tone System

During the years 1914 to 1920, Schoenberg finished very few works as he tried to develop a more systematic method of organizing atonal music. In the early 1920s, he finally developed what he called the "method of composing with twelve tones." He partly applied this new technique in the *Five Piano Pieces*, Op. 23, and the *Serenade*, Op. 24, and then fully elaborated it in the *Suite* for piano, Op. 25. All were composed from 1920 to 1923. These and some other works of the 1920s are less subjective and expressionistic than Schoenberg's earlier and later music. They use traditional forms (sonata form) and eighteenth-century dance types (the minuet and trio, gavotte, and gigue).

The twelve-tone system enabled Schoenberg to write more extended compositions than he had when using free atonality. In 1928 he composed the monumental *Variations for Orchestra,* and in the years 1930 to 1932 he wrote the opera *Moses und Aron,* which is based entirely on a single tone row. Though he never finished the third act of this great masterpiece, the opera has an overwhelming impact. From the time of his arrival in the United States in 1933 to his death in 1951, Schoenberg used the twelve-tone system in many rich and varied works, including the *Violin Concerto,* Op. 36 (1936), the *Fourth String Quartet,* Op. 37 (1936), the *Piano Concerto,* Op. 42 (1942), and the cantata *A Survivor from Warsaw,* Op. 46 (1947). We'll study his cantata, but let's first look briefly at some basic principles of Schoenberg's technique.

The **twelve-tone system** offers the composer a new way of organizing pitch in a composition. It is a twentieth-century alternative to tonality. The twelve-tone system gives equal importance to each of the twelve chromatic tones, rather than emphasizing one central tone as the tonal system does. The twelve-tone method is a systematized form of atonality. It grew out of Schoenberg's desire to structure his music *"consciously* on a unifying idea."

In a twelve-tone composition, all pitches are derived from a special ordering of the twelve chromatic tones. This ordering or unifying idea, is called a **tone row, set,** or **series.**[4] The composer creates a unique tone row for each specific piece. The choice of rows is practically limitless, since there are 479,001,600 possible arrangements of the twelve chromatic tones. The tone row must be constructed with great care because it vitally affects the total sound and is the source of every melody and chord in a piece. Here is an example of a row, the one used by Schoenberg in his *Suite* for piano, Op. 25:

E	F	G	Db	Gb	Eb	Ab	D	B	C	A	Bb
1	2	3	4	5	6	7	8	9	10	11	12

Notice that no pitch occurs more than once within a row. This prevents any single tone from receiving too much emphasis. An entire composition is built by manipulating a single twelve-tone row. The row may be presented in four basic forms: forward (original form), backward (retrograde), upside down

---

[4]Because of the systematic use of a *series* of tones, the twelve-tone method is also referred to as "serial technique."

(inversion), and backward and upside down (retrograde inversion). The retrograde (backward) form simply presents the original tone row in reverse:

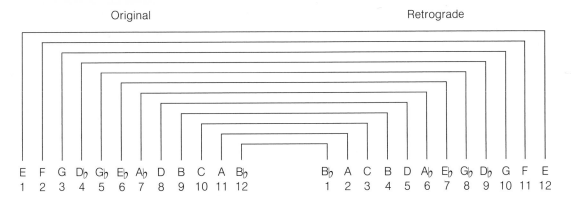

The inverted (upside down) form keeps the original sequence of intervals between tones, but the intervals move in the opposite direction. For example, the original row begins by moving *up* a half step from E to F. The inversion begins by moving *down* a half step from E to E♭.

The retrograde inversion (backward and upside down) presents the tones of the inversion in reverse:

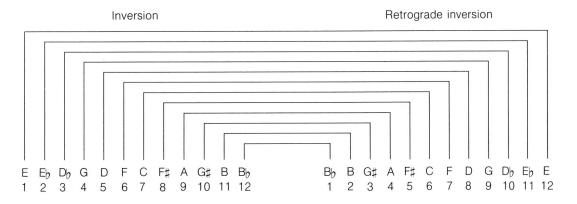

A tone row may be shifted to any pitch level. That is, it may begin on any of the twelve chromatic tones while keeping the original pattern of intervals. This applies to all four forms of the row: original, retrograde, inversion, and retrograde inversion. Since a row may begin on any one of twelve pitches and exist in four forms, there are forty-eight (twelve times four) possible versions of a row. This gives the composer a great deal of flexibility.

Each tone of a row may also be placed in any register, allowing an infinite variety of melodic shapes to be drawn from a single row. For example, given a row that begins with tones E–F–G, a composer could have the tones move upward by step, or he could have the E leap up to a high F and the F leap down to a low G.

This further increases the flexibility of the system and may partially explain why so many twelve-tone melodies have unusually wide leaps. The tones of a row may be presented one after another, to form a melodic line, or at the same time, to form chords. Here is the same row treated in two different ways.

We'll now study two works by Schoenberg: the "freely" atonal *Five Pieces for Orchestra*, Op. 16 (1909), and the twelve-tone cantata, *A Survivor from Warsaw*, Op. 46 (1947), composed almost forty years later.

Five Pieces for Orchestra, Op. 16 (1909)

"I can promise you something really colossal, especially in sound and mood," wrote Schoenberg to composer and conductor Richard Strauss after completing *Five Pieces for Orchestra*, Op. 16, in 1909. These revolutionary pieces were the first atonal works for full orchestra. Though Schoenberg calls for an especially large orchestra, he treats it as a group of soloists. (In 1949, Schoenberg rearranged the *Five Pieces* for a conventional orchestra.) Many novel orchestral effects are exploited, and instruments are often used at the top or bottom of their ranges. The pieces, especially the third, embody Schoenberg's concept of a **tone-color melody** (*Klangfarbenmelodie* in German), a succession of varying tone colors used as a musical idea in a composition. The third piece, *Summer Morning by a Lake: Colors* (also called *The Changing Chord*), is based on subtly shifting tone colors of a gradually changing chord. Schoenberg wrote in the score that "the change of harmonies should occur gently, without emphasis on instrumental entries, so that only a difference in tone color is perceived."

Schoenberg added descriptive titles after he composed the music. Each piece is quite brief; at the time, Schoenberg unconsciously felt the need to "counterbalance extreme emotionality with extraordinary shortness." The first two pieces, *Premonitions* and *Yesteryears*, show contrasting sides of Schoenberg's musical personality.

Premonitions (*Vorgefühle*)

An amazing amount of musical activity takes place in the two-minute span of *Premonitions*. It is "just an uninterrupted change of colors, rhythms, and moods," according to Schoenberg. The constant intensity and desperate energy of *Premonitions* are typically expressionistic.

The piece consists of two connected sections: an introductory part lasting about half a minute, and a main part three times as long. The introduction sounds fragmentary and has a bewildering succession of musical ideas in different tempos, tone colors, dynamics, and registers. As though holding his full resources in reserve, Schoenberg uses only a few instruments at any one time. First, muted cellos introduce an abrupt upward motive (short-long-long, short-long-long):

The entire piece is built from rhythmic and melodic transformations of this idea.

The second part of *Premonitions* is rhythmically more continuous; it becomes increasingly complex in both texture and sound.

The cellos begin with a steady succession of rapid notes. They have a three-note figure that is repeated as a background ostinato throughout the piece.

The sound becomes increasingly loud and dense as more and more melodic fragments are piled on top of one another. After an ear-splitting climax, the texture thins, and the volume decreases. *Premonitions* ends with a snarling chord

Five Pieces for Orchestra, Op. 16 (1909)

423

played by trombones and tuba. (The effect results from flutter-tonguing; each brass player rapidly rolls the tongue as if pronouncing *d-r-r-r.*) This chord is sustained in the background throughout most of *Premonitions,* and it unifies the flow of free associations in the piece.

Yesteryears (Vergangenes)

This slow, lyrical piece evokes a feeling of brooding over the past. As its title might suggest, *Yesteryears* is somewhat more traditional in harmony and form than the other pieces. It has a great variety of delicate and beautiful tone colors. Its dynamics are subdued; instruments are often muted. Except for a brief moment at the climax, the entire orchestra never plays simultaneously. Instead, groups of soloists engage in complex polyphonic conversations. Ostinatos play an important role in *Yesteryears.* Several different repeated figures are piled on top of one other to form different layers of sound. You'll easily recognize the ostinato played by the celesta because of its distinctive bell-like sound.

    Yesteryears has three parts: an opening, an extended middle section, and a brief conclusion. The piece becomes increasingly complex in texture; it begins in relatively simple homophony, but becomes more and more polyphonic. The texture is most dense at the end of the middle section, which has the greatest variety of tone colors and the most intricate polyrhythms. The conclusion of *Yesteryears* is truly a "remembrance of things past": all the earlier motives are recalled softly.

LISTENING OUTLINE
To be read while music is heard

Yesteryears *(Vergangenes)* from *Five Pieces for Orchestra,* Op. 16 (1909), by Arnold Schoenberg

2 piccolos, 2 flutes, 2 oboes, English horn, 2 clarinets, bass clarinet, 2 bassoons, contrabassoon, 4 horns, 2 trumpets, 4 trombones, tuba, xylophone, cymbals, triangle, harp, celesta, violins 1, violins 2, violas, cellos, double basses

Moderate tempo

(About 5½ min)

1   *a.* Legato melody, *p,* solo muted cello; clarinet and English horn continue melody; brief pause.

   b. Celesta, *p,* accompanies soft woodwinds and muted trumpet, which share interwoven melodic lines.
   c. English horn, *p,* opening of legato melody; low trombone phrase, *pp;* briefly held chord.

2   a. Solo muted viola, *pp*, presents new motive which is softly imitated by other solo instruments; complex polyphonic texture; celesta, *pp*, high violins.

Solo viola

pp

b. Celesta, *pp*, flutes, then staccato bassoons simultaneously play different repeated motives (ostinatos); soft, short solos in harp and muted violin.

c. Muted viola melody returns; polyphonic texture becomes more complex; crescendo to climax, *f*, entire orchestra. Decrescendo, tempo slows down; sustained string harmonics.

3   Oboe, *p*, opening legato melody; flute and celesta ostinatos; soft recollection of previous motives by solo instruments; sustained orchestral chord, *pp*.

A Survivor from Warsaw, Op. 46 (1947)

A dramatic cantata for narrator, male chorus, and orchestra, *A Survivor from Warsaw* deals with a single episode in the murder of six million Jews by the Nazis during World War II. Schoenberg wrote the text himself, partly basing it on a direct report by one of the few survivors of the Warsaw ghetto. Over 400,000 Jews from this ghetto died in extermination camps or of starvation, while many others perished during a heroic revolt against the Nazis in 1943. The narrator's text is spoken in English, except for some terrifying Nazi commands which are shouted in German. The narrator's part is a kind of *Sprechstimme,* the novel speech-singing developed by Schoenberg. The rhythms of the spoken words are precisely notated, but their pitch fluctuations are indicated only approximately.

I cannot remember ev'rything,   I must have been un-conscious most of the time;

Besides English and German, the text includes Hebrew. These were the three languages of Schoenberg's life: German, his native tongue; English, his adopted language in America; and Hebrew, the language of the faith to which he returned. The six-minute cantata builds to an overwhelming conclusion when the male chorus sings in unison the Hebrew words of the prayer *Shema Yisroel* ("Hear, O Israel"). For centuries this has been the prayer of Jewish martyrs in their last agonized moments.

A Survivor from Warsaw is a twelve-tone composition written in 1947 when Schoenberg was seventy-two. Its tense, expressionistic style recalls the composer's orchestral piece *Premonitions,* written almost forty years earlier. The music vividly sets off every detail in the text.

A Survivor from Warsaw opens with a brief orchestral introduction that captures the nightmarish atmosphere as Nazi soldiers awakened the Warsaw

A Survivor from Warsaw, Op. 46 (1947)

425

Jews for transport to death camps. We hear a weirdly shrill reveille in the trumpet and fragmentary sounds in the military drum and high xylophone.

During the narrator's opening lines, Schoenberg already prepares for the concluding Hebrew prayer. As the narrator speaks of "the old prayer they had neglected for so many years," a French horn softly intones the beginning of the melody that is later proclaimed by the chorus.

An especially vivid musical description comes when the narrator describes how the Nazis counted their victims: "They began again, first slowly: One, two, three, four, became faster and faster. . . ." The music itself becomes faster and louder, building to the powerful entrance of the chorus. The sung Hebrew contrasts dramatically with the spoken English and German that came before, and it is the first extended melody in the work.

> I cannot remember everything. I must have been unconscious most of the time; I remember only the grandiose moment when they all started to sing, as if prearranged, the old prayer they had neglected for so many years—the forgotten creed!
>
> But I have no recollection how I got underground to live in the sewers of Warsaw so long a time.
>
> The day began as usual. Reveille when it still was dark—get out whether you slept or whether worries kept you awake the whole night: you had been separated from your children, from your wife, from your parents, you don't know what happened to them; how could you sleep?
>
> They shouted again: "Get out! The sergeant will be furious!" They came out; some very slow, the old ones, the sick men, some with nervous agility. They fear the sergeant. They hurry as much as they can. In vain! Much too much noise, much too much commotion and not fast enough!
>
> The Feldwebel shouts: *"Achtung! Still gestanden! Na wird's mal, oder soll ich mit dem Gewehrkolben nachhelfen? Na jut; wenn Ihr's durchaus haben wollt!"* ("Attention! Stand still! How about it, or should I help you along with the butt of my rifle? All right, Jew, if you really want to have it!")
>
> The sergeant and his subordinates hit everyone: young or old, strong or sick, guilty or innocent—it was painful to hear the groaning and moaning.
>
> I heard it though I had been hit very hard, so hard that I could not help falling down. We all on the ground who could not stand up were then beaten over the head.
>
> I must have been unconscious. The next thing I knew was a soldier saying, "They are all dead!" Whereupon the sergeant ordered to do away with us.

There I lay aside half conscious. It had become very still—fear and pain—Then I heard the sergeant shouting: *"Abzählen!"* ("Count Off!")

They started slowly, and irregularly: One, two, three, four, *"Achtung."* The sergeant shouted again: *"Rascher! Nochmals von vorn anfangen! In einer Minute will ich wissen wieviele ich zur Gaskammer abliefere! Abzählen!"* ("Faster! Once more, start from the beginning! In a minute I will know how many I am going to send off to the gas chamber! Count off!")

They began again, first slowly: one, two, three, four, became faster and faster, so fast that it finally sounded like a stampede of wild horses, and all of a sudden, in the middle of it, they began singing the *Shema Yisroel.*

Shema Yisroel Adonoy elohenoo Adonoy eḥod. Veohavto es Adonoy eloheḥo beḥol levoveḥo oovoḥol nafsheḥo oovoḥol meodeḥo. Vehoyoo haddevoreem hoelleh asher onoḥee metsavveḥo hayyom al levoveḥo. Veshinnantom levoneḥo vedibbarto bom beshivteḥo beveteḥo oovelehteḥo baddereḥ ooveshoḥbeḥo oovekoomeḥo. ("Hear, O Israel, the Lord our God the Lord is One! And thou shalt love the Lord thy God with all thy heart, and with all thy soul, and with all thy might. And these words, which I command thee this day, shall be in thy heart. And thou shalt teach them diligently unto thy children, and speak of them when thou sittest in thy house, and when thou goest on the way, and when thou liest down, and when thou risest up.")

Technical Postscript

A Survivor from Warsaw is built from the following twelve-tone row: F♯-G-C-A♭-E-D♯-B♭-D♭-A-D-F-B. The opening of the choral melody uses two different transformations of the row: the original form shifted four half-steps higher (B♭-B♮-E-C-A♭-G-D-F-D♭-F♯-A-E♭) and the inverted form shifted nine half-steps higher (E♭-D-A-C♯-E♯-F♯-B-G♯-C-G♮-E♭-B♭).

A Survivor from Warsaw, Op. 46 (1947)

427

At the opening of the work, Schoenberg uses the first six notes of the original form in the first trumpet and violins, and the first six notes of the inversion shifted five half-steps higher in the second trumpet and contrabasses (Cb–Bb–F–A–C♯–D).

Basic Terms

If you aren't sure what each of the following words means, look back at the text, where they appear in bold type. Additional information about some of them can be found by checking the index.

atonality   tone row (set, series)
Sprechstimme   tone-color melody
twelve-tone system

[9] ALBAN BERG

Alban Berg (1885–1935), a student of Schoenberg, wrote music that is a unique synthesis of traditional and twentieth-century elements. He combines Romantic sounds and time-honored forms with the techniques of free atonality and the twelve-tone system. A wide audience has been attracted by the lyrical warmth, vivid tone colors, and theatrical qualities of Berg's compositions.

Like his teacher, Berg was born in Vienna. At nineteen, he began studying privately with Schoenberg and continued working with him from 1904 to 1911. After serving in the Austrian army during World War I, he became codirector (with Schoenberg) of the Society for Private Musical Performances in Vienna. The goal of the society, which lasted from 1918 to 1921, was to "give artists and music-lovers a real and exact knowledge of modern music" through repeated and well-rehearsed performances.

Berg first attracted international attention in 1925, when his opera *Wozzeck* premiered in Berlin. Though the opera's atonality baffled many critics, *Wozzeck* made such a powerful impression on the public that it was soon performed throughout Europe and in the United States.

Perhaps because of chronic ill-health, Berg did not perform or conduct and composed relatively few works. From the time he finished *Wozzeck* (1922) until his death at the age of fifty, his works include the *Chamber Concerto* for piano, violin, and thirteen winds (1925), the *Lyric Suite* for string quartet (1926), the opera *Lulu* (1929–1935, orchestration not completed), and the *Violin Concerto* (1935). Let's now turn to Berg's best-known work, *Wozzeck*.

Wozzeck (1917–1922)

Wozzeck is the tragic story of a soldier who is driven to murder and madness by a hostile society. An antihero obsessed by strange visions, Wozzeck is persecuted by his sadistic captain, used as a guinea pig by a half-demented doctor, and betrayed by his mistress Marie. Wozzeck stabs Marie to death and drowns while trying to wash her blood from his hands.

Berg's musical imagination was fired in 1914 when he saw *Woyzeck*, a play by the German dramatist and revolutionary Georg Büchner (1813–1837). Though written in the early 1830s, the play is amazingly modern in its starkly realistic dialog and disconnected scenes that recall the technique of some recent movies. Berg adapted the play into an opera while in the Austrian army in World War I. His traumatic army experiences may well have deepened his sympathy for Wozzeck.

The opera's nightmarish atmosphere makes it a musical counterpart of expressionist painting and literature. Berg conveys the tensions and torments of the unconscious through harsh dissonances and grotesque distortions. The music's range of emotions and styles is tremendous. Though most of *Wozzeck* is freely atonal—it does not use the twelve-tone system—major and minor keys occasionally add contrast. The vocal line includes speaking, shrieking, *Sprechstimme*, distorted folk songs, and melodies with wide leaps that are difficult to sing. The gigantic orchestra closely parallels the dialog and stage action. Descriptive effects include vivid orchestral depiction of the moon rising, frogs croaking, and water engulfing the drowning Wozzeck. Berg's music rapidly shifts between very high and very low registers, between *ffff* and *pppp*.

Wozzeck has three acts, each with five scenes. Connecting the scenes are short orchestral interludes that comment on the preceding action and serve as preparation for what is to come. As in the music dramas of Wagner, there is a continuous musical flow within each act, and characters are associated with specific musical ideas. A novel feature of *Wozzeck* is that the music for each scene is a self-contained composition with a particular form (passacaglia, sonata form, etc.) or of a definite type (military march, lullaby). The five scenes of the last act—which we'll study—are organized as (1) variations on a theme, (2) variations on a single tone, (3) variations on a rhythmic pattern, (4) variations on a chord, and (5) variations on continuous running-notes. But Berg did not intend for the listener to concentrate on or even be aware of these unifying techniques. He wanted the audience to be caught up in the opera's dramatic flow. Before Act III, Wozzeck has been driven to desperation by his mistress's infidelity and by a savage beating from the man who slept with her.

Wozzeck (1917–1922)

Act III

Scene 1: Marie's room

In the touching first scene of Act III, Wozzeck's unfaithful mistress Marie reads the story of Mary Magdalene from the Bible and laments her own weakness. Berg dramatically highlights Marie's anguish by having her alternate between speech and song. When Marie reads or tells a story to her child, we hear *Sprechstimme;* when she expresses her anguish, we hear jagged, hysterical phrases that are sung.

Berg also contrasts tonality and atonality for dramatic effect. When Marie relates a fairy tale to her son ("And once there was a poor wee child"), Berg uses Romantic harmonies in the clearly defined key of F minor. For Berg, this key symbolized "the vanished world of the fairy tale."

Scene 2: A path near a pond

Wozzeck stabs Marie to death while walking along a forest path near a pond. In an almost impressionistic way, the orchestra depicts the eerie night-time sounds in a forest. Wozzeck's obsession with Marie's murder is symbolized by the note B, which appears throughout the scene in different registers and in various instruments. Most of the time the tone is barely audible. But when Wozzeck pulls out his knife and kills Marie, the B is forced into the listener's consciousness through relentless timpani strokes. The obsessive B becomes overpowering during the orchestral interlude following the murder, when there are two ear-splitting crescendos on this note. Between the crescendos, drums hammer out a rhythmic pattern that will be repeated and developed in the next scene.

(This rhythm can be represented as long-long, short-long, long, short-short-long.)

Scene 3: A tavern

At a tavern, Wozzeck, almost insane, desperately struggles to forget his crime. Dissonant and distorted dance music is heard from a tiny on-stage piano that is supposed to sound out-of-tune. Marie's friend Margret sings a weirdly distorted folk tune for Wozzeck. When she notices his bloody hands, Wozzeck flees in terror.

Scene 4: A path near a pond

Wozzeck returns to the scene of the crime to dispose of his knife. Berg's orchestra vividly evokes the dark forest scene as a background to Wozzeck's anguished shrieks. Rising harp tones suggest the blood-red moon coming up through the clouds. Wozzeck goes mad and drowns in the pond while trying to wash the blood from his hands. Soft chromatic slides depict the engulfing water as the Captain and the Doctor, Wozzeck's oppressors, indifferently comment that someone is drowning. As Wozzeck drowns, the slides become slower and narrower in range.

The long orchestral interlude that follows is a deeply moving expression of grief for Wozzeck's tragic fate. It recalls the musical themes associated with his life. Berg described it as "a confession of the author stepping outside the dramatic events of the theater and appealing to the public as representing mankind." For this outpouring of compassion, Berg returns to tonality (the interlude is in D minor) and the musical language of late Romanticism.

Scene 5: A street before Marie's door
Children are playing in front of Marie's house; bright sunshine brings glaring contrast to the darkness of the preceding scenes. One of the children cruelly tells Wozzeck's son: "Hey! Your mother is dead." The boy rides off on his hobby horse with the other children to see the body. The orchestra is reduced in size to produce delicate sounds that match the children's high voices, and a continuous rhythm symbolizes their utter indifference. The opera does not end with a conclusive chord. It simply breaks off as though to suggest that the tragedy could begin again.

Scene 1

(*Marie's room. It is night. Candlelight. Marie, alone with her child, is sitting at the table, turning the pages of the Bible and reading.*) — Viola, *p.* imitated by cello.

Marie

"*Und ist kein Betrug in seinem Munde erfunden worden . . ."*	"And out of His mouth there came forth neither deceit nor falsehood . . ."	Spoken (*Sprechstimme*).
Herr-Gott! Herr-Gott! Sieh' mich nicht an!	Lord God! Lord God! Look not at me! (*She turns the pages.*)	Sung, *f.*
		Brief pause. High violin, *pp,* imitated by high cello.
"*Aber die Pharisäer brachten ein Weib zu ihm, so im Ehebruch lebte. Jesus aber sprach: 'So verdamme ich dich auch nicht, geh' hin, und sündige hinfort nicht mehr.'"*	"Wherefore the Pharisees had taken and brought to Him an adulterous woman. Jesus said to her: 'Thus condemned shall you not be. Go forth, go forth in peace, and sin no more.'"	Spoken, *p.*
Herr-Gott!	Lord God! (*She covers her face with her hands. The child presses up to Marie.*)	Sung, *f.*
Der Bub' gibt mir einen Stich in's Herz. Fort!	The boy looks at me and stabs my heart. Be off! (*Pushes the child away.*)	

Wozzeck (1917–1922)

431

Das brüst' sich in der Sonne!	Go proudly in the sun- light! (*Suddenly, more gently.*)	
Nein, komm, komm, her! Komm zu mir!	Ah, no! Come here! (*Draws him closer.*) Come to me.	
"Es war einmal ein armes Kind und hatt' keinen Vater und keine Mutter . . . war Alles tot und war Niemand auf der Welt, und es hat gehungert und geweint Tag und Nacht. Und weil es Niemand mehr hatt' auf der Welt . . ."	"And once there was a poor wee child and he had no father, nor any mother . . . for all were dead, there was no one in the world, therefore he did hunger and did weep day and night. Since he had no one else left in the world . . ."	Spoken. Romantic harmonies.
Der Franz ist nit kommen, gestern nit, heut' nit . . . Wie steht es geschrie- ben von der Magdalena? . . .	But Franz has not come yet, yesterday, this day . . . (*She hastily turns the pages of the Bible.*) What is written here of Mary Magdalene? . . .	Sung.
"Und kniete hin zu seinen Füssen und weinte und küsste seine Füsse und netzte sie mit Tränen und salbte sie mit Salben!"	"And falling on her knees before Him and weep- ing, she kissed His feet and washed them, and washed them with her tears, annointing them with ointment!" (*Beats her breast.*)	Voice alone. Solo strings, *pp*, join.
Heiland! Ich möchte Dir die Füsse salben! Heiland! Du hast Dich ihrer erbarmt, erbarme Dich auch meiner!	Savior! Could I anoint Thy feet with ointment! Sav- ior! As Thou hadst mercy on her, have mercy now on me, Lord!	Crescendo.
		Orchestral interlude, trombones, *ff*. Decrescendo.

Scene 2

(*Forest path by a pond. Dusk is falling. Marie enters with Wozzeck, from the right.*)

Low tone, B, in
background,
p.

	Marie	
Dort links geht's in die Stadt,	The town lies over there.	
's ist noch weit. Komm	It's still far. Let's hurry!	
schneller!		

	Wozzeck	
Du sollst dableiben, Marie.	You must stay awhile,	
Komm, setz' Dich.	Marie. Come, sit here.	

	Marie	
Aber ich muss fort.	But it's getting late.	

	Wozzeck	
Komm. Bist weit gegangen,	Come! (*They sit down.*) So	
Marie. Sollst Dir die Füsse	far you've wandered,	
nicht mehr wund laufen. 's	Marie. You must not	
ist still hier! Und so dunkel.	make your feet so sore,	
—Weisst noch, Marie, wie	walking. It's still, here in	
lang' es jetzt ist, dass wir	the darkness.—Tell me,	
uns kennen?	Marie, how long has it	
	been since our first meet-	
	ing?	

	Marie	
Zu Pfingsten drei Jahre.	At Whitsun, three years.	

	Wozzeck	
Und was meinst, wie lang' es	And how long, how long	
noch dauern wird?	will it still go on?	

	Marie	
Ich muss fort.	(*Jumping up.*) I must go!	

	Wozzeck	
Fürchst Dich, Marie? Und	Trembling, Marie? But you	Upward harp
bist doch fromm? Und gut!	are good (*laughing*) and	glissando, *pp.*
Und treu!	kind and true! (*He pulls*	
	her down again on the seat;	
	he bends over her, in deadly	
Was Du für süsse Lippen	*earnest.*) Ah! How your	
hast, Marie! Den Him-	lips are sweet to touch,	
mel gäb' ich drum und die	Marie! (*Kisses her.*) All	
Seligkeit, wenn ich	heaven I would give,	
	and eternal bliss, if I	
Dich noch oft so küssen	still could sometimes	
dürft! Aber ich darf nicht!	kiss you so! But yet I	
Was zitterst?	dare not! You shiver?	Xylophone taps,
		pp.

	Marie	
Der Nachttau fällt.	The night dew falls.	

Wozzeck (1917–1922)

433

Wozzeck

Wer kalt ist, den friert nicht mehr! Dich wird beim Morgentau nicht frieren.

(*Whispering to himself.*) Who cold is, you who shiver, will freeze no more in cold morning dew.

Marie

Was sagst Du da?

What are you saying?

Wozzeck

Nix.

Nothing.

(*A long silence. The moon rises.*)

Brasses, *pp*, rising tones.

Marie

Wie der Mond rot aufgeht!

How the moon rises red!

Wozzeck

Wie ein blutig Eisen!

Like a blood-red iron! (*He draws a knife.*)

Obsessive timpani strokes. Crescendo.

Marie

Was zitterst? Was willst?

You shiver? (*She jumps up.*) What now?

Wozzeck

Ich nicht, Marie! Und kein Andrer auch nicht!

No one, Marie! If not me, then no one! (*He seizes her and plunges the knife into her throat.*)

Marie

Hilfe!

Help! (*She sinks down. Wozzeck bends over her. She dies.*)

Decrescendo.

Wozzeck

Tot!

Dead! (*He rises to his feet anxiously, and then rushes silently away.*)

Orchestral interlude, crescendo on tone B. Drums beat obsessive rhythm. Second orchestral crescendo on B.

Scene 3

(A tavern. Night. Badly lit. Girls, among them Margret, and apprentices are dancing a wild and rapid polka. Wozzeck is seated at one of the tables.)

"Out-of-tune" piano.

Wozzeck

Tanzt Alle; tanzt nur zu, springt, schwitzt und stinkt, es holt Euch doch noch einmal der Teufel!

Dance, all you, dance away! Leap, sweat and reek. For some day soon he'll fetch you, the Devil! *(Dashes down his glass; then, shouting down the pianist.)*

Es ritten drei Reiter wohl an den Rhein,

Three riders came riding up to the Rhine,

Bei einer Frau Wirtin da kehrten sie ein.

And went to my hostess to taste of her wine.

Mein Wein ist gut, mein Bier ist klar,

My wine is good, my beer is clear,

Mein Töchterlein liegt auf der . . .

My daughter dear lies on her . . .

Verdammt! Komm, Margret! Komm, setz Dich her, Margret! Margret, Du bist so heiss. Wart nur, wirst auch kalt werden! Kannst nicht singen?

Be damned! *(jumps up.)* Come, Margret. *(Dances a few steps with her, then suddenly stops.)* Come, let's sit down, Margret. *(Leads Margret to his table, and pulls her onto his lap.)* Margret, you're hot as fire. *(Presses her to him; lets her go.)* But wait till you're cold also! Can't you sing, girl?

Margret

In's Schwabenland, da mag ich nit,

To Swabia I will not go,

Und lange Kleider trag ich nit,

And your long dresses I'll not wear,

Denn lange Kleider, spitze Schuh,

For trailing dresses, pointed shoes,

Die kommen keiner Dienstmagd zu.

Do not belong to servant girls.

Distorted folk-like melody accompanied by "out-of-tune" piano.

Wozzeck

Nein! keine Schuh, man kann auch blossfüssig in die Höll'

(Flaming up.) No! Wear no shoes! For one can bare-

geh'n! Ich möcht heut raufen, *   * footed go to hell-fire. I
raufen . . . *   * want to wrestle, wrestle . . .

Margret

Aber was hast Du an der *   * But what is that there on
Hand? *   * your hand?

Wozzeck

Ich? Ich? *   * Mine? Mine?

Margret

Rot! Blut! *   * Red! Blood!

Wozzeck

Blut? Blut? *   * Blood? Blood!

(*People gather round Margret and Wozzeck.*)

Margret

Freilich . . . Blut! *   * Surely . . . blood!

Wozzeck

Ich glaub', ich hab' mich ge- *   * I think, I must have, I've *   * Gradual cre-
schnitten, da an der rechten *   * cut it sometime, on my *   * scendo.
Hand . . . *   * right hand . . . *   * Voices to-
*   * gether.

Margret

Wie kommt's denn zum Ellen- *   * How comes it then on
bogen? *   * your elbow?

Wozzeck

Ich hab's daran abgewischt. *   * I've wiped my hand on it
*   * there.

Apprentices

Mit der rechten Hand am *   * His right elbow wiped
rechten Arm? *   * with his right hand?

Wozzeck

Was wollt Ihr? Was geht's *   * What do you mean? That's
Euch an? *   * my affair.

Margret

Puh! Puh! Da stinkt's nach *   * Pooh! Pooh! It smells of
Menschenblut! *   * human blood!

Wozzeck

Bin ich ein Mörder? *   * Am I a murderer?

Apprentices

Blut, Blut, Blut, Blut! *   * Blood, blood, blood, blood!

Girls

Freilich, da stinkt's nach Men- *   * Surely, it smells of human
schenblut! *   * blood!

Wozzeck

Platz! oder es geht wer zum Teufel!	Off! Or else someone pays the Devil! (*Rushes out.*)	
		Orchestral interlude, *ff*. Snaredrum roll.

Scene 4

(*Forest path by the pond. Moonlit night as before. Wozzeck staggers on hastily, and then stops as he searches for something.*)		Winds, *p*, repeated chord.

Wozzeck

Das Messer? Wo ist das Messer? Ich hab's dagelassen . . . Näher, noch näher. Mir graut's! Da regt sich was.	Where is it? Where has the knife gone? Somewhere here I left it . . . Somewhere here, somewhere. Oh! Horror! There something moved!	Spoken.
Still! Alles still und tot . . . Mörder! Mörder! Ha! Da ruft's. Nein, ich selbst. Marie! Marie! Was hast Du für eine rote Schnur um den Hals? Hast Dir das rote Halsband verdient, wie die Ohrringlein, mit Deiner Sünde! Was hängen Dir die schwarzen Haare so wild? Mörder! Mörder! Sie werden nach mir suchen . . . Das Messer verrät mich! Da, da ist's. So! Da hinunter. Es taucht ins dunkle Wasser wie ein Stein.	Still! All is still and dead! . . . Murder! Murder! Ah, who cried? No, 'twas me. (*Still searching, he staggers forward a few more steps, and comes on the corpse.*) Marie! Marie! What is that so like a crimson cord round your neck? And was that crimson necklace well earned, like the gold earrings: the price of sinning! Why hangs your fine black hair so wild on your head? Murder! Murder! For me they'll soon be searching . . . That knife will betray me! (*Seeks it feverishly.*) Ah! It's here! (*At the pond.*) Down to the bottom! (*Throws the knife in.*) It sinks through deep dark water like a stone.	Shouted.

Wozzeck (1917–1922)

437

(The moon comes up blood-red through the clouds.)

Rising harp
tones, *pp.*

Aber der Mond verrät mich . . . der Mond ist blutig. Will denn die ganze Welt es ausplaudern?!—Das Messer, es liegt zu weit vorn, sie finden's beim Baden oder wenn sie nach Muscheln tauchen. Ich find's nicht . . . Aber ich muss mich waschen. Ich bin blutig. Da ein Fleck . . . und noch einer. Weh! Weh! Ich wasche mich mit Blut! Das Wasser ist Blut . . . Blut . . .	See how the moon betrays me . . . the moon is bloody! Must then the whole wide world be blabbing it?—The knife there, too near to the shore! They'll find it when bathing, maybe when they are mussel-gathering. (*He wades into the pond.*) It's gone now. I ought to wash my body. I am bloody. Here's a spot . . . and here . . . something. Woe! Woe! I wash my-self with blood! The water is blood . . . blood . . . (*He drowns.*)

Water music.
Upward or-
chestral slides,
pp. Rhythm
gradually
slows.

(After a short time the Doctor enters, followed by the Captain.)

Captain

Halt!	Stop!	Spoken.

Doctor

Hören Sie? Dort!	(*Stands still.*) Do you hear? There!

Captain

Jesus! Das war ein Ton.	Heavens! There was a sound. (*Stands still.*)

Doctor

Ja, dort!	(*Pointing to the pond.*) Yes, there!

Captain

Es ist das Wasser im Teich. Das Wasser ruft. Es ist schon lange Niemand er-	It is the water in the pond. The water calls. It is a long time since anyone

trunken. Kommen Sie, Dok-   was drowned. Come,
tor! Es ist nicht gut zu hören.   Doctor, this is not good
to hear. (*He tries to drag
off the Doctor.*)

Doctor

Das stöhnt . . . als stürbe ein   (*Stands still and listens.*) It
Mensch. Da ertrinkt Jemand!   groans . . . like a dying
man. There's someone
drowning!

Captain

Unheimlich! Der Mond rot   It's uncanny! The moon is   Celesta.
und die Nebel grau. Hören   red, and the mist is
Sie? . . . Jetzt wieder das   grey. Do you
Ächzen.   hear? . . . That groaning
again.

Doctor

Stiller, . . . jetzt ganz still.   It's getting softer . . . and
now quite gone.

Captain

Kommen Sie! Kommen Sie   Come away! Quick! (*Drags
schnell.*   the Doctor off with him.*)

Extended orches-
tral interlude.

Scene 5

(*Street before Marie's door. Bright morning. Sunshine. Children are playing and shouting. Marie's child is riding a hobby-
horse.*)

Children

Ringel, Ringel, Rosenkranz,   Ring-a-ring-a-roses, all fall
Ringelreih'n!   down!
Ringel, Ringel, Rosenkranz,   Ring-a-ring-a-roses, all . . .
Rin . . .

(*They stop, and other children come rushing on.*)

One of them

Du Käthe! . . . Die   Katie! . . . Marie . . .
Marie . . .

Second Child

Was is?   What is it?

First Child

Weisst' es nit? Sie sind schon   Don't you know? They've
Alle'naus.   all gone out there.

Third Child

Du! Dein Mutter ist tot!   (*To Marie's child.*) Hey!
Your mother is dead.

Wozzeck (1917–1922)

439

Marie's Child

Hopp, hopp! Hopp, hopp!   (*Still riding his horse.*) Hop,
Hopp, hopp!   hop! Hop, hop! Hop
                                 hop!

Second Child

Wo is sie denn?   Where is she now?

First Child

Draus' liegt sie, am Weg,   Out there, on the path by
neben dem Teich.   the pond.

Third Child

Kommt, anschaun!   Let's go and look! (*All the
                           children run off.*)

Marie's Child

Hopp, hopp! Hopp, hopp!   (*Continues to ride.*) Hop,
Hopp, hopp!   hop! Hop, hop! Hop,
                            hop! (*He hesitates a mo-
                            ment, and then rides off
                            after the other children.*)

                                                       Music breaks
                                                       off.

[10] ANTON WEBERN

Neglected during his lifetime, Anton Webern (1883–1945) did not live to see his music influence composers throughout the world during the 1950s and 1960s.

He was born in Vienna, the son of a mining engineer. As a young man, he composed constantly and studied piano, cello, and music theory. At eighteen, he entered the University of Vienna and later earned a doctorate in music history. While at the university, he studied composition privately with Arnold Schoenberg.

After finishing his studies with Schoenberg, Webern earned a modest living conducting various orchestras and choruses. His career was solid but unspectacular. His most important position was as director of the Vienna Workers' Symphony Concerts, where traditional and contemporary compositions were performed for a working-class audience. Rare performances of his own works were usually met with ridicule.

Webern was a shy man, devoted to his wife and children. A Christian mystic, he loved to commune with nature while mountain climbing in the Austrian Alps. "It is not the beautiful landscape, the beautiful flowers in the usual romantic sense, that move me," he wrote to his friend Alban Berg. "My object is the deep, bottomless, inexhaustible meaning in all. I love all nature, but most of all that which is found in the mountains."

With the rise of Nazism in Austria in 1934, Webern's orchestra and chorus—sponsored by the Social Democratic party—were dissolved. In 1938, when Nazi Germany annexed Austria, Webern lost his job with the government radio, and his music was banned. He was forced to eke out a living by proofreading for his Viennese publisher.

While Webern's life seems ordinary enough, his death was a bizarre tragedy. Toward the end of World War II, he took refuge from the bombing of Vienna in the small Austrian town of Mittersill. His daughter lived there with her husband and three children. In 1945, victorious American soldiers occupied the town; on the night of September 15 they arrested Webern's son-in-law, who was suspected of dealing in the black market. During the questioning, Webern and his wife—who were unaware of their son-in-law's activities—went into the bedroom where their grandchildren were sleeping. Later, Webern stepped outside the house to smoke a cigar without disturbing the children. Minutes later, an American soldier left the house and bumped into Webern in the darkness. Nervous and in a hostile foreign country, the soldier mistakenly thought he was being attacked. He fired three shots, and Webern was dead.

Webern's Music

Poetic lyricism pervades Webern's music, which is amazingly original in its brevity, quietness, and concentration. Webern distills a musical universe into miniatures lasting only two or three minutes; every single tone is of such crucial importance that the listener experiences time with a new intensity. Schoenberg aptly observed that Webern "expressed a novel in a single gesture, a joy in a breath."

Rarely has a composer achieved such worldwide influence on the basis of so little music; virtually all of Webern's mature music is on only four long-playing records. Choral works and songs make up about half of his output. The rest is music written for chamber orchestra or small chamber groups (as in the *Quartet* for clarinet, tenor saxophone, violin, and piano, Op. 22; 1930). Webern's first atonal works date from 1908 to 1909, around the same time as Schoenberg's. He adopted the twelve-tone system in the late 1920s, not long after his teacher developed it.

Webern exploited Schoenberg's idea of a "melody built of tone colors." His melodic lines are "atomized" into two- or three-note fragments which are presented in constantly changing tone colors and registers. He forces us to focus on the tone color, dynamic level, and register of each note.

At first his music may seem like isolated wisps of sound, but repeated hearings reveal that the fragments add up to a unified whole.

The texture of Webern's music is delicate and transparent; usually not more than a few solo instruments play at once. In his twelve-tone works, there is often strict polyphonic imitation among the lines of the texture. This technique

Webern's Music

441

may well reflect Webern's profound knowledge of Renaissance choral music, in which polyphonic imitation is so important. Texture, tone color, and dynamics play a crucial role in creating form in Webern's music.

Composers in the 1950s and 1960s used Webern's special way of manipulating a tone row as a musical point of departure. They were fascinated by his use of texture, tone color, dynamics, and register as unifying elements, and they often imitated the deceptively "cool" sound of his later music. Works that appealed to very few during Webern's lifetime have become a source of inspiration after his death.

Five Pieces for Orchestra, Op. 10 (1911–1913)

Webern's unique style is fully revealed in these early atonal works, composed before he adopted the twelve-tone system. These five "expressions of musical lyricism," as Webern called them, are among the shortest orchestral compositions ever written. The fourth piece is only 6 ⅓ measures long and lasts less than thirty seconds. Webern's chamber orchestra of eighteen soloists includes unconventional instruments like the mandolin, guitar, cowbells, and harmonium (a small organ with metal reeds). Each piece is scored for a different number and combination of instruments.

Melodic fragments are whispered by ever-changing solo instruments and framed by poetic silences. Tone-color melodies replace "tunes" in this music. There are few notes, but each is crucial. The tempo constantly fluctuates. Brasses and strings are usually muted.

Aware that his music required an open-minded listener, Webern was delighted when the fourth piece of the set appeared on the children's page of the *Christian Science Monitor* along with pictures of the instruments used. "If the so-called adults, the grown-ups, had as few prejudices as children," he wrote, "then everything would be quite different."

1. Very calm and tender

Changes of texture help create the form of this quiet miniature, which lasts only about thirty seconds. It opens with a single melodic line, then becomes more complex as several lines are presented at once. Then the original monophonic texture returns. The opening melodic line is a clear example of a tone-color melody; the first seven pitches are assigned a variety of timbres:

Pitch 1:	harp, muted trumpet
Pitch 2:	celesta, harp harmonic, viola harmonic
Pitch 3:	harp, flute flutter-tongue
Pitches 4–6:	glockenspiel
Pitch 7:	celesta trill

2. Lively and tenderly animated

Lasting less than a half a minute, this piece quickly moves from a soft beginning to a climactic *ff* ending that features high woodwinds, horn, trumpet, and glockenspiel (a set of metal bars struck by two hammers).

3. Very slow and extremely calm

With its bell sounds coming as though from far off, this piece has a feeling of solitude and eerie stillness. The dynamics never rise above *pp*. The sustained bell-like sounds—produced by mandolin, celesta, guitar, harp, glockenspiel, cowbells, chimes, and harmonium—are heard both at the beginning and at the ending. This creates a vague A B A' effect. Melodic fragments in ever-changing solo instruments are set apart from one another by brief moments of near silence.

LISTENING OUTLINE

To be read while music is heard

Third Piece (1913) from *Five Pieces for Orchestra,* Op. 10 (1911–1913), by Anton Webern

clarinet, muted horn, muted trombone, harmonium, mandolin, guitar, celesta, harp, bass drum, snare drum, chimes, cowbells, violin, muted viola, muted cello

Very slow and extremely calm

(About 1½ min)

1   *a.* Pulsating bell-like sounds, *ppp.*
     b. Violin, *pp,* pulsating bell-like sounds, *ppp.*
     c. Muted horn, *pp,* chimes, *ppp.*
2   Quicker notes in clarinet. Muted viola.
3   *a.* Pulsating bell-like sounds, *ppp.*
     b. Muted trombone, *ppp*; pulsating bell-like sounds, *ppp.* Snaredrum roll, extremely soft.

4. Flowing, extremely tender

The shortest piece in the orchestral repertory, this touching miniature demands the utmost concentration. Its few notes are all soft and in a fairly high register. The pulse and meter are barely perceptible. The piece is scored for clarinet, mandolin, celesta, harp, and snare drum, as well as the following muted instruments: trumpet, trombone, violin, and viola. While most of the instruments have sustained or repeated tones, tiny melodic fragments are played by the mandolin, trumpet, trombone, and violin.

5. Very flowing

This is scored for twenty instruments, more than any other piece of the set. Webern begins with a few rarefied sounds but moves to a piercing climax at

Five Pieces for Orchestra, Op. 10 (1911–1913)

443

the exact center of the piece. The dynamics quickly return to *pp*, and the piece ends with an "extremely tender" note on the viola and a faint tap on the celesta.

[11] BÉLA BARTÓK

Béla Bartók (1881–1945), whose music is infused with the spirit of East European folk song, was born in the Hungarian town of Nagyszentmiklós. When Bartók was seven, his father died and his mother was forced to move with her son from town to town while she earned a living as a schoolteacher. She gave him his first lessons on the piano, an instrument which played an important role in his career. For twenty-seven years (1907–1934), Bartók taught piano at his alma mater, the Budapest Academy of Music, and gave recitals throughout Europe.

During the early 1900s, Bartók was influenced by the nationalist movement that swept Hungary. He came to love the music of Hungarian peasants, and he spent most of his free time in tiny villages recording folk songs on a cylinder phonograph. Bartók became a leading authority on the peasant music of the Magyars, Rumanians, Slovaks, Turks, and the Arabs of North Africa. Soon his own music was profoundly affected by the folk music he knew so well.

Though Bartók was recognized early as an important composer abroad, he was neglected in Hungary. For a time after 1911, he even refused to play in Hungary because of "the indifference and animosity" of his countrymen. It was only after the successful Budapest premiere of his ballet *The Wooden Prince* in 1917 that Bartók's music gained acceptance in his homeland. During a tour of the United States in 1927 to 1928 one newspaper headline warned readers: "Hungarian Modernist Advances upon Los Angeles to Convince Scoffers." By 1939 he was able to gleefully report to his son that "Since 1934, I have worked almost exclusively upon commissions!"

Hitler's rise posed a serious problem for Bartók, who was violently anti-Nazi. After Germany's annexation of Austria in 1938, he wrote a friend: "There is the imminent danger that Hungary will also surrender to this system of robbery and murder. How I could then continue to live or—which amounts to the same thing—work in such a country is quite inconceivable." Bartók did not allow his music to be performed in Germany or on any radio station that could be heard in Germany or Italy.

In 1940, Bartók finally emigrated to the United States, where he spent the last five years of his life. This was a bleak period for him; he had little money, was in poor health, and felt isolated and neglected. "My career as a composer is as much as finished," he wrote in 1942. "The quasi-boycott of my works

Caught up in the nationalist movement that swept Hungary, Bartók spent most of his free time in tiny villages recording folk songs on a cylinder phonograph (G. D. Hackett).

by the leading orchestras continues. . . ." For three years he stopped composing. He held a position as a research scholar in folk music at Columbia University, but the grant ended before he could finish his work. In 1943, his health declined alarmingly. After his weight fell to eighty-seven pounds, he entered a New York hospital, where he unexpectedly received a commission for the *Concerto for Orchestra*, his best-known work. The success of its first performance in 1944 resulted in a series of commissions for the once-ignored composer. Tragically, Bartók had only a year to live and could write just two more compositions, the *Sonata* for solo violin (1944) and the *Third Piano Concerto* (1945).

Soon after his death in New York in 1945, Bartók became one of the most popular twentieth-century composers.

Béla Bartók

445

Bartók's Music

"I do not reject any influence," wrote Bartók, "whether its source be Slovak, Rumanian, Arab, or some other; provided this source be pure, fresh and healthy." But he emphasized that the "Hungarian influence is the strongest." Bartók evolved a completely individual style that fused folk elements, classical forms, and twentieth-century sounds. He believed that peasant music helped liberate him from the "exclusive rule of the major or minor system." Most folk melodies, he observed, "adhere to the old church modes or the ancient Greek modes and certain still older modes (especially pentatonic), and moreover display extremely free and varied rhythmic structures and changes of meter. . . ." Bartók arranged many Hungarian and Rumanian folk tunes, often giving them highly dissonant accompaniments. In most of his works, however, Bartók does not quote folk melodies; he uses original themes that have a folk flavor. His aim was to "assimilate the idiom of peasant music so completely" that he could "forget all about it and use it as his mother tongue."

Bartók's genius found its most characteristic expression in instrumental music. He wrote many works for piano solo, six string quartets, other chamber music, three concertos for piano, one for violin, and several compositions for orchestra. Embracing a wide range of emotions, Bartók's music is deeply expressive. Fast movements can convey a primitive brutality or the vitality and swing of a peasant dance. Slow movements often suggest feelings of bleakness and profound pessimism. They frequently contain atmospheric, almost impressionistic music suggesting nocturnal insect noises and the chirping of birds. Such mysterious passages are known as Bartók's "night music."

Bartók revitalized and reinterpreted traditional forms such as the rondo, fugue, and sonata form. He unifies the contrasting movements of a composition by bringing back a theme in transformed versions. He also creates formal unity by beginning and ending a movement in the same way. For example, the second movement of the *Concerto for Orchestra* (1943) opens and closes with a solo on the side drum. Polyphonic imitation and motivic development often generate tension and excitement.

Bartók always organized his works around a tonal center. But within this tonal framework, he often used harsh dissonances, polychords, and tone clusters. In some of his late works, however, he returned to a more traditional and less dissonant vocabulary. Bartók's music is rhythmically characterized by a powerful beat, unexpected accents, and changing meters. The irregular meters and asymmetrical rhythmic patterns of East European folk music are used imaginatively. (See Bartók's *Six Dances in Bulgarian Rhythm* in section 1.)

Bartók was also imaginative in his use of tone colors, particularly of percussion instruments. In works such as *Music for Strings, Percussion and Celesta* (1936) and the *Sonata for Two Pianos and Percussion* (1937), he drew unusual sounds from the xylophone and timpani. Bartók was especially fond of glissandos on the timpani (this sliding effect is produced by a pedal mechanism). Like many twentieth-century composers, Bartók drew percussive, drumlike sounds from the piano as well.

Bartók's six string quartets are widely thought to be the finest since those of Beethoven. The works abound in exciting glissandos and pizzicatos that produce a "snap" when the string rebounds against the fingerboard. But Bartók's string quartets are more than a collection of novel sounds; they reflect the composer's profundity and nobility.

Concerto for Orchestra (1943)

The commission which led to the *Concerto for Orchestra* was offered to Bartók in 1943, while he was hospitalized in New York City. Serge Koussevitsky, the conductor of the Boston Symphony Orchestra, offered him a thousand-dollar commission for a new work. While recuperating at Saranac Lake, New York, Bartók was able to work "practically day and night" on his new composition. He finished it in six weeks. The *Concerto for Orchestra* was an enormous success at its premiere in Boston in 1944 and has since become Bartók's most popular work.

"The general mood of the work," wrote Bartók, "represents, apart from the jesting second movement, a gradual transition from the sternness of the first movement and the lugubrious death-song of the third, to the life-assertion of the last one." Bartók explained that the unusual title "Concerto for Orchestra" reflects the work's "tendency to treat the single orchestral instruments in a *concertant* or soloistic manner."

Written for an orchestra of virtuosos, this dazzling showpiece is Romantic in spirit because of its emotional intensity, memorable themes, and vivid contrasts of mood. Though its melodies were original with Bartók, they have a distinct folk flavor. The concerto is an example of Bartók's mellow "late" style, which is characterized by more frequent use of traditional chords. In all five movements, time-honored procedures like A B A, sonata form, and fugue are fused with twentieth-century rhythms and tone colors.

First Movement: *Introduction* (Andante non troppo); Allegro vivace

The concerto begins with an extended slow Introduction based on two melodic ideas that grow in intensity as they are varied. Low cellos and double basses mysteriously introduce the first idea, a short phrase that climbs and then falls. The cello phrase returns twice, each time ascending higher before it descends. The flute then softly introduces the second thematic idea, an exotic-sounding figure that circles around a single tone. This theme also returns twice. First it is varied and expanded by the trumpets playing very softly, and then it is transformed into a passionate outcry by the strings.

The Allegro vivace is a type of sonata form. Themes are broken into fragments that are shifted among different instruments. In this movement there are frequent alternations between fast, powerful sections featuring strings and brasses and slower, calmer sections in which woodwinds are most prominent.

The assertive opening theme of the exposition is marked by the rapidly changing meter so typical of twentieth-century music.

Concerto for Orchestra (1943)

447

Its descending second phrase is an inversion, or upside-down form, of the ascending first phrase.

Before the contrasting second theme enters, the trombone plays a somber phrase. This has an important role later in the movement. The atmosphere of the Middle East is evoked by the plaintive second theme, which is first played by the oboe. It features an alternation between two tones, and it has a static, dronelike accompaniment that is common in folk music.

In the development section, the trombone motive from the exposition grows into an exciting brass fanfare. It is polyphonically imitated among the trombones, trumpets, French horns, and tuba. The recapitulation of the movement is unusual because the second theme comes before—rather than after—the first theme. The Allegro vivace ends decisively with the trombone motive, played in unison by all the brasses.

LISTENING OUTLINE
To be read while music is heard

Concerto for Orchestra (1943) by Béla Bartók

First Movement: *Introduction* (Andante non troppo); Allegro vivace

Sonata form

piccolo, 3 flutes, 3 oboes, English horn, 3 clarinets, bass clarinet, 3 bassoons, 4 horns, 3 trumpets, 3 trombones, tuba, timpani, cymbals, 2 harps, violins 1, violins 2, violas, cellos, basses

(About 9 min)

Andante non troppo
INTRODUCTION

1 *a.* Low strings, *p*, ascending and descending phrase. High string tremolo, *pp*, flutes.

    b. Low strings, *p*, phrase ascends higher, then descends. High string tremolo, *pp*, flutes.
    c. Low strings, phrase ascends still higher, then descends.

2 *a.* Flute, *p*, new phrase. Strings, *p*.

    b. Trumpets, *pp*, new phrase varied and extended. Strings in background.

    c. Violins, *f*, new phrase transformed into forceful melody.

    d. Crescendo, bass motive repeated faster and faster, leading into

Allegro vivace
EXPOSITION

First theme   1   *a.* Violins, *f*, main theme. Fast tempo. Violin melody becomes slightly softer. Crescendo to *f*.

    b. Trombone motive, *mf*. Flute, *p*, descending melody.

Second theme   2   *a.* Oboe, *p*, folklike melody, slower tempo. Strings and harp accompany.

    b. Folklike melody repeated and extended by clarinets, flutes, *p*. Strings and harp accompany.

DEVELOPMENT

     1   Orchestra, *f*, fragments of main theme in imitation. Allegro vivace. Crescendo to *ff*.

     2   Clarinet, *p*, new legato melody, slower tempo. Melody extended by English horn, flute, *p*.

     3   Strings, *ff*. Brasses, trombone motive in imitation. Allegro vivace. Orchestra, *fff*, high sustained tone.

RECAPITULATION

Second theme   1   *a.* Clarinet, *p*, folklike melody, slower tempo. Strings and harp accompany.

    b. Folklike melody repeated and extended by flutes, oboe, *p*. Strings and harp accompany.

    c. Low strings alternate with higher woodwinds. Crescendo and accelerando to

First theme   2   Orchestra, *ff*, main theme. Allegro vivace. Brasses, *ff*, trombone motive ends movement.

Second Movement: *Game of Pairs* **(Allegretto scherzando)**

In A B A' form, the jesting second movement is a "game" involving different "pairs" of woodwind and brass instruments. The instruments of each pair move in parallel motion and are separated by a distinctive pitch interval. In the opening section (A), a chain of five melodies is played consecutively by pairs of bassoons, oboes, clarinets, flutes, and muted trumpets. The contrasting middle section (B) is a hymnlike melody softly played by brass instruments. When the opening section returns (A'), it has a more active accompaniment. The incisive sound of a side drum (without snares) is prominent throughout the movement. It plays syncopated solos at both the beginning and the end, as well as in the hymnlike middle section.

LISTENING OUTLINE
To be read while music is heard

Concerto for Orchestra (1943) by Béla Bartók

Second Movement: *Game of Pairs* (Allegretto scherzando)

A B A' form, duple meter ($\frac{2}{4}$)

2 flutes, 2 oboes, 2 clarinets, 3 bassoons, 4 horns, 2 trumpets, 2 trombones, tuba, timpani, side drum, 2 harps, violins 1, violins 2, violas, cellos, basses

(About 6½ min)

A	1	Solo side drum (without snares), *mf.*
	2	Two bassoons, *p*, accompanied by pizzicato strings.
	3	*a.* Two oboes, *p*, in higher register. Pizzicato strings accompany.
		b. Low strings, pizzicato, while oboes sustain tones.
	4	*a.* Two clarinets.
		b. Low strings, accented notes.
	5	*a.* Two flutes, *mf*, in higher register.
		b. Low strings, pizzicato, while flutes sustain tones.
	6	Two muted trumpets, *p*. Muted string tremolos, *pp*, in background.
B	1	*a.* Brasses, *mf,* hymnlike legato melody. Side drum accompanies.
		b. Horns, *p*, conclude hymnlike melody and sustain chord.
	2	Oboe, flute, and clarinet, *p*, lead to
A'	1	Two bassoons, *p*, opening melody. Staccato bassoon in background.
	2	*a.* Two oboes, *p*, in higher register. Clarinets and strings in background.
		b. Low strings, pizzicato, while oboes sustain tones.
	3	*a.* Two clarinets. Flutes and strings in background.
		b. Low strings, accented notes.
	4	*a.* Two flutes, *mf*, in higher register. Woodwinds and strings in background.
		b. Low strings, pizzicato, while flutes sustain tones.
	5	Two muted trumpets, *mf*. Harp glissandos and muted string tremolos in background.
	6	Woodwinds, *p*, repeated chord; solo side drum, decrescendo, ends *Game of Pairs.*

Third Movement: *Elegy* (Andante, non troppo)

Bartók thought of this deeply moving music as a "death song." The Elegy is based largely on themes from the slow Introduction to the first movement. Mysterious opening bars—similar to those of the Introduction—lead into a section of "night music." A misty, nocturnal atmosphere is evoked by soft harp glissandos, splashes of woodwind sound, chirps from the piccolo, and a mournful oboe line.

The central section of the Elegy is louder and more melodic than the rest. High violins proclaim a theme that was played softly by trumpets in the Introduction to the first movement. A folklike melody is then introduced by violas and repeated, at a higher pitch, by woodwinds. The Elegy ends as it began, with misty "night music" and faint chirps from a piccolo.

Fourth Movement: *Interrupted Intermezzo* (Allegretto)

There is an amusing story behind the title of this movement. While working on his *Concerto for Orchestra*, Bartók heard a radio broadcast of the Seventh Symphony by Soviet composer Dimitri Shostakovich. Bartók found one of its themes to be so silly that he decided to parody it. In the middle of the movement, which is outlined A B A–interruption–B A, we hear this tune in the clarinet mocked by vulgar and noisy "interruptions" from the entire orchestra.

The Interrupted Intermezzo begins with a wistful folklike melody (A) played by the oboe.

Constant alternation between $\frac{2}{4}$ and $\frac{5}{8}$ meter makes the tune delightfully irregular. The strings play an ardent, expansive melody (B). After the "interruption," there is a return of both melodies in reverse order, and the movement ends abruptly and humorously.

Fifth Movement: *Finale* (Presto)

The Finale, in sonata form, sounds like a frenzied dance. An opening horn motive introduces a fiery "perpetual motion" theme in the violins. Tension drops when Bartók introduces a quiet woodwind episode, and the tempo slows. But the dancelike mood and rapid tempo are soon resumed when a trumpet introduces a fanfare theme with staccato repeated notes.

Concerto for Orchestra (1943)

451

Presto

f

The fanfare theme is immediately imitated by a second trumpet, but in inverted, or upside-down, form. After a gentle harp passage, the fanfare theme is further developed in a fuguelike section, first by the strings, then by the whole orchestra. The shortened recapitulation ends with brasses proclaiming a slowed-down form of the fanfare theme.

[12] CHARLES IVES

American composer Charles Ives (1874–1954) wrote startlingly original music that was far ahead of its time. He was born in Danbury, Connecticut, the son of a bandmaster who loved to experiment with unusual sounds. "Pa taught me what I know," Ives later recalled. He learned to play many instruments and to follow the "rules" of harmony and counterpoint. But his father also encouraged independence of mind and ear by instructing ten-year-old Charles to sing a tune in one key while being accompanied in another. At thirteen, Ives held a regular job as church organist, and his compositions were performed publicly. Still he was prouder of his ability as a baseball player than of his musical skill. When asked what he played, he gruffly replied "Shortstop!"

When he was twenty, Ives entered Yale University to study musical composition. His conservative teacher, Horatio Parker, frowned on his musical experimentation. Faced with choosing a profession on graduating, Ives decided that he could keep his music "stronger, cleaner, bigger, and freer" if he did not try to make a living out of it. He knew that his unconventional music would not be popular, and he did not want to raise a family that might "starve on his dissonances." Ives therefore went into the insurance business, starting out as a clerk in a New York firm. Eventually he founded a successful insurance agency and became very wealthy. A creative businessman, Ives invented the concept of "estate planning" and wrote a textbook widely used by insurance agents.

Ives composed furiously each day after business until two or three in the morning and on weekends and holidays. During the years he composed, he was isolated from the music world; none of his major works was publicly performed. Musicians for whom he occasionally played his compositions

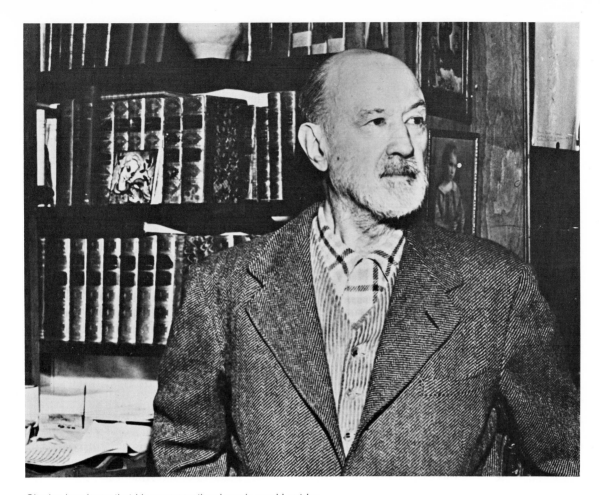

Charles Ives knew that his unconventional music would not be popular, and he did not want to raise a family that might "starve on his dissonances" (Frank Gerratana, Omikron).

commented: "It is not music," "It makes no sense," or "How can you like horrible sounds like that?" They urged him to write more conventionally. His wife—a clergyman's daughter appropriately named Harmony—believed in his genius and supported his refusal to compromise. Completely unknown, his scores accumulated in the barn of his Connecticut farm.

America's participation in World War I from 1917 to 1918 dampened Ives's creative urge. "I did practically nothing in music. I did not seem to feel like it," he recalled. "We were very busy at the office at this time with the extra Red Cross and Liberty Loan drives, and all the problems that the War brought on." Then, in October 1918, shortly before the end of the war, the forty-four-

Charles Ives

year-old Ives had a heart attack from which he never completely recovered. He composed almost nothing after 1921. Instead, he began to make his compositions known to the public.

From 1920 to 1922, Ives privately printed his monumental *Concord Sonata* for piano, his explanatory *Essays before a Sonata*, and a collection of *114 Songs* and sent them to musicians, critics, and libraries. At first, the volumes aroused little more than ridicule. ("It was the fate of many of them," wrote Henry Cowell, Ives's biographer, "to be used to adjust the height of the piano bench in the studios of more than one" well-known musician.) Gradually a few young composers and performers recognized that Ives was enormously original. In 1939, when Ives was sixty-four, his *Concord Sonata* (1909–1915) aroused an ovation at its first complete New York performance. By the 1940s, many thought Ives to be America's first great composer. In 1947 he won a Pulitzer Prize for his Third Symphony (1904–1911), written some forty years earlier. Newspapers and magazines all over the country took up the story of the businessman who had lived a secret life as a composer. Ives's typically gruff reaction to the Pulitzer Prize was, "Prizes are for boys. I'm grown up."

A few years before his death, Ives received a letter from Arnold Schoenberg's widow, who had found the following note among her husband's papers: "There is a great Man living in this Country—a composer. He has solved the problem how to preserve one's self and to learn. He responds to negligence by contempt. He is not forced to accept praise or blame. His name is Ives."

Ives's Music

Though experimental and far ahead of their time, Ives's compositions are rooted deeply in the folk and popular music he knew as a boy: revival hymns and ragtime, village bands and church choirs, patriotic songs and barn dances. Ives was inspired by the "unconventional" features of the American tradition: the village fiddler playing slightly out of tune, the cornetist a fraction ahead of the rest of the band, the church organist accidentally holding one chord while the choir sings another. While earlier American composers made folk material conform to academic "rules," Ives reveled in its irregular rhythms and asymmetrical melodies. His polyrhythms, polytonality, and tone clusters grew out of the music he knew.

To evoke nostalgic memories, Ives often quotes snatches of familiar tunes—"Yankee Doodle," "Columbia, the Gem of the Ocean," "America"—along with revival hymns and college songs. These snatches are not merely quoted but are developed and integrated within his music. Even the titles of his works evoke Ives's New England heritage: the Second Piano Sonata is subtitled "Concord, Mass. 1840–60"; its movements are "Emerson," "Hawthorne," "The Alcotts," and "Thoreau." We'll study one movement from a set of orchestral pieces entitled *Three Places in New England.* His large and varied output includes five symphonies and other orchestral music; music for piano, chorus, and chamber ensembles; and over two hundred songs. Many of his instrumental works have philosophic or descriptive programs.

A boyhood incident seems to have had an important influence on Ives. Two bands playing different music passed each other as they marched by him in different directions. Their dissonant clash fascinated the young boy. In later works Ives simultaneously presents musical events that seem unrelated: two bands play in different keys, consonant chords are set against dissonant chords; conflicting meters and rhythmic patterns are intertwined.

Ive's music shows a wide range of emotions, styles, and musical techniques. It includes mild-sounding consonant chords and ear-splitting dissonances that caused his contemporaries to think of him as a crank. Ives scorned those who couldn't take dissonance. "Beauty in music," he wrote, "is too often confused with something that lets the ears lie back in an easy chair." Once, when dissonant music of his friend Carl Ruggles was hissed at a concert, Ives jumped up and shouted, "You goddamn sissy. . . . When you hear strong masculine music like this, get up and use your ears like a man!" Interested only in satisfying his inner ear, Ives created music that is extraordinarily difficult to perform. "The impossibilities of today are the possibilities of tomorrow," he wrote.

The Unanswered Question for Chamber Orchestra (1906)

The Unanswered Question depicts the human search for life's meaning. This brief but highly original work for chamber orchestra has a philosophical program. The music represents a "Cosmic Landscape" in which eternal silence is broken by vain attempts to answer the "Perennial Question of Existence." To convey this idea, Ives calls for an unconventional performing group composed of a trumpet, four flutes, and muted strings which are placed off stage or away from the other instruments. Each tone color is assigned a completely different kind of music, so that there are three separate layers of sound and rhythm functioning simultaneously. The strings have soft, slow, hymnlike music that represents silence. Mostly consonant, the string chords move serenely and are unaffected by what is played by the trumpet and flutes. Seven times during the piece, the trumpet intones the same short phrase that represents "the Question." This questioning phrase is indefinite in key and does not harmonize with the string chords. To the trumpet phrase, the flutes reply six times with harsh dissonances as they "hunt for the invisible answer." Each flute reply is louder and faster in tempo than the one before, growing from *p* and *adagio* to *ffff* and *presto*. The last response is the longest and shrillest as the flutes "seem to realize a futility and begin to mock 'the Question.'" At the end, the flutes make no further attempt to answer the trumpet's question, and the strings fade into silence.

Putnam's Camp, Redding, Connecticut (1903–1911) from *Three Places in New England* (1903–1914)

Three Places in New England is a set of three movements for orchestra that evokes American history, life, and landscape. Completed in 1914, it was not performed until 1930, when it was booed and hissed in Boston. Today, it is one of Ives's most popular works and a landmark in American music.

Putnam's Camp, Redding, Connecticut (1903–1911) from *Three Places in New England* (1903–1914)

455

The daring and brilliant second movement, *Putnam's Camp, Redding, Connecticut,* is a child's impression of a Fourth of July picnic. Ives recaptures his boyhood memory of two marching bands clashing dissonantly as they play different tunes. He quotes many fragments from once well-known marches by John Philip Sousa (1854–1932), the American composer nicknamed the "March King." Snatches of patriotic songs and folklike tunes written by Ives contribute to the piece's popular flavor.

In his preface to this score, Ives wrote, "Near Redding Center, Conn., is a small park preserved as a Revolutionary Memorial; for here General Israel Putnam's soldiers had their winter quarters in 1778–1779." One Fourth of July, "a child went there on a picnic held under the auspices of the First Church and the Village Cornet Band." The child wanders "away from the rest of the children past the camp ground into the woods. As he rests on the hillside of laurel and hickories, the tunes of the band and the songs of the children grow fainter. . . ." He falls asleep and dreams of the discouraged American soldiers breaking camp, marching out "with fife and drum to a popular tune of the day. Suddenly a new national note is heard. Putnam is coming over the hills from the center,—the soldiers turn back and cheer. The little boy awakes, he hears the children's songs and runs down past the monument to 'listen to the band' and join in the games and dances."

Putnam's Camp is in three sections (A B A') that parallel the descriptive program. The first, marked "quick step time," captures the gaiety and confusion of a Fourth of July picnic in a nineteenth-century town. After a raucous, highly dissonant introduction, the strings play the main theme, a vigorous march that begins with conventional harmonies.

Such abrupt shifts between harsh dissonances and mild-sounding consonances are typical of Ives and are heard throughout *Putnam's Camp.* The piano, woodwinds, and brasses begin to compete for the listener's attention, and soon it sounds as though two bands are playing against each other. The mood becomes even more comic when a parody of the opening phrase of "Yankee Doodle" is quickly played by the trumpet, flute, and violins.

After more orchestral confusion, the music gradually becomes softer and slows to a halt, depicting the child falling asleep.

A mysterious high chord in the strings ushers in the middle section, which depicts the child's dream. Repeated piano and drum beats that seem out of phase with the rest of the orchestra begin one of the boldest parts of the score. Ives creates the impression of two bands playing at different tempos. (One band employs strings and woodwinds; the other has piano, drums, and trumpet.) Here the conductor must beat four bars with one hand against three bars in the other. The bands merge, and we hear a flute playing "The British Grenadiers," a favorite tune of the Revolutionary army.

The riotous concluding section creates deliberate melodic and rhythmic confusion as the main march theme is combined with "The British Grenadiers" and other fragments. *Putnam's Camp* ends with an ear-splitting dissonant chord. (In some recordings, the raucous sounds at the end drown out Ives's quotation from "The Star-Spangled Banner" in the last two bars.)

AARON COPLAND [13]

Aaron Copland (b. 1900), a leading American composer, was born in Brooklyn in 1900 of Russian-Jewish immigrant parents. "No one ever talked music to me or took me to a concert," he recalled of his boyhood. "Music as an art was a discovery I made all by myself." At fifteen he decided to become a composer. He studied with a competent but conservative teacher who discouraged contact with "modern" music. This only made the forbidden fruit more attractive. Copland showed only his academic exercises to his teacher, keeping his more original efforts to himself.

In 1921 Copland went to France, where he was the first American to study composition with Nadia Boulanger. This extraordinary Frenchwoman was sympathetic to modern musical trends and became the teacher of several generations of American composers. Both Mlle. Boulanger's teaching and the stimulating atmosphere of Paris—where expatriates like Picasso, Stravinsky, and Ernest Hemingway felt at home—were to have a lasting influence on Copland's music.

When he returned to New York after three years in Paris, Copland was "anxious to write a work that would immediately be recognized as American in character." For Copland in 1925 "American" meant jazz. In his *Music for the Theater* (1925), a work for small orchestra, elements of the blues and ragtime are combined with an approach to rhythm and harmony that is like Stravinsky's. Copland's "jazz period" lasted only a few years. During the early 1930s he composed serious, highly dissonant works that were accessible only to

Aaron Copland

457

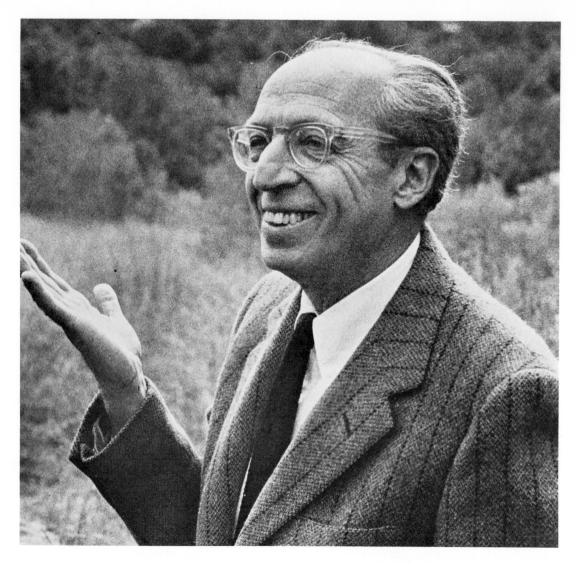

Aaron Copland (John Ardoin, Omikron).

sophisticated listeners. Compositions like the extraordinary *Piano Variations* (1930) convey starkness, power, percussiveness, and intense concentration.

In the late 1930s, Copland modified his style again, writing more accessible works for a larger audience. To understand this shift, recall that the 1930s brought the Great Depression; artists throughout the world were appalled by the economic misery surrounding them. To many composers, it seemed futile to write merely for a sophisticated elite, and they simplified their music to reach a wider audience. "I began to feel an increasing dissatisfaction with the relations of the music-loving public and the living composer," Copland later explained. Most concertgoers, he felt, could not grasp complex, highly dissonant music and wanted to hear only familiar music by Beethoven and Brahms. "It made no sense to ignore them and to continue writing as if they did not exist. I felt that it was worth the effort to see if I couldn't say what I had to say in the simplest possible terms." Copland drew on American folklore for his ballets *Billy the Kid* (1938), *Rodeo* (1942), and *Appalachian Spring* (1944). The use of jazz, revival hymns, cowboy songs, and other folk tunes helped make Copland's name synonymous with American music. His scores for films such as *Of Mice and Men* (1939) and *Our Town* (1940) brought his music before a mass public, as did patriotic works such as *A Lincoln Portrait* (1942).

Copland accomplished the difficult feat of writing simple, yet highly professional music. The texture of his music is clear and transparent. There are slow-moving, almost motionless harmonies that seem to evoke the openness of the American landscape. While strongly tonal, his works embody twentieth-century techniques such as polychords, polyrhythm, changing meters, and percussive orchestration. Since 1950, Copland has used serial technique—the manipulation of a tone row or series—in such work as *Connotations* for orchestra (1962). This composition recalls the austere, uncompromising style of Copland's music during the early 1930s. Like Stravinsky, who also turned to serial technique during the 1950s, Copland used a tone row to create music that is completely personal in style.

Aside from his extraordinary compositions, Copland made other valuable contributions to music in America. He directed composers' groups, organized concerts of American music, lectured around the country, wrote books and magazine articles. At the request of the U. S. State Department, he was a musical ambassador to South America, where he talked with many composers and listened to their works. For twenty-five years, he taught young composers every summer at the Berkshire Music Center in Tanglewood. And at fifty, Copland began yet another career, that of conductor. He has conducted over fifty orchestras—primarily in his own music—throughout the world.

Appalachian Spring (1943–1944)

Appalachian Spring originated as a ballet score for Martha Graham, the great modern dancer and choreographer. It took Copland about a year to finish the music. At the time he thought, "How foolhardy it is to be spending all this time writing a thirty-five-minute score for a modern-dance company, knowing how short-lived most ballets *and* their scores are." But Copland arranged parts of the ballet as a Suite for full orchestra (originally the ballet used only thirteen instrumentalists) that won important prizes and brought his name to a large public. Today, *Appalachian Spring* is widely performed both as a ballet and as a concert piece.

The ballet concerns a "pioneer celebration in spring around a newly built farmhouse in the Pennsylvania hills" in the early 1800s. The rhythms and melodies are American-sounding and suggest barn dances, fiddle tunes, and revival hymns. But Copland uses only one actual folk tune in the score—a

Appalachian Spring
(1943–1944)

Copland composed the music for Martha Graham's ballet
Appalachian Spring (Arnold Eagle).

Shaker melody entitled, "Simple Gifts." (The Shakers were a religious sect established in America around the time of the Revolution. They expressed religious fervor through shaking, leaping, dancing, and singing.) *Appalachian Spring* is bright and transparent, has a clear tonality, and is basically tender and calm in mood. The score's rhythmic excitement comes from delightful syncopations and rapid changes of meter. As in many twentieth-century works, the orchestra contains a piano and a large percussion section, including xylophone, snare drum, wood block, and glockenspiel. The eight sections of the suite follow each other without pause and are described in Copland's synopsis of the score.

Section 1: "Very slowly. Introduction of the characters (bride, groom, a neighbor, revivalist preacher and his flock), one by one, in a suffused light." The peaceful open countryside is evoked by quiet dynamics, sustained harmonies, and evenly flowing rhythms.

Section 2: "Fast." Strings and piano in unison suddenly begin a joyful dance tune that is American in flavor.

"A sentiment both elated and religious" grows as the dance tune is combined with a solemn hymnlike melody in the *ff* winds. The section ends calmly; strings softly sing the hymnlike melody, while the flute recalls the dance tune.

Section 3: "Moderate. Duo for the Bride and her Intended—scene of tenderness and passion." Gentle woodwind solos frame an intense dissonant passage for muted strings.

Section 4: "Quite fast. The Revivalist and his flock. Folksy feelings—suggestions of square dances and country fiddlers." Off-beat accents produce a delightfully humorous effect. After a brief pause, a slow transition begins with an "eloquent" *ff* passage and leads to

Section 5: "Still faster. Solo dance of the Bride—presentiment of motherhood. Extremes of joy and fear and wonder." Breathless motion and rapid syncopations create excitement.

Section 6: "Very slowly (as at first)." A high solo violin begins this "Transition scene to music reminiscent of the Introduction." Again, the peaceful countryside is evoked.

Section 7: "Calm and flowing. Scenes of daily activity for the Bride and her Farmer-husband." There are five variations on the Shaker melody, "Simple Gifts." The theme is introduced by a clarinet.

Appalachian Spring
(1943–1944)

Variation 1: An oboe presents the theme "a trifle faster" and in a higher register.

Variation 2: Against high sounds in the piano and harp, the violas play the theme at half its previous speed. Then the violins and cellos in turn imitate the theme, creating a polyphonic texture. A brief transition leads to

Variation 3: Trumpets and trombones proclaim the theme at twice the previous speed, against rapid notes in the strings.

Variation 4: Woodwinds quietly play the second part of the theme at "a trifle slower" tempo than the preceding variation.

Variation 5: The first part of the theme is majestically played *fff* by the full orchestra.

Section 8: Moderate. "The Bride takes her place among her neighbors." After a hushed passage for muted strings marked "like a prayer," there is a quiet recollection of the hymnlike melody. The neighbors leave and the bride and groom are left "quiet and strong in their new house."

[**14**] MUSICAL STYLES SINCE 1950

Since World War II, we have lived with instant communication—television, computers, and space satellites provide access to a virtually unlimited flow of information. We have been bombarded by an incredible variety of stimuli. And there is a constant demand for novelty. New styles in fashion and painting rapidly spread and then disappear.

In music as well, emphasis has been on novelty and change. Musical innovations since 1950 have been even more far-reaching than those of the earlier 1900s. There have been many new directions, and the range of musical styles and systems is wider than ever. As American composer Hugo Weisgall has observed, "Many composers today change their musical points of view with astonishing rapidity, composing this way and that, moving easily from complete traditionalism into the 'avant' *avant garde.*"

Accurately describing the recent past is a difficult task. Yet any overview of music since 1950 must include the following major developments:

1. An increased use of the twelve-tone system.
2. The composition of music in which tone color, texture, dynamics, and rhythm are as important as pitch.

3. The spread of *chance music*, where a composer chooses pitches, tone colors, and rhythms by random methods, or allows a performer to choose much of the musical material.
4. The development of electronic music.
5. A greater exploitation of noiselike sounds.

Since 1950, long-playing records and audiotape have spread new musical ideas far and wide.

Increased Use of the Twelve-tone System

A striking development after World War II (1945) was the gradual abandonment of tonality in favor of the twelve-tone system. From the early 1920s—when Schoenberg invented the system—to about 1950, most composers still wrote music with a tonal center. Few were attracted to the new method because it was associated with Schoenberg's expressionist style, which went out of fashion. During the 1950s, however, the twelve-tone system was adopted by many composers, including Stravinsky, who had been the leading composer of tonal music.

What contributed to this dramatic shift? In Europe, the end of the war brought a strong desire for new musical beginnings. During the Nazi years, composers had been denied access to the twelve-tone works of Schoenberg and Webern; when peace came, they were eager to explore unfamiliar musical territory. In the United States, twelve-tone music was now available on long-playing records, and complex scores became easier to study.

But the most important reasons for the shift to the twelve-tone system were the resources of the system itself. Composers discovered that it was a compositional technique rather than a special musical style. Musicians as different as Bach, Mozart, and Chopin had all used the tonal system, and a comparable diversity of style was possible within the twelve-tone system. The new method also had the advantage of stimulating unconventional approaches to melody, harmony, and form. As Aaron Copland expressed it recently, "I began to hear chords that I wouldn't have heard otherwise. Heretofore I had been thinking tonally, but this was a new way of moving tones about. It freshened up one's technique and one's approach."

Many composers of the 1950s and 1960s chose to write music that was stylistically reminiscent of Anton Webern, Schoenberg's disciple. They created "pointillist" music in which melodic lines are "atomized" into tiny fragments that are heard in widely separated registers and framed by moments of silence. Webern's style answered the needs of the post-World War II generation. His music had a lean, "modern" sound, while Schoenberg's was considered too "Romantic" and traditional in form. The French composer Pierre Boulez (b. 1925) spoke for many of his generation in 1952 when he unfavorably compared Schoenberg's alliance with "the decadence of the great German Romantic tradition" with Webern's reaction "against all inherited rhetoric."

Extensions of the Twelve-tone System: Serialism

During the late 1940s and early 1950s, the techniques of the twelve-tone system came to be used to organize dimensions of music other than pitch, such as rhythm, dynamics, and tone color. Recall that in early twelve-tone music the system was used primarily to order *pitch* relationships. All the pitches of a twelve-tone composition would be derived from a single tone row, or series. After 1950, a series of twelve durations (rhythmic values), dynamic levels, or tone colors also could serve as a unifying idea. A rhythmic or dynamic series might be manipulated like the series of twelve tones. The use of a series, or ordered group of musical elements, to organize several dimensions of a composition is called **serialism.** The leading proponents of serialism include Milton Babbitt (b. 1916) of America, Karlheinz Stockhausen (b. 1928) of Germany, and Olivier Messiaen and Pierre Boulez of France. While their methods led to a totally controlled and organized music, the actual sound—in certain cases—could seem random and chaotic. The music's complex relationships are often difficult to perceive.

Chance Music

The 1950s witnessed not only serialism but an opposite approach known as *chance* or *aleatory* music (from the Latin *alea,* or "game of chance"). In **chance music,** composers choose pitches, tone colors, and rhythms by random methods such as throwing coins. They may also ask performers to choose the ordering of the musical material, or even to choose much of the material itself. For example, a composer might write out brief passages of a composition but ask the performer to play them in any desired order. Or a composer might indicate a group of pitches but direct the performer to invent rhythmic patterns.

The most famous and influential creator of chance music is the American John Cage. At the very beginning of this book we mentioned his silent "composition" entitled 4'33" (1952), which requires the performer *not* to make a sound for four minutes and thirty-three seconds. The "music" is made up of the unintentional sounds that an audience might produce in this time span. "I try to arrange my composing means," explains Cage, "so that I won't have any knowledge of what might happen. . . . My purpose is to eliminate purpose." For Cage, "The purpose of this purposeless music would be achieved if people learned to listen. Then when they listened they might discover that they preferred the sounds of everyday life to the ones they would presently hear in the musical program. . . . That was all right as far as I was concerned." Cage's approach is also illustrated by his *Imaginary Landscape No. 4* (1951), for twelve radios. The score gives precise directions to the performers—two at each radio—for manipulating the dials affecting wavelength and volume. Yet all the indications in the score were chosen by chance means. They show no regard for local station wavelengths or the time of performance. "At the actual performance of *Imaginary Landscape*," reported one member of the audience, "the hour was later than anticipated before the work's turn came on the program, so that the instruments were unable to capture programs diversified enough to present a really interesting result." This is not surprising, since Cage chose the wavelengths and dynamics by throwing dice.

With Cage's work as an example, serial composers such as Pierre Boulez and Karlheinz Stockhausen introduced elements of chance into their compositions during the mid-1950s. Stockhausen's *Piano Piece No. 11* (1956) has nineteen short segments of music printed on a large roll of paper that measures 37 by 21 inches. The segments can be played in any order, and the performer is instructed to begin with the fragment that first catches the eye. The piece is likely to be different each time it is played.

Chance music makes a complete break from traditional values in music. It asserts, in effect, that one sound or ordering of sounds is as meaningful as another. To most listeners, a piece of chance music is more often significant as an idea than as a collection of actual sounds. Some composers may be attracted by the sheer novelty of chance music, by its ability to shock and attract attention. Others are influenced by Oriental philosophies such as Zen Buddhism, which is not structured according to Western concepts of logic. Finally, some composers may want to give performers a major part in the creative process.

Electronic Music

Since the development of tape studios, synthesizers, and computers in the 1950s and 1960s, composers now have potentially unlimited resources for the pro-

Karlheinz Stockhausen's *Etude II* was the first published electronic score (Universal Edition, London).

duction and control of sound. Electronic music is as diverse as nonelectronic music. Its spectrum includes rock, chance music, and serial compositions.

Electronic instruments let composers control tone color, duration, dynamics, and pitch with unprecedented precision. Composers are no longer limited by human performers. For the first time, they can work *directly* in their own medium—sound. There is no more need for intermediaries, the performers. The audiotape of a composition *is* the composition. Thus, a composer alone is now responsible for putting into music the subtle variations of rhythm, tone color, and dynamics that once rested with the performer.

Many composers have felt a need to "humanize" their electronic music by combining it with live performers. This can be done in several ways. Some pieces use live performer(s) and taped sounds. The taped sounds may be electronic pitches or noises, or they may be previously recorded sounds of live performers. In some cases, performers may be involved in a duet with themselves, or with electronically manipulated versions of their own performances. In combining live performers with taped sounds, composers face the problem of synchronizing sounds that change from performance to performance—those of live musicians—and the taped sounds, which don't vary.

There are also works for traditional instruments and electronic synthesizers that are performed "live." Traditional instruments are also "electrified" through amplification. Composers use "electric" pianos and violins.

Electronic music is important not only in itself, but in its influence on musical thought in general. Electronic instruments have suggested new sounds and new forms of rhythmic organization. "These limitless electronic media," said Milton Babbitt, "have shown us new boundaries and new limits that are not yet understood—the very mysterious limits, for example, of the human capacity to hear, to conceptualize, and to perceive. Very often we will specify something and discover that the ear can't take in what we have specified. . . . The human organism simply cannot respond quickly enough, cannot perceive and differentiate as rapidly and precisely as the synthesizer can produce it and as the loudspeaker can reproduce it."

"The Liberation of Sound"

Composers today use a wider variety of sounds than ever, including many that were once considered undesirable noises. Composers have achieved what Edgard Varèse called "the liberation of sound . . . the right to make music with any and all sounds. . . ." Electronic music may include environmental sounds like thunder or electronically generated hisses and blips. But composers also may draw novel sounds from voices and nonelectronic instruments. Singers are asked to scream, whisper, laugh, groan, sneeze, cough, whistle, and click their tongues. They may sing phonetic sounds rather than words. Composers may treat their vocal text merely as a collection of sounds and not attempt to make the meaning of the words clear to the audience.

Wind and string players tap, scrape, and rub the bodies of their instruments. A brass or woodwind player may hum while playing, thus creating two pitches

Vladimir Ussachevsky, professor of music at Columbia University, at the controls of the sound mixing panel of the electronic composer (Columbia University).

at once. A flutist may click the keys of the instrument without producing a tone; a pianist may reach inside the piano to pluck a string and then run a chisel along it, creating a sliding sound. To communicate their intentions to performers, composers may devise new systems of music notation, because standard notation makes no provision for many noiselike sounds. Recent music scores contain graph-like diagrams, new note shapes and symbols, and novel ways of arranging notation on the page. But composers are not the only ones to invent unusual sounds. Often the players themselves discover new possibilities for their instruments. Many modern works have been inspired by the discoveries of inventive performers.

The greatest expansion and experimentation has involved percussion instruments. In many recent compositions, percussion instruments outnumber strings, woodwinds, and brasses. Traditional percussion instruments are struck with new types of beaters made of glass, metal, wood, and cloth. Unconventional instruments now widely used include tom-toms, bongos, slapstick, maracas, guiro, and vibraphone.

In the search for novel sounds, increased use has been made of **microtones,** intervals smaller than the half step. Small intervals like quarter tones have long been used in non-Western music, but they have only recently become an important resource for Western composers. Electronic instruments have stimulated this development, since they are not restricted to conventional scales and do not force players to unlearn performance habits.

"The Liberation of Sound"

467

Composers such as Krzysztof Penderecki (b. 1933) create sounds bordering on electronic noise through tone clusters, groups of closely spaced tones played together. Clusters are unlike traditional chords in that one usually does not hear individual tones but a mass, block, or band of sound. Composers may achieve a sense of growth or change by widening or narrowing such a band, or by making it more or less dense.

The directional aspect of sounds—how they are projected in space—has taken on new importance. Loudspeakers or groups of instruments may be placed at opposite ends of the stage, in the balcony, or at the back and sides of the auditorium. In electronic compositions like Varèse's *Poème électronique* (1958) and nonelectronic works like Elliott Carter's *Double Concerto* for harpsichord and piano with two chamber orchestras (1961), sounds are made to travel gradually in space, passing from one loudspeaker or player to another.

Mixed Media

Electronic music often has visual counterparts such as slide projections, films, light shows, gestures, and theatrical actions. One such mixed-media presentation was Varèse's *Poème électronique,* which combined electronic sounds with images projected on walls. But multimedia works are not confined to electronic music. Chance music and other types of recent music sometimes require performers to function as actors as well as sound producers. We shall observe theatrical movement on and off stage when we consider *Ancient Voices of Children* (1970), by George Crumb. Mixed-media presentations generally are intended to break down the ritual surrounding traditional concerts and to increase communication between a composer and the audience. Support for multimedia presentations comes from composer Richard Maxfield:

I view as irrelevant
the repetitious sawing on strings and
baton wielding spectacle
we focus our eyes upon during a
conventional concert.
Much more sensible
either no visual counterpart
or one more imaginatively selected
such as lighting
cinema, choreography
fireworks
trees. . . .

Rhythm and Form

Rhythm and form have undergone some of the most striking changes in music since 1950. Earlier in the century, composers often changed meters or used unconventional ones such as $\frac{7}{8}$ and $\frac{5}{8}$. Today, some composers abandon the concepts of beat and meter altogether. This is a natural outcome of electronic music, which needs no beat to keep performers together. In nonelectronic music, too, the composer may specify duration in absolute units like seconds rather than relative units like beats. In some recent music, there may be several different speeds at the same time.

More than ever, each piece of music follows its own laws, and its form grows out of its material. Many composers no longer write music in traditional forms like A B A, sonata form, or rondo. Indeed, form may be on-going, with little or no obvious repetition of material.

Basic Terms

If you aren't sure what each of the following words means, look back at the text, where they appear in bold type. Additional information about some of them can be found by checking the index.

serialism   microtone
chance music (aleatory music)

MUSIC SINCE 1950: [**15**]
FIVE REPRESENTATIVE
PIECES

Sonata for Flute, Oboe, Cello, and Harpsichord (1952), by Elliott Carter

Elliott Carter (b. 1908) is an American composer recognized as a major figure in contemporary music. He first attracted international attention when his *String Quartet* No. 1 (1951) won first prize at a composition contest held by the city of Liège in Belgium in 1953. Since then, he has produced an imposing series of instrumental works, including two other string quartets (1959, 1972), the *Variations for Orchestra* (1955), the *Double Concerto* (1961), the *Piano Concerto* (1966), and the *Concerto for Orchestra* (1969). Carter does not belong to any compositional "school" but has evolved a personal style that we'll study in his *Sonata for Flute, Oboe, Cello, and Harpsichord* (1952).

"The *Sonata*," explains Carter, "was commissioned by the Harpsichord Quartet of New York. My idea was to stress as much as possible the vast and wonderful array of tone-colors available on the modern harpsichord. . . . This aim of using the wide variety of the harpsichord involved many tone colors which can only be produced very softly and therefore conditioned very drastically the type and range of musical expression, all the details of shape, phrasing,

Sonata for Flute, Oboe, Cello, and Harpsichord (1952), by Elliott Carter

469

rhythm, texture, as well as the large form." Carter has said that at the time of composition in 1952, "it seemed very important to have the harpsichord speak in a new voice, expressing characters unfamiliar to its extensive Baroque repertory."

Each of the four instrumental parts has a separate, highly individual identity, like a character in a drama. As Carter put it, "I regard my scores as scenarios, auditory scenarios, for performers to act out with their instruments, dramatizing the players as individuals and participants in the ensemble. . . . To me the special teamwork of ensemble playing is very wonderful and moving, and this feeling is always an important expressive consideration in my chamber music."

The texture of Carter's sonata is complex and polyphonic; several different, apparently unrelated things go on at once. Each of the simultaneous instrumental parts has individualized rhythms and melodic gestures. The music has many tempo changes that are precisely regulated. Carter developed a technique called **metrical modulation,** which has been defined as "a means of going smoothly, but with complete accuracy, from one absolute metronomic speed to another, by lengthening or shortening the value of the basic note unit." The three movements of the sonata are not in traditional forms; they have a feeling of purposeful improvisation.

First Movement: *Risoluto* (Determined)

"The music starts, *Risoluto*," writes Carter, "with a splashing dramatic gesture whose subsiding ripples form the rest of the movement." After the opening, the harpsichord often plays a succession of even notes while the other instruments comment with short phrases or single tones. This brief movement ends calmly with a high tone from the harpsichord.

Second Movement: *Lento*

Carter described the second movement of his sonata as "an expressive dialogue between the harpsichord and the others with an undercurrent of fast music that bursts out briefly near the end." The *Lento* opens with a one-note theme: the tone G is played softly in turn by the flute, oboe, cello, and harpsichord. Soon, other tones grow out of the G, and longer phrases unfold. A long section follows, in which the harpsichord repeatedly alternates with the three other instruments playing together. At first the harpsichord's assertive phrases are answered timidly by the other instruments, but soon the other instruments also begin to sound determined. A change from Lento to a very fast tempo brings the first extended passage for all four performers at once. Toward the end of this seven-minute movement, the slow tempo returns, along with some of the opening thematic material. The *Lento* concludes on the same tone it began with, but now the G is played loudly, rather than softly.

Third Movement: *Allegro*

The last movement uses the rhythmic pattern of the *forlana,* a Baroque dance associated with the gondoliers of Venice. It is a carefree dance in $\frac{6}{8}$ meter with dotted rhythms. Carter writes that he "draws out of the characteristic rhythmic cell of that dance all sorts of rhythmic changes." The movement has many different dance rhythms, and often one fades into another.

Threnody for the Victims of Hiroshima, by Krzysztof Penderecki

During the late 1950s a group of avant-garde composers unexpectedly emerged in Poland. For years all artistic experimentation had been actively discouraged by the Soviet government and by other regimes of Eastern Europe. However, after the revolt against Stalinism in 1955–1956, the new Polish government encouraged cultural independence and free artistic expression in films, painting, theater, and music. Composers had at their disposal well-trained performing groups and electronic music studios. The best-known younger Polish composer is Krzysztof Penderecki (b. 1933).

Penderecki was a young boy when the Nazis occupied Poland and massacred most of its Jewish population. Although not threatened personally, Penderecki felt great compassion for the victims. "That great war crime," he wrote, "has undoubtedly been in my subconscious mind since the war, when, as a child, I saw the destruction of the ghetto in my small native town of Debica." His compassion for human suffering has been expressed in works like the *Dies irae* (1967), to the memory of the victims of Auschwitz, and the *Threnody for the Victims of Hiroshima.* In these works, and in his well-known *St. Luke Passion* (1963–1965), Penderecki draws spectacular and novel sounds from voices and conventional instruments. He often calls for tone clusters, glissandos, noiselike and percussive effects, and choral hissing, laughing, shouting, and whistling.

Penderecki's Threnody, or song of mourning, is an almost unbearably intense work; its sounds are not intended to be "pleasant." Fifty-two string instruments—violins, violas, cellos, and double basses—produce a wide variety of noiselike sounds that often seem to come from electronic generators. Many of these sounds are tone clusters. At the beginning of this nine-minute work, shrill clusters are produced by ten groups of instruments playing "the highest note of the instrument (no definite pitch)." At the end of the piece, a huge cluster that sounds like the roar of a jet engine is produced by all fifty-two strings playing pitches a quarter-tone apart. Penderecki often uses slides or glissandos to make the clusters expand and contract. Noiselike sounds are also produced by tapping on the body of the instrument and bowing on the tailpiece.

There is no feeling of beat in this music. The duration of its various musical events is indicated in seconds at the bottom of the score. The Threnody is divided into six sections. Some feature sustained sounds, while others contain a variety of rapid percussive attacks. Noiselike sounds are so predominant that

Threnody for the Victims of Hiroshima, by Krzysztof Penderecki

471

a definite pitch at the beginning of section two is very striking. An overall sense of coherence is produced by the general similarity of the first and last sections, as well as by the climactic character of section four.

LISTENING OUTLINE
To be read while music is heard

Threnody for the Victims of Hiroshima for 52 strings (1960) by Krzysztof Penderecki

24 violins, 10 violas, 10 cellos, 8 double basses

(About 9½ min)

1   *a.* Shrill, sustained clusters, one entering after the other.
    b. Suddenly soft.
    c. Pizzicatos. Soft, rapid squeaks. Increased rhythmic activity.
    d. Clusters fade out, squeaks and pizzicatos remain.
2   *a.* Single sustained tone surrounded by squeaks.
    b. Only sustained tone remains. Tone moves down a half step.
    c. Upward and downward glissandos (slides). Single, sustained tones expand into clusters, clusters contract into single tones.
    d. High sustained tone.
3   *a.* Low, sustained cluster, *p.* Higher sustained cluster, *f.* Other clusters join.
    b. Glassy sounds slide upward. Decrescendo into silence.
4   *a.* Quick attacks of single tones build to very wide and loud cluster.
    b. Low, roaring cluster. Slides. Low cluster narrows to single, sustained cello tone. Decrescendo into 5-sec pause.
5   Disconnected pizzicatos, tremolos, blips, scratches at various dynamics and registers. Percussive sounds lead to
6   *a.* High sustained clusters, crescendo. Low clusters with high squeaks. Suddenly soft.
    b. Sustained cluster like jet roar. Sound gradually fades into silence.

Ancient Voices of Children (1970), by George Crumb

During the late 1960s, American composer George Crumb (b. 1929) became prominent with a series of works that were acclaimed highly by both audiences and critics. His music is personal and emotionally intense; it is distinguished by an imaginative use of novel and delicate tone colors. Currently, Crumb teaches composition at the University of Pennsylvania.

    Like much of his recent music, Crumb's *Ancient Voices of Children* is set to poetry of Federico Garcia Lorca, the great Spanish writer who was murdered in 1936 during his country's civil war. "I have sought musical images," wrote Crumb, "that enhance and reinforce the powerful, yet strangely haunting imagery of Lorca's poetry. I feel that the essential meaning of this poetry is concerned with the most primary things: life, death, love, the smell of the earth, the sounds of the wind and the sea."

    Ancient Voices of Children is a cycle of five songs with two instrumental interludes. The work is written for mezzo-soprano, boy soprano, oboe, mandolin, harp, percussion, and "electric piano." (A normal grand piano is amplified by means of contact microphones attached to its sounding board.) Three percussionists command a wide variety of instruments, including such unconventional ones as tuned tom-toms, Tibetan prayer stones, and Japanese temple bells. The pianist also plays a toy piano (in the fourth song); the oboist, a harmonica (fourth song); and the mandolinist, a "musical saw" (an ordinary saw played with a double-bass bow).

"Perhaps the most characteristic vocal effect in *Ancient Voices*," writes Crumb, "is produced by the mezzo-soprano singing a kind of fantastic vocalise (on purely phonetic sounds) into an amplified piano, thereby producing a shimmering aura of echoes." (A *vocalise* is an extended melody sung without a text, only on vowels.) Gradually fading sounds are produced by gongs, harp, vibraphone, and marimbas—among other instruments—and contribute to the vaguely Oriental atmosphere. The composer wants us to savor individual tone colors; in many passages, only a single instrument or voice is heard.

Ancient Voices is theatrical in character and has already been used as ballet music by several companies. A boy soprano singing off stage heightens the drama. Even the instrumentalists play a dramatic role, occasionally being required to sing, shout, or whisper. "In composing *Ancient Voices of Children*," Crumb explains, "I was conscious of an urge to fuse various unrelated stylistic elements . . . a suggestion of Flamenco with a Baroque quotation . . . or a reminiscence of Mahler with a breath of the Orient." We'll focus on the last three songs of the cycle.

"From where do you come, my love, my child?" ("Dance of the Sacred Life-Cycle")

The most spectacular part of *Ancient Voices,* this central song uses the characteristic rhythm of a bolero, a Spanish dance in triple meter. The song opens with a soprano solo on phonetic sounds, sung into the amplified piano. Then the percussionists begin an ostinato in bolero rhythm that continues throughout the piece. They make a gradual crescendo and descrescendo, and progress from whispering to shouting, then back to whispering. Each of the poem's three stanzas has a half-sung question and answer by the two vocalists, a decorative oboe phrase, and an exuberant soprano melody.

¿De dónde vienes, amor, mi niño?	From where do you come, my love, my child?
De la cresta del duro frío.	From the ridge of hard frost.
¿Qué necesitas, amor, mi niño?	What do you need, my love, my child?
La tibia tela de tu vestido.	The warm cloth of your dress.
¡Que se agiten las ramas al sol	Let the branches ruffle in the sun
y salten las fuentes alrededor!	and the fountains leap all around!
En el patio ladra el perro,	In the courtyard a dog barks,
en los árboles canta el viento.	in the trees the wind sings.
Los bueyes mugen al boyero	The oxen low to the ox-herd
y la luna me riza los cabellos.	and the moon curls my hair.

Ancient Voices of Children (1970), by George Crumb

¿Qué pides, niño, desde tan lejos?	What do you ask for, my child, from so far away?
Los blancos montes que hay en tu pecho.	The white mountains of your breast.
¡Que se agiten las ramas al sol	Let the branches ruffle in the sun
y salten las fuentes alrededor!	and the fountains leap all around!
Te diré, niño mío, que sí,	I'll tell you, my child, yes,
tronchada y rota soy para ti.	I am torn and broken for you.
¡Cómo me duele esta cintura	How painful is this waist
donde tendrás primera cuna!	where you will have your first cradle!
¿Cuándo, mi niño, vas a venir?	When, my child, will you come?
Cuando tu carne huela a jazmín.	When your flesh smells of jasmine flowers.
¡Que se agiten las ramas al sol	Let the branches ruffle in the sun
y salten las fuentes alrededor!	and the fountains leap all around!

"Each afternoon in Granada, a child dies each afternoon"

This is the shortest song of the cycle; it is marked, "Hushed, intimate; with a sense of suspended time." In the background is a sustained chord produced very, very softly by the marimba, by percussionists who hum and sing, and by the harmonica. Just three simple phrases are sung by the soprano. Then the toy piano plays a brief quotation from a song by Bach. The song was originally meant for Bach's wife, Anna Magdalena, and its original text began with the words "Be thou but near, and I contented will go to Death, which is my rest." The toy piano gradually slows down, "like the clockwork of a toy running down," and stops just before the cadence. This poetic use of a musical quotation symbolizes a child's death.

Todas las tardes en Granada,	Each afternoon in Granada,
todas las tardes se muere un niño.	a child dies each afternoon.

Instrumental Interlude: "Ghost Dance"

Crumb makes a mandolin sound like an Oriental instrument by having its player move a glass rod along the E string, producing slides between tones. Marked "eerie, spectral," the mandolin melody is accompanied by three percussionists who whisper and softly play maracas, gourd rattles from Latin America.

"My heart of silk is filled with lights"

This musical setting seems to reflect the poetic lines "with lost bells" and "I will go *very far* . . . to ask Christ the Lord to give me back my ancient soul of a child." The song is permeated with bell- and chimelike sounds. Distance is conveyed by an unaccompanied oboe solo played "timidly with a sense of loneliness." The melody is a quotation from the concluding ("Farewell") movement of *Das Lied von der Erde* ("The Song of the Earth," 1908), by the late nineteenth-century composer Gustav Mahler. The oboist slowly walks off stage, from where we again hear his distant melody. Toward the end of the song, the boy soprano slowly walks on stage, and both vocalists sing into the amplified piano. We hear recollections from the opening song of the cycle, and the music fades into silence.

Se ha llenado de luces	My heart of silk
mi corazón de seda,	is filled with lights,
de campanas perdidas,	with lost bells,
de lirios y de obejas.	with lilies, and with bees,
Y yo me iré muy lejos,	and I will go very far,
más allá de esas sierras,	farther than those hills,
más allá de los mares,	farther than the seas,
cerca de las estrellas,	close to the stars,
para pedirle a Cristo	to ask Christ the Lord
Señor que me devuelva	to give me back
mi alma antiqua de niño.	my ancient soul of a child.

Composition for Synthesizer (1960–1961), by Milton Babbitt

American Milton Babbitt (b. 1916) is a leading composer and theorist of twelve-tone music and a major figure in the development of electronic music. A brilliant teacher who is now Conant Professor of Music at Princeton University, Babbitt has profoundly influenced many young composers. He was the first composer to extend serial principles of organization to all musical dimensions—rhythm, dynamics, and tone color, as well as pitch. Not only are all the pitches in a Babbitt work derived from a tone row, but all the rhythms are drawn from a "durational row," a series of rhythmic values. His earliest works to use such techniques of serialism date from the late 1940s: *Three Compositions for Piano* (1947), *Composition for Four Instruments* (1947–1948), and *Composition for Twelve Instruments* (1948).

Babbitt's desire to precisely control every aspect of his music attracted him to the possibilities of electronic music. Since 1959 he has made extensive use of the RCA Mark II synthesizer, an enormous machine that fills an entire wall at the Columbia-Princeton Electronic Music Center in New York City. "If you know how to specify it, any sound that can be passed by a loudspeaker can be created by this machine," Babbitt has explained. "I could synthesize the equivalent of a recorded violin sound if I knew exactly what the relevant dimensions of such a violin sound are." Through the RCA synthesizer, composers can precisely control the pitch, duration, tone color, and dynamic level of sounds. Using a mechanism like a typewriter, composers punch their musical specifications into a wide roll of paper that is fed into the synthesizer. The

Composition for Synthesizer (1960–1961), by Milton Babbitt

475

sounds produced may then be recorded on audiotape. The RCA synthesizer is very complex, and few composers other than Babbitt have used it. (He is a trained mathematician as well.) The synthesizer is not "played" as one plays an organ or a piano, and composers may spend many hours with the machine to produce a few minutes of music. Babbitt has used the RCA synthesizer to produce works such as *Vision and Prayer* for soprano and synthesized accompaniment (1961); *Philomel* for soprano, recorded soprano, and synthesized tape (1963); *Ensembles for Synthesizer* (1962–1964); and *Composition for Synthesizer* (1960–1961), which we'll now study.

In *Composition for Synthesizer* both pitch and rhythm are governed by serial organization. Here is the basic twelve-tone row: G–E–A♭–E♭–B–C–D–A–B♭–D♭–F–G♭. Babbitt has written that the *Composition* is less concerned with "new sounds and timbres" than with the control and specification of rhythm made possible by the RCA synthesizer. Electronic music, he explains, provides "a means of controlling rhythm in all its aspects, including speed and flexibility of pitch succession and time rate of change of dynamics, something that was never afforded a composer before." Though some noiselike sounds are heard in *Composition for Synthesizer*, most of the sounds have definite pitches.

The opening 45 seconds of *Composition* clearly show Babbitt's skillful use of contrasting textures and registers. There is a regular alternation between gonglike chords and melodic fragments, which are shifted to different registers, changed in speed, and presented in backward (retrograde) and upside-down (inverted) form. The texture becomes more and more complex as the number of melodic lines increases from one to four. This increasing complexity can be seen in the following outline:

1 *a.* Gonglike sustained chord stated twice.
   b. One staccato melody.
2 *a.* Sustained chord stated twice.
   b. Two staccato melodies.
3 *a.* Sustained chord.
   b. Low legato melody joined by two higher staccato melodies.
4 *a.* Sustained chord.
   b. Two very low melodies joined by two higher staccato melodies.

Many trill-like figures are heard in the section that follows. Their speed and evenness could only be achieved through electronic means.

Synchronisms No. 6 for Piano and Electronic Sounds (1970), by Mario Davidovsky

Mario Davidovsky (b. 1934), an Argentinian composer now living in the United States, is well known for compositions in which electronically synthesized sounds are combined with one or more conventional instruments. Live musicians, whose interpretations vary each time, are synchronized with audiotape, a "performance" that never changes.

In *Synchronisms No. 6,* which won a Pulitzer Prize in 1971, the piano and electronic sounds are integrated through similarities of pitch, rhythm, dynamics, and tone color. The electronic sounds—of definite and indefinite pitch—were produced through the resources of a tape studio and a Buchla synthesizer. Davidovsky explains that the electronic part "should perhaps not be viewed as an independent line, but rather as if it were inlaid into the piano part."

The opening of *Synchronisms No. 6* shows how one sound can grow out of another. A single piano tone, G, is joined imperceptibly by an electronic G, which gets louder. The piano tone itself seems to increase in volume, something that normally is impossible. Often during the piece, the electronic sounds change the acoustical characteristics of the piano by affecting the way in which its tones begin and die away.

It is fascinating to listen to the interplay between piano and taped sounds. Staccato piano tones may inspire electronic clicks and pops of indefinite pitch. Scurrying rushes of electronic sounds are imitated by rapid piano passages. Staccato and sustained sounds are often combined both on the piano and on the tape.

After about 5½ minutes in which the continuity is rarely broken, *Synchronisms* is punctuated by climactic piano octaves and a long pause. A reflective epilog then recalls earlier moments in the piece. Slow, quiet piano chords lead into an eerie, atmospheric section in which tones are allowed to reverberate by means of the damper pedal. High, very soft fluttering sounds in the piano are accompanied by tiny electronic blips. The dry, staccato tones that follow bring *Synchronisms No. 6* to a witty conclusion.

Synchronisms No. 6
for Piano and
Electronic Sounds
(1970), by Mario
Davidovsky

JAZZ

In the New Orleans jazz band, the front line provided melodic material, while the rhythm section kept the beat and added harmony. King Oliver, second from right, is shown here with his Creole Jazz Band in 1923, including Louis Armstrong, third from right, and Lillian Hardin Armstrong, at piano (The Bettmann Archive).

[1] THE "AMERICAN" ART FORM

For the roots of a music as American as jazz, we must look back hundreds of years to the culture of Africa.

We know that people were kidnaped from Africa as early as 1619 and brought as slaves to America. They were the cheapest agricultural labor available to the plantation owners, and they brought to America a musical culture that was totally different from the white European culture familiar to most Americans today. We will see how this musical culture was adapted (by force and the need to survive) to the American slave culture and how, under hostile, oppressive conditions, it became the parent of the most original American art form, improvised jazz.[1]

The Slave in America

In Africa, music was religious and functional. It played an everyday role in African culture, and all members of the culture were included in its performance, whether a prayer to a harvest god or a song to celebrate a victorious battle. Music was not "art" in our Western sense; it was not performed in a concert hall for an audience that sat quietly to listen. Instead, it was an integral part of the African lifestyle.

In America the Africans entered a bewildering world where their language, religion, traditions, and music were suppressed. The practice of African religion became punishable by death in many places in the South. The slave had to find a new way to express spiritual feelings. Christianity was all that was available, and the Africans turned to it. They adapted themselves to the new religion musically by taking familiar African melodies and changing the words to fit the English Christian mold. But the rhythms, harmonies, and vocal inflections remained African. Transplanted to a foreign soil, the Negro **spiritual** took root—the first example of Afro-American music.

The key word in the development of this music is *inflection*. African dialects, essentially musical in sound, rise and fall in pitch and have a great variety of tone color (made by soft attacks and sharp releases). The slaves learned English by imitating the sounds around them. This new language was important in two ways. First, it signaled the process whereby the Africans began their slow assimilation into American life. Second, it let the slaves express themselves to peers without being understood by white people.

[1]Several examples of music discussed in this section are included on Record V, Side 2 of the five-record set accompanying *Music: An Appreciation* (see Appendix VI). An excellent recorded anthology of jazz is *The Smithsonian Collection of Classic Jazz* (distributed by W. W. Norton and Company, Inc.). A brief discography of jazz is given in Appendix III.

While the slaves created a new verbal communication, they retained their unique mode of musical communication, one that the slaveowners feared: the sound of *drums.* In Africa the drum was the basic music instrument, providing very strong beats, rhythms, and polyrhythms. It signaled such actions as waking in the morning, greeting visitors to the village, and attacking enemies; it was used to accompany dancers, workers, and funeral processions; and it was used in a highly sophisticated way to communicate messages over long distances. But what terrified the white men was that the drum could incite great passion and, possibly, riot and revolt. In slave America, drums were prohibited, too.

Nevertheless, the slaves found spiritual supplement to their field work through the **work song.** In Africa, work songs were common and usually reflected the rewards of labor. The song was happy because the work was for personal or tribal gain. But a slave in America received no rewards, and the work song became a rhythmic reference to the work at hand; its tempo and beat came directly from the work. Often the songs were little more than a cadenced shout or "holler" that was repeated over and over until the work was finished for the day. The important elements of the work song were that it was personal and that it was often improvised. In combination, these elements form the essence of jazz—the ability to express ideas and feelings in a musical framework at the moment they are experienced. And if the work song had no particular form except the repetition of material, we can find in it the beginnings of a most significant music, the "blues."

The Blues

When emancipation finally came, it was traumatic. By the time of its proclamation, the plantation owners' goal had been reached: for blacks, Africa was no longer a frame of reference; slavery was. With the Emancipation Proclamation black people became American Negroes, and they were "free." But after so many frustrating years, former slaves found that freedom was a myth. They could, more or less, travel where they wanted, but they couldn't get much work, their political power was minimal, and they were generally denied the opportunity of education. Yet, in the search for "freedom" and the "promised land," they entered parts of American life to witness things previously withheld— railroads, cities, saloons, stagecoaches, Indians, seaports, poker, police, whorehouses, and venereal disease could be theirs as much as white people's. And from such life experiences they drew a wealth of material for the blues.

Above all, the **blues** are personal—they speak about real situations and real feelings (something a slave could never show to an outsider). Now the former slaves had new personal experiences to draw from, and their songs began to speak of earthly pleasures, not just heavenly ones.

These early blues were very simple in melodic content and resembled the work song, with one melody being repeated over and over again. Since there was no set form, a blues could be three or fifteen bars (measures) long; each

The Blues

481

blues singer had his or her own story to tell and took as much time as needed to tell it. Regional styles developed so that you could tell where singers came from by how they sang the blues. But no matter what area of the country the singers were from, they more and more sang about an American life experience.

Roots are hard to trace when they become smothered or entangled. And though African origins had been obscured by around 1900, the blues had developed into a standard poetic and musical form, a form that has not yet changed. Personal experience was still the basis for the blues, but improvisation became an important feature. The poetic form was simple: one line was sung and repeated, and a different line closed the three-line stanza:

> I woke up dis mornin an' my head felt bad.
> I woke up dis mornin an' my head felt bad.
> I was dreamin' 'bout my baby an' what a time we had.

The singer improvised as many lines as he or she could for each blues, telling more about the event with each stanza. The same melody was used for the first two lines, and a slightly different one for the last.

The musical form of the blues is based on a harmonic progression that is usually twelve bars in length. Known as the **blues progression,** this harmonic structure involves only three chords, the tonic, dominant, and **subdominant** (the triad based on the fourth note—*fa*—of the scale). The chord pattern of the twelve-bar blues can be outlined as: tonic (4 bars)–subdominant (2 bars)–tonic (2 bars)–dominant (2 bars)–tonic (2 bars). The music is usually in $\frac{4}{4}$ time.

dreamin' 'bout my baby   an' what a time we had.

This twelve-bar harmonic progression is repeated several times. (Such a formal and harmonic structure used as the basis of a jazz improvisation is known as a **chorus.**)

Within this simple form, blues singers fill the measures with an endless variety of details about life. Similarly, instrumentalists fill the measures of the blues form with different types of content. Both vocal and instrumental melodies feature "blue" notes, which are produced by lowering or "flatting" the third, seventh, or fifth notes of the scale. And along with such "bent" notes, slides between pitches contribute to the distinctive quality of a blues melody. Sometimes new melodies go with the basic chords, and sometimes the melodies imply new chords; rhythms often don't fall on the beat but are syncopated; and several people may "speak" their story at the same time. From such variety a new music was created in New Orleans, Louisiana, and was called *jazz*.

Basic Terms

If you aren't sure what each of the following words means, look back at the text, where they appear in bold type. Additional information about some of them can be found by checking the index.

spiritual
work song
blues
blues progression
subdominant
chorus

NEW ORLEANS Jazz [**2**]

By 1900 New Orleans was a major urban area in the United States, a world trade center dealing in such goods as coffee, sugar, bananas, lumber, and petroleum. Steamboats traveled the Mississippi River carrying these goods from small towns and villages to the Gulf city. The steamboats also carried the various ethnic inhabitants of New Orleans. Black, Indian, French, and English-speaking groups conducted their business in this thriving scene according to a predictable and orderly rule: the bosses were white, and the workers were black, Indian and poor white.

Culturally, each group was segregated, and each had its own activities. Europeans reflected the cultures of their homelands: they sought high fashion, refined cuisines, concerts, theater, formal dancing. The white American scene varied from medicine shows, rodeos, and burlesques to band concerts (popular after the Civil War). Black culture was strongly represented by the church, the revival of African drumming and dance (performed openly since emancipation), minstrel shows, and the blues.

Although these ethnic groups were segregated by color and economic class, their cultural activities crossed boundaries and influenced each other. Minstrelsy, for example, was picked up by white entertainers who toured rural areas doing skits and songs in "blackface." This kind of exploitation reached an international level by 1927, when the first talking movie brought Al Jolson to the screen in blackface as *The Jazz Singer.* And George Gershwin became famous as a "jazz composer" in 1923 with *Rhapsody in Blue,* a composition scored for large symphonic orchestra which bears little resemblance to improvised jazz other than in its imitation of jazz instrumental sounds. The conductor of its premiere, Paul Whiteman, became known to most Americans as the "King of Jazz."

In the cultural trade-off that occurred in New Orleans, European music influenced black music in two basic ways: Formal study of the "great masters" resulted in *ragtime;* and adaptation of European instrumental techniques (and instruments like the trumpet, clarinet, and trombone) resulted in *jazz.*

Ragtime

Ragtime music is primarily played on the piano. Most "rags" have a formal musical structure, syncopated melodies, and recognizable compositional techniques. "Maple Leaf Rag" by Scott Joplin (1868–1917) was published before this century opened (1899), and is still one of the most famous of all ragtime compositions.

A grab bag of cross-cultural influences, "Maple Leaf Rag" brings together marching music, polkas, saloon ballads, and Scott Joplin's early formal keyboard study with a German music teacher. Perhaps its most important characteristics are that it was "acceptable" to society; it was notated and published to be performed by anyone—black or white—with the necessary talent; and, most important, no matter how often it is performed, it "stays the same." This was something new for music that had grown out of the black experience in America. It can't be said about the early instrumental jazz in New Orleans.

Jazz

484

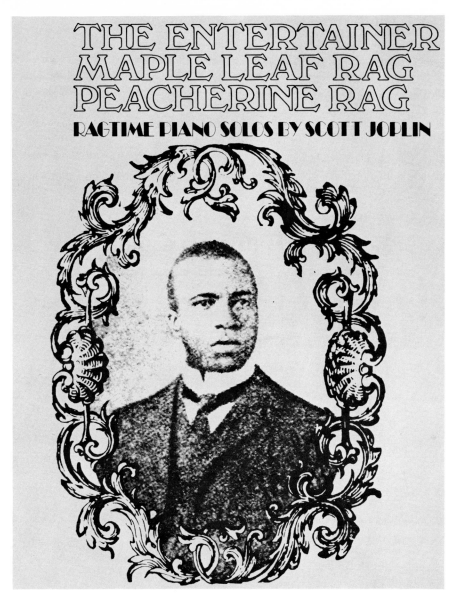

The "Maple Leaf Rag" is a grab-bag of
cross-cultural influences—marching music,
polkas, saloon ballads, and Scott Joplin's early
formal keyboard study (Omikron).

LISTENING OUTLINE

To be read while music is heard

"Maple Leaf Rag" (1899), by Scott Joplin

A-flat major, $\frac{2}{4}$ meter, A A B B A C C D D form

piano

(About 3 min)

1   The sixteen measures of the A section employ three compositional techniques:

    a. Syncopated melody in the right hand and a strong, single-note–chord rhythm ("oom-pah") in the left hand:

Tempo di Marcia

    b. Shift of register: a melodic fragment is played at different octaves:

    c. Repetition of an entire phrase an octave lower:

The entire A section is repeated.

2   The B section has sixteen measures and makes use of similar techniques, but it has a new melody and bass line. The B section is also repeated.

3   The entire A section is repeated.

4   The C section, too, has sixteen measures. In this section the music modulates (changes key) to the subdominant, a technique typical of ragtime. The right hand has a new melody that uses a combination of single notes and chords to give a rich texture. The left hand accompaniment is fuller because of the greater distance between the note and chord.

The C section is repeated.

5   In the sixteen measures of the final section, D, the music modulates back to the original key of A flat. There is a new melody and bass line similar to those of sections A and B. After section D repeats, the piece ends with a final cadence.

Jazz

Musical instruments were not unknown to blacks. The banjo, originally from Africa, was found in minstrel shows; the guitar accompanied the blues; the piano and organ were used in church; and the tambourine and other rhythm instruments, with various drums, were always part of the black music scene. However, when blacks picked up European instruments, their immediate frame of reference was not the concert hall but the *concert band.* By 1910 American bands and bandmasters such as John Philip Sousa had begun to have a tremendous impact on the development of jazz.

   The New Orleans jazz band was, in instrumentation, a smaller version of the Sousa band. The **front line** (instruments that played melodic material) usually included a cornet (a smaller, quieter trumpet), clarinet, and trombone.

Jazz

487

The cornet played the lead melody, while the clarinet played an *obligato,* or free melody, winding around it. The trombone added a third melody which was more restricted and outlined chords much as the pianist's left hand does in a rag, but with more sophistication. The **rhythm section** kept the beat and supplied harmony or chords; it usually included a chord instrument (banjo, guitar, or piano); a single-note low instrument (tuba or bass fiddle); and a percussionist. The music they played was highly polyphonic—all the more remarkable because they improvised it.

For early jazz instrumentalists, improvisation began as a dubious practice. Often only one person in the band (usually the cornet player, or the leader) had a good ear for melodies, some formal music training, and the ability to read music. He or she taught the music to the other musicians, playing it over and over until each could play it. The others, in turn, would try to "follow the leader." We can't know what the early attempts sounded like because they were not notated, but we do know that in some way these musicians tried to imitate what they called a "Sousa sound." They ended up translating a *vocal* concept of music (the spirituals, work songs, blues) to an *instrumental* concept. To do so, they used the forms—but not always the content—of band music, ragtime, popular songs, hymns, and the blues. This free hodgepodge of ideas, forms, instruments, and techniques produced a music so distinct and original that no one knew what to make of it. The day's "eminent critics" found it primitive, vulgar, and ugly. The second-class status of its performers was transferred to the music itself: finding its way to no concert halls, jazz found only one sympathetic environment in the Storyville section of New Orleans, the red-light district.

Storyville was a section of gin mills, saloons, gambling joints, whorehouses, and other establishments eager to satisfy a willing customer. Each "joint" had a piano player or a small band. The patrons didn't much care what the musicians played, as long as they created the "right atmosphere." So musicians were free to experiment. Piano players improvised material to add to original ragtime. They combined it with pop tunes and the blues to create a new style of piano playing called **stride,** a fluid and inventive music with improvisation as its basis. The other musicians also found new ways to handle their roles, every night creating music within the stationary frameworks they began with. In this exciting atmosphere of changing ideas and influences, the first *real* "King of Jazz" found his court.

Louis Armstrong

On July 4, 1913, a thirteen-year-old boy was arrested for shooting a gun in festive Storyville. His enthusiasm for the country's birthday was enhanced because it was his birthday, too. He had lived his first thirteen years in this fast-moving New Orleans atmosphere; he was to spend the next few in a reform school, the Colored Waifs' Home. There Louis Armstrong (1900–1971) learned to play the cornet.

Jazz

Bessie Smith, one of the most influential blues singers (CBS Records).

When released from the home, Armstrong began his early "professional" training—on the Mississippi riverboats. Storyville was closed in 1917, and the only jobs that black musicians could find were with minstrel shows or on the boats. Besides cargo, the riverboats had saloons, dance halls, and gambling casinos, where you could hear New Orleans jazz.

Chicago developed as a trade center and became the new home of jazz. By 1925 it was Armstrong's home too. He worked in Chicago and New York with, among others, King Oliver (his first trumpet idol), Bessie Smith (perhaps the greatest known blues singer), and Fletcher Henderson (a bandleader who featured Armstrong). His rising popularity with the jazz audience brought him the attention of record companies. In 1925, in Chicago, Armstrong made his first recordings for Columbia Records.

If there is such a thing as a "classic" New Orleans band, "Louis Armstrong and His Hot Five" were it. They included Armstrong (cornet), Johnny Dodds (clarinet), Kid Ory (trombone), Johnny St. Cyr (banjo), and Lil Harding (piano; she later became Lil Armstrong). The early Hot Five recordings are certain proof that Armstrong was the first great jazz musician. (See the listening outline for "Hotter Than That," in the Elements section.)

Armstrong's influence on musicians playing New Orleans style jazz was great, and his contributions provided new roots for later generations of jazz musicians. Because of him, their growth and creativity were advanced.

Basic Terms

If you aren't sure what each of the following words means, look back at the text, where they appear in bold type. Additional information about some of them can be found by checking the index.

ragtime	rhythm section
front line	stride

[3] SWING

Viewed from any angle, 1933 was an eventful year in the United States. The Roaring Twenties were out, and the Great Depression was painfully in. Franklin Delano Roosevelt began the longest presidency in American history. Segregation split the country—openly in the South, less so in the North. Welfare rolls got longer, and unemployment increased rapidly. Theaters featured both movies and live shows. Most homes had a radio. While Bing Crosby "crooned" and Boris Karloff offered "Frankenstein," W. C. Fields and the Marx Brothers convulsed an audience that craved escape. Greta Garbo and Marlene Dietrich proved they were the most desired women in films, and John Barrymore was the leading matinee idol of the time.

In the midst of such events, jazz went into its first major upheaval. Less was being heard from New Orleans, and more was coming out of Kansas City. Swing, a new style of jazz, was developing.

We saw in section 2 that New Orleans music was polyphonic, mostly improvised and generally performed by small bands. A typical **swing band,** however, included a *saxophone section* (two altos, two tenors, and a baritone); *trumpet and trombone sections,* each with three or four musicians; and a *rhythm section* with a piano, bass (which replaced the tuba), drums, and guitar (instead of banjo). Such big bands needed music that was composed and arranged—a sharp contrast to the free-wheeling improvisations of the small New Orleans bands. With swing, the bandleader became more of a personality and show-man, leaving the serious musical chores to an unknown musician behind the scene, the composer-arranger. Swing music makes room for solo performers, but its main emphasis can be heard in the often slick, popular arrangements of tunes like "I Got Rhythm," "When You're Smiling," and "I'm a Ding-Dong Daddy." The most accessible musical element in these—aside from the obvious melody—is the use of the *riff*.

A **riff** is a short melodic idea that is repeated many times to correspond to the harmonic background and form of the tune being played. It generally creates tension and excitement. For example, in a typical arrangement of a twelve-bar blues, the rhythm section might play one chorus and be followed by the saxophone section playing a chorus of a riff. The next chorus would keep these elements and add a riff by the trombone section. And the last chorus would include all three of these elements plus a trumpet-section riff. This block-building of riffs produced a "roaring" sound which did, in fact, generate energy and excitement. But the emphasis on sound often hid the work of individual musicians in the band. Soloists still improvised, but the ensemble playing was arranged.

Swing music was a different style of music from New Orleans jazz, but it served the same master: mood and atmosphere were still more important than musical substance to the general audience. Although the music scene changed from whorehouses and gin mills to large dance halls and ballrooms, the audience still expected something special for the price of admission. Most swing bands obliged.

Each band had its costume. They might be dressed in a version of bellhop uniforms, dinner jackets, or tuxedos. Male singers tried to look as virile as possible, and females concentrated on being sexy. The band was set up to give an impression of being a well-balanced, well-organized outfit with "class."

Most swing bands staged battles between instruments. Two musicians would compete in a cutting contest to determine (nightly) who was "king." They stood in front of the band and improvised on a tune that was played in a fast tempo. The audience crowded around the bandstand and cheered their favorites. The winners of cutting contests were judged by standards such as how loud or how fast they played, or how long they could hold a note. But the emphasis on the surface aspects of playing music helped to erode the very thing they were after. Many soloists took the audience's cheers more seriously than the

Swing

In the swing era, bandleaders took on titles to enhance their images. The Count Basie Orches-

music, and they based their improvisations on crowd-pleasing devices. It was difficult for a musician to develop his art in such a "right" atmosphere. To do so, he had to forget about the audience and what it could or couldn't understand; he gave up the reward of recognition and expressed what he must, with whatever originality and subtlety he was capable of.

Lester "Pres" Young

In the swing era, it was a custom for bandleaders to take on titles that would enhance their image. *Duke* Ellington, *Earl* Hines, and *Count* Basie were three members of the "royal" family. Lester Young (1909–1959) was only a saxophone tra is shown here in 1940 (Brown Brothers).

player in Count Basie's band (1936–1941), but somewhere along the line he earned a title that was unusual in such aristocratic company. He was "elected" president—*Pres* Young.

Young was born in New Orleans in 1909. He came from a musical family and first played the drums. But he gave them up because they were too heavy to carry to *gigs* (jobs); then he started playing the alto saxophone. At eighteen he left home to join a band in which he played baritone sax for a while, then tenor sax, and, occasionally, the clarinet.

Little is known about Young's early career. He worked around Kansas City with Walter Page's "Blue Devils," King Oliver (Louis Armstrong's early idol), and Fletcher Henderson (whose band was one of the best). At the time, the

Lester "Pres" Young

493

king of tenor sax was Coleman Hawkins, who played with a very big rich tone, a wide vibrato, and an aggressive style with fast runs and a strong beat. Hawkins might generally be characterized as a "stomper." His kind of saxophone playing was what the audience, and musicians too, had come to expect and want. When they heard Pres Young play, they were dismayed, disappointed, and hostile.

Young played with a tone that was light, but it varied greatly depending on the nature of his improvisation. His rhythmic sense was extraordinarily subtle—the beat was a reference point that he skated around, sometimes hitting it, sometimes hitting the space between beats. He avoided fast, flashy playing and concentrated on exploring each sound's possibilities by using different inflections for different attacks. While many swing-era soloists played short, choppy phrases and repeated notes to end up sounding like a series of riffs, Pres's solos were extremely lyrical with long, flowing melodic lines. When he did use repeated notes, he invented "false" or "alternate" fingerings so that they sounded different each time. And he saved the vibrato for the end of a series of notes, an afterthought, rather than using it as part of his general sound. In short, Pres Young wanted every sound he made to have meaning.

By the time Young joined Count Basie in 1936 he was already a puzzling figure. He was not particularly liked by audiences; worse, he had to overcome the biases of other musicians. He sat with his instrument at a peculiar angle at the end of the saxophone section, almost purposefully detached from the rest of the band. He fought the nightly "battle of the saxes" with Herschel Evans, another tenor-sax man, who played in the Coleman Hawkins style.

By today's standards, Young's solo time was limited. He worked out in introductions; he would play four or eight bars here and there, backgrounds for vocalists, and one or two choruses in numbers that featured him. This was a most difficult setting for improvisation, and Young's first recordings in 1936 show some of his greatest work. They were made in the less restrictive and more appealing setting of a five-piece band. Along with the blues, the standard form used for improvisation was the thirty-two-bar A A B A form. In this form, contrasting material is in the B section, called the **bridge,** or **release.** In this section soloists usually dispensed with the melody and used the harmony and form to guide their improvisations.

Young was in the army from 1941 to 1944, and when he came out he was a changed man. The jazz scene, we'll soon see, had also changed, and Young was "behind the times." His sound more and more took on the Hawkins characteristics, rather than the delicate, subtle style he developed before 1941. It was a tragic transformation. After 1944 Young's creativity was a feeble shadow of what it once was. Like Louis Armstrong, Young led the way for later musicians and was, in fact, "rediscovered" in the late forties. And, like Armstrong, his reputation ironically increased as his playing and improvisational abilities diminished. He became a lonely, unhappy person whose health and emotional state deteriorated until his death in 1959. His originality was never fully appreciated.

Jazz

494

Lester Young's career and life point to a turn jazz had taken which would affect the lives of nearly all its artists: jazz had become a business.

LISTENING OUTLINE

To be read while music is heard

"Lady Be Good" (1936), by Lester "Pres" Young and Count Basie

Carl Smith (muted trumpet), Lester Young (tenor sax), Count Basie (piano), Walter Page (bass), and Jo Jones (drums)

Fox trot, A A B A (32 bars), $\frac{4}{4}$ meter, G major

(About 3 min)

1. Full chorus (thirty-two bars). Basie (piano) plays four bars of the original Gershwin melody, then continues to improvise. He repeats a fragment of the familiar melody near the end of his solo. Notice the extremely sparse use of his left hand, in sharp contrast to the style of the ragtime players. Also notice that Basie plays short single notes and chords in the upper register with his right hand. The bass plays an outline of the harmony on every beat, and the drummer plays on the cymbals, using other drums for occasional accents. This chorus is more of a rhythm section solo than a piano solo.
2. Two choruses (thirty-two bars plus thirty-two bars). Compare Young's solo (tenor sax) with the original melody.

Pres' improvised solo (first 16 bars)

original melody "Lady Be Good"

3　One chorus; trumpet (muted) solo with Young "riffing" in the background. The trumpet solo exhibits the short fragment style.

4　Bridge (B section): rhythm section plays as in the beginning.

5　Last eight bars (A section): trumpet plays same riff till end. Young repeats a single phrase, but it sounds different each time.

Pres' last 8 bars

Billie Holiday

Few women in jazz have been instrumentalists. Most have sung. And the jazz vocalist is *most* accessible to the audience because they both speak the same language. Whether a woman sang well or not, she was generally regarded as property. She was what the customer paid for. And she was expected to sing, be sexy, and give an impression that she was "available." Who can wonder that so many jazz women have led confused and tragic lives?

It's no secret that Billie Holiday (1915–1959) was a one-time prostitute, a heavy drinker, and a heroin addict. "Decent" folk never let her or the public forget it. What is often overlooked, though, is that after 1942 no jazz singer's style escaped the influence of Billie Holiday. Her first recordings with Benny Goodman in 1933 ("Your Mother-in-Law's Son" and "Riffin' the Scotch") give little indication of the original style she showed only three years later. In the early recordings it's hard to find much difference between her work and that in any commercial "novelty" number of the swing era. But in 1936 her great work began, and it continued until 1946, when she received recognition and financial reward.

Billie Holiday's early recording dates were informal, to say the least. She sang mostly pop tunes with the standard A A B A, thirty-two-bar form and an occasional blues. Decisions were made about the key, introductions, number of choruses, endings, who played or sang where and for how long; then the microphones were turned on and the musicians did a "take." With little or no rehearsal, most of Holiday's early recordings were made in one or two takes

Jazz

496

with a small band. These low-paying, nonroyalty recordings are spontaneous, relaxed, and deeply personal.

Most vocalists sang the music as it was written, with little variation. Not Billie Holiday. She improvised like an instrumentalist within the framework of the lyrics and form. She would bend notes, sing words like *love* and *baby* with an endless variety of inflection, add little cries at the ends of some words, and change the original melody to suit herself. She would lag behind the beat so that at times she sounds "off beat" or "out of tempo." None of it was an accident. Holiday sang like a horn. Her strongest influence came from Lester Young, whom she liked to have play "pretty solos" behind her when she sang. Young made many of the early recording dates and did, in fact, contribute some of his greatest solos as well as a most sensitive accompaniment. Holiday and Young improvised together at the same time. They never tried to outdo each other, but rather were happy to share the music in a loving, noncompetitive way.

After 1946, Billie Holiday's career was characterized by two songs that became "hers": "Strange Fruit," a bitter poem describing racist conditions in the South, and "God Bless the Child," a singer's analysis of the ruling class. By this time she was known as "Lady Day" (a name Young gave her) and "The Lady with White Gardenias" (she wore them in her hair). All of this had little to do with Holiday's music. The imagemakers were at it again, and they succeeded. There's no need to list the details of suffering in the later part of Billie Holiday's life. Words from her autobiography, *Lady Sings the Blues,* just about sum up her situation: "You can be up to your boobies with white satin, with gardenias in your hair and no sugar cane for miles, but you can still be working on a plantation."

The swing era halted abruptly when the United States entered World War II in December 1941. Many jazz musicians enlisted or were drafted, and it became increasingly hard to put together personnel for a band. More and more vocalists were featured, and instrumental solos—improvised or set—became less frequent. Throughout the war, swing bands played at service clubs and at concerts for soldiers. Unfortunately for the evolution of jazz, the bands gradually became mere accompanists for singers destined to be the "name acts" of the next decade's entertainment industry. Ella Fitzgerald, Frank Sinatra, and Doris Day all started as swing-band vocalists. The split and distinction between jazz artists and jazz entertainers had begun.

Basic Terms

If you aren't sure what each of the following words means, look back at the text, where they appear in bold type. Additional information about some of them can be found by checking the index.

swing band   bridge (release)
riff

Basic Terms

[4] BEBOP AND MODERN JAZZ

In the 1940s jazz musicians developed a complex new style called **bebop** (or **bop**). It was an abstract music that required attentive listening and was not meant to "entertain." To its early audiences, bebop seemed to lack melody, organization, and a clearly defined beat. Bop drummers did not play all four beats of the bar on the bass drum, as in swing style. Instead, they used the other drums for very asymmetrical accents sometimes called "dropping bombs," and played a constant rhythm on the ride cymbal. This took away the listener's familiar frame of reference—the beat—since the drummer wasn't stating the beat but only referring to it.

There is, in fact, as much organization in bebop as in swing or New Orleans music. The *forms* are exactly the same: the twelve-bar blues and the thirty-two-bar A A B A. The boppers kept the basic harmonic structure of the forms, but they composed a new melody (called a "line" or "head") to substitute for the original pop tune. These lines served as recurring themes between improvisations. The elaborate melodic improvisations contained tones that suggested substitute chords. A "substitution" is a chord or series of chords that refers to the original chord or chords; it has either additional or altered notes that usually correspond with the melody. Complex bebop harmonies were generated by the horn players' melodies.

Charlie "Bird" Parker

Bebop was not only a new style of music, but a distinct lifestyle as well. Shades, berets, and goatees were the "official" dress, and "hip" or "jive" talk was the vernacular. The man who epitomized this revolution and was, in fact, its musical and spiritual leader was Charlie "Bird" Parker (1920–1955).

Parker was born in Kansas City. He played baritone horn in the school marching band but soon switched to alto saxophone. By fifteen, he was a high school dropout, a professional musician, and a heroin addict. He worked around Kansas City and there heard Lester Young play with the Basie band. Young was Parker's most profound early influence. Parker then lived in New York for some time. Along with trumpet player Dizzy Gillespie, he became a standard figure in the Harlem jam sessions. Both he and Gillespie worked with Earl Hines in a traditional swing band until they were fired for playing their "weird" music.

The first bebop records were made in late 1944 and early 1945 for the new and exclusively jazz Savoy record company. Parker recorded as a sideman with Tiny Grimes, with Dizzy Gillespie, and finally under his own name. Most of these recordings had typically (for bebop) deceptive titles like "Billie's Bounce" (twelve-bar blues), "Thriving on a Riff" ("I Got Rhythm"), "Ko Ko" (a strange version of "Cherokee"), "Donna Lee" ("Back Home Again in Indiana"), "Hot House" ("What Is This Thing Called Love?"). These records had a hostile reception, with critics using such glowing adjectives as "comical," "ugly," "squealing," "honking," and "non-" or "antimusic."

Lyricism, intensity, and timing were the three major elements of Parker's style. His melodic line was extremely long and used intervals that implied so many substitutions that the harmonic background of the original tune was changed forever. He had a great sense of humor and quoted melodies from outside the jazz repertoire in the middle of his improvisations. The *Habanera* from Bizet's opera *Carmen* and "Popeye the Sailor Man" were two favorites. He combined many different articulations so that the beginning of a phrase might be slurred (smooth or legato), while the end of the phrase might be sharp and detached. Parker played double- and triple-time rhythms fast and clean. When his records are slowed down to half speed, very definite melodies can be heard in place of the rapid rhythms. Parker could play with great tenderness ("My Old Flame," 1947) or explosive passion ("Parker's Mood," 1945). He *always* played with feeling. And many of his endless ideas were improvised within the simple structure of the twelve-bar blues.

After 1950, Parker headed the way of many other great jazz improvisers. His health and emotional state worsened. He tried to commit suicide. He tried to kick his habit but couldn't succeed. Charlie Parker died in 1955. The death certificate listed his age as fifty-three; but he was thirty-four years old.

Charlie Parker brought jazz improvisation to heights never before achieved. The audience, however, was more interested in music that was immediately accessible. Rock 'n' roll and folk music unquestionably became the sound of the fifties, and there was little that jazz players could do about it. They tried to inject new blood into jazz from outside influences, and by 1960 jazz was played under many titles: funky, soul, gospel, Latin, Afro-Cuban, bebop, cool, East Coast, West Coast. Many albums were released as the "jazz version" of hit shows and movies. All of this attracted little attention, and by the beginning of the sixties the moans could be heard that jazz was dead.

John Coltrane

John Coltrane (1926–1967) and Sonny Rollins were the two most influential saxophone players after 1955. Coleman Hawkins had inspired both of these aggressive tenor sax players. While Rollins was still perfecting his post-bop style, Coltrane left bebop and emerged as the new spiritual leader of modern jazz.

Coltrane's first break came while he was with the Miles Davis Quintet, 1955–1957. This band played bebop standards, nonjazz standards ("Bye Bye Black Bird"), and the blues. The driving force behind the band was the rhythm section: Red Garland (piano), Paul Chambers (bass), and "Philly" Joe Jones (drums). They provided a solid background for Coltrane's solos, which were characterized by a bebop rhythmic feeling, melodic lines punctuated by "cries" in the upper register, and some use of double-time passages. Perhaps his most outstanding characteristic is that—unlike Young, who created new melodies

John Coltrane

John Coltrane left bebop to emerge as the new spiritual leader of modern jazz (United Press International).

on top of simple harmonies—Coltrane "ran the changes," creating patterns that extended the harmonies. This new approach to improvising was fully realized when he left the Davis Quintet in 1958. Substitution, in the bebop sense, had meant altering the chord progression to fit the soloist's melodic line. But Coltrane's "Giant Steps" goes beyond this and starts out with substitutions as the original harmonies. The harmonic vocabulary is complex in this tune, and Coltrane changes chords every two beats.

On the record album *Live at Birdland* (1963), Coltrane plays tenor and soprano saxophones. The "cries" from his early period have turned into *screams* with the piercing sound of the high-register soprano sax. He plays more fast runs, and instead of the complicated changes of "Giant Steps," he uses a simple three-chord background for harmonic support. He goes back to the long-forgotten modes (dorian, lydian, and others) for a melodic frame of reference. The rhythm section sounds more like a polyrhythmic percussion section. McCoy Tyner (piano) plays crashing chords and pedal points: Jimmy Garrison (bass) plays short melodies instead of a steady beat and (on later records) strums the bass like a guitar; and Elvin Jones (drums) literally smashes the cymbals and creates constant barrages of sound while providing an intense *in tempo* foundation for the solos.

With Coltrane's death in 1967, jazz completed a full cycle. Today jazz is heading toward a fusion with rock music. This seems inevitable, with more and more rock bands playing jazz and with jazz musicians using rock tunes and forms for improvising. Only time can tell whether the fusion will produce artists whose creativity matches that of the musicians we have briefly examined here.

Basic Term

If you aren't sure what the following word means, look back at the text, where it appears in bold type.

bebop (bop)

Basic Term

ROCK

1 Rock 'n' Roll

2 Rhythm and Blues

3 Rock

Their early work gave little indication that the Beatles would ignite a blaze that would sweep the world (Omikron).

[1] ROCK 'n' ROLL

In the early part of the twentieth century, children were expected simply to assume the attitudes of their parents. Teenagers were seen as young adults. Their clothes, while youthful in appearance, were similar to what older people wore. And their responses to similar situations were like their parents'. For example, in the late 1940s, both mother and daughter swooned—Mom over Clark Gable and daughter over Frank Sinatra. Both Dad and junior spent hours under the hood—Pop with the family car and junior with an old jalopy. Mom, apple pie, and Archie and Jughead were symbols of the American way.

By 1955, teenage life in America took a standard direction: high school, dating and going steady, the prom or the hop, graduation, and adulthood. Most people viewed these young people as happy, hard-working, athletic, and church-going; in short, they were the hope of the future.

The movie *Blackboard Jungle* shocked everybody. Here was a portrayal of teenagers who talked back to teachers, who didn't want to learn, who attempted rape, and who responded to discipline by trying to beat two teachers to death. While *Blackboard Jungle* focused on an urban school setting and a group of "juvenile delinquents," it nonetheless revealed feelings toward authority that became the new symbols of teenage rebellion. The film's portrayal of musical attitudes was prophetic, too. When an involved teacher tries to "reach" his class by playing a treasured collection of rare jazz records, the students respond by laughing at the "old-fashioned" music; in a game of "catch," they smash the records, one by one.

Bill Haley and the Comets

The theme song for *Blackboard Jungle* was "Rock Around the Clock," by Bill Haley and the Comets. The song was simple: it sang of twenty-four-hour party time. Its musical form was simple, too: twelve-bar blues without alterations. Haley was a guitarist and singer from the country-western field. After selling over one million copies of "Rock Around the Clock," he became the leader of the new teenage music. His music was extraordinarily simple. And he was a rather bland-looking man with a constant grin. What, then, was the rage about? For the first time, music spoke to, about, and for teenage life, with no references to the adult world. As far as teenagers were concerned, now they had something that was completely theirs. This fact did not escape the watchful eyes of the recording industry.

Rock 'n' roll was, is, and probably always will be a business.[1] Its main objective is to make money. And the quickest way to do that is to find out

[1] An example of music discussed in this section is included on Record V, Side 2 of the five-record set accompanying *Music: An Appreciation* (see Appendix VI). A brief discography of rock 'n' roll, rhythm and blues, and rock is given in Appendix III.

The movie *Blackboard Jungle* revealed feelings toward authority
that became the new symbols of teenage rebellion. Its theme
song was ''Rock Around the Clock,'' by Bill Haley and the
Comets (United Press International).

what audiences want to hear and mass-produce it. The rock 'n' roll formula
is simple: The music is twelve-bar blues, or a ballad (love song). Melody,
harmony, and even lyrics are subordinate to the beat. Unlike jazz drummers,
rock 'n' roll drummers never vary the beat or rhythmic pattern. There is no
subtlety, or need for it. The second and fourth beats of a four-beat measure
are accented by the snare drum.

Costumes and staging became an integral part of the rock 'n' roll formula.
Haley and the Comets, for example, imitated the adult world by wearing
tuxedos, the costume of establishment entertainers like Dean Martin and Bob
Hope; but the tuxedos were of blazing colors—fire-engine red, chartreuse,
glittering gold. Solos were staged to emphasize physical movement, rather than
musical content. For example, the keyboard player half jumped up and down
while playing; Haley used the neck of his guitar to emphasize whatever riff
he was playing; the saxophone player performed while lying on his back; and
the bass player laid his instrument on its side and used it as a mattress while
he pulled the strings as hard as possible. This was all part of the show.

Rock 'n' Roll

505

If togetherness had been the American family image during the thirties and forties, alienation became the image for teenagers in the mid-fifties. "Don't bug me" and "Just leave me alone" were main themes of teen life. They were aimed at the adult world, and they sprang from years of repressed anger. From the movies, a new antihero emerged. Marlon Brando led a roaming motorcycle gang in *The Wild Ones.* He was alienated, angry, and tough. He rode a fast bike and wore a black leather jacket and boots and spoke in one-syllable words. This image found its way into rock 'n' roll. Once and for all, the adult world was confronted with what it never spoke about in public: sex.

Elvis Presley caught the essence of the early rock 'n' roll sexual revolution (United Press International).

Elvis Presley

Elvis Presley (b. 1935) caught the essence of the early rock 'n' roll sexual revolution. On stage, there was no doubt about the focus of attention. He offered sex appeal. While his view of women was hardly liberated, "You Ain't Nothin' But a Hound Dog" kept women swooning. "Love Me Tender" offered a softer, warmer, almost affectionate side that contrasted with his blatant sexuality. Presley changed his costume to "superflash"—pink suits—and drove a gold Cadillac. In a rock 'n' roll revival show in 1972, his fans still came to see him, helping him retain the title "Elvis the Pelvis."

RHYTHM AND BLUES [2]

Rhythm and blues is black music that was being played long before disc jockey Alan Freed invented the term "rock 'n' roll." Sex and alienation were well known to rhythm and blues musicians, but their songs about such subjects seldom made it to the pop charts in the established white world. Rhythm and blues material was often picked up by groups who released "acceptable" versions that met the demands of the larger, more profitable white audience.

The **rhythm and blues** formula is different from rock 'n' roll, even though their goals were similar. For example, the typical ballad by a rhythm and blues group includes a lead singer in an extremely high register with other singers providing background harmony, much like a madrigal ensemble or a barbershop quartet. The bass singer repeats the end of phrases in a deep spoken voice, adding a wide contrast of pitch range and an almost sermon-like quality to the lyrics. The Platters were a typical rhythm and blues group of this period. Their two big hits, "Only You" and "The Great Pretender," followed this formula.

Little Richard

If Elvis was blatant, Little Richard (b. 1932) was outrageous. His big hits were "Tutti Frutti," "Keep a-Knockin'," and "Long Tall Sally." His lyrics were essentially meaningless. Instead of singing, he screamed at the top of his lungs. He pounded the piano as hard as he could. And he didn't do dance steps, but jumped—up, down, and sideways.

Other stars in the early days of rhythm and blues include Bo Diddley, Jerry Lee Lewis, Screamin' Jay Hawkins, and Chuck Berry. Most groups rose to fame and lost it in a very short time, a characteristic of pop music.

Soul

In the early sixties, black pop music returned to its roots and fused jazz, blues, gospel, and rhythm and blues. The result was called **soul.**

Soul

507

Gospel roots inspired Aretha Franklin's early material; she led the choir in her father's Baptist church (Chester Higgins, Rapho/Photo Researchers).

James Brown's music was designed to transform an audience into a massive electrical charge that could be defused only after the final curtain was brought down (Omikron).

Soul
509

Ray Charles

Ray Charles (b. 1932) cut his first records in 1954. At that time he was a "crooner" in the tradition of Nat King Cole. By 1960, he discarded that image with one of the first big soul hits, "What'd I Say?" This song differed from what was being heard in several ways. First, Charles really could play the piano and the alto sax, in a manner born in blues and bebop. His use of a horn section for background riffs was right out of the swing era. His background group of women, the Raelets, provided harmony as well as choreography. The vocal and instrumental solos are broken by a call-and-response section like that in a gospel service. There are breaks as in New Orleans jazz. And the drummer plays double-time rhythm on the bell of the cymbal, while tom-toms give an effect of African drumming.

Aretha Franklin

Aretha Franklin (b. 1942) led the choir in her father's Baptist church. Deep gospel roots inspired her early material. When she signed with Atlantic records in 1967, she began creating the title Soul Sister Number One.

Like Ray Charles, Aretha Franklin can play the piano; in addition, her powerful voice projects volume and quality without theatrics. "You're All I Need to Get By" has a rhythm section of piano, electric bass, electric guitar, tambourine, and drums; it could be found in a church or in Madison Square Garden. There is a string section and a small background group of women vocalists. Aretha Franklin sings solo, unfolding the simple lyrics of an old and familiar love story. That's how she starts. By the last chorus, she is more like a gospel preacher shouting a message over the choir singing in four-part harmony. Her shouts, unlike Little Richard's, are melodic lines with a great deal of inflection. In "Respect," Franklin gets to the heart of soul. The opening lines ("What you want, baby I got. What you need. You know I got it. All I'm askin' for, a little respect") exhibit Aretha Franklin, gospel singer, in a definitely nonsacred role. The rhythm section's background is reminiscent of the most powerful rhythm and blues records. There is no variation, merely a riffing saxophone section and a vocal group. The strings are gone. The soul of a singer is laid bare.

James Brown

With Aretha Franklin at the heart of Soul is Soul Brother Number One: James Brown (b. 1928). "Hot Pants," "Make It Funky," "Call Me Super Bad," and "The Sex Machine" are numbers made up of funk, earthiness, and sweat. He gives a show from beginning to end. His group of women vocalists and his band focus on him, the star. Wearing capes and throwing cufflinks to the audience, he collapses at the microphone, only to be revived by cheers that bring on more frenzied dancing and cause him to collapse and repeat the

Rock

510

routine. The band riffs, while the women dance and sing in the background. The beat is always present, driving constantly, without variation or subtlety. This is pure energy music designed to transform an audience into a massive electrical charge that can be defused only after the curtain is brought down.

ROCK [3]

Rock music of the early sixties (the white counterpart of soul) returned to parts of the rock 'n' roll formula of the mid-fifties for inspiration. But unlike rock 'n' roll, rock severed all ties with the adult establishment and became independent. A brief dance craze, which started in New York, helped pave the way for the constantly evolving revolution of rock.

Chubby Checker did the twist, and a new trend was set. Of course, the music was not much (the usual twelve-bar blues with a riff theme), nor was Chubby's singing. But the dance described by the lyrics found avid fans in every area of society. The overwhelming surprise about the twist was that it was accepted and even adopted by the adult world. Teenagers had become a political class with great influence. The youth culture had become a marketable commodity.

Pop trend setters have generally come from the United States. Pop, rock 'n' roll, rhythm and blues, and soul are American. Yet the two most successful rock groups of the sixties—the Rolling Stones and the Beatles—come from England.

The Rolling Stones

The Rolling Stones illustrate rock's most basic qualities. They discard any image associated with causes. No Brando or James Dean here. They are angry, detached, and exclusive. Their dress varies from T-shirts to Superman costumes. Their music is *loud.* The decibel level they reach (along with other rock groups) is so high that prolonged exposure to it can result in deafness. Rock groups take full advantage of technological advances in amplification.

Mick Jagger is, perhaps, the most fascinating pop star. He exudes sexuality. His bumps and grinds with the microphone and his wriggles and shakes make Elvis Presley and Little Richard look tame. He whips his long hair around his sweating face, propelling his body to higher and higher energy levels. Although sex is unquestionably flaunted, the gender is unspecified. Energy is all-consuming. "Get Off My Cloud," "Sympathy for the Devil," and "Street-fighting Man" sum up the Rolling Stones' philosophy: What's mine is mine; I'll sell my soul for it and fight to the death to keep it.

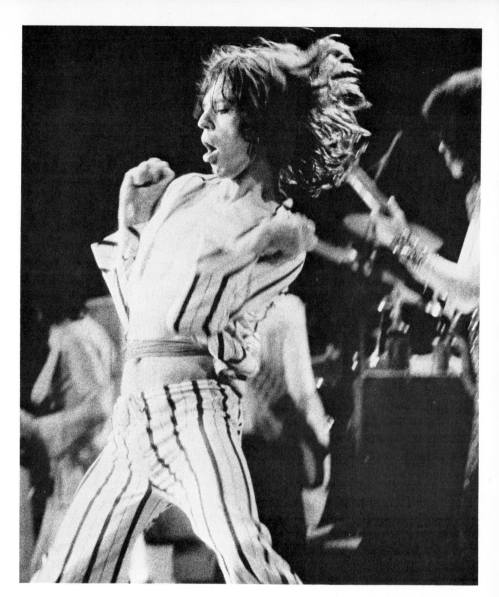

Mick Jagger and the Rolling Stones at a 1975 concert in New York City (Nancy Ney, Globe).

The Beatles

The Beatles, also from England, were the biggest of the pop groups. John Lennon, Paul McCartney, George Harrison, and Ringo Starr revolutionized pop music. Their early work was basic rock-formula music: simple lyrics, guitars, the beat, uniforms, a catchy group name, and, of course, their hairstyles. "I Wanna Hold Your Hand" and "I Wanna Be Your Man" gave little indication that the Beatles would ignite a blaze that would sweep the world.

One reason for the Beatles' huge success was their openness to outside influences. The American folk singer and poet Bob Dylan was their first

Rock

influence. Dylan had nothing musical to offer the Beatles. But lyrics are the essence of folk music, and Dylan could write lyrics. Like the Rolling Stones, he was angry; but, far from being detached, he wrote songs about human feelings. "Blowin' in the Wind," "It's a Hard Rain," and "It's All Right, Ma," are antiwar songs dealing with oppression, atomic holocaust, senseless killing, and wasted human life. Dylan was personal, something pop music had never quite been before. Lennon and McCartney (the main Beatle songwriters) were affected. "Yesterday" is their lament about the difficulties of love between people. The beat is soft. The song has a real melody and harmonic progressions that were new in pop music. "Eleanor Rigby" is about human loneliness. Not only is the beat gone, but so are the guitars. A string quartet provides the only background. Obviously, the barriers between teenage and adult life were slowly being destroyed.

A second strong influence on the Beatles was Eastern spirituality. The combination of these influences led to their most outstanding album, *Sgt. Pepper's Lonely Hearts Club Band.* The forms, melodic and harmonic content, and instrumentation are original.

The title tune, for example, begins as basic rock. But soon a trombone or baritone horn interlude becomes part of the background and is integrated with the basic rock introduction. An electric harpsichord and bass and drastic tempo and instrumentation changes add novelty to the psychedelic "Lucy." And "When I'm Sixty-four" is right out of a 1920s British vaudeville revue. A rhythm section, two clarinets, and chimes provide the background for this questioning look at old age.

"Within You Without You" is George Harrison's contribution. He plays the sitar (which he studied with Indian master Ravi Shankar) and sings a long winding melody about love, salvation, and peace. A small group of unison strings are added to the tambura and tabla. (These Indian instruments are described on pp. 529–531.)

In the seventies, there are fewer easy labels. Everyone literally does his or her own thing. Business is still business, but it's no longer everything. Trends and teenagers still change rapidly, and their stars rise and fall. Along with revived interest in jazz and improvisation, electronic music is now available to those with technical and financial resources to experiment with sophisticated equipment. "Country-and-western" and bluegrass music remain very much alive. All the kinds of music from 1955 on are performed by one group or another. Young musicians are searching for inspiration among sources as widely varied as Charles Mingus, Modest Mussorgsky, Karlheinz Stockhausen, and secular music of the Middle Ages.

Basic Terms

If you aren't sure what each of the following words means, look back at the text, where they appear in bold type. Additional information about some of them can be found by checking the index.

 rock 'n' roll   rhythm and blues   soul   rock

NON-WESTERN MUSIC

The *koto* was brought from China via Korea to Japan. Today, it is probably the most popular of all Japanese musical instruments (Omikron).

[1] MUSIC IN ORIENTAL AFRICA

Background

Euro-American interest in non-Western music has a long history.[1] At the Paris World's Fair in 1889 and 1900, not only were non-European musical instruments exhibited, but live concerts of Indian, Indonesian, and Arabic music were included as well. These concerts were performed by musicians highly regarded in their own countries.

Debussy was one of the observers who was highly impressed by the dramatic sound of the Indonesian gong-chime orchestra. He was one of the first European composers to see what non-Western music could contribute to European music. From the music he heard, Debussy extracted non-Western techniques such as parallelism, new melodic patterns, and use of only one set of motivic materials. Non-Western music inspired him to use woodwind instruments for elaborately decorated and continuous solo passages in order to create a dream-like mood. *Prélude à ''L'Après-midi d'un faune,''* first performed in 1894, demonstrates Debussy's attempt to integrate some of these non-Western idioms into Western compositions. A similar trend was established by other European composers who grafted non-Western musical techniques onto their European compositions.

Methods of Learning

The development of music in most European cultures has always depended on the works of composers; in fact, it is generally true that the history of music in the West is the history of composers. As a *script tradition,* a tradition which documents information in writing, European scholarship attempts to explain and preserve music with its recognizable esthetic theories, modes of expression, performance practices, traits, and elemental formulas. Music is generally learned from and transmitted through books and printed scores.

Non-Western music, on the other hand, has generally been transmitted from one generation to the next by the direct educational method of *oral tradition.* Since music creation is communal and often spontaneous, there is no emphasis on the historical role of the composer. The musicians of the non-Western world often commit an astounding repertory of music and information to memory; this musical material is transmitted by word of mouth from one generation to another. A song, a proverb, a story, and making or playing an instrument are learned by rote through a process of imitation or learning-by-doing.

Non-Western Music

[1]Examples of non-Western music are included on Record V, Side 2 of the five-record set accompanying *Music: An Appreciation* (see Appendix VI). A brief discography of non-Western music is given in Appendix III.

Music in Oriental Africa

The music of Oriental African countries is in many ways similar to the music of the Islamic cultures. The musical instruments also have a definite resemblance to the instruments of the so-called Arab world. The north African countries—particularly Egypt, Tunisia, Morocco, and Algeria—have come under the Islamic sphere of influence. The Oriental style extends to many of the northeastern countries around the horn of Africa, including Ethiopia, Somalia, and Sudan. Use of melodic instruments, solo performance, melodic elaboration and decoration, spontaneous song-text improvisation, heterophonic texture, and emphasis on poetry predominate in the Oriental African zone.

North Africa

Usually no mention is made of Egypt in studies that deal with Africa. However, it is important to realize that Egypt, an African nation, was one of the most important centers of world civilization and exerted a decisive influence on the cultures of the Occident and the Orient. Egyptian ideas in the fields of astronomy, acoustics, and music spread along with Egyptian conquests.

Influences never operate in one direction only. The Egyptian heritage has also been bombarded with alien influences. Egyptians took up musical ideas, performance practices, and musical instruments from the neighboring African, Mediterranean, and Asiatic cultures with whom they came in contact. Today the music and instruments of ancient Egypt have either undergone drastic changes or have disappeared entirely. The numerous paintings on walls and inside tombs that have remained to this day depict a sophisticated musical heritage in ancient Egypt.

Very little is actually known about Egyptian music before the advent of Islam, a relatively recent religious movement that dates from the birth of its founder Mohammed (c. 570–632). In addition, very little is known about Arab culture itself before the advent of Islam. Scholars generally agree that the Arab outlook on life prior to Islam was secular and hedonistic. In fact, the period from the first to the sixth century is known in Arabic history as the "Days of Ignorance."

With the Islamic invasion of north Africa in the seventh century, the Muslim cultural practices took firm roots and flourished in Egypt. Thus many of the instruments of the Islamic world are popularly used in the performance of modern Egyptian music. It is not at all surprising that Egypt is one of the four major branches of modern Muslim classical music traditions. (The other three are Iran, Tunisia, and Turkey.)

The first Muslim invasion of Tunisia occurred in 668. The original inhabitants of this country, the Berbers, were converted to Islam. By 713 Muslim armies had established themselves in most of north Africa and had advanced and conquered Spain.

The Muslim states in Spain were known as Al-Andalus. "Andalusian" once referred to the highly sophisticated Muslim culture that flourished in Spain.

Music in
Oriental Africa

517

Music became very important in the kingdoms of Al-Andalus, and musicians received patronage. Hispano-Arabic elements were blended in the Andalusian school of music. This school produced famous musicians who were able to transmit a high caliber of artistic performance to the latter generations that fled to live in north Africa. Religion has always served as the most important unifying factor in Muslim tradition, and so the Muslims of north Africa have maintained close cultural ties with Al-Andalus. In fact, when at last the Christian *reconquista* of Spain took over the Andalusian cities from the thirteenth century until the end of the sixteenth century, the Muslim inhabitants gradually fled to north Africa. These refugees in Tunisia, Morocco, and Algeria maintained and cultivated the Moorish-Andalusian style. Today Andalusian music refers to this classical music tradition which flourished in north Africa, and particularly in Tunisia.

Northeast Africa

Semitic tribes from South Yemen migrated across the Red Sea to northeastern Africa in the first and second millenniums B.C. *Ag'azian* and *Habesha* were the two important South Arabian emigrant groups that arrived in what is now Ethiopia. A form of orthodox Judaism came to Ethiopia from Yemen, where it once flourished among South Arabian tribes. The musical practices of the Ethiopian *Fellasha*, or the so-called "Black Jews," are highly reminiscent of the Hebrew chant.

Ezana, an Ethiopian monarch, accepted the Christian faith in 330 and made it the state religion. Music was considered the best medium for religious expression and the acquisition of the ascetic state. Mystic practices were started both by Egyptian and Ethiopian members of the Orthodox Christian Churches. These mystic practices gave birth to chanting of slow sacred songs accompanied by sistra (metal-rattle), drums, and dances, just as they are performed today. Ethiopian Orthodox Church music still uses *Diggua*, a treatise on education and a collection of sacred hymns, compiled by the Ethiopian ecclesiast St. Yared in the sixth century. The Muslim invasion of the sixteenth century, however, destroyed almost all of the important books of this sacred tradition and helped advance the secular patriotic song form known as *shilela*.

The Main Instruments of Oriental African Music

Since melodic elaboration is the most important trait of this musical zone, many melodic instruments are found. **Chordophones,** instruments that produce sound by means of a vibrating string or strings, play the most important role in the performance of music in Oriental African cultures. **Aerophones,** wind instruments, come second; **membranophones,** instruments that produce sound by means of a stretched membrane or skin over a frame, are third; and **idiophones,** solids that produce sound when beaten, are last.

The *'ud* is widely used in the musical performance of most Oriental African cultures (The Metropolitan Museum of Art, Gift of Dr. George C. Valliant, Miss Marian Valliant and Mrs. Benjamin Tenney, Jr., in memory of Mr. Louis D. Valliant, 1944).

Chordophones

Early Egyptian paintings in the museum at Cairo depict lutes played by women. Although the active role of women in musical entertainment has gradually disappeared along with imperial patronage, it is obvious that lute-type instruments, which generally resemble the modern banjo or guitar and are played with a plectron or quill, existed in pre-Christian times.

The short-necked lute *'ud* is the foremost instrument of Islamic music in general. The Tunisian *'ud* has five strings—three of which are made of gut, and the other two of wire. Although the *'ud* is not popularly played among the non-Islamic societies such as that found in Ethiopia, it is an instrument very widely used in the musical performances of most Oriental African cultures.

The two-stringed fiddle of north Africa known as *rbab* is almost identical in construction and function with the Ethiopian fiddle known as *masinKo*. The Islamized Tuaregs of the Sahara have a one-stringed fiddle called *amzhad*, or *imzhad*, which is used to accompany highly ornamented love songs. The *masinKo* also has one string.[2]

A zither which has gained recognition as an important instrument of virtuosity is the *kanun*. It has seventy-two strings. In north Africa, it is played with picks that are fitted to the index fingers. The closely related *santur* of Iran, on the other hand, is played by two beaters. This dulcimer is of interest because it is the ancestor of such Western instruments as the piano.

Lyre types are largely found in northeast African cultures. In the countries east of the Nile, there are lyres which have bowl-shaped sound resonators such as the Ethiopian *krar*. This bowl-lyre of northeast Africa usually has six gut strings which are played either by muting or strumming. The ancient rock paintings and frescoes in Sudan show musicians playing harps and lyres during the kingdoms of Nubia and Merewetiks. The lyre's historic and important musical role in these cultures strongly indicates interaction among the northeast African kingdoms. The box lyre *begena*, which has eight to ten gut strings, is found today only in Ethiopia. Etymologically the bowl-lyre is known as *kinnor* in Hebrew, *Kinnara* in Arabic, *ginera* in Egypt, and *lyra* in Greek. Differences in function between the bowl and box lyres also occur. The first is a secular instrument, while the latter accompanies religious poetry on solemn occasions.

Aerophones

The *nei* and the *zorna* are the main aerophones of Oriental African music. The *nei* is a simple bamboo flute. Probably the oldest bamboo flutes, the *sibs*, have been found in Egypt along the river bank of the Nile. One of the oldest records, in one of the tombs in the Gizeh Pyramid (about 2000 B.C.), depicts a band of seven flute players accompanying a vocalist. Today bamboo flutes have the widest distribution in the world. However, differences exist from region to region in the construction, in the length and width of the bamboo, and in the methods of tone production. Variations also exist in the number of holes and the distances between the finger-holes. The Ethiopian *washint* often has four to five holes, while the Tunisian *nei* often has seven holes. It is very important to realize that these musical instruments are home-made, usually by the performers themselves; they are not factory-produced. Consequently, they are not uniform in structure. The size of the finger-holes, for example, largely depends upon the size of the flute and the size of the performer's fingers.

[2]Today many of these fiddles are replaced by European violins, particularly in urban localities such as Tunis, Cairo, and Addis Ababa.

The *zorna* is a double-reed instrument of the oboe type. It usually has seven holes. It plays an important musical role in village social and ceremonial functions such as weddings, births, and other days of celebration. In Sudan, it is known as *Al Kaita,* and it is closely associated with a social dance called the *zihee.* In addition, the shrill, high sound of the *zorna* has been associated with animal mesmerism. A street *zorna* player charming a basketful of snakes is a common sight today in north Africa.

Membranophones

The prevalent notion held by most Euro-Americans that rhythmic instruments constitute most of the music of all African peoples is erroneous. African music is characterized by great diversity. Vocal music predominates in the Oriental African cultures. In solo performances, the melodic instruments already discussed often imitate the style of vocal improvisation, ornamentation, and decoration. As a result, rhythmic instruments are not very common in this zone.

The few potentially rhythmic instruments are often used in nonmusical activities. Double kettle drums known as *naqqara* are used in north African kingdoms, as among the Tuaregs of the Sahara. These drums symbolize the king's power; they were left standing near the throne. The Ethiopian kettle drum *negarit,* a court instrument, accompanied every imperial proclamation or announcement before the advent of technological communication. In fact, the name *negarit* is derived from the word *negere,* which means "talked" or "proclaimed."

Another drum, the *kebero,* should be mentioned as an instrument which accompanies religious chanting. It is mainly a processional drum used to accompany the music of important religious celebrations. The role instruments play in a culture should be seriously considered. The *negarit,* for example, is an instrument of the palace, while the *kebero* belongs to the church. The north African tambourine called *tar* is another membranophone which is used in the rhythmic sections of Andalusian classical music. The *tar* has jingling metal plates that are fitted to its body.

Idiophones

Idiophones are often used in sacred music and other nonmusical, semireligious activities. The spheric jingle, which is popularly found throughout Oriental Africa, is known by various names: *al-gulgul, schkelkil* (Egyptian), *al-qalaquil* (Sudan), and *quachil* (Ethiopia). In the provincial old Coptic (Egyptian) and Ethiopian churches, the *quachil* is still attached to the censer or sometimes to the sacred robes of the priests and deacons. This is reminiscent of the biblical jingles worn by priests to protect them from deadly spirits when they entered sacred places. Instruments made of metal, particularly iron, are reputed to have votive power. The Egyptian and Ethiopian *sistra* are often sounded by priests to drive away evil spirits that lurk around the churches. Children wear jingles

The Main Instruments of Oriental African Music

and bells around their necks to ward off the evil eye. Hence, some instruments are played for purely musical purposes, and others fulfill extramusical objectives, such as medicine, magic, and symbolism.

Music and Musicians in Oriental Africa

The Oriental African zone is inhabited by diverse ethnic groups, each with its own tradition. The Jews, the blacks, and the Berbers are only three groups who live in this zone. There are also diverse musical styles, forms, and types.

Music is often performed by hereditary professional musicians or craftsmen called *Gnawas* and *Essawas* in most of Islamic North Africa. In Ethiopia they are called *Azmari*. Since the attitude of society toward musicians is most unfavorable in Oriental Africa, most musicians are members of a guild, brotherhood, or an association in order to protect or advance their mutual interests. For example, the Sudanese musicians, the *Griots*, have formed their own brotherhood which has segregated them as a special caste of musicians from the rest of society.

Music, vocal or instrumental, sacred or secular, is often monophonic: there is a single melody without harmony. A single melody may also be performed in several different versions at the same time; this is called group **heterophony.** Vocal music takes precedence over instrumental music. In fact, Oriental African cultures show a high degree of sophistication and artistic vitality in poetry and verse. **Zajal** is an important north African vocal form which uses classical poetry set to music. **Fondu** consists of song types that use texts in the idiomatic language of the common people and are all chanted by a chorus. The northeast African **shilela,** a type containing songs of war and patriotism, is performed by a single singer. The Andalusian **nuba,** made up of sections or movements, is one of the most important forms. Usually, a *nuba* starts with an improvised instrumental prelude in an unmeasured rhythm. Unlike the first section, the second includes rhythmic instruments and is performed by an ensemble in very slow tempo. The third section is an unornamented chant. The fourth section is an instrumental interlude in a fast-moving duple meter. A virtuoso performer usually plays the fifth section solo. The sixth section is a joyous ornamented chant in a lively triple meter. The last section, the finale, is always very fast and lively, and it is performed with great fervor as the climax of the *nuba*.

Basic Terms

If you aren't sure what each of the following words means, look back at the text, where they appear in bold type. Additional information about some of them can be found by checking the index.

chordophones	idiophones	*fondu*
aerophones	heterophony	*shilela*
membranophones	*zajal*	*nuba*

MUSIC IN [2]
SUB-SAHARAN AFRICA

The term *sub-Saharan Africa* refers to an enormous zone which includes practically all the cultures south of the Sahara Desert. Music forms an integral part of the societies' activities in this zone; thus it has to be studied in the context of diverse traditions. Society consists of four groups: (1) the gods and goddesses, (2) the ancestors, (3) the humans—living and dead, and (4) the natural world. Hence, music is closely associated with the various phases of culture, such as poetry, religion, drama, magic, and dance. Its function is largely utilitarian and ritualistic.

Music is played in rituals concerned with warding off evil spirits. Most sub-Saharan African societies traditionally believe in polytheistic religions. Music, poetry, and dance are performed to celebrate the days of the various deities. Gods are appeased by sacrifices and songs. Wearing masks and re-enacting life situations in a form of a drama, particularly in times of adversity, enhance peace and harmony. Medicine men heal the sick by singing songs and performing prescribed dances. In Ghana, the priest-healer chants special *Klamas* (memory aids) to the god of medicine to aid him in discovering a curative herb. The curative and therapeutic values of music are gradually gaining recognition outside Africa, particularly in the United States, where music is used in hypnosis, musical therapy, and psychiatry.

Funerals are often accompanied by music and dance. As a tribute both to ancestors and the living, the dead body is lavishly entertained before it enters its last resting place. Similarly, specific song types are performed on the naming day of a baby. These songs are accompanied by dance and are performed a week after the baby's birth; the sex of the infant determines what songs are used. Music plays a significant role in initiation rites and ceremonials. Sub-Saharan music includes a large repertory of lullabies and children's songs.

Other song types express complaint or social commentary. These songs are concerned with interrelationships between the sexes, the social and political classes, and the individual and the family.

Musical experience permeates the whole course of human life in sub-Saharan Africa. Music is not only an esthetic experience but a way of life as well. There are hunting songs, ballads, songs of litigation, songs of obscenity, drinking songs, and many other types which are used for specific occasions such as weddings, hangings, and activities of secret societies. Some songs teach youth the male and female codes and mores of society; others are sung to correct unruly behavior. There are even songs claimed to attract termites.

Sub-Saharan African Musical Instruments

Since it is beyond the objectives of this book to include by name the great variety of musical instruments found in Africa, only a few, considered to be

Sub-Saharan African
Musical Instruments

523

most representative, will be discussed. These will hopefully give the reader an understanding of the music and instrumental resources of the cultures in sub-Saharan Africa.

Idiophones

Idiophones, the most common type of instrument, are widely distributed throughout sub-Saharan Africa. Untuned instruments include metal and gourd rattles, bells, clappers, friction sticks, cymbals, and an endless variety of scraped and stamped idiophones. There are also idiophones such as the xylophones and the *mbira* which combine the rhythmic potentials of percussion and the melodic possibilities of tuned instruments.

The *mbira* may generally be considered an idiophone. European travelers and missionaries have mistakenly called it "Kaffir's piano," "thumb piano," and "African piano." It has also been known by different African names such as *sanza, sansi, kalimba, likembe, lukembi, mbila, kasansi,* etc. The problem of nomenclature is particularly difficult with this instrument, due to the many languages and dialects spoken by the peoples of Africa. And there is as much diversity in the construction, type, and function of the *mbira* as there is in nomenclature. However, all *mbiras* usually have a wooden soundboard, a number of metal keys, a sound amplifier, and a buzzing tone quality. The number of keys greatly varies from as few as four to more than twenty.

Although widely distributed throughout Africa, the *mbira* is most often found among the peoples living in and around Zambia, Rhodesia, and Mozambique. The peoples of these regions are historically known for their metal crafts-manship. The *mbira* is the foremost instrument of the Shona people of Rhodesia. Rhodesians have often used the *mbira* as an important instrument in music concerned with rituals, when it accompanies singing. Most *mbira* players like to sing story songs, epics, and ballads while accompanying themselves.

The type of xylophone with calabash resonators is found in most of sub-Saharan Africa. However, it is not used by the peoples of Madagascar, nor is it found among the Yoruba people of West Africa. This xylophone is commonly known as *marimba,* particularly among the Bantu of Rhodesia. As most African instruments are homemade, variations often occur. The size and shape of this xylophone type vary, and it has anywhere from ten to about twenty keys. Xylophones without resonators are most often encountered in solo or ensemble performances. In southeastern Africa, the xylophone orchestra is common, particularly among the Chopi.

Membranophones

Membranophones are second in importance to idiophones. There are single- and double-headed drums. Different types, sizes, and shapes exist—for example, there are cylindrical, bottle-shaped, conical, and pressure drums. These may be tuned (played in sets) or untuned. Although wood is commonly used

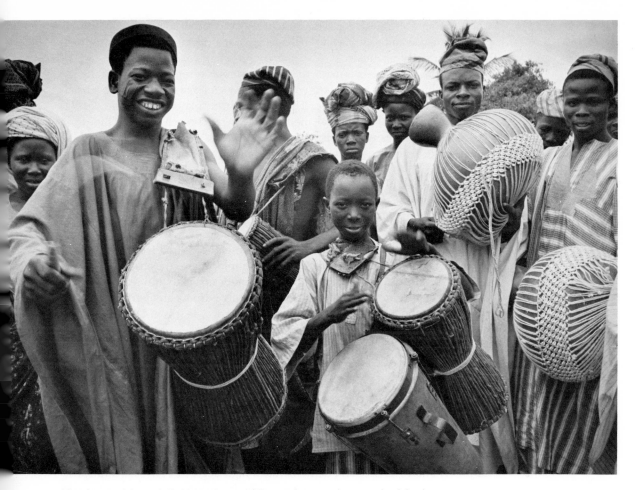

Nigerian musicians on their way to a wedding perform on drums and calabash gourds. African music is closely associated with such aspects of culture as poetry, religion, drama, magic, and dance (Marc and Evelyne Bernheim, Woodfin Camp).

in the making of drum frames, there are also drums made of clay, metal, tortoise shells, or gourds. Ox hide, calf, goat, elephant, or lizard skin may be used to cover the frame, depending on the geographic location and availability of the animal.

Drum making is almost always accompanied by ceremony. A tree has to be chosen in an appropriate location. Before it is cut down, libations have to be poured to placate the spirit inhabiting the tree. Then the body of the drum will be prepared by the experienced hands of a specialized wood-carver and his apprentices. Following the prescriptions of oral tradition, a symbol, often an "eye" that stares in the direction of the drummer, will be carved on the

Sub-Saharan African
Musical Instruments

525

wooden frame of the drum. This watchful "eye," according to tradition, will prevent misuse and foul play as well as enable the drummer to commune with the patron deity of music.

The *atumpan* of Ghana is made following a similar ceremony. The installation of a new chief cannot take place without a new *atumpan* and its active participation in the ceremonial music. The master drum plays in three modes: (1) the dance mode, (2) the signal mode, and (3) the speech mode. This drum accompanies dances when it is played in the dance mode. It also plays in the signal mode when leading other instruments in ensemble performance. Following the high-low pitches of the tone language, the *atumpan* expresses poems, proverbs, praises of the chief, and the valor of warriors. In sub-Saharan Africa, instrument makers and musicians are respected members of their societies. This is unlike the Oriental (Islamic) African musical practice, where musicians constitute a lower and despised caste of craftsmen.

Large instrumental ensembles that perform complex and frenzied rhythms are most characteristic. In Burundi, for example, there are ensembles made entirely of drums, with as few as three or as many as twenty trained drummers. The largest court ensemble consists of twenty-five drums and performers. The drum is a symbol of authority in sub-Saharan Africa, as it is in Oriental Africa.

[3] THE MUSIC OF INDIA

India's art music is particularly appealing because of its lack of affectation and its ability to create a spiritual climate. The performers approach their art with simplicity and reverence and demonstrate a high degree of physical and spiritual enjoyment. Indians conceive music as the language of the gods performed by humans. Rabindranath Tagore, an Indian scholar-musician, tells us that Indian music represents the emotions of the soul in the presence of nature. It is not, therefore, hard to understand why the performance of music requires an attitude and an atmosphere similar to the attitude of religious worship.

The Melodic Principle of Indian Music: *Raga*

Since music is *not* an international language, we have not established a universal vocabulary to explain the musical theories and practices of cultures around the world. Terms, concepts, and principles exist in one culture that are entirely unknown in another. The Euro-American languages, for example, have no analogous term for the Indian *raga,* or for the concepts embodied in it. **Raga** directly applies to the melodic principles of Indian music. It has also a psychological implication; some ragas (or melody types) are reputed to invoke moods of happiness, while others are involved with emotions of sadness, love, and patriotism.

Furthermore, certain ragas may be played on solemn occasions, while others are saved for festive days. There are morning, afternoon, and evening ragas. The degree of artistic elaboration on a given raga varies from simple to the most refined melodic formulas, depending on the performer's technical ability, musicianship, attitude, and the general atmosphere under which the performance takes place.

Performance of a raga includes improvisation and ornamentation. Improvisation is a complex process of spontaneous recreation of sound on a theme. It is best achieved through a form of instantaneous contemplation, tonal organization, and performance. The tonal, temporal, and spatial aspects of sound have to be conceived and executed in terms of the performer's experiences. In other words, meaningful sound relationships are made between what has been, is, and will be played. Most Indian performers depend largely on their meditational and religious experiences. Improvisation requires a favorable atmosphere and proper attitude. Incense is burned; the room where the performance takes place is decorated; the performer places in front of him a momento or a picture of his favorite guru (master-teacher) for inspiration. Correct intonation has to be maintained at all times. India possesses one of the oldest continuous musical traditions in the world, and the technique of improvisation has reached one of the highest peaks of refinement through rigorous training, dedicated practice, and absolute discipline of mind and body.

The Tonal Elements of Indian Music

The octave is a sound interval found in all musical cultures of the world. Unlike the European tempered tone system, which divides the octave into twelve equal semitones, the Indian octave is divided into twenty-two microtonal intervals, each nearly a quarter-tone. These intervals are called **scruti.** Indian musical theory also recognizes the existence of scale types made of these *scruti.* Five-tone (pentatonic) and six-tone (hexatonic) scales are very common. Seven-tone (heptatonic) scales are also popular in the art music of India. What the Hindustani (northern Indians) call *raga Bilava,* for example, is comparable to the European major scale. It is, however, very important to remember that the European tone system is based on scientific subdivision of tones into absolute pitches, while India's entire theory and sound conception have largely depended on the performance practices and knowledge transmitted through generations of oral tradition. Consequently, many of these theoretical intervals, sound conceptions, performance practices, and esthetic principles must be understood in the context of Indian culture.

Indian singers use tone syllables that are comparable to the European system of *do-re-mi-fa-sol-la-ti-do.* Indian tone syllables, or **svara,** are *sa-ri-ga-ma-pha-dha-ni-sa.* Indian vocalists often improvise with perfect intonation from simple to

The Tonal Elements
of Indian Music

527

complex melodic passages using the *svara* only. This technique of improvisation by the permutation of tone syllables is called ***svara-prastara.***

The Temporal Principle of Indian Music: *Tala*

Tala refers to the organization of beats into aurally recognizable patterns of time. As is the case in European music, Indians use what they call the **matra**, or beat, as the basic time unit. A succession of two regular beats forms a duple meter or *guru*. *Guru* consists of an accented first and an unaccented second beat. A succession of three regular beats forms a triple meter or *pluta*. *Pluta* consists of an accented first beat and two unaccented or weak beats. Indians also have another meter known as *laghu* which consists of only one accented beat.

Indian melodies are often set to *tala,* or accompanied by rhythmic instruments. In such cases, two or all of the above meters are combined or added to form a metric cycle. For example, *guru + guru + laghu + laghu* can form a metric cycle of a *tala* that consists of six beats, as follows:

Six-beat metric cycle

$$1 \quad 2 \mid 1 \quad 2 \mid 1 \mid 1 \mid = \text{total of six beats}$$

This ingenious process of combining time organizations to form metric cycles of the *tala* is widely practiced by Indian performers, particularly by drum players, and is known as **additive meter.**

To guarantee accurate performance, Indian singers visually keep the metric cycle of the *tala* by means of hand gestures known as *kriva.* Sometimes they clap their hands or snap their fingers, according to the accented and unaccented beats that form the metric cycle. In an unaccompanied free-rhythmed solo passage, the singers also indicate the tonal directions of the melodic passages by means of expressive hand gestures. The hand is raised when the tones of the melody ascend and vice versa. Wagging the head with the vibrating and trilling tones is a common practice which adds to the enjoyment of Indian music.

The Instruments of Indian Music

Musical instruments of India are classified into four groups: the idiophones (*ghana*), membranophones (*avanaddha*), aerophones (*susira*), and chordophones (*tata*).

Tata (Chordophones)

Indian musical performances, vocal or instrumental, are supported by a continuous drone sounded on an instrument called a *tambura*. The tambura is a long-necked lute without frets; its four strings are tuned to the tonic and dominant drone tones. To create a drone the strings are continuously plucked. A drone based on the tonic and dominant tones helps the improvising performers to maintain a constant point of reference in general tonal relationships. Tamburas are used exclusively to produce a sustained drone; they never play melodies.

The *sitar*, a lute type, is the most popular of all Indian instruments. It consists of seven strings over movable metal frets; melodies are played on these seven strings. The sitar has additional strings to sound the drone required of all Indian art music. In other words, the sitar is a self-supporting instrument and can perform without the tambura, though the presence of the tambura is always preferred. The secondary drone strings resonate by sympathetic vibration when the main melodic strings are plucked. These secondary, or sympathetic, strings add shimmering overtones as an element of decoration as well. The sound chamber of the sitar is made of a gourd. A second round gourd, which might be mistaken for a sound resonator, is attached to the back of the neck of this instrument. It chiefly serves to keep the neck off the floor when the instrument is not in use, and it is an element of structural decoration as well. Its function as a sound chamber is minimal, since it does not directly come in contact with the vibrating strings.

The *vina* is the Carnatic (southern Indian) equivalent of the Hindustani (northern) sitar. The *vina*, a long-necked plucked lute, is also held across the lap of the seated performer. Only four strings are used to play melodies; it has an additional three to four strings which are used as sympathetic strings. Though not as popular as the sitar outside of its native habitat, the vina is definitely the older of the two and the most popular instrument of Carnatic classical music.

The *sarod* is another Hindustani stringed instrument. Traditionally it has a larger sound chamber than the sitar, and it is played with an ivory plectrum.

The Instruments of Indian Music

529

The *sitar* (top) and *vina* (bottom) are two popular lute-type instruments of India (Omikron; The Metropolitan Museum of Art, Gift of Alice E. Getty, 1946).

The sarod has a total of twenty-five metal strings. Melodies are played on eight main strings, while the rest are sympathetic strings of secondary importance.

Susira (Aerophones)

The seven-holed bamboo flute and a double-reeded oboe type are the two most important wind instruments of India. Indians call the bamboo flute *venu*. The double-reeded oboe is found in both northern India, where it is known as *sahnai*, and southern India, where it is called *nagasvaram*. Although the *sahnai* is played by many rustic performers, it has in recent years been elevated to the status of a concert instrument.

Avanaddha (Membranophones)

A pair of tuned drums plays an important role in Hindustani art music. The pair of drums is played by one performer. The high-pitched drum, known as *tabla*, is played by the right hand; the tabla is often tuned to the tonic tone (after the *tambura*). The low-pitched drum, known as *banya*, is played by the left hand. In the hands of a skilled performer, this pair of tuned drums can play intricately syncopated and improvised passages without ever losing count of the metric cycle of the *tala*.

The *mrdanga* is also a tuned barrel-shaped drum; it belongs to Carnatic tradition. The smaller of the two faces has the higher pitch and is tuned to the tonic. Generally the larger the face of a drum the lower the pitch, and vice versa. The larger of the two faces plays the part of a bass drum. The *mrdanga* is both a solo and an accompanying instrument. The players undergo a long period of arduous training and demonstrate great skill by performing complex improvised passages, similar to the virtuosity of the *tabla-banya* performers of Hindustani tradition.

The above two kinds of membranophones are frequently encountered in most performances, but India has a great variety of other tuned and untuned drums.

Ghana (Idiophones)

Music, poetry, dance, and drama are closely integrated in Indian tradition. Instruments of the idiophonic class often appear with music that accompanies dance and drama. Dancers wear metal jingles or small bells on their wrists and ankles to accentuate their movements while dancing. A small hand drum with metal jingles, similar to the European tambourine, often accompanies dance music; this instrument is called *kanjira*.

The Music

Most Indian music is vocal; instrumental music often duplicates the vocal techniques, generally imitating a vocal style of performance. Musical theory and the theory of language are considered to be two parallel branches of one general science of sound. Consequently, poetry and melody are closely linked. The Indian singer is also a poet.

Indian musicians have many performing styles. Among the most important is *alap*, a vocal exposition. It is played at the beginning of a concert. *Alap* introduces the thematic material in a slow, free-rhythmed, and unornamented style of singing. The melodic possibilities of the tones are carefully explored, and the tonality is accurately established. Indian singers often use meaningless syllables when performing an *alap*; obviously melodic elaboration and improvisation are enhanced by avoiding metrically structured poetry.

Khyal is probably one of the most popular song forms of Indian music. Basically, it is a form of improvisation on a theme. Unlike the *alap*, the melodies are set to *tala* or meter. It uses poetry, it is played at a moderate tempo, and it is lavishly ornamented.

The great repertory of Indian music exists in oral tradition; the composers are often unknown. There are also works of relatively recent origin, largely song forms, that are attributed to composers. These works are not notated in the form of a European score; they have been passed down through the master-student method of transmission. Indian musicians are trained to commit to memory an astonishing amount of material. One of the most important composers of the seventeenth century, Purandara Dasa, was reputed for his 475,000 songs. Indian tradition has bestowed upon Purandara the titles of "Saint" and "Father of Karnatic Music." The list of the most important composers includes the three South Indians Swami Tyagaraja, Muttu Swami Dikshitar, and Shayama Sastri. These three were all born in the same village and lived in the eighteenth century; they are collectively known as "the musical trinity."

Tyagaraja was responsible for a religiously inspired multisectional song form known as *kriti.* The *kriti* is considered one of the most important forms, and no South Indian concert or recital would be complete without at least one. The kriti has three sections: a short intricate composition used as a basis for improvisation usually in free rhythm; a strictly measured section accompanied by a drum (*mrdanga*); and a lively improvised section on a strictly measured and accompanied music which explores the characteristics of both the raga and tala. The song texts or poetry of the *kriti* have philosophical and religious orientations. The word *religious* has different connotations in India from those found in African and European traditions. "When we say 'religious song,' says Ravi Shankar, "we are not necessarily speaking of songs of a spiritual and holy nature, but rather of songs whose central characters are religious figures, such as Shiva, Krishna, or Rama. These godly characters are portrayed as human beings, with all the pathos, humor, and love of mortals. The songs can be rendered either with religious intention or as a narrative of the gods' adventures."

Indian gods and goddesses have been personified, and many of them are associated with specific musical instruments. For example, Saraswati, the goddess of knowledge, is often depicted playing the vina—the instrument of philosophers and a very difficult instrument to master. Krishna, who is considered an incarnation of the god Vishnu (the Creator), is associated with the bamboo flute venu—the instrument of love and charm.

Basic Terms

If you aren't sure what each of the following words means, look back at the text, where they appear in bold type. Additional information about some of them can be found by checking the index.

raga	*matra*
scruti	additive meter
svara	*alap*
svara-prastara	*khyal*
tala	*kriti*

KOTO MUSIC OF JAPAN [4]

In this section our study will be confined to one instrument, its music, and its role in Japanese culture—the **koto.** We will discuss the instrument and its cultural implications in the context of Asian music.

The *koto* is a thirteen-stringed Japanese zither. The strings are stretched over an oblong and hollow sounding board about six feet long, ten inches wide, and two inches deep. Traditionally the strings were made of threaded silk; a few professionals still follow this practice. But today the silk strings have generally been replaced by nylon ones, which are cheaper and more accessible. A movable bridge called *ji* is inserted between each string and the sounding board. Traditionally the thirteen bridges were made of ivory, but today plastic is commonly used. The thirteen strings are tuned by means of these thirteen movable bridges. The strings are numbered from one to thirteen, and counting must always start with the string farthest from the player. Obviously, the koto strings produce a total of thirteen tones. Melodies are played on the tuned strings found above the bridges to the right side of the player facing the koto.

The koto performer wears three ivory plectrons called *tsume* around thumb, index, and middle fingers of the right hand. Plucking, shaking, scraping, and striking the strings of the koto with the ivory plectrons enable the player to produce a wide range of dynamic contrasts, tonal colors, and other technical skills and sound effects including Japanese glissandos, tremolos, trills, and glides. The fingers of the left hand are basically used to apply pressure on the strings below the bridge on the left side of the player, particularly when changes in pitch or timbre are required. Heavy pressure raises the pitch of

Koto Music of Japan

533

The *koto*.

the string, and vice versa. Changes in timbre can be accomplished by a slight pull of the string with the left hand. The fingers of the left hand are also used to pluck the melodic strings in passages with short and detached (pizzicato) tones. Since most composers of koto music are also koto performers, the finger techniques and the hands to be used are prescribed by the composers themselves in precise notational symbols.

Koto: Historical Background

Historically, the Japanese koto is derived from the ancient Chinese zither called *ch'in.* Unlike the koto, the ch'in is without bridges and has only seven strings. The ch'in is still considered the most famous of all Chinese traditional instruments. Intercultural borrowing among Chinese, Korean, and Japanese peoples has created numerous traits commonly found in all three cultures. In Korea, for example, we find a twelve-stringed zither called *kayakeum.* Similar to the Japanese koto, the Korean kayakeum has movable bridges. Historically, Japan and Korea have undergone long periods of Chinese political and cultural domination. As a matter of fact, Japanese musicians were trained either in China or Korea in the early part of Japanese history; Chinese and Korean musicians were also imported to play Japanese court music.

The koto was brought from China via Korea to Japan in the ninth century by a musician named Fujivara Sadatoshi. Until the end of the fifteenth century, the koto was used to accompany Japanese court music. It was also used to accompany Buddhist rituals and ceremonials in Japan. In the sixteenth century, the koto began to be used as a solo instrument. A priest composer-performer named Kenjun Morota is credited with having composed the first solo piece. A school of koto playing evolved called *Tsukushi-goto,* named after the town where he had lived.

Koto music gained status as important Japanese music during the Edo period (1615–1868); the Japanese gave it the name **sokyoku** ("koto music"). During this period, Japan closed its doors to the outside world and followed a strict policy of isolation. The repertoire of *sokyoku* that flourished in this period forms the bulk of the compositions heard today as masterpieces of Japanese art music.

Systems of Koto Tuning

There are three main systems of tuning the thirteen strings of the koto. These tuning systems are (1) *oshiki-cho,* (2) *hira-joshi,* and (3) *kumoi-joshi.* Indicating the koto string numbers under each note, the equivalent tones of these tuning systems are presented on European staff notation as described below.

Oshiki-cho Tuning

Koto strings: 1 2 3 4 5 6 7 8 9 10 11 12 13

Oshiki-cho tuning is the oldest and least used today. It belongs to the school of koto playing that first flourished in *Tsukushi-goto.* Note, however, that there are only five different pitches in this tuning: E, F♯, A, B, C♯. It is thus a pentatonic tuning. These five tones are distributed systematically among the thirteen strings of the koto. The first string's pitch is duplicated by the fifth string; other pairs of strings that are tuned an octave apart are 2 and 7, 3 and 8, 4 and 9, 5 and 10, 6 and 11, 7 and 12, and 8 and 13. The tonal center of this tuning system is E.

Hira-joshi Tuning

Koto strings: 1 2 3 4 5 6 7 8 9 10 11 12 13

Hira-joshi is a tuning system that evolved during the Edo period (1615–1868). Its invention is ascribed to a famous blind musician, Yatsuhashi Kengyo (1614–1685). Most of the koto masterpieces by Yatsuhashi and his followers are composed for this particular tuning. Even today, it is the most frequently used of the three tuning systems.

The differences between *hira-joshi* and *oshiki-cho* occur on strings 4, 6, 9, and 11. Only these four strings are tuned a semitone (or half-tone) lower in *hira-joshi* than in *oshiki-cho.* All the other strings are tuned alike. Obviously, Yatsuhashi modified the older *oshiki-cho* by lowering its fourth, sixth, ninth, and eleventh strings a semitone and giving it a new name—*hira-joshi*. Consequently, a semitone occurs in *hira-joshi* between strings 3-4 (B-C) and 5-6 (E-F); and again an octave higher between strings 8-9 (B-C) and 11-12 (E-F). This occurrence of minor seconds, or semitone intervals, gives the *hira-joshi* tuning its musically distinctive character.

Hira-joshi also has only five pitches, E, F, A, B, and C. It is one of the pentatonic scales.[3]

Kumoi-joshi Tuning

Koto strings: 1   2   3   4   5   6   7   8   9   10   11   12   13

Kumoi-joshi, in turn, is derived from the *hira-joshi* tuning. It is the most recently developed koto tuning.

The differences between *hira-joshi* and *kumoi-joshi* concern strings 3, 4, 8, 9, and 13. In *kumoi-joshi,* strings 3, 8, and 13 are tuned a semitone lower than in *hira-joshi;* strings 4 and 9 are tuned one whole tone higher than in *hira-joshi.* This is the basic *kumoi-joshi* tuning; many variants exist.

The koto—an instrument formally tuned to pentatonic scales—is often used for musical passages with heptatonic, chromatic, and other intricate microtonal sound structures and subtle melodic nuances.

Schools for Koto: The Composers and Their Music

Buddhism came to Japan from China via Korea around the middle of the sixth century. (Originally Buddhism came to China from India, but it had more adherents in China, Korea, and Japan than in its native land.) Confucianism also had a firm foothold in Japan by the late seventh and eighth centuries. Music—particularly vocal music in the form of chanting—then served to advance the spiritual and religious culture of scholarly priests. The Japanese freely borrowed elements from Chinese music until the Edo period (1615–1868). Although not directly imitated or exactly duplicated, the Japanese music culture until this period was definitely designed and built after Chinese models.

Tsukushi-goto School

Kenjun Morota (1547–1636), the founder of the school of solo performance, was himself a Buddhist priest. He was also known for composing the first purely

[3] Since *hira-joshi* has semitone intervals (between E-F and B-C), it is technically called a hemitonic pentatonic scale. A five-tone scale without semitones, such as *oshiki-cho,* is an anhemitonic pentatonic scale.

instrumental variation form, as well as many solo vocal forms with *koto* accompaniment. As was mentioned, this school is known as **Tsukushi-goto,** after the town where Kenjun lived. The *oshiki-cho* tuning system belongs to *Tsukushi-goto.* The music of *Tsukushi-goto* was strongly religious and ceremonial, as its artistic objectives were to serve Buddhist priests, the Japanese aristocracy, and the upper class.

Yatsuhashi School (*Yatsuhashi-ryu*)

As early as the fourteenth century, Japan had a vocational agency to educate the blind. By the seventeenth century, this agency had become a center of professional training. Somewhat equivalent to present-day unions, the specialized guild of blind men, known as *todo-shokuyashiki*, protected and advanced the interests of its members. The guild also prepared sightless men in music, acting, acupuncture, and massage. It granted titles and diplomas, teaching licenses, and professional stage names. The koto became the favored instrument among sightless musicians. Those highly qualified virtuoso performers and teachers were given the official licensing title of *Kengyo,* or master of koto.

Yatsuhashi-Kengyo (1614–1685), the famous blind master of koto, is considered the founder of modern koto music. This school is called **Yatsuhashi-ryu** ("Yatsuhashi school") after him. The *hira-joshi* system of tuning is also credited to him. In contrast to *Tsukushi-goto,* which had a religious orientation, *Yatsuhashi-ryu* was a school of secular or popular koto music. The Japanese refer to it as *zoku-so* or "unreligious" koto music. Obviously, *Yatsuhashi-ryu* appealed to the common people, while *Tsukushi-goto* belonged exclusively to the religious and upper-class intellectuals. The Chinese musical influences dominated *Tsukushi-goto.* In fact, the *oshiki-cho* type of pentatonic scale is still popularly played in the traditional music of contemporary China. *Yatsuhashi-ryu* evolved through the spirit of nationalism of the Edo period. The style of performance, the sound material, and the esthetics in general were created to express the Japanese artistic personality.

Ikuta School (*Ikuta-ryu*)

The **Ikuta-ryu** was founded by the composer-performer Ikuta-Kengyo (1655–1755). It was the second secular school of koto, the first being *Yatsuhashi-ryu.* *Ikuta-ryu* is today one of the two most popular schools; the other is *Yamada-ryu.*

Ikuta retained the characteristics of *Yatsuhashi-ryu* and maintained the *sokyoku* style; that is, the koto was used as a solo instrument. In addition, Ikuta composed pieces where the koto played important parts in small ensembles, or at times utilized it as an instrument of accompaniment. Ikuta developed the *Ji-uta* form—an art song for voice, koto, and *sangen* (a three-stringed plucked lute). *Ikuta-ryu* also advanced the *tegoto-mono* form—a series of art songs (usually three) connected with one another by virtuoso instrumental interludes.

Schools for Koto:
The Composers
and Their Music

A master *koto* performer of the Ikuta School (Erik Borg).

Yamada School (*Yamada-ryu*)

Yamada-Kengyo (1757–1817), another composer-performer and a member of the Guild of Blind Men, belonged to the Edo period. He derived the principles of *Yamada-ryu* from the other two branches of secular music. New types of scales, including the *kumoi-joshi,* were popularly used in the compositions of *Yamada-ryu.* Besides retaining all the existing forms and performance styles, he introduced and developed a new narrative vocal style (*joruri*), in which the koto played an important part. He is also credited for having improved the structure of the koto, modified the sitting position of the koto performer, and changed the shape of the ivory plectrons worn by the performers.

Koto Music

Rokudan (*No Shirabe*)

Rokudan is one of the most popular compositions in the repertoire of Japanese music today. It is a composition for solo koto ascribed to Yatsuhashi-Kengyo. It is also the most representative of Japanese absolute music.

Rokudan is composed in a variation form known as *dan-mono* or *shirabe-mono*. The **dan-mono** form consists of several sections, or movements. Most compositions in the *dan-mono* form have titles that indicate the number of sections. In this case, *roku* means "six" and *dan* means "sections." Hence, *Rokudan* consists of six interrelated sections.

Almost all *dan-mono* compositions, including *Rokudan*, are played in *hira-joshi* tuning. All *dan-mono* compositions have duple metric structures. Gradual increase and change in tempo, long ritards, and elastic or stretched rhythm are only a few important temporal characteristics of the *Rokudan*. Melodic ornamentation is also an important trait. The musicianship of a performer is often judged by his skillful ability to use ornaments and other subtle melodic and rhythmic nuances.

Basic Terms

If you aren't sure what each of the following words means, look back at the text, where they appear in bold type.

koto	*Yatsuhashi-ryu*
sokyoku	*Ikuta-ryu*
oshiki-cho tuning	*Yamada-ryu*
hira-joshi tuning	*Rokudan*
kumoi-joshi tuning	*dan-mono*
Tsukushi-goto	

Bibliography

The following selected books have been used in preparing this chapter on non-Western music. Mantle Hood's *The Ethnomusicologist* (New York: McGraw-Hill, 1971); Ashenafi Kebede's *The Music of Ethiopia* (Ann Arbor: University Microfilms, 1971); William P. Malm's *Music Cultures of the Pacific, the Near East, and Asia* (Englewood Cliffs, N.J.: Prentice-Hall, 1967) and *Japanese Music and Musical Instruments* (Rutland, Vt.: E. Tuttle Co., 1959); David P. McAllester ed. *Readings in Ethnomusicology* (New York-London: Johnson Reprint Corp., 1971), and especially Robert Brown's article "India's Music" in the same book; Alan P. Merriam's *The Anthropology of Music* (Evanston, Ill.: Northwestern University Press, 1964); G. H. Nketia's *Music and Dance in Ghana* (Ghana: University of Ghana Press, 1965); Curt Sachs' *The Rise of Music in the Ancient World* (New York: Norton, 1943); Ravi Shankar's *My Music, My Life* (New York: Simon and Schuster, 1968); and Henry G. Farmer's *A History of Arabian Music to the XIIIth Century* (London: Oxford University Press, 1967).

APPENDIXES

Appendix

[I] CHRONOLOGY

MIDDLE AGES (450–1450)

Musicians	Artists and Writers	Historical and Cultural Events
		Sack of Rome by Vandals (455)
		Reign of Pope Gregory I (590–604)
		First Crusade (1096–99)
Perotin (late 12th century)		Beginning of Notre Dame cathedral in Paris (1163)
		King John signs Magna Carta (1215)
	Dante (1265–1321)	
	Giotto (1266–1337)	
Guillaume de Machaut (c. 1300–1377)		
	Boccaccio (1313–1375)	
	Chaucer (c. 1343–1400)	Hundred Years' War (1337–1453)
		The Black Death (1348–1350)

RENAISSANCE (1450–1600)

Musicians	Artists and Writers	Historical and Cultural Events
Guillaume Dufay (c. 1400–1474)		Fall of Constantinople (1453)
Josquin des Prez (c. 1440–1521)	Leonardo da Vinci (1452–1519)	Gutenberg Bible (1456)
		Columbus discovers America (1492)
	Michelangelo (1475–1564)	
	Raphael (1483–1520)	Martin Luther's ninety-five theses (1517)
	Titian (c. 1477–1576)	
	François Rabelais (c. 1494–c. 1553)	
Andrea Gabrelli (c. 1520–1586)		
Giovanni Pierluigi da Palestrina (c. 1525–1594)		Council of Trent (1545–1563)
Roland de Lassus (1532–1594)	Michel de Montaigne (1533–1592)	
William Byrd (1543–1623)		
Thomas Morley (1557–1603)	Cervantes (1547–1616)	Elizabeth I, Queen of England (1558–1603)

542

Musicians	Artists and Writers	Historical and Cultural Events
	William Shakespeare (1564–1616)	
		Spanish Armada defeated (1588)
Thomas Weelkes (1575–1623)		

BAROQUE (1600–1750)

Musicians	Artists and Writers	Historical and Cultural Events
		Jamestown founded (1607)
Claudio Monteverdi (1567–1643)		
	Peter Paul Rubens (1577–1640)	
Heinrich Schütz (1585–1672)		Thirty Years' War (1618–1648)
	Gian Lorenzo Bernini (1598–1680)	
	Rembrandt (1606–1669)	
	John Milton (1608–1674)	
Jean-Baptiste Lully (1632–1687)	Molière (1622–1673)	Louis XIV reigns in France (1643–1715)
	Baruch Spinoza (1632–1677)	
Arcangelo Corelli (1653–1713)		
Henry Purcell (c. 1659–1695)	Jonathan Swift (1667–1745)	Newton, *Principia Mathematica* (1687)
François Couperin (1668–1733)		
Antonio Vivaldi (1678–1741)		Louis XV reigns in France (1715–1774)
Johann Sebastian Bach (1685–1750)	Jean Antoine Watteau (1684–1721)	
George Frideric Handel (1685–1759)		

CLASSICAL (1750–1820)

Musicians	Artists and Writers	Historical and Cultural Events
	Voltaire (1694–1778)	
	Benjamin Franklin (1706–1790)	Publication of the French *Encyclopedia* begins (1751)
Christoph Gluck (1714–1787)	Jean Jacques Rousseau (1712–1778)	
		Seven Years' War (1756–1763)
Carl Philipp Emanuel Bach (1714–1788)		Winckelmann's *History of the Art of Antiquity* (1764)
	Immanuel Kant (1724–1804)	
Joseph Haydn (1732–1809)		
	Goya (1746–1828)	
	Jacques Louis David (1748–1825)	

543

Musicians	Artists and Writers	Historical and Cultural Events
	Johann Wolfgang von Goethe (1749–1832)	Louis XVI reigns in France (1774–1792)
Wolfgang Amadeus Mozart (1756–1791)		American Declaration of Independence (1776)
Ludwig van Beethoven (1770–1827)		French Revolution begins (1789)
		Eli Whitney invents cotton gin (1792)
		Napoleon becomes First Consul of France (1799)
		Battle of Waterloo (1815)

ROMANTIC (1820–1900)

Musicians	Artists and Writers	Historical and Cultural Events
	William Wordsworth (1770–1850)	
	J. M. W. Turner (1775–1851)	
Carl Maria von Weber (1786–1826)		
Gioacchino Rossini (1792–1868)		
Franz Schubert (1797–1828)	Heinrich Heine (1797–1856)	
	Eugène Delacroix (1798–1863)	
	Honoré de Balzac (1799–1850)	Revolutions in France, Belgium, Poland (1830)
Hector Berlioz (1803–1869)	Victor Hugo (1802–1885)	
		First Reform Bill in Britain (1832)
Felix Mendelssohn (1809–1847)	Edgar Allan Poe (1809–1849)	
Frédéric Chopin (1810–1849)		Revolutions of 1848; Marx and Engels, *The Communist Manifesto* (1848)
Robert Schumann (1810–1856)		
		Darwin's *Origin of Species* (1859)
Franz Liszt (1811–1886)		American Civil War (1861–1865)
	Charles Dickens (1812–1870)	
Richard Wagner (1813–1883)		Franco-Prussian War (1870)
Giuseppe Verdi (1813–1901)		
César Franck (1822–1890)	Fëdor Dostoevsky (1821–1881)	
Anton Bruckner (1824–1896)		
Bedřich Smetana (1824–1884)	Leo Tolstoy (1828–1910)	
Johannes Brahms (1833–1897)	Édouard Manet (1832–1883)	
Georges Bizet (1838–1875)	Paul Cézanne (1839–1906)	

544

Musicians	Artists and Writers	Historical and Cultural Events
Modest Mussorgsky (1839–1881)		
Peter Ilyich Tchaikovsky (1840–1893)	Claude Monet (1840–1926)	First group exhibition of Impressionists in Paris (1874)
Antonin Dvořák (1841–1904)	Stéphane Mallarmé (1842–1898)	
Giacomo Puccini (1858–1924)	Friedrich Nietzsche (1844–1900)	Bell invents telephone (1876)
Gustav Mahler (1860–1911)		
	Vincent Van Gogh (1853–1890)	
Richard Strauss (1864–1949)		Spanish-American War (1898)

TWENTIETH CENTURY

		Freud, *The Psychopathology of Everyday Life* (1904)
Claude Debussy (1862–1918)	Wassily Kandinsky (1866–1944)	Einstein, special theory of relativity (1905)
	Henri Matisse (1869–1954)	
	Marcel Proust (1871–1922)	
Arnold Schoenberg (1874–1951)		First World War (1914–1918)
Charles Ives (1874–1954)		Russian Revolution begins (1917)
Maurice Ravel (1875–1937)		
Béla Bartók (1881–1945)	Pablo Piccaso (1881–1973)	
	James Joyce (1882–1941)	Beginning of Great Depression (1929)
Igor Stravinsky (1882–1971)		
	Franz Kafka (1883–1924)	
Anton Webern (1883–1945)		Hitler Chancellor of Germany (1933)
Edgard Varèse (1883–1965)		
Alban Berg (1885–1935)		
	T. S. Eliot (1888–1965)	Second World War (1939–1945)
Sergei Prokofiev (1891–1953)		
Paul Hindemith (1895–1963)		
Roger Sessions (b. 1896)		
George Gershwin (1898–1937)	William Faulkner (1897–1962)	
	Henry Moore (b. 1898)	
	Ernest Hemingway (1899–1961)	
Louis Armstrong (1900–1971)		

Musicians	Artists and Writers	Historical and Cultural Events
Aaron Copland (b. 1900)		
	Willem de Kooning (b. 1904)	
Dmitri Shostakovich (b. 1906)	Jean Paul Sartre (b. 1905)	
Elliott Carter (b. 1908)	David Smith (1906–1965)	
Olivier Messiaen (b. 1908)		Atomic bomb destroys Hiroshima (1945)
John Cage (b. 1912)		
Hugo Weisgall (b. 1912)		Korean war begins (1950)
Benjamin Britten (b. 1913)	Jackson Pollock (1912–1956)	
Billie Holiday (1915–1959)	Albert Camus (1913–1960)	
Milton Babbitt (b. 1916)	Andrew Wyeth (b. 1917)	
Charlie Parker (1920–1955)	Alexander Solzhenitsyn (b. 1918)	
Pierre Boulez (b. 1925)	Roy Lichtenstein (b. 1923)	
John Coltrane (1926–1967)	Norman Mailer (b. 1923)	
Karlheinz Stockhausen (b. 1928)	James Baldwin (b. 1924)	American involvement in Vietnam increases dramatically (1965)
George Crumb (b. 1929)		
Krzysztof Penderecki (b. 1933)		American astronauts land on moon (1969)
Mario Davidovsky (b. 1934)		
		Resignation of President Nixon (1974)
		End of American involvement in Vietnam (1975)

Appendix

[II] READING LIST

GENERAL

Apel, Willi. *Harvard Dictionary of Music,* 2nd ed. rev. Cambridge, Mass.: Harvard University Press, 1973.

Apel, Willi, and R. T. Daniel. *The Harvard Brief Dictionary of Music.* Cambridge, Mass.: Harvard University Press, 1970.

Baker's Biographical Dictionary of Musicians, 5th ed. (ed. Nicolas Slonimsky), New York: Schirmer, 1958 with 1971 supplement.

Crocker, Richard. *A History of Musical Style.* New York: McGraw-Hill, 1966.

Grout, Donald Jay. *A History of Western Music,* rev. ed. New York: Norton, 1973.

Grove's Dictionary of Music and Musicians, 5th ed. (ed. Eric Blom), 10 vols. New York: St. Martin's Press, 1970.

Hughes, David G. *A History of European Music.* New York: McGraw-Hill, 1974.

Kamien, Roger (ed.). *The Norton Scores: An Anthology for Listening,* 2 vols. New York: Norton, 1970.

Lang, Paul Henry. *Music in Western Civilization.* New York: Norton, 1941.

Appendix

Raynor, Henry. *A Social History of Music: From the Middle Ages to Beethoven.* New York: Schocken, 1972.

Tovey, Donald Francis. *The Forms of Music.* Cleveland, Ohio: Meridian, 1963.

I. ELEMENTS

Backus, John. *The Acoustical Foundations of Music.* New York: Norton, 1969.

Carse, Adam. *The History of Orchestration.* New York: Dover, 1964.

Castellini, John. *Rudiments of Music.* New York: Norton, 1962.

Cooper, Grosvenor W., and Leonard Meyer. *The Rhythmic Structure of Music.* Chicago: University of Chicago Press, 1960.

Donington, Robert. *The Interpretation of Early Music.* New York: St. Martin's Press, 1963.

Harrison, Frank, and Joan Rimmer. *European Musical Instruments.* New York: Norton, 1964.

Meyer, Leonard B. *Emotion and Meaning in Music.* Chicago: University of Chicago Press, 1956.

Mitchell, William J. *Elementary Harmony,* 3rd ed. Englewood Cliffs, N.J.: Prentice-Hall, 1965.

Sachs, Curt. *The History of Musical Instruments.* New York: Norton, 1940.

Schwarz, Elliott. *Electronic Music: A Listener's Guide.* New York: Praeger, 1973.

Shapiro, Meyer. "Style," in *Aesthetics Today,* ed. Morris Philipson. New York: Meridian, 1961.

II. MIDDLE AGES

Heer, Friedrich. *The Medieval World.* New York: World, 1963.

Huizinga, J. *The Waning of the Middle Ages.* New York: Doubleday, 1954.

Reese, Gustave. *Music in the Middle Ages.* New York: Norton, 1940.

Sachs, Curt. *The Rise of Music in the Ancient World.* New York: Norton, 1943.

Seay, Albert. *Music in the Medieval World.* Englewood Cliffs, N.J.: Prentice-Hall, 1965.

Strunk, Oliver (ed.). *Source Readings in Music History: Antiquity and the Middle Ages.* New York: Norton, 1965.

III. THE RENAISSANCE

Blume, Friedrich. *Renaissance and Baroque Music.* New York: Norton, 1967.

Burckhardt, Jacob. *The Civilization of the Renaissance in Italy.* New York: Washington Square Press, 1958.

Lowinsky, Edward E. "Music in the Culture of the Renaissance," in *Renaissance Essays,* ed. Paul Oskar Kristeller and Philip P. Wiener. New York: Harper and Row, 1968.

Reese, Gustave. *Music in the Renaissance,* rev. ed. New York: Norton, 1959.

Strunk, Oliver (ed.). *Source Readings in Music History: The Renaissance.* New York: Norton, 1965.

IV. THE BAROQUE PERIOD

General

Bukofzer, Manfred F. *Music in the Baroque Era.* New York: Norton, 1947.

Palisca, Claude V. *Baroque Music.* Englewood Cliffs, N.J.: Prentice-Hall, 1968.

Strunk, Oliver (ed.). *Source Readings in Music History: The Baroque Era.* New York: Norton, 1965.

Specific Topics

Grout, Donald. *A Short History of Opera,* 2nd ed. New York: Columbia, 1965.

Kerman, Joseph. *Opera as Drama.* New York: Vintage, 1956.

Newman, Ernest. *Great Operas: The Definitive Treatment of their History, Stories, and Music,* 2 vols. New York: Vintage Books, 1958.

Newman, William S. *The Sonata in the Baroque Era.* New York: Norton, 1972.

Pauly, Reinhard G. *Music and The Theater: An Introduction to Opera.* Englewood Cliffs, N.J.: Prentice-Hall, 1970.

Weisstein, Ulrich (ed.). *The Essence of Opera.* New York: Norton, 1969.

Individual Composers

Bach

David, Hans T., and Arthur Mendel (eds.). *The Bach Reader,* rev. ed. New York: Norton, 1966.

Geiringer, Karl, with Irene Geiringer. *Johann Sebastian Bach: The Culmination of an Era,* New York: Oxford, 1966.

Corelli

Pincherle, Marc. *Corelli: His Life, His Work.* New York: Norton, 1956.

Handel

Lang, Paul Henry. *George Frideric Handel.* New York: Norton, 1966.

Larsen, Jens Peter. *Handel's Messiah: Origins, Composition, Sources.* New York: Norton, 1972.

Monteverdi

Schrade, Leo. *Monteverdi, Creator of Modern Music.* New York: Norton, 1969.

Purcell

Zimmerman, Franklin B. *Henry Purcell, His Life and Times.* New York: St. Martin's, 1967.

Vivaldi

Pincherle, Marc. *Vivaldi: Genius of the Baroque.* New York: Norton, 1962.

V. THE CLASSICAL PERIOD

General

Blume, Friedrich. *Classic and Romantic Music.* New York: Norton, 1970.

Pauly, Reinhard. *Music in the Classic Period,* 2nd ed. Englewood Cliffs, N.J.: Prentice-Hall, 1973.

Rosen, Charles. *The Classical Style: Haydn, Mozart, Beethoven.* New York: Norton, 1972.

Wellesz, Egon and Sternfeld, Frederick (eds.). *The Age of Enlightenment: 1745–1790* (vol. 7 of the *New Oxford History of Music*). London: Oxford University Press, 1973.

Specific Topics

Newman, William S. *The Sonata in the Classic Era.* New York: Norton, 1972.

Ulrich, Homer. *Chamber Music,* 2nd ed. New York: Columbia, 1966.

Individual Composers

Beethoven

Anderson, Emily (ed. & tr.). *The Letters of Beethoven,* rev. ed. New York: St. Martin's, 1964.

Arnold, Denis, and Nigel Fortune (eds.). *The Beethoven Reader.* New York: Norton, 1971.

Grove, George. *Beethoven and His Nine Symphonies.* New York: Dover, 1962.

Kerman, Joseph. *The Beethoven Quartets.* New York: Knopf, 1967.

Sonneck, O. G. (ed.). *Beethoven: Impressions by His Contemporaries.* New York: Dover, 1967.

Thayer, Alexander W. *Life of Beethoven,* rev. ed. (ed. Elliot Forbes). Princeton, N.J.: Princeton Univ., 1973.

Tovey, Donald F. *Beethoven.* London: Oxford Univ. Press, 1963.

Haydn

Geiringer, Karl. *Haydn, a Creative Life in Music,* rev. ed. Berkeley, Cal.: University of California Press, 1968.

Landon, H. C. Robbins: *The Symphonies of Joseph Haydn.* London: Rockcliff and Universal Edition, 1955; supplement, 1961.

Mozart

Anderson, Emily (ed.). *Letters of Mozart and his Family,* 2 vols., 2nd ed. (eds. A. Hyatt King and Monica Carolan). New York: St. Martin's, 1966.

Dent, Edward. *Mozart's Operas: A Critical Study,* 2nd ed. London: Oxford Univ. Press, 1960.

Einstein, Alfred. *Mozart: His Character, His Work.* New York: Oxford Univ. Press, 1945.

VI. THE ROMANTIC PERIOD

General

Abraham, Gerald. *A Hundred Years of Music,* 3rd ed. Chicago: Aldine, 1964.

Blume, Friedrich. *Classic and Romantic Music.* New York: Norton, 1970.

Einstein, Alfred. *Music in the Romantic Era.* New York: Norton, 1947.

Hugo, Howard E. (ed.). *The Portable Romantic Reader.* New York: Viking Press, 1960.

Loesser, Arthur. *Men, Women and Pianos: A Social History.* New York: Simon and Schuster, 1954.

Longyear, Rey M. *Nineteenth-Century Romanticism in Music,* 2nd ed. Englewood Cliffs, N.J.: Prentice-Hall, 1973.

Newman, William S. *The Sonata Since Beethoven.* New York: Norton, 1972.

Stevens, Denis (ed.). *A History of Song.* New York: Norton, 1961.

Strunk, Oliver: *Source Readings in Music History: The Romantic Era.* New York: Norton, 1965.

Individual Composers

Berlioz

Barzun, Jacques. *Berlioz and the Romantic Century,* 2 vols., 3rd ed. New York: Columbia University Press, 1969.

Berlioz, Hector. *Memoirs* (ed. and tr. David Cairns). New York: Knopf, 1969.

Brahms

Gal, Hans. *Johannes Brahms: His Work and Personality.* London: Weidenfeld and Nicolson, 1963.

Geiringer, Karl. *Brahms: His Life and Works,* 2nd ed. New York: Oxford, 1947.

Chopin

Hedley, Arthur. *Chopin.* London: J. M. Dent, 1947.

Dvořák

Clapham, John. *Antonin Dvořák, Musician and Craftsman.* New York: St. Martin's, 1966.

Liszt

Searle, Humphrey. *The Music of Liszt.* New York: Dover, 1966.

Sitwell, Sacheverell. *Liszt.* New York: Dover, 1967.

Perényi, Eleanor. *Liszt: The Artist as Romantic Hero.* Toronto and Boston: Atlantic, Little, and Brown, 1974.

Mendelssohn

Werner, Eric. *Felix Mendelssohn: A New Image of the Composer and His Age.* New York: Free Press, 1963.

Mussorgsky

Calvocoressi, Michael D. *Modest Mussorgsky, His Life and Works.* Fair Lawn, N.J.: Essential Books, 1956.

Puccini

Hughes, Patrick Cairns. *Famous Puccini Operas,* 2nd rev. ed. New York: Dover, 1972.

Schubert

Brown, Maurice J. E. *Schubert: A Critical Biography.* New York: St. Martin's Press, 1958.
Brown, Maurice J. E. *Schubert Songs.* Seattle, Wash.: University of Washington Press, 1969.

Schumann

Brion, Marcel. *Schumann and the Romantic Age.* New York: Macmillan, 1956.
Schumann, Robert. *On Music and Musicians.* New York: Norton, 1969.

Smetana

Large, Brian. *Smetana.* New York: Praeger, 1970.

Tchaikovsky

Abraham, Gerald. *The Music of Tchaikovsky.* New York: Norton, 1974.
Weinstock, Herbert. *Tchaikovsky.* New York: Knopf, 1973.

Verdi

Toye, Francis. *Giuseppe Verdi, His Life and Works.* New York: Vienna House, 1972.

Wagner

Goldman, Albert and Evert Sprinchorn (eds.). *Wagner on Music and Drama: A Compendium of Richard Wagner's Prose Works.* New York: Dutton, 1964.
Newman, Ernest. *The Life of Richard Wagner,* 4 vols. New York: Knopf, 1933–1946.
Newman, Ernest. *The Wagner Operas.* New York: Knopf, 1949.
White, Chappell. *An Introduction to the Life and Works of Richard Wagner.* Englewood Cliffs, N.J.: Prentice-Hall, 1967.

VII. THE TWENTIETH CENTURY

General

Austin, William, *Music in the Twentieth Century.* New York: Norton, 1966.
Machlis, Joseph. *Introduction to Contemporary Music.* New York: Norton, 1961.
Salzman, Eric. *Twentieth-Century Music. An Introduction,* 2nd ed. Englewood Cliffs, N.J.: Prentice-Hall, 1974.
Slonimsky, Nicolas. *Music Since 1900,* 4th ed. New York: Scribner's, 1971.
Stuckenschmidt, H. H. *Twentieth Century Music.* New York: McGraw-Hill, 1970.
Vinton, John (ed.). *Dictionary of Contemporary Music.* New York: Dutton, 1974.

Specific Topics

Chase, Gilbert. *America's Music,* rev. 2nd ed. New York: McGraw-Hill, 1966.
Cope, David. *New Directions in Music.* Dubuque, Iowa: Brown, 1973.
Hitchcock, H. Wiley. *Music in the United States: A Historical Introduction,* 2nd ed. Englewood Cliffs, N.J.: Prentice-Hall, 1974.
Meyer, Leonard B. *Music, The Arts, and Ideas.* Chicago: University of Chicago Press, 1969.
Music Educators Journal. November, 1968 (issue devoted to electronic music).
Schwarz, Boris. *Music and Musical Life in Soviet Russia, 1917–1970.* New York: Norton, 1972.

Schwarz, Elliott. *Electronic Music: A Listener's Guide.* New York: Praeger, 1973.

Individual Composers

Babbitt
Babbitt, Milton. "Who Cares If You Listen?" *High Fidelity,* VII, 2 (February, 1958).

Bartók
Stevens, Halsey. *The Life and Music of Béla Bartók,* rev. ed. New York: Oxford, 1967.

Berg
Reich, Willi. *Alban Berg.* New York: Harcourt, Brace & World, 1965.

Cage
Cage, John. *Silence.* Cambridge, Mass.: M.I.T. Press, 1971.

Carter
Edwards, Allen. *Flawed Words and Stubborn Sounds: A Conversation with Elliott Carter.* New York: Norton, 1972.

Copland
Berger, Arthur. *Aaron Copland.* New York: Oxford University Press, 1953.
Copland, Aaron. *Copland on Music.* New York: Norton, 1963.

Debussy
Lockspeiser, Edward. *Debussy: His Life and Mind,* 2 vols. London, Cassel, 1962, 1965.

Ives
Cowell, Henry and Sidney Cowell. *Charles Ives and His Music.* New York: Oxford University Press, 1969.
Ives, Charles. *Essays Before a Sonata and Other Writings* (ed. Howard Boatwright). New York: Norton, 1962.
Kirkpatrick, John (ed.). *Charles E. Ives: Memos.* New York: Norton, 1972.

Schoenberg
Reich, Willi. *Schoenberg, a Critical Biography.* New York: Praeger, 1971.
Schoenberg, Arnold. *Letters* (ed. E. Stein). New York: St. Martin's Press, 1965.
Schoenberg, Arnold. *Style and Idea.* New York: Philosophical Library, 1950.

Stravinsky
Craft, Robert. *Stravinsky, Chronicle of a Friendship: 1948–1971.* New York: Vintage, 1973.
Stravinsky, Igor. *An Autobiography.* New York: Norton, 1962.
Stravinsky, Igor. *Poetics of Music.* New York: Vintage, 1956.
Stravinsky, Igor and Robert Craft. *Conversations with Igor Stravinsky.* New York: Doubleday, 1959.
Stravinsky, Igor and Robert Craft. *Retrospectives and Conclusions.* New York: Knopf, 1969.
White, Eric Walter. *Stravinsky, the Composer and His Works.* Berkeley, Cal.: University of California, 1966.

Webern
Kolneder, Walter. *Anton Webern: An Introduction to His Works.* Berkeley, Cal.: University of California, 1968.

VIII. JAZZ

General

Feather, Leonard. *The Encyclopedia of Jazz,* rev. ed. New York: Horizon, 1960.
Schuller, Gunther. *Early Jazz: Its Roots and Musical Development.* New York: Oxford University Press, 1968.
Southern, Eileen. *The Music of Black Americans: A History.* New York: Norton, 1971.

Reading List

551

Sterns, Marshall. *The Story of Jazz.* New York: Oxford University Press, 1970.

Williams, Martin. *Where's the Melody? A Listener's Introduction to Jazz,* rev. ed. New York: Pantheon, 1968.

Specific Topics

Blesh, Rudi. *Shining Trumpets,* 2nd ed. New York: Knopf, 1958.

Blesh, Rudi and Harriet Janis. *They All Played Ragtime,* 4th ed. New York: Oak Publications, 1971.

Charters, Samuel B. *The Country Blues.* New York: Rinehart, 1959.

Keil, Charles. *Urban Blues.* Chicago: University of Chicago Press, 1966.

Williams, Martin. *Jazz Masters in Transition, 1957–1969.* New York: Macmillan, 1970.

IX. ROCK

Eisen, Jonathan (ed.). *The Age of Rock: Sights and Sounds of the American Cultural Revolution,* 2 vols. New York: 1969, 1970.

Gillett, Charles. *The Sound of the City,* 2nd ed. New York: Dell, 1972.

Goldstein, Richard. *The Poetry of Rock.* New York: Bantam Books, 1969.

Roxon, Lillian. *Rock Encyclopedia.* New York: Grosset and Dunlap, 1974.

X. NON-WESTERN MUSIC

General

Hood, Mantle. *The Ethnomusicologist.* New York: McGraw-Hill, 1971.

Malm, William P. *Music Cultures of the Pacific, the Near East, and Asia.* Englewood Cliffs, N.J.: Prentice-Hall, 1967.

Merriam, Alan P. *The Anthropology of Music.* Evanston, Ill.: Northwestern University Press, 1964.

Nettl, Bruno. *Folk and Traditional Music of the Western Continents.* Englewood Cliffs, N.J.: Prentice-Hall, 1965.

Sachs, Curt. *The Rise of Music in the Ancient World.* New York: Norton, 1943.

Specific Topics

Brown, Robert E. "India's Music," in *Readings in Ethnomusicology* (ed. David P. McAllester). New York-London: Johnson Reprint Corp., 1971.

Malm, William P. *Japanese Music and Musical Instruments.* Rutland, Vt.: E. Tuttle Co., 1959.

Nketia, J. H. Kwabena. *The Music of Africa.* New York: Norton, 1974.

Shankar, Ravi. *My Music, My Life.* New York: Simon and Schuster, 1968.

Appendix

 DISCOGRAPHY

The most useful catalog of recorded music is the *Schwann Record and Tape Guide,* published monthly by W. Schwann Inc., Boston, Mass. Standard discographies of Medieval and Renaissance music are James Coover and Richard Colvig's *Medieval and Renaissance Music on Long-Playing Records,* Detroit, Information Service Inc., 1964, and *Medieval and Renaissance Music on Long-Playing Records: Supplement, 1962–1971,* Detroit, Information Coordinators, 1973. Basic jazz discographies are Brian Rust's *Jazz Records, 1897–1942,* 2 vols., London, Storyville Publications, 1970, and Jorgen Grunnet Jepsen's *Jazz Records,* 11 vols., Copenhagen, Nordisk Tidsskrift and K. E. Knudson, 1942–62, 1963–70.

Appendix

The following is a brief guide to recordings of music and musical instruments discussed in Part II. *Middle Ages*, III. *The Renaissance*, VIII. *Jazz*, IX. *Rock*, and X. *Non-Western Music*. (Appendix VI lists the compositions included in the five-record set accompanying *Music: An Appreciation*.)

II. MIDDLE AGES

Alleluia: Dominus dixit—Archiv Produktion 2533 131
Perotin: *Alleluya Nativitas*—Bach Guild BG 656
Gherardello da Firenze: *Tosto che ll'alba*—Pleiades P-250
Machaut: *Je puis trop bien*—Pleiades P-250
Machaut: *Notre Dame Mass*—Bach Guild 5045

III. THE RENAISSANCE

Josquin des Prez: *Ave Maria . . . virgo serena*—Telefunken SAWT 9480-A
Palestrina: *Pope Marcellus Mass*—Archiv Produktion 198 153
Weelkes: *As Vesta Was*—Turnabout 34017
Morley: *It Was a Lover and His Lass*—RCA LSC-3131
Andrea Gabrieli: *Ricercar in the Twelfth Mode*—MCA 2511

VIII. JAZZ

An excellent jazz anthology is the six-record set, *The Smithsonian Collection of Classic Jazz* (distributed by W. W. Norton & Co., New York, N.Y.).
Scott Joplin: *Maple Leaf Rag*—Biograph BLP 1006Q
Bessie Smith: *Lost Your Head Blues*—Columbia G 31093
Louis Armstrong: *Hotter Than That*—Columbia CL 851
Lester Young, Count Basie: *Lady Be Good*—Epic SN 6031
John Coltrane: *Giant Steps*—Atlantic At. S-1311
John Coltrane: *"Live" at Birdland*—Impulse S-50

IX. ROCK

Ray Charles: *What'd I Say*—Bluesway BLS-6053
Aretha Franklin: *You're All I Need to Get By*—Atlantic SD 8295
The Beatles: *Sgt. Pepper's Lonely Hearts Club Band*—Capitol SMAS 2653

X. NON-WESTERN MUSIC

Music in Oriental Africa

'Ud (side 1, bands 2–5), *rbab* (side 1, band 7), *kanun* (side 1, band 6), *nei* (side 1, band 1), *zorna* (side 1, band 8), *zajal* (side 2, band 1), *fondu* (side 2, band 5), *nuba* (side 2, band 4): *Tunisia* (UNESCO Collection)—Bärenreiter Musicaphon BM 30 L 2008
MasinKo (side 2, band 4), *krar* (side 2, band 4), *washint* (side 1, band 1), *shilela* (side 1, band 5): *Ethiopia: Azmari Music of the Amharas*—Anthology AST 6000
Begena (side 1, band 1): *Musique traditionelle d'Éthiopie*—Vogue CLVX-164
Kebero (side 1, band 5): *The Music of Ethiopia* (UNESCO Collection)—Bärenreiter Musicaphon BM 30 L 2304

Music in Sub-Saharan Africa

West African funeral dirge (side 1, band 2): *Ewe Music of Ghana*—Asch AHM-4222
Music claimed to attract termites (side 2, band 4): *Musique Centrafricaine*—Ocora 43
African wedding music (side 2, bands 7–8): *Bulu Songs from the Cameroons*—Ethnic Folkways Library p 451
Mbira (side 1, band 4): *The African Mbira: Music of the Shona People of Rhodesia* (Explorer Series)—Nonesuch H-72043

Xylophone (record 2, side 2, band 4): *Anthology of Music of Black Africa*—Everest SDBR-3254/3

Atumpan (side 2, band 1): *Africa East and West*—(produced by the Institute of Ethnomusicology, U.C.L.A.) I.E. Records IER 6751

African drum ensemble (side 2, band 5): *Musique du Burundi*—Ocora 40

The Music of India

Tala played on *tabla-banya* (side 2, band 1); *sitar* (side 1, band 1): *Ravi Shankar at the Monterey International Pop Festival*—Liberty WPS-21442

Tambura (side 1, band 1), *vina* (side 3, band 1), *sarod* (side 2), *venu* (side 3, band 2): *The Anthology of Indian Music, Vol. I*—World Pacific Records WDM-6200 WDS-26200

Nagasvaram (or *shanai*): *Shanai*—Odeon MOAE 113

Mrdanga (side 2, band 2): *Classical Indian Music*—Odeon XPEIX-704, MOAE-149

Music with *kanjira* accompaniment (side 1, band 1): *India II* (UNESCO Collection)—Bärenreiter Musicaphon BM 30 L 2007

Alap: India III (UNESCO Collection)—Bärenreiter Musicaphon BM 30 L 2018

Khyal (side 1): *Khansahib Abdul Karim Khan*—Odeon MOAE-144

Kriti (side 2, band 1): *Ragas from South India*—Folkways FW-8854

Koto Music of Japan

Koto: 18th Century Traditional Music of Japan—Everest 3306, *Classical Japanese Koto Music*—Everest 3206, *Japanese Koto Classics: Shinichi Yuize Koto Master*—Nonesuch Explorer Series H-72008

Rokudan: Japan III (UNESCO Collection)—Bärenreiter Musicaphon BM 30 L 2014

Appendix

[IV] TONE COLOR AND THE HARMONIC SERIES

What we perceive as a single musical tone is actually a mixture of a number of different tones heard at the same time. The pitches making up a single musical tone are called *harmonics* (or *partials*). To understand what harmonics are, recall that a musical tone is produced by a vibrating body, such as a string or air column.

A string vibrates not only in its entirety but also in segments such as halves, thirds, fourths, fifths, and so on. These vibrating segments produce faint tones that are higher in pitch than the *fundamental tone* (or first harmonic), produced by the string vibrating as a whole. The halves produce a tone twice the frequency of the fundamental tone, the thirds produce a tone three times the frequency of the fundamental tone, and so forth. The entire group of component pitches is called the *harmonic series*. Here are the first sixteen harmonics of the tone C.

1 2 3 4 5 6 7 8 9 10 11 12 13 14 15 16

(The 7th, 11th, 13th, and 14th harmonics—indicated by black notes—are markedly out of tune with the scales used in Western music.)

A tone's color or timbre is determined by the number and relative intensity of its harmonics. For example, an oboe tone has almost all the harmonics, but a clarinet tone lacks the even-numbered harmonics.

String players can produce audible harmonics—high, whistle-like tones—by lightly touching the string at certain points. A light touch half-way along a string's length produces the second harmonic, which is an octave higher than the fundamental tone.

KEY SIGNATURES [V]

C major   G major   D major   A major   E major
A minor   E minor   B minor   F# minor   C# minor

B major   F# major   C# major
G# minor   D# minor   A# minor

F major   B♭ major   E♭ major   A♭ major   D♭ major
D minor   G minor   C minor   F minor   B♭ minor

G♭ major   C♭ major
E♭ minor   A♭ minor

Key Signatures

555

[VI] RECORD SELECTIONS

The following compositions are included in the five-record set accompanying *Music: An Appreciation:*

Record I - Side 1

MIDDLE AGES

Alleluia: Dominus dixit

THE RENAISSANCE

Josquin des Prez: *Ave Maria . . . virgo serena*

THE BAROQUE PERIOD

Bach: Brandenburg Concerto No. 5 in D Major, First Movement
Bach: Prelude in C Minor from *The Well-Tempered Clavier*, Book 2
Bach: Organ Fugue in G Minor ("Little" Fugue)
Bach: Cantata No. 140, *Wachet auf*, Fourth Movement: Tenor Chorale

Record I - Side 2
Bach: Suite No. 3 in D, Air
Bach: Suite No. 3 in D, Gigue
Bach: Mass in B Minor, *Crucifixus*
Handel: *Messiah*, "Ev'ry valley shall be exalted"
Handel: *Messiah*, "For unto us a Child is born"
Handel: *Messiah*, "Hallelujah Chorus"

THE CLASSICAL PERIOD

Haydn: Symphony No. 94 in G Major ("Surprise"), Second Movement

Record II - Side 1
Mozart: Symphony No. 40 in G Minor, K. 550, First Movement, Fourth Movement
Mozart: *Eine kleine Nachtmusik*, K. 525, Third Movement: Minuet
Mozart, *Don Giovanni*, Act I
    Introduction
    Leporello's "Catalogue Aria" (*Madamina*)
    Duet: *Là ci darem la mano*

Record II - Side 2
Beethoven: Symphony No. 5 in C Minor, Op. 67, First, Second, Third, Fourth Movements

Record III - Side 1
Beethoven: String Quartet in C Minor, Op. 18, No. 4, Fourth Movement: Rondo

THE ROMANTIC PERIOD

Schubert: "The Erlking"
Chopin: Prelude in E Minor for Piano, Op. 28, No. 4
Chopin: Prelude in C Minor for Piano, Op. 28, No. 20
Chopin: Polonaise in A-flat Major, Op. 53
Mendelssohn: Concerto for Violin and Orchestra in E Minor, Op. 64, First Movement

Record III - Side 2
Berlioz: *Fantastic Symphony*, Fifth Movement: *Dream of a Witches' Sabbath*
Tchaikovsky: *Nutcracker Suite, Dance of the Reed Pipes*
Smetana: *The Moldau*

Record IV - Side 1
Wagner: *Lohengrin*, Prelude to Act III
Wagner: *The Twilight of the Gods,* Act III, Immolation Scene (Conclusion)
Puccini: *La Bohème:* Act I, Scene between Rudolfo and Mimi (From Mimi's entrance
    to the conclusion of the act)

Record IV - Side 2

THE TWENTIETH CENTURY

Debussy: *Prelude to "The Afternoon of a Faun"*
Stravinsky: *Firebird Suite,* Finale
Stravinsky: *The Rite of Spring*, Part I, Introduction and *Dances of the Youths and Maidens*
Stravinsky: *Symphony of Psalms,* First Movement
Webern: *Five Pieces for Orchestra,* Op. 10, Third Piece

Record V - Side 1
Schoenberg: *A Survivor from Warsaw,* Op. 46
Bartók: *Concerto for Orchestra,* First Movement
Ives: *The Unanswered Question*
Varèse: *Poème électronique*

Record V - Side 2

JAZZ

Scott Joplin: *Maple Leaf Rag*
Bessie Smith: *Lost Your Head Blues*
Louis Armstrong: *Hotter Than That*
Lester Young, Count Basie: *Lady Be Good*

ROCK

Ray Charles: *What'd I Say*

NON-WESTERN MUSIC

Yoruba Dance Music, Nigeria
Ravi Shankar: *Maru-Bihag* for sitar, tambura, and tabla
Mitsuzaki Kengyō: *Godan-Kinuta* for two kotos, opening section

Record Selections
557

ACKNOWLEDGMENTS

Text

Gherardello da Firenze, *Tosto che ll'alba* from Instituto Italiano di Cultura, New York, N.Y.

Machaut, *Je puis trop bien* from Archibald Davidson and Willi Apel, eds., *Historical Anthology of Music* (Cambridge, Mass.: Harvard University Press, 1954), p. 245.

Josquin des Prez, *Ave Maria . . . virgo serena* from *Josquin des Prez, Motets, 1490–1520* (Telefunken Decca, SAWT 9480, Hamburg, Germany).

Bach, *Cantata No. 140* from Gerhard Herz, trans., R. Kamien, ed., *The Norton Scores* (New York: W. W. Norton, 1970), pp. 173–175.

Handel, *Julius Caesar,* Act III, from R. Kamien, ed., *The Norton Scores* (New York: W. W. Norton, 1970), p. 112.

Monteverdi, *The Coronation of Poppea,* Act III, from Joseph Kerman and Ugo Tessitore, trans., *The Coronation of Poppea* (Wellesley, Mass.: Cambridge Records, CRSB 1901, 1967), p. 41.

Mozart, *Don Giovanni* from William Murray, trans., *Don Giovanni* (Angel Records, DL 3700, Capital Records, 1961).

Schubert, "The Erlking" and "You My Soul" from *The Ring of Words* edited by Philip L. Miller. Reprinted by the permission of Doubleday & Company, Inc.

Schubert, *Gretchen at the Spinning Wheel* from S. S. Prawer, ed. and trans., *The Penguin Book of Lieder* (Copyright S. S. Prawer, 1964), pp. 33–34.

Schubert, "Dedication" from *Myrtles* from Philip L. Miller, ed., *The Ring of Words* (New York: W. W. Norton, 1973), pp. 265, 267.

Berlioz, *Fantastic Symphony.* English translation from *Symphonie Fantastique* (New York: Edition Eulenburg), p. III.

Mussorgsky, *Boris Godunov,* Coronation Scene, from Louis Biancolli, trans., *Boris Godunov* (RCA Victor, LM 6403, 1952).

Smetana, *The Moldau* from Brian Large, *Smetana* (New York: Praeger, London: Duckworth & Co. Ltd. 1970), p. 273. John Clapham, *Smetana* (London: Dent & Sons Ltd., 1972), p. 77.

Verdi, *Rigoletto,* Act III, from William Weaver, *Seven Verdi Libretti* (New York: W. W. Norton, 1974), pp. 54–61.

Puccini, *La Bohème,* Act I, from William Weaver, trans., *La Bohème* (Capital Records, Seraphim 6038, 1952).

Wagner, *The Twilight of the Gods,* Act III, from G. M. Holland, trans., *The Twilight of the Gods* (Copyright 1965. The Decca Record Company Limited, London. Exclusive U.S. Agents, London Records, Inc., New York, N.Y. Used by Permission.)

Schoenberg, *A Survivor from Warsaw* from Arnold Schoenberg, *A Survivor from Warsaw* (Hillsdale, N.Y.: Boelke-Bomart, 1949).

Crumb, *Ancient Voices of Children* from Federico Garcia Lorca, *Selected Poems.* (Copyright 1955 by New Directions Publishing Corporation. Reprinted by permission of New Directions Publishing Corporation).

Berg, *Wozzeck,* Act III. English translation from Eric Blackall and Vida Harford, *Wozzeck* (Copyright 1923 by Universal Edition A. G. Wien R 1951 for the German text and Copyright 1952 by Alfred A. Kalmus. London for the English trans. Used by permission in both cases).

Music Examples

Debussy, *The Sunken Cathedral.* Copyright 1910, Durand et Cie. Used by permission of the publisher, Elkan-Vogel, Inc., sole representative, United States.

INDEX

The symbol (LO) following page numbers indicates that there is a Listening Outline within the given pages.

561

569

standard instrumental sections in, 14, 120, 192
Orchestra pit, 135
Orchestral piece, Op. 10, No. 3 (Webern), 378
Orchestration, 267
Orfeo (Monteverdi), 136, 138
Organ, 11, 25, 10
described, 27
in Middle Ages, 80
Organ Fugue in G Minor ("Little" Fugue) (Bach), 130–131
Organ point, defined, 130
Organum, 89–91
defined, 89
Oriental music (*see* African music, Oriental; Asian music)
Ory, Kid, 490
Ostinato, 399
defined, 384
examples of, 383, 409
Otello (Verdi), 342, 343
Overture:
concert, 305
French, 160
opera, 135, 305
Overture 1812 (Tchaikovsky), 305
Overture to *A Midsummer Night's Dream* (Mendelssohn), 298, 300

Paganini, Niccolò, 270, 291
Page, Walter, 493
Pagliacci, I (Leoncavallo), 352
Pagodes (*Pagodas*) (Debussy), 377
Palestrina, Giovanni Pierluigi da, 104–106
Pope Marcellus Mass, 105–106
Paris International Exhibition, 377, 388, 389, 516
Parker, Charlie "Bird," 498–499
Parker, Horatio, 452
Parsifal (Wagner), 364
Passacaglia, 340, 377
(*See also* Ground bass)
Patronage:
aristocratic, 100, 121–124, 126, 136, 152, 194–196, 209–212, 219, 240, 242
church, 100, 121–124, 152–154
Esterházy family and, 209–212
and middle-class market, growth of, 195, 208, 269–270
opera-house, commercial, 121, 123
town, 121–124
(*See also* Musicians, social status of)

Pedal point, defined, 130
Pelléas et Mélisande (Debussy), 388–389, 391
Penderecki, Krzysztof, 468, 471
Dies irae, 471
St. Luke Passion, 471
Threnody for the Victims of Hiroshima, 471–472(LO)
Pentatonic scale, 527, 537
described, 390
hemitonic and anhemitonic, 536n.
in koto music, 535–537
Percussion instruments, 11, 14
in African music, 25, 481, 484, 521, 524–526
in Asian music, 25, 377, 531
of definite and indefinite pitch, 24
described, 24–25
in jazz and rock, 25, 498, 505, 510
in twentieth-century music, 25, 377, 378, 446, 467, 498
(*See also* Membranophones; *and* specific instruments)
Performance, 71–76
conductor and, 72–74
evaluation of, 75
performer and, 71–72, 206–207
recorded and live, 74–75
Performing, 10–33
instruments, 11–33
voices, 10–11, 33
Pergolesi, Giovanni Battista, 378, 399
Peri, Jacopo, 136
Perotin, 90, 377
Alleluya Nativitas, 90–91, 94
Petrushka (Stravinsky), 381–382, 386, 396, 398, 400–404(LO)
"Petrushka chord," 399
Philharmonic societies formed, 270
Phrases, described, 46–48
Pianissimo (*pp*), defined, 5
Piano, 3, 12, 26, 207, 244, 270, 378, 466, 487, 520
Chopin and, 286–288
in Classical era, 191, 207
described, 25
electric, 473
as harpsichord replacement, 191
improved, 267
Liszt and, 270, 291–294
octave tones, 4, 39, 41–42
and pitch notation, 39–42
in Romantic era, 267, 268, 270
stride playing style, 488
Piano (*p*) defined, 5
Piano Concerto (Copland), 377
Piano Concerto in D Minor, K. 466 (Mozart), 235–239(LO)

Piano Piece No. 11 (Stockhausen), 465
Piano Sonata in F Minor, Op. 57 ("Appassionata") (Beethoven), 253–257(LO)
Piano trio, 208
Piano Variations (Copland), 458
Picasso, Pablo, 372, 375, 395–398, 404, 405, 457
Piccolo, 18, 19, 267
Pictures at an Exhibition (Mussorgsky), 305, 316
Pierrot lunaire, Op. 21 ("Moonstruck Pierrot") (Schoenberg), 419
Pipe organ (*see* Organ)
Pissarro, Camille, 387
Pitch:
defined, 2
definite and indefinite, 3, 24
notation, 38–42
organization (*see* Key; Tonal system)
principles of, 2–4
Pitch range, 101, 267
defined, 4
of instruments (*see* specific categories of instruments)
and register, 12
of voices, 4, 10, 133–134
Pizzicato, defined, 15
Planer, Minna, 361–362
Platters, The, 507
Plucked-string instruments, 15, 88
non-Western, 513–515, 518–520, 529–531, 533–534, 537
(*See also* String instruments; *and* specific instruments)
Poco più animato, defined, 339
Poe, Edgar Allan, 260
Poème électronique ("Electronic Poem") (Varèse), 28–29, 31(LO), 468
"Pointillist" music, 463
Polonaise:
Chopin and, 288, 290
defined, 390
Polonaise in A-flat Major, Op. 53 (Chopin), 290
Polychord, defined, 380
Polyphonic texture, 69–70(LO)
described, 60–61
medieval development of, 89–91, 94–95, 101
Renaissance, 101–103, 105, 442
Polyrhythm, defined, 383
Polytonality, defined, 381
Ponte, Lorenzo da, 222
Pope Marcellus Mass (Palestrina), 105–106

572

575

579